H: Holy of Holies (inside the Temple)

I: Priest's apartments

J: Court of the Gentiles

K: Entrance and exit to Huldah or South Gates

L: Herod's Basilica (Royal Portico)

M: Western Porticoes

BEHOLD
THE MAN

GERALD N. LUND

THE
Kingdom
AND THE **Crown**
VOLUME THREE

BEHOLD
THE MAN

SHADOW
MOUNTAIN

Library of Congress Cataloging-in-Publication Data

Lund, Gerald N.
    Behold the man / Gerald N. Lund.
      p.   cm.— (The kingdom and the crown ; v. 3)
    Includes bibliographical references.
    ISBN 1-57008-853-5 (alk. paper)
     1. Jesus Christ—Fiction.   2. Bible. N.T.—History of Biblical events—Fiction.   I. Title.

PS3562.U485 B44 2002
813'.54—dc21
                                                                   2002012028

Printed in the United States of America   72076-6993
Publishers Printing, Salt Lake City, Utah

10   9   8   7   6   5   4   3   2   1

SYNOPSIS OF VOLUME ONE

Fishers of Men opened as Marcus Quadratus Didius, a tribune in the Roman legions, comes to the family of David ben Joseph, a wealthy merchant from Capernaum. The Holy Land has been under the total and often brutal rule of the Roman Empire for almost a century. The corrupt system of Roman tax collection encourages corruption, and David ben Joseph has gone to Damascus to try to raise money to pay an exorbitant assessment. His wife, Deborah, is already deeply embittered against the Romans. When she was fifteen years old, her family was caught up in a rebellion against Rome. Several, including her father, were killed, and her mother died in the months following as they were forced to hide through the winter in the mountains. This hatred for everything Roman has been passed on to her son, Simeon, twenty-one, who leads a band of "Zealots." When Marcus Didius learns that the family does not have the money for their taxes, he refuses to accept their pleas for additional time and tries to arrest them. Simeon resists and is nearly killed. David, his father, returns barely in time to rescue his wife and daughter from being sold into slavery. It is against this backdrop of violence and injustice that the story unfolds.

As a young man some thirty years before, David ben Joseph was in the shepherd fields of Bethlehem. He saw the angels and heard the glorious announcement that the Messiah had been born. So when word comes to the Galilee that a man named John the Baptist claims to be the forerunner for the Messiah and has designated a carpenter from Nazareth as that Messiah, David is anxious to learn more. Then Jesus comes to Capernaum and calls David's partners in the fishing business as followers—Simon Peter and his brother, Andrew. David decides to investigate further. He is convinced almost immediately that Jesus is the Christ, or the promised Messiah, and soon is able to convince the rest of his family—all except for Simeon. Simeon finds the teachings of Jesus highly offensive. Loving your enemies and turning the other cheek seems antithetical to all the true Deliverer would stand for. Simeon's refusal to follow Jesus alienates Simeon from his family.

However, in time, Simeon cannot help being drawn to Jesus by the simple impact of his teachings and the increasing evidence of his remarkable power. After watching Jesus instantly and completely restore a man's twisted and withered hand and then feed five thousand people with five small loaves of bread and two fish, Simeon can no longer say that Jesus is an ordinary man. This realization does not bring Simeon peace, however. Now he is torn between his old loyalties to the Zealots and his desire to become a follower of Jesus of Nazareth.

Mordechai ben Uzziel is one of the richest and most powerful men in Jerusalem. An aristocratic Sadducee and member of the Great Council there, he is anxious to make accommodation with Rome in order to maintain peace and protect the base of power he and the other Jewish leaders hold. His eighteen-year-old daughter, Miriam, is pampered, coddled, and accustomed to a life of comfort and luxury. But she is also filled with a strange sense of unrest. She sees that her father's religion consists mostly of outward trappings, and she searches for deeper meaning in life. On a trip to the Galilee, she and her father are rescued from the hands of a vicious bandit, Moshe Ya'abin, by Simeon and his band of Zealots. Though Miriam feels a great sense of obligation to Simeon for this, her father does not. Because the Zealots threaten war with Rome, Mordechai sets up an intricate plot with Pontius Pilate, the Roman governor of Judea, to draw the Zealots into a trap.

As the story unfolds, Miriam also comes in contact with Jesus of Nazareth. She is on the Temple Mount when he drives out the money-changers. Later she watches him deal compassionately with a woman taken in adultery. Though she knows little about him, she determines to learn more. To her surprise, her father is furious when he hears of her desire and forbids any further contact.

Then Miriam accidentally learns of her father's plan to draw the Zealots into the trap. A seemingly isolated wagon train of arms will be sent to decoy the Zealots into the Joknean Pass; then waiting Roman legionnaires will swoop down and kill them. Knowing that Simeon and the others who saved her life will most likely die, Miriam decides she cannot simply stand by. She goes to the Galilee and tells Simeon everything.

This puts Simeon in a terrible dilemma. Just prior to Miriam's coming, Simeon had told his band of men that he would not lead them in the raid against the Romans. Because of his commitment to follow Jesus, he has decided he must turn from his life of violence. But when he learns of Mordechai's treachery and the danger to his men, there is no choice. He and his father ride to the Joknean Pass. Ironically, in order to stop a massacre, Simeon has to save the Romans, led by Tribune Marcus Didius, the very man who epitomizes all that Simeon once hated. Driven by a desire to do what is right, Simeon intervenes and saves the Roman column, but in doing so, one of his men is killed, and another, Yehuda, his closest friend and second-in-command, is captured.

The book closes as, in an agony of conscience, Simeon realizes that his commitment to be a disciple of Jesus has come only at a terrible price to those who trusted in him.

Synopsis of Volume Two

After the tragedies at the Joknean Pass, Simeon is wracked with guilt over Yehuda's capture and Daniel's death. Though time is of the essence, he is immobilized by indecision, struggling to merge his old role as a Zealot leader with his new role as a peaceful disciple of Jesus. How can he "love his enemies" when those same enemies have imprisoned his friends? Knowing that by rushing into action with a sword he would betray his newly made baptismal covenants, Simeon concocts several more subtle plans to free Yehuda from prison. His first plan involves disguising a group of Zealots as Roman guards and delivering forged papers from the governor for Yehuda's release. When complications arise, Simeon abandons that plan and prepares to bribe Pilate with gold to buy Yehuda's freedom.

Pilate is not so easily swayed, however, and underlying his acceptance of the deal is his own plan to capture Simeon and force him to reveal the name of the person who betrayed the Romans at the Joknean Pass. Late one evening, Marcus arrives with Yehuda and the other prisoners at the rendezvous point. The deed is done, the trap is sprung, and Marcus returns to present Pilate with the gold *and* a new prisoner—Simeon.

Miriam is in similar straits—though in a prison of a different kind. Her relationship with her father, Mordechai, has been strained since the events at Joknean Pass. She is worried about the repercussions if her father were ever to find out that she was responsible for informing Simeon of the trap at the pass. Treading carefully around his increasingly volatile moods, she dares not protest too much when he announces they will be moving to Rome for an indeterminate length of time until the bandit Ya'abin can be captured or subdued. Miriam rejoices when Mordechai agrees to let her stay with Ezra until the move, for she knows that she will then be free to travel to the Galilee and listen to the teachings of Jesus. Her joy is increased tenfold as she, Livia, and Simeon enter the waters of baptism.

Miriam, Simeon, and the others have been able to spend more time with Jesus and to hear some of his most profound teachings—the parables of the soils, the good Samaritan, and the lost sheep. As Jesus performs some of his most memorable miracles, including stilling the stormy sea with a word, walking on the water, and healing the demonic boy, his influence and reputation spreads throughout the region.

Miriam is visiting Simeon's family when they receive word of his capture; and Miriam knows she must take steps to save him—if she can—as it is her identity that he is protecting. She arrives in Caesarea ahead of her father and pleads with Pilate to set Simeon free. When Pilate refuses, she suggests an alternative plan: release Simeon and Yehuda with orders to capture and subdue Ya'abin within a certain amount of time. If they succeed, they go free; if they fail, they are at the mercy of the Romans. Pilate agrees to the plan, and Simeon and Yehuda are released to hunt down Ya'abin in the Judean wilderness.

Mordechai and Miriam move to Rome. Marcus joins them while he is on leave. The blossoming relationship between Miriam and Marcus deepens; he asks Mordechai for Miriam's hand in marriage. And Marcus hires a man to track down Livia's brother, Drusus, who had been sold into slavery when he was a child. Drusus is found and the siblings are reunited.

Tensions continue to rise between Mordechai and Miriam as he plots the destruction of Jesus, and she hides the fact that she has been baptized. When events force her to reveal to her father not only her baptism but also her role in the Joknean Pass incident, Mordechai disowns her. He leaves Miriam and Livia in Rome under house arrest and returns to Jerusalem with Marcus.

Meanwhile, Simeon and Yehuda have embarked on a series of psychological sneak attacks designed to demoralize Ya'abin's forces. After months of baiting the Desert Fox, they deliver the final blow by luring Ya'abin into a blind canyon, where the Romans swoop down on their prey. Marcus toys with the idea of allowing Simeon to be killed in the trap as well, but his centurion, Sextus, essentially defies him and rescues Simeon. Flushed with victory, Marcus boasts to Simeon that he is engaged to Miriam.

Simeon, unable to believe Marcus's boast, journeys with Ezra to Rome, where he discovers the truth for himself: Miriam does not want to marry Marcus, and she and Livia have been plotting for some time to return to Jerusalem. Simeon and Ezra help them escape from Rome, and during the journey home, Simeon and Miriam proclaim their love for each other.

LIST OF MAJOR CHARACTERS

The Household of David ben Joseph, Merchant of Capernaum
    David: Simeon's father, 47[1]
    Deborah bat Benjamin of Sepphoris: Simeon's mother, 45
    Simeon: Second son of David and Deborah, ardent Zealot, 22
    Ephraim: Simeon's older brother, married to Rachel, 26
    Rachel: Ephraim's wife, 23
    Leah: Simeon's sister, 17
    Joseph: Simeon's youngest brother, 11
    Esther: David and Deborah's granddaughter, daughter of Ephraim and Rachel, 5
    Boaz: David and Deborah's grandson, son of Ephraim and Rachel, 3
    Amasa: David and Deborah's grandson, son of Ephraim and Rachel, 3 months
    Aaron of Sepphoris: Deborah's brother, Simeon's uncle, a dedicated Pharisee, 40
    Hava: Aaron's wife, 38

The Household of Mordechai ben Uzziel of Jerusalem
    Mordechai: Miriam's father; leader of the Sadducees, member of the Great Sanhedrin of Jerusalem, 43
    Miriam bat Mordechai ben Uzziel: Mordechai's only daughter, 19
    Livia of Alexandria: Miriam's servant and friend, 21
    Drusus Alexander Carlottus: Livia's brother who was sold into slavery, 18

---

[1] Ages are given as of A.D. 31.

Ezra of Joppa: Sandal maker, married to Lilly, 32

Lilly: Ezra's wife, cousin to Miriam's deceased mother, 29

The Household of Yehuda of Beth Neelah

Yehuda: Simeon's friend and partner in the Zealot movement, a farmer, 26

Shana: Yehuda's sister, 19

Samuel: Shana's husband, 26

Other Prominent Characters

Jesus of Nazareth: Carpenter and teacher, 31

Mary of Nazareth: Mother of Jesus[2]

Simon Peter: Fisherman, one of the Twelve Apostles called by Jesus

Andrew: Simon Peter's brother, one of the Twelve

James and John: Sons of Zebedee, partners in fishing with Peter and Andrew, both apostles

Matthew Levi: A publican in Capernaum, called to follow Jesus, also one of the Twelve

Luke the Physician: A disciple of Jesus in Capernaum

Mary Magdalene: A follower of Jesus from Magdala on the Sea of Galilee, from whom Jesus cast out seven devils

Martha, Mary, and Lazarus of Bethany: A family close to Jesus with whom he sometimes stayed while in the Jerusalem area

Caiaphas: High Priest, chief of the Great Sanhedrin

Azariah the Pharisee: Leader of the Jerusalem group and titular head of the Pharisees, 51

---

[2]Ages for actual Bible characters are not given here since they are not known (other than the age of Jesus), though suggestions about their ages may be included in the novel itself.

Caleb the Pharisee: Second to Azariah in the hierarchy of the Pharisees, 48

Menachem of Bethphage: Mordechai's closest ally on the council, 40

Joseph of Arimathea: A wealthy member of the Great Sanhedrin in Jerusalem, a secret follower of Jesus

Nicodemus: A moderate voice on the council, follower of Jesus

Zacchaeus: A publican in Jericho

Jephunah ben Asa: A wealthy man in Jerusalem who owns the "upper room," 39

Asa the Beggar: The man born blind

Pontius Pilate: Procurator of Judea

Marcus Quadratus Didius: Roman tribune, 26

Diana Servilius: Marcus's wife, 19

Sextus Rubrius: Roman centurion, about 51

GLOSSARY

NOTE: Some terms which are used only once and are defined in the text are not included here.

Bath or *bat* (BAHT)—Daughter, or daughter of, e.g., Miriam bat Mordechai, or Miriam, daughter of Mordechai.

Ben (BEN)—Son, or son of, as in Simeon ben David or Simeon, son of David. An Aramaic translation of *ben* is *bar*, as in Peter's name, Simon Bar-jona, or Simon, son of Jonah (Matthew 16:17), and *bar mitzvah*.

Beth (BAIT; commonly pronounced as BETH among English speakers)— House of, e.g., *Bethlehem*, House of Bread; *Bethel*, the House of God.

Beth Chatanim—(BAIT hah-tah-NEEM*) "House of the bridegrooms"; common hall in larger communities used for weddings, much like a modern reception center.

Chuppah (HOO-pah*)—Covering, the canopy used during a wedding ceremony.

Erev tov (AIR-ev TOHV)—Good evening.

Ezer knegdo (AY-zur KNEG-doh)—Help meet; in Hebrew, literally to meet one's equal or match.

Goyim (goy-EEM)—Gentiles, literally in Hebrew, "nations"; a word used for anyone not of the house of Israel; in modern times, one who is not a Jew; singular is *goy*.

Kadash (kah-DAHSH)—Holy, set apart or consecrated.

Ketubah (keh-TOO-bah)—"Instrument of covenant," specifically the prenuptial agreements or contracts of betrothal.

Kiddushin (kid-doo-SHEEN)—Ceremony of betrothal; from *Kadash*, which conveys the idea that the future bride is *consecrated* to her future husband.

Lailah tov (LIE-lah TOHV)—Good night.

*The Hebrew "ch" is a guttural "h" sound similar to the German "ch," made as though one were clearing one's throat.

Lulav (LOO-lahv)—Plume of gathered palm fronds, willow branches, and stems of myrtle; used during specific rituals of the Feast of Tabernacles.

Mazal tov (MAH-zahl TOHV)—Good luck; an expression used to congratulate people at weddings or other celebrations.

Menorah (commonly men-ORE-rah, but also men-ore-RAH)—A candlestick; usually refers to the sacred, seven-branched candlestick used in the tabernacle of Moses and later in the temples.

Pesach (pay-SOCK)—The Hebrew name for Passover.

Praetorium (pree-TOR-ee-um)—Official residence of the Roman governor or procurator or other high government official.

Publicani (poo-blee-KHAN-ee)—Latin for "public servant"; the publicans of the New Testament were hired by Romans to serve as the tax assessors and collectors in local districts.

Rosh Hashanah (ROSH hah-SHAWN-ah; also ROSH hah-shawn-AH)—The Jewish New Year; the beginning of the civil year.

Sanhedrin (san-HED-rin)—The ruling council in various towns and cities; the Great Sanhedrin in Jerusalem was the supreme governing body of the Jews at this time.

Shabbat (sha-BAHT)—Hebrew name for the Lord's day; the source of our word *Sabbath*.

Shalom (shaw-LOWM)—"Peace"; used as a greeting and a farewell.

Sukkot (sue-COAT)—The Feast of Tabernacles.

Talmud (TALL-mood)—A collection of sacred writings and commentaries written by learned rabbis and Hebrew scholars of the Torah over many generations.

Tefillin (teh-FEE-lin)—Greek for "phylacteries"; small leather cases worn by observant Jews on the left bicep and on the forehead during prayers and other rituals; these cases contained tiny scrolls with selected scriptures written on them.

Todah rabah (toh-DAH rah-BAH)—Thank you very much.

Torah (TORE-ah)—The writings of Moses; the first five books of the current Old Testament.

Via Maris (VEE-ah MAR-ees)—The Way of the Sea; famous highway following the eastern Mediterranean coastline from Egypt to Syria.

Yeshivas (yeh-SHEE-vahs)—Jewish schools that taught the Law of Moses.

Yom Kippur (YAHM kee-PUHR)—The Day of Atonement, the most sacred and solemn of all Jewish holy days.

Pronunciation Guide for Names

Readers may wish to use the common English pronunciations for names that have come to modern times, such as David. The Hebrew pronunciation is for those who wish to say them as they may have been spoken at the time of the Savior. Any such pronunciation guide must be viewed as speculative, however; we simply do not know for certain how Hebrew names were pronounced in antiquity.

Abraham—In Hebrew, ahv-rah-HAM
Anna—ahn-AH
Azariah—ah-zeh-RAI-ah
Bethlehem—English, BETH-leh-hem; Hebrew, BAIT lech-EM
Beth Neelah—BAIT nee-LAH
Bethsaida—English, BETH-say-dah; Hebrew, BAIT sah-EE-dah
Caesarea—see-zar-EE-ah
Capernaum—English, ka-PUR-neh-um; Hebrew, kah-fur-NAY-hum
Chorazin—khor-ah-ZEEN
Daniel—dan-YELL
David—dah-VEED
Deborah—deh-vor-AH
Ephraim—ee-FRAI-eem
Esther—es-TAHR
Eve—hah-VAH
Galilee—English, GAL-leh-lee; Hebrew, gah-LEEL or gah-lee-YAH
Ha'keedohn—ha-kee-DOHN
James—Same as Jacob, or yah-ah-KOHV in Hebrew
Jerusalem—ye-roosh-ah-LAI-eem
Jesus—Hebrew form of the name is Yeshua (yesh-oo-AH), which is the same as the Old Testament *Joshua*; Greek form is hee-AY-soos.
John—Hebrew form of the name is Johanan (yo-HAH-nahn)
Joknean Pass—yohk-NEE-an
Joseph—yo-SEPH

Leah—lay-AH
Miriam—meer-YAM
Mordechai—mor-deh-KAI
Moshe Ya'abin—mohw-SHEH ya-ah-BEEN
Mount Hermon—hur-MOHN
Mount Tabor—English, TAY-bur; Hebrew, tah-BOHR
Ptolemais—TOHL-eh-mays
Rachel—rah-KHEL
Samuel—shmoo-EL
Sepphoris—seh-PHOR-us
Shana—SHAW-nah
Simeon—shee-MOHN
Simon—see-MOHN
Yehuda—yeh-HOO-dah; other forms, Judah or Judas

CHAPTER 1

DON'T COUNT YOUR CHICKENS UNTIL THEY'RE HATCHED.

—Aesop, from the tale of the milkmaid and the pail

I

JERUSALEM, THE TEMPLE MOUNT
30 OCTOBER, A.D. 31

Mordechai ben Uzziel was bored.

The meeting of the Great Sanhedrin, the supreme council of Jerusalem, was well into its third hour, and there was no indication that the end was anywhere in sight.

He suppressed a sigh, shifted his weight in the ornately carved chair, and let his eyes move down the four rows of massive columns that formed the Royal Portico on the Temple Mount. The forty monolithic pillars in each row were like a gigantic frozen forest.

Say what you would about King Herod the Great, Mordechai thought. He was godless, brutal, and ruthless—but he was a builder of things of incredible magnificence. The temple complex he had created in Jerusalem was his finest creation, rightly judged by many to be one of the great man-made wonders of the world.

"Does the Father of the House of Judgment find all of this unworthy of his attention?"

The sneer in Azariah's voice brought Mordechai sharply back to the chambers of the council. In the Great Sanhedrin, the chief or president of the council was usually the current high priest. That was Caiaphas, at present. The second in command, who served as vice-president and sat at the president's right hand, was called the Father of the House of Judgment—it was his duty to see that all judgments pronounced by the court were proper and in keeping with the law. Caiaphas had appointed Mordechai to that position because of Mordechai's skills in working with the fractious and difficult body. So Mordechai was officially the Father of the House of Judgment, but council members rarely used that ponderous and pompous title.

On the president's left hand sat the third officer of the court, he who was called the Sage, or the Wise One. His role was to see that all judgments were administered with wisdom and judiciousness. What a joke, Mordechai thought. Azariah, chief of the Pharisaical party in Jerusalem and therefore titular head of Pharisees everywhere, could be described with many words, but judicious was not one of them.

Mordechai leaned forward and smiled at his fellow council member and long-time political enemy. "Actually, Azariah," he said blandly, "I was just musing. Do you suppose that if every empty word you Pharisees have uttered here today were a grain of wheat, this hall would be filled to the rafters by now?"

Azariah stiffened, his face flaming, his side curls bobbing softly. Mordechai's comment brought gasps from the other Pharisees as well, but the Sadducees responded with open snickers. Then someone—perhaps Menachem of Bethphage, Mordechai's closest ally on the council—answered the question in a voice heard by all. "At least that much, and perhaps half the Kidron Valley as well."

Azariah shot to his feet, eyes bulging. "Outrage!" he cried. "Insult! Honorable president, an apology is in order here."

Mordechai leaned forward. When he spoke, it was lazily and with barely disguised contempt. "I concur," he said. "And I accept the apology from our esteemed Sage."

That brought a roar of laughter from the group, while Azariah went from bright red to mottled purple. "You dare—You think it was *I* who—" He stopped as he realized that Mordechai was deliberately baiting him.

"All right, brethren," Caiaphas broke in. "That's enough." His tone of voice made it plain he was more amused than offended by the interchange.

Azariah slowly sat down again, motioning to colleagues who had also leaped to their feet to do the same. Mordechai watched him, not without a touch of admiration. His recovery was swift and complete. Judicious might not be a word Mordechai would use to describe Azariah, but he was shrewd, cunning as a hungry fox. Only a fool would count him out too quickly.

Mordechai turned back to Caiaphas, his patience gone. "Honorable President, the issue before this council is what to do about the man called Jesus of Nazareth. Our esteemed colleague prattles on about how the Pharisees have shamed this wandering rabbi on numerous occasions, and yet—"

"He is not a rabbi!" Azariah cut in coldly. "He has no training in the intricacies of the Torah. He is an unlearned village peasant. How dare you dignify him by using the sacred title of 'teacher,' or 'master'?"

"*I* don't call him rabbi," Mordechai shot right back, "*the people do!* They flock to him by the thousands. Instead of discrediting him, every time you Pharisees confront him he makes you look like fools, and the people love him all the more."

Azariah was on his feet again, as were several of his colleagues. Mordechai leaped up as well, roaring like a bull. "The time for talk is over! All of Galilee is aflame with the news of this man. The Romans are growing nervous. Would you sit here and endlessly debate while our whole nation is at peril?"

4

Caiaphas stood and raised both hands. Gradually the uproar subsided to an angry rumble. "Mordechai is right," he said when he could
be heard again. "The time for debate is past. Our purpose today is to
devise a plan for dealing with this rogue once and for all." He shot
Azariah a withering look. "Enough words. It is time for action."

"Objection!"

The half circle of seventy men turned toward the far left side of
the circle. Joseph of Arimathea was on his feet. Mordechai inwardly
winced. As one of Jerusalem's wealthy and powerful men, Joseph
should have been squarely in the camp of the Sadducees, but he never
was. Nor did he align himself with the Pharisees. He kept himself independent of both the major parties. His was one of the most respected
of the moderate voices on the council.

"Yes," Caiaphas said, obviously surprised by this development.
"What is it, Joseph?"

"No legitimate charges against Jesus have been brought before this
council."

"He is a blasphemer!" Azariah shouted.

"Because he refuses to accept the doctrine of the Pharisees?"
Joseph asked calmly. "I suspect there are many on the council who
would be in similar peril if that were the case." Then his voice sharpened. "This tribunal was created to deal with violations of the law, not
differences of opinion or interpretations of our faith. Let me hear the
charges against this man before we talk about what plan of action we
must devise to destroy him."

Azariah leaned forward slightly, his eyes narrowed into dangerous
points of light. "Has our noble colleague become a follower of this
Jesus?"

The older man swung around. "Let me hear the charges against
this man," he said slowly. "That is the way of the council. Neither
mumbled accusations nor childish hand-wringing are sufficient. Show
me a crime, or let us move on to more important matters."

"Hear, hear!"

Mordechai turned. That declaration had come from the man three seats down from Azariah. Nicodemus was a Pharisee, but another of the moderates on the council. He and Joseph of Arimathea often stood with each other on important issues.

Mordechai watched the two of them through lidded eyes. Was Azariah right? Both of these men were sympathetic to the Nazarene. Were they his followers as well? Would they dare risk their seats on the Great Sanhedrin to trot after the man? This would bear careful watching.

The council had fallen into shambles. Members shouted at each other. Some waved their hands wildly, seeking recognition from Caiaphas. Azariah was spitting out something venomous at Joseph of Arimathea, and two of the other leading Pharisees had rounded on Nicodemus.

Mordechai grabbed the walking stick beside his chair and brought it down with a sharp crack across the back of his chair. Instantly, all noise stopped and every face turned to him. Several registered shock.

"Enough!" he bellowed. "We speak not of taste here. We speak of treason. We speak of rebellion—rebellion that the Romans will not tolerate. This man could cost us everything we have worked so carefully to reconstruct these past three decades." He let his eyes swing around the circle, daring anyone to disagree. One by one, the council members sat down again.

"We have made important strides with the Romans, but how can we bear the continuing humiliation?" He looked down at Caiaphas, who was listening intently. "The Roman procurator still holds the sacred vestments of the high priesthood because a group of rabble rousers thought they could challenge the might of Rome. And now our esteemed leader must go to a *Gentile*"—he nearly spat out the word—"each time he needs the robes of the priesthood to officiate on the high holy days."

There were nods and angry mutterings at that, as Mordechai knew there would be. Some thirty years before, after the great rebellion in the Galilee led by Judah of Gamla, the Romans took control of the priestly vestments as a reminder of who was really in charge. Few things grated on the nerves of the people more deeply than this.

"It would be too much to say that the current governor is our loyal friend," he went on, "but he *is* listening to us. He is willing to let us rule ourselves, as long as we can show that we will not tolerate what Rome fears most—an uprising in one of her provinces."

"Jesus is not going to start any rebellion," Joseph of Arimathea broke in. "He preaches just the opposite: love, forgiveness, tolerance."

"A brilliant ruse," Mordechai said darkly. "And what's to stop him from suddenly arming the thousands who flock to him? One word and he could spark a Zealot wildfire that could consume us all."

"That is not what he is teaching," Joseph answered stubbornly. "So far he has said and done nothing that is illegal, not even under Roman law."

Mordechai watched his fellow council member for several seconds. Yes, he thought. They were going to have to watch this one very closely. But unfortunately, the point he was making was exactly right. It was maddening. Technically, Jesus had done nothing they could use to take action against him. Mordechai sat back down, every eye upon him. "What he is or is not doing is only part of the picture," he pointed out. "What matters is that the Romans are nervous. They don't like it when a man can draw thousands of followers to him, especially in the Galilee—whether he is peaceful or not."

He swung on Azariah, his voice hardening again. "And whining about whether or not he agrees with what you or I teach isn't going to solve the problem. Our president and high priest has asked that we stop talking and come up with a plan of action. I would suggest it is time to do exactly that."

"Of course," Azariah said, his voice cool. "The Sadducees are

always for action and care little for the spiritual aspects of a question."
He went on smoothly, as Mordechai visibly started at the insult. "And
surely the esteemed Father of the House of Judgment"—his voice fairly
dripped sarcasm—"is not trying to rush through this discussion so as
to escape the embarrassment of having a member of his own household be a disciple of this imposter."

Gasps of shock and cries of anger broke out on every side, but
Mordechai didn't move. He fought to keep his face impassive even as
the fury exploded within him. So Azariah knew. In Rome, when
Miriam had told her father about being baptized, one of his first
thoughts had been about how the council would react to the news. But
in the five months since his return from Rome, nothing had come up.
No one had even hinted about Miriam's betrayal, and he had begun to
hope that no one knew. He cursed himself for being so blind. Of course
Azariah would know. He had people reporting to him from everywhere. He had simply been waiting for the right time to spring this on
his old enemy.

"It is obvious," he said calmly, surprised that his voice revealed
none of the rage inside him, "that Azariah knows about my daughter,
Miriam. Unbeknownst to me, and contrary to my specific counsel,
Miriam went north to the Galilee last year and was duped by this Jesus.
She was baptized. She became a follower of the Galilean preacher."

He saw the shaking of heads, heard the sympathetic clucking of
tongues, and hated it. "That was when I decided to take her to Rome
to escape the influence of this man. She will not be returning for a very
long time." What Mordechai said wasn't strictly true—he and Miriam
had fled to Rome to escape possible retaliation by Moshe Ya'abin. But
the council didn't know that.

Heads nodded in understanding. The faces of a few allies showed
genuine sorrow and empathy for his predicament. What man had full
control over his children? But he also saw the gloating, the pure joy
behind the eyes of his enemies. So the mighty Mordechai had a chink

in his armor. It wouldn't have surprised him to see some of them rubbing their hands in open glee. How embarrassing for him! How *wonderfully* embarrassing for him!

He took a quick breath. "This only underscores the urgency of our task. I don't know what power this man from Nazareth has over people. I don't understand what draws the masses to him like moths to the open fire of the lamp. But as a father, and as a leader in Israel, I know this: he presents a direct and current danger to our families, to our religion, to our nation. And I, for one, would suggest we stop our babbling and do something before more tragedies happen and more souls are lost."

He sat down, no longer looking at the council members, no longer thinking about the politics of the situation. He was thinking of Miriam and her betrayal. No, not betrayal. *Betrayals.* She had thwarted what should have been a stunning success at the Joknean Pass. She had sneaked off to the Galilee to hear Jesus. She had been baptized as one of his followers. She refused to accept betrothal to Marcus Didius. Was there no end to it?

Azariah rose slowly. His face was downcast. His mouth, nearly buried in the thickness of his beard, feigned deep sorrow. "Our hearts go out to our brother Mordechai. We feel the extent of this tragedy in his family. Would that all children honored their parents as God, blessed be his name, has commanded. But such is not so."

Mordechai looked up, watching him, hating him. *You think you have won something important this day, you old jackal, but I shall not forget. And when the time is right . . .*

"So while we vehemently disagree on many issues," Azariah continued, "my colleague, Mordechai ben Uzziel, and I agree on one thing. Jesus must be stopped. This interloper, this fraud, this blasphemer must be brought to heel." He looked to Caiaphas. "Honorable President, I suggest that we proceed under your wise direction to seek a solution to our shared concern."

II

JERUSALEM, UPPER CITY

Mordechai was still seething as his litter-bearers rounded the corner and entered the street that led to his palace. For all of Azariah's unctuous words about finding a solution, the council had spent two more hours of deliberation but moved no closer to any definitive action.

He let out a soft exclamation of disgust. *Deliberation?* More like the babbling of idiots whose bellies were filled with too much wine. Five hours all together, and if anything they were further from a solution than when they started.

And now Mordechai had a new problem. Azariah was going to use Miriam's defection to try to undermine Mordechai's influence. He knew that as surely as he knew it was raining. And that knowledge left him as chilled as the weather.

He lifted one hand and pulled the curtain back slightly. Sundown was at least another hour away, but the sky looked more like the final moments of twilight. The clouds were heavy and dark. This was the season of what the Jews called the early rains, the rains that came in the fall and softened the ground for the winter planting. The latter or spring rains would come in a few more months. Today's rain came in a cold, driving storm that would help fill the cisterns of the city before it moved across the Jordan and fizzled out over the vastness of the great Arabian Desert.

He dropped the curtain and fell back against the cushions. Azariah was an enemy to be reckoned with. Mordechai couldn't simply brush him aside as a sputtering old fool. He would give careful thought as to how to counter this parry. Perhaps, with some wise planning,

Mordechai might help Azariah be scorched by the very flames he hoped to turn against . . .

The carriage lurched to a halt, jostling Mordechai roughly. He sat up as he heard the slap of sandals on wet paving stones. He pulled back the curtain, instantly feeling the drops of rain against his arm. His head litter-bearer, a powerful Idumean who also served as a bodyguard, appeared. His hair was plastered to his head and his tunic was black, soaked through to the skin.

"Yes, yes!" Mordechai snapped. "What is it? Get on with it."

"Master, there are Romans ahead. It looks like they are waiting outside the gate of your courtyard."

That brought Mordechai forward sharply. "Romans?"

"Yes, sire." He turned, wiped quickly at his eyes with the back of his hand, and peered ahead intently. "I'd say eight or ten men. And there is an officer with them."

Mordechai considered that only for a moment, then waved a hand. "We have nothing to fear from Romans."

"Yes, sire. As you wish."

"Forward. Let's see who it is."

III

"Well, well," Mordechai said, as he slipped his sandals off and straightened again. "Had I known you were here, I would have gladly left the council early."

Marcus Quadratus Didius stepped forward enough for Levi to shut the door behind him. He removed his helmet and ran his fingers through his short-cropped hair. Mordechai's chief household servant stepped forward quickly and took the long red cape from the tribune's shoulders. It was already dripping water from the bottom of the fabric.

"Take that in and spread it before the fire," Mordechai commanded. Levi took the helmet as well and started out. Mordechai turned back to Marcus. "I'm sorry. You should have come inside to wait."

"Your servant invited us into the courtyard," Marcus said, waving it away, "but—" He grinned briefly. "It is good for the soul to stand in the driving rain from time to time. It toughens a man. Actually, we had been there for only a short time. I was debating about coming back later when you arrived."

"Levi!"

The servant had disappeared around the corner at the end of the long hallway. A moment later, he reemerged. "Yes, Master?"

"As soon as you've seen to some food and wine for us, make sure that the tribune's men are brought in before the fire and given something to eat as well."

"Aye, Master. I have already sent Malachi to see to that, and to the tribune's horse as well."

"No, just wine for me and my men," Marcus called out. Then to Mordechai: "We can't stay long. We have to be back to the Antonia Fortress by nightfall."

Mordechai waved a hand at the servant, and Levi disappeared again.

"Come," Mordechai said, motioning toward the banquet hall. "There's a fire in there as well. The wine will be here shortly."

They walked together into the spacious room. One wall was nearly filled with a massive marble fireplace; its fire crackled in welcome. Both men moved over and stood beside it. Mordechai stretched forth his hands and rubbed them together, watching the Roman out of the corner of his eye. Marcus was a striking man, made all the more so by the officer's uniform. He was twenty-six, if Mordechai remembered right. Son of a rich and powerful family in Rome, he carried the air of confidence and competence that only that kind of life could breed. His face was tanned, his jaw line firm, his cleft chin smooth shaven. His eyes were a deep green and very compelling. Even though his hair was short, it still showed a slight curl around the base of his neck. He was thoroughly Roman in bearing and appearance. Why couldn't Miriam see what kind of man he was and the opportunity she was throwing away? Mordechai thought bitterly.

"So," Mordechai said after a moment, pushing that last disturbing thought aside, "this is a welcome surprise. I heard you had gone to Damascus."

"I returned last week." He hesitated, then looked squarely at Mordechai. "A surprise, yes. But welcome?" He shook his head. "Sorry. I fear I am the bearer of bad news."

"Oh?"

"Very bad."

"Don't tell me that Pilate has withdrawn permission for you to accompany me to Rome." He forced a quick laugh. "It would be a little awkward to hold a wedding without the bridegroom."

"Miriam is gone."

"Oh?" Mordechai said in surprise. "Gone where?"

"Gone!" Marcus said flatly. "Disappeared."

Mordechai rocked back. "*What?*"

"It's been a month now," Marcus said, shaking his head. "The letter from my father arrived day before yesterday. I came up from Caesarea immediately."

Mordechai moved over to one of the heavily padded chairs and sank down slowly. "Kidnapped?" he asked after a moment, his voice low.

Turning his back to the fire, Marcus shook his head. "Doubtful. Father waited three days. There was no demand for ransom. And the servant girl and her brother are gone as well. They would be of no value to a kidnapper."

Mordechai just stared at him, trying to force his mind to comprehend what he heard.

"A man came to Miriam's apartment one afternoon, claiming to be her cousin. The guards refused to let him see her."

"A cousin?"

"Yes. The guards said he spoke with a guttural accent. They guessed he was from one of the eastern provinces." He let that sink in. "A few days later, while Miriam and the other two were in the Roman Forum, a street vendor approached them. Just as the guards were moving in to make sure nothing was wrong, they were accosted by this same so-called 'cousin,' who cleverly delayed them for a minute or two. When they broke free, Miriam and the vendor and the others were gone."

"Gone?" He muttered something that Marcus missed. Then: "I thought you said the men we arranged to watch her were the very best." There was no mistaking the edge to his voice now.

"They were," Marcus said evenly. "They—"

There was a knock on the door; then it swung open. It was Levi holding a tray with a pitcher of wine and two silver goblets. He almost spoke, but at the look on Mordechai's face he moved quickly to the table, poured the wine, then backed out of the room as silently as he had come. Marcus left the fire and came and took one of the cups. He drank deeply before meeting Mordechai's gaze.

"My father has asked that I convey to you his deepest regrets. You entrusted this matter into his hands, and he has failed you. But the deed was done with much cunning. Father immediately sent soldiers to watch the port at Ostia, and also Puteoli, down the coast. He has launched a massive search in the city and round about."

He drank again, draining the cup, then set it down. "They're not going to find them, Mordechai. This was too cleverly done."

Mordechai was clearly shaken to the core. "Who?"

Marcus shook his head. "Come on, Mordechai. Do you really have to ask? This cousin was described as lean of build, thin-faced, with startlingly blue eyes and a dark beard."

Mordechai sat back slowly, jaw rigid, eyes narrowing into tiny slits. "Ezra?"

Marcus nodded. "Yes. I met him and his wife when they brought Miriam to Caesarea before your departure for Rome."

Mordechai had not touched his goblet. "But why—" He visibly jerked. "*Simeon!*"

Marcus refilled his cup but drank no more from it. "The guards said that the street vendor was dressed as an old man in rags, but they're sure that was a disguise. They said he was lithe and moved like a cat."

He shook his head slowly. It was Simeon. It had to be.

"The day we captured Ya'abin in the wilderness of Judea, I told Simeon that Miriam and I were to be wed." Marcus stopped as the color faded from Mordechai's face. "I did so because I wanted him to know that she was spoken for. I had a feeling that Simeon might have an interest in your daughter."

Mordechai was as pale and gray as the skies outside the window. He suddenly looked very old. He was a big man who had enjoyed a life of too much food and too little physical activity. His hair was thinning and seemed to have more gray than when Marcus last saw him. His beard, as always, was neatly trimmed. Heavy dark brows gave him a perpetual look of sternness. He bore power well, and Marcus knew from experience he was not afraid to wield it.

"My father is sparing no expense in trying to find them, and I expect additional word to arrive shortly. But I am satisfied in my mind. Miriam's gone and won't be back. Not to Rome."

The Sadducee only nodded. Marcus could see the veins in his neck throbbing, but his face had become expressionless. Then Mordechai rose to his feet. "Tell your father that I do not hold him accountable in this matter. He did all that any honorable man could have done."

Marcus inclined his head slightly. "He will be pleased to know that you feel that way."

"If you receive any further word, I would appreciate knowing of it."

"Of course." He set the cup down. "I have already told Pilate that our trip to Rome is no longer required. He said to convey his deepest regrets to you as well."

It was like Mordechai was off in another room. He nodded, but it was barely perceptible.

Marcus took a quick breath. "I have been asked by the governor to convey something else to you."

That brought the older man's head up. "Asked or commanded?" he said after a moment.

Marcus spread his hands blandly. "With Pilate, does it matter?"

"What is it?"

"The governor knows of your concerns about this Jesus and also of the Zealot threat in the Galilee."

"Yes?" The word came out slowly, and Marcus could see the wariness in Mordechai's eyes.

"Pilate appreciates your concerns for these matters and concurs fully—"

"But?" Mordechai asked bluntly.

"Since Simeon and Yehuda calmed the Zealot factions as a condition for their release from prison, things have been quiet up north. The governor is not fooled by that, of course, but for now he doesn't want anything disturbing the *status quo*." He tipped his head slightly. "You are familiar with that Latin phrase?"

"Of course," Mordechai snapped. "And what of this Jesus?"

"A definite concern to us all," came the reply, "and Pilate expects that the Great Council will carefully determine how best to solve the problem."

"But?" Mordechai said again, barely disguising his disgust.

"Pilate has other things on his mind now. He is anxious to finish the aqueduct. The legate from Syria is coming to Caesarea in a few months. There is much to be done in preparation. He asked that I make it clear that no action is to be taken without his express permission. Not against Jesus, not against the Zealots."

"How nice," came the soft reply. It was another stinging blow in a day of one blow after another. And then he had an additional thought. "And what are *you* going to do, Marcus?"

"Me? About what?"

Mordechai shot him a derisive look.

"About Miriam?" Marcus's mouth tightened. "Before any of this happened, I had about concluded that this marriage was not to be."

"So Pilate told you too," Mordechai said, almost relishing the words. "You are to do nothing as well."

Marcus only looked at him for a long moment, then turned. "I must be on my way. Thank you for the wine and the use of your fire."

IV

Two hours later, Mordechai still sat in the library, his face dark, his mood even blacker than the stormy night that gripped Jerusalem. His thoughts were cold, methodical, determined.

At one point, he wondered if he could still feel any love for Miriam after all she had done to him. But the answer came almost instantly. She was still his daughter, his only child. In actuality, the proof of his love was his growing determination to do whatever was required to save her from herself. And this time he wouldn't leave it in the hands of others.

There was a soft knock on the door. Mordechai looked up. "Yes."

Levi opened the door, and a man stepped inside. "This is Gedaliah of Motzah," Levi said. "The man you wanted." Then he shut the door behind him, leaving the two men alone.

Mordechai stood. "Did my servant tell you what it is I need?"

"Something in the Galilee, he says, carried out with the greatest of discretion."

"The greatest." Mordechai eyed the man carefully, taking his measure. "I need you to find out about a person. A woman. This could require you to be away from home for some time. Perhaps a month. Maybe more."

Gedaliah shrugged. "I am engaged in a project for another week. I could leave immediately thereafter. Would that be too late?"

Mordechai continued to look him up and down for a long moment. "Haste in this matter will only work to our detriment." He motioned to a chair. "Sit down."

CHAPTER NOTES

The information on the Great Sanhedrin in Jerusalem, including its organization and how it functioned under the Romans, is drawn from several sources (Hastings, pp. 827–28; Fallows, 3:1522–23; Buttrick, 4:214–18).

CHAPTER 2

MY SON, HEAR THE INSTRUCTION OF THY FATHER, AND FORSAKE
NOT THE LAW OF THY MOTHER: FOR THEY SHALL BE AN ORNAMENT
OF GRACE UNTO THY HEAD, AND CHAINS ABOUT THY NECK.

—*Proverbs 1:8–9*

I

CAPERNAUM
9 NOVEMBER, A.D. 31

David ben Joseph, the leading merchant of Capernaum, closed the heavy books, sat back, and put his hands behind his head. "Done," he said.

Deborah nodded. "Good." She paused. "And?" She had spent a lot of time entering and tallying various records, but the summary, the grand total of everything, her husband always did himself.

He stood and went to her, putting an arm around her. "It was a good year. As Malachi the prophet promised, the Lord has opened the windows of heaven in our behalf."

"As always," she said with an answering smile.

"The three gold talents we gave Simeon to give to Pilate took a hefty bite from our profits, of course, but even considering that, we did well. Very well."

"Shall we pay our tithes tomorrow then?"

"Yes. It shouldn't take long to calculate them now."

"And what about something extra for Ephraim?"

"Of course." He looked out the door and into the warehouse. They couldn't see Ephraim at the moment, but they could hear him in a far corner, helping unload casks filled with olives that had come in a few hours before.

"Good. He has become as much a partner as a son, hasn't he."

David nodded thoughtfully. "I could turn the whole thing over to him and not worry about it for a moment."

"And Leah?"

His eyes instantly softened at the thought of his only daughter. "Yes, of course. We shall add generously to her dowry." Pleasure filled his eyes. "She is so quick. Last week I showed her how to calculate the volume of olive oil in those huge clay jars. She asked one, maybe two questions, and then she had it."

"Life has been good to us, David." She leaned her head against him. The best thing that had ever happened to her was standing right there beside her. How had she, the bitter, orphaned daughter of a Zealot leader, ever come to marry such a gentle, good, and prosperous man? Deborah's father had been a leader in the rebellion that swept the Galilee thirty years before when the Romans tried to increase taxes. Her father, uncle, and several other family members had been caught and crucified. She, her mother, and her younger brother, Aaron, had fled to the hills. Before the winter was over, her mother had died of consumption. Left at fifteen to care for Aaron, Deborah had become a passionate supporter of the Zealot cause and a virulent enemy of all that was Roman. Then, less than a year later, David had somehow found her.

She looked up at him. He had turned forty-seven in the spring, two years older than she was. Those years were starting to show. His beard, short and carefully trimmed, was dark, but there was now gray around his temples. At the corner of his blue eyes, the lines were obvious. Good, she thought. They matched her own.

He looked down at her. "What are you thinking?"

He was a full hand-span taller than she was. She touched his cheek with her hand and went up on tiptoe. "Thank you," she whispered, and kissed him.

He looked surprised.

"Thank you for these last thirty years."

He smiled and kissed her back. "The best decision I ever made," he said. "I was thinking about that the other—"

A soft banging sound cut him off. They turned toward the door of the office. The sound had definitely come from the warehouse, but from somewhere in the back, not where Ephraim and his crew were working.

David cocked his head slightly. "That almost sounded like someone was—"

It came again, perhaps a little louder than before.

"—knocking." He gave Deborah a quick look, then started for the door. She followed him.

"Did you hear that?" It was Ephraim. He was coming down the main aisle of the warehouse toward them.

"It sounded like it came from the back door," David said, turning in that direction.

The back wall of their main warehouse in Capernaum butted up against the city wall. When the warehouse had been constructed, there had been a small, little-used gate through that wall. David had framed the opening and placed a heavy metal door in it, thinking they might have use for it from time to time. He might have saved himself the trouble. The door opened onto a footpath that was rarely used. In a year or two, undergrowth had covered that portion of the wall and all but obscured the gate. In fact, the only one who ever used it was . . .

Deborah had passed him, having broken into a half-run. "Simeon!"

Bam! Bam! Bam! This time the sound was loud, insistent.

"Coming!" David shouted. He and Ephraim hurried to keep up with Deborah.

Mother, father, and son came to a halt in front of the door, each a little breathless. David gave his wife one last quick look, then stepped forward and lifted the heavy bar. The metal hinges screeched softly in protest as he pulled the door open.

It was late afternoon and, though in shadow from the under-growth, the doorway was clearly illuminated. Deborah took one look, gave a squeal of joy, and launched herself through the doorway. "Simeon!"

II

"Leah! Leah!"

The cry brought Leah up sharply. She, along with several other young women from the village, were at the edge of the sea doing the week's washing. She stood as Joseph, her youngest brother who was eleven, came flying recklessly toward her.

She felt a sudden jab of fear. "What?"

He threw up his arms in a gesture of triumph. "Simeon's back!" he shouted.

She leaped to her feet. "Really? Does he have Miriam?"

Joseph motioned vigorously for her to follow. "Of course. Come! Come quickly."

III

In the small living quarters above the shop of Ezra the Sandal-maker, Lilly hummed softly to herself as she cleaned up after her simple midday meal. As she passed the small crib beside the table, she stopped, marveling once again at the miracle that lay before her. Little Miriam was asleep after nursing greedily half an hour before. She lay on her back, one hand across her chest, the other above her head, her long dark lashes softly touching her cheeks. Her chest rose and fell slightly as she breathed.

Lilly's eyes softened as she thought back to the day of her baptism, now almost a year and a half ago. Jesus had startled her when he gripped her hand in greeting. "I understand you are as Sarah and Hannah of old," he said. Then with a soft smile he had added, "Eventually, both received the wish of their hearts." Though her heart had leaped within her, she had not dared hope that he was telling her that her barrenness, like that of these two great women of old, would be taken away. But wonder of wonders, a few months later she began to sense a change in her body, a change she had never before experienced.

She felt tears well up behind her eyelids at the memory of the moment when she knew what those changes meant. She bowed her head and closed her eyes, offering once again a brief but profound prayer of thanks.

A noise brought her head up sharply. Her eyes flew open as she swung around. A narrow set of stairs at the back of the sandal shop provided access to their living quarters. Ezra had built a door at the bottom of those stairs to close them off from the shop. The leather hinges had a peculiar squeak to them whenever the door opened. It was her way of knowing when Ezra was on his way up.

But Ezra was gone. The sandal shop had been closed for over two months.

She heard the soft sound of sandals on stone. She could distinguish his step from every other. One hand flew to her mouth. "Ezra!" She reached the door just as it swung open.

Ezra stepped inside, smiling tiredly. "*Shalom*, Lilly."

IV

Ephraim, oldest son of David and Deborah, burst into the small courtyard at the front of his home. The gate slammed back against the wall with a sharp crack.

His firstborn was seated on a step near the house, playing with a doll. Esther gave a low cry and jumped, startled. "Papa!" Then she gave him a stern look. "You frightened me!"

Ephraim moved swiftly across to her. "I'm sorry, Esther. Where's Mama?"

Boaz stepped out of the shadows of an archway. "Mama is in garden, Papa." Boaz was three now, and starting to talk quite clearly.

"Has she got the baby with her?"

Esther shook her head. "Amasa is asleep, Papa. Me and Boaz are listening for him."

Ephraim nodded, not surprised. Their son, born just two weeks before Lilly's little girl, was barely over three months old. There were only two things Amasa cared about: eating and sleeping. If the first was taken care of, the second happened automatically. "Esther, I'll get the baby. You go get Mama." As she stood, he stepped to her and took her by the shoulders, bending down to look into her eyes. "Uncle Simeon's home, Esther. They just got back."

The dark eyes widened, first with shock, then with exultation. "Really!" The doll slipped from her hands, totally forgotten.

"Yes, and he has Miriam and Livia. They're safe."

Boaz trotted over. "Livie?" he exclaimed.

Ephraim laughed and swept him up in his arms. "Yes, Livia is here too. Come. Let's go get Mama and the baby. We're all going to meet at Grandma and Grandpa's house."

V

It was a joyous reunion that evening in the home of David ben Joseph. It was a clear night, but cool, with a brisk wind coming down off the Galilean highlands. It was cool enough that they met inside the house rather than staying out in the courtyard.

Only the immediate family were there, along with Ezra and Lilly. There would be time later for inviting friends and neighbors to welcome the travelers home. The two new mothers, Rachel and Lilly, nursed their babies and put them to bed, making everyone promise not to start the story until they returned. Esther and Boaz, with the wonderful adaptability of children, had already accepted the fact that Simeon was back, and Miriam and Livia with him. Sensing an extended period of grown-up talk, they went to a back room where they could play quietly and not disturb the adults. They invited Joseph to join them, but he would have none of it. Simeon was a hero to his youngest brother, and there was obviously a tale of adventure to be told.

They gave no thought to food. Not until everyone had heard the report. They placed the four travelers—Simeon, Ezra, Miriam, and Livia—in a row, then sat around them in a half circle.

"All right," David said, once everyone was settled, "start at the beginning. Tell us everything."

VI

When the final detail of the journey had been completed and the final question asked, everyone finally seemed to relax.

"There is no question but what the Lord went with you, Son," Deborah said to Simeon. And then to Miriam: "We are so sorry that your father has taken such a harsh stance. I can't believe he would make you a virtual prisoner in your own house."

Miriam just nodded. She couldn't bring herself to talk about it further. It was far too painful.

"I thought you'd have to fight with the guards," Joseph said, clearly disappointed. He had been hoping for an account of swordplay, open battles, and daring escape. Dressing up as an old candle vendor hardly stirred his imagination.

Simeon reached out, sensing that the disappointment in his youngest brother was real and not to be made light of. "Actually, Joseph, if we had attacked the guards something might have gone wrong, and we would have risked Miriam and Livia and Drusus getting free."

"You didn't tell us how you found Drusus," Leah said. "What happened?"

"Well," Miriam answered, "believe it or not, it was Marcus who found him and purchased his freedom. That was still when he thought he was going to marry me." She blushed a little. "Of course, I knew nothing about all of that."

Simeon pulled a face at the thought of Marcus. "Jesus told us to love our enemies. I guess what Marcus did for Drusus makes that a little easier to do."

"But where is he then?" Leah persisted.

Livia's face fell. "As you may remember, I am originally from Macedonia. I—"

"I thought you were from Alexandria," Joseph butted in.

She smiled. "I was in Egypt when Miriam's father purchased me from the slave markets—that's why everyone has called me Livia of Alexandria—but I grew up in Macedonia. Anyway, when we reached Athens, Drusus decided he wanted to stay. Being Greek, he felt like he had come home at last." She sighed. "I tried to tell him how wonderful it would be down here, that he would grow to love it, but I couldn't convince him."

"He's known little else besides slavery," Miriam added. "I tried to teach him some Aramaic so he could adjust to life here more quickly, but Athens was just too much for him to resist. There was a man at one of the inns where we stayed who was looking for an apprentice in the building trades. That was all it took. Drusus agreed immediately when the man made the offer." She didn't have to say how much that had hurt Livia. It showed on her face even now, several weeks after brother and sister had been forced to part again.

Livia forced a wan smile and looked at Leah. "Actually, I was hoping he would come so that he could get to know you, Leah. He is so gentle in spirit and sensitive, just as you are. I think you would have become great friends. And, of course, I really wanted him to meet and come to know Jesus."

"Perhaps in the future," Simeon said. "If the apprenticeship doesn't work out, we told him to write and let us know."

The room fell silent, each person lost in private thought. A sense of gratitude rested on all of them. Finally, Deborah stirred. "I'll bet you're famished. When did you last eat?"

Simeon quickly raised a hand. "Mother. There's one more thing before we finish."

She settled back. "What is it?"

"I—" He took a breath, glancing quickly at Miriam, who had gone very still. As he looked at her, he had to stop. At this moment, with her face radiant as she waited expectantly, she was more beautiful than he could ever remember. Her dark hair, still tousled from a day on the trail, now fell partway down her back. Her dark eyes shone with happiness. Her skin was bronzed by a month on the road. It made him a little dizzy to think how close he had come to losing her.

He turned and looked at his mother. "Well, we have something to tell you and father."

Deborah leaned forward. Her eyes flitted back and forth between her son and Miriam, seeing the looks passing between them.

"Go on," Ezra grinned, nudging Simeon. "You can do it."

Simeon stood and, to the surprise of his parents, Ephraim, and Leah, moved over to stand beside Miriam, laying a hand on her shoulder. She looked up, smiled, then took Simeon's hand.

Deborah's eyes widened perceptibly. Leah drew in a quick breath, staring at them both. Rachel's and Lilly's eyes were riveted on them too. David leaned forward, as intent on the pair as was his wife. Joseph, sensing that he was missing something, looked puzzled.

"Well," Simeon continued, "after the terrible blunder I made with Miriam that first night in Rome, I knew I had to do something to show that I was truly sorry for being such a fool. I thought of every possibility, but—" He stopped again, smiling down at Miriam.

"But he found the perfect way," Miriam said, her eyes shining.

Simeon drew his shoulders back, and he looked directly at his mother, then at his father. "I told Miriam that if she would forgive me, I would spend the rest of my life trying to make her happy."

Leah leaped to her feet, clapping her hands together. "You're betrothed?"

"Well," Simeon drawled, barely suppressing a grin himself, "not formally, but Miriam agreed that if Mother and Father approved, that's our next step."

"When?" Leah squealed.

They looked at each other, but Simeon shook his head when Miriam indicated he should answer. "No, you tell them."

She gave a sigh of deep happiness. "Well, in Rome I met this foul-smelling old man trying to sell me some Hanukkah candles. I immediately fell in love with him, so we decided it would only be fitting if we were betrothed the day before Hanukkah begins." Her face grew suddenly anxious. "If you don't think that is too soon. That's less than a month away."

"Too soon?" Deborah wanted to tip her head back and shout. "How could there be a more wonderful time for a betrothal than Hanukkah?"

VII

Livia sat on the floor watching with deep affection as Rachel's two children played with small wooden blocks made by their grandfather. Esther, sensing her gaze, looked at her with a questioning glance.

"It's been so busy since we returned, Esther, that I haven't had a chance to hold you. Will you come see me for a moment?"

Rachel's firstborn stood and came forward shyly. Her eyes were wide with pleasure, but her face was quite somber, which was so like her.

"You have grown so much since I last saw you," Livia said, putting her arms around her. "You're six now?"

She gave a hint of a smile. "Almost," she said. "Mama says in four more months."

"I think you're a full hand taller than when Miriam and I last saw you," Livia said. "And your hair is getting so long now. It's beautiful."

Finally the smile moved fully to Esther's face, and she snuggled in against Livia's body. "Thank you, Livia," she said demurely.

Boaz jumped up, bothered that he was being ignored. He ran to her side. "Livie! Livie!" He tugged at her sleeve.

Livia moved Esther to one side, picked Boaz up, and sat him on her lap. "Yes, Boaz. And you've grown too. You're not a little boy anymore."

"I know. I big now," he said proudly. "'Cause I three."

"I know you are. I think you've grown to be twice as big since I last saw you."

He grinned mightily. Esther was only a hand taller. He was twice as big! He settled back again, then looked up into Livia's face. "Did you see bears, Livie?"

She laughed aloud. She had forgotten his fascination with bears. "Actually, we did," she said.

Esther's eyes grew large. "Really?"

"Did they eat you?" Boaz cried in alarm.

"No," Livia said, struggling to maintain a straight face. "These were bears in cages. Some soldiers pulled them along in a victory parade. They captured them in a place called Germania."

Esther was as interested as her brother. "Real bears?" she asked.

Livia smiled at their interest. "Yes, real bears. They run wild in the forests there. And they had wolves, too."

"Oh," Boaz said, greatly impressed.

"What's this about wolves?" Rachel asked as she came into the room.

Livia laughed softly. "I was just telling Boaz about some of the things we saw in one of the victory parades in Rome."

"Livie saw bears, Mama!" Boaz said in awe.

"Did she really?" she said. She came over and took Boaz by the hand. "Come, children," she said affectionately. "The baby's asleep again. We need to help Granmama and Aunt Leah with supper."

VIII

10 November, a.d. 31

It was past midnight when Miriam came quietly down the stairway from the upper hallway. Her bare feet made only a whisper on the tile floor and stairs. She held her sandals in one hand. The temperature had dropped several degrees, even within the house, and she knew that though the courtyard was protected from any wind, it would not be a night for bare feet.

Moving carefully in the near-total darkness, she crossed the main entryway and slipped out the front door, shutting it carefully behind her. She looked around for a moment at the darkened courtyard, then sat down and pulled on her sandals. As she stood again, she drew her woolen shawl around her shoulders. It wasn't bitterly cold, but she was glad she had been wise enough to bring it.

For a moment, she considered staying in the courtyard, but as she looked up and saw the quarter moon and the brilliant night sky above her, she opted for the roof. She ran lightly up the stone stairs along the courtyard wall. The moon gave just enough light for her to see. She walked over to one of the benches and sat down, drawing her knees up beneath her.

She had barely settled herself when she heard the soft sound of footsteps. In surprise, she stood again just in time to see the dark shape of a head appear on the stairway.

"Miriam?"

"Leah? Is that you?"

"Yes." Simeon's sister finished her ascent and went over to her.

"What are you doing still up?"

Leah walked over and took a bench facing her. "I couldn't sleep. I heard your door open and you going down the hall. So why are *you* still awake?"

Miriam sat down again, directly across from Leah. How she loved this young woman who soon was to become her sister-in-law. Lovely of face and figure and so gentle and sweet in spirit, Leah was a delight. There was no giddiness in this one, no silliness like there was in so many of the girls Miriam had grown up with in Jerusalem. Already slightly taller than her mother, Leah had taken after her father. And that, Miriam thought, was a legacy anyone could be proud to claim.

Then she realized Leah was waiting for an answer. "I think this evening has had a little too much excitement for a girl like me."

Leah leaned forward and touched her hand briefly. "We are so happy for you and Simeon, Miriam. So happy."

"I'm glad. I've been worried about what your family would say."

Leah reared back, incredulous. "You're not serious."

"Yes, I am. I wasn't sure exactly how all of you would react to the news." She laughed softly. "I was pretty sure of *your* response, but in light of what's happened with my father, he could very likely make trouble for your family. And I come from such a different background than your family and—"

Leah stopped her with a merry laugh.

"What?"

"It's Simeon who should have been worrying. If he *hadn't* asked you, we would have sent him back to prison in Caesarea until he came to his senses."

"Really?" Miriam felt a rush of pleasure.

"Of course. Mother and I talked about it a lot after he left for

Rome. One day even Father surprised us by saying something about it."

"Like what?"

Leah shrugged. "I don't know, something like, 'Do you think Simeon knows what a wonderful woman Miriam is?'"

Miriam was deeply touched. "Coming from your father, that means a great deal to me."

"And Rachel told us that Esther has been praying for several months now that God would let Simeon know that you wanted to marry him."

"She knew that?" Miriam exclaimed.

Leah laughed softly. "Perhaps 'know' is too strong a word, but that is certainly what she wanted. You saw her reaction when Simeon told her."

"Yes. It brought tears to my eyes." She took a deep breath. "Oh, Leah, I am so happy."

"Me too. I still can't believe that you're going to be my sister."

"But this will only make it official. I feel like we've been sisters from the moment we first met."

"I know."

The younger woman leaned back, gazing up at the crescent moon low in the sky. "I can hardly wait for the betrothal. Do you really need to wait a full year after that before you are married? I know it is the traditional thing to do, but after all you've been through, do you think you want to wait that long?"

"Both Simeon and I need time to get ready," Miriam said. "After all, I don't have a life anymore. What few things I did own were all left behind in Rome. I had some money of my own, but Father confiscated all of that."

"I know, but—"

"And Simeon feels bad that he has been gone so much these past few years. He feels like he hasn't done his share in your family's business. Ephraim and your father have had to carry the majority of the load."

"I really liked what he proposed today, and I think Father did too. With him speaking fluent Latin, he can deal with Roman merchants in areas where neither Father nor Ephraim feel comfortable. He'll soon be pulling his full weight. No one is worried about that."

"I think so too," Miriam agreed, "but *soon*, not now. I'm just thankful that Ezra and Lilly are living here in Capernaum now. That gives Livia and me a place to live until we can get a place of our own. And—" She shook her head. "Anyway, we'll be fortunate if we are ready in a year. I have nothing for a dowry."

"Simeon doesn't care about that."

"But I do. I want to bring something to this marriage besides myself. If we can get ready before a year, we'll marry sooner, but we won't know that for several months."

"Papa is talking about having both you and Livia help us at the warehouse. That will help you with your dowry."

Miriam was genuinely surprised. "When did he say that?"

"He and Mama were talking about it when I went in to say good night. In Papa's mind, it's all settled. You are fluent in Latin, and Greek is Livia's native language. The rest of us can get along in either tongue, but more than half of the documents we have to deal with are in one or the other of those languages, and your fluency will be valuable. And if Simeon goes out and brings in more trade, well, you are going to earn your salary. Papa says he is going to talk with you in the morning about it."

A great relief washed over Miriam. Several times on their journey, Simeon had brushed aside her concerns about how she would live, saying his family would take care of that. But she didn't want to be put on a dole, and neither did Livia. That was important to them.

"I can read some Greek," Leah said, "but I would love to learn

Latin. I know only a few phrases now. I suggested something else our family could hire you to do: tutor me in Latin."

"I would love to. But not for hire." As if there was not enough joy already, now she and Livia might have a way to support themselves. Miriam reached out and took her hand. "It is so good to be back, Leah. It's like I've never been gone, like Rome was just a dream and now I've finally awakened again."

CHAPTER 3

THERE IS A FRIEND THAT STICKETH CLOSER THAN A BROTHER.

—*Proverbs 18:24*

I

ON THE SHORES OF THE SEA OF GALILEE, NEAR CAPERNAUM
11 NOVEMBER, A.D. 31

As Livia, Miriam, and Simeon hurried along behind Peter, Simeon looked up at the leaden skies. They would surely bring rain before midday, he thought. "Are you sure it's all right if we disturb him?" he asked the chief apostle. "If Jesus needs some time alone, we can see him later." Peter gave him a look like that of a parent to a child who doesn't listen well. "I told you. I know you asked to see him. But he specifically asked if he could see you this morning."

"Does he know all that has happened?" Miriam asked.

"Most of it," Peter said. "Deborah tells Anna, Anna tells me, I tell Jesus." He grinned. "It's a pretty efficient system, all in all. We were in Bethsaida yesterday," he went on, "but the first thing we heard on our return was the news that you were back and that your mission was successful. Jesus seemed very pleased."

"I'm glad he'll see us," Livia said. "It's been over a year since Miriam and I last heard him preach."

"Yes," the burly fisherman replied, "and much has happened in that time. On the other hand, nothing has changed. He still mingles with every class of society. He still teaches the people in simple but powerful words. He still drives the Pharisees mad because he won't give them the honor they so *richly* deserve." The last was said with faint irony.

He turned to Simeon. "And speaking of the Pharisees, does your Uncle Aaron know that you are back?"

"No. Mother and I were talking this morning about perhaps going to Sepphoris to see Aaron."

"I'm surprised he continues to live there," Peter said.

"Why is that?" Miriam asked.

"There's a strong Roman influence there," Simeon answered, knowing why Peter responded as he had. "The Romans call the city Diocaesarea. It's actually the administrative center for the Galilee. The garrison there is larger than the one here in Capernaum."

"That does seem strange for Aaron," Livia mused, "knowing how the Pharisees avoid any contact with the Gentiles."

Simeon's mouth twisted into a little frown. "That's one of the things that makes the Pharisees so remarkable." The sarcasm was heavy in his voice. "Any contact with a Gentile and Aaron will spend a full day purifying himself. But he is a very skilled potter, and besides the fact that Sepphoris is the largest city in the Galilee—and therefore the best possible market for his goods—the Romans particularly like what he produces. They are his best customers."

"Really?" Peter said in surprise. "So he deals with them?"

"Never directly, of course. He always uses others to actually work with the Romans, so he never comes in contact with them personally. But I guess the garrison is a very lucrative market for him. So he gets rich off the very people he despises."

He felt a sudden stab of shame. "On the other hand, when I was imprisoned in Caesarea, Aaron didn't hesitate for one minute to put himself at risk to speak up in my behalf. In all that has happened since my release, I've not had a chance to thank him properly for that. That's another reason for going to see him."

"I think the letter he sent had an influence on Pilate," Miriam broke in. "I was there the day the governor received the delegation of Pharisees that came to the palace. That night Pilate told us he was disgusted with their demands, but I think it worried him a little. The Pharisees hold a lot of sway with the people."

"That they do," Peter said. "That they do." He said nothing more. They were approaching a thick stand of willows that stretched for almost a quarter of a mile along the shoreline of the Sea of Galilee, just east of Capernaum. The path they were on looked like it went right up to the undergrowth, then abruptly stopped. But as they drew closer, Simeon saw in the gray light that there was an opening in the thicket.

As they reached it, Peter stopped for a moment. "This is a favorite spot for Jesus. He can usually come here and have some time to himself." Then he turned and moved forward.

The brush was thick, and they had to keep their hands up before their eyes, but in a moment it had opened up onto a narrow strip of shoreline that was completely sheltered from the land. In high-water years, this stretch of beach would probably be immersed, but in a normal year such as this the strip between willows and water was ten or fifteen feet wide. A few stones lay here and there on the ground, but mostly the beach held smooth sections of small gravel broken by numerous patches of low bunch grass. They immediately saw a figure squatting near the water's edge a few paces away.

At the sound of their footsteps, Jesus stood, turned, and lifted a hand in greeting. Peter motioned them forward. "You know the way out now," he said.

"You're not staying?" Simeon asked in surprise.

"Not unless he asks me to," the fisherman replied. "Anna needs some things done around the house."

As the apostle started back toward the path, Jesus called out to him. "Thank you, Peter."

Peter waved a hand and disappeared. With Simeon in the lead, the three of them moved forward. Jesus was dressed in a heavy woolen tunic. His beard was neatly trimmed and carefully combed. His eyes looked gray, almost black in the muted light, but they were warmly welcoming. His hair, also neatly cut, hung to his shoulders.

"*Shalom,* Master," Miriam said as she came up to him.

"And peace to you, Miriam of Jerusalem." He smiled at Livia. "And to you, Livia of Alexandria."

"Good morning, Master," Livia said.

He and Simeon clasped hands for a moment. "Welcome back," Jesus said. "It is good that your success brings these two safely back to us."

"We were fortunate," Simeon said. "God was with us."

Jesus nodded and motioned to a spot near the willows where the grass was fairly thick. "Let us sit for a time." As they settled themselves, Jesus looked at Miriam. "I understand that you are to be betrothed."

She colored slightly, but smiled. "Yes. The day before Hanukkah begins."

"A most appropriate time."

"If you are here in Capernaum then, we would be honored if you and the Twelve would join us for the ceremony," Simeon said.

"Deeply honored," Miriam added quickly.

"Thank you. Your family has done much to further the work of the kingdom, Simeon. And Peter, Andrew, James, and John are more like sons to your father than fishing partners. The honor would be ours."

"Wonderful," Simeon said.

Jesus turned to Livia. "I am told that your brother was found and rescued from slavery."

"Yes, for which we are deeply grateful. But he chose to remain among our own people in Achaia, which saddens me."

"But he is free."

"Yes," Livia said. "That is the most important thing."

Jesus nodded. "As the Psalmist says, 'God crowns us with his loving kindness and tender mercies.'"

Livia was struck by the aptness of the metaphor. "He certainly has in our case."

"Amen," Simeon said fervently.

Jesus turned back to Miriam. "And what of your father, Miriam?"

The gentleness in his voice caused tears to spring to her eyes. "He no longer claims me as his daughter. We have become completely estranged."

"And your mother is gone too, as I remember."

"Yes, she died when I was six."

"Peter tells me that the cause of this difficulty with your father is partly because you have chosen to follow after me."

Miriam's head dropped, but she nodded. "There were other things as well, but when I told him Livia and I had been baptized and that I fully accepted you as the Messiah, he went into a fury. It even seemed that he was going to strike me."

Jesus nodded slowly. "Do you remember what I said to you on that day you were baptized?"

She nodded instantly. "You said that those of our own households may become our enemies. Yes, I have thought of that many times. I thought I understood what you meant then, but it has since taken on a much deeper meaning. To my father, I am as one who is dead."

Sorrow filled his eyes. "It is a difficult thing, Miriam, but sadly such is sometimes the case. Yet you have chosen the better part."

Simeon started. Those were precisely the same words Jesus had said to Martha of Bethany when she wanted him to chastise her sister, Mary, for not helping her to serve supper. "Mary has chosen the better part." It was a superlative compliment, and he turned to see if Miriam had fully understood. She had. She was too overcome to speak, as the tears overflowed and ran down her cheeks.

Jesus half turned, looking out across the water, which was gray as slate from the overcast skies. "My doctrine angers the leaders of the Jews, both Pharisee and Sadducee. They say that I bear witness of myself and therefore my witness cannot be true. But they are like blind men leading others who are blind. And if the blind lead the blind, then both shall fall into a ditch."

The three said nothing, watching the face of the Master closely, realizing that he was doing what they had hoped he would do when they came, and that was to teach them.

"Be not afraid of them who kill the body but after that have no more that they can do to you. But I give you warning whom you shall fear. Fear him which, after he has killed you, has the power to thrust both body and soul down to hell."

Then he turned to Miriam again. "But even as I say these things unto you, remember that which I have said before. Your enemies may be those of your own household, but I have commanded you to love your enemies, to bless them that curse you, to do good to them who hate you, and to pray for them who despitefully use you and persecute you."

Miriam's lips were moist and her eyes wide as the import of his words sunk into her heart. This was her father he was speaking about. She bowed her head. "Yes, Lord, I understand."

"There is a way to find solace in such times as these," Jesus said. "Simeon has heard me teach this before, but now I say unto you and Livia, whosoever hears my sayings and *does* them, I will liken him unto a wise man who built his house upon a rock. And the rain descended, and the floods came, and the winds blew, and beat upon that house; and it fell not, for it was founded upon a rock.

"And every one that hears these sayings of mine, and does them not, shall be likened unto a foolish man, which built his house upon the sand. And the rain descended, and the floods came, and the winds blew, and beat upon that house; and it fell, and great was the fall of it."

He stopped, and for a moment the only sound was the quiet lapping of the water against the shore. Miriam's eyes were burning again. She felt like she had come through a terrible storm. She was battered and torn, but she was still standing. She shook her head. *More than just standing.* She had lost her father but found Simeon. She had left the traditions of the Sadducees and found the doctrine of truth. She no longer had a home in Jerusalem, but she had a better home here in the Galilee.

She bowed her head slightly. "Thank you, Master," she whispered. "You have heard the cries of my heart and brought me peace."

II

CAPERNAUM

12 NOVEMBER, A.D. 31

The morning had been unusual for Simeon. He had remembered that there were still eight Roman uniforms hidden among the stacks and bales and barrels, purchased in Damascus in one of his empty-headed schemes to free Yehuda from prison. He immediately took them out and burned them. They were a dangerous thing to have around, and Ephraim was glad to see them gone.

But if the morning had been out of the ordinary, the afternoon was profoundly mundane. Normally, one of the laborers at the warehouse cared for their horses and pack asses, but things were slow now that the harvest was in, and his father had not required his extra workers today. After working for a while in the warehouse, Simeon had volunteered to take care of the animals.

The women of the family were at Ezra's sandal shop, cleaning out a small storeroom in the back where Livia and Miriam would stay until the marriage took place. Ezra and Lilly and the baby lived above the shop itself, so Livia and Miriam would occupy the spare room on the ground floor.

It felt good to Simeon to be alone. Since his return with Miriam and the announcement of their betrothal, a steady stream of friends, neighbors, and fellow disciples had come to the house to offer congratulations. So he welcomed the opportunity to work in solitude, speaking softly to the animals as he forked hay into their mangers and dumped barley in the troughs.

He spread one last bucket of barley, patted the head of the mare as she moved forward to eat. As he stood there, he heard a noise. He backed out of the stall and saw a man standing in the doorway of the stable. Simeon recognized him instantly. "*Shalom*, Sextus Rubrius."

"*Shalom*, Simeon ben David."

Simeon moved forward and extended his hand. As they clasped arms in the Roman manner, Simeon realized that he had not seen this Roman centurion since the day of the capture of Moshe Ya'abin. That was more than five months before. "I thought you were in Jerusalem," Simeon said.

"I was until three days ago. The governor fears that with lessening tensions here in the Galilee, the garrisons in the north may be growing sloppy." Sextus shrugged in that enigmatic way he had that said a lot without revealing anything. "We arrived just last evening."

"Welcome back."

"Thank you. I'll be here a few days, then I'm going to Sepphoris, where our main garrison is. I'll probably stay there until spring, then transfer to Jerusalem in time for Passover and stay there until I return to Rome."

Simeon's eyebrows lifted. "Rome?"

"Yes. I will complete my thirty years of service in about eighteen months. I'll be going home again."

It occurred to Simeon that he knew very little about this Roman with whom he had become friends and allies. Was he married? Did he have children? He felt a little blush of shame that he had never taken the opportunity to inquire about such things. "Are things well with you then?" Simeon asked.

"Yes. And with you?"

"Well, thank you."

Sextus smiled openly. "That's what I understand. Congratulations. Your father told me this morning about your upcoming betrothal."

Simeon felt a sudden jab of fear. Had Marcus heard of Miriam's disappearance? Surely. And he would surely guess who had freed her and where she was going. Had he sent his most trusted officer up to learn if she was in Capernaum? But Simeon pushed the concerns away. Nothing amiss showed in the man's eyes, and Simeon trusted him deeply. Yes, he was a Roman legionnaire whose first duty—on pain of death—was always to Rome. But on the other hand, they had developed a relationship of mutual trust and respect. And it wasn't as though Miriam's return could be hidden. Word of her rescue and of the betrothal was all over the Galilee. Simeon's face relaxed into an easy grin. "I think my mother was beginning to despair that I would ever marry."

"I have met this Miriam briefly on one or two occasions, once in Jerusalem on the Temple Mount, and once when I came to your house to give your father the news of your arrest by Pilate. She is a lovely and gracious woman."

"Thank you."

"I must be off. I'm inspecting the garrison this morning." He smiled with obvious relish. "I need to put the fear of Zeus into a few legionnaires. They've gotten lazy in my absence."

Simeon smiled back. "I'd like to watch that."

"I—" Sextus was suddenly all business again and yet hesitant for some reason.

Simeon watched him steadily, knowing there was something more than amiable well wishes behind this visit.

Sextus cleared his throat. "I thought it might be of interest to you to know that there is a stranger in town."

Simeon set the bucket down slowly. "Oh?"

"They tell me he's a Judean, and from his accent, probably from Jerusalem or nearby."

A chill ran through Simeon's body. "And do you know what this stranger is doing in Capernaum?"

"Not for sure," Sextus answered. He seemed to be choosing his words carefully. "He has not come to us. In fact, he seems to be taking care to avoid us, but he's going about asking questions."

"What kind of questions?" Simeon already knew the answer.

Sextus gave a soft grunt. "First of all, he says he represents someone on the Great Sanhedrin in Jerusalem. He uses that as leverage to get people to talk to him. I am told that he is quietly asking questions about you and your family."

Mordechai! It had to be Mordechai. So it had begun. Simeon felt sick.

There was the tiniest hint of a smile behind the Roman eyes. "Of course, you know how these stubborn Galileans are about outsiders, especially those who come from Jerusalem."

That took Simeon aback somewhat. That was true. Galileans were normally open, warm, and hospitable, but Jerusalemites looked down their collective noses at their country cousins from the north. In fact, the rabbis had a saying: "Jerusalem is wheat, Galilee straw, beyond

Jordan, only chaff." He gave Sextus a wry look. "Are you saying he's not having much success?"

"Thus far, word is, he is getting very frustrated."

"Is there any chance this person was sent by some of your people?" Simeon asked.

"You mean Tribune Didius?" Sextus asked bluntly.

Simeon nodded. "Or Pilate."

"None." He almost said more, but duty held him back. Marcus Didius had spoken of Miriam's disappearance to Sextus, and it was obvious his commander harbored some deep resentment against Simeon. But he had also given the centurion specific orders to carry to the Galilean garrisons: If Miriam was there, she was to be left alone. The same for Simeon ben David.

Simeon's mind was working swiftly. "Would you characterize this man as potentially dangerous?"

"No," came the quick reply. "He is, however, well-financed. I'm told he is willing to pay handsomely for information. And that seems to be his primary mission at the moment: to gather information. I'm sure he will eventually learn what he wants to know. Money can do that, as you know."

Yes. That made sense. That's how Mordechai would begin. Simeon bobbed his head. "Once again I am in your debt, Sextus. Thank you."

Sextus Rubrius gave a curt nod. Among men of good will, debts were incurred, paid, incurred again. It was the way of life.

Sextus carried a scar in his leg. He had received it at the Joknean Pass when Moshe Ya'abin had broken his word and tried to massacre a full Roman cohort. When Sextus had gone down with an arrow in his leg, another bandit came at him, swinging a sword. It was Simeon's shaft out of the darkness that had saved him. On the other hand, though Simeon didn't know this, Sextus had repaid the debt some time later when he had essentially disobeyed an order to not throw ropes down to Simeon's band, trapped in a box canyon by a very angry

Moshe Ya'abin. If he hadn't, the Zealots would have been massacred. Strangely, instead of feeling released from his sense of obligation, Sextus actually felt a deeper bond with this man and his family.

He watched the younger man, marveling still that this lithe figure that moved like a cat and had the courage of a lion had voluntarily turned his back on the Zealot life. And yet, in a way, it wasn't surprising. Sextus himself had been powerfully influenced by the one known as Jesus of Nazareth. The presence of the man was impossible to ignore. A year before, when Sextus had been stationed in Capernaum, he had, on more than one occasion, stood near the edge of the crowds so he could listen to the man. And when his servant had taken deathly ill one day, Sextus had gone to his friend, David ben Joseph, to see if he would intervene with Jesus. There had been none of the expected disgust and revulsion in Jesus' eyes when he had stood face to face with a Roman. Instead, Jesus had spoken a word and the miracle had happened.

Sextus pulled out of his thoughts, straightening. "Well, best wishes to you and your bride-to-be. How soon after the betrothal will you be married?"

"Probably a year, as is customary," Simeon said, only half listening.

"You Jews," Sextus grunted, almost smiling. "Most Romans don't even wait for the betrothal to consummate the marriage," he said dryly. "Like I say. Strange customs."

Simeon chuckled at that. "Well, in my case, I've been running around the countryside for so long, it's time I came back and became part of the merchant business. Right now I couldn't support a rabbit, let alone a wife and family."

"Your father said you were going to see what you could do to expand your trade into such areas as Damascus, Jerash, and maybe even Alexandria."

"That's right. And we're going to start in Tiberias and try to expand our trade there significantly. Ephraim doesn't like to go there.

Leah loves the city, but she obviously can't go in and deal with suppliers. With my Latin, I could do a lot more than we've done. Tiberias is a huge market, less than ten miles away, and though we've had success there, we think we can do much more."

"Sounds like this is more than just a way to make a place for you in the family business."

"I hope so. I want to be able to finally pull my own weight and not leave it to Father and Ephraim to do all the work. Miriam and I figure it will take six months to a year to get enough money to start a home. If we can do it sooner than a full year, we'll marry then."

"I wish you and Miriam the best." Sextus turned and walked out of the stable again. But just as he exited into the sunlight, he stopped and looked back. "Not suggesting that you would have any reason to be concerned about this stranger, of course," he drawled softly. "But he is taking lodging at the Inn of the Golden Horn."

"I am deeply obliged to you, Sextus Rubrius," Simeon said, slapping his arm across his chest in the salute of a Roman soldier. Sextus nodded, saluted back, and then was gone.

CHAPTER NOTES

Jesus' quotation from the Psalmist is found in Psalm 103:4. The statement that "Mary has chosen the better part" comes from Luke 10:42. The King James Version says, "Mary hath chosen that good part"; the statement that "Mary has chosen the better part" is found in the New Revised Standard Version. Jesus' teachings on building one's house on a rock come from Matthew 7:21–29.

CHAPTER 4

HE THAT HATH EARS TO HEAR, LET HIM HEAR.

—*Matthew 11:15*

I

CAPERNAUM

15 NOVEMBER, A.D. 31

Livia, Miriam, Deborah, and Leah were standing inside the largest stall in Capernaum's main marketplace, a stall dedicated completely to women. The shop, open on the south end and made of thin wood partitions, was maybe five paces across and fifteen deep. But Deborah had been right in suggesting that this would be the best place for Livia and Miriam to refurbish the wardrobes they had left behind when they fled from Rome.

There were dozens of outer robes hanging from overhead ropes. Some were made of simple, but practical, light-brown homespun material; others were made of more expensive linen and embroidered with bright colors and intricate patterns. The inner "shirts," or light cotton underclothing worn beneath the main dress, were discreetly stacked on a table in the corner. From pegs on one wall hung shawls, headdresses, and veils—some of linen so fine it was like looking through slightly clouded water, others made of heavy dark wool with slits only for the eyes, nose, and mouth. These were used by the married women from the wandering tribes that ran sheep in the highlands of the Golan. Only their husbands were permitted to look upon their faces, so when they came into town, they wore these heavier veils.

Another long table carried various footwear, from winter boots that came halfway up the calves to soft sandals designed for wear inside the home. There were baskets of bracelets, headbands, and other jewelry. The shopkeeper, who knew Deborah well, hovered discreetly in the background, sensing that this could be a profitable day for him.

Livia stood to one side, near the entrance. She had made her purchases quickly—a habit borne of a lifetime of living simply—then stepped back, not wanting to rush Miriam.

Suddenly she lifted her head. Across the half-crowded marketplace, a moving figure had caught Livia's eye. He towered above the other people and was impossible to miss. She leaned forward, peering intently; then a smile broke across her face. She turned and called into the shop. "Miriam. Look. It's Yehuda."

All three of the other women turned, their eyes scanning across the square. At that moment, Yehuda saw them as well. He lifted a hand, waved, and called something to them.

Deborah turned to the shopkeeper, pointing to the growing pile on his counter. "Hold these," she said. "We'll be back."

"But of course."

The four of them moved outside as Yehuda reached them. "*Shalom*, Deborah," he boomed happily. "*Shalom*, young Leah."

"Good morning, Yehuda," Deborah said with a broad smile. "This is a most pleasant surprise."

The burly giant turned slightly. "And *shalom* to you, Miriam and Livia. So it is true. You're back."

Miriam reached out and took his hand warmly. "Yes. We arrived just a few days ago."

He looked at Deborah and clucked his tongue. "That lout of a son of yours didn't even bother to send me word."

"Actually," Miriam said, feeling a need to defend Simeon even though she knew Yehuda was only half serious, "we talked about going to Beth Neelah to see you, but then . . ." She bit her lip and dropped her eyes.

Deborah explained quickly about the stranger who had come to Capernaum and the decision by David and Simeon to go to Jerusalem.

Yehuda scowled. "I'm sorry, Miriam. Your father is not a man to take defeat lightly—but Simeon will know what to do."

"So how did you hear we were back?" Livia asked.

"But I didn't," he grumped, obviously playing to his audience. "I brought Shana down last night. As I'm sure you've heard, she and Samuel are now betrothed. Samuel has an aunt here—Zipporah, wife of Jebu the baker—who will help her with the wedding preparations." He pulled a face. "I don't understand why she thinks I can't do that for her."

As they laughed, he went on. "It's no place for a man, I'll tell you, not when they're getting ready for a wedding. So I went to the warehouse to see if there was any word of my old friend and companion, Simeon ben David. And lo, Ephraim tells me he's been back for several days."

Leah broke in, looking at her mother. "Do you need me? I'd love to see Shana again."

"Go," her mother said. "And invite her to take the midday meal with us. Yehuda is going to eat with us, aren't you." It wasn't a question.

He shook his head. "Is it any wonder that your brother is the way he is?" he said to Leah. "He gets his determination from his mother." Then he inclined his head to Deborah. "It would be an honor, as always."

Leah hurried away. "I'll see you at home then," she called over her shoulder.

"I asked Ephraim how Simeon did it," Yehuda said, speaking to Miriam and Livia again, pulling at his thick, dark beard as he spoke. "How he got you two out of Rome. But he told me I needed to hear the whole story from you two."

Deborah laid a hand on Miriam's shoulder. "You and Livia take Yehuda home where you can talk. I'll finish our purchases and also stop at the butcher and get some meat."

II

Yehuda pushed back and patted his stomach. "Wonderful, as always, Deborah. Thank you. I feel as though I have added the weight of a talent around my waist since entering through your door."

They laughed at that. There were just the four of them—Deborah, Livia, Miriam, and Yehuda. Leah had sent word that Shana was busy with wedding preparations and had invited Leah to eat with her family rather than taking time to go to Deborah's house.

Livia watched Yehuda with veiled interest. He was a big man, much taller than she was, and there was no softness in that body. His life as a vineyard keeper, coupled with his forays throughout the Galilee with his band of Zealots, kept him in fine physical shape. On the journey from Rome, Simeon had spoken more than once of his good friend and comrade. He described him as both fearless and fearsome—and yet surprisingly gentle by nature. Livia and Miriam had seen the fearless side of him two years earlier, in the highlands of Samaria. Miriam's father had been leading a delegation from the Sanhedrin to the Galilee to meet with Zealot leaders. One morning their camp had been attacked by Moshe Ya'abin. Suddenly two men had stridden into camp, outnumbered roughly ten to one, and convinced Ya'abin that they had an army hidden on the hillside. In actuality, it turned out that there had been only five of them. The bluff had worked though, and Ya'abin had surrendered.

That night she had seen the other side of Yehuda. The two Zealots took the delegation to the village of Beth Neelah in the hills around Nazareth. There Yehuda had shown himself to be a giant but tender-hearted bear, roaring with delight as the villagers welcomed him home, rumbling with pleasure as he greeted his sister, Shana, dancing like a sprite to the lilting sounds of a flute. Livia colored slightly as she remembered how he had come to her that night and persuaded her to dance with him. It had been a moment of great pleasure as they became as one, feet and hands moving in perfect time to the music.

"Come," Deborah said, interrupting Livia's thoughts. "It will turn cool once the sun goes down, but it is pleasant in the courtyard for now. We can talk out there."

Yehuda got to his feet. "I can't stay long. I told Zipporah to do what is necessary to have a proper wedding for Shana. Now I am not so sure that was wise. I'd better go see what they are up to." He shook his head. "And we have to leave in the morning again."

"So soon?" Deborah exclaimed.

"There is much to do back home," he said, pulling a face. "I only came down because Shana was getting worried about not having everything ready." He grinned at Livia and Miriam. "For some reason, she thinks I'm not sensitive to these things."

"Will you come back for supper?" Deborah said, clearly disappointed. "And Shana too. And if you need a place to stay while you're here, Simeon's room is open. And Shana can sleep with Leah."

He hesitated. "Well, Zipporah invited us to stay there, but her house is small. Let me speak with her and Shana. Thank you for the invitation."

"We'll come with you," Miriam said, getting to her feet as well.

She said it brightly, though she really wasn't looking forward to meeting Shana again. Simeon's betrothal to Yehuda's sister was in the past now, but it would still be a little awkward. But Miriam had seen in Livia's eyes the disappointment that Yehuda was leaving.

"Simeon will be sorry that he missed you," Deborah said, her disappointment showing too. "They just left three days ago, so we don't expect them back for a few more days."

"Well, you tell that little fox that he owes me a visit and an apology. I have a score to settle with him. And not just that he didn't come and tell me he was back."

"Oh?" Deborah and Miriam both said it together.

He looked directly at Livia as he spoke. "If I had known he was going to Rome to get the two of you, I would have gone with him. He needs a cuff across the back of the head for thinking he can run off and do something like that without me."

"You would have come?" Livia asked in soft surprise.

"Of course. I owe as much to you and Miriam as Simeon does. The ravens would have picked my bones clean long ago if you two hadn't come to Caesarea and devised that plan for getting us out of prison."

Now it was Deborah who felt like Simeon needed defending. "Simeon felt bad that he had already taken you away for almost a year to hunt Ya'abin. He didn't feel like he should ask you to leave again."

"Well, he was wrong, and a few knocks on the head are in order."

"I'll tell him that," Deborah chuckled. "Once he gets home again, I'll tell him he has to get up there and take his punishment."

Yehuda screwed his face into such a look of little boy anticipation that the women burst out laughing.

Suddenly Yehuda reared back. "Hey! Here's a thought. Miriam, why don't you and Livia and Leah come to Beth Neelah with Shana and me today? You, too, Deborah, if you can get free. And young Joseph, of course. Stay for a week or so; then Simeon and David can come up and bring you all home again."

That took them all by surprise. Miriam considered the idea for a moment, but then shook her head. "I would love to see Beth Neelah again, but I am to be betrothed in just about three weeks. There is much to do in that time to get ready."

"Perhaps after the betrothal," Deborah said, agreeing with Miriam's practical response.

His face fell. "What about Leah? It would do Shana so much good to have her spend a few days with us. There just aren't any other young women of her age in the village."

Deborah nodded almost immediately. "She is a big help to us, but it would be good for both of them. I think we could get by—as long as she is back in time for the betrothal."

Miriam's eyes turned to Livia, and she thought of one night on their journey from Rome. Simeon had begun talking about Yehuda. Curious, Livia had plied him with numerous questions. Miriam had even teased her about it later, delighted when Livia blushed to the roots of her hair. *Of course*, Miriam thought. "What about you, Livia?" Miriam finally said. "Why don't you go?"

She almost jumped in surprise. "Me?"

"Yes."

"But you said there is so much to do." Livia said it hesitantly, almost reluctantly. Behind Livia's words, Miriam thought she could hear the unspoken message, "Persuade me that it is all right if I accept."

"In addition to Deborah and me," Miriam rushed on, "we have Lilly and Rachel to help. We'll be fine."

"But—"

"A splendid idea," Yehuda boomed. "Splendid. Then Simeon will *have* to come up to see us." He looked at Miriam. "And you come with him."

"Of course. Simeon needs to see his Uncle Aaron, and Sepphoris is not that far from Beth Neelah." She turned to Livia. "What do you say?"

There was no question but what Livia was torn, but finally she shook her head. "I don't feel good about leaving all of you at such a busy time."

Yehuda immediately backed off, hiding his disappointment. "I understand."

"Come," said Miriam, deciding that she had pushed enough, "we'll at least go with you to find Shana."

III

"Look," Miriam exclaimed, pointing up ahead to a large crowd by the side of the road. "I wonder if Jesus is teaching."

"Oh," Livia said, "I'm sure he is. We know he's still here in Capernaum."

Yehuda slowed his step. "We can go another way."

Livia turned. "Let's stop for a moment and hear him."

The big man was instantly shaking his head. "Not for me, thank you."

"Come on, Yehuda," Miriam teased. "He's not going to baptize you."

"I really need to see if Shana needs help."

"Shana will do just fine with Leah and Zipporah," Miriam retorted. "Please. You have to remember that Livia and I have been away for over a year. We haven't had a chance to hear him much."

"That's fine," Yehuda said. "You go and hear him. I'll go find Shana." Then, suddenly, his eyes narrowed and a shrewd look came into them. "Tell you what," he said. "I'll come and listen to Jesus if Livia will come to Beth Neelah with me and Leah and Shana."

It was hard to tell who was more shocked by that offer, Livia or

Miriam or Deborah. The other two women turned to stare at Livia. Her cheeks colored deeply. "I—"

Miriam laughed aloud. "Livia, think about it. This may be our only chance to save this lost and wandering soul."

"But I—" She stopped again. There was no mistaking the look on her face. Though caught completely by surprise, she obviously wanted to accept the offer.

Deborah urged her as well. "It's your duty," she said solemnly, "no matter what the cost. There's no other way to bring the light of the gospel to this hardened and impenitent heart."

Yehuda grinned broadly. "There you go," he said. "What an opportunity."

Livia finally lowered her head, smiling shyly. "All right."

He sighed wearily. "What a man won't do to get a woman to change her mind. All right. Let's go."

As they started forward, Livia shot Miriam a questioning look. *Had she done the right thing?* Livia was a little surprised by her own boldness to say yes.

Miriam made sure Yehuda wasn't watching, then mouthed the words, "Yes! Good for you!"

IV

ON THE SHORES OF THE SEA OF GALILEE, NEAR CAPERNAUM

Jesus, as was often his custom, had chosen a place on a low hillside. That put him slightly higher than his listeners, which allowed his voice to carry to them better. The storms that had swept over the

Galilee the last two days were gone. A few scattered clouds remained, like ships drifting lazily across a perfectly blue sea, but the sun was warm and the air crystal clear after the rains.

Deborah stopped to talk to someone, while Miriam, Livia, and Yehuda found a place where they had a clear sight of Jesus and sat down. Jesus had seen them approaching and smiled briefly at them as they got settled.

Yehuda looked around. "It looks like everyone in Capernaum is here," he whispered.

"More than that," Miriam said. "If people know he's going to be teaching, they come from surrounding villages as well. Bethsaida, Magdala, Chorazin."

More people were hurrying to find a place, and Jesus waited until everyone was settled. Finally the people quieted, and he stepped forward and began. "I would speak a parable unto my disciples," Jesus began without preamble. "There was a certain rich man, which had a steward. And the same was accused unto him that he had wasted his goods."

Livia found herself nodding. Sometimes Jesus used concepts or words with which she wasn't familiar, Aramaic not being her native language, but this was clear to her. A steward was a person who had responsibility for something but was not the owner; he was one the master would trust to run his affairs, like a chief servant. He often even controlled much of his master's finances.

"And he called the steward unto him," Jesus went on, "and said unto him, 'How is it that I hear this report of you? Give me an account of your stewardship, for you may no longer be my steward.' Then the steward said within himself, 'What shall I do? for my lord will take away from me the stewardship. I cannot dig. To beg I am ashamed.'"

"The man is obviously guilty as charged," Yehuda growled, surprised at the twist the story had just taken.

"And," Jesus went on, "then the steward said, 'I am resolved what to do so that, when I am put out of the stewardship, the people I have served may receive me into their houses.' So he called his lord's debtors unto him, and said unto the first, 'How much do you owe unto my lord?' And the man said, 'An hundred measures of oil.' And the steward said unto him, 'Take your bill. Sit down quickly and write fifty and I will endorse it.'

"Then the steward said to another man," Jesus continued, "'And how much do you owe?' And the man said, 'An hundred measures of wheat.' And the steward said unto him, 'Take thy bill and write fourscore, and I shall validate it.'"

"The man is an outright thief," Yehuda rumbled. Around them other people were shaking their heads. This was a strange story to come from the Master's lips.

Jesus waited for a moment to let what he had said sink in. Then he calmly went on. "And the lord commended the unjust steward because he had done wisely."

Miriam rocked back a little. What was that?

Yehuda was staring at Jesus in equal disbelief.

Jesus went on, raising his voice to be heard over the murmuring. "The children of this world are in their generation wiser than the children of light. And so I say unto you, make to yourselves friends of the mammon of unrighteousness that, when you fail, they may receive you into everlasting habitations. If therefore you have not been faithful in the handling of unrighteous mammon, who will commit to your trust the true riches?"

Jesus stopped, partly because the buzz of sound was swelling quickly.

"Did you hear what I just heard?" Yehuda asked the two women. "Jesus is praising this thief?"

Miriam didn't know what to say. It certainly sounded like that to her, and yet surely the Master was not commending dishonesty. To her great relief, a movement caught her eye, and she turned to see Deborah coming to join them.

"Did you hear that?" Miriam asked, as Deborah sat down beside them.

She nodded, unperturbed. "I did."

"Well?" Yehuda demanded. "Is this what your Jesus teaches?"

Deborah looked to where Jesus was standing. He was simply waiting, comfortable with giving the people time to talk about what he had just said. "David and I heard him give this parable to a small group once before," she said. "He didn't commend the steward's dishonesty, Yehuda. He commended his shrewdness. And remember, it wasn't Jesus who praised the man, it was the master in the story, the same who had been cheated."

"What is the difference?" Yehuda demanded.

Before Deborah could answer, a man stood up near the front of the group. His long, ornate robes instantly marked him as a Pharisee. He was waving a hand, trying to get Jesus' attention. "Let's talk after," Deborah said, and they turned to watch.

When the Pharisee spoke, his voice was sharp and challenging. "Master, you speak folly. You speak as though accumulating any worldly goods is evil. A man has to seek the things of the world at least to some degree or he cannot care for his family. He cannot purchase a home or food and clothes."

"As if that matters to you," Deborah murmured.

"Who is that?" Miriam asked, surprised by her future mother-in-law's cold reaction.

"His name is Amram," Deborah said, speaking low. "He is a wealthy Pharisee who has been a vocal critic of Jesus. David says if ever there was a covetous man, a man who loves riches, it's Amram. And knowing how rare it is for your father to speak negatively of anyone, that says quite a bit."

Jesus was looking at Amram, and he wasn't smiling. "You and

others of the Pharisees may try to justify yourselves before men, but God knows your hearts. That which is highly esteemed among men is an abomination in the sight of God."

"Abomination! How dare you?" Amram shouted. "You cannot know what is in our hearts."

Jesus seemed completely unperturbed by the outburst. He turned away from Amram to address the crowd again. "There was a certain rich man, which was clothed in purple and fine linen and fared sumptuously every day."

Another parable, Livia thought. This wasn't making it any easier for Yehuda.

"And there was a certain beggar named Lazarus, which was laid at his gate. He was full of sores and longed to be fed, even if it were only the crumbs which fell from the rich man's table. Moreover, the dogs would come and lick his sores."

Livia pulled a face. What a grim picture! She stole a look at Yehuda and was pleased to see that he was listening carefully.

"And it came to pass that the beggar died and was carried by the angels into Abraham's bosom."

Livia shot Miriam a look. Abraham's bosom? What an odd expression.

"I'll explain in a minute," Miriam whispered.

"And the rich man also died," Jesus continued, "and in hell he lifted up his eyes, being tormented. And he saw Abraham afar off, and Lazarus was in his bosom. And the rich man cried, 'Father Abraham, have mercy on me. Send Lazarus that he may dip the tip of his finger in water and cool my tongue, for I am tormented in this flame.'

"But Abraham said, 'Son, remember that in your lifetime you received the good things of life, but Lazarus received evil things. But now, he is comforted and you are tormented.'"

There was not a sound. The simple tale had been drawn. In just a few words a dramatic image had been evoked, and every person could clearly visualize what Jesus was saying.

"'And besides that,' Abraham continued, 'there is a great gulf fixed between us, so that they which would pass from here to where you are, cannot. Neither can they who are with you pass to us.'

"Then the rich man said, 'Then I pray thee, therefore, Father Abraham, that you would send Lazarus to my father's house, for I have five brothers there. Send Lazarus to warn them, lest they also come into this place of torment.'"

Jesus slowly turned back so that he was facing Amram, who was still on his feet. "And Abraham said unto the rich man, 'They have Moses and the prophets. Let them hear them.' And the rich man said, 'Nay, Father Abraham, that will not change them. But if one went unto them from the dead, they would repent.'"

Jesus paused. Amram shrank back a little before that unflinching gaze. "And," Jesus concluded, emphasizing the words with great care, "And Abraham said to him, 'If they hear not Moses and the prophets, neither will they be persuaded even if one rose from the dead.'"

V

"All right, Deborah," Yehuda said, "let's hear you explain why dishonesty is commended." He said it with a teasing smile, but his eyes clearly indicated he was serious about the question. Jesus had finished, and the crowd was breaking up.

"And I have another question," Livia said, before Deborah could respond. "What is this about Abraham's bosom?"

"That one is easy," Yehuda said. "I'll answer that one for you, if Deborah can answer the other one for me."

Deborah smiled. "You first."

Yehuda grew more serious. "To be in Abraham's bosom is our way of saying that when you die and enter the life after this, you will be in paradise."

"Why?" Livia asked.

"Well, first, you know how Abraham is revered as the father of the faithful."

"Yes, I am familiar with that."

"So when he died he clearly went to paradise. To be in Abraham's bosom means that you are in paradise too."

"Oh," Livia said. "So the rich man ends up in hell—what in Greek we call *Hades*—but the beggar is in paradise."

"Just so," Yehuda said enthusiastically. "An image which I find quite pleasing, being a poor man myself." He turned to Deborah. "But the first parable is very troubling."

Deborah sighed. "Yes, the first story. It does seem a little strange, but here are some thoughts David and I had as Jesus told it before." She smiled briefly. "I wish David were here. He sees so much more than I do when Jesus teaches."

"I find you also do very well, Deborah," Miriam said. "So tell us what you're thinking. To be honest, the first story caught me by surprise too."

"Well, for one thing," Deborah said, "the two stories are closely tied together."

"How?" Yehuda shot right back.

"Think about the unjust steward for a minute," Deborah said. "Why did he go to those two debtors and offer to falsify the accounts?"

"Because he was a crook," Yehuda said bluntly. "And Jesus commended him for it."

"No," she said patiently. "First of all, Jesus said that the man's master commended him. And, as I said, he didn't commend his dishonesty, he commended his shrewdness because he had done wisely."

"I think you're splitting hairs," Yehuda grunted.

"But that was not really my question," Deborah said, ignoring his response. "Why did the steward go to those two men? Why did he choose *them* over others?"

Livia began to nod slowly. "He must have known that they would agree to the deceit."

"Yes, and what else?"

Miriam finally saw what she thought Deborah was after. "Because he hoped that once he lost his position—which he clearly knew was going to happen—these men would help him."

Deborah turned and gave Yehuda a knowing look. "Do you agree?"

His eyes were thoughtful. "Yes, I see that."

"What was the steward most afraid of when he thought he might lose his position with the Master?"

"He did not want to be poor," Yehuda answered without hesitation. "He was too proud to beg and didn't want to dirty his soft white hands digging ditches."

"Very good. Or to put it another way, he was worried about his future, right?"

Both Miriam and Livia were nodding.

"So let's not talk about his honesty for a moment. Let's talk about how shrewd he was in trying to prepare for his future. He made lasting friends with these men by offering them gain. Would you say he 'did wisely' as Jesus suggested?"

"I suppose," Yehuda said, half grudgingly, half intrigued.

"Now, think for a moment what Jesus taught us after the story was over. What did he say?"

Miriam answered first. "He said that the children of the world are wiser than the children of light."

"And," Livia added, "that we should make friends for ourselves with the mammon of unrighteousness. That seemed really strange to me."

Deborah sat back, trying to think how best to say it. "That's right.

Mammon is another word for worldly riches. So think for a moment about the rich man and Lazarus. What if the rich man had not ignored Lazarus every time he went in and out of his house? What if he had fed him and given him clothes? Or taken him to a physician to cure his sores? Would that have made a difference in how the parable was told, do you think?"

"Of course," Yehuda said.

"When the rich man died, he would have had friends in the next world," she said slowly, letting her words sink in. "Lazarus would have spoken up in the rich man's behalf. Abraham would have been pleased with what he had done."

Livia's mouth had opened slightly as the meaning became clear. "And thus the rich man would have used his wealth to prepare for his future."

Deborah gave her a warm smile. "Which would be a very shrewd and wise move, don't you think? When Jesus said that we should make friends with mammon, I think he was saying that we should make friends for ourselves by *using* righteously the mammon that is so often used unrighteously. We can help people here who will be our friends after death, people who will speak in our behalf."

Miriam saw it too. She looked at Yehuda to see if he understood it as well. She tried to make it even clearer. "The steward, who was a child of the world, was wise enough to try to prepare for his future. We, the covenant people, who are supposedly the children of light, need to be concerned about preparing for what lies in our future, especially what will happen to us after we die."

The three women watched Yehuda closely. He didn't want to, but he did have to admit that it now made sense. And he could see how the two stories were interconnected.

"That's why Amram was angry," Deborah pointed out. "He understood exactly what Jesus was saying. He is a Pharisee, who more than all others claim that God is first in their lives. But his whole focus is on accumulating worldly wealth. So he is not as wise as the unjust steward. He is not using his wealth to prepare for eternity."

Yehuda blew out his breath. "All right, I see it. And it does make sense. But why does Jesus have to make things so obscure? I'm a simple, unlearned man. I like it better when people just come right out and say what they mean."

Deborah laughed and punched him softly on the arm. "First of all, I think his message was very clear. Second, Yehuda of Beth Neelah, if you are a simple, unlearned man," she laughed, "then we are but babes still in swaddling clothes. You are as shrewd and cunning as that unjust steward."

He winced, feigning great pain. "How can you say such a thing?" he yelped.

"Because you got Livia to agree to come to Beth Neelah with you and Leah and Shana," she said, poking him again. "Now that's about as shrewd as it comes."

Chapter Notes

The parable of the unjust steward is found in Luke 16, as is the parable of Lazarus and the rich man (Luke 16:1–31). The latter story is often referred to as "Lazarus and Dives," *dives* being the Latin word meaning riches.

Of the expression, "Abraham's bosom," Fallows explains: "There was no name which conveyed to the Jews the same associations as that of Abraham. As undoubtedly he was in the highest state of felicity of which departed spirits are capable, 'to be with Abraham' implied the enjoyment of the same felicity; and 'to be in Abraham's bosom' meant to be in repose and happiness with him. The latter phrase is obviously derived from the custom of sitting or reclining at table which prevailed among the Jews in and before the time of Christ. By this arrangement, the head of one person was necessarily brought almost into the bosom of the one who sat above him. . . . The guests were so arranged that the most favored were placed so as to bring them into that situation with respect to the host" (Fallows, 1:28).

CHAPTER 5

AND IN TERROR THEY DEEMED THE THINGS WHICH THEY SAW,

TO BE WORSE THAN THAT UNSEEN APPEARANCE.

—*Wisdom of Solomon 17:6*

I

JERUSALEM, UPPER CITY

16 NOVEMBER, A.D. 31

Mordechai ben Uzziel was glad he had decided to walk home from the house of Caiaphas, high priest of Jerusalem. The feast had been long, sumptuous, and raucous. He had drunk too much wine, and his knees felt a little wobbly when he got up from the table. But the cold, crisp air had cleared his brain, and he felt much better as he approached the gate to his courtyard. There was a perfect half moon, and he could see some distance along the street in both directions. He hoped his bearers had told Levi he was coming so someone would be ready at the gate to let him in.

As he approached the door and reached for the thick brass knocker, to his surprise the door abruptly swung open. "Good evening, Master."

"Levi! You startled me."

"Sorry, sire. I had come to secure the gate and looked out and saw you coming. So I waited."

Mordechai ignored the sudden pounding in his heart. "Thank you."

"You have company, sire."

Mordechai's eyes narrowed. "At this hour?"

"He's been here for some time, Master."

He swore under his breath.

"He wouldn't give his name," Levi rushed on. "Said he has a matter of important business with you." He lowered his voice. "A Galilean, judging from his accent. He's very nicely dressed, sire, and he's carrying a considerable sum of money. I hefted the bag onto the table for him, and it must contain several hundred shekels."

That piqued Mordechai's interest and explained why Levi had been willing to let a stranger into the house.

Inside, Mordechai allowed his steward to remove his cape and winter boots. He held up one foot, then another, and Levi put on the slippers made of calf's leather and soft wool. Then he started toward the library.

"Would you need anything of me further, sire?"

"Not unless I call you." Then he considered that. "But don't go to bed until I say. I'm not sure what this man wants."

"Of course, Master. I shall be in my room."

Mordechai opened the door and went inside the large room that served as his library and office at home. The man seated on the marble bench stood immediately. Mordechai noted the leather bag on the table. It was fat and round.

"*Erev tov,*" the stranger said.

"*Erev tov,*" Mordechai answered, with a flash of anger. At this hour—it was well into the second watch of the night—*Lailah tov,* or good night, was a more appropriate greeting than "good evening." But he pushed the thought away as he studied the man's face. He looked vaguely familiar, and yet Mordechai knew he had never met him before. He had an excellent memory for faces. The man was about his own age, solidly built, with little sign of fat. His hair and short beard were sprinkled with gray, and he had clear blue eyes. It was the eyes that looked familiar to him. But Levi had been right. His robes and outer cloak bespoke a man of considerable means.

"My servant tells me you have business with me. Do I know you?"

The man gave a quick smile. "Well, yes and no." He withdrew a rolled parchment from his robe. "This will explain everything, I believe."

Definitely from the Galilee, Mordechai noted. The accent was unmistakable.

The man stepped forward and handed the roll to Mordechai. "If you don't mind," he went on, as Mordechai took it and examined the wax seal, "I've left two items in your courtyard that will be important in our discussion. May I have your permission to retrieve them while you read the document?"

"I can have my servant—"

"No." He smiled enigmatically. "In this case, I think it better if I bring them in myself." Without waiting for an answer, he turned and left the room.

Mordechai watched him go, still puzzled by what was proving to be a highly unusual meeting. He moved behind the table and sat down. As he started to break the wax seal, his eye fell again on the large brown bag resting in front of him. He reached across and hefted it, grunting at the unexpected weight. Levi was too conservative. It felt more like a thousand shekels—not an insignificant amount, even to a man as wealthy as Mordechai ben Uzziel. His curiosity only deepened as he broke the seal, unrolled the scroll, and smoothed it on the table.

To his surprise, the document was written in elaborate classical lettering, very formal, very impressive. Then his brow furrowed as he saw the title:

KETUBAH

Mordechai's mouth pulled down. The word meant "marriage contract" or "marriage license." Its primary purpose was to record the groom's financial and other obligations to his bride. In a world where a man could divorce his wife without her consent, this gave the woman a guarantee of some financial security in the case of divorce or the death of her husband.

But why would this man be handing him a *ketubah?* It only heightened his sense of strangeness and a growing concern that something was not right. He leaned forward and began to read.

Be it known to all men everywhere, through the formal declarations of this ketubah, which are duly witnessed by those whose signatures appear below, that I, Simeon ben David ben Joseph, of Capernaum . . .

Mordechai visibly jerked. *Simeon ben David!* Instantly his eyes narrowed, and his face darkened. *He* had something to do with this?

. . . That I, Simeon ben David ben Joseph . . .

His head came up again, and he stared at the door. Simeon, son of David, son of Joseph. *David ben Joseph!* No wonder the man looked familiar! It was Simeon's father. The resemblance was not striking, but it was there. And the eyes. How could he have missed that? They were Simeon's eyes. He should have seen that at once.

Anger exploded inside him. He started to raise his voice to shout for Levi, but then his eyes were drawn downward again.

. . . I, Simeon ben David ben Joseph, of Capernaum, do hereby declare before the Holy One of Israel, blessed be his name, and to all the world, my intentions to betroth myself on the 5ᵗʰ day of Tevet (in the Latin calendar, also known as the seventh day of December), to Miriam bat Mordechai ben Uzziel, formerly of Jerusalem, more recently of the city of Rome . . .

He shot to his feet, nearly overturning the table. *Miriam! Simeon and Miriam!* He gave a strangled cry of fury and started for the door.

Then he stopped, remembering the short Roman sword he kept hidden in a lower cabinet behind the table. First that, and then he would rouse the servants.

Before he reached the table, however, the sound of the door opening spun him around. "*You!*" he spat in utter disgust.

Simeon smiled thinly. "But surely you were expecting me, Mordechai ben Uzziel." The tone was calm, which only added to the sense of being mocked.

Mordechai swore, reaching for the cord that would ring the bell in Levi's quarters.

"I wouldn't do that," Simeon said quietly.

Though he didn't move, Mordechai's hand dropped, and he stepped back quickly. "Where is my daughter?"

"In Capernaum. She is staying with your cousin Lilly and her husband, Ezra. As you already know, I'm sure, they live in Capernaum now. A member of their family drove them out of Joppa when they chose to stand by his daughter in a time of need."

His eyes never left Simeon's face. "So it *was* you that kidnapped her."

Simeon's eyes went cold. "No, Mordechai, you are the one who took Miriam prisoner. Ezra and I only freed her."

"I want her back!"

"She's your daughter, not a dog or a sheep that you've lost."

The rage almost blinded Mordechai. He took a step toward the other man, fists clenching and unclenching. "I'll have you—" He stopped. Two other figures had appeared at the door.

David ben Joseph came into the room. He held a man by the elbow, a man whose hands were tightly bound with cords. There was also a rope around his ankles, short enough that he had to hobble to move forward.

Mordechai drew in a sharp breath when he saw who it was . . .

Gedaliah of Motzah, the man he had sent to the Galilee to learn if Miriam was there.

Simeon turned and in two quick movements slashed the man's ropes. "Go," he commanded. "You can settle with your employer later."

The man rubbed his hands, looking back and forth between Simeon and Mordechai. "It would not be wise to show your face in Capernaum again," Simeon murmured. "Not for any reason. Not for a very long time."

Gedaliah swallowed hard, then looked at Mordechai. Mordechai jerked his head, and the man backed out the door. A moment later they heard the front door open and shut again, and the man was gone. David pulled the door to the library shut and then came forward to stand beside his son. "Did you have a chance to examine the document?" he asked amiably.

Mordechai strode to the table and picked it up. "Is this your idea of a joke? You want *my* permission to marry my daughter?"

Simeon kept his voice even. "We are not here seeking permission. Miriam and I are to be betrothed in about three weeks. She wanted you to know that, and we wanted you to have the *ketubah* so you would know that all things will be done in order."

"I forbid it. I'll have the betrothal annulled."

David shook his head. "Miriam is of age. Your permission, while desirable, is not legally required. Should the details be made known of how you treated her in Rome—seizing her mail, restricting her freedom against her will, and even confiscating those assets that are legally hers—I think even the Great Council would condemn your actions and give her permission to pursue her own way in life now. The Law is quite clear on such issues."

"You dare to think you could take action against me in my own council?" he roared.

"It is not *your* council, Mordechai," Simeon shot back. "It is the council of the people. But I fear that you and others like you have forgotten that long before now."

Mordechai flung the scroll aside. "I will not sign it. Now get out!"

Simeon bent down and picked up the parchment, rolling it up again and tossing it on the table. "We have a duplicate *ketubah* in Capernaum. All the necessary signatures have been secured. This was a courtesy only, in keeping with your daughter's desire not to do something without your knowledge."

"I have no daughter. The daughter I once had is dead to me."

"As you will," Simeon answered.

"Get out," Mordechai said coldly, "or I will call for help."

"We brought the dowry as specified in the *ketubah*. One thousand shekels. A most generous dowry, considering the circumstances." Simeon glanced at the bag on the table. "In keeping with the statutes, should something ever happen to dissolve the marriage, Miriam is entitled to the full amount back from you, along with any income derived from investing the same."

Mordechai swung around. With one vicious sweep of his arm, he sent the heavy bag off the table. It hit the ground with a tremendous thud. The leather split down the sides, and silver shekels skittered across the marble floor in every direction. "There is your dowry," he raged, panting heavily. "Now get out of my house!"

Simeon didn't even glance down. "I hope you mean what you say, Mordechai ben Uzziel." His voice was like the whisper of steel across silk. "If Miriam is dead to you, then you will make no more effort to interfere with her life."

"Are you threatening me?" he thundered.

It was David who answered. "We would call your attention to the law of the land, as well as the law of our God. A man not only has the right but the solemn duty to protect and care for his family. Miriam will soon be a part of our family. As her betrothed husband, Simeon would be less than a man if he did not deal with any possible threat to his wife. As Miriam's father-in-law, my rights now become equal to yours. My fortunes are nothing compared to yours, but know this: I would spend every shekel I own and can borrow to bring you to answer to the law."

"I'll have your heads for this," Mordechai snarled, so livid he could hardly speak.

Simeon gave a soft, almost sad laugh, which only made it all the more menacing. "That is exactly what Moshe Ya'abin once said to me."

Mordechai's mouth opened and then shut again. The fire within him was burning white hot, but the mere mention of that name cut off the next outburst even as it formed on his lips. And in the back of his mind, he also knew that David was right. With all of his influence, he might not be able to win this one. In some cultures, women had no rights before the law. Not so for Judaism.

Simeon moved forward one step, and in spite of himself, Mordechai shrank back. "It was over a year ago, Mordechai, that you were under threat of death from Moshe Ya'abin. As you know, I was freed by the governor to eliminate that threat to you and to him." He sighed wearily. "I don't believe in empty threats, Mordechai. And I want nothing more than to live in peace. But even though it took us almost one full year, eventually Moshe Ya'abin was brought to justice. He now lies in the grave because he made the mistake of thinking he was beyond the laws of God and the reach of man."

Simeon's voice grew very quiet. "Should something happen to Miriam, or even threaten her peace and safety, I would consider myself under obligation to see that justice is done."

"Get out!"

"Make no mistake," Simeon said with cool deliberation. "This is done with here and now, Mordechai, or you shall never know peace again."

Something in the combination of Simeon's eyes and the coldness

of his voice sent a shiver through Mordechai. After the capture of
Ya'abin, Marcus Didius had given Mordechai a full report of how
Simeon had done it. It was a brilliant campaign. Flawless. Frightening
in its implacability. He swallowed quickly, suddenly remembering
Pilate's warning to stay out of the Galilee and to put any thoughts of
retaliation aside. His eyes dropped, and he knew that for now he had
lost. But time would pass, and things would change.

Simeon watched the older man, struck suddenly by the awareness
that in a short time this man would become his father-in-law. The
thought filled him with a sharp pang of sorrow. When Mordechai said
nothing more, Simeon motioned to his father, and they both left the
room, not bothering to shut the door behind them.

II

SEPPHORIS, IN THE GALILEE
22 NOVEMBER, A.D. 31

Sepphoris lay about four miles north of Nazareth, near the center
of a fertile valley where copious springs provided an abundance of fresh
water. To the south, the Nazareth Ridge rose about fifteen hundred feet
above the site, providing a beautiful backdrop for the city. It was little
wonder that the Romans chose this as the place to create a major presence in the Galilee.

Simeon, Miriam, David, and Deborah were traveling alone. With
the betrothal coming so quickly, they had even left young Joseph with
Ephraim and Rachel. They had left very early and pushed hard. Now,
as they made their way through the city, Simeon was reminded of

Rome. They passed an aqueduct bringing water into the city, a mausoleum, theaters, temples, luxurious homes. What was it about these Romans that made them bring their culture, their architecture, their religion, their traditions and impose them upon the local populations?

They moved through the main part of the city, passing the walled, fortress-like garrison where dozens of soldiers milled about or stood guard. Then, in a matter of a few blocks, they were in neighborhoods completely Jewish, different enough that it seemed as if they had not only come miles but changed countries completely.

Aaron's house was on one of the finer streets, but it was not by any means the most impressive in that block. It was two stories high, with a small courtyard in front. There was no fountain there, which was surprising in a city with virtually unlimited supplies of water and where most courtyards held elaborate marble fountains.

Aaron was an enigma in many ways, Simeon decided. Born in a fiercely independent family that hated Rome with the intensity of a she-bear protecting her young, Aaron's uncle was the famous Judah of Gamla, founder of the Zealot movement. Thirty-some years before, Cyrenius, newly appointed legate of Syria, called for a census. The people rebelled. Not only were the taxes based on the census grossly unfair, administered through the corrupt and venal system of *publicani,* or tax collectors, but much of the money went directly to the emperor. This was an affront of enormous proportion to the Jews, who vehemently eschewed any form of idolatry, because the emperor was worshiped by many as a god. The Galilee exploded in open rebellion.

Eventually it took three full legions to put the revolt down. Two thousand Jews were either killed in battle or crucified by the victorious Romans. When it was over, Aaron and Deborah were alone.

Deborah had come out of that experience fired with passion. The Zealot cause was her cause, and, through her encouragement, Simeon had taken it up as well. Only when she had come to believe in Jesus had those fires finally been banked.

But Aaron had chosen a different path. He turned to the strict, demanding code of the Pharisees, embracing it with the same amount of passion his sister felt for the cause of freedom. He started late in the *yeshivas*, the schools that taught young men the Law of Moses, but he quickly surpassed his classmates in expertise, knowledge, and dedication.

Where Simeon's mother was self-effacing, Aaron was haughty. Where Deborah was tolerant of divergent views, Aaron treated anything outside of Pharisaism as near heresy. Instead of Deborah's deep and gentle warmth, much of which had been gained before tragedy struck the family, Aaron could exhibit a condescending coldness that stung like the flick of a whip. For the previous several years, whenever Simeon and Aaron were together, they went at each other like their tongues were swords and their minds battering rams. That always saddened his mother, even though she often sided with Simeon against Aaron's rigidity.

He looked up from his thoughts. His mother was seated between him and his father on the seat of the cart. She was watching him steadily. "What?" he asked.

"No battles today. Please."

Simeon laughed softly. Had his feelings shown so clearly on his face? "I won't, Mother. I only want to thank him for what he did and invite them to the betrothal."

"Good. When you two fight, it upsets Hava as much as it does me."

"I promise," Simeon said, lifting his hand to signify as much.

"We can't stay that long anyway," David came in. "Not if we're going to make Beth Neelah by nightfall."

"I know," Deborah replied. "Aaron will be disappointed."

"No," David said dryly, "Hava will be disappointed. Aaron will be relieved."

"Now listen, you two," she scolded, trying to sound severe. "I mean it. No arguments."

"Aunt Hava is wonderful," Simeon noted with exaggerated innocence.

"Simeon." There was warning in Deborah's eyes, and she was no longer teasing.

He raised both hands, this time in defense. "I promise, Mother. I'll be nice."

III

"And so," Simeon concluded, taking a quick breath, "since I was in the wilderness of Judea for so many months, I never had a chance to really thank you, Uncle Aaron. What you did in bringing that letter to the governor not only showed your concern, but it put you at risk too. I didn't know until just a little while ago that you actually went inside the Praetorium and talked with the governor face to face."

Aaron was toying with one of his *peyot*, the long side curls that were a mark of piety and thus were especially favored by the Pharisees. Somewhere in the thickness of his beard there was half a smile, and his dark eyes twinkled. "Actually, the hardest part was the month of purification it took after that before I could feel clean again."

Simeon nearly choked. Aaron was joking with him! Embarrassed by Simeon's sincerity, he was trying to make light of what he'd done. Simeon could hardly believe it.

"Well," Miriam said, "as I said before, my father and I were there in Caesarea that night. After you left, we had supper with Pilate and he told us about your visit. He was still muttering about it. He didn't like you interfering, but I think it was a factor in influencing him to strike a bargain with Simeon."

"Whether it was or wasn't," Hava said, watching her husband with open pride, "we are grateful to the Holy One, blessed be his name, for

working things out as he did." She turned to Miriam. "And now this."
Her smile filled her whole face. "We are so happy for you two."

"Thank you, Hava," Miriam said.

"Will you be coming down for the betrothal then?" Simeon asked.
"It will be the day before Hanukkah."

"Of course."

Simeon suddenly had an idea. When he had been betrothed to
Shana, more than eighteen months before, the ceremony had taken
place in Beth Neelah, Shana's village. Shana's uncle, Rabbi Nahum,
had performed the betrothal ceremony. Normally the groom chose the
wedding officiator, and Sepphoris was only a few miles from Beth
Neelah, but at that point Simeon wouldn't have considered asking his
Uncle Aaron to officiate. Thus, Rabbi Nahum had been asked. The
only thing that saved Simeon was the fact that Nahum was a relative
of Shana's, but Aaron had let his sister know he had been deeply hurt
that he hadn't even been considered.

"We have a request," Simeon said. "We were wondering if you
would perform the ceremony for us."

Aaron almost jumped. His eyes widened as he peered at Simeon.

"You are a rabbi, Uncle Aaron. We need a rabbi to perform the
ceremony. Who better than you?"

Even Deborah was staring at her son. She had planned to suggest
that Aaron be asked but was still working up the nerve to do so. "Yes,"
she said quickly, "who better than you, Aaron?"

Simeon looked at Miriam.

She didn't wait for his question. "We would be very pleased," she
said warmly. "In fact, it would be an honor to have it be someone in
the family."

Then came the second surprise of the afternoon: Aaron's eyes
were glistening. "I am the one who would be honored," he said. "Most
honored. Thank you."

Deborah was a little misty-eyed herself. What had just happened was a small step toward healing some deep breeches, and she was very pleased. "Then you'll stay with us for the festival as well?" she asked, speaking to Aaron and Hava. "We would love to have you in our home again."

"Actually," Aaron began, then turned and looked at his wife. She nodded for him to go on. "Actually, that would work out very nicely for us. You see, we are moving to Jerusalem."

"What?" Deborah nearly shot off her chair.

Pleased with himself for his little surprise, his head bobbed quickly. "Yes. We planned to leave here and celebrate Hanukkah in Capernaum on our way down. We have decided that we are too far removed from the main center of Pharisaism up here." He gave them a wry smile. "Jerusalem would change that somewhat."

"Aaron has been invited by Azariah, the chief of all the Pharisees, to become part of the community there," Hava said, her eyes shining with pride. "He even hinted that perhaps there might be a seat on the Great Council."

"Hava," he said, half chiding her. "He didn't say that."

"But he hinted at it," she replied.

There was no mistaking the pleasure on Aaron's face. "Yes, he hinted at it."

"But . . ." Deborah was still dumbfounded. "What about your pottery business?"

"Hava's brother will take over things here. He's done most of the selling to the Romans anyway. I'll just have to see whether I have time to start a shop down there."

"You'll love Jerusalem," Miriam said. "I used to spend hours just walking the streets."

Aaron twisted both side curls around his fingers, his way of showing either great agitation or deep satisfaction. "It is time we moved to where there are more of our own." He rolled his eyes in mock horror. "Oh! The influence here. One can hardly walk down the street here without bumping into a Roman, a Greek, or a Phoenician. I spend half my life in the ritual bath purifying myself."

"Congratulations are in order then," David said. "We wish you well."

"And you also," Aaron said, looking at Simeon. "It is certainly time that you were getting married. Past time," he added.

It was said without malice, and Simeon smiled. "My parents would emphasize the word *past.*"

Aaron turned to Miriam. "I understand you, too, are a follower of Jesus of Nazareth."

The comment was so unexpected that Miriam just looked at him for a moment. Instantly, there was tension in the room. "I . . ." Then her head came up. "Yes. My friend and I were baptized before we left for Rome."

"May I ask why?"

"Aaron," Deborah broke in, "we don't want to get into all of that today. We have to leave soon."

He waved his sister away. "I'm not being critical, merely curious. I would like to know what it is about Jesus that appeals to people, especially one who was raised in the house of a Sadducee. I am determined to try to better understand him."

"So you can stop him?" Simeon said shortly.

Deborah shot Simeon a warning glance, but Aaron ignored the comment. "So?" he asked, still addressing Miriam.

"I first saw him in Jerusalem, on the Temple Mount. He was incensed when he saw what the money changers and the other sellers had done there. Noise, filth, a terrible smell. And the dishonesty as they changed money for the people. I've always hated that part of the festivals."

"Ah, yes," Aaron said softly. "I heard of this incident. And you were there?"

"Yes, just a few feet away. He was magnificent. Even the temple police didn't dare stop him."

"That is one of the few times we Pharisees would be in total agreement with what Jesus did. The Sadducees turn a blind eye on those doings because a goodly share of the profits goes directly into their purses."

Since Aaron had mentioned only moments before that Miriam's father was a Sadducee, it seemed clear that his comment was likely a jab at her. She almost responded that, according to her father, the Pharisees quietly took their cut as well—but then decided to let it pass. She decided instead to further answer his question about Jesus. "Then my friend, Livia, and I came up here to the Galilee. We heard Jesus teach. What he said was so simple, so reasonable. It was like I had finally found a treasured book I had lost many years before." She shrugged. "I don't know how else to describe it."

"Interesting," Aaron said.

Simeon was watching their interchange cautiously. Aaron was a master of setting verbal traps. He would entice you in with an innocent face, then slam the door shut with great relish. But he seemed genuinely curious.

"I once thought I wanted to be a Pharisee," Miriam said.

"Really?" Simeon, his mother, and Aaron all said it at the same time.

"When I was fifteen. I could see that my father and his associates used religion mostly as a cloak they wore when it was convenient."

"Well said!" Aaron exclaimed.

"But," she went on, knowing she was going to lose his approval but needing to say it anyway, "I found Pharisaism too confining, too stifling. All the rules. All the minutia. I'm sorry, but that's how it was for me."

"The burden of the Law is too heavy for some," Aaron said, not taking offense. "And where one feels a burden, it is difficult to see beauty."

Mystified, Simeon shot a glance at his mother. What was going on with Aaron today? Where was the Pharisee who bristled at the slightest criticism of his beliefs?

"When I listened to Jesus," Miriam went on, "it was liberating, not stifling. It was like he was removing shackles rather than handing me more. I had never felt so free. I had never heard anything that felt so right."

"Interesting," he said again. "Others I have spoken to use similar words to describe their feelings."

"Am I hearing this correctly?" Deborah blurted. "You have been asking people about why they believe in Jesus?"

Aaron tipped back his head and laughed, his ample girth bouncing merrily. "I have surprised my sister? Wonderful." Then he sobered and leaned forward earnestly. "Believe it or not, I am convinced that we can learn a few things from this Jesus about how to have greater influence with the common people. Some of my colleagues vigorously disagree with me on that, but I feel it strongly. We are finding that we too often offend people because they perceive us as being rigid and unbending."

"Really?" Simeon said with an absolute straight face.

His sarcasm went right past Aaron. "Yes, I'm sorry to have to admit to that, but it is true. In actuality, we have only two serious objections to Jesus," he said. "The first and most obvious is that he is always condemning us. He tells the people we are hypocrites and that we don't love God."

His eyes were suddenly spitting sparks. "We—I!—find that highly offensive. To disagree with our teachings is one thing. To question our devotion, our love of God? That is quite another."

"Aaron," Deborah started, but he cut her off with a wave. Surprisingly, as quickly as his anger had flared, it was gone again.

"The second thing," he said, still addressing Miriam, "is how he goes about teaching. We don't expect everyone to agree with us. We are used to differing opinions. But why won't Jesus come into the synagogues or the *yeshivas* and debate the Law with us? Debate is the very lifeblood of the *yeshivas*. Someone proposes an interpretation of the Law; then everyone goes at it with all the energy and determination they can muster. Even some of the greatest of our sages disagree with how the Law should be interpreted."

"That is not Jesus' way," Simeon said quietly, not making it a question.

"No, it is not!" Aaron snapped back. "And that is exactly the problem with him. He speaks as if there is no other possibility. He speaks as if he is the ultimate authority. If he were a renowned sage or had spent a lifetime studying under one of the great masters, then maybe he could make such pronouncements. But no! He sits atop some lofty intellectual mountaintop, hurling down his pronouncements as if they were the only truths in all of existence."

The four visitors looked at one another, and something passed between them. Finally, David turned to his brother-in-law and said what they were all thinking. "Yes," he said, "you have captured it exactly. It is almost like he is the Son of God or something."

Aaron's eyes narrowed suspiciously. "That comes dangerously close to blasphemy, David," he said.

Deborah stood up before anything more could be said. "We really must be off, Aaron. We want to reach Beth Neelah before nightfall. We need to join up with Leah and Livia and get back home. There is much to do before Hanukkah arrives." She turned to Hava. "It is so good to see you again. Come whenever you like; there will always be a place for you in our home."

Then she took her brother's hand. "Thank you for being willing to perform the ceremony, Aaron. We'll see you before Hanukkah then?"

He gave her a sharp look, realizing she had shut off any further comments about blasphemy, but then only nodded. "Yes, before Hanukkah."

CHAPTER NOTES

The *ketubah,* or premarital contract between the groom and his intended bride, was described in some detail in *Fishers of Men,* pp. 182–84 (see also Jacobs, pp. 41–43; Bloch, 34–35).

The marking of time in Judea at this point in history was also described previously, but a brief review here might be helpful to the reader. (1) Unlike our day, which begins at midnight, the Jewish day was measured from sundown to sundown. Thus, the evening is always the first part of the new day, and the afternoon the last. We see remnants of this system in Christmas Eve and New Year's Eve, both of which precede the actual holiday. (2) The work day was divided into twelve "hours" of equal length, beginning roughly at 6:00 A.M. and ending at 6:00 P.M. Therefore, the third hour of the day would be approximately 9:00 A.M. for us, and the eleventh hour about 5:00 P.M. Since the amount of daylight varies with the seasons, the "hours" in summer would be longer than the "hours" of winter. (3) The night was divided according to the Roman custom of "watches" or the amount of time during which guards stood watch. There were four watches of about three hours each. The first watch would generally run from 6:00 to 9:00 P.M., the second from 9:00 P.M. to midnight, and so on.

The tax rebellion that led to the formation of the Zealot movement began about A.D. 6. After the death of Herod the Great, his kingdom was divided between his two sons, Archelaus and Antipas, both of whom functioned under Roman patronage. The new arrangement of the kingdom called for a change in the tax system that had existed under Herod. To implement this new order of things, the legate of Syria, Sulpicius Quirinius (the New Testament spelling is Cyrenius—see Luke 2:2) ordered a census of the province. This not only involved counting people but also cataloging resources. (This form of census, or taxing, is referred to twice by Luke, in Luke 2:1–2 and Acts 5:37.)

Though the Jewish population mostly hated the Herods, at least they were nominally Jewish. But under the new system, tribute would go directly to Rome. That alone was bad enough, but Augustus Caesar had encouraged a growing cult who said the emperor was divine. In the minds of the more fanatical opponents of the tax or tribute, this meant that by paying taxes they would be directly supporting idolatry.

In an effort to combat the tribute, a man named Judas from the Galilee led a rebellion that quickly mushroomed into a full-scale war. Though the rebellion was eventually crushed by the Romans, the seeds had been planted. The rebels took upon themselves the name of Zealot (from Numbers 25:11). The Zealot movement ebbed and flowed until A.D. 66, when another Jewish revolt broke out, ending in the destruction of Jerusalem in A.D. 70. (See Brandon, 15:632–34.)

CHAPTER 6

WHO CAN FIND A VIRTUOUS WOMAN?

FOR HER PRICE IS FAR ABOVE RUBIES.

—*Proverbs 31:10*

I

BETH NEELAH, IN THE UPPER GALILEE

22 NOVEMBER, A.D. 31

The home of Yehuda of Beth Neelah was not a large one, but it was neatly kept—thanks mostly to Shana. They sat before the fire, mellow and relaxed after a plain but generous meal. There were just the seven of them—Simeon and Miriam, Deborah and David, Livia, Leah, and Yehuda. Shana and Samuel had been present for the supper but left immediately after. They said they were expected by Samuel's family. But, in addition, there was still some strain in having Shana and Simeon together again. So Shana and Samuel excused themselves and went to spend the evening with Samuel's family.

Yehuda was in an expansive mood and had been a consummate host. He was now reminiscing on the first time Livia and Miriam had visited Beth Neelah.

"I remember it well," Miriam said with a rueful laugh. "My feet were so blistered I wondered if I would ever walk again."

Yehuda grinned at her. "I remember it too. I asked you to dance with us, and you gave me this feeble excuse about your feet being too tender."

"Feeble?" Miriam cried. "Thanks to Simeon, we had marched almost thirty miles that day. I was in agony. I still have scars on my feet from some of the larger blisters."

The big Galilean glanced at Livia quickly, then turned back to Miriam. "Do you remember what happened next?"

"Perfectly. I'll never forget how you and Livia danced that night."

Simeon was nodding, smiling softly with the memory. "I remember now. Daniel played the flute. You astonished all of us, Livia. In a matter of minutes, it seemed as though you had been dancing with the villagers for years. It was amazing."

"It was a beautiful night in a beautiful place," Livia admitted softly.

Miriam looked at her friend. "So have you danced again since you got here?"

Livia's fair skin instantly glowed red. "Only twice," she murmured, shooting a quick look at Yehuda.

"And?" Miriam pushed.

"Let us just say," Yehuda answered for her, "that her visit to Rome did not diminish her ability nor add any weight to her feet."

Leah smiled. "The villagers say she dances as though she was born here. That's a high compliment indeed."

Miriam watched her friend with interest and was glad she had pushed Livia to make the trip to Beth Neelah. She seemed very happy to be here.

Deborah stirred. "Well, we were up and on the road very early this morning. And we have to leave early again tomorrow. We'd better go to bed."

Yehuda frowned. "You just arrived a bit ago. Surely you can stay one full day."

Deborah shook her head. "The betrothal is in two weeks. We left Joseph with Ephraim. And now with Aaron and Hava and their children coming, there are things I need to do to get the house ready."

He grimaced, but nodded. "I understand."

"You will be coming down?" Simeon asked.

"Of course. I had become so convinced you'd never find a woman who could stand to live with you that I wouldn't miss this for anything in the world."

Laughing at Simeon's expression, Yehuda stood too. "Deborah, you and David will take my bed. Shana is staying with Samuel's cousin, so Livia, Leah, and Miriam will take her room. I'll bring in another mat." He looked at Simeon. "For you and me, it's the stable."

"That will be better than a lot of places we have slept in lately," Simeon said. "But then, on second thought, I haven't had to listen to you snoring either. That's the real reason I didn't ask you to go to Rome with Ezra and me." He looked at Miriam and Livia. "It's like sleeping next to a working gristmill."

Quick as a cat, Yehuda leaped, grabbing Simeon in a headlock, then twisted sharply, driving him to his knees.

"Ow!"

"What say you, Miriam? Would you have me do away with this impudent pup once and for all and save you much sorrow and heartbreak?"

Though the others were laughing, Miriam pretended to look perplexed, troubled by the question.

"Hey!" Simeon yelped. "Let's hear a protest of some kind from over there, please."

Miriam gave a pained sigh, then: "Oh, Yehuda. What's a woman to do? The arrangements are all made. And, believe it or not, his mother still loves him. I guess I'll just have to learn to live with him."

II

"Simeon?"

"Hmm?"

"You're surely not asleep already. We just lay down."

"No, I'm not asleep. But I'm ready to be. I'd forgotten how soft a pile of hay can be."

"There's something I want to talk to you about."

"All right."

Yehuda sat up, pulling his knees up beneath his chin. In the darkness of the stable, Simeon could barely make out his shape. "Something serious."

"I'm listening."

"If you laugh, I'll bust your nose."

Simeon threw off the blanket and sat up too. They both were still fully clothed; they knew it was going to get chilly before the night was over. "I'm listening," he said again, this time completely serious.

There was a long silence; then he heard an expulsion of breath in the darkness. "You're going to think this is crazy."

"From you? Don't be silly. You've never done anything crazy in your life. Why would you—"

"I want you to speak in my behalf."

"What?"

He spoke slowly, emphasizing each word. "I want you to speak in my behalf. To Livia."

Whatever else flashed through Simeon's mind, it was not a desire to laugh. He was completely dumbfounded. "What do you mean, speak to her in your behalf?"

"Come on, Simeon," he snapped. "You know exactly what I mean. She has no father or mother. I can't just approach her directly. That wouldn't be right. Your family is as close to a true family as anyone she has."

"Are you saying . . . ?" He stopped. He couldn't say it. It was too fantastic, too completely unexpected.

"I want you to ask Livia if she would ever . . ." A soft explosion of air sounded in the darkness; then the words came out in a rush. "Look. I know that what has happened to you and Miriam—to come to love each other before you're even betrothed—is wonderful. But it's certainly not typical when most marriages are arranged through the parents or a matchmaker. You know that all too often the two parties don't even meet until the day of the betrothal. My parents didn't, and yet, eventually, they came to love each other. So it's not like—"

Simeon's hand shot out and grabbed Yehuda's arm. "Slow down! I'm still trying to catch up here."

A low rumble sounded, but nothing else.

"You want me to ask Livia if she will *marry* you?"

"No. Well, yes, but that's far too much to hope for. I would like you to speak to her and see if she would at least consider me as a possible suitor." When Simeon didn't answer, Yehuda gave a miffed grunt. "Do you find that possibility so unbelievable?"

"No, I—in fact, Miriam and I have talked about whether there might ever be something between you two. But—"

Yehuda chuckled softly. "But old Yehuda caught you by surprise on this one, right?"

"That's putting it mildly."

"I find Livia to be a remarkable woman, Simeon. I've thought that from the first time we saw her and Miriam in Samaria. But since she's been here, my eyes have really been opened. She's intelligent, kind, gracious, gentle—"

"You don't have to convince me of that."

"I had about decided that I might never find someone, but now . . ." His voice trailed off in the darkness. After a long moment of silence, he spoke again. "So? Will you speak in my behalf, or do you need some more time to think about it?"

Simeon laughed. "You just punched me in the stomach, my friend. At least give me a moment to catch my breath."

"Take whatever time you need."

The silence stretched on for a considerable length; then Simeon cleared his throat. "Let's suppose for a moment that Livia says yes. When do you think the betrothal might take place?"

There was a long silence before Yehuda spoke. "If I had my way," he quietly said, "we would get betrothed and married the same day."

He must have heard Simeon's quick intake of breath. "I know, I know. But I'm getting old, Simeon. I'll be twenty-seven next summer. Some men my age have eight and nine-year-old sons. I don't care what people might say. I don't care if she doesn't have a dowry." Then he sighed. "But that's only me speaking. If she'll have me, I'll agree to whatever she thinks is appropriate. If she wants to wait a year, then we'll wait a year."

Simeon was hesitant. "I need to be honest with you, Yehuda. There are a couple of concerns I have."

"Let me guess. The first is the fact that I am a Zealot, a man of war. The second has to do with Jesus."

"You really *have* been thinking about this, haven't you."

"I've thought of little else this past week."

"If I speak to Livia in your behalf, I'll have to be honest with her as well."

"I wouldn't have it any other way."

"As you said, Livia is a gentle woman. She is quiet and introspective by nature."

"And I'm loud and brash and—"

"Are you going to let me talk or do I need to put a rag in your mouth?"

"Sorry," he mumbled.

"You are a Zealot, Yehuda, not just in mind but in heart. And now that I have withdrawn from our band, you are a leader of Zealots. I'm not sure Livia can live with that. It's not just the danger. It's the constant hate, the desire for revenge that never goes away. It's nights lying awake knowing that you may not come back. It's bands of men in her kitchen plotting rebellion. It's knowing that your sons will want to be just like you."

He looked at his friend in the darkness. "I'm not being critical, Yehuda. Why do you think I waited so long for marriage? I didn't feel like I could ask a woman to live with that. I only finally agreed to marry Shana because she is as much a Zealot as you and I are."

"I know," came the quiet reply. "I know full well that what you say is true."

"And?"

Again there was silence in the stable. Simeon waited, knowing Yehuda was deciding how best to say what he had to say.

"You won't believe this, but I'm tired, Simeon. You and me, we've been at this business now for . . . what? Six? Eight years?"

"About that."

"This last year I spent with you out chasing Ya'abin really affected me: the nights without sleep, day after day riding in a bitter cold rain, eating food that a jackal wouldn't touch, always looking over my shoulder to see who's coming, going to bed with a spear in one hand and a sword in the other, never sleeping."

There was a shuffling sound in the darkness as Yehuda shifted his weight. "It has felt so good to me these last few months to be home, to have my only worry be about my grape vines."

Simeon didn't know what to say. He knew this man too well to suspect this was just a ploy to win Livia's hand. And he could feel the weariness in Yehuda's soul as he spoke.

"I know you find this hard to believe, Simeon, but I mean it. I'm ready to hang up my bow too. Oh, if there were a major eruption, if the Romans invaded the Galilee, or something like that, I couldn't just stand by idly. But then, who could? I suspect even you would take arms again to protect your family."

"Yes, I would."

"Yesterday, as I made up my mind to talk to you about all of this, I realized that I was glad Livia can't live as a Zealot's wife. I'm ready for a change."

"She really has affected you, hasn't she," Simeon said in wonder. "And I can tell Livia that you are willing to make that commitment to her?"

"Yes."

Simeon blew out his breath, still reeling a little.

"So, let's talk about the other issue," Yehuda said.

When Simeon answered, there was a sadness in his voice. "Livia doesn't talk much about her feelings, but she believes deeply that Jesus is all he claims to be."

"I know that. But you and I disagree about this as well. Would it be fair to say that in spite of our differences, I have respected your right to feel as you do? I haven't made our relationship contingent on your putting aside how you believe, have I?"

"No, you haven't."

"I can fully respect Livia's beliefs. I will not ridicule them or try to convince her she is wrong. The question is, can she extend that same respect to what I believe? Will she object if we raise our children as good Jews?"

Simeon instantly shook his head, then remembered that Yehuda couldn't see him in the darkness. "That would surprise me very much. I know Livia isn't Jewish by birth, but she at least partially accepted our religion back in Jerusalem. She never formally converted, but I don't think she finds it objectionable."

"I know," Yehuda murmured, "but that was before she became a disciple of Jesus."

"Yehuda," Simeon said earnestly, "Jesus has not asked us to put aside the Law. In fact, he says that he has come to *fulfill* the Law. Miriam and I fully plan to raise our children as his followers *and* good Jews. We will continue to go to synagogue. We will circumcise our sons, honor the dietary laws, keep the other requirements set down by Moses. I assume Livia feels the same."

"If she does, then I can accept her being a follower of Jesus."

"And raising your children to be followers of Jesus?"

He thought for a moment, then grunted. "Yes, that too. I have to admit that following after this man does seem to make one a better person."

Simeon stood up. "Then I shall speak in your behalf, Yehuda of Beth Neelah.

"When?"

"Knowing women, I doubt very much they are asleep yet either. We really can't delay our return to Capernaum any longer. I'll go talk to her right now. That will give her tonight to think about it; then hopefully by morning, you will at least have an idea of her response."

"I would like that," he admitted. "I've been like a cat passing through a village full of dogs these last few days."

Simeon laughed. It was an image that didn't fit his friend very often.

"Well?" Yehuda said after a moment.

"Well what?"

"Why are you still standing there? Go!"

III

23 NOVEMBER, A.D. 31

It was going to be a beautiful day in the Galilee. The sun was not up yet, but the sky was cloudless, and the golden glow of morning was spreading across the land. Yehuda stood behind the toolshed, washing his face and hands in a small stone cistern. He stopped and spun around at a sound behind him. Nothing was there. "Like a cat in a village of dogs," he muttered to himself.

Simeon had returned to the stable about an hour after going to find Livia. All he could and would say was that Livia was astonished by what he had said, and she certainly wouldn't sleep much that night.

Not that Yehuda had either. He had tossed and turned and fretted for hours. But he must have finally dozed off for a brief time, because Simeon had slipped out of the stable without waking him.

"Yehuda?"

He jumped and swung around. Simeon was standing there, face impassive.

Wiping his hands on his tunic, he rushed forward. "Yes? Have you seen her? Have you talked with her this morning?"

"Let's walk."

Yehuda felt his stomach twist sharply. He hadn't very often seen Simeon this grave. "Tell me," he said, falling into step beside him. "Was she offended by my boldness?"

When there was no answer, he swung away, bitter and angry with himself. "I should have waited. Another month or so and she could have gotten to know me better and—"

"Not only do you snore like a wild boar," Simeon cut in, "but you can't wait even one minute, can you?"

"I—"

"Can you hold your questions for another fifty paces so we can talk undisturbed?"

"Come on, Simeon. I'm dying. I haven't slept all night."

Simeon just sighed, like a father who despairs of ever having his son come to his senses. They had walked well into the rows of vines, out of sight of the shed and the house. Simeon stopped, looked around, then sat down on a low wall made of stones, indicating that Yehuda should do the same.

"All right," Yehuda said immediately, "just tell me. Don't try to sweeten it up with honey. I've pretty much accepted it already."

"Oh," Simeon said in amusement, "I'm not sure that's true."

"Why?"

"Well, first off, she told me you totally ruined the night for her. She hasn't been to bed at all. She spent hours walking and thinking. She also said she spent a long time on her knees."

The thick dark eyebrows lifted hopefully. "So she didn't just burst out laughing?"

"Are you ready for this?" Simeon asked slowly, enjoying prolonging his friend's agony.

"I don't know if I am or not," came the murmured reply.

A slow, deep smile stole over Simeon's face. "I told you last night that it was like you had punched me in the stomach. But that was nothing compared to what happened with Livia when I talked to her."

"Yes, and? What did she say?"

"She has agreed to your proposal for marriage."

Yehuda shot to his feet. "Really?" Then his brows lowered darkly. "You wouldn't joke about something like this, would you?"

"No, Yehuda, I wouldn't joke about something like this."

The big man turned and faced the east, where the sun was just peeping over the hills. His head tipped back, and he closed his eyes.

"That's not all." Simeon went on, enjoying this more than

anything he could remember in a long time. "Not only does she agree to the idea that you should be betrothed and married the same day, but she doesn't want to wait very long. She wants to return here with you after you go down to Capernaum for Hanukkah and our betrothal. She would like the marriage to take place immediately after that."

Yehuda turned slowly, gaping at his friend. "She said that?"

"Yes, she did. She said that was what took her most of the night to decide. She knew immediately that she wanted to marry you. But she's afraid that you will think her unseemly for wanting to move so quickly."

That really took Yehuda aback. "Unseemly?"

"You have to remember that though Livia has lived among us for six years or so, she is not one of our people. She hasn't grown up with our customs or our traditions. But she is fully familiar with our custom of waiting a year, and she is hesitant for your sake to violate it—even though you brought it up. At the same time, she is getting older, as you are. Most girls are married by sixteen in Greece, the same as here. And she is twenty-one. She was beginning to think she might never marry. So if you would not find it offensive—and she wanted me to stress that point—that is her proposal."

Yehuda looked as if a wall had just fallen on him. Simeon laughed right out loud at the expression on his friend's face. "I told you it's been a night of surprises."

"She really said all that?"

"She did," Simeon said with a grin. "So, do you feel her boldness is unseemly?"

"Unseemly? Are you mad? That is the most wonderful thing I have ever heard. It's more than I could have hoped for in my wildest imaginings."

Simeon nodded slowly, then stood up next to his long-time friend. "Do you know what's strange, Yehuda?"

"What?"

"Last night I was afraid Livia was going to ask me if I thought this was the right thing for her to do. I didn't want to have to tell her that I had serious reservations about it."

"You didn't tell me that last night."

"I did in my own way," Simeon corrected him. "But . . ." He shook his head slowly, his eyes taking on a faraway look. "When she told me how she felt, instantly I knew it was right. For you. For her. I knew it as surely as I know I love Miriam."

He stuck out his hand and gripped Yehuda's tightly. "So, congratulations, my friend. Now let's go. There is a very anxious woman waiting by the shed to learn what you have to say to all of this. And we have some pretty incredible news to break to the rest of the family."

CHAPTER 7

THIS IS NOW BONE OF MY BONES, AND FLESH OF MY FLESH: SHE
SHALL BE CALLED WOMAN, BECAUSE SHE WAS TAKEN OUT OF MAN.
THEREFORE SHALL A MAN LEAVE HIS FATHER AND HIS MOTHER, AND
SHALL CLEAVE UNTO HIS WIFE: AND THEY SHALL BE ONE FLESH.

—*Genesis 2:23–24*

I

CAPERNAUM
24 NOVEMBER–6 DECEMBER, A.D. 31

With their return from Beth Neelah, the women of the family of
David ben Joseph of Capernaum launched into feverish preparations
for the betrothal of Miriam and Simeon. Some things had already been
done before they went up to Sepphoris and Beth Neelah, but Livia's
plans to marry Yehuda immediately following Hanukkah changed
everything. Now preparations for that were added to the other.

In actuality, the primary purpose for the traditional year of
betrothal was to allow both the bride and the groom time to prepare
themselves to start their own household. It also allowed the parents of
both families to have sufficient time to prepare for the wedding feast.
Weddings and betrothals, even in the smallest villages, were eventful
affairs, carrying religious, cultural, and communal significance.

According to the Torah, or the writings of Moses, the first marriage had been performed by God himself. Adam and Eve set the pattern for all of their posterity to follow. It was a joyous time, one calling for extended and intense celebration.

No one in the family questioned Livia's decision to marry so quickly. Her announcement that morning in Beth Neelah had been met with genuine joy and complete support. But Livia had no family except Drusus, who was not there. So Miriam and the family of David ben Joseph took her under their wings as if she were their own.

Leah, Miriam, and Lilly set to work to help Livia pull together at least the minimal personal dowry that every woman was expected to bring to her marriage: kettles for the cooking fire; pots, jars, bowls, and dishes for eating; larger vessels for wine and oil; bed linens and, if possible, a new straw mattress; sufficient clothing to start a new life; table coverings and towels.

Deborah, Rachel, and Hava (once she and Aaron arrived from Sepphoris) worked on the elaborate kit of cosmetics required for the wedding ceremonies, the wedding garments, and the appropriate jewelry for both women. For the actual purchase of the wedding garments, every woman in the household, including five-year-old Esther, accompanied Miriam and Livia, spending all day before a final decision was made.

David, Simeon, Ephraim, and Ezra worked on the practical side of the betrothal feast. Traditionally, betrothal ceremonies were held in the home of the bride's parents. In Miriam's case, that was not possible, so the most logical substitution was David's home. However, David ben Joseph was an influential and highly respected man in Capernaum. He had associates in the trade from many surrounding areas who would come to honor the family. Simeon's band of brothers from the Galilee would come down as well. And if Jesus came, which he planned to do, dozens of others would come with him, whether they knew the family or not. There was no way that the ceremony and celebration could be held at David's home.

So the decision had been a simple one. They would secure the *Beth Chatanim*, or "house of the bridegrooms." Though originally that title referred to the actual house that belonged to the groom and which would become the home of the newly wedded couple, most larger communities now had a public place in which betrothals and weddings could be held. Not only did these places include a spacious hall that could accommodate large crowds, but most *Beth Chatanim* also had a *chuppah* room. *Chuppah* was the covering, or canopy, under which the actual ceremony took place. If it was a marriage and not a betrothal, the *chuppah* room could also serve as the bridal chambers.

David and his three sons, along with Ezra, set to work preparing the hall. Fortunately, winter was a time when much of the harvest had already been shipped out of the warehouses, making available dozens of low tables normally used to keep the sacks of grain off the floor. Since people ate in a semi-reclining position, they then had to borrow, buy, or rent hundreds of pillows and mats on which the guests could eat. They rounded up sawhorses and long planks and created a dozen or more serving tables. Stools for the musicians; dishes sufficient to feed hundreds; great vats of wine; and sacks of spices, grains, dried peas, beans, and other legumes were brought in until it began to look as though there would be no room for the people themselves.

The fresh food, and especially the meat, would have to wait until the day of the celebration, but Ephraim and Simeon went to more than a dozen merchants and made arrangements to have food delivered to the *Beth Chatanim* early on the morning of the betrothal. Bakers all around the city were paid to bring their loaves of bread hot from the ovens once the feasting began. While Ephraim and Simeon were out purchasing the food, David secured several servants to help with the feast, in addition to the part-time servants who came in to help Deborah from time to time.

As sundown of the day before Hanukkah approached, things gradually quieted. The flurry of activity lessened somewhat, and all was in readiness.

II

At sundown, which marked the beginning of the next day, specially invited guests began to gather in two places. The male friends and relatives of the bridegroom went to the *chuppah* in the *Beth Chatanim*. The female friends and relatives of the bride went to the home of David and Deborah. Since Miriam had no parents in Capernaum, Deborah's house had become the designated home for the betrothed.

In keeping with customs that stretched back hundreds of years, the evening began with Deborah holding forth at her home for the women of the family and their closest friends. As soon as everyone had arrived, Deborah led Miriam to a stool in the center of the room. There she was seated, with the expectation that she would not speak or actively participate in the activities that followed. The task for the women of the family—in this case, Deborah, Hava, Livia, Rachel, Leah, and Lilly—was to prepare Miriam to meet her husband-to-be. Esther, her dark hair woven with ribbons, flitted around the circle with uncharacteristic excitement, taking in every detail.

It was an elaborate ritual, carefully orchestrated so as to last several hours. Its purpose was simple. The bride was to be arrayed in her wedding attire. Her hair was carefully combed and brushed, then crowned with garlands of olive and grape leaves. Cosmetics were carefully applied by women expert in the craft. Finally, jewelry that signified the richness of their lives was added piece by piece. All the while, as Miriam sat silently, the women kept up a running chatter of praise, extolling the virtues and beauties of the betrothed as if she were not there listening to every word.

While this was going on, a similar celebration was taking place for the bridegroom. Normally this was held in the groom's house, the home where he would take his bride to live once the marriage was completed. Since Simeon had not yet secured such a house, David had arranged for them to use the canopy chamber. Here, too, the invitation to attend was limited to an inner circle of immediate family members or close friends. In this case, this included Jesus, Peter, Andrew, James, John, and the rest of the Twelve, as well as Luke the Physician. An invitation had been sent to Sextus Rubrius, but he had been stationed at Sepphoris and sent back word that he would not be allowed to leave. But he sent his warmest congratulations and an exquisitely wrought silver bowl as a gift.

Tables were spread with food and wine, while the men helped Simeon to put on his finest robes. Unlike the bride, a groom was not expected to sit passively through this experience. Simeon was the center of focus, but he walked around, mingling with the guests, laughing and talking in a convivial manner. Ephraim read a poem he had written praising Simeon's exploits, including his years as a Zealot captain, his imprisonment in Caesarea, the conquest of Moshe Ya'abin, and the successful trip to Rome. He had a wry sense of humor and put in a few jabs at his younger brother that kept the guests, especially Yehuda, laughing and applauding. Yehuda made a similar tribute—but to Simeon's surprise, he could not make it through without having to stop three or four times to compose himself. Simeon was deeply touched.

Wine flowed freely, though moderately. It was considered very poor taste for anyone to become intoxicated at such a time of joy. As the night wore on, the exuberance and enthusiasm began to wear down. By the time midnight approached, the women had finished their work of adornment and had run out of things to say. They sat around, some talking quietly, some dozing off, waiting for the signal that the time for the ceremony had come. At the *chuppah*, things were slowing as well. Finally, Simeon gave his father a questioning look. "Are we ready?"

"We are if you are," David said.

Immediately, everyone except family members and Yehuda arose and went to a corner table. Jesus and Peter took the lead, with Andrew, James, and John—David's former partners in the fishing business—right behind. The five of them lit small hand lamps that had been previously prepared and stepped out into the night. The rest of the male guests followed. David waited until the last one had gone, then shut the door behind them. As the procession began to spread the word to the waiting throngs, the men of the family turned to other responsibilities of the night.

The appearance of the men with their lamps and torches was the signal the city had been waiting for. A few people had gathered outside the *Beth Chatanim* waiting for just this moment. They held out their own hand lamps as the chamber guests came out, and one by one the lamps were lit. A line quickly formed behind the five in the lead, each person holding a lamp above his or her head and waving it slowly back and forth. "It is time!" they cried. "The betrothed is ready! Prepare to meet the bridegroom!"

The cry leaped from mouth to mouth, rooftop to rooftop. People poured out of their houses to join the procession, hands thrusting out to get their lamps lit as well. The column would continue to swell as it wound its way to the home of David and Deborah, gathering up the party of women waiting there. By the time it returned to the *Beth Chatanim*, it would become a veritable river of dancing lights, and the cries would rise to fill the night. "The bridegroom is waiting. Prepare to meet the bridegroom!"

Meanwhile, back in the *Beth Chatanim*, the men of the family set to work. Fetching of the bride and bringing her to the *chuppah* would take half an hour or more, and things had to be in perfect readiness when she came. Simeon sat on a chair quietly. He was not expected to help with the menial work on this night. Once the effects of the evening's celebration had been cleared away, Uncle Aaron went to one corner and carefully donned his prayer shawl. It was a beautiful piece of handwoven, pure white linen, large enough to cover his head and spill down his back almost to the waist. His *peyot*, or side curls, danced softly as he adjusted it carefully over his head. The covering of the head was a sign of humility. To approach God with a bared head was to suggest that one was not willing to submit to his authority and majesty. Thus wrapped, Aaron also symbolically shut out the world so he could officiate as God's representative without distraction.

While Aaron was thus engaged, the men took seats around Simeon. David turned to Yehuda. "Yehuda of Beth Neelah. I should like you to place your chair alongside Simeon's. Soon you will be married, and what I have to say as Simeon's father is for both of you."

Yehuda, looking a little flustered, stood, moved his chair beside his friend, and sat down again. Then with great solemnity, David moved over to stand in front of the two of them.

"Simeon, before the coming of your betrothed, I should like to speak of the sacred nature of what you are about to do."

Simeon nodded gravely. There was no easy familiarity of a family member now. David regarded his role as spiritual advisor to his son very seriously, which was exactly as it should be.

"Tonight is the night of your betrothal. In the Law of Moses, this is considered to be as binding as marriage itself. It is a serious commitment that you will make this evening. Only death or a formal bill of divorcement can dissolve your betrothal. Betrothal carries all of the attendant obligations of marriage except for the rite of cohabitation."

Simeon nodded, his face somber.

David took a breath, looked around once to make sure everyone was appropriately attentive, and then went on. "Now, for the both of you, as you know, the first marriage of all marriages was performed by God himself, between Father Adam and Mother Eve. Not only is this proof of the sanctity of marriage and its centrality for all mankind, but there is much in the account thereof which provides instruction for us.

"When Adam was placed in the Garden of Eden, he was alone. After a time, the Lord God, blessed be his name, made a profound declaration. Said he: 'It is not good for man to be alone.'"

He leaned forward, as earnest as Simeon could ever remember seeing him. "Consider on that statement for a moment, Simeon and Yehuda. That is a divine declaration. 'It is not good for man to be alone.'"

David let that sink in, his eyes challenging them to ponder the import of those words. Then he went on. "After declaring that it is not good for man to be alone, the Holy One of Israel made a second, most significant declaration. He said, 'I shall make an help meet for him.' That is a most instructive term, 'help meet.' In the original Hebrew of the sacred writ, the phrase is *ezer knegdo*. Some have translated that phrase to mean a *helper* or a *help mate*. That is not true to the deeper meaning of the phrase. *Helper* would imply a superior role for men and a helping or inferior role for women. Many feel that way, of course, and treat their wives as chattel, but that is not what the Creator of us all declared. *Knegdo* means to 'meet' or to have two things brought together. But it carries a much deeper connotation, where one finds something that is equal to something else. In other words, a *help meet* is a person who helps us 'meet ourselves,' like looking into a mirror and seeing yourself."

Both Yehuda and Simeon were listening intently. They knew the words of course, but they had not heard it defined in exactly this way.

"What then follows is the creation of Eve. And here, too, there is much for us to learn from the sacred word. You know it well. The Lord God caused a deep sleep to come upon Adam, and he took from his side a rib, and from that rib he created woman."

Simeon's father smiled thoughtfully. "I've wondered if the Lord couched this account in imagery to teach us important truths. It is a widespread supposition, for example, that men have one less rib than women, a fact that Luke, our physician here, assures me is not the case. But be that as it may, what do we learn from the story of the rib?"

Simeon tentatively raised a hand. "I've heard it said that woman was taken from Adam's side because it is closest to his heart, suggesting that she should walk beside him always."

"Yes, I'm sure that is part of it. If Eve had been taken from Adam's head, then she would rule over him. If she were taken from his foot, he would rule over her. If from his hand, she would be only a tool to do his bidding. To be taken from the side is beautiful imagery and teaches us much about how we are to treat our wives. But I think there is something much more profound than that."

The two men waited expectantly, not yet seeing what it was David was suggesting.

"Once Eve was created from the bone taken from Adam, what follows in the account?"

"The commandment for them to become one flesh," Yehuda replied.

"Yes. Think about that. Adam now has a help meet, or in other words, he has finally met his equal. And the Lord now says, 'Therefore'—in other words, because I have created woman and brought her to you—'Therefore shall a man leave his father and his mother and shall *cleave* unto his wife.' "

David ben Joseph stopped and turned his head. In the distance, as though barely a whisper, the first cries of the approaching wedding party could be heard. He turned back quickly. "Think of that interesting choice of verbs for a moment. Normally, 'to cleave' means to cut asunder, to split into two parts. We speak, for example, of the camel having a cloven hoof. But in our language, that word also carries the opposite meaning. It means to put back together two things that have been separated, to join them so tightly one to the other it is as if there was no original separation.

"And here, my two young sons, is the key to understanding how God views this sacred relationship between a man and a woman. Adam had something cut away from him, cloven from his side. He was missing something. He was not whole any longer. So what is the solution? How does a man become whole again?"

"By cleaving to our wives," Simeon said in wonder.

"Yes. By cleaving to the only creation that is truly equal to us. And when we cleave together—or better, cleave *back* together—we become whole once again. We become not two, but one—one in flesh, one in mind, one in spirit. Then and only then, can man be fully complete."

Simeon was struck with another thought. No wonder his mother and father loved each other as they did. This was the basis for that love: total respect for each other, viewing themselves as different but of equal importance.

Behind David the cries of the approaching crowd were rapidly swelling. They would soon be at the *Beth Chatanim*.

He turned for a moment to listen, then hurried on. "This is why our religion does not believe the joining of male and female is an act only for the procreation of children. Of course, that is an important part of it, but the act of human intimacy between a man and a woman was designed by God as a way to bind man and woman together into a perfect oneness."

David bowed his head slightly. "This is what we learn from the marriage of Adam and Eve. You two have found yourselves wonderful women, the perfect help meets. Tonight we shall begin the process that will reunite you, Simeon, to Miriam, so that eventually, you can become one flesh, one in the sight of God."

III

Simeon stood with Miriam, side by side and holding hands, still beneath the canopy. Merriment and celebration swirled all around them. Others repeatedly came up to them and shook their hands, or they called out and raised their cups.

Simeon squeezed Miriam's hand. "Thank you," he whispered.

"For what?" she said in surprise.

"For not throwing me out the window that night in Rome. For being willing to marry a fool."

"Simeon," she said, her eyes glowing with happiness as she looked up at him, "it was I who was foolish that night."

"You are the best thing that has ever happened to me," he said. "You are my Eve. You are my perfect help meet."

That startled her for a moment; then she smiled softly. "Thank you."

"Remind me when things quiet down to tell you what Father told us tonight. Then you will better understand what I mean by that."

"All right."

"I love you, Miriam bat Mordechai ben Uzziel."

There were sudden tears of joy in her eyes. "And I love you, Simeon ben David ben Joseph. More than I could ever possibly express in words."

"*Mazal tov!*" somebody cried. "Good luck to you."

Not letting go of Miriam's hand, Simeon turned and raised his cup of wine. "Thank you." The people drifted away again, and he turned back to her. "I have only one wish for tonight," he said.

"What?"

"May this coming year fly by as swiftly as the eagle, be as fleeting as the shadow of a bird, pass as quickly as the flying arrow."

"Amen," Miriam whispered, squeezing his hand tightly. "Amen and amen."

IV

Beth Neelah, in the Upper Galilee
17 December, a.d. 31

"*Mazal tov!*" Simeon lifted his wine cup high, saluting his friend.

"*Mazal tov!*" roared the villagers of Beth Neelah in response.

"Thank you," Yehuda said. He stood at Livia's side beneath the canopy erected in the main square of the village. His face fairly glowed with happiness.

Miriam stepped forward and kissed Livia on the cheek. "I thought I was happy on the night of our betrothal, but I think I am just as happy for you tonight," she whispered.

Livia fought back tears. "If it weren't for you and Simeon, none of this would have ever happened."

Simeon overheard and said, "No, this was the hand of the Lord. Miriam and I were just instruments in his hand to help it along."

Yehuda reached out, grasping Simeon on the back of his neck and shaking him gently. "Instrument or direct cause, I know not," he said huskily. "But thank you, old friend. Thank you for all of it."

CHAPTER NOTES

The phrase "help meet," found in Genesis 2:18, is often translated or quoted as "help *mate*" or "helper." But the original phrase carries the meaning of correspondence or equality (see Wilson, p. 271). As Clarke states it: "*Ezer knegdo* [means] a help, a counterpart of himself, one formed from him, and a perfect resemblance of his person. If the word be rendered scrupulously literally, it signifies one *like* or *as himself*, standing *opposite to* or *before him*. And this implies that the woman was to be a perfect resemblance of the man, possessing neither inferiority or superiority, but being in all things *like* and *equal* to him" (Clarke, 1:45).

The customs associated with betrothal were described in great detail in volume one and so were not included in the same detail here (see the footnote for chapter 8 in *Fishers of Men*, p. 187).

At the time of Christ, there were wedding halls—what we today would call reception centers—in the larger communities in the Holy Land (Bloch, p. 30).

It is not clear how early the traditional salutation of *mazal tov*, or "good luck," came into common use, but it was inserted here because it is so well known today.

CHAPTER 8

IF THE MIGHTY WORKS, WHICH HAVE BEEN DONE IN THEE, HAD BEEN
DONE IN SODOM, IT WOULD HAVE REMAINED UNTIL THIS DAY.

—*Matthew 11:23*

I

BETH NEELAH, IN THE UPPER GALILEE
4 SEPTEMBER, A.D. 32

"Livia." Yehuda straightened, shooting his wife a warning glance.
"Leave the baskets to me."

Livia wiped at her forehead with the back of her hand. "You are
like an old dog with burrs in its coat, Yehuda. Stop fussing. I am just
fine." With a toss of her head, she lifted the basket filled with clusters
of red grapes and carried it over to the cart, half loaded for the trip to
the winepress.

"I should have made it a condition of the *ketubah* that you would
be more obedient to the counsel of your husband," he grumbled.

"Then you would have had a cow for a wife and not a woman."

He laughed in spite of himself, slid the knife he was using to cut
the grape clusters into a sheath, and walked over to her. He took
the empty basket from her hands, tossed it aside, and took her by the
shoulders.

She cocked her head at him. "If you are going to kiss me, hold me tighter. If you are going to lecture me about obedience, then get back to work."

He kissed her.

Livia kissed him back, lingering much longer than he did. When she pulled back, her eyes were soft. "Thank you for being concerned," she murmured. "But really, hard work will only make my body stronger." A momentary look of pain darkened her features. "I know it's been almost a year, Yehuda, but that's not a long time. Not for some women."

"I'm not worried," he said lightly, though in actuality his concerns were growing. Shana and Samuel had been married several months after they had, and Shana was four months with child. "My own parents didn't have me until they had been married almost two years."

"And you were certainly worth waiting for," she teased.

He laughed. "They wondered there for a while."

She grew more serious. "Really, Yehuda. I feel wonderful. I think the life of a vineyard keeper's wife completely agrees with me."

He was instantly sober too. "I worried a lot about that before I decided to ask you to marry me," he said. "You've lived in large cities your whole life. It pleases me greatly that you love it here as much as I do."

"I do, Yehuda," she said, reaching up to lay her hand on his cheek, partially covering his thick beard. "I have never been more happy."

"Nor I," he agreed.

"All right you two," a voice from behind them barked. "You're supposed to be working out here, not mooning into each other's eyes."

They both swung around. "Simeon!" Livia cried in delight.

"Well, well," Yehuda exclaimed in pleased surprise. "A stranger in our midst."

Simeon turned, cupping a hand to his mouth. "They're back here!"

As Livia and Yehuda started moving between the rows of

grapevines, Miriam and Leah came out of the olive grove that bordered the vineyard.

"Miriam!" Livia broke into a run.

Miriam did the same. "*Shalom, shalom*, Livia!"

II

They were seated on two stone benches beneath a huge, old gnarled olive tree. Yehuda and Simeon sat on the one, half turned so they faced each other. Livia and Miriam sat shoulder to shoulder on the other, hands clasped tightly. Leah had stayed with them for a few minutes, but when Yehuda announced that Shana was with child, Leah set off to see her old friend. Though it was still only mid-morning, the sun was getting hot, proof that while summer might be ending there was very little softening of the temperature as yet.

Miriam reared back, looking Livia up and down. "Look at you. You're so brown."

Livia looked down at her arms. Her light summer tunic had a sleeve that came barely to the elbow. "I know. I like it. Mother always said my skin was too pale."

She had a small, triangular scarf tied over her head. It was dark brown and accentuated her light blond hair and blue eyes. She looked radiant, assured, fully at peace. Miriam smiled. "This being the wife of an old bear must agree with you."

"Hey!" Yehuda yipped in protest.

Miriam laughed lightly. "It's a good thing she looks so happy, Yehuda. I was prepared to give you a lecture about treating her right."

"Me? How about giving *her* the lecture? I can't get her to slow down even a little."

Livia smiled. "I can handle the old bear except when he starts smothering me by being too much of an overprotective husband."

"Good for you," Miriam said to the big man.

Yehuda gave his wife a triumphant grin.

"How soon will Shana's child come?" Simeon wondered.

"In the spring," Livia answered. "She and Samuel are very happy."

"We'll have to go and congratulate her," Simeon said.

"So what about you two?" Yehuda asked Miriam. "Are you still planning on getting married at Sukkot?"

"We are," she said happily. "Simeon had to come up to Sepphoris, so we thought we'd stop and let you know it's on for sure. Also, we have a question for you."

Simeon looked at Yehuda. "Do you plan to go up to Jerusalem for *Sukkot?*"

Yehuda gave a quick nod. "If we can get the harvest in and the grapes pressed."

"No ifs," Livia corrected him. "We're doing well. Everything will be done. We are going."

"Good. Miriam and I have talked about being married in Bethlehem just before the Feast of Tabernacles begins."

"In Bethlehem?" Yehuda repeated. He hadn't expected that.

"At my cousin Benjamin's home. We don't want a large ceremony. We'll invite only the family and a few close friends. Benjamin and his wife, Esther, weren't able to come for the betrothal last year, so they are very pleased. Also, Uncle Aaron and Aunt Hava are now in Jerusalem too, as you know. Aaron would like to perform the marriage for us." He shrugged. "The more we thought about it, the more sense it made to be married there."

Livia and Yehuda looked at each another for a moment, then both nodded. "That should work fine for us," Livia said.

"Good," Simeon said. "If you couldn't be there, we would make different plans."

"I think that's a wonderful idea," Livia said. "I'm looking forward to being in Jerusalem again. How soon will you be leaving?"

"Actually," Miriam answered, "we plan to leave next week."

"Next week?" Yehuda said in surprise. "Why so soon? *Sukkot* is not for another month."

Simeon responded. "Well, first off, it turns out that Jesus has decided that he and the Twelve are leaving next week. He wants to take his time going up, cross over Jordan, and travel through Perea, perhaps doing some teaching there. Which is fine with us. Besides getting to journey with him, it will get us to Jerusalem a few days ahead of the feast. That works well for Mother, who wants to be there to help Esther get ready."

"We've been so busy this last while, and Simeon's been gone so much," Miriam was explaining to Livia. "We haven't been able to spend much time with Jesus. Simeon's parents decided that it was a good opportunity for all of us. We'll finish bringing in the harvest, then leave the warehouse in charge of Phineas, David's chief steward. That will give all the family an opportunity to spend some time with Jesus as we go up to Jerusalem for *Sukkot*."

"Will you try to see your father?" Livia asked.

Pain twisted Miriam's mouth, and she looked away. "No." When they had gone to Jerusalem for Passover in the spring, she had considered it, but Simeon talked her out of it. They had heard nothing from him, and in Simeon's mind it would not be well to stir up old emotions.

Simeon blew out his breath, half in disgust, half in sorrow. "Uncle Aaron writes us from time to time. He is, of course, in the middle of things there and is often at the meetings of the Great Council. In one of his letters, he said that Mordechai still forbids anyone to speak Miriam's name in his presence and refuses to talk about her in any way."

"I had hoped," Livia said softly, "that after almost a year and half, he might start to soften."

"Softness is not a quality that Mordechai ben Uzziel has culti-vated," Yehuda growled, frowning darkly. "He's not going to bend. He's too proud."

Miriam still looked at the ground. "Maybe once we are married and have children, he will soften."

No one said anything. Obviously they were not as hopeful as she was.

Yehuda, having seen the pain in Miriam's eyes, decided to change the subject. He stood up. "Why don't you two go on back to the house with Livia? I'll finish cutting this row of grapes; then I'll come on in too."

"I'll help you," Simeon said, standing as well.

"I can finish," Livia started to say, but Yehuda waved her away. "If Simeon hasn't grown too soft living the life of a wealthy merchant, I'll put him to work. We'll see you in about an hour."

III

"Tell me about Drusus, Livia."

Livia turned. They were in the room that served as kitchen and eat-ing room, starting preparations for the midday meal. "What about him?"

"You've heard from him, I suppose."

"Oh, yes," she said. "He writes every two or three months."

"He's still in Athens?"

She nodded. "His first year of apprenticeship as a builder is com-pleted, and he seems happy. He even talked about coming to see us in another year, perhaps."

"That would be nice," Miriam said.

"And what of Leah?" Livia said. "As you know, I had hopes that she and Drusus might become kindred spirits. Does she have any prospects for marriage?"

"Actually," Miriam answered, "there is something developing. There is a family in Capernaum that have been longtime associates of David and Deborah. They have a son named Jonathan. He and Leah have been friends since childhood. His father hinted to David the other day that they would be interested in seeing if something might be arranged."

"And Leah would find that acceptable?"

"I think she is quietly pleased, but it's still too soon to say for sure."

"Good for her. She is such a jewel."

"And how are things here for you?"

"Wonderful."

Miriam smiled. "I didn't mean between you and Yehuda. That is obvious. And I'm so happy for you, Livia. But how are things in Beth Neelah? Sometimes small villages can be so tight-knit."

She shrugged diffidently. "I'm pretty much accepted now. And it's getting better all the time. Some of the men, especially those who used to be in Simeon's and Yehuda's band, are convinced that I'm the one who forced Yehuda to turn away from being a Zealot. There's still some resentment, but not much."

"And what does Yehuda say to that?" Miriam wondered.

"No one dares say anything to his face. He's very protective of me. And—"

At that moment the door opened, and Yehuda stuck his head in. Livia turned in surprise. "It will be about another quarter of an hour before the food is ready." She laughed. "Actually, more than that. Miriam and I have been talking."

"I know, but Simeon and I just had an idea."

"What?"

"He's going to help me finish cutting grapes this afternoon and in the morning. Then all we'll have to do is take them to the winepress. Since tromping grapes in the press is so slippery, I think you'd better not help with that task. You could fall and hurt yourself."

"Yehuda, I will be—"

He was grinning broadly. "So why don't you go to Jerusalem with Miriam and Simeon and the family?"

Her mouth dropped open.

His grin only broadened. "I mean it. Once the wine is done, I'll come and join you in Bethlehem for the wedding."

"Really?" The thought of being with Jesus for almost a month was very tempting.

"Yes, really. Don't think about it. Just do it."

"Oh, Livia," Miriam said, "that would be wonderful. We'll stay up every night talking like we used to do."

"Are you sure?" She was searching her husband's eyes.

"I'm sure," he said, soberly. "It's what you've wanted. And since we're going anyway, why not go now?"

"Thank you, Yehuda. Thank you very much."

Now the smile split his face, and he turned to Miriam. "I think she loves me," he boomed. Then he laughed aloud, in that boyish way he had. "And can you blame her?"

Miriam laughed in pure delight as he waved a hand and shut the door again.

IV

CAPERNAUM

11 SEPTEMBER, A.D. 32

To a bystander, what was happening in the large, open field just outside Capernaum might have looked like a generous mixture of chaos, pandemonium, and bedlam. But in actuality, except for the children who ran hither and yon, screeching shrilly as they played hide-and-seek among the baggage and the animals, the activity was really quite well organized and moving ahead with remarkable precision.

It would be a fairly substantial caravan that headed south to Jerusalem. There were close to a hundred people all together. In one way, that was good. Whether they took the road through Samaria or went down through the Jordan River Valley and through Jericho, there was always danger from brigands and robbers. The larger the party traveling together, the less the risk of attack.

And yet the journey would provide challenges, too. Since this trip to Jerusalem involved staying through the full week of the Feast of Tabernacles, which was still nearly a month away, there was the problem of feeding and bedding a very large group, including babies and numerous children, for an extended time. But it was the time of the harvest, and food was plentiful right now. Each village along the way would welcome the chance to sell to passing groups.

Most of the disciples closest to Jesus were there. The Twelve and their families, of course, were in the thick of organizing things. But also present were Luke the Physician, and Mattathias, a loyal friend. As Simeon looked around, he recognized most of the people. Then, with a start, he realized how many of those in the group had felt the healing touch of Jesus. There was Joachin the leper, whole and cleansed for more than a year and now back at his trade. Mary of Magdala had been possessed of evil spirits. Now she hurried about, smiling and laughing and playing with the children. Joanna, whose husband was chief steward for the family of Herod in Tiberias, had been cured of her infirmity in one day. Near one of the donkeys, Jairus, former ruler of the synagogue in Capernaum, was working with his wife and young daughter. She was the young maid who had actually died before Jairus could bring Jesus to her. "Maid, arise," Jesus had said. And she arose. There was Ruth, widow of Yohanan the weaver. She was an older woman who for twelve years had been afflicted with an issue of blood, a continual hemorrhaging that drained her of all energy and health. One day, in desperation, she pressed through the crowd, hoping to but touch the hem of Jesus' robe. In an instant, she had been cured of what no physician had been able to staunch before. And there was Elah ben Reuben, who had been struck down with a paralyzing infirmity that left him bedridden. When friends had tried to get him to Jesus, there had been too many people in the house for them to gain entry. So they had carried Elah up to the roof, removed some of the tiles, and lowered him down to Jesus. That day Elah had picked up his bed and carried it home, perfectly well again.

It was not a caravan in the traditional sense, with camels and donkeys laden with goods for trade. There would be only about two dozen donkeys, and these were owned by individual families. They would primarily carry bedding, tents for the women and smaller children, some dried food supplies, and a few other necessities. Other than that, most people would walk. Smaller children would occasionally ride atop their father's shoulders or be nestled into the packs on the backs of the animals, but the pace was leisurely enough that they too walked much of the time. That was one reason for leaving so far in advance of the time of the festival.

If he pushed it, a man on horseback could make the seventy-mile trip from Capernaum to Jerusalem (eighty miles if one went by way of the Jordan Valley to avoid Samaria) in about two and a half days. A caravan would take closer to six, assuming it made no significant stops along the way. This group planned to be on the road for as much as two weeks, depending on where Jesus decided to go. They would stop for midday meals and camp each night around sundown. If a problem of any kind arose, they might stop for half a day or more to take care of it.

Family caravans were not the best mode of travel if one was in a hurry, but having family along was part of the excitement of a pilgrimage. For the children, even older ones, it was a grand adventure. Even the adults looked forward to the pilgrimages, for it brought a change from the daily grind of life and an opportunity to participate in the grand festivals of Judaism.

David ben Joseph looked around, letting his eyes stop where Jesus stood a few paces away. This was the hub of the greatest amount of activity. He could see Peter making the rounds, checking everything for the last time. David turned to his family. "I think it's time we got everyone together. It looks like they're almost ready."

"Has anyone seen Esther in the last while?" Rachel asked.

Simeon turned to his sister-in-law. "I saw her a few moments ago over with Peter and Anna's family."

Ephraim gave one last tug on the rope, making sure the pack on their donkey was secure and straightened. "I'll go find her," he told his wife.

Their younger brother, Joseph, appeared from out of nowhere. "I know where Peter is," he said. "I'll get her." And he was off. Though twelve now and soon to be considered an adult, on this day he was pure boy again, and his excitement was hard to contain.

"Hurry!" Rachel called after him. "It's almost time to go."

Since Rachel was helping Ephraim pack and Lilly was doing the same with Ezra, Livia and Miriam had taken the mothers' two babies and were seated on a blanket watching the activity. Boaz, Rachel's second child, sat beside them. He was so pleased to have Livia with him that he chose her over playing with the other children. The two babies were both walking now. Lilly's little Miriam, now thirteen months old, stood on the other side of Livia, one hand resting on her arm. Amasa, Rachel's youngest and two weeks older than little Miriam, swayed back and forth on unsteady feet, watching the activity around him with wide eyes.

They were very different, these two. Miriam was a tiny thing and was going to be a miniature of her mother, a fact that brought Lilly continuing delight every day. Amasa was a heavy boy, with fat cheeks, thighs like the legs of a stool, and a triple chin. He was mellow in temperament, rarely cried, and was always quick to smile at anyone who would pay him the slightest attention.

Deborah, satisfied at last that their things were ready, went over to where the babies were. She reached down and picked up Amasa. "There's my boy," she said. "Are you ready to go?"

His face split in a grin at the sight of his grandmother, and he made some sound which she took to be assent. Ephraim went over too. He poked his son in the ribs, and Amasa squealed aloud, arching his back. He was very ticklish. "This one is always ready to go," Ephraim said. "He likes to be in the middle of things."

Miriam got to her feet and held out her arms for her namesake. Little Miriam immediately lifted her arms, and Miriam picked her up. "We're ready when you are, Lilly."

Rachel looked around. "Where is Esther?" But even as she asked the question, she saw Joseph threading his way toward them, Esther in tow.

"Esther," Ephraim said, "I want you to stay close now. We're almost ready to go."

"Yes, Papa."

They heard a shout and turned toward Peter. He had his arms in the air, motioning people in. "If you could all gather in, I think it's time."

They did, parents calling to their children and taking their hands.

Peter waited until he was completely surrounded and the group quieted. "It looks like all is in readiness," he said. He had a deep voice that had a tendency to boom out, and there was no problem with anyone hearing him. "Family heads, be sure you have everyone accounted for before moving out."

All around, the older members of the group nodded. Once they started on the march, there would be no effort to keep individual families together. The group was like one large family anyway. The children would gather into rough age groups to play and be together. Whichever family was closest to a given group would keep an eye on them. Most of the men would move out to the head of the column, watching for problems and setting the pace. The women would likewise gather in groups to visit as they walked. The caravan was really much like a rolling village, with family groups taking precedence only at meal times and at night.

"As you all know," Peter said, "we will be taking the Jordan Valley route, and there is a good chance we may cross over into Perea. It has been some time since Jesus visited there, and he would like to take this opportunity to do so again."

Jesus spoke up. "We'll see what happens. It may be that we'll go into Perea after the festival. I would like to spend some time there either now or before Passover."

Simeon looked at his father in surprise. Passover was seven months away. Was Jesus saying he wouldn't be returning to Capernaum until after that? David shrugged. That was news to him as well.

Peter spoke again. "We have no set time to be in Jerusalem, except to arrive in time for *Sukkot*, so we'll take it day by day. Are there any concerns before we start?"

It was Luke who spoke up. He stood beside Andrew, Peter's brother, and James and John, the sons of Zebedee. "We are going to be with you, Master," he said. "It doesn't matter to us what you decide."

There was an instant murmur of agreement. Jesus seemed pleased and nodded to them all.

"We shouldn't have any problems on the road," Peter went on, "but once we stop in a town or village, you know what will happen. As soon as the multitudes know Jesus is with us, they will come out by the hundreds."

"Or thousands," Andrew said.

"Yes, or thousands. The Master will take time to teach them, and when he does, we'll try to move away from our camp a ways to protect you from the crowds. But that may not always be possible. Therefore, when those times come, you will want to watch the children, especially the little ones. The crush of people can get pretty heavy at times."

That was wise counsel, and everyone was nodding again. Peter turned to Jesus, clearly wanting to know if there was anything else he wished to say. Jesus was thoughtful for a moment, then moved up to stand beside Peter. Parents leaned down and motioned their children to be silent. Very quickly, there was no sound but the breeze rustling the leaves of the trees around them.

As he looked around on these friends, all of whom were trusted and loved, Jesus grew very somber, almost sorrowful. Finally his shoulders lifted and fell, as if he were trying to shrug off a burden. "My time has now come. I set my face steadfastly toward Jerusalem."

Again Simeon gave his father a quick look. What did that mean? They were all going up to the capital. David still looked as perplexed as Simeon.

"John the Baptist came among the people, and they knew him not. And they did unto him whatsoever they wished."

People looked at each other in surprise. John the Baptist had been beheaded by Herod Antipas almost a year and half earlier.

"Likewise, shall the Son of man suffer of them."

That created even more of a stir. The Son of man was a title the Master sometimes used to refer to himself. People looked at each other in dismay. Was he saying . . . ? But that couldn't be. Simeon glanced at Peter. The big fisherman had his head partly down. He was clearly troubled by what Jesus had said, but he didn't seem surprised.

Suddenly Jesus half turned, looking back toward the main part of town. Then his head lifted, and he seemed to be scanning the hillsides that rose northward from Capernaum, golden brown after a long summer of no rain. "Woe unto thee, Chorazin," he said in a loud voice.

Simeon started. Chorazin was a town constructed almost entirely of black basalt stone in the hills a few miles north of Capernaum.

Jesus turned even more, looking eastward beyond Capernaum, along the shoreline of the sea. "And woe unto to thee, Bethsaida. If the mighty works which have been done in you had been shown in Tyre and Sidon, they would have repented in sackcloth and ashes long ago."

Everyone gave the others strange looks. Tyre and Sidon were Phoenician seaport cities, Gentile cities famous for their worldliness and wickedness. What did this mean?

He released a long sigh, filled with pain. Simeon saw Jesus' head turn so he was looking directly at the nearest houses of the town. "And thou, Capernaum, which are exalted unto heaven, thou shalt be brought down to hell. For if the mighty works which had been done in thee had been done in Sodom, it would have remained until this day."

Simeon winced. Sodom and Gomorrah had become the ultimate metaphor of wickedness. Those cities had been destroyed in one day when Abraham could find no righteous among them. And Capernaum was worse than that?

And then he thought of what he had noticed just a few moments before. All around him stood living evidence of the miraculous power of Jesus. Joachin the leper; Elah ben Reuben; Ruth, widow of Yohanan; Mary Magdalene; Jairus's daughter. Simeon realized that right here, before his very eyes, was one example after another of the "work" that Jesus had done in this area. And there were those who were not with them this day. A blind man, healed with a touch. A man from Chorazin who had come to the synagogue one morning, one hand drawn back within his robes so that people wouldn't see its withered, twisted deformity. Somewhere he carried out his occupation, whatever it was, and now he did it with two strong, healthy hands. The servant of Sextus Rubrius had been healed from a distance when Sextus had told Jesus that he wasn't worthy to have the Master come to his home.

And what of that which had helped to finally turn Simeon's hardened heart around? On a hillside west of Capernaum, Simeon had watched with his own eyes as five loaves of bread and two fishes had been blessed, then passed to more than five thousand people. When the people had all eaten, twelve baskets filled with leftovers were brought back in.

If the mighty works which have been done in you had been shown in Tyre and Sidon, they would have repented in sackcloth and ashes long ago. Yes, he thought. If Sodom had seen such marvels happen in their streets, what then? If Rome or Athens or Alexandria had been witness to such wonders, would the majority of their citizens have gone on about their business as if nothing had happened?

Jesus slowly turned back to the crowd. There was sorrow in his eyes. "I say unto you, in the day of judgment it shall be more tolerable for the land of Sodom, and for Tyre and Sidon, than it shall be for Capernaum, for Chorazin, for Bethsaida."

He stopped then, looking drained, stepped back, and turned to Peter. "We can go when you are ready."

CHAPTER NOTES

As has been stated in earlier volumes, arranging the events of Christ's life into chronological order is very difficult to do. Many so-called "harmonies" of the Gospels have tried to do this, and none are in complete agreement with each other. Not that it makes a significant difference. The power of Jesus lies in *what* he said and did, not *when* he said or did it. Most harmonies do agree that the last months of Jesus' life were spent in what is often called "the Perean and later Judean ministry." John seems to tie the beginning of that ministry to the Feast of Tabernacles (John 7:1–3), which was held in October.

Many of the cities, towns, and villages in the Holy Land today occupy the same sites they did in the time of Christ, though often the names have changed or been modified. Ironically, though Chorazin, Bethsaida, and Capernaum were thriving towns situated on sites one would expect to be conducive to continued occupation, there are no villages at any of the three sites today. Some find that interesting in light of Christ's condemnation of these villages because of their lack of response to his ministry (see Matthew 11:20–24; Luke 10:13–15).

Just a note about the way in which the characters in the novel speak of "going up" to Jerusalem. To modern readers, "up" and "down" is usually determined by the orientation of our maps, with north being at the top. Thus, from Montana one goes "down" to Arizona, while Arizonans would go "up" to Montana. To the Jews, one always went "up" to Jerusalem. This was partly because Jerusalem sits at about 2,600 feet above sea level in the tops of the central ridge of mountains that dominate Israel. Even when considering the north and south, along the spine of the mountains, Jerusalem is higher than the immediate land surrounding it. So as one approached the city, one would literally go up.

But the use of the expression "going up" indicated far more than simply elevation. Jerusalem was the capital city. It was the center of culture, learning, and religion. Here the temple, the heart and soul of Judaism, crowned one of Jerusalem's highest hills, gleaming golden-white in the sun, like a beacon to all the world. So to go to Jerusalem was to ascend upward—physically, emotionally, culturally, and, most importantly, spiritually. "Going up" to Jerusalem is frequently used in both the Old and New Testaments (see, for example, 1 Kings 12:28; Isaiah 2:3; Matthew 20:18; Mark 10:33; Luke 18:31; Acts 15:2).

CHAPTER 9

I

ON THE ROAD TO JERICHO

12 SEPTEMBER, A.D. 32

"Uncle Simeon. Tell me a story before I go to bed."

Rachel, who was laying out blankets on the ground, swung around. "Esther! It is past your bedtime. Boaz is already asleep. You have stalled long enough."

The large black eyes didn't even glance in her mother's direction. In the firelight, they only grew larger, more imploring, and more beautiful. "Please, Uncle Simeon. Please, Aunt Miriam."

Simeon turned to his sister-in-law. "Now, how are we supposed to resist something like that?"

Rachel just shook her head. "She is shameless, you know. She knows that she can twist the three of you like a thread around her finger."

Simeon nodded, smiling at his niece. "I know, but it *is* our first night on the road. Little girls—young women!"—he quickly corrected himself, before she could react—"need something to calm them down after all the excitement."

Esther snuggled in between Miriam and Livia, who put an arm around her. "We'll make it short," Livia promised Rachel.

Rachel sighed, not really displeased, and bobbed her head. "All right. But then, Esther, you promise that you will go right to bed when it's done?"

"Yes, Mama." It was said humbly, but the gleam of triumph in her eyes was unmistakable.

Simeon laughed. "So what story would you like to hear?"

"Queen Esther!" came the instant reply.

"Of course," Miriam said, hugging her tightly. "What else would it be?"

II

Simeon was lying back, propped up on one elbow. He watched Miriam, her face tinged with just a hint of gold from the low firelight. She was sitting, arms folded on her knees, staring into the fire. They were alone now. Livia had taken Esther to her family and had stayed to talk.

"What are you thinking?" he asked.

She turned, slightly startled, then smiled. "Actually, I was thinking about what Queen Esther's uncle said to her when he was trying to convince her to go to the king and plead for him to save her people."

"'And who knoweth,'" Simeon began to quote softly, "'whether thou art come to the kingdom for such a time as this.'"

"Exactly," Miriam murmured. "And surely it was so. To have a

Jewess in such a position of influence in the royal court of Persia that she could save her people, that had to be the hand of the Lord."

"No question about it. She was a woman of uncommon beauty and remarkable courage. The Lord surely raised her up for that very purpose." He reached out and touched her arm. "I picture her to be like someone else I know."

Miriam smiled. "Hardly anything like Queen Esther, but thank you anyway." She turned her head to where Ephraim and Rachel were preparing for bed beside their sleeping children. "What will our little Esther see in her lifetime? What things has the Lord in mind for her?"

"It is a sobering question," Simeon replied. "For one thing, she will grow up being a disciple of the Master. She already has as much faith in him as anyone does."

"Yes, and that seems strange, doesn't it. We came to know Jesus in our adulthood. She and Boaz and little Miriam and Amasa will all grow up knowing him from the beginning."

"And our children as well."

She nodded happily. "That, too. What a difference it will make to them. What a great blessing that will be to them."

"What blessing is that?"

They both turned as a figure appeared out of the night. Simeon sat up, half turning. "Peter? *Erev tov!*"

"And good evening to you two. May I join you?"

"Of course." Simeon moved closer to Miriam to make a place for him. The chief apostle sat down beside them, sighing wearily as he did so.

"I thought Mother and Father were with you," Simeon said.

"They are, or were. They're with Anna and Mary Magdalene and Joanna. I decided I would take one last look around camp to make sure everything is all right."

"And?"

He chuckled. "You can tell it's our first day on the road. Half the camp is already asleep."

"What about Jesus?" Miriam asked.

"He's off by himself somewhere. We asked everyone to let him have some time alone." He looked at Miriam. "So what blessings were you talking about as I came up?"

"Oh, we were talking about these children who will grow up knowing Jesus from the very beginning."

"We told Esther the story of Queen Esther," Simeon explained. He chuckled. "For the hundredth time at least. And we were just wondering if the Lord has something special in store for our Esther, just as he did for Queen Esther."

"But of course," Peter said. "She will be part of the new kingdom of God."

"That's just what I was saying," Miriam responded, pleased to know her thoughts were similar to their old friend's.

"And what will the kingdom be like in twenty-five or thirty years?" Peter mused. "Look how many have come to believe in just these last two years. Give it thirty more years, and Jesus could have a following of tens of thousands."

Miriam was struck with that thought. "Wouldn't that be wonderful? It could influence the entire country."

"All of Israel even," Peter agreed.

That reminded Simeon of something that had been bothering him all day. "Have you got a few minutes?" he asked. "Or do you have to get back?"

"No, I'm fine. It feels good to sit for a while."

"Tell me about what Jesus said this morning as we were preparing to leave."

Peter turned himself a little so he faced them more directly. "About Chorazin and Capernaum?"

"Yes. That and his other comments. It was almost like he was saying good-bye. Like he wasn't coming back."

Peter looked at him sharply. "Why do you say that?"

Simeon shrugged. "I don't know. It was just a feeling I had. That comment about the Son of man having to suffer as John the Baptist did. Was he talking about himself?"

Peter didn't answer for a long time; then his mouth pulled down. Absently, he began to stroke his beard, deep in thought. "I'm worried, Simeon."

"Why?"

"Well, first of all, we weren't supposed to go up to Jerusalem for *Sukkot* this year."

Simeon began to nod. "That's what Father said you had told him a few weeks ago. So what happened?"

"It was really strange. Mary, his mother, came down with the rest of the family a week or so ago."

"Yes, I remember that."

"The brothers asked Jesus if he was going up to the feast. He said no. By that time we knew there was talk of possible trouble in Jerusalem, and so we were pleased to hear that."

"Are his brothers still having a hard time accepting Jesus for what he is?" Simeon wondered.

Peter's mouth pulled down again as he nodded.

"Not Mary, surely," Miriam exclaimed.

"Oh, no," Peter replied hastily. "Mary knows exactly who and what her son is. But his brothers . . ." He shook his head. "There's no animosity there, or anything like that. It's just . . . well, I can see why. I mean, it would be hard to believe that the Messiah had come right into your own family. That he was the older brother you grew up with, wrestled with, shared a sleeping room with, ate with every day. That would be strange."

"And yet surely they've seen him work," Miriam said. "Surely they've witnessed some of his miracles."

"Yes, they have. And in fact, that's why they pressed him to go to Judea. They want him to let the disciples there see what he does. 'If you work in secret,' they told him, 'how can you hope to be known openly. Go, show yourself to the world.'"

"And what did Jesus say to that?" Simeon asked.

"That's one of the things that worries me," was the response. "He said something like, 'My time is not yet come. Your time is here, so you go up to the feast. But my time is not yet.'" He exhaled slowly. "Then his next words really chilled us all. He said, 'The world cannot hate you, but it hates me, because I testify that its works are evil.'"

"Whew!" Simeon said. "Those are strong words."

"Yes," Peter said, "and it clearly frustrated them. We learned just a few days ago that the family had taken Mary to Jerusalem. Then, to our surprise, Jesus announced that we would be going up there after all."

"In spite of the danger?" Miriam asked softly.

"In spite of everything. He has agreed to go up secretly, but we are going."

"Secretly?" Simeon gave a short, mirthless laugh. "With the crowds he draws, the Sanhedrin will know he's coming before we ever reach the city."

"I know," Peter said glumly.

"Do you think he's afraid that . . ." Miriam couldn't bring herself to say the words.

"Afraid? No. Does he think that he's in danger?" He nodded vigorously, rubbing at the dirt with the palm of his hand. "Definitely."

"And you couldn't convince him not to go?" Simeon asked, already knowing what the answer was.

Peter stared into the fire for a long time before answering. When his head finally lifted, he looked very grave. "Let me share with you something that happened not long ago," he said. "We haven't talked much about this, and it's so personal that I don't like to talk about it, but it helps to answer your question."

Both Miriam and Simeon sat back to listen.

"We had gone north," Peter began, his voice soft and far away, "up in the area of Caesarea Philippi. You've been there, Simeon. It's where the springs of Pan are."

"Yes, I know it well." At the southern base of Mount Hermon, copious springs burst forth from the ground, forming one of the sources of the River Jordan. It was a beautiful spot, and much earlier, the Greeks had turned it into a center for the worship of Pan, their god of forest and pasture, flocks and shepherds. In recent times, Herod Philip, son of Herod the Great, had built a Roman city there and named it Caesarea in honor of the Emperor Tiberias. It was called Caesarea Philippi to distinguish it from the Caesarea on the coast.

"One afternoon, out of nowhere, Jesus asked us a question," Peter continued. "He asked us who men thought he was. We knew what he was thinking—there were many theories about his identity. I think it was Andrew who said that some people were saying that he was John the Baptist come back from the dead. Others claim he is Elijah. We've even heard that some believe he is the prophet Jeremiah returned from the grave."

"And what did he say to that?" Miriam asked.

"He seemed interested in those reports, but then he looked squarely at us and said, 'But whom do *you* say that I am?'" Peter seemed far away. "It was the strangest thing. Suddenly it was like I had a fire erupt inside of me. I looked right at him and said, 'Thou art the Christ, the Son of the Living God.'"

"Well said," Simeon half whispered. He had been thinking how he would have answered. Peter's reply said it all.

"That seemed to please him," Peter admitted. "Looking right back at me, he said, 'Blessed are you, Simon, son of Jonah, for flesh and blood have not revealed this to you, but my Father which is in heaven.' And then he told us some things about the kingdom that I shall not speak of at this time."

"That must have been a marvelous experience," Miriam breathed, thoroughly caught up in the words of the fisherman.

"It was." He hesitated. "But it was what happened a short time thereafter that I wish to speak of." He stopped, his eyes troubled in the firelight. "It wasn't long after that. He started telling us he had to go to Jerusalem." His head dropped. "He said he had to go there and suffer many things of the elders, the chief priests, and the scribes."

Miriam looked down and briefly closed her eyes in pain. One of those elders was her father.

"This time there was no hinting, no skirting around things. He told us straight out that he would be killed, but that he would be raised again the third day."

"Killed!" Miriam cried out. It was one thing to talk about arrest or imprisonment, but death? A cold chill swept through her body, causing her to shudder.

Simeon had likewise gone cold. "Then why are you letting him go? We have to stop this."

"Let me finish," Peter murmured.

"Sorry," Simeon said.

"I felt exactly as you did. We were all shocked, but I was horrified to hear him talk like that. I grabbed his arm and began to rebuke him. 'Lord,' I said, 'this thing be far from you. This shall not be.'"

He stopped. Simeon and Miriam didn't speak, just watched Peter's face twist with shame.

"Jesus turned on me," the apostle went on, speaking slowly and with pain. "His eyes were blazing. 'Get thee behind me, Satan,' he said."

Miriam's head came up in astonishment. "He called you Satan?"

"He did, and in the same tone I used just now. 'Thou art an offense unto me,' he went on. 'You savor the things of man more than you do the things of God.'"

He looked at them directly. "You can imagine how that hit me. It was so unexpected, so utterly shocking, that I fell back a step. His eyes never left me. They bored into me like twin lances of fire. It is a rebuke I shall never forget."

He stopped, and they all fell silent. Peter stared into the fire, the memory still searing his consciousness.

"But why?" Simeon finally asked. "Why would that make him angry? You were just trying to protect him."

"I'm not completely sure. We haven't spoken of it again." He looked at Simeon. "Remember the day when Jesus sent me to catch the fish with the tribute money in its mouth?"

"Of course. I'll never forget that day."

"If you'll remember, he gently rebuked me then too. I had taken it upon myself to speak for the Master, to tell him what he had to do." He gave an exclamation of disbelief. "Me! A common fisherman, telling the Son of God how to solve a problem! The audacity of that even now takes my breath away."

He slowly shook his head. "On this day, I did it again. He was telling us what had to happen, what God's will for him was, and I tried to tell him that it could not be."

His hands came together and began to twist. "I was speaking out of love, but I was not speaking God's will. I was speaking Satan's, for it is Satan who tries to stop him from working his Father's will. I hope never to do that again."

Again there was silence as they considered what they had just heard. Finally, Miriam spoke. "So you think he will be killed?" The horror of it strained her voice even to say it.

"I don't know. I just know that we will trust him to do what is right. And we have already decided, the twelve of us. We are never going to leave his side. If there is any way to protect him, then we shall do it."

"I shall do the same," Simeon said.

"I know," Peter answered forlornly, "but will it make any difference?"

III

NORTH OF JERICHO

13–16 SEPTEMBER, A.D. 32

As the caravan traveled southward from the Sea of Galilee, they moved down the valley of the Jordan, passing by and through various cities, towns, and villages. At the Yarmuk River ford, a few miles south of the Sea of Galilee, they crossed to the east side of the Jordan and traveled in the province of Perea for a time. But when they reached the Jabbock River, where Jacob had wrestled with an angel some two millennia before and had his name changed to Israel, they crossed back again to the west side of the Jordan.

From both sides of the river, people poured out in great multitudes to see and hear the Master. This slowed their progress considerably, and as Rosh Hashanah approached, they were still several days' travel from Jerusalem.

No one minded. This was exactly what they expected. Every day became a feast of its own. Jesus would stop and teach the people the doctrines of the kingdom. Then, invariably, someone would bring a child who was sick, or an aged and infirm father or mother. Soon there would be a line, and those traveling with Jesus had the opportunity to witness for themselves, time after time, again and again and again, the incredible power and majesty of the Son of God. Philoteria, Gadara,

Jabneel, Ramoth, Jabesh-gilead, Tabbath, Coreae—villages that Simeon had never even heard of emptied as word spread of the approach of the man from Nazareth.

One unforeseen blessing for the company was that they were showered with every evidence of welcome and hospitality. Almost every night, the mats spread on the ground were filled with the richness of the fall harvest. Every night Jesus was invited to have supper at the home of this person or that, and he often ended up at more than one place for the evening.

As they approached Jericho, the largest and most important city in the Jordan Valley, it was the day before the Sabbath. They camped a short distance north of the city while it was still early in the afternoon, and parents bustled around preparing both their children and their meals for the day of rest. The plan was to welcome *Shabbat* quietly and without fanfare. But two hours before the sun went down, a delegation from the city came out to the camp. They found Jesus and graciously invited him to bring some of his group into the city to observe the Sabbath at the synagogue there. He immediately accepted. About half the group decided to stay in camp and watch over their goods. The rest set out barely fifteen minutes later.

IV

JERICHO

Jericho was a prosperous city. Not only did it sit astride one of the primary trade routes connecting two major north-south highways, but it also had three very profitable sources of income. All around the city were the famous date plantations once owned by Herod the Great. This crop was so lucrative that Herod and Queen Cleopatra of Egypt had almost gone to war over the vast groves of date palms.

Then there were the balsam orchards. Lying just a few miles north of the Dead Sea, Jericho's climate was hot and dry, even in the winter months, and the land along the Jordan was fertile. It provided the perfect environment for growing the tree, whose sap was tapped and dried. Like incense, balsam sap was highly valued for use in perfumes and other costly cosmetics. Balsam sold for twice the amount one could obtain for an equal weight of silver.

The third source of income, and an equally profitable trade item, was salt. Just south of the city lay the saltiest body of water known to man. The shores were white, and when the water was channeled into shallow ponds it would evaporate and leave thick layers of brilliant white crystals. Salt was the universal currency in the Roman Empire. In addition to its value in flavoring food, it had preservative powers. Meat, dried and salted, would last for months. Fish packed in barrels of salt water were shipped all over the world.

So valuable was this commodity that Roman soldiers were often paid with bags of salt, which they could then use for themselves or trade with as much ease as if they had been paid in gold coins. From that practice came the word "salary," from the Latin *salerium*, or "salt money."

With such profitable commerce, it was not surprising that the synagogue at Jericho was a large one. Simeon supposed that Jericho had more than one synagogue—probably several, given the size of the city. But he guessed that people from the other synagogues had heard of Jesus' coming, for as large as this building and its courts were, by the time they arrived every space was already filled with people. But the benches inside had been kept empty, and the Galileans quickly filled the large room.

Though special deference was shown to Jesus—he was placed beside the ruler of the synagogue on the chief bench, or front row, on the male side of the room—the celebration was carried out with no special mention or specific attention paid to him. It proved to be the standard Sabbath evening service, giving the travelers a pleasant opportunity to rest and reflect.

But when the meeting was over and the people were exiting the building, all of that changed.

The family of David ben Joseph came together in the courtyard in front of the synagogue. The women's side of the synagogue was closest to the door, and so Livia, Miriam, Deborah, Leah, Rachel, and Lilly exited first and moved to one side to wait for the men. In a moment, Simeon, his father, Joseph, and Ezra appeared. Ephraim had stayed back in camp with several others to watch the children and guard the camp.

As they rejoined the women, Simeon turned to watch Peter, Andrew, and the other apostles come out into the evening air. Moments later Jesus came through the door. He was flanked on both sides by the ruler of the synagogue and several of the leading Pharisees. Simeon watched with some curiosity. Normally Pharisees meant conflict. They were constantly challenging and testing Jesus, but thus far this inter-change had remained amiable. The ruler of the synagogue seemed a little haughty and somewhat condescending to Jesus, but most of the group seemed genuinely pleased to have such a famous guest. Simeon guessed that there would be an invitation for the Master and a few of his closest associates to spend the evening with some of these men.

Then Simeon felt a hand on his arm. He turned to look at Miriam, who had come up beside him. "Look," she said softly.

He turned to follow her gaze and saw the crowd moving back to make way for someone just coming into the courtyard area. In addition to the faint moonlight, there were several small lamps hanging from hooks on the outer walls of the synagogue, so the light was good enough for Simeon to see immediately what had drawn Miriam's reaction. A stooped figure half hobbled, half shuffled through the gateway from the street. For a moment, Simeon couldn't tell if it was a man or a woman.

Others had also seen the figure too and were watching as well. Quickly the courtyard quieted.

"Poor thing," Miriam murmured. Everyone was stepping back, making a path.

The "poor thing" turned out to be a woman. For a moment, Simeon thought she was a hunchback. It looked as though through some terrible accident of birth, she had been cursed with a deformed spine. But as she drew closer, he could see it was worse than that. The pitiful creature was bent over to the point where her upper torso was nearly parallel to the ground. She had to lift her head at a twisted angle to see directly in front of her. And through the fabric of her thin summer robe, Simeon saw that the spine was not only bent, but twisted horribly as well. Every movement was tortured, labored, requiring a supreme effort on her part.

The assembled people were completely still. Eyes flicked from the woman to Jesus. This was the man who, it was said, could heal the sick and the infirm. But this . . . could it be possible?

"Her name is Huldah," someone behind Deborah whispered.

Every eye followed the painful, labored movement of this pitiful creature. She was not headed directly toward Jesus but angling toward a side door, as if she sought to go into the synagogue now that everyone else had come out.

"Woman!" The voice of Jesus was commanding but filled with compassion. The term he used was one of deep respect and honor. Startled, those in the courtyard turned to look at their famous visitor.

The shuffling movement slowed, and the head lifted, turning to search for the source of the voice. Now Simeon could see her face. It was wrinkled and gnarled, like the bark of the olive tree. It was a face that had known much suffering. There was sudden fear in the wrinkled eyes. Her head dropped again, and she kept moving, perhaps thinking that the call had been for someone else.

Jesus moved in her direction, leaving the others to stare after him.

His steps intersected her path. "Woman," he said again, more softly. "I would speak with thee."

Again the head twisted and looked up at him. It was not possible for her to straighten enough to look Jesus directly in the face.

Jesus went down into a crouch so he could look her in the eye. "How long have you been stricken with this infirmity?" he asked.

"Eighteen years, my Lord."

"That is long enough. Woman, thou art loosed from thine infirmity." As people all around gasped and gaped, Jesus reached out his hands and laid them upon her shoulder. For a moment, all seemed frozen in time. Then he stepped back.

Miriam's fingers dug into Simeon's arm, but he was barely aware of it. Slowly, the woman's head came up again—only now it was not just turned to one side. She looked straight ahead, and as if pulled by that motion, her back slowly straightened. Up she came, her body lifting, the spine lifting, straightening, flexing all in one smooth, fluid movement.

"Praise be to God!" Simeon heard someone whisper in awe.

The face of the woman was something that Simeon would not forget for the rest of his mortal life. As quickly as the shifting flames of a fire, her bewilderment turned to astonishment, astonishment turned to wonder, and wonder gave way to joy. Her hands shot up and covered her mouth as her eyes widened. Suddenly tears were streaming down her cheeks. She gave a gasp of such amazement and joy as Simeon had never before heard.

Jesus watched all of this with a gentle smile. Suddenly the woman was overcome with the realization of who Jesus was. With a strangled sob, she dropped to her knees, throwing her arms around the legs of the Master, pressing her face against his robes. "Thank you, Lord," she cried. "Thank you for your mercy."

Miriam was sobbing, her face in her hands as she stared at the woman at Jesus' feet. Deborah and Leah were clinging to each other. Livia stood transfixed, her eyes burning and her lip trembling.

"Hosanna!" someone shouted. "Blessed be the name of Jesus!"

Yes! Simeon felt like leaping to the top of the wall. Where was the shofar that would sound for *Rosh Hashanah* in only a week? Someone needed to let forth a blast on the trumpet that would tell the entire world what had just happened.

He turned and took Miriam in his arms, feeling his own eyes blurring.

"Master!" The voice was sharp and hard, filled with indignation.

Simeon turned to see the ruler of the synagogue rushing forward. The man's face was twisted with shock and horror. Jesus turned slowly to face him. "Yes?"

"Master, have you forgotten yourself? It is the Sabbath day. What have you done?"

"He has loosed a poor soul from her infirmity," a woman answered. "Huldah is freed."

"Leave him alone," someone near the back shouted. "It is a miracle!"

The ruler rose to his full height, only the more inflamed by the shouts. His eyes were blazing. "Are there not six days in the week in which men ought to work?" He swung on Huldah, whose head was fully erect now. She looked at him as if he were mad.

He was nearly so. Several of the other Pharisees were also muttering angrily, though some stood gaping, shocked into silence. But the ruler of the synagogue was fast approaching apoplexy. He was stammering as he shook his fist at her. "You should have come here on one of the other six days of the week if you wanted to be healed. Not on a Sabbath day!"

With lowering brows, Jesus faced the man. His mouth had drawn into a tight line. "You hypocrite!" he said. "Does not the Law of Moses say that we can loose an ox or an ass from the stall on the Sabbath day in order to take them to water? Should not this woman, who is a daughter of Abraham, who has been bound, lo, these eighteen years, likewise be loosed?"

An angry cry went up from the crowd, but it was not directed at

Jesus. They were shouting at the Pharisee, who was trembling with out-rage. "You would condemn such an act?" one of the onlookers cried in utter disbelief.

"Leave her alone!" a woman shouted.

"It is a miracle!"

"God be praised!"

For a moment, the ruler stood there, looking as if he might launch himself at either Jesus or the woman. But there was still enough ratio-nality in the midst of the rage that he understood that any further action on his part would trigger the wrath of the crowd around him. With a harrumph of utter disgust, he pulled his robes around him and stalked away. Several of the Pharisees fell into step behind him. There were jeers and catcalls as they disappeared through the gate, their minds as twisted and deformed as the woman's back had been just minutes before.

Jesus watched them go, then turned to face the woman who, still on her knees, wept quietly before him. Smiling softly, he reached down and touched her shoulder. She looked up, her cheeks wet, her eyes swollen. His smile deepened as he looked into her eyes. Then, without a word, he motioned to Peter and the others and started for the gate.

V

JERUSALEM

21–23 SEPTEMBER, A.D. 32

The month of Tishri, the seventh month in the sacred Jewish cal-endar, actually had three festivals or holy days within it: the Feast of Trumpets, the Day of Atonement, and the Feast of Tabernacles.

The Feast of Trumpets was also called the Day of Blowing. It occurred on the first day of the month, which corresponded to the Roman mid-September. This celebration was held in compliance with the commandment found in the book of Leviticus: "In the seventh month, in the first day of the month, shall ye have a sabbath, a memorial of blowing of trumpets, an holy convocation." Since the first of Tishri was considered the beginning of the civil year, this festival also came to be known as *Rosh Hashanah*, or "the beginning of the year." In a word, it was the Jewish New Year.

Ten days later came the Day of Atonement, or *Yom Kippur*. This was the most solemn and sacred of all the high holy days. On this day, the high priest underwent an elaborate purification ritual to prepare himself to enter the holy of holies in the temple—the only time all year when anyone was allowed into that inner sanctuary. There he made atonement for the sins of all Israel. It was a time of mourning for the sins and imperfections of all Israel.

Five days following *Yom Kippur* came the beginning of *Sukkot*, or the Feast of Tabernacles. This was the harvest holiday and lasted a full week. It was one of the required pilgrimage festivals, meaning that all adult males among the Jews who were able were expected to go to Jerusalem to celebrate the feast. Passover and Pentecost were the other two pilgrimage festivals.

At *Sukkot*, the mourning for sin during *Yom Kippur* turned into the joy of thanksgiving. Fasting gave way to feasting. Sackcloth and ashes were laid aside and replaced with colorful robes and brilliant headdresses. Israel's sins were atoned for and forgiven; the harvest was in. It was time for merriment and rejoicing.

By the time of *Rosh Hashanah*, the caravan of disciples making its way southward from the Galilee had arrived in Jerusalem, just in time to observe the holiday. It was commanded to be "an holy convocation," and so no servile work could be performed on this day, which included travel. They were grateful to be able to conclude their journey, even though it had been more leisurely than taxing. And, with the rest of their people, they prepared themselves to greet the new year.

Chapter Notes

We know that before he ever arrived in Jerusalem for the last Passover of his mortal life, Jesus was telling his disciples that his death was imminent and that he was going to Jerusalem to be killed (see, for example, Matthew 16:21; 17:10–12; Luke 17:25). The experience at Caesarea Philippi, including the sharp rebuke of Peter's well-meaning objection, is told in greatest detail in the Gospel of Matthew (Matthew 16:13–23; see also Mark 8:27–33).

It is John who tells us that Jesus specifically knew that the Jewish leaders were plotting his death and thus told his family that he would not be going up to Jerusalem for the Feast of Tabernacles (see John 7:1–9). We are not told why he later changed his mind and went (see v. 10). John also explains that at this time "neither did his brethren believe in him" (John 7:5). Though we are not told how this happened or when, we know that eventually Jesus' brothers were converted, for they were present with their mother at a meeting following Christ's resurrection (see Acts 1:14). One of them, James, became an apostle after Christ's death (see Galatians 1:19).

For reasons that are not entirely clear, the civil year in the Jewish calendar started in the fall, while the sacred, or religious, calendar began in the spring. Tishri is the seventh month of the sacred calendar. The first day of that month came to be viewed as the beginning of the new year. Today, some two thousand years later, *Rosh Hashanah*, or the Jewish New Year, is still celebrated by Jews across the world each autumn.

The story of the healing of the woman who had suffered with an infirmity for eighteen years is found only in Luke's Gospel (Luke 13:11–17). Though it is usually placed in the time of the Perean and later Judean ministries, which occur late in the ministry of Jesus, we do not know exactly where it took place. But it did take place on the Sabbath, creating a violent reaction from some who witnessed it. The record does say just a few verses later that Jesus "went through the cities and villages, teaching, and journeying toward Jerusalem" (Luke 13:22); for this reason, that healing is placed just before the Feast of Tabernacles in this account.

CHAPTER 10

ROME HAS SPOKEN. THE CASE IS CONCLUDED.

—*Augustine*, St. Augustine Sermons, *Bk. 1*

I

CAESAREA

1 OCTOBER, A.D. 32

"Sit down, Marcus."

"Thank you, Excellency."

Once Marcus was seated, Pilate sat on a marble seat facing his commander. "Welcome back."

"Thank you. I very much appreciate your kindness in letting me go to Rome."

Pilate gave a short laugh. "A man ought to be there for his own wedding."

Marcus smiled back at him. "One would think so."

"Well, you have a lovely bride. And your family has made a good marriage."

"Thank you. The Servilius family is a noble and honorable one. It is a privilege to join their name with that of the Didius family."

And politically, it was an important step upward, Pilate thought. The Servilius family was well connected to the emperor, and Lucas

Pontus Servilius was one of the most powerful voices in the Senate. Though Marcus had another two years of service in Judea, it would not surprise Pilate to see the legate of Syria promote Marcus to prefect of the legion, second in command to the general himself. He made a note that he would have to treat Marcus with even greater respect than he had hitherto done. It was always well to have friends in high places.

"So how have things been in my absence?"

Pilate considered the question for a moment, frowning somewhat. "Stable, for the most part, but there have been a few skirmishes in the Galilee. Nothing major—some running attacks on a couple of columns, a few wagons pillaged. Enough to make me nervous that our time of peace up there isn't going to last much longer."

"What action has been taken?"

"That's what I want to talk to you about. I have been thinking a great deal about our problem in the Galilee. We tried to solve it once and for all two years ago, but the fiasco at the Joknean Pass put an end to that."

Marcus felt a sudden lurch of anxiety. Pontius Pilatus, procurator or governor of Judea, was an efficient and adequate ruler of a very unruly province. He was no better and no worse than dozens of other such rulers who used their friends and influence to wrangle positions of power and, as a result, to make themselves wealthy. But in the six years of his reign, Pilate had made two strategic blunders that had almost cost him his position. The first had happened before Marcus was posted to the province, but he had heard about it in great detail more than once. The Jews had a strict prohibition—it was one of their so-called Ten Commandments—against worshiping graven images. The Roman legions carried their standards on poles topped with figures of the Roman eagle, or in some cases, images of the emperor. Since the emperor was considered divine by official declaration, the Jews considered the standards to be idols. Previous procurators had learned that these standards were highly offensive to the Jews and so put them away or kept them hidden when they marched into Jerusalem or other major Jewish cities.

On his arrival, Pilate had acted more like a man of senatorial rank even though he was only of the Equestrian, or Knights, order. When Pilate had been told about this peculiarity of the Jews, he haughtily decided he was not about to let some silly superstition dictate to him what he could and could not do. He marched the troops into Jerusalem with the banners fully exposed and then set them up in the Antonia Fortress. The uproar was both instantaneous and widespread. Six thousand Jews marched to Caesarea and demanded that the standards be removed. Furious at such arrogance, Pilate herded them into the Hippodrome, surrounded them with his soldiers, and gave them two choices: go home and forget this nonsense, or die. Six thousand Jews lay down on the ground and bared their throats. Knowing that a massacre of the populace over something so trivial as this would not set well with Rome, particularly as his first official act, the governor, humiliated and infuriated, had no choice but to back down.

The second, and perhaps even more damaging incident, had taken place just last year. The population of Jerusalem sometimes swelled to more than a million people during the great festivals, particularly Passover, or *Pesach*, as the Jews called it. This taxed the water resources of the city beyond their capacity. Pilate devised a simple solution for the problem. He decided to build another aqueduct to bring water into Jerusalem from some springs fifteen or twenty miles south of the city. No one disputed the need and all agreed it was a worthy project.

Where Pilate made his mistake was in objecting to the idea that the funds for such an extensive project should come from his own resources. He was still completing the great aqueduct that would bring water from Mount Carmel to Caesarea, and his funds were stretched to the limit. So he hit upon another solution. Millions of *sesterces* poured into the temple treasury every year. In the Law of Moses, every adult male—not just those living in the province, but every Jewish man living anywhere in the empire—was required to pay a so-called temple tax. Nor was that all. At the great pilgrimages, tens of thousands of people tossed contributions into the large chests placed inside the Court of the Women on the Temple Mount. This too was a source of enormous revenue, especially for the Sadducees, who controlled the high priesthood and the temple funds.

Had Pilate been wise enough to go to the Great Council and put the problem to them, they might have agreed to help fund the project, since it would directly benefit the city. But that implied some kind of equality between Jew and Roman, a concept that galled Pilate deeply. So he simply expropriated the money from the sacred treasury.

Once again his actions triggered an immediate and violent reaction. At the Feast of Pentecost, great crowds gathered around the Antonia Fortress when they learned Pilate had come to Jerusalem for the feast. He went out and tried to reason with them, but, as crowds often do, they became abusive—jeering, catcalling, crying out insults. His puffed-up ego was pricked, and he once again decided that these impossible Jews needed to be taught a lesson.

The following day, as the people again gathered, Pilate sent hundreds of his soldiers into the crowds in disguise, with weapons hidden beneath plain brown robes. Their orders were to teach the perpetrators a lesson, but to keep their response restrained. When the crowd became unruly, Pilate commanded them to disperse. Again the hecklers began. Someone even had the audacity to throw rotten fruit at the procurator. Pilate gave the prearranged signal, and his men threw off their robes. But there was no way to distinguish between the innocent and the guilty, and once the soldiers were unleashed, there was no stopping them. They fell upon the people and slew a great number of them; some reports said as many as a thousand.

Outraged, the Great Sanhedrin wrote a protest to the emperor. Through the legate of Syria, the person to whom Pilate directly answered, the emperor had sent back a sharp rebuke. What was the governor thinking? Ruling Judea was difficult enough without deliberately provoking the people. In essence, the emperor was putting Pilate on notice. One more miscalculation and there would be a new procurator in Judea.

Marcus eyed the governor carefully. Surely he had not cooked up another one of his grand schemes. But of course Marcus said nothing, merely waited.

"If we don't respond to these initial incursions," Pilate was saying, "it will only embolden them. And we can't strike back at them in their own territory without launching a major campaign."

"I agree."

Pilate's face was mercurial, growing more agitated with every word he spoke. "But I'll wager that half the Galilee will be here for the Feast of Tabernacles, including a good share of the Zealots."

So here it comes, Marcus thought. He does have a plan, and he'll want me to make it work. "Yes?" he asked cautiously.

"So do something while they're here."

Marcus nearly choked. "What would you like me to do, Excellency?"

Pilate swung on him, suddenly cold. "Has getting married addled your brain? How do I know what? You're the tribune. Do whatever it takes. But by the gods! I want those Zealots to know they've been hit, and hit hard. Do you understand me?"

Marcus, completely taken aback by the outburst, nodded curtly. "I do."

"I want to hear your plan by tomorrow at this time."

Marcus fought to keep his face impassive. He and Diana had only arrived at Caesarea and disembarked from the ship two hours before. They had been three full weeks on board, and Marcus was tired. But he was also wise enough to know that none of that mattered. For now, even a tribune with important family connections had no choice but to give unquestioning obedience to his commander. He stood. "I'll get to work on it right away." He saluted by slapping one arm against his chest and started for the door.

Pilate didn't move. He was brooding darkly, staring at the floor. At the sound of the door opening, he looked up. "Welcome back, Marcus. And congratulations."

"Thank you, Excellency."

"Bring your Lady Diana for supper tonight. We'd all like a chance to get to know her."

"Yes, Excellency."

II

JERUSALEM, UPPER CITY
4 OCTOBER, A.D. 32

"Sire?"

Mordechai looked up. "Yes, Levi?"

"You have a guest, sire. It is the Roman tribune."

"Marcus Didius?" That was a surprise.

"Yes, sire. And he has a woman with him."

Mordechai rose swiftly. "Show him in." As Levi moved away, Mordechai began to sweep the papers and books off the table and into a chest. He removed a key from the chain around his neck, locked the chest securely, then pushed it out of sight under the table.

He heard footsteps coming down the marbled hall and walked toward the door. It opened as he reached it, so he stepped back.

Levi was there. He half bowed, sweeping out his arm in a gesture of introduction. "Sire, may I present Tribune Marcus Quadratus Didius, along with his wife, Lady Diana Cornelia Arria Servilius Didius."

Mordechai barely hid his surprise—not that Levi could rattle off the full name with ease, since that was expected of a chief steward, but that she had been introduced as Marcus's wife. Mordechai bowed low. "Lady Didius, this is a most distinct honor. Welcome to my home. And, of course, to you as well, Marcus Didius."

"Thank you," Marcus said. His wife inclined her head slightly in acknowledgment but said nothing. She was beautiful, almost regal. Mordechai guessed she was several years younger than Marcus, probably near twenty. Her hair, long and dark brown, glistened like oiled wood. Her eyes were not particularly large, but close set and a striking green. She had a tiny nose and a small but well-formed mouth. Her slender body was almost that of a young girl, with a tiny waist. Her skin was like polished alabaster and without flaw. One look told Mordechai that here was a woman of class, wealth, and sophistication.

"Levi, fetch us some wine," Mordechai said, moving back into the room and inviting them to follow.

Marcus raised a hand. "Thank you, but no. We've just arrived from Caesarea and came straight here. Diana is very tired, and I am to meet the commander at the Antonia Fortress in just over an hour." He turned to his wife. "Would you wait in the courtyard, Diana? You'll find it quite pleasant, and I have a matter to discuss with Mordechai. It will take only a few moments."

"Of course," she said. She looked at Levi, obviously surprised to be dismissed so quickly, then followed him back out into the hall.

Marcus shut the door and moved forward. "Sorry to be so abrupt. We were delayed coming through the Beth Horon Pass yesterday and have arrived later than anticipated. Perhaps we can come again once the feast is over. I would like you to get a chance to know Diana."

"Unless you have to return to Caesarea immediately following the end of the feast, I should like to sponsor a banquet in your honor, to introduce your wife to Jerusalem society."

"Thank you, we would like that." Marcus was genuinely pleased. He had not been fishing for an invitation.

"I must say, this is a surprise. I only heard a week or so ago that you had gone back to Rome. Now here you are with a new wife."

"Yes. By the beginning of the summer, I had completed my third year of duty here in Judea. When my father wrote to Pilate and told him they had arranged a marriage with the Servilius family, Pilate immediately granted me three months leave."

"She's very lovely."

"Yes, in more ways than one. Her father is a senator who served as legate of Belgica for a time. So while she may look delicate and fragile, she is used to postings outside of Rome."

"Ah," Mordechai said, duly impressed. He was not an expert on the Roman Empire, but he knew enough to know that Belgica, a province on the northern frontiers of the empire, was of strategic importance to the emperor. Diana's father must be a very powerful man indeed. Which meant Marcus had catapulted several notches upward in terms of power and influence. Mordechai filed that away in his memory. "Then we must be certain the banquet is fitting for one of her station," he said smoothly.

"She would be most appreciative," Marcus responded, with a slight incline of his head. "As would I."

Mordechai knew it was time for the pleasantries to be done. "You spoke of a matter of business," he suggested.

Marcus nodded curtly. "Yes. I bring a request from Pilate."

That was not a great surprise, though he couldn't imagine what it might be. "Go on."

Marcus drew a little closer. "This is for your ears only. No one, not even your most trusted associates on the council, can know of this."

"I understand."

Marcus's hand went up, and he rubbed his face. His chin was covered with a light stubble—something unusual for Marcus—and he looked tired. "There may be trouble on the Temple Mount."

"Oh?" Mordechai said slowly. "What kind of trouble?"

"We're not sure, and it could prove to be nothing."

Mordechai waited. If it was going to be nothing, it would never have been brought up.

"Pilate is looking for an excuse to come down hard on the Zealots. We assume there will be a lot of Galileans here for *Sukkot*."

"Many," Mordechai agreed.

"If something does start, it would be helpful if your temple guards were . . . uh . . . shall we say, occupied elsewhere."

"I see." Mordechai's mind was racing. "Will this be a deliberate provocation, and if so, has a time and place been determined?"

"Nothing is fully set. If it does happen, it will likely be near the end of the feast, on the last day or two. I will be able to give you at least one day's warning."

Mordechai felt uneasy. This was too vague, too undefined. And Marcus wasn't telling him everything. He could see that in his eyes. And then a disturbing thought popped into his mind. "There isn't going to be another raid on the temple treasury?" he asked darkly.

"No, no," Marcus said quickly. "No, it's nothing like that."

Mordechai grunted but said nothing. Along one wall of the Court of the Women, the first of the inner courts of the temple, stood thirteen large chests. Here the visitors to the temple made their offerings. Nine chests were for obligatory offerings required by the Law of Moses, and four were marked for strictly voluntary offerings. It was a traditional part of the Feast of Tabernacles to open the great chests and empty them. The contents of all thirteen chests taken together represented a staggering sum. It would be a tempting target for someone as venal and shortsighted as Pilate.

Marcus evidently sensed Mordechai's uneasiness. He lowered his voice and leaned forward. "Pilate acknowledges that the whole aqueduct project was an error of judgment. We have the strictest orders to leave the temple coffers alone."

The Sadducee relaxed a little. The mistake had been a costly one for Pilate and had nearly lost him his governorship. But neither was Mordechai completely comfortable with what Marcus was proposing. "It will be very awkward to have the temple guards absent on the last days of the feast. First of all, that is the time when the crowds are greatest. Second, we would be fools to move the treasury without an escort."

Marcus frowned, not in disagreement, but because it complicated his problem.

"Why not wait until the day following the feast?" Mordechai proposed.

Marcus lifted one eyebrow. "Won't the Galileans start home?"

"Not usually. They take another day or two to pack things up."

"You're sure?"

"Yes, and there's another reason. The first and last days of the festival are considered by us to be holy days of convocation; they are the most sacred days of the feast. Not only will the crowds be heavy, but even the most radical of the Galileans will tend to be more restrained on such a day. There is a good chance they would avoid any violence, if at all possible. But the day following the last day of the feast there would be no such reluctance, and they will play right into our hands."

Marcus nodded. He had been three years in this country, and he still had much to learn about this peculiar religion and the effects it had on the people. "Then, tentatively, we shall plan on the day following the last day of the feast."

Then he decided he needed to further relieve some of Mordechai's anxiety. "Things are stirring in the Galilee again," he explained. "Twice we've had columns attacked around Sepphoris. Nothing major, just little skirmishes, but still disturbing. Pilate wants to teach them a lesson, nip this in the bud."

"Why not just go after them up there?"

"You know the answer to that," Marcus responded. "There are a dozen or more separate bands who are rarely together in the same place. They melt away into the forests. Every person you pass up there is a potential enemy, every village a potential ambush."

There was no disputing that, Mordechai thought. "But they will all likely be here in Jerusalem," he mused thoughtfully. He began to nod. That did have its possibilities. "You'll need more than the contingent of soldiers you usually have at the Antonia. This could easily get out of hand, knowing what hotheads the Galileans are."

That came as no surprise to Marcus, and he was already taking steps to prepare for that very contingency. The number of soldiers kept at the Antonia Fortress, which guarded the northwest corner of the Temple Mount, was always doubled during the big festivals anyway. He had brought another two hundred men with him, and over the next few nights another five hundred would slip in under cover of darkness. That would bring the garrison up to almost fifteen hundred men. When that many poured out of the Antonia Fortress, it would catch the Galileans totally off guard.

Of course, he said none of that to Mordechai. Part of his hesitancy was that he himself wasn't yet sure exactly how he was going to pull this off. "Our plan is to see if we can't somehow entice the primary Zealot leaders to one place where we can take them: Jesus Barabbas, Yehuda of Beth Neelah, Gehazi of Sepphoris, Yohanan the Blind." He gave a momentary, wry smile. "An odd name for a Zealot leader."

"He lost one eye in an ambush by a squad of your soldiers about six years ago, I'm told." Then Mordechai said, "But not Yehuda."

"Why not?"

"You haven't heard? Yehuda no longer leads that band. I understand he married Livia, the servant of my—" He caught himself. "A former servant in my household."

Marcus had not heard that. "Livia? The Greek girl?"

"Yes. Yehuda has publicly renounced his life as a Zealot."

"Well, well," Marcus said, completely surprised. "So who has taken over the leadership?"

"A man named Samuel. He's Yehuda's brother-in-law. But our sources say that the group is still waiting to see which leader rises naturally to the top."

"And what of Miriam?" Marcus asked.

Mordechai's face instantly darkened. "We do not mention that name in this house any longer."

Marcus took that without comment. In actuality, he found this whole thing with the Jews declaring their unfaithful children to be dead to them quite macabre and totally ridiculous. In Rome, if a child utterly disobeyed the authority of the father, you didn't pretend they were dead, *you put them to death!* But he was curious and so he ignored the older man's warning. "Did she finally marry, then?"

"The last I heard, which was almost a year ago, she was betrothed."

The last he heard? Marcus doubted that. If the Great Council had such excellent intelligence on the Zealots, he would know exactly what was happening with his daughter. "To Simeon ben David?"

"Yes."

"I knew it," Marcus said. "After Simeon helped her escape from Rome . . ." He frowned. "Maybe getting him out of prison to chase after Ya'abin was a mistake."

"No," Mordechai snapped. "But letting him go free once you had Ya'abin trapped, that was the mistake. I tried to warn you."

Marcus realized his error in bringing up Miriam. He shouldn't have tried to needle the man. But Mordechai's petulance at Marcus for not letting Simeon be killed in the wilderness of Judea irritated

Marcus. Still, he decided to let it pass. "Well, Diana is waiting. I'd better go."

Mordechai walked out with him into the hall and toward the main entrance. Then an idea took form. "Jesus is a Galilean," he said.

Marcus slowed his step. "What's that?"

"Jesus of Nazareth is from the Galilee."

The Roman stopped, staring at Mordechai. "Yes, he is," he finally said. "But he's not going to be drawn in with the Zealots."

"Would you give it some thought? Perhaps there is a way."

Marcus nodded, but he had already considered that and rejected it. Jesus was a man of peace. Every source Marcus used had told him that.

"There is one other you might consider," Mordechai said.

"Who is that?"

"Simeon ben David is also a Galilean." He paused. "And they *are* here for *Sukkot*."

Marcus nearly laughed aloud. So much for Mordechai's claim that he did not know what Miriam was doing. But he thrust that aside and began to consider what lay behind Mordechai's words. Memories of Simeon ben David still rankled Marcus. He carried a scar on his fore-arm from their first encounter. Simeon had been the one primarily responsible for their defeat at the Joknean Pass. And if it hadn't been for Simeon, Miriam could have been his.

Now that he was married to Diana, Marcus was honest enough with himself to realize that marriage to a Jewess, beautiful and intel-ligent though she might be, would have been a mistake. Mordechai was a man of wealth and influence, but only in Palestine. He was nothing compared to the Servilius family. But it still annoyed him that Simeon had snatched her away before Marcus had determined she wasn't the one for him. And the man's arrogance was insufferable. He looked squarely at Mordechai, "If Simeon was in the right place at the right time . . ." He shrugged.

"It's possible," Mordechai said, his eyes hooded but smoldering darkly. "It would have to be carefully done. As though he accidentally got swept up in things. There could be no hint that the Great Council had anything to do with this."

"If your guards are occupied elsewhere," Marcus said with a dry smile, "it would be 'those filthy Romans.' Who could blame you?" In this case, what Mordechai was asking for would be easy enough to arrange. After all, Yehuda was Simeon's closest friend. Simeon had risked his life once before to free him from prison. "Do you know where Simeon is staying?"

"They always stay with his father's cousin in Bethlehem."

"What about Yehuda and this brother-in-law of his?"

Mordechai shook his head. "I don't know about them. The Zealots are much more careful when they come here. They know we don't like them, and they know that you would love to get your hands on them."

"But Simeon probably knows where Yehuda is staying?"

"Undoubtedly."

"Let me think on it," Marcus concluded. "But I suspect we can accommodate your needs while we solve our own problem."

Mordechai grunted in satisfaction. "Let me know for sure what day you decide. I'll need a full twenty-four hours to make sure our soldiers are elsewhere."

"I shall see to it," Marcus said. He extended his hand, and they shook briefly.

Mordechai walked to the main door and opened it wide. "Plan on a banquet following the end of the festival. Perhaps we shall have more to celebrate than your recent marriage."

Marcus laughed. It was good doing business with someone who knew what he wanted and was willing to pay for it.

III

BETHLEHEM

5 OCTOBER, A.D. 32

It was a glorious day for a wedding, and everything to this point had gone well. Now came the most solemn moment of all. Aaron motioned for the couple before him to take their place in front of the canopy. It was much smaller than the one they had stood beneath for their betrothal; Benjamin's courtyard in Bethlehem could not accommodate something quite that grand. Simeon actually preferred it. It seemed to fit the more intimate and limited scope of the wedding. As Simeon and Miriam left their escorts—Livia for Miriam, Yehuda for Simeon—and came forward, the crowd hushed.

Simeon was clothed in richly embroidered robes, with gold trim and silver chains for sashes. On his head was a gold-plated diadem. On this day he was a king, about to be wed to his queen. This made them both as royalty.

Miriam wore a white linen dress that came to the floor, with long cowled sleeves. The material was trimmed around the bottom of the skirt and the sleeves with a ribbon of deep blue. The dress was held together at the shoulder with golden brooches purchased from a gold-smith in Damascus. Her veil was of heavy silk, designed to hide her face from all until the marriage was consummated. The whiteness of the dress and veil emphasized Miriam's light olive skin and jet-black hair. In the ten months since the betrothal, Miriam's hair had grown a full hand-span longer and now fell halfway down her back. It shone like oiled ebony in the sunlight.

To each side, and slightly behind them, stood Ephraim and Rachel's two older children. Esther, now six, stood behind Miriam, her arms filled with garlands of flowers. Anyone not knowing the relationship might have mistaken them for sisters, they were so much alike. Boaz was on the other side, standing beside Simeon. Grandma Deborah had found a seamstress to make him an elaborately decorated robe as well, and he looked like a miniature bridegroom. He was taking his role very seriously and looked straight ahead. Just looking at the two children brought smiles to everyone's faces.

Aaron took one step forward. The hush deepened. For a moment, he just looked at them; then he smiled. "Thank you," he whispered.

Then he took a breath and raised his voice for all to hear. "It is time for the ceremony of *nisu'in*, or the formal marriage. As you know, Simeon ben David, when you were betrothed, both you and Miriam participated in the ceremony of *kiddushin*, or consecration to each other. When something is set aside and consecrated to the Lord God of Israel, blessed be his name, it becomes *kadash*, or holy. Therefore it is forbidden for any other use. The giver can no longer claim it as his own property."

Simeon nodded solemnly.

"On that night, Miriam bat Mordechai of Jerusalem became *kiddushin*, consecrated and sacred to you. Tonight she becomes your wife and from henceforth is forbidden to all other men, and you to all other women. Do you understand this?"

Simeon wanted to look at Miriam as he answered, but that was not the custom. He looked at Aaron and nodded. "Yes."

Aaron half turned. "Miriam of Jerusalem, earlier you covenanted to become *kiddushin*. On this night, that becomes your permanent state. Do you willingly accept that as your new condition in life?"

"Yes."

"Simeon ben David," Aaron said, turning to his nephew again. "Would you take your place beneath the canopy?"

Simeon stepped away from Miriam, moving beneath the overhanging linen.

"Miriam," Aaron said, gesturing with his hand, "you take your place on the right hand of Simeon."

As she did so, he intoned, "In the Psalm of David, it states, 'Upon thy right hand did stand the queen.'"

A murmur of approval rippled through the crowd as the couple stood together.

"In the Book of Genesis," Aaron went on, very grave, "we learn that Rebekah was brought from Haran as a bride for Isaac. As the caravan approached the home of Abraham, Rebekah saw Isaac working in the field. When the servant told her that this was her bridegroom to be, it is written that, 'Rebekah took a veil and covered herself.'"

With that, the small company in the courtyard erupted. They cried out the words of blessing given to Rebekah by her family as she left her home to join her betrothed in a far-off land. "Be thou the mother of thousands of millions. Let thy seed possess the gates of those who hate thee."

Suddenly a shower of wheat fell across the bride and groom, thrown by the guests from every corner of the court. A symbol of fertility, the grain was a visual representation of the wish for many children, the same wish that had just been expressed in the triumphant shout.

Nearly glowing himself, Aaron motioned for the couples to face him again. "You may present the *ketubah* to your bride."

Simeon withdrew the scroll on which their marriage contract was written. He had first given this to her in the betrothal ceremony. Now it was finalized. He extended it toward Miriam. "Miriam bat Mordechai, with this *ketubah* and the money and goods promised therein, I hereby wed myself to thee by the laws of Moses and of Israel."

Miriam reached out and took it, shyly smiling at him for the first time. "Amen!" the assembled guests exclaimed.

Then came one of the most sacred of moments. The prophet Jeremiah had once written that a woman should "compass" a man. It was assumed by the scribes that this meant that she was to court him, but it was also taken literally in the wedding ceremony. Moving in a stately manner, Miriam began making slow circles around Simeon. As she completed the first circle, she repeated the first of three expressions of betrothal found in the prophet Hosea's writings: "I betroth thee unto me forever."

She began the second encirclement. "I betroth thee unto me in righteousness, in judgment, in loving kindness and in mercy."

Simeon watched her as she started around the third time. "I betroth thee unto me in faithfulness," she said, "and thou shalt know the Lord."

With that, Aaron walked to a nearby table, lifted a silver pitcher of wine, and filled a cup. He lifted it high above his head and offered a short benediction. Then he walked back and handed the cup to Simeon. He nodded for Simeon to proceed.

Looking over the edge of the cup to the veiled face, Simeon took one swallow. "With the sharing of this cup, we signify the sharing of our lives together in this marriage."

He handed it to Miriam, who lifted the cup under her veil and took a sip as well, all the time her eyes never leaving his. "Amen," she said.

"Amen!" roared the crowd. Aaron took back the cup.

With a smile that filled his whole face, Simeon took one step forward so that he was directly in front of her. He took both of her hands and squeezed them softly.

"Amen and amen!" shouted the family.

"Amen and amen," shouted the assembled guests.

"Amen," Simeon whispered, and squeezed her hands again.

CHAPTER NOTES

Pontius Pilatus, or Pilate, as we call him in English, served as procurator (or governor) of Judea for about ten years, beginning his reign in A.D. 26. His role in the crucifixion of Christ has made his name famous, but outside of the New Testament, there are very few contemporary accounts of his administration. However, Flavius Josephus, the Jewish historian who lived in the first century of the Christian era, does give an account of two political blunders Pontius Pilate made with the Jews, both of which are cited here (see Josephus, xviii, iii, 1).

In Exodus 30:12–13, the law required every adult male Israelite to pay half a shekel tax for maintaining the sanctuary, which at first was the tabernacle, then later was the temple. In Matthew 17:14–27 we learn that "they that received tribute money" accused Jesus of not paying this tax. This shows there was some formal mechanism for collecting the tax, at least in the Holy Land. How this was done in other areas of the empire we are not told.

This tax was not paid to Rome, but to the Jewish leadership who controlled the temple. At the time of Jesus, this was the Sadducees. Josephus does not tell us exactly how Pilate took the money from the Jewish funds, only that he did so.

Jesus Barabbas is listed by Marcus here as one of the Zealot leaders. In the New Testament, he is known only as Barabbas (*bar* and *ben* in Hebrew both mean "son of"; see Wilson, p. 404). One of the old manuscripts mentions him as Jesus Barabbas. Since Jesus (*Yeshua* in Hebrew) was a common name in the time of Christ, many commentators believe this was likely his full name. We do know that Barabbas was being held for insurrection and murder (see Mark 15:7), which makes him a likely candidate for being a Zealot (Clarke, 3:270).

Though it is hard to specify exactly what marriage customs prevailed at the time of Christ, what is described here comes from what information we have about Jewish weddings; some such traditions are very old (see Bloch, pp. 33–36). It is widely known today that at Jewish weddings a goblet or glass is broken at the end of the ceremony. This serves as reminder of the loss of the temple in A.D. 70, the idea being that even at times of great joy Jews remember the tragedy that occurred so many years before. Since the temple had not been destroyed at the time of the novel, that of course could not have been part of the ceremony described in this story.

CHAPTER 11

AND THE MULTITUDES THAT WENT BEFORE, AND THAT FOLLOWED,
CRIED, SAYING, HOSANNA TO THE SON OF DAVID: BLESSED IS HE THAT
COMETH IN THE NAME OF THE LORD; HOSANNA IN THE HIGHEST.

—*Matthew 21:9*

I

JERUSALEM, ANTONIA FORTRESS
6 OCTOBER, A.D. 32

Tribune Marcus Quadratus Didius walked slowly, head down, hands clasped behind his back. Beside him, but not speaking, walked his senior centurion, Sextus Rubrius.

"Time's running out," Marcus said abruptly, stopping to face his grizzled old officer. "The feast starts tomorrow, and I'm no closer to resolving all the details to our plan than I was when I met with Mordechai."

Sextus hesitated, then decided that his commander wanted his counsel, even though he had not asked Sextus a specific question. "You are wise to be cautious, sire. You have seen the crowds. The Feast of Tabernacles is a joyous festival for these people. Often the crowds surpass even those that come for Passover."

"Yes, and that is a concern. I want to start a riot, but it has to be a controlled riot, one that we can use for our own purposes. If it gets out of hand, we could end up in a very nasty situation."

"Agreed," Sextus said. "In that, Mordechai is right. We must wait until the feast is over. There will still be many people in the city, but they won't be thronging the Temple Mount as they do for the daily ceremonies."

"But how do I entice the Zealot leaders in to the mount? It is not worth the risk involved if we aren't able to seize our primary targets. That's where I'm stumped. I have three different plans, but each is so elaborate and has so many ifs to it, I cannot feel good about them."

"The Zealots will be extremely wary," Sextus said. He had grave reservations about this whole scheme of Pilate's, but he would never say that. It didn't matter what he thought. The governor had given a command; it was up to them to carry it out.

"Exactly," Marcus growled.

They were walking through the large assembly area inside the walls of the Antonia Fortress, approaching the gate on the south wall that led from the fortress directly onto the Temple Mount. It stood open, and they could see the vast throngs pouring out of the Court of the Women following the daily ritual of offering water. Marcus frowned. "What kind of people offer water to their gods?"

Sextus turned in surprise. "What was that, sire?"

"Never mind." Marcus gestured toward the gate, and they walked out into the crowds.

They moved slowly, Marcus barely aware of how the crowd parted before them, shooting nasty glances in their direction. He was lost in thought again, and Sextus chose not to interrupt him. They moved westward, walking parallel to the north side of the temple. There the crowds began to thin.

Marcus stopped, his head coming up. About twenty paces ahead of them, a young man stood apart from the people passing by. His head was tipped up, staring at the massive building in front of him. For a long moment, Marcus gazed at the man, his brow furrowing. "That young man looks vaguely familiar to me," he said, half to himself.

Sextus had already noted where Marcus was looking. "I don't recognize him, sire."

Marcus stared at him, searching his memory. Then he snapped his fingers. "I remember now. He looks very much like—" He peered more closely, then shook his head. "No, it's not."

"Very much like whom?" Sextus inquired.

"A young slave I found in Rome. He was brother to Miriam's servant girl, Livia. I purchased his freedom for him."

Still not absolutely positive that it wasn't the same person, Marcus moved forward, with Sextus close behind. Suddenly the young man saw them staring at him. His dark eyes flashed momentary hostility; then he turned away, moving off swiftly. But Marcus had seen enough. It wasn't the same young man.

Then he had a thought. "Did Livia's brother come to Capernaum with her?"

Sextus shook his head. "I understand he stayed in Athens when they passed through on their way back from Rome. I've not heard anything since."

Marcus started forward again, his mind going back to the original problem. Then, abruptly, he stopped. "Wasn't she once a slave too?" he asked. Then, without waiting for an answer, he said, "Yes, of course. She and her brother were slaves in Alexandria. They belonged to a man who lost everything. She was sold to Mordechai and the brother went elsewhere." Marcus's mind was racing. "And then Mordechai gave Livia her freedom when she became Miriam's servant."

Marcus suddenly whirled on his centurion. "And you know this Livia, right?"

"Not well, but I—"

"But you know her by sight?"

"Yes, sire."

"It is likely she has come up for the feast, no?"

"Yes, especially if Yehuda comes. They're married, you know."

"I know."

"I see no reason why she wouldn't be here."

"Sextus, I want you to return to the fortress immediately. Remove your uniform and dress in the robes of a simple country man."

One of Sextus's eyebrows shot up. Marcus was grinning with enthusiasm. He finally had the beginnings of a plan.

"Get out among the people. Spend all day out here. Every day of the feast if you have to. Watch for Livia and Yehuda. If you see either of them, then follow them. I want to know where they are staying during the feast."

Sextus nodded, but his eyes were clouded. "Sire, it might be dangerous if you were to try to capture Yehuda in the city. The people—"

"No, no." He cut Sextus off with a wave of his hand. "It's Livia I'm interested in. Once we know where they are staying, we can have her followed whenever we wish."

"Oh?" Sextus said slowly, more puzzled than ever.

Now Marcus's smile was wickedly malicious. "Yes, Rome can't have runaway slaves walking around without fear of arrest. It could lead to all sorts of problems."

"But you said that Mordechai purchased her freedom."

Marcus feigned great surprise. "Now who told you a thing like that?"

II

JERUSALEM, THE TEMPLE MOUNT

7 OCTOBER, A.D. 32

The Feast of Tabernacles was distinguished from other festivals in three primary ways: the dwelling in *sukkot* (small, temporary booths called tabernacles), the palm branches and the fruit, and the ritual offerings in the temple.

The dwelling in booths, made of various tree branches, served to remind the people of the time when Israel wandered in the wilderness dwelling in tents. The waving of the palm branches and the fruit signified their acceptance of Jehovah as their king. The rituals in the temple represented the pouring out of the Holy Spirit upon the people and the light of God that resulted.

For the seven days and nights of the Feast of Tabernacles, families were expected to take their meals and sleep each night in booths which they erected on the flat roof tops of their houses or in their courtyards. The children thought this a grand adventure, and their excitement added to the joyousness of the celebration. The adults, while perhaps not reveling in the experience, saw it as a solemn reminder of when life was much more austere. But it was more than that. The wilderness wandering had been a time for renewing ancient covenants with Jehovah. So each year Israel was to remember those days in the wilderness and once again renew their promises of obedience to Jehovah.

The second feature of the feast, the waving of the palm branches and the fruit, was closely tied to the first. Since *Sukkot* occurred in the fall, when the ingathering of the harvest was complete, it was also a thanksgiving festival. In the Torah, celebrants were instructed to "take the fruit of goodly trees, branches of palm trees, and the boughs of trees and the willows of the brook" and carry them in their hands. The "fruit of goodly trees" was interpreted to mean the citron, a pale yellowish fruit much like a lemon but larger and with a thicker rind. It was carried in the left hand. The "branches"—palm fronds, willow branches, and stems of myrtle—were tied together to form long, festive plumes. These were carried in the right hand. This plume, or *lulav*, as it was called in Hebrew, was waved back and forth during specific rituals of the feast. All but the smallest children were expected to have their own *lulavs* and join in the ceremony.

The waving partially represented the joy of the people for another bounteous harvest. But in addition, the citron and the *lulavs* represented the welcoming of Jehovah as Israel's king. Just as an earthly king was greeted by his subjects with the waving of banners, so the Heavenly King was greeted with an undulating sea of green branches and cries of welcome.

The third unique aspect of the Feast of Tabernacles involved two very solemn rituals. The first was called the "pouring out." The second was the lighting of the four great *menorahs*, or lampstands, in the Court of the Women.

On the opening day of the feast, following the evening sacrifice, a procession of priests descended from the Temple Mount to the Pool of Siloam, a distance of perhaps a quarter of a mile south of the temple. There sufficient water for the rituals of all seven days of the feast was collected in a golden vessel. As the procession returned to the temple complex, it was met by vast crowds, who then followed it into the inner courts of the temple. At the great altar of sacrifice in the Court of Israel, the officiating priest then poured out the water into an orifice on the altar, which orifice was made especially for that purpose. This "pouring out" was interpreted to represent the Spirit of God being poured out upon Israel so that God's work of salvation would be realized. In keeping with a charge from the prophet Isaiah, at that point a great shout would be offered up.

"Praise ye Jehovah," Isaiah had commanded them to say. In Hebrew, the word for praise was *hallel*. When coupled with *Yah*, a shortened form of Jehovah, the phrase became *Hallelujah!* So as the stream of water poured out upon the altar, a mighty shout went up, accompanied by the *lulavs* waving back and forth in great sweeping arcs. "*Hallelujah!* Praise ye Jehovah!"

Immediately after the pouring out came the lighting of the great *menorahs*. The entire Temple Mount was huge, covering an area of about thirty-five acres. Most of that space was taken up by the Court of the Gentiles and the surrounding porticoes, which provided shade from the sun. Directly in the center of this great courtyard was the temple itself, with its inner courts. The first and largest of the inner temple courts was the Court of the Women. Its name was derived from the fact that women could enter it without restriction, but they could not go into the next court, the Court of Israel, unless they were participating in the sacrificial rites.

It was in the Court of the Women that four massive golden candelabra, or lampstands, stood, one in each corner. Massive was hardly an adequate word for them. These *menorahs* towered upwards as high as a five-story building. They were eight or nine times the height of a grown man. In fact, their height was so great that the bowls actually stood above the top of the walls of the inner courts, enabling the *menorahs'* light to fill the entire Temple Mount.

The thick central shaft of each lampstand branched out at the top to hold four large golden bowls, each of which could hold about four gallons of olive oil. The wicks for each bowl were made from the worn-out breeches and sacred garments of the priests. Each morning during the feast, young men of priestly descent climbed ladders especially made for this purpose. They refilled each bowl with oil and lay in the new wicks. By the time the "pouring out" of the water was finished, full darkness had descended upon the city. The night air was then split with three shrill blasts, as priests with silver trumpets announced what was about to happen. The throngs instantly fell silent, anticipating what was about to happen.

Priests and Levites appeared, filing out from the Court of Israel to descend fifteen steps into the Court of the Women. Four priests carrying torches appeared first. These torches had been ignited, not from just any fire, but from the flames of the great altar of sacrifice. Hundreds of other priests followed, carrying lutes and lyres, trumpets, cymbals, psalteries, drums, and other musical instruments. The night erupted with music. This was not a solemn, silent ritual, but one of tremendous joy. Weaving, dancing, and singing, the procession filled the court as the people stood back and looked on, *lulavs* waving back and forth in time to the music. The four priests with torches climbed the great ladders.

As the priests climbed higher and higher, the music swelled into a great crescendo. In perfect synchronization, sixteen bowls of oil were set ablaze. In that instant, the entire Temple Mount was thrown into sharp relief, bathed in the golden glow of lamplight. So bright were the flames of the four *menorahs* that details on the Mount of Olives, across the Kidron Valley to the east, could be clearly seen.

As the light pushed back the darkness, the crowd once again let forth a mighty shout. Jehovah had come. The King of Israel had returned to his own house. The *lulavs* swayed back and forth wildly. "*Hallelujah! Hallelujah!* Praise be to the Lord. Praise ye Jehovah!"

III

"Uncle Simeon?"

"Yes, Esther?"

"What are they doing now?"

Rachel started to shush her daughter, but Simeon went down on one knee beside her. He sensed this was not just a petty question from a bored child. She clutched her palm frond carefully, making sure to keep it vertical. Boaz had given his to his mother until the time came when he actually needed it. He was clearly bored. But Esther was taking everything very seriously. Now six, and bright as a silver button, she was old enough to begin to sort out the complexities of the rituals. She recognized that what was happening on this day was different from what she had witnessed a few days before. That was perceptive, for this was the last day of the feast, and there were significant differences.

They stood at the gate that led from the Court of the Women into the Court of Israel. In this second court, much of which was filled by the great altar of sacrifice, there was no more room for any people. Usually children did not enter those sacred precincts anyway, so the family had gone early enough to get a place on the top step. There they could see into the next court and observe what was happening.

Simeon turned Esther to face him. She was so beautiful, with her large dark eyes, jet-black hair, and perfect features, and so earnest at the moment. "Since this is the last day of the feast, the priests go around the altar seven times, instead of once, before pouring out the water. Can you think why that might be?"

Her brow furrowed. "Joshua marched around Jericho seven times and made the walls fall down," she ventured tentatively.

Simeon was pleased. "That is exactly why. Today we are reminded that in some future day God will make the walls of unbelief tumble to the ground. Then Israel can go in and possess the land and let the world know of the one true God."

"Oh," she said, nodding slowly.

Simeon felt a light punch on his shoulder and turned to see Boaz, his eyes wide as he stared upward. "Are the walls going to fall down?" he asked anxiously. He inched in closer to Simeon. Simeon swept him into one arm. "No, Boaz. They're just pretending. That's how it will be someday a long time from now."

Ephraim suddenly stood beside his son. "We're fine, Boaz. Nothing is going to happen."

Just then the mournful sound of a flute began. The circle of priests stopped, and one of them moved toward the ramp that led to the top of the altar.

"Do you know who that is?" Simeon whispered into Esther's ear.

"The high priest."

"That's right. His name is Caiaphas." Shifting the fruit and palm branch to his left hand, he scooped her up and straightened so she could see better. Ephraim lifted Boaz up, and his mother handed him back his *lulav*, a much shorter version of the plume than the adults had.

Simeon felt a touch on his arm and turned to see Miriam smiling at him. Her eyes were filled with love and appreciation. He stepped closer so their shoulders were touching. He had to keep reminding himself that this was his wife standing beside him. What had seemed like an eternity had finally passed, and they had been man and wife for two full weeks.

As Caiaphas reached the top of the altar, the crowd went still. The sun was down, and the courtyards were completely in shadow. In a few more minutes, it would be full dark. The *lulavs* held in every hand were raised to the vertical but hung motionless for the moment. Another flute joined in, then another.

"Raise your hand!" the crowd shouted as Caiaphas moved into position. He did so, raising the pitcher in his hand high so all could watch as he poured the water into the special opening. The moment he was done, the circle of priests began the *Hallel*, half sung, half chanted, the words taken from the psalms of King David.

"*Hallelujah!* Praise ye Jehovah!"

"*Hallelujah!*" answered the crowd, and the *lulavs* began to sway.

"Praise, O ye servants of Jehovah. Blessed be the name of the Lord from this time forth and for ever more."

"*Hallelujah! Hallelujah!*" Simeon was surprised to hear Esther perfectly match the pitch of the priests as she cried out her praises. She was waving her *lulav* back and forth with so much energy that Simeon had trouble holding her and waving his *lulav*, too.

"Who is like unto Jehovah who dwelleth on high?" chanted the priests. "Tremble thou earth, at the presence of the Lord. *Hallelujah!* all ye nations. Praise him, all ye people!"

"*Hallelujah! Hallelujah! Hallelujah!*"

"O work then now thy salvation, Jehovah," the priests chanted. "Save us now, we beseech thee, O Lord."

A new cry then burst forth from the people. "Save now" in Hebrew was *Hoshianah* or *Hosanna*.

"*Hosanna!*" cried the people.

"Save us now, we beseech thee, O Lord," chanted the priests.

"*Hosanna! Hosanna! Hosanna!*" Above their heads the mass of green swayed like a vast forest being stirred by a mighty wind.

"Blessed is he that cometh in the name of the Lord," chanted the priests.

That was a direct reference to the coming of the Messiah, and, if possible, the shout was even greater than before. "*Hosanna! Hallelujah!*"

Only a heart of the coldest stone could not be stirred by this moment. There was nothing like it in all of Israel. They were welcoming their Messiah, the King of Israel. When he came, the lamb would lie down with the lion. The sword would be thrust into the fire of the smith and hammered into a pruning hook. There would be no more war. No more tyrants. No more slavery, suffering, or sin. No wonder every throat shouted out with unrestrained joy.

Now the flutes were barely discernible, and the priests had to almost shout the chants to make themselves heard. Once again there was a shrill blast of trumpets. Once. Twice. Thrice.

"This is the day which the Lord has made," shouted the priests, continuing the *Hallel*. "We will rejoice and be glad in it. Thou art my God, and I will praise thee. Thou art my God, and I shall exalt thee. O give thanks unto Jehovah, for he is good, and his mercy endureth forever."

From beneath the waving mass of palm, willow, and myrtle, ten thousand voices rose in one mighty hymn of praise and petition.

"*Hallelujah! Hosanna! Hosanna! Hosanna!*"

As the sound died away, echoing off the walls of the courtyard, no one moved. The *lulavs* slowed, then stopped, held at the vertical.

In that moment of silence, a single voice rang out, as piercing and compelling as if a trumpet had sounded. "People of Israel, listen to me."

Every head turned. Simeon drew in his breath sharply, but a much greater sound of shock swept the crowd. Jesus was standing just inside the Court of Israel.

"It's the prophet from Nazareth," someone called.

"It's the Messiah!" a woman shouted, her voice shrill. "Look, the Messiah has come!"

Caiaphas stiffened, his face going a deep scarlet.

"*Hallelujah!* Praise God. The Messiah has come."

It was an electrifying moment. Whenever Jesus appeared, it caused a stir, but stepping forth at the very moment the *hallelujah* shout echoed in the temple courts stunned everyone.

Jesus raised his hands. The noise stopped almost instantly.

"If any man thirst," he called out, his voice loud enough to be heard by all, but strangely calm, "let him come to *me* and drink."

Everyone began shouting at once. There was no mistaking his meaning. They had just witnessed the "pouring out," the bringing of water from the Pool of Siloam. Even the older children understood that those waters symbolized the pouring out of the Spirit. *God's Spirit!* That could come from only one source: God himself, who could minister his Spirit through the Holy Messiah. If Jesus had stepped forward and declared, "I am the Messiah," his intent couldn't have been any clearer.

"What is the meaning of this!" It was the voice of Caiaphas. He had come to the edge of the altar and was peering down at Jesus, his face as red as the bloodstains on the tables of sacrifice.

Jesus looked up at him with no change of his expression. If he had heard the high priest it did not show on his face. There was such a regal majesty in his bearing that gradually the crowd became quiet again. No one moved. Every eye was on him.

Finally Jesus turned away from the altar and looked around at the sea of faces staring at him. A man standing directly in front of him raised an imploring hand. "Tell us, good sir. Art thou the Messiah?"

Again there was no change in his expression. Jesus did not look directly at the man, only at the faces around him. "He that believeth on me, as the scriptures saith, 'From deep within him shall flow rivers of living water.'"

At the citation of the passage from Isaiah, there was a strangled cry from Caiaphas. He turned and, robes flying, raced down the ramp.

He disappeared from Simeon's view for a moment, then reappeared flanked by five priests, all of them looking very angry. Caiaphas then snarled something at the temple guards who lined the back wall, as mesmerized as everyone else by what was happening. They jumped guiltily and, spears lowering, started moving toward Jesus. At that same moment, perhaps because they saw what was happening, Peter, Andrew, and the rest of the Twelve pushed out of the crowd. They formed a protective half circle between Jesus and the oncoming guards.

"He blasphemes!" cried one of the priests.

Whether it was the words of Jesus, his calm majesty, or the fact that he now had several very determined-looking men in front of him was not clear, but the guards stopped, their spears lifting again. They looked at each other in consternation, but no one took a further step toward the man from Nazareth.

"Seize him!" Caiaphas roared at them. "He blasphemes the name of God."

"No!" shouted a voice from somewhere beyond Jesus. "Leave him alone. This is the great prophet promised by Moses."

"Yes!" It came from a dozen voices.

"He is the Messiah!" It was the same woman as before.

"*Hallelujah!*" went up the cry. A few palm fronds began to wave back and forth.

Caiaphas stopped, shocked to the core.

In an instant, the crowd took up the chant. "*Hosanna! Hosanna!*" The whole courtyard filled with waving *lulavs*. If this *was* the Messiah, it was the most stunning moment in Israelite history. The King had come and was here, in the flesh, standing right before their very eyes.

In seconds the *hallelujahs* and *hosannas* crescendoed to a thunderous ovation.

"Cease this!" a voice roared when there was a momentary break. "Cease this madness this instant!"

Miriam's hand shot out and grabbed Simeon's arm. Her fingers dug into his flesh. Simeon didn't have to ask why. Even as he recognized that bull voice, his eyes picked out Mordechai ben Uzziel pushing his way through the circle of priests. Dressed in white robes of the priest-hood, signifying the role of the Sadducees as supervisors of the priestly function, he had not stood out before. This was the moment Miriam had been dreading for a week. They had not yet seen her father in the crowds. But here he was, his face bristling with rage.

Surprised by this new development, the crowd noise dropped quickly but did not cease entirely. Palm fronds fluttered and slowed.

"This man is from Nazareth," Mordechai shouted. "He is from the Galilee. How can you say that he is the Messiah? Does the Christ come out of Galilee?"

"No!" Caiaphas answered loudly, recovering quickly enough to see the brilliance of what Mordechai was doing.

"Of course he doesn't," Mordechai shot right back. "The prophet Micah tells us that the Messiah comes of the seed of David and will come out of Bethlehem, the city of David."

"But he *is* from Bethlehem," Deborah said, looking at her husband, knowing of the experience he and Benjamin had shared in the shep-herd fields some thirty or more years before.

David nodded. "But very few people know that."

The question had its effect on the crowd. The prophecy of Micah was one of the best known of all promises concerning the coming of the Messiah. "The Messiah cannot come from Nazareth," a woman standing near the priests called out. She was probably a wife of one of those in the circle. "How can this Jesus be the Promised One?"

"Listen to him speak," another person shouted from the crowd. "Look at the mighty works that he performs. Surely he is *that prophet*." The expression was significant. Moses had prophesied that a great prophet would be raised up and that he would be like unto Moses. The rabbis universally interpreted that prophet to be the Messiah.

But Mordechai's intervention had its effect, throwing the people into confusion. While some started to shout and wave their plumes again, many others were shaking their heads doubtfully. People began to turn to each other, putting forth one view or the other. The courtyard was bedlam.

"Seize him!" Simeon heard Mordechai hiss to the waiting guards. Simeon's hand dropped to his belt, where he kept his dagger. If Jesus needed help . . .

Even as he saw the guards straighten and grasp their spears again, he swung around, poised to sprint to Jesus' side. But before he could move, he pulled up, gaping. Jesus was gone! He had melted into the crowds, and the Twelve had evidently followed after him.

Simeon turned slowly to Miriam. The man who had just publicly announced that he was the source of the true living water, the man who had all but directly proclaimed himself as the Messiah, was gone.

CHAPTER NOTES

The Feast of *Sukkot*, or Tabernacles, is still celebrated by Jews around the world today. The practice of constructing small booths, or tabernacles (*sukkot* in Hebrew), served as a reminder of Israel's wandering in the wilderness for forty years. Small booths made of palm, willow, and myrtle branches were erected on the flat roofs of the houses. During the festival week, families took their meals in the *sukkot* and slept in them unless the weather became extremely bad. This festival began on the first full moon of autumn when the olive, wine, and vegetable harvests were completed. It lasted one full week. Because it celebrated the harvest, it was also known as the Feast of Ingathering, a holiday similar to our Thanksgiving. Since it was one of the three pilgrimage festivals, all Jews were expected to celebrate the holy days in Jerusalem, if possible. (See Edersheim, *The Temple*, pp. 176–87; Buttrick, s.v., "Booths, Feast of," 1:455–57; Backhouse, pp. 16–21).

The various scriptures connected to the Feast of Tabernacles referred to in this section include Deuteronomy 1:32–33; Leviticus 23:39; Psalm 113:1–2; and Isaiah 12:3–4; 9:3.

Though we have explained the use of the name of God in an earlier volume, it may be helpful to review that information here. Since Hebrew was not originally written with vowels, it is not certain how the sacred name of God (made up of four consonants, JHVH) was pronounced anciently. (Since the Y and J were similar sounds, the four consonants are sometimes shown as YHVH.) The King James Version of the Bible wrote it JeHoVaH. Modern scholars often make it YaHVeH or YaHWeH. Since this series uses the King James text of the Bible, we have used Jehovah as it is found there.

The name became so sacred to the Jews anciently that they chose not to pronounce or write it. Instead they substituted the word *Adonai,* or Lord, whenever they came upon the name. Out of respect for that tradition, the King James translators translated the name as "Jehovah" in only four places in the Old Testament (plus three additional instances where *Jehovah* is used in a compound word), even though it is used thousands of times in the Hebrew. In all other cases, they, too, substituted the word *Lord.* However, to distinguish it from the conventional use of "lord" (for example, "My lord, the king"), they rendered it with small capital letters: LORD. (An example of both uses of Lord can be seen in Psalm 110:1.) So while the first part of the *Hallel* (the entirety of which is drawn from Psalms 113 to 118) is rendered in the King James Version as "Praise ye the Lord" (Psalm 113:1), in Hebrew it is "Praise ye Jehovah," or *Hallelujah.*

It is John who tells us that it was on the "last day, that great day of the feast" that Jesus stepped forward and declared himself to be the living water (John 7:37–44). Edersheim believes he stepped forward at the very moment the ceremony of the "pouring out" of the waters of Siloam was concluded and that it was this that had such a profound impact on the crowd (Edersheim, *The Temple,* pp. 183–84).

We are not told who raised the objections and cited the prophecy about the Messiah coming from Bethlehem (see Micah 5:2), but it did result in a "division among the people." Then, John tells us, "And some of them would have taken him; but no man laid hands on him" (John 7:43–44).

As explained in an earlier volume, the title of "Christ" (from the Greek *Christos*) and "Messiah" (from the Hebrew *Meshiach*) have an identical meaning, viz., "the Anointed One." So when the crowd cried out, "This is the Christ" (John 7:41), they were saying that Jesus was the Messiah.

CHAPTER 12

I AM THE LIGHT OF THE WORLD: HE THAT FOLLOWETH ME SHALL NOT

WALK IN DARKNESS, BUT SHALL HAVE THE LIGHT OF LIFE.

—*John 8:12*

I

JERUSALEM, IN THE COURT OF THE WOMEN ON THE TEMPLE MOUNT

14 OCTOBER, A.D. 32

Normally, the lighting of the four great *menorahs* immediately followed the "pouring out" of the waters of Siloam. But on this night, half an hour passed before things got underway again. People milled about, still talking of the electrifying experience they had just witnessed. The name of Jesus was on every tongue.

While they waited, Rachel told Ephraim she was going to take the children home. She and Lilly had left their babies—now almost fifteen months old—with a young woman in Bethlehem. If they stayed through all of the festivities associated with the lighting of the lamps, it would be well after midnight before they would get back.

But Simeon sensed there was more to their desire than just wanting to get back to care for their babies. After the near miss between the temple guards and Jesus, Rachel was afraid there was a chance there would be trouble. Ephraim agreed, coming to the same conclusion, and said he would go with her and the children. Joseph, Simeon's younger brother, surprised them all by saying he would go with Esther and Boaz. Then Lilly decided she would go too. She had waited too long for little Miriam to risk having something happen to her mother, she said. For all the joy, for all the festive spirit of the feast, history suggested that things had a way of getting out of hand very rapidly. The riot that followed Pilate's attempt to finance an aqueduct from the temple treasury was still fresh in everyone's memory.

Aunt Esther and Uncle Benjamin (Simeon always called them that, even though they were his cousins) went too. Since they were the hosts in Bethlehem, Esther felt an obligation to be there if everyone else was returning to her home. In the end everyone left except David and Deborah, Leah, Miriam, and Simeon. Deborah tried to convince Leah to go too, but she wouldn't hear of it.

As they said their good-byes and moved away, David looked around. Since this next rite took place in the Court of the Women and not the Court of Israel, the top of the staircase—which was fifteen steps higher than the Court of the Women—provided a perfect vantage point. David saw an available place there, and they moved to that location. As they waited, they said little. Full darkness had settled over Jerusalem. Small oil lamps mounted on the inside of the walls provided some light, but only in a limited circle right around each lamp.

Simeon watched sadly as Miriam restlessly scanned the crowd. Her face was lined with pain. Simeon reached out and took her hand. "He won't be here yet," he said gently. "If he is still around, he'll come in with the procession of the priests."

"I know," she said. Her voice was flat and lifeless. What had happened just minutes before had left her deeply shaken. She was almost positive that her father had seen her, and yet he had not given her the slightest acknowledgment. She had not seen him for a year and a half, and she had hoped at least for some small sign of softening. But any hopes of that were now dashed. Worse, the pure hatred she had seen in his eyes when he was looking at Jesus left her with no hope of any future reconciliation.

David, watching the interchange between his son and daughter-in-law, decided to change the subject. "I hope Jesus has left the Temple Mount completely. I don't see the guards back yet. They're probably still out looking for him, and that's a good sign."

Leah was clearly worried. "Surely Peter and the others will take him to safety."

Simeon was tempted to say something, but he thought better of it when he remembered Peter's account of how Jesus had rebuked him when he tried to protest any mention of possible trouble.

All around them, people had formed into small groups. They talked quietly as they waited for the next stage of the celebration. The Court of the Women was filled to capacity, and the overall sound was like a muted roar of anticipation. Here and there snippets of words rose above the noise: "Messiah." "Blasphemy." "Pharisees." "King." "Prophet." "Arrest him."

"Father!" It was a sharp whisper from Leah. They all turned to look at her, but her head was turned away. She was looking intently toward the gate that led into the Court of Israel. Instantly they saw what she was looking at. Uncle Aaron was coming toward them, pushing his way through the crowds.

"Oh, oh," Leah said softly.

"No fights," Deborah said quickly. "Not here."

Simeon nearly quipped that Aaron might have a say in that, but Aaron was nearly on them, so Simeon bit back his retort.

"*Shalom*, Aaron," Deborah said. "I expected you to be here somewhere."

"Deborah. David. I'm glad I found you."

To Simeon's surprise, Aaron's face showed great distraction but not necessarily anger. Simeon had expected him to be incensed over what had just happened.

Then Aaron seemed to realize that his sister and brother-in-law were not alone. "Oh," he said, almost startled. "*Shalom*, Leah. *Shalom*, Simeon. Miriam." He inclined his head slightly toward them.

"Good evening, Uncle Aaron," Miriam responded.

"Are Hava and the children with you?" Deborah asked.

His eyes had already moved away, and only after a moment did he look back. "What was that?"

"Hava," David said. "Is she here tonight?"

"Oh." He half turned, waving one arm in the direction from which he had come.

Deborah peered at him. "Are you all right, Aaron?"

He started to nod, then looked around anxiously, as if fearing someone might be watching. "There's not much time. The lighting ceremony is about to begin." One hand shot out, and he clasped Deborah's arm. "I have to ask you a question."

"Aaron," Deborah started, "if it's about what just happened with Jesus, I—"

He gave an impatient flutter of his hand. "I don't want to talk about that. I need to ask you something."

"What?"

"You came up to Jerusalem with Jesus?"

"Yes."

"You were with him the whole time?"

David was puzzled. "Not every moment, but each day, yes."

"Were you in Jericho with him?"

Simeon was curious too. Something was eating at his fastidious uncle. "We were, Uncle Aaron. Why do you ask?"

Again he looked around furtively. Then, still holding onto Deborah's arm, he turned her so they were no longer facing the crowd, but inward to the wall separating the two courts.

"Hava has a brother there," he said after a moment, as though he had suddenly come awake.

"Oh, yes," Deborah said. "I had forgotten that." She was completely baffled. She had met this brother only once, at Aaron's wedding many years earlier. He was an overseer on one of the big date plantations, as she remembered. Was Aaron offended that they hadn't visited with him while they were there?

"His wife's mother—" He stopped, lifting one hand and passing it over his eyes. He suddenly looked very tired. His beard seemed to droop, and his side curls barely moved.

Deborah's face showed concern. "Is there a problem?"

His hand dropped. In the near darkness, softened only by the waning moon and the faint lamplight, his face was deep in shadow. Deborah couldn't see his expression, but he seemed almost haunted.

"What is it, Aaron?" she asked more firmly. "What is the matter?"

He took a deep breath; then it came out in a long, painful sigh. "Hava's brother's mother-in-law is a wonderful woman. Sweet and gentle and kind. She's lived with her daughter for many years . . ." He blinked, as if still trying to sort something out in his mind. "Ever since she became crippled. It was horribly painful for her and over time left her completely deformed."

Deborah's hand flew to her mouth; behind her, Leah gasped.

"So you *were* there?" Aaron exclaimed.

"Oh, Aaron. We had no idea she was related to you."

"Were you there?" he said, almost sharply. "Were you there when Jesus . . ." He couldn't say it. He just shook his head.

"Yes, Aaron," David said quietly. "We were there, only a few feet away. We saw what happened."

But again Aaron was far away. "We haven't been down to see them for a while. We've been so busy since coming to Jerusalem. We send them money to help out, of course."

The family waited, sensing what was coming.

"A few weeks ago, we received a letter from Hava's brother in Jericho. He said something had happened to Grandma Huldah—that's what we all call her. He said he couldn't explain it in the letter and urged us to come to Jericho immediately."

"And you went?" Deborah asked softly.

"We just got back two days ago." His eyes had a haunted look.

"And Huldah was fine," Deborah finished for him softly.

He finally looked at them. "Yes." It was said with complete awe. "She has no pain. She walks perfectly upright, something that hasn't happened for nearly twenty years."

"You should have been there, Uncle Aaron," Leah said. "We saw Jesus do it. He held out his hand toward her and said something about loosing her from her infirmity, and then suddenly this look of wonder came into her eyes, and she slowly straightened herself upright." Tears had come to Leah's eyes. "It was wonderful, incredible." She let out a quick breath. "Unbelievable."

"That is what she said too," he whispered.

"Then rejoice in it, Aaron," David said, reaching out and gripping his shoulder. "How wonderful that something like that should come into Hava's family."

"But it was the Sabbath!" he cried. His voice was anguished, almost tortured. "Why does he do such things on the Sabbath? He did the same thing in Capernaum when he healed the man with the withered hand."

Deborah was incredulous. "What does that matter, Aaron? He healed them! He made them whole! What better work to do on the Sabbath than that?"

Before Aaron could answer, they heard a piercing blast of trumpets. They whirled around to see. Near the gate between the two courts, the three priests with trumpets had appeared again, the long silver instruments pressed to their lips. Another shrill blast broke out. It was the signal. The ceremony for the lighting of the *menorahs* was about to begin.

Aaron looked bewildered for a moment, then fell back a step. "I have to go," he said.

"Aaron?" Deborah started to say more, but he spun around and disappeared into the crowd.

II

As they marveled at what had just taken place with Aaron, Miriam suddenly let out a cry of joy. "There's Yehuda!" She raised a hand and began to wave. "And Livia."

Turning in the direction she was pointing, they were pleased to see Yehuda, who towered above most of the crowd, coming toward them, Livia in tow. It was a thrill for Miriam to see her friend within the restricted precincts of the temple for the first time. After her marriage to Yehuda, Livia had decided to formally convert to Judaism, seeing no conflict between that and her belief in Jesus. She had completed the process just a few months before.

The last of the three blasts of the trumpet pierced the air, the sound echoing off the enclosed walls. That told them that in the Court of Israel the priests were assembling, lighting the torches that would be used to ignite the *menorahs* in the Court of the Women. The noise of the crowd lessened somewhat as the third and final blast of trumpets echoed off the courtyard walls. It would be another two or three minutes before the procession actually appeared.

The two from Beth Neelah reached the family, and Miriam threw her arms around her longtime friend. "Oh, Livia, it is so good to see you. I have looked for you every day since the wedding but could never find you. Are you all right?"

"Of course." Livia turned and hugged Leah and Deborah as Yehuda shook hands with Simeon and David. "I've looked for you too," she said, "but with the crowds, I guess we just missed each other. I've been here almost every day. I've wished we had set a time and place to meet."

The crowd had grown much quieter, their eyes turned toward the gateway. Simeon moved closer to his old friend and companion in battle. "I heard a rumor yesterday."

"Oh?"

"I heard that Jesus Barabbas paid a visit to Beth Neelah."

Yehuda frowned darkly. "Your sources of information are still very good."

"So it's true?"

"Yes, about a month ago."

"And?"

Yehuda looked around. With the throngs, they could too easily be overheard. "Let's talk about it later."

"Well," Deborah said, turning from Livia to Yehuda, "it is good to see you. We came early this afternoon to get a place. We still have some food and a little wine in the basket there."

"We're fine," Yehuda said.

"Speak for yourself," Livia said. "I'm famished."

Yehuda feigned a groan as Deborah laughed and reached for the basket that contained what they had not eaten. "Can you believe this?" he said. "We ate just before we left."

"That was two hours ago," Livia retorted, removing the cloth and taking out a large chunk of cheese. Then she looked at Miriam and blushed.

Miriam's hand shot out and grasped Livia's arm. "You're not . . . ?"

The color deepened, and Livia nodded. "I think so."

"But—" They had last seen each other just over a week before, and Livia had not even given a hint.

Livia smiled shyly. "We're just beginning to suspect."

If they hadn't been where they were, Miriam would have squealed out loud. Instead she threw her arms around Livia. Leah and Deborah moved in for congratulations as well.

Simeon gave Yehuda a huge smile.

His friend grinned back. "Yes. We can't be sure at this point, but it sure looks like we're going to have a baby," he whispered. "In the late spring."

Then before they could say anything more, the sound of flutes could be heard. The procession of the priests was coming.

III

As it turned out, Jesus did not come back for the lighting of the *menorahs*. At least he didn't come into the Court of the Women where the lighting actually took place. Nor did they see Miriam's father again. Or Aaron. The lighting ceremony went off without any further interruptions, and once the blazing lights had thrown much of the city of Jerusalem into near daylight, the crowds left the Court of the Women and went out into the vast expanse of the Court of the Gentiles. David ben Joseph and his family went out with them.

After the illumination of the *menorahs*, worshipers typically stayed on the Temple Mount for a good part of the night. Especially on this, the last night of *Sukkot*, there was a reluctance to bring things to an end. In a day or two the people would pack up and return to lives that were, for the most part, pretty uneventful. So tonight they lingered on, wandering around the various courts, visiting with friends and family, sometimes praying, often just walking slowly, enjoying the pleasant coolness of the evening. David and Deborah decided they would leave the rest of the night to the young people. They left the Temple Mount through the south gate, heading for the road that led to Bethlehem.

Leah, feeling somewhat awkward with the two married couples, went with her parents.

The four who remained strolled along in a leisurely fashion. Miriam and Livia went out slightly ahead of the men, talking animatedly about how it seemed that Livia would soon be a mother, as well as Simeon and Miriam's plans for their new home when they returned to Capernaum. Simeon deliberately slowed his step so he could talk to Yehuda without being overheard.

"Tell me about Samuel," he said. "I hear he's leading the band now."

Yehuda nodded, somewhat gloomily. "Not only that, but he thinks he's got to prove himself to them. They attacked a Roman patrol here a few weeks ago."

"So it was them," Simeon said. He had heard of the raid but hoped it wasn't true. "So, what about Barabbas?"

"What about him?"

"He's a bad one, Yehuda. Samuel's not linking up with him, is he?"

"No. That's what he wanted, of course. When I heard he had come, I talked to Samuel. I told him the same thing you would have told him. Barabbas wants to be king, even if it's only over a hundred men. If anyone joins his group, it has to be on his terms. And his terms are that he's the leader, no questions asked."

"In some ways he reminds me of Ya'abin. He can be pretty ruthless."

"Well," Yehuda said, "I talked to Samuel. That's about all I can do. He doesn't take kindly to my advice now, especially about being a Zealot. We get along fine in every way except that. He still thinks we both betrayed the cause."

"That's no surprise. I wouldn't—"

Miriam stopped short, then spun around. "Simeon. That's your Uncle Aaron."

He stepped beside her to see where she was looking. She was right.

Angling across their path, perhaps ten or fifteen paces ahead of them, a group of men were hurrying toward Solomon's Porches on the east side of the Temple Mount. In the brightness shed by the great lamps, Simeon could easily distinguish his uncle, side-curls bobbing in rhythm with those of the other Pharisees as he hurried along, clutching his skirts up a little so they wouldn't impede his hurried stride. Then Simeon heard Miriam quickly take in her breath. "Look, Simeon. He's with Azariah."

Simeon had already recognized the portly figure of the chief of the Pharisees.

"Where are they off to in such a hurry?" Yehuda asked with a frown.

It was not just the Pharisees who were in a hurry. A crowd of people was following close behind, with others joining in even as Simeon and the others watched.

"Jesus!" Livia said suddenly. "It has to be Jesus!"

"Come on," Simeon said, knowing she was right.

Yehuda grabbed for Livia's hand as she started forward. "No, Livia. We don't need to get involved."

She turned to him. "Yehuda," she said evenly, "While we have been here, I have not once asked you to find Jesus. I want to hear him. If you don't, I understand. Tell me where you will be, and I will meet you later."

Miriam looked at her friend with wide eyes. This was the woman who had once been so shy and timid that she didn't even dare to meet Miriam's father's eyes when he looked at her. Then she suppressed a smile. Yehuda looked as if he had sat on a thorn. Not waiting for his response, Livia started forward.

With an exasperated sigh, Yehuda shook his head and muttered something under his breath, but he fell in behind her. The four of them moved into the surging crowd that was swelling rapidly with every passing moment.

IV

The complex that held the temple and the inner courts was raised above the main plaza of the Temple Mount, or Court of the Gentiles, by six or eight feet. Twelve steps made of long slabs of stone led from the main terrace to the temple courts. Of the nine gates that gave entry into the temple courts, the grandest and most elaborate was the Gate Beautiful, which faced the east and served as the temple's primary entrance. Five massive pillars held a corniced roof that sheltered the gate from the weather. Both pillars and roof had been constructed of gleaming white marble, which contrasted sharply with the golden brown sandstone used in the walls. The gate itself was a wonder to behold. Made of richly ornamented Corinthian brass, the two doors were so massive that it took twenty men to open or close either side.

It was at the entrance to the Gate Beautiful that Jesus had chosen to stand. It was a good choice. Not only was he elevated above the crowds so he could be clearly heard, but with the gates open, he was bathed in the golden glow of the lamps coming from the Court of the Women.

As Simeon, Miriam, Yehuda, and Livia reached the edge of the crowd, which already numbered in the hundreds, they stopped. Azariah and his entourage disappeared into the throng, calling out roughly for the people to move aside. In a few moments, Azariah appeared on the steps, moving up three or four of them so he could be seen, but he remained a few steps below the level where Jesus waited. Aaron must have stayed at the base of the stairs, because Simeon could no longer see him. Then Simeon saw Peter and Andrew. They too were on the stairs but also below the Master, flanking him on either side, looking like bodyguards prepared to fend off any possible attack. Simeon looked around anxiously and felt a lurch of concern when he saw rows of spears off to one side, above the heads of the crowd. The temple guards were there, but they were standing back.

For another full minute, Jesus just stood there, watching the crowd grow quickly, swelling outward in a half circle from where he stood. Azariah was obviously agitated but seemed unwilling to do anything until Jesus took some action. Finally, Jesus raised his hands and the crowd quieted. He dropped his hands again and began to speak.

"I am the light of the world." His voice rang out clearly and carried easily to all who were there. "He that follows me shall not walk in darkness but shall have the light of life."

The words died out. No one moved. Every eye was on the figure standing there at the gate. It was a dramatic moment. In the glow from the four great *menorahs* behind him, Jesus was almost in silhouette, backlit by the brilliance coming through the Gate Beautiful.

Simeon felt Miriam take his hand and turned to looked at her. She was not looking at him, but at Jesus, her face golden in the lamplight. Her eyes also glowed with joy and satisfaction. And then it struck him. Just as Jesus had chosen the moment of the "pouring out" to declare that he was the source of living water, now, illuminated by the brilliant glow of the four great lampstands, he had declared himself to be the ultimate source of light.

He was about to whisper that insight to Miriam when a movement caught his eye. Azariah had taken two steps upward to stand directly in front of Jesus.

"You bear record of yourself," Azariah said in a loud voice, which even at a distance carried an evident sneer. "In the Law, it is written that the testimony of two is required to establish truth. Therefore your record cannot be true."

A murmur raced through the crowd. The Pharisees had not come to listen but to challenge. They didn't dare try to take Jesus—he was far too popular with the people—but they would use the Law to show this upstart preacher to be the imposter he was.

"Though I bear record of myself," Jesus answered with perfect equanimity, "yet my record is true, for I know from whence I came and whither I go." He looked directly at Azariah. "But you cannot tell from whence I come or whither I go, for you judge after the flesh, but I judge no man."

Azariah swelled up angrily, but before he could speak, Jesus went on, speaking now to the people. "And yet if I do judge, my judgment is true, for I am not alone, but I and the Father that sent me." He turned back to Azariah, whose face was growing darker with every word. "What you say is right. It *is* written in our law that the testimony of two men establishes truth. But I am not the only one who bears record of me. I am one that bears witness of myself. But the Father that sent me also bears witness of me."

A second Pharisee moved up to stand beside Azariah. Miriam said in a low voice. "That is Caleb. He is considered second only to Azariah in the hierarchy."

"You say that your father will bear witness of you?" Caleb asked rudely. "Where is your father that we may hear him? I don't see anyone."

Jesus answered in that same unruffled voice. "You neither know me, nor my Father. If you knew me, you would have known my Father also."

Azariah threw up his hands in disgust. "What kind of answer is that?" he asked the crowd.

If he hoped for a supportive reaction, he was disappointed. There was an angry muttering from several in the crowd, and it was clear it was not directed at Jesus. "Leave him alone," someone shouted. "Let him speak."

"Go home, Pharisees," cried another. "Let us listen to a man of truth."

"Send the old brood hen home," Yehuda growled, referring to the chief Pharisee. He was not necessarily impressed with what Jesus had said, but he had no patience with Azariah's pompousness.

Before Simeon could answer, Miriam tugged on his sleeve. He turned back to see that his Uncle Aaron had joined Azariah and Caleb. Simeon groaned inwardly as Aaron moved closer to Jesus. However, he did not appear to be as angry as the other two leaders. "May I ask a question of you?" Aaron said.

Jesus nodded.

"Who are you?"

It was said with such plaintive longing that Simeon was startled. This was not an accusation; it was a question from one who was confused. He remembered the look on Aaron's face as they had discussed the healing of the old woman.

"Even the same that I said unto you in the beginning" came the answer.

Aaron stood there, seeming unsure of what that meant. "I have not been with you from the beginning," he finally answered.

"I have many things to say and to judge of you," Jesus responded, looking not just at Aaron but at Azariah and Caleb and the group of Pharisees that had accompanied them. "He that sent me is true; and I speak to the world those things which I have heard of him."

"He's speaking of his Father," Livia said softly.

"I know," Miriam said, "but Aaron and Azariah don't know that."

Aaron stood for a moment longer, then backed down again, disappearing from their view, looking more confused than ever.

Jesus lifted his head and spoke to the people. "When you have lifted up the Son of man, then shall you know that I am he."

That got an instant reaction. "I am he" could mean only one thing. *I am the Messiah.* It was as though a shock wave went through the assembly.

"Then shall you know that I do nothing of myself. I speak these things only as my Father has taught me. And he that sent me is with me. The Father has not left me alone, for I do always those things that please him."

"I thought his father was dead," Yehuda whispered to Livia.

"He's not speaking of his earthly father," she answered. "He's talking about his Heavenly Father."

Azariah was fuming. This was ridiculous. He pulled at his side curls angrily, then started to say something, but another cry from the crowd cut him off. "It is the Messiah," an older woman sang out. "*Hallelujah! Praise God!*"

"Speak on, Jesus," someone else shouted. "We believe you. Don't stop."

"Blessed be the mother that carried you in her womb," cried another female voice.

"Tell us what we should do, Rabboni," a man immediately in front of Simeon and the others shouted. "Teach us."

Jesus half turned, away from Azariah and toward the group that was calling out to him. "If you continue in my word, then are you my disciples indeed, and if you are my disciples, you shall know the truth, and the truth shall make you free."

"What?" Azariah roared. "What was that you said? We are Abraham's seed and were never in bondage to any man."

"Other than being captives to the Assyrians," Yehuda remarked dryly. "And the Babylonians. Not to mention the Greeks, the Egyptians, and a few Romans here and there."

Simeon smiled. There was a rich irony in Azariah's protest. Just to the north of them loomed the dark shape of the Antonia Fortress, a constant reminder even here on the Temple Mount that Judea was a vassal state of the Roman Empire.

Jesus turned back to face Azariah, but he didn't say anything.

The old Pharisee was so outraged he was almost sputtering. "How dare you say that you can make us free?"

The Master leaned forward slightly, speaking easily to the man confronting him, yet his voice carried clearly to all who watched. "You say that you are Abraham's seed, and yet you seek to kill me because my word has no place in you. I speak that which I have seen with my Father, and you do that which you have seen with your father."

Caleb moved up the last couple of steps to stand behind his leader. Seeing that, Peter and Andrew started to close in as well, but Jesus held up his hand, and they stopped.

"Abraham is our father!" Caleb screamed shrilly.

"If you were Abraham's children," Jesus said simply, "you would do the works of Abraham. But now you seek to kill me, a man who has told you the truth. This is not something that Abraham did."

Both Pharisees rocked back, shocked by the direct accusation. Then Azariah turned to appeal to the crowd. "The man is mad. No one here is seeking to kill him."

Jesus went on as if Azariah hadn't spoken. "You do the deeds of your father."

Azariah raised a fist and shook it in Jesus' face. The implication was that if they were not Abraham's seed, they were not legitimate children of Israel. "We are not born of fornication. We have one Father, even God."

For the first time, there was a touch of coldness in Jesus' voice. "If God were your Father, you would love me, for I came from God. Why will you not understand what I say? Even because you will not hear my word. Why? Because you are of your father the devil, and the lusts of your father is what you do."

Azariah fell back a step, his mouth working, his fingers clenching and unclenching. "The devil? You say our father is the devil?"

"O my!" Miriam breathed. "Now that's about as straight as I have ever heard."

But Jesus wasn't through. "Because I tell you the truth, you won't believe me. Which of you convicts me of sin? What proof have you? And if I say the truth, why do you not believe me? He that is of God is willing to hear God's words. You refuse to hear them because you are not of God."

By this point, Azariah was livid. He couldn't get a word out. He just stood there, trembling with rage. Caleb whirled about and shouted at the crowd. "Say we not well that this man is a Samaritan and has a devil? What further evidence do you need?"

"I have not a devil," Jesus cried out, his voice sharp and ringing clearly. "But I honor my Father, and you do dishonor me. Verily, verily, I say unto you, if a man keeps my saying, he shall never see death."

In that moment, Azariah saw that what Caleb had just tried was the only hope left to them. This man was an outrage, a blasphemer, and an accuser. Nothing they could say would get through to him. Their only hope lay with the crowd.

He turned his back on Jesus, hands out, imploring. "Now we know for sure that this man has a devil. He says that if any man keeps his sayings, he will never see death. But Abraham is dead. Others of the prophets are dead. What does he mean, if a man keeps his saying, he shall never taste of death?"

The crowd had fallen silent at the last interchange. Many of the people there were like Yehuda. They didn't like the arrogance and self-righteous superiority of the Pharisees, but most of the common people believed that the Pharisees were closer to God and that their teachings were more in harmony with his will than the aristocratic Sadducees, or even the Essenes, those extreme ascetics who had completely withdraw from the world and formed their own community on the shores of the Dead Sea. Jesus was not just criticizing the excesses of the Pharisees, which would have won him a lot of support. He had called them the children of Satan. He had just said as plainly as tongue could tell that they were not of God. Suddenly many in the crowd were confused and uncertain.

Azariah, as shrewd and quick as any man could be, sensed the change in mood and pressed in eagerly. He whirled back to face Jesus.

"Are you saying that you are greater than our father Abraham, who is dead? Do you claim to be greater than Isaiah and Ezekiel and Jeremiah and the other prophets, all of whom are dead? What are you trying to make of yourself?" he finished incredulously.

Jesus looked thoughtful yet totally uninfluenced by the passions all around him. "Your father Abraham rejoiced to see my day: and he saw it, and was glad."

Azariah hooted in pure contempt. "You are not yet fifty years old, and you claim that you have seen Abraham?"

For one electric moment, the crowd seemed to hold its breath. Jesus waited, as calm as if he were seated on a hillside by himself, enjoying a summer's day. Then, more gravely than he had said anything up to that point, he went on. "Verily, verily, I say unto you . . ." There was a long pause. Not a sound filled the courtyard. And then it came. *"Before Abraham was, I am."*

It was as though a tidal wave had slammed into the crowd. Everyone rocked back, faces registering disbelief. When Moses had been called of God on Mount Sinai to deliver the children of Israel, he had asked the Lord, "When I come to the people and tell them that the God of their fathers has sent me to deliver them, they will ask me your name. What shall I tell them?"

And the voice of God answered Moses, saying, "I AM THAT I AM. Thus thou shalt say unto the children of Israel. Say that I AM has sent you unto them."

In Hebrew, that most sacred and holy of all names was written as *Jehovah*. Jehovah meant literally, *I Am! I exist!* And rightly so. Of all the false gods worshiped in a thousand places across time and in a thousand nations of the world, which could say, "I am. I do truly exist"?

What was so utterly shocking was that Jesus had just invoked that sacred name in such a way that it clearly had reference to himself. It was not some vague, obscure comment. Virtually everyone there understood exactly what he had just said, which was, in effect, "Before Abraham was, I was. I am the I AM. *I am Jehovah.*"

For a moment, Simeon, as shocked as everyone else, thought Azariah was going to have a stroke right there on the spot. But instead, Azariah's face went as dark as death, and he gave one strangled cry. "He blasphemes. He makes himself as God. Stone him! Stone him!"

It was fortunate that they were in a paved court. People began scrambling, looking for a loose paving stone or anything else they might lay their hands on to throw at this man who had just committed sacrilege. In one instant, some members of the crowd joined together in an angry mob. Many others, who just minutes before had shouted their support of Jesus, now looked bewildered. Would a man of God blaspheme the name of God in such a manner?

Azariah ran to the northern edge of the stairs, waving frantically. Simeon saw the row of spears start to move. The old Pharisee was summoning the temple guards. Once again, Simeon's first reaction was to spring to Jesus' defense. "Stay here," he cried to Miriam. But as he started shoving his way through the crowd, which was now in full chaos, he suddenly stopped. The top of the staircase was empty except for Azariah, who was shouting for the guards to hurry. Where Jesus had been standing just moments before, there was nothing. Peter and Andrew were gone. Only Azariah and Caleb were there. Caleb was still haranguing the crowd, chanting: "Stone him! Stone him! Stone him!" Azariah was waving for the guards to hurry.

As the line of spears reached the bottom of the steps below Azariah, he turned back pointing. "Seize him!" he shouted. Then he froze when he saw that no one was there. His enemy was gone. Once again Jesus had slipped away and disappeared into the crowd.

CHAPTER NOTES

Having the woman whom Jesus cured of an infirmity be related to Aaron is obviously a fictional device of the author's. However, it does serve to remind us that, while rarely given names, these were actual people, with families and friends and lives of their own.

John gives us the lengthy account of the events connected with the Feast of Tabernacles (John 7–8), and he specifies that they happened on the "the last day, that great day of the feast" (John 7:37). In the New Testament, the story of the woman taken in adultery (John 8:1–11) is inserted between the "living waters" account and the "light of the world" passages. However, most scholars agree that this story is a later insertion into John's Gospel. It breaks the sequence of the festival account and is not found in the more ancient manuscripts (see Dummelow, p. 788; Guthrie, pp. 945–46). That is not to imply that the account of the woman is spurious. The account is very ancient and well attested to. It is its placement in John that is questioned. For this reason, this author treated the story of the woman taken in adultery in an earlier volume and not here.

Since the lighting of the lampstands immediately followed the "pouring out" ceremony, it is reasonable to assume that the two interchanges between Jesus and the Jewish leaders happened at roughly the same time.

The deeper significance of Jesus' statement, "Before Abraham was, I am," is lost in the English translation. It seems like a harmless, almost obscure, passing comment to modern readers. But it highly offended the Jews. John describes their reaction in this manner: "Then took they up stones to cast at him" (John 8:59). Blasphemy was a capital offense under the Mosaic Law, and the specified form of execution was stoning. The implication seems to be that Jesus' comment was viewed as blasphemous. But why?

In the original Greek of the New Testament manuscripts, the phrase which is translated as "I am" in English is *ego eimi*. That is exactly the same phrase used in a Greek version of the Old Testament (the Septuagint) where God says that his name is "I AM" (Exodus 3:14).

Various commentators have noted the importance of what Jesus said. "It is important to observe the distinction between the two verbs ["Abraham was" and "I am"]. Abraham's life was under the condition of time, and therefore had a temporal beginning. . . . Jesus' life was from and to eternity. Hence the formula for *absolute, timeless* existence, *I am (ego eimi)*" (Vincent, 1:456).

"Christ seems here to declare Himself to be the Jehovah, or the I AM of the O.T., the eternal, self-existent Creator" (Dummelow, p. 790).

What Jesus was saying was essentially this: "I am from all eternity. I have existed before all ages. You consider in me only the person who speaks to you, and who has appeared to you within a particular time. But besides this human nature, which ye think ye know, there is in me a Divine and eternal nature. Both, united, subsist together in my person. Abraham knew how to distinguish them. He adored me as his God; and desired me as his Savior. He has seen me in my eternity, and he predicted my coming into the world" (Calmet, as cited in Clarke, 3:582).

Is it a surprise, then, that these Jews who refused to see Jesus for who he really was were greatly offended by the simple declaration, "I am"?

CHAPTER 13

YOU ARE NOT A BETTER JUDGE THAN GOD, OR WISER THAN THE MOST
HIGH! LET MANY PERISH WHO ARE NOW LIVING, RATHER THAN THAT
THE LAW OF GOD WHICH IS SET BEFORE THEM BE DISREGARDED.

—*2 Esdras 7:19–20*

I

JERUSALEM, IN THE CHAMBERS
OF THE SANHEDRIN ON THE TEMPLE MOUNT
14 OCTOBER, A.D. 32

The Great Council normally did not seat themselves during festivals, but this was an emergency. Mordechai sat in his seat beside Caiaphas, silently fuming. He started to rise. "Where are they?" he burst out.

Several in the council turned their heads at the sound of his voice. Azariah, chief of the Pharisees and Mordechai's chief antagonist on the council, gave him an oily smile. "Patience, my dear Mordechai. They'll bring him."

As if only waiting for that comment, there was a sudden scuffing of sandals on marble. Everyone turned. A column of eight men, two abreast, spears held at attention, had entered beneath the massive columns of the Royal Porches and were marching toward them.

Mordechai leaned forward, peering eagerly, then sat down heavily. "They don't have him," he grunted.

Beside him, Caiaphas uttered a low imprecation. Dismay and disgust were written clearly on Azariah's face.

The men stopped behind the double circle of stone chairs, which marked the back edge of the council's chambers. The captain came forward, removing his helmet, clearly fearful.

"Where is Jesus?" Caiaphas demanded. "Why have you not brought him?"

The man fumbled a little, turning his helmet nervously in his hands. "Excellency, we—" His eyes dropped. "Excellency, never did any man speak as this man does."

Mordechai shot to his feet. He had expected some weak excuse about not being able to find Jesus again after he disappeared into the crowds. But this? This was unthinkable.

Before he could speak, though, Azariah spoke for him. "Are you also deceived?" he roared.

The man didn't look up, just stared at the ground. Behind him, his men were also looking away.

"Rabbi," the captain said to Azariah, "the people, there are many who accept him as the Messiah. If we had tried to take him, there would be—"

But Azariah was still enraged by the first comment. "Have any of the rulers of the Pharisees believed on this man?" He was seething. "Do you see any man here saying—" His voice became a singsong whine—"'Never did any man speak as this man does.' You fool! The people don't know the Law. No wonder they are dazzled by this fraud."

"I should like to speak."

Mordechai turned, as did Caiaphas. Nicodemus, another of the leaders of the Pharisees, had stood. Mordechai frowned. He had long suspected that Nicodemus and Joseph of Arimathea, both members of the council, were at least sympathizers of Jesus, if not outright disciples.

However, if he was, Nicodemus was too timid to let his feelings be known. He knew that he risked his seat on the Sanhedrin.

"Say on," Caiaphas said reluctantly, obviously guessing what might be coming.

"Does our law judge a man before it hears him? It seems as though this council is bent on convicting Jesus of crimes we are not sure he has committed. Let us hear him and learn what it is he does."

Mordechai, still on his feet, looked at Caiaphas, who nodded for him to speak. "Are you a Galilean too, Nicodemus?"

"Of course not," the Pharisee replied, unruffled.

"Then may I remind you of something?" Mordechai said coldly. "Search the Law. Search the writings. Search the prophets. And you will find that out of Galilee comes no prophet."

Nicodemus looked as if he wanted to respond, but there was nothing to say. He had been in the temple when Mordechai used that same argument to tame the crowd. Even the most unlearned knew of Micah's clear declaration. Nicodemus took his seat and looked down.

Mordechai shook his head, glaring at the other man. Then, knowing he wasn't going to change Nicodemus's mind, he looked up and down the faces of the rest of them. His voice went dangerously quiet. "We are facing the greatest crisis this council has faced in a hundred years. You saw what happened there tonight. The *hallelujahs*. The *hosanna* shout. The wild waving of the *lulavs*. That wasn't just a moment of joyous ecstasy. The people weren't just momentarily carried away."

Suddenly his voice blasted out, startling several. "This man put himself forth as the Messiah! Azariah was able to convince a few of them that he's a fraud and a blasphemer. But most of the people are like a stupid flock of sheep. We're lucky the Romans weren't there to see all of this."

Nicodemus rose again.

"*No!*" Mordechai bellowed. "Hear me out. Pilate won't hesitate for one moment. If he thinks there's going to be a rebellion, this council will be disbanded in the snap of a finger. Maybe you want to rot in a Roman jail, Nicodemus, but I do not."

No one spoke.

Mordechai didn't look at Caiaphas to get his approval for what he said next. He swung on the captain of the guard. "Have you ever seen the pit prison in the palace of our high priest?" he demanded, his voice suddenly icy.

The man blanched. "Yes, sire."

"If you ever want to see your wife again, then you find this man, and you bring him to us. Someone is going to occupy that cell before this feast is over. Either it will be this imposter who threatens our very nation, or it will be the clumsy fools who don't have the courage to take him. Do you understand me?"

The man was already backing up, as were the other guards with him. "Yes, sire."

"Then get out of here, and don't come back here empty-handed again."

II

Mordechai flicked a finger at Menachem of Bethphage as the council broke up and emptied back out into the Court of the Gentiles. Menachem, a fellow Sadducee, was Mordechai's protégé and staunchest supporter on the council.

Mordechai waited until it was just the three of them—Caiaphas, himself, and Menachem—then leaned forward. Even though Caiaphas was the high priest and titular head of the Great Sanhedrin, everyone, including Caiaphas, understood who really controlled the council. As Menachem sat down with them at the table that stood at the head of the council chambers, Caiaphas leaned back, clearly content to let Mordechai lead out.

"Brethren," Mordechai said, speaking low in case anyone was lurking behind the pillars, "though it infuriates me, I fear the captain is right. You saw the reaction tonight. If we try to take him during the festival, we may cause an eruption that will do our cause irreparable harm."

"But—" Caiaphas started. Then he thought better of it and shook his head.

"There are other things stirring," Mordechai said. "This goes no further than this circle. Not under any circumstances. Understood?"

Their nods reflected deep gravity. Mordechai didn't tell them about the visit of Marcus Didius to his palace. He spoke in generalities. He told them that there were rumors of trouble, that the governor might use this opportunity to try to take some of the Zealot leaders. They were instantly concerned. He went on swiftly.

"I have quietly sent word to the Romans that the greatest source of rebellion is Jesus of Nazareth. If the Romans take him, the people won't dare try to stop them." He smiled tightly. "And if we lose a few hundred Zealots in the process, that won't break our hearts either, will it."

"The Romans have a way of letting things get very messy," Caiaphas said darkly.

"Yes, they do, but unless our bold and fearless captain of the guard"—that was said in utter contempt—"is wise enough to take Jesus when there are not a lot of people around, it could get very messy for us."

"True," Menachem said. "If the Romans take Jesus, then we can't be held responsible."

Mordechai pulled at his lip. "I'm going to try to find out more about what's going on. But—" He looked around again and dropped his voice even more. "I am going to station the temple guards somewhere away from the Temple Mount for the next day or two. If there are any questions, I need your support."

"Why would you want to do that?" Caiaphas asked. Then understanding dawned. "Ah," he said.

"The farther away we are from what happens, the better it will be for us."

"Very good," Menachem said.

Mordechai leaned forward. "Brethren, you saw what happened tonight. I don't have to tell you, it sent chills up and down my spine. This man could raise an army of ten thousand with a single word. He has got to be stopped." He sighed. "And when it is over, it must be the Romans who take the blame."

III

JERUSALEM, IN THE COURT
OF THE GENTILES ON THE TEMPLE MOUNT

Almost an hour had passed since Jesus had been at the Gate Beautiful. Miriam, Simeon, Yehuda, and Livia were seated on one of the many low benches scattered around the edges of the Court of the Gentiles. The crowds had thinned somewhat, but many people were still walking around. The four friends had not spoken of what had happened with Jesus. Miriam was dying to know what Yehuda was thinking about it all, but didn't dare ask. Nor did Simeon seem inclined to broach the subject.

"Will you be leaving after the Sabbath then?" Miriam asked.

212

Yehuda nodded. "Yes, in two days. And you? Will you stay here for a while with Jesus?"

Simeon answered. "We're going to stay a few days longer to help Uncle Benjamin and to strengthen some of our trading relationships. We'll be heading back to Capernaum after that."

"But not with Jesus?" Livia said.

Simeon shook his head. "Father talked to Peter yesterday. Jesus is thinking of going into Perea again, maybe even staying until Passover next spring."

"Wise move," Yehuda said.

Miriam was surprised. "Why do you say that?"

Yehuda was very sober. "When Jesus started talking about the Pharisees trying to kill him, I thought perhaps he had been out in the sun a little long. Azariah is a pompous old fool, but he's about as dangerous as a setting hen kicked off her nest. Or so I thought. But when Jesus accused him and the rest of the Pharisees of being children of the devil . . ." He shook his head in awe. "It's a wonder they didn't kill him on the spot."

"I've watched old Azariah many times in the council," Miriam agreed. "I've never seen him as incensed, as totally livid as he was today." She bit her lip. "It's true that as an individual Azariah is not a threat. But he is a powerful voice on the council, and the council can be very dangerous."

"Either way," Yehuda went on, "Jesus had better get out of Jerusalem, or he won't last until the end of the month."

Miriam found this conversation very depressing and decided to change the subject. "Will you be coming up to the temple again, after the Sabbath but before you leave?" she asked Livia.

Livia looked to her husband. He shrugged. "I promised Samuel to go and look at some new vines for the vineyard. You don't have to go."

"Then, yes," Livia said, answering Miriam. "I would like to hear Jesus again if he's still here."

"As would I," Miriam said, pleased. "The men have promised to help Uncle Benjamin mend some rock walls in the pasture before we leave, so I'm free. Let's meet at the Gate Beautiful. Shall we say about the third hour?"

"Wonderful. I'll see you then."

They all stood, but before they could say their farewells, someone called out. "Simeon!"

They turned to see who it was, but Simeon had already recognized Aaron's voice. Feeling a spurt of anxiety, he and the others turned. Aaron came bustling up. This time his demeanor was not one of perplexity or distraction, but open irritation and anger.

"Where's your mother?" he demanded before he even reached them.

"They left right after the lighting," Simeon answered. "Mother was tired."

He muttered something, clearly disappointed. "So she didn't hear any of that?"

"Any of what?" Simeon said wearily, already knowing exactly what he referred to.

"Did you hear it?" he said. "Were you there?"

"Yes, Aaron, we were there."

"Well?"

"Well, what?"

He stared at his nephew in astonishment. "What more do you need? Surely you cannot follow a man who commits open and public blasphemy."

"It is only blasphemy," Simeon retorted tartly, "if Jesus is *not* the Messiah."

It was as if something poisonous had crawled inside Aaron's robe.

He had a look of horror as he shuddered and fell back. "You, too!" he exclaimed.

"Yes, Aaron, me too."

"Careful, nephew," he said tightly. "The penalty for blasphemy is death. The council has already called an emergency session. They will not hesitate to take action against anyone who dares to violate the Law."

Miriam was thinking of her father. She had sat in on council meetings many times, taking notes for him. She knew how that body worked. And suddenly she understood something. "The council really does want to kill him, don't they."

"Don't be ridiculous."

"I wasn't," she shot right back. "What Jesus said to Azariah is true. They want to kill him because he speaks the truth."

He raised a fist above his head, not to strike her, but to emphasize how deeply he was shaken. "A woman is not exempt from the demands of the Law," he hissed. "Take care, Miriam, daughter of Mordechai. Even your father cannot protect you from a charge of blasphemy."

"My father is the last one who would try to protect me," Miriam answered slowly.

"And what of your Grandma Huldah?" Livia suddenly asked.

Aaron half turned, rocking back. "What?"

"I've been told how you spoke of the healing of the woman named Huldah. Doesn't that suggest that Jesus may indeed be the Messiah, as he claims to be?"

Aaron raised his hands, as if warding off an attack. "You, too?" he cried hoarsely. He started backing away. "Take care, Simeon," he warned. "You are climbing a very slippery slope. And the rest of you, too. This has got to be stopped."

With that, he turned and plunged into the crowd again, disappearing from their sight.

IV

As they moved slowly across the great courtyard, heading for the western gate that would take them off the Temple Mount, the four friends did not speak. Aaron's diatribe had left them all with a sour taste in their mouth.

"Did you know that Jesus has talked about dying here in Jerusalem?" Simeon said unexpectedly.

"I know. That's why he must go," Livia said. "You have to tell him that, Simeon. He has to leave."

"And have Jesus rebuke me like he did Peter? No, thank you." And then, even more seriously, he added. "He's the Messiah, Livia. Don't forget that. No one is going to kill him."

Yehuda snorted softly but said nothing.

Livia ignored her husband's skepticism. "Yes," she said, suddenly relieved. "We have to remember that, don't we."

"Of course, that doesn't mean God can't use us as instruments to help protect him. Either way, we can't lose hope."

Yehuda began a retort, but once again they were interrupted by a voice calling out to them. "There you are. Good!"

They turned to see Luke the Physician coming swiftly toward them. "What is it, Luke?" Simeon asked.

"Peter asked that I find as many disciples as possible and have them come to Jesus."

"He's still here?" Simeon exclaimed.

"Yes. He's back near the Gate Beautiful again."

"Have the temple guards—"

"We haven't seen them," Luke cut in, "but Peter's worried. He's convinced the only hope is to have enough people around that they won't dare to arrest him."

"All right," Simeon said without hesitation. Luke raised a hand, then hurried away to find others.

Simeon turned. "Miriam, perhaps you'd better go with Yehuda and Livia. I can come and get you when this is over."

To his surprise, it was Yehuda who shook his head as vigorously as Miriam did. When he saw Simeon's expression, he spoke in clipped words. "I don't agree with what Jesus teaches," he said, "but he has a right to speak his mind. He's done nothing worthy of being arrested by those frogs on their lily pads who pass themselves off as our rulers. I'm coming with you."

"We're coming too," Miriam said, her voice brooking no disagreement. "As Luke said, the more people who are there to support Jesus, the less chance the guards will try something."

V

JERUSALEM, AT THE GATE BEAUTIFUL ON THE TEMPLE MOUNT

Luke was right. Jesus was standing in almost the same place where he had been when Azariah and Caleb faced him. The crowd had become smaller, but it still ran into the hundreds. Simeon angled in from one side, pushing his way forward until he was close enough to act swiftly, if needed. Jesus was speaking quietly with a group of men standing on the steps. Peter was behind him but turned at seeing movement and saw Simeon. He smiled and walked swiftly over to them.

"Luke found you?"

"Yes," Simeon answered. "Is everything all right?"

Peter shook his head, frowning deeply. "For now, I suppose. But frankly I'm worried. As you saw tonight, Jesus has some powerful enemies."

"At least one," Yehuda observed dryly. "That old lizard Azariah."

Peter stuck out his hand. "Agreed. How are you, Yehuda? And Livia? It's good to see you again. How is life as the wife of a vineyard keeper?"

"Absolutely wonderful," Livia answered.

"And how are you two old married people doing?" Peter asked Miriam.

She smiled as broadly as Livia had. "Wonderful."

"How is Jesus, Peter?" Livia asked anxiously. "Is he being careful? I'm sure the whole Sanhedrin is up in arms tonight."

"He's . . ." He hesitated, searching for the right word. "Determined. We've stopped trying to get him to be careful. He just gives us that look."

"You're staying in Bethany?" Simeon asked.

"Yes, at Mary's house. Which is good. Jesus is completely comfortable there. He can have time alone, if he wants. And Lazarus has been good to protect us from too many of the inquisitive."

Simeon turned and looked around at the crowd. He was pleased to see many faces he recognized, some from Capernaum, some from the Upper Galilee that he had gotten to know during his years as a Zealot.

Peter saw what he was doing and did the same. "It should be all right. Most of these are friends, or at least sympathizers."

"That's good," Simeon said with a nod. This was not a crowd that would shrink away from any sign of trouble.

"Master?"

They all turned. Jesus was still standing on one of the lower stairs. He too turned to see who had spoken.

"I'd better go," Peter said. "Thank you for coming."

As Peter moved off, Simeon and the others followed, pressing in closer to where Jesus stood. Meanwhile, there was a disturbance in the crowd, and people began to fall back. Then two men appeared. The first was slightly ahead of the other, leading him by the hand. Then, in the light from the great lamps, Simeon saw why. The man was obviously blind. His head was turned upward at a slight angle, and sightless eyes peered from beneath half-closed lids.

Miriam caught her breath, and Simeon turned to look at her. "I know this man," she said.

"The blind one?"

"Yes." She looked at Livia. "We used to see him when we came up to the Temple Mount. He would sit at one of the gates, asking for alms."

"Of course," Livia said. "I remember now. We gave him money once or twice."

Miriam nodded.

As the two men came up to Jesus, the crowd quieted. Were they about to witness another miracle?

The first man bowed low in respect. "Master," he said. "We would ask a question of you."

Jesus' head bobbed slightly. "Yes?"

Simeon was expecting a request for help for the man, so their question surprised him. "Who did sin? This man, or his parents, that he was born blind?"

Jesus looked at the man who stood before him. The blind man's head tipped back, as if he were trying to look at Jesus, but other than that he didn't speak or move.

Then Jesus answered. "Neither has this man sinned, nor his parents. This has come upon him that the works of God should be made manifest in him."

The blind man's companion looked puzzled.

Jesus went on. "While it is day, I must work the works of him that sent me. The night is coming when no man can work." He looked around, as if looking for the darkness that was currently being held back by the four great *menorahs*. "As long as I am in the world, I am the light of the world."

Miriam leaned forward. She felt a sudden thrill shoot through her. Horrified at the thought that this man had never had sight, she had just been wondering what it would be like to have known only darkness. A whole life of darkness. She felt a shiver ripple through her body, a shiver of anticipation. Now, at this very moment, the man stood before the Light of the World.

To everyone's surprise, Jesus stepped down from the stair to the main level of the court and dropped to one knee. His head bowed, and he spat on the ground. He spat again, then reached down and seemed to be picking something up.

"What is he doing?" Yehuda whispered.

No one answered, because no one could see for sure. Then he stood, and they saw what he had been doing. Though they were on the Temple Mount and everything was paved with stone, here and there, especially in the corners or around the base of the stairs where the wind would eddy, were small piles of dirt and debris. Jesus had found such a place. He had spit into the dirt, then scooped the muddy mixture into the palm of his left hand. Heads craned as people tried to see better what was happening.

Jesus turned to the blind man. "Come forward," he said quietly.

The man shuffled forward one step. Jesus reached out and took his hand, squeezing it with a slight pressure. The man knelt before him, bowing his head. Jesus reached out with his right hand and lifted the man's head to fully face him. Gently, he touched the eyes with his fingertips, closing the lids as though he were bidding him to sleep. Then with great tenderness, Jesus dipped his forefinger in the muddy paste and smeared it over one of the man's eyes. The man jumped slightly at that first touch but immediately steadied again. Jesus repeated the process for the other eye.

The blind man looked as if he wore two eye patches. Jesus examined his handiwork for a moment, then stepped back. "Go," he said, speaking to the man's companion. "Have him wash in the Pool of Siloam."

VI

A half dozen or so of the crowd followed after the two men to see for themselves what would come of this strange occurrence, but the rest stayed with Jesus. Perhaps, like Simeon, they wanted to remain there to protect him if something developed.

The Pool of Siloam was normally about a ten-minute walk south of the Temple Mount. Leading a blind man, it would take somewhat longer. A full half hour passed, and nothing happened. Still no one left. Jesus stood quietly talking with Peter and the Twelve. Everyone seemed content simply to wait patiently.

Finally, Livia could bear it no longer. She had to ask the question that was on everyone's mind. "Why the mud and spittle on his eyes?" she asked her companions. "Have you ever seen him do that before?"

Simeon shook his head.

Miriam's head came up slowly as a thought flashed into her mind. "In the 'pouring out' ceremony, the waters of the Pool of Siloam represent the Spirit of God."

Livia's eyes widened. Simeon looked at his wife in surprise.

"The man's eyes are covered with the dust of the earth. Now he goes to Siloam to wash that away with God's spirit."

Simeon began to nod, watching Yehuda out of the corner of his eye. He would have gladly given a hundred shekels to know what was going on in his friend's mind, but Yehuda's face was impassive. He didn't react to Miriam's suggestion at all. They fell silent again, waiting to see what would happen.

Finally, they heard a commotion behind them, and the crowd turned. Across the courtyard, weaving in and out of the crowds, a man was running toward them. As he got closer, he cried out, waving his arms. "I see! I see!"

Stunned, the crowd fell back, opening a path for him. People began murmuring and pointing. It was the blind man, and he was trotting along unassisted by anyone. The front of his tunic was dark, obviously wet and muddy. Several paces behind him, his companion appeared, trying to keep up.

As one, the crowd turned back to see what Jesus would do. Then a disappointed cry went up. Jesus was gone. When everyone had turned to watch the return of the man, Jesus had quietly left. Peter and the others had gone as well.

The man who had spent his life in darkness and begging for his livelihood, stopped, looking around. "Where is the man who touched my eyes?"

"He's gone," someone said. "He was here just a moment ago, but he's gone."

The man's shoulders slumped in dejection, then immediately straightened again. He turned to the crowd, searching their faces eagerly, like a man coming off a long fast and finally seeing a table filled with food. "I see you!" he said in wonder. "I can see you."

Miriam was blinking rapidly, trying to clear her eyes. She felt someone beside her and turned to see Livia, tears streaming down her cheeks. They held each other joyfully.

Simeon looked at Yehuda. His friend was staring at the man, looking dazed. Simeon touched his longtime friend on the shoulder. "Well, Yehuda," he said slowly, "now you have seen for yourself what Jesus can do. And what are you going to do with that?"

CHAPTER 14

I

JERUSALEM, IN THE CHAMBERS OF THE
SANHEDRIN ON THE TEMPLE MOUNT
14 OCTOBER, A.D. 32

"We shall now hear from the Father of the House of Judgment."

Caiaphas sat down, and Mordechai ben Uzziel stood. "Father of the House of Judgment" was a ponderous title, but what it really meant was that he was the second in authority to the high priest, the vice-president of the Great Council, as it were. Fortunately, Caiaphas, who was often a doddering old fool but loved the posturing he could do as head of the council, knew this night was too much for him.

Mordechai looked slowly around the council, seated in a double row that formed a half circle around him. "Brethren, I need not tell you that we face a grave crisis. The fact that we are meeting a second time within a few hours, and that during a high festival, is evidence enough of that. Thank you for coming on such short notice."

There were nods and a few murmurs. Not all seventy members of the council had been found, but there were fifty or more, enough for the council to proceed. Mordechai waited for a moment, but no one said anything. That was a miracle in itself. Normally this group was so independent and refractory that one could barely say "Good evening" without someone taking exception to it.

"First," Mordechai said, "before we get to the critical issue at hand, I have an item of information. As you have probably heard, thievery in the areas around the gates of the city has increased of late, especially during this last week. We have had several complaints."

In reality, there had been a few reports of petty theft, but nothing out of the ordinary, especially during a large festival such as this. But word of these had been played up, in keeping with Mordechai's instructions, so he was not surprised to see several nod at his announcement.

"Therefore—and this information is for your ears only and is not to be repeated—starting at dawn tomorrow, we have asked the temple guards to secrete themselves in various places around the main gates into the city. We shall see how many of these thieves we can catch with their hands in our purses."

Caleb the Pharisee raised a hand. Mordechai acknowledged him with a flick of his hand.

"How many will that leave for the Temple Mount? There will still be a lot of people here."

"Only half a dozen will remain on the Mount." Which was actually six more than Mordechai was really going to leave there.

Another man, one of Mordechai's fellow Sadducees, rose slowly, frowning. "And what if this Jesus shows up again? There could be trouble. Half a dozen won't be enough."

Menachem of Bethphage leaped up. "The guards haven't been able to find Jesus yet. We think he has been frightened off. I move that we support our esteemed leader's suggestion."

Mordechai went on, pleased to again hear numerous murmurs of assent. He gave them a crafty smile. "If this charlatan does try to return, well, he will have to enter through one of the gates now, won't he. It should be a simple matter to detain him for examination."

The group laughed shortly, and Menachem and the other man sat down again. As they did so, Mordechai was momentarily startled. There were always a few people standing behind the council members. Generally they were trusted assistants or other support staff. Now among them Mordechai saw a face that looked familiar. It was one of the men standing behind Azariah and Caleb. It was . . . He thought hard. He had seen him before, standing as he was now, behind the head of the Pharisaical party. He was assisting the leadership of the Pharisees. One of those whom Azariah had taken under his wing to groom for a future seat on the council. Mordechai started to turn away, still somewhat troubled. That was not all. There was something more. . . .

He stiffened as it came to him. The man's name was Aaron. He was brother-in-law to David ben Joseph of Capernaum. He felt a hot flash of anger. If his report was correct, this was the man who had actually performed the marriage of his daughter to Simeon ben David.

Azariah half rose. "Yes, yes," he snapped, jerking Mordechai out of his thoughts. "Our concern here tonight is not temple guards. There are far more serious problems to deal with. Let's get on with it."

Mordechai gave Aaron one last look. He knew he couldn't hold the marriage performance against this man. Simeon was his nephew. It would be expected of him. Nevertheless, this one would bear watching.

Mordechai forced himself to focus on the matter at hand. Though Azariah was his usual irritating self, his sneering comment had deflected any further questions about why Mordechai was moving the guards off the Temple Mount. So Mordechai nodded. "My esteemed colleague is right, of course," he said unctuously. "We have a more critical matter to deal with."

Just then there was the sound of footsteps. Mordechai straightened and turned. It was one of servants of the council. Before Mordechai could ask, he pointed back in the direction from which he had just come. "We've got him, sire."

"Excellent. Bring him in." This was what he had been waiting for, the primary reason the council had been reconvened and the reason Mordechai had been stalling for time.

Every head turned as four temple guards appeared, marching a middle-aged man with graying hair between them.

Mordechai indicated with a wave of his hand where he wanted him, and the guards brought the man forward. Then they stepped back out of the circle, taking up their station behind the second row of council members.

Mordechai took the man's measure quickly, fighting not to let contempt show on his face. The man's tunic was dusty and soiled. His sandals were worn, with one strap broken, and his feet were nearly black with dirt. Yet the Sadducee couldn't help but feel a deep uneasiness as he looked the man. He had recognized him instantly, of course. It *was* the blind beggar, just as reported. Mordechai had seen this man countless times around the temple courts. He felt his stomach lurch a little, as can happen when one looks into an open wound he hadn't expected to see. Where before the man's eyes had been half closed, hiding sightless orbs beneath the lids, now they were fully open. The man was looking around with interest, studying the faces around him, looking up in wonder at the massive pillars of the Royal Portico. The eyes were clear and showed obvious intelligence. *What had happened here?*

A low buzz broke out as the council leaned forward. "Quiet!" Mordechai said sharply. Then, as his command was obeyed, he turned to face the man. "State your name."

"I am Asa the Beggar."

"The one who supposedly was blind until today?"

The man gave him an odd look. "Supposedly?" he said slowly. His hands came up, the fingers almost touching his eyes. "I see, where before I was blind. If that is 'supposedly,' then yes, I am he."

Mordechai winced. "Supposedly" had slipped out without thinking. He motioned to the beggar. "Stand forth and answer some questions."

The man took a step forward, looking nervous.

"You say your eyes have been opened. How was this done?"

"A man that is called Jesus made clay with his hands and anointed mine eyes. Then he said unto me, 'Go to the Pool of Siloam, and wash.' I went and washed, and as I did so, I received my sight."

"Where is this man?" Mordechai demanded.

"I know not. When I returned to thank him, he was gone."

That corresponded to what had already been reported to Mordechai. Azariah was on his feet again, and Mordechai nodded for him to speak. "This happened just a short time ago?" he asked the beggar.

The man turned to face his new interrogator. "An hour, perhaps two. No more."

"And did you know that this, being a feast day, is a Sabbath day?"

"Of course, yes."

"Tell us again. What did this man do to you?"

"He put clay upon my eyes, and I washed, and I do see."

"And where did he get this clay?"

"He spit into some dirt on the pavement and then scooped it into his hands."

Azariah turned and gave a sharp look at his colleagues. "So he made it himself?"

"Yes."

"On the Sabbath day? This man mixed clay on *Shabbat*?"

The man nodded, sensing trouble. The Pharisees in the circle were all giving him dark looks. No righteous man would violate the strict laws of the Sabbath.

Caleb stood up beside his mentor. "Then this man cannot be of God, because he keeps not the Sabbath day."

Joseph of Arimathea, also a Pharisee and seated three places down from Azariah, shot to his feet. "If Jesus is a sinner, as you say, how can he do such miracles?"

"Yes! Answer that!" someone else cried out. Mordechai's brows lowered. In a moment, the council was in chaos. This was not good. Uproar in the council was not unusual, but this was an issue with tremendous impact. The man that stood before them was not a stranger to them. He had been a beggar on the Temple Mount for more years than anyone could remember. Everyone knew personally of his blindness, and now he stood before them, his eyes opened, turning to look at them when they spoke. If Mordechai felt shaken by this incontrovertible reality, it should be no surprise that the rest were as well.

He let the shouting and yelling run on for almost a full minute; then he let out a roar. "Enough! Sit down!"

It took a while, but gradually order returned. Then, before Mordechai could continue, Nicodemus spoke. "Asa the Beggar? What do you say of him, he that opened your eyes?"

There was not the slightest hesitation. "He is a prophet."

Any control Mordechai had regained was instantly gone again. Men rose to their feet up and down the row, shouting at each other, shaking their fists in the air. Mordechai picked up a thick walking stick he kept beside his chair for this very purpose and brought it down with a resounding crack on the marble table. "*I said enough!*"

One by one, the council members sat down again, all except Azariah. Mordechai watched his longtime enemy, knowing that in this situation they were allies, strange as that might seem. "The leader of the Pharisees may speak," he said.

"I am not sure this man was born blind, as he claims," Azariah mused. "Perhaps—" His voice rose sharply as others started to protest.

"Perhaps, like others who make their living by begging, this man has hidden his true abilities for all these years to elicit greater sympathy. Perhaps he just pretended to be blind."

Asa the Beggar was dumbfounded.

"Ridiculous!" Joseph of Arimathea exclaimed. "What proof does our esteemed leader have for such an accusation?"

But it was Asa who answered. "My parents are here. Ask them."

Mordechai's eyes narrowed. His parents? He didn't like the sound of that. But it was too late. "Bring them forth," Nicodemus cried.

"Yes, let us hear of this matter from them," said another.

Heads turned as two people stepped forward from behind the guards. They were both elderly. The woman's hair was almost pure white. The man was balding, but what was left of his hair and beard were heavily streaked with gray. They moved forward until they stood by their son. The mother reached out and took his hand, clearly very much frightened by these proceedings.

There was no choice but to question them. Mordechai motioned to the old man and woman. "Is this your son?"

The father spoke. "It is." It was barely heard.

"Speak up, man!" Mordechai barked. "Let the council hear you."

"It is," he said more loudly.

"And he has had problems with his eyesight in the past?"

To his surprise, it was the mother who spoke, and her voice was surprisingly strong. "Problems?" she said in amazement. "He came out of my womb blind."

Another murmur swept the group, and Mordechai shot them a withering look. Then he looked at the woman. "Did he have any sight at all?"

"None. Not ever."

He thought about asking additional questions about the man's past, but decided against it. Every answer was only going to play into the hands of his opponents. He decided to take another tack. "If you say he was born blind, how then does he now see?"

For a moment, husband and wife looked at each other. They might be poor and unlearned, but Mordechai could tell they were not stupid. They knew that the body before which they stood was the most powerful in Jerusalem. Finally it was the mother who spoke. With an enigmatic shrug, she said, "All we know is that this is our son, and that he was born blind. By what means he now sees, we know not."

"Or who opened his eyes," the father added, "we know not that either. He is of age. Ask *him*. He can speak for himself."

It was a crafty reply and somewhat of a rebuke. Parents could be made to speak for their children only if they were still under the legal age of adulthood. Asa the Beggar was long past that. Had the parents heard that the Great Council had already decreed that anyone who believed in Jesus as the Messiah could face excommunication from the synagogue? Was that why they were sidestepping his questions?

The woman was watching Mordechai, careful, but no longer afraid. "He is of age," she repeated. "Ask our son."

Mordechai waved them away, wishing that Azariah hadn't tried the ploy of discrediting the man. He motioned to the beggar. "You have clearly had something wonderful happen to you, and for that, we rejoice with you in your good fortune. But the man you say did this is a sinner. Give *God* the praise, and you are free to go."

For a long moment, Asa didn't answer. His face was thoughtful, his mouth pursed. Then his head came up. "Whether this man is a sinner or no, I cannot say. But one thing I know. Whereas I was blind, now I see."

"How?" Azariah shouted. "How did he open your eyes?"

The beggar turned slowly to face the chief Pharisee. "I have told you already, and you would not hear. Why do you ask me again? Would you also be one of his disciples?"

If it hadn't been so deadly serious, and such a devastating question,

Mordechai would have laughed right out loud at the expression on Azariah's face.

The old Pharisee straightened to his full height, his face like a thundercloud. "You may be a disciple of this Jesus, but we are disciples of Moses. We know that God spake unto Moses, but as, for this man, we know not from whence he is."

Asa slowly shook his head. "Then this is a marvel. He has opened my eyes—eyes that have never before seen—but you say that you know not from whence he is." He looked around at the encircling faces. "We know that God does not hear sinners. Only if a man be a worshiper of God and does his will, only then will God hear him. Since the world began it has not been heard that any man opened the eyes of one that was born blind. If this man were not of God, he could do nothing."

That sent several men to their feet at once, but Azariah left his seat and strode forward, his jaw as hard as stone. "Would you, who was altogether born in sin, seek to teach us?" He spun around to look at Mordechai. "Away with this man. He reviles the Law of Moses and this council. Excommunicate him!"

"Hear! Hear!" Caleb yelled. "Cast him out of the synagogue. He reviles the Law."

Menachem was up too. "Excommunicate him! Away with this sinner."

Mordechai sat back. There were a few shouts of protest, but they were feeble. The man had played right into their hands. He let it roll on for several moments, then stood. Gradually the council quieted. "Charges have been laid against this man," he said. "Charges of a most serious nature. Charges worthy of having him cast out of the synagogue."

Asa the Beggar said nothing. His parents stood back, faces torn with pain, but the man stood with his head high.

"Do you wish to recant?" Mordechai asked. "Do you wish to renounce the words you have spoken which revile the Law?"

"I have spoken only the truth," Asa said. "I did not speak against the Law."

Mordechai shook his head sadly. He looked up and down the council. "You have heard it from his own mouth. All who would speak for excommunication, let it be known now."

All but two or three hands shot upward. There was no need to call for those against. It was an overwhelming majority. "Done!" said Mordechai.

II

Jerusalem, in the Court
of the Gentiles on the Temple Mount

It was nearing midnight, and the crowds on the Temple Mount had thinned considerably. Asa the Beggar walked slowly along with his mother and father. They had come out of the Hall of the Council, stung by the injustice of what had transpired and the swiftness with which their lives had changed. To be cast out of the synagogue in the homeland of the Jews, a society dominated by religious life, was a bitter blow and would have far-reaching effects.

But it was more than that. Asa had made his living—a meager one to be sure, but one that allowed him to survive—by begging. But he was no longer blind. Now even that was taken from him. What would he do? He was the sole support of his aged parents. What would they do?

Their step slowed. A group of men was angling across the court-yard, still lit by the flames of the great lampstands, directly towards them. Asa felt himself tense. Had the council already determined to take further action?

"It's all right," his father said in a low voice. "They are Galileans."

Asa had noted that they were dressed far differently than the men who had just confronted him, but he had no basis for judging a man from his dress or appearance.

The group stopped a few feet away, except for the man in the lead. He came forward and stood before Asa. Asa searched his face, won-dering who he was.

"We have heard that the council has cast you out of the syna-gogue," the man said.

Asa started. He did not know the face, but he had heard that voice before, on this very night. "You have heard the truth," he answered sadly.

"Do you believe on the Son of God?" was the next question.

"Who is he, Lord, that I might believe on him?" His heart had started to race, for he knew that this was the man who had covered his eyes with mud, then sent him to the Pool of Siloam.

Jesus answered in a low voice, filled with warmth. "You have both seen him and heard him. It is he that is talking with you now."

A cry of joy rose from his throat, and Asa dropped to his knees. "Lord, I believe! Thank you." He bowed down, his face touching the ground in front of the Master's feet.

Jesus reached down and lifted him up. He turned and smiled at the man's parents, who were looking on in wonder. "For judgment I am come into this world," he said, speaking to Asa again, "that they which see not, might see, and that they which see, might be made blind."

"Are we blind then?"

Jesus turned. A single Pharisee, previously unnoticed, had been following Asa and his parents. He came forward. Jesus looked more closely at him. "You are Aaron, brother of Deborah, wife of David ben Joseph."

Aaron started guiltily. He had hoped to remain anonymous. "Yes."

"And your question?"

"You seem to speak of the Pharisees. Are we blind also? Is that what you meant by what you just said?"

When Jesus spoke it was in a voice heavy with sorrow. "If you were blind, you would have no sin. But you say, 'We see.' Therefore your sin remains."

Aaron stared at him. This man was such an outrage. And such a wonder. "I—"

But Jesus had already turned away. His disciples moved in around him, and they walked off, the blind man and his parents in the midst of them.

For a long time, Aaron watched the disappearing backs. His face was expressionless, and yet inside he was filled with turmoil. Some time before, he had witnessed Jesus restore a man's withered hand. Though incensed that it had been done on the Sabbath, Aaron had been deeply shaken by it. As time went on, though, he pushed it out of his mind. Then came the healing of Grandma Huldah's misshapen back. How did he ignore that? Now a man who had been born blind had full vision. He didn't agree with Azariah, much as he would have liked to. The evidence was incontrovertible. This man who had never been able to see, now saw. And it was Jesus who had done this for him.

Then anger flooded back in again. Jesus had declared himself to be the I AM. Aaron shuddered. All of his life, he had studied the Law. He could close his eyes and cite page after page of the Torah without the slightest error. Of the more than six hundred commandments laid down by Moses, the gravest of them all was to honor God and give him reverence. This man, this nobody from Nazareth, had taken the most sacred and solemn of all titles upon himself. Even now, it filled Aaron with an inexpressible horror to think of it.

Then suddenly, the words of Asa the Beggar rose in Aaron's mind. They had struck him like a blow in the council meeting. They struck him like a blow again now. "Since the world began it has not been heard that any man opened the eyes of one that was born blind. If this man were not of God, he could do nothing."

Aaron turned. With head down, he walked slowly back the way he had come.

III

JERUSALEM, ANTONIA FORTRESS
16 OCTOBER, A.D. 32

Marcus looked up as a knock sounded on the door. He motioned at the slave who was scraping him down with the strigil, and the young man leaped to answer the door. Marcus felt a flash of irritation. It was a standing order that no one was to bother him while he was in the baths.

The baths were part of a strict regimen with him, especially when he was in Jerusalem and constantly battling boredom. Each morning he arose with the sun, went to the small *gymnasium* normally used by the legionnaires for wrestling matches or other games of physical prowess, and worked himself into a hard sweat for half an hour or more. The *gymnasium* was small, as were the baths that were part of the same complex, but he made do with both.

Once he was perspiring heavily, Marcus would undress and enter one of the rooms adjacent to the *calderium*, or hot baths, where the surrounding steam heated the cubicles to high temperatures. This process was called the dry bath because he didn't actually immerse himself in water. He stayed there until the sweat poured out from his body even more copiously than during his exercises.

From there he moved into the *calderium* itself, sprinkling almost scalding hot water from a large tub onto his body and having it scraped with the strigil, a tool with a curved, blunt blade shaped to fit the contours of the body. This not only cleansed the pores, but it also scraped off any dry, dead layers of skin. Using the strigil required skill and so Marcus always brought his personal slave from Caesarea to perform that function.

Once the scraping was complete, he would move into the *tepidarium*, a small pool where the water temperature was about the same as his body's. Here he would lie motionless, allowing himself to gradually cool down. Finally, he would take a quick plunge in the *frigidarium*, an experience that always left him gasping but thoroughly refreshed physically, mentally, and emotionally. After that—the whole ritual took about an hour—he was ready for the day. Interruptions were not appreciated.

Steam was rising off the *calderium* in great clouds, and it took a moment for Marcus to see the figure standing at the door. "Yes, yes," he snapped. "What is it?"

There was movement; then Sextus appeared. Immediately, Marcus waved the slave away. The man exited quickly, shutting the door behind him. "The news had better be good, Sextus," Marcus grumped. "The feast is over. The birds are going to fly the nest tomorrow or the next day."

"It is good news, sire," Sextus said. "A runner just came in. The report is proving to be accurate. After spending a quiet Sabbath yesterday, Yehuda and his brother-in-law left the house early and headed east toward Bethany or Bethphage. They were overheard talking about new grapevines, sire. Livia seems to be preparing to depart the city tomorrow or the next day. As arranged with Miriam, today she will be going to the Gate Beautiful for the two of them to have one last visit before leaving."

"There's no mistake about that?" he said, relaxing a little. This was the news he was looking for.

"No, sire. The young man we had watching them was only a few feet away when Livia and Miriam made the arrangements."

"And they are to meet at midday?"

"That is what they said. We still have two watchers at the house. If the woman goes anywhere else, we shall know it immediately."

Marcus picked up the strigil and began scraping down his thighs. They had trailed Livia to a small house in the quarter of the city near the Damascus Gate. If worse came to worst, he could have soldiers there in a quarter of an hour or less. Finally, he looked up. "We'll use Miriam to take the word to Simeon, but she cannot be anywhere around when we first take Livia. Mordechai, for all his bitterness about his 'dead' daughter, would never forgive us if something should happen to her."

"I have given instructions that she is to be detained, sire."

The tribune considered that as he wiped the instrument on a towel, then began scraping his other leg. "Well done, Sextus. Keep me informed. And have the men ready."

"Yes, sire." Sextus saluted, turned on his heel, and started away. Then he stopped, half turning. "Sire?"

"Yes?"

"Sire, as you know, I have spent many years in Capernaum since coming here. In that time I have become friends with the family of David ben Joseph."

"Yes?" Marcus's voice now carried an edge.

"I will do as you command, sire, but I would appreciate it if another could take this woman."

For a moment, Marcus wanted to throw the strigil at him. What did he care about such things? Since when did a Roman officer put friendship above duty? "It's that, or I'll have you lead the squad that goes after the Zealots. That could prove far worse."

"With your permission, sire, I would prefer the latter."

Marcus muttered something indistinguishable, then finally nodded. Sextus was a loyal soldier. He had even saved Marcus's life once. "All right then," he snapped. "Permission granted. But *you* will see to the detaining of Miriam. I don't want anything to go wrong there."

There was no expression on the older man's face, but Marcus sensed his dismay.

"Very good, sire," Sextus said. He touched his chest with his right fist, disappeared into the clouds of steam, and shut the door behind him.

CHAPTER NOTES

John, whose Gospel has over 90 percent of its content unique to him, is the only one who gives the account of the man born blind (see John 9). Though some details had to be added to make the novel flow, these were minimal. The elements of the story, including the making of the clay, the washing in Siloam, being brought before the Sanhedrin, and his later meeting with the Savior, are all as given in the Gospel record.

While we know that the Sanhedrin operated within some restrictions, there is some evidence that proper procedures were not always followed.

Gymnasium was a Greek word taken from *gymnos*, which meant "naked." The Greeks had glorified the human body and thus often raced or wrestled or threw the javelin in the nude in special buildings created for just that purpose. Though Rome had borrowed the name, they had not made it a practice to follow the same customs.

CHAPTER 15

THOSE WHOM THE GODS LOVE DIE YOUNG.

—*Menander*, Dis Exapaton, *frag. 4*

I

JERUSALEM, IN THE COURT OF THE GENTILES
ON THE TEMPLE MOUNT, NEAR THE GATE BEAUTIFUL
15 OCTOBER, A.D. 32

Livia walked slowly back and forth along the *soreg*, or Wall of Partition. She stopped as she reached one of the marble plaques mounted to one of the stone panels. She knew what it said almost by heart but read it again. It was in written in Greek: "No stranger is to enter within this wall around the temple and enclosure. Whoever is caught will be responsible for his own death, which will ensue." Similar plaques could be found about every twenty paces, next to every opening in the wall. The *soreg* ran completely around the temple.

Though Livia had been a Jewess for several months, it still bothered her. Yes, the temple precincts were holy, but why should only Gentiles be targeted for exclusion? Why should only they risk capital punishment if they walked on that sacred ground? Though Livia had never personally witnessed it herself, Miriam had told her that there was no quicker way to start a riot on the Temple Mount than to take a Gentile past the *soreg*.

And what about the Jew who is unholy? She blew out her breath. These people and their exclusiveness. She was a convert to their religion and thus no longer under the ban, but she was Greek. She was, by blood, one of the *goyim*, or Gentiles. Why should blood be the basis for exclusion from the Lord's house? If the signs read: "Let *all* who are unholy not pass beyond this wall," then she would have no quarrel with the practice. But they did not.

Realizing she was only being petulant, she turned, walked quickly down to the first opening in the partitions, and passed through. When she reached the steps that led up into the Gate Beautiful, she stopped and looked around. Still no Miriam. She glanced up at the sun. It was halfway up in the sky, signifying it was close to the third hour. She might be a little early, but not that much. Well, Bethlehem was much farther away than the Damascus Gate. Miriam would naturally take longer to arrive.

II

JERUSALEM, IN THE COURT
OF THE GENTILES ON THE TEMPLE MOUNT

"Is that the woman?"

Sextus nodded. "She is not to be harmed. Not even touched. Understood? Just delayed."

The sergeant nodded curtly. "Yes, centurion."

Motioning for the other men to follow, the sergeant straightened his spear and started off, cutting at an angle so he would intercept the woman the officer had pointed out to him.

Miriam was not paying attention to the crowds around her. She was drinking in the wonder of the marvelous temple complex. Tomorrow she and the family would start back north. They would not return to Jerusalem until Passover, roughly six months away. She missed the city. She loved the Galilee, but this was her city. From the time she could walk, she had made her way through it. She loved the crowded markets, the streets jammed with vendors with every imaginable thing for sale. She loved the way the stone walls of every building turned to gold when the sun lowered in the sky. She loved the hills, rising and falling sharply wherever one walked. And most of all, she loved the magnificence of the Temple Mount and its splendor. She could walk in its courts for hours and be totally enthralled. She marveled anew each time she went there, and now she was drinking it all in again so the memory would last her for the next six months.

She stopped as she suddenly realized someone was blocking her way. Her eyes widened slightly when she saw it was a squad of eight soldiers in full uniform. Looking away quickly, she turned aside.

"Hold!" the lead man called.

She stopped. His voice had been commanding, but not angry. "Me?" she asked in surprise.

The man gave a quick nod. "I would ask you some questions, m'lady," he said politely. He was not much older than Miriam and spoke in rough Aramaic. She experienced a momentary sense of fear, but then pushed it aside. His face showed no hostility. In fact, for a Roman soldier, he was being especially polite.

"Yes?" was all she could think of to say. Without realizing it, she answered him in Latin.

A little surprised, he went on in Latin himself. "You are a resident of Jerusalem?"

"I used to be. Now I live in the Galilee. In Capernaum."

"So you know this city well?"

"Of course. I lived here most of my life."

"Then we have need of your services for a short time." The man seemed to have become more hesitant.

"What do you mean?"

"We are from Caesarea and do not know Jerusalem. Our commander has asked that we inspect the arched bridge that leads to the Temple Mount. There is a report of possible damage to the arch. Could you be so kind as to show us where that might be?"

She turned and pointed. "See the arched doorway at the west end of the Royal Portico? You go through there, then down some steps, and it takes you right to the gate that leads to the bridge."

He shifted his weight, somewhat embarrassed. "I'm sorry, m'lady, but our commander is anxious for our report. Could you show us the way?"

Miriam shook her head. "I have an appointment. I'm already late."

The man's eyes never left her. "I must insist," he said, "otherwise, we would come into disfavor with our commander, who is a surly and mean-spirited man."

Some of the other soldiers chuckled at that.

Miriam's mind worked quickly. By law a legionnaire could stop any citizen of the country where they were stationed and ask him or her to carry his pack for up to one Roman mile. Taking them there would cost her another five minutes, but was it worth the risk of angering them if she refused? So far they had been a model of courtesy.

"Once I show you, may I go?"

"Of course. We can find our own way back."

She nodded and started to turn. Just then the young soldier turned his head and looked back, as if seeking some kind of approval. Miriam started. There, fifteen or twenty paces away, stood a Roman officer. He turned away quickly when he saw her looking at him, but it wasn't quickly enough. She had already recognized him. It was Sextus Rubrius.

"Is that your commander?" she asked, suddenly suspicious.

The young man didn't turn to look again. "No, m'lady." He motioned for her to start moving before she could say anything more. "Please. We'll follow you."

III

JERUSALEM, AT THE GATE BEAUTIFUL ON THE TEMPLE MOUNT

Livia was sitting on the steps that led up to the Gate Beautiful, one hand up to shade her face from the brightness of the sun. She had thought about going inside the court but decided that Miriam would be looking for her out here. So she idly watched the passing people and thought about what she still needed to do in order to be ready for their departure tomorrow.

A movement caught her eye. Over the heads of the crowds, she saw a red plumed helmet moving horizontally across her line of vision. It was followed by a dozen or more plain helmets. They were outside the Wall of Partition, of course, and so ten or fifteen paces from where she sat. She watched curiously as the crowd began to part, muttering at the sight of the passing legionnaires. Then Livia started. The people were moving back, and she could see the column and then its leader more clearly.

At that same moment, the tribune's head turned, and he saw her. One hand flew up. "Halt!" he barked to his men.

As the men came to a stop, Livia saw that there were sixteen of them—four quaternions, as the Romans called them. "Livia? Livia of Alexandria? Is that you?"

She rose slowly to her feet. "Good morning, Tribune Didius," she called.

He smiled in pleased surprise, then motioned for her to come over to him. He was near the *soreg* and so could come no closer.

She hesitated, not sure this was wise; but then she decided that perhaps they could exchange a brief greeting, and he would be gone again before Miriam arrived. Miriam definitely would not want to see Marcus Quadratus Didius. Not now. Not here. Forcing a smile, she ran lightly down the steps and closed the distance between them.

<hr>

IV

JERUSALEM, IN THE COURT
OF THE GENTILES ON THE TEMPLE MOUNT

<hr>

Miriam was thoroughly perplexed. They had barely reached the arched doorway leading down to the southwest gate when the young sergeant abruptly changed his mind. "Thank you, m'lady" he said. "We can find it from here. Sorry to have been a bother."

Somewhat irked at the man's behavior, she merely nodded and started back the way she had come. Halfway across the Court of the Gentiles, she stopped, surprised to hear the rhythmic crunch of sandals on pavement. Through the scattered people, she saw the eight men trotting in quick step along the western edge of the court. They were headed north in a path that would take them behind the temple and back to the Antonia Fortress. So they hadn't gone to the gate after all. How strange.

She shrugged it off and hurried on, knowing that Livia would be starting to wonder where she was.

V

"So Miriam is married now, I hear."

Livia nodded cautiously. Marcus was smiling, and there didn't seem to be any animosity in the question. "Yes, just two weeks ago, in Bethlehem."

"Ah, yes," he chuckled. "This strange thing with Jewish betrothals and a year of waiting."

Livia said nothing.

"And you as well, I'm told."

"Yes."

"And how is Yehuda? As bullheaded as ever?"

"I don't find him that way at all," she said coolly.

"I was married just a few months ago myself. To the daughter of Senator Servilius. Will you tell Miriam?"

Livia couldn't hide her surprise. "I will. Congratulations."

Marcus turned, his eyes searching across the great plaza. Then he turned back. "Well, how pleasant to see you. Give my regards to Miriam and Simeon. And Yehuda, of course."

"Of course." She felt immense relief. There was something very odd about this whole encounter.

Marcus half turned, then turned back. "Say," he said, "am I not remembering correctly that you were once a slave? In Alexandria, if my mind serves me right."

Livia went very still. "Yes. Mordechai ben Uzziel purchased my freedom for me almost eight years ago when I became Miriam's personal servant."

"I apologize," he said, not in any way looking apologetic, "but we have been asked to be on the lookout for runaway slaves. Do you have your papers of manumission?"

The color drained instantly from Livia's face. "I—Well, no. I—" She was stammering like a frightened child. "It's been eight years. And I am married to a citizen of this country now. I am not required to carry papers."

"Freed slaves are required to have their papers with them at all times," Marcus said. Any warmth in his voice had disappeared.

"That's not true," she cried. "You've never said anything before when I was in your presence."

"Guards, seize this woman. We shall hold her until her papers are produced."

"No!" Livia gasped, as two men leaped forward and grabbed her by the arms. "You know I was freed."

He clucked disapprovingly. "I would be derelict if I let personal acquaintance influence me from doing my duty."

Then, again to her surprise, he looked away, scanning the crowd. Several people had stopped and were watching curiously, but he wasn't looking at them. It was as though he was expecting someone.

"Please, Tribune Didius, I beg of you."

He didn't so much as glance at her. Then there was a soft grunt of satisfaction. Livia turned to see what he was looking at. Her knees almost buckled. Miriam was pushing her way toward them, her head turning back and forth, searching.

Miriam stopped dead at the sight that awaited her. "Marcus?" she exclaimed. Then her jaw went slack, and her eyes widened in horror as she saw Livia held fast between two soldiers.

"Miriam," Marcus said stiffly. "I wondered if you might not be here in Jerusalem."

"Livia?" She started forward, then stopped again, turning to Marcus. "What is going on?"

"Your slave does not carry papers of manumission."

"*What?*"

"He says they are going to arrest me for not having proof of my freedom on me," Livia cried. "Tell him, Miriam. Tell him my freedom was purchased by your father. Tell him I am married."

"This is ridiculous." She swung on the man she had once felt affection for. "What is the meaning of this? You know she has been legally freed."

"Do I?"

"You know that my father—" She stopped. Once again there was the sound of sandals slapping on pavement. Then eight men appeared from around the corner of the temple. Miriam fell back a little. It was the same eight men who had left her a few minutes before. They had simply circled around the back of the temple and now came to join their comrades. They were puffing from their exertion.

"Why are you doing this?" Miriam demanded, feeling hot anger shoot through her. "Freed slaves are not required to carry their papers with them. Not here in Judea."

"They are now," he said icily. He waved toward the guards. "Take her back to the fortress. And watch yourselves." He turned to join his men.

"Marcus!" Miriam was pleading now. "She is with child. Have some mercy."

"The child of a slave is considered to be a slave as well," he said shortly. "If she has papers, I suggest you present them to me before morning. Otherwise, we shall take her and any others we may find back to Caesarea."

"But her papers are in Beth Neelah."

"Then you had better send a fast rider," he said mockingly. "You have about eighteen hours, and then she'll be gone."

VI
JERUSALEM, ANTONIA FORTRESS

The arrest took place somewhere around the third hour of the morning. By the sixth hour, or midday, the first of a very angry crowd had started to gather. Now in midafternoon, five or six hundred men were gathered outside the south gate of the Antonia Fortress in the Court of the Gentiles, most of them Galileans. And they were working themselves into a fine fury. Farther back—much farther back—a larger crowd had gathered to watch. That had worried Marcus at first, but it was clear that was all they were—curious onlookers drawn by the smell of possible violence.

"Well?" Marcus said.

They were standing on the walls, half hidden behind one of the parapets, looking down on the mob. Sextus answered without delay. "You've already seen Simeon and Yehuda for yourself."

"Yes. And Simeon's father too."

"That is his older brother with them," Sextus said without expression. "Ephraim."

Marcus stifled the urge to shout aloud in triumph. He had fretted for so long over this, worried about what Pilate would do if he couldn't find a way to carry out his orders. And it had turned out to be so easy. He had almost given in to the urge to tell Miriam to be sure to complain to Simeon about Livia's arrest, but he hadn't. He knew that wasn't necessary. She must have gone straight to him, though, and Simeon surely went and found Yehuda out looking at grapevines. So easy!

"What about the others?"

"Most of the key Zealot leadership is here," Sextus answered.

"I've seen Gehazi of Sepphoris, Elihu of Gadara, Yohanan the Blind, Jesus Barabbas. The young one there to the left of Simeon is Samuel, Yehuda's brother-in-law. He's supposedly taken over Simeon's old group, but he's still pretty inexperienced."

Marcus felt a grudging admiration. This was Yehuda's problem. He wasn't even a Zealot any longer, yet his former comrades came without hesitation. Good thing the Jerusalemites didn't stick together like that, or there could be real trouble. "I think we might change that today," he said.

"Even though they're armed," Sextus continued, "they're here to negotiate. They would never try a frontal assault on the fortress. If we don't give them Livia back, they'll probably see if they can take her while we're on the road somewhere."

Marcus merely grunted. Sextus was right, of course, except for one thing. Marcus had no plans to negotiate, and he certainly didn't plan to let them ambush him on the road. Then he remembered his conversation with Mordechai. "And Jesus? Is he out there?"

Sextus shook his head. "I've not seen him or any of his closest disciples. Perhaps it is true, as we heard, that they have already left for Perea."

Marcus shrugged. It was rare that one got every single thing he wished for. Well, the Sanhedrin could worry about that later. "We can't wait any longer."

Marcus looked down into the central courtyard of the fortress. It stood empty in the afternoon sun, but in the shadows of the over-hanging walkways he saw the glint of spears. One century was hidden just to the left of the gate. Another was just to the right. Along the back wall, two more centuries stood poised and ready. None of them could be seen by the Galileans because the outer gate was closed.

He turned, still taking stock. Hidden in the barracks were nearly two additional cohorts. Along the catwalks, crouched down so they couldn't be seen from below, two hundred bowmen with full quivers waited his signal to leap to their feet. All together he had over fifteen hundred men. These oafish peasants would never know what hit them.

"All right then," he said softly. "Have the men in readiness." He spun around and headed for the ladder leading down to the courtyard.

VII

Jerusalem, in the Court
of the Gentiles on the Temple Mount

Simeon stood in front of the group of Zealots, facing the south gate of the towering fortress. A ring of legionnaires three men deep guarded the entrance, spears at the ready. There were forty or fifty of them. Their faces were hard, but Simeon thought he detected a trace of fear in their eyes.

Suddenly there was a loud creaking sound, and one of the gates swung partially open. Through it Simeon saw that the courtyard of the Antonia was empty. He grunted to himself. No wonder the legionnaires were nervous. Marcus was probably scrambling to find reinforcements, only now realizing he had made a serious mistake.

"Do you want me to try to talk with them?" Simeon asked. He looked at Yehuda, but he spoke loud enough for everyone to hear. Around him was the single greatest threat to Rome in the region. Virtually every band of Zealots had gathered when the cry for help went out.

"Talk to them?" Jesus Barabbas sneered. "Talk to them about what? They're not going to give her back. I say we leave now, make it look like we lost our nerve, then hit them hard at the Beth Horon pass."

Gehazi then spoke up; he was the oldest of the leaders and therefore the closest to an acknowledged head among men who were all fiercely independent. "It may come to that," he said, obviously not relishing the thought. "But talking should come first. The word we have is that Pilate's not looking for trouble right now. I think this is all a mistake."

"Maybe if we went to Mordechai," Yehuda started. But then he bit it off and shook his head bitterly. Mordechai wasn't about to offer any help in this, not for a servant girl, not for the one who encouraged Miriam in her defection from her father. He turned to Simeon. "Your Latin is the best. Maybe now, seeing the kind of numbers we can muster, they'll be willing to talk. Tell them we can have the papers here in a few days." His jaw clenched. "But they need to know, Simeon. Livia is not going to Caesarea tomorrow."

"I have a concern." They turned. It was David, Simeon's father, who had spoken. "The captain is Tribune Marcus Didius."

"So?" Gehazi asked.

"He knows Livia. In fact, he purchased freedom for her brother in Rome. There was never any question about Livia's papers before."

"So what has that got to do with anything?" Barabbas retorted. "What are you saying?"

"For some reason, this is a deliberate provocation," David said. "There has been no word of a search for runaway slaves."

"Well," Barabbas shot back, "if it's provocation they're looking for, then I say, let's show them what provocation means to a Zealot." Several others in the circle emphatically agreed.

"Go!" Yehuda barked at Simeon. "Let's see what happens."

As Simeon moved up to the circle of troops, they stiffened,

spears dropping to point at his belly. "I wish to speak to your tribune," he said in flawless Latin. "Tell him Simeon ben David of Capernaum wishes to confer."

"I am here." The gate opened another two feet, and Marcus stepped into view. "Let him pass."

The front of the circle opened. Simeon hesitated for a moment. Suddenly there flashed into his mind memories of the night when he had stood on the aqueduct outside of Caesarea. He had gone to negotiate with Marcus Didius on that night too, and it ended up with both him and Yehuda rotting in a cell in Caesarea. But it was too late to change his mind now. He moved through the line of soldiers, which immediately closed back when he passed. Marcus stepped back inside, and Simeon followed.

"So," Marcus said, openly disgusted, "you are part of this little insurrection? I thought you had become a follower of that pacifist from Nazareth."

"Why are you doing this?" Simeon asked quietly. "Of all men, you know Livia is not a runaway."

"You really don't understand?" He started walking slowly. Simeon glanced around. He saw two sentries posted at the stairs to the main building, but nothing more. He fell in beside the tribune.

"Think about it, Simeon ben David," Marcus said. He was speaking as if to a child. "If you are right about what I know, and of course you are, then why would I do such a thing?"

"If this is some cheap way of getting back at me, why use Livia? She was not responsible for what happened between me and Miriam."

Marcus laughed derisively. "You think that's it? That it's only a desire for petty revenge? Ah, Simeon, you disappoint me. You've lost your edge, my friend."

"What will it take to get Livia back? Money? Is that what you're after?"

"Oh," Marcus said softly, "much more than that. And you? Why you're just sauce on the pudding."

Suddenly Simeon, whose eyes were darting this way and that, saw something that made his blood run cold. All around the inside of the walls of the Antonia were board catwalks, designed so soldiers could defend the walls in time of war. Beneath those overhangs, everything was in shadow. But a movement had caught his eye. As he turned and peered more closely, he saw rank after rank of soldiers in the shadows. They were standing at attention, shields up, swords and spears in hand. Hundreds of them.

He spun around, a shout rising in his throat, but instantly Marcus was on him. His arm shot out and clamped around Simeon's neck, cutting off his cry. At the same time, Marcus pressed a dagger hard against his ribs. Simeon gasped at the sudden sharp pain in his side. "Take this man!" Marcus called urgently. Four men leaped from the shadows and grabbed Simeon by the arms.

"Will you never learn?" Marcus said mockingly. Then he raised his head. "Attack!" he bellowed. "Take them!"

As Simeon gasped, all along the upper catwalks bowmen leaped up and leaned out over the walls, notching their arrows. Thwung! The sound of a hundred bowstrings being loosed at the same moment sounded like a bell struck with a muffled hammer. The courtyard, deadly quiet before, exploded into action. With a mighty roar, the waiting soldiers burst from the shadows, their hobnailed sandals pounding like hail on an empty barrel. Five men leaped to the two gates and swung them fully open.

Simeon could only gape as he was dragged backward out of their way. There were easily a thousand Romans in the attack. He jerked his head to one side. "Ambush! Run!" A heavy blow struck him on the back of the head, and he went down, brilliant colors flashing before his eyes.

"Fool!" the soldier growled. "Keep your mouth shut!"

VIII

Yehuda nervously watched Simeon and Marcus as they disappeared behind the gates. The murmur of their voices died. "Careful," he muttered. "Watch him, Simeon."

He turned and saw that David and Ephraim were watching just as intently as he was and that their eyes were just as worried as his must be. He felt his skin begin to crawl. Something was wrong.

David started angling off to one side so he could keep his son in sight longer as he receded through the narrow opening. Ephraim followed his father. That simple act probably saved their lives. As they moved away from the main body of men, suddenly there was a shout. Their heads swept upward as movement caught their eye. A hundred bowman—two hundred! maybe more!—lined the parapets. The sunlight momentarily flickered as hundreds of arrows passed overhead.

Men screamed and went down. "To arms!" someone shouted in Aramaic. David thought it was Gehazi's voice. He didn't turn to see. He grabbed Ephraim's tunic and jerked him forward. "Run!" he shouted. "For the porches."

Like every other wall of the temple courtyards, covered porticoes lined the wall that abutted the Antonia Fortress, offering shade and rest from the Judean sun. The two men dashed ahead, weaving back and forth. Bone- and metal-tipped arrows began pinging off the paving stones around them. With a diving leap, they vanished into the deep shadows and out of the line of fire.

They dropped to a crouch behind one of the pillars, then turned to stare in horror. Legionnaires were streaming out of the fortress, swords flashing in the sun. The Galileans fell back, screaming and shouting, pulling together to form a defensive ring. But the Romans were like a flash flood overrunning an earthen dam. The Galileans' naked flesh was no match for naked steel, metal shields, and leather armor. Bodies were falling everywhere. Men on both sides were stumbling over them as they fell on one another. Arrows still filled the air. The din was deafening. Screams, shrieks, and curses joined the clang of swords. Farther away, a roar of terror went up as the crowd of onlookers who had come to watch panicked and stampeded away.

"A vicious trap," David gasped between breaths. "This was their plan all along."

"We've got to get Simeon," Ephraim cried.

"No!"

Ephraim stared at him.

"Not yet. The Galileans are falling back. They're pulling the Romans with them. Give them a minute and perhaps the fortress will be emptied."

IX

The moment the guards took Simeon from his grasp, Marcus sprinted forward, shouting at his men. He shot through the gate and into the Court of the Gentiles, Sextus right behind him. He stopped, shouting at the top of his lungs, directing the men as they poured out into the courtyard. He raced back and forth, leaping in to slash and parry, then falling back to assess their progress.

In moments, there were fifty bodies on the ground. Sixty. Very few of them were in uniform, he noted with satisfaction. Blood was everywhere. The Galileans were falling back with heavy losses.

"Sextus!"

The centurion sidestepped a sword thrust and clubbed the man on the side of the head. As the man went down hard, Sextus swung around. "Here, sire!"

Marcus pointed. "Take some men around the flank. Cut them off. I don't want any getting out the main gate."

"Yes, sire." The centurion leaped forward, shouting at his men to follow.

Marcus didn't wait to see how they fared. He moved in to help a soldier who was desperately fighting against two Galileans. Behind them, Marcus saw something that gave him great satisfaction. A man was falling back under the onslaught of three legionnaires. He was big and heavily bearded. He looked as if he had gone totally, utterly mad. It was Yehuda of Beth Neelah.

X

Jerusalem, under the Northern Porticoes on the Temple Mount

David watched, feeling sick. This was a massacre. He looked toward the gate that led into the Antonia Fortress. There were no more soldiers coming out now. The battle line was slowly moving away from them, toward the entrance to the Court of the Women. The Galileans had recovered somewhat and were putting up a furious resistance. Their reputation for valor had not been lightly won. Bitter hand-to-hand combat was raging everywhere David looked. But they were still falling back under the press of sheer numbers. The closest soldier was now a full hundred paces from the gate. David could see no one watching the gates. There was no need to. The battle was moving east and south, in front of the Court of the Women, and it was being won.

He looked at Ephraim. "One more minute; then we'll go."

XI

JERUSALEM, ANTONIA FORTRESS

Any legionnaire worthy of the title hated being left behind in the heat of battle. They wanted to be in the thick of it. The four men who had taken Simeon from Marcus quickly bound his wrists in front of him. They dragged him beneath one of the overhanging catwalks and pushed him to the ground. Later he would be taken to a prison cell, but now their comrades needed every sword they could get. Telling the youngest of them to watch the prisoner, they ran off with a shout to join the battle.

Simeon stifled a groan as he carefully rolled onto his side. His head felt like it had been split right down the middle. When he moved too quickly, his vision blurred a little. From his position under the catwalk, he could see into the courtyard. Where before there had been a rush of men, now it was empty. His guard stood out in the sunlight, trying to see what was happening through the gate.

Careful not to make any sound, Simeon turned his head, looking for his belt with the sword and dagger. He couldn't see it anywhere. Inching his way backwards, keeping an eye on the young soldier, he moved deeper into the shadows. Finally he bumped against the wall. He waited for a moment, but the guard was too engrossed to notice what was going on behind him.

Simeon pushed himself into a sitting position, then tested his bonds. The man who tied his wrists may have been hurried, but he had done a good job. The ropes were cutting into Simeon's flesh, and they were too thick to cut with anything but a knife. Bracing his back against the wall, he pulled himself up onto his feet. He looked around and then stepped behind a door that stood partially open. Inside, he saw a storage room filled with sacks of grain.

"Hey!" he shouted.

The guard whirled. He stared at where Simeon had been; then, with a cry, he whipped out his sword. He dashed forward, squinting against the brightness of the sun, then moved deeper into the shadows, his eyes sweeping back and forth. Simeon waited until he had nearly passed the door, then stepped out. Both fists swung in a vicious arc, catching the man squarely in the jaw. The man gave a strangled cry and went down.

In an instant, Simeon was on the guard's back, trying to get his hands over the man's head so he could control him. But it wasn't necessary. The man lay still. There wasn't so much as a groan.

Glancing quickly into the courtyard to make sure no one else had come, Simeon stood. Though it was awkward with his hands tied, Simeon grabbed the man by his wrists and dragged him into the storeroom and shut the door. Removing the man's dagger from his belt, Simeon propped it between his feet and began to saw back and forth on his bonds.

Three minutes later, Simeon walked out of the room and shut the door. He stopped at the edge of the shadow to search the courtyard once more. He adjusted his breastplate and helmet—they were a little large, but not noticeably so, he hoped—then he took a quick breath and stepped out into the sunshine. Without looking back, he headed across the courtyard toward the main door of the great fortress. He rounded a corner. There, as he had hoped, he saw only two sentries.

"What's happening?" one sentry demanded. "Were you out there?"

"It's a rout!" Simeon said in Latin, giving them the victory sign. "There must be a thousand Galileans already dead. And the rest are on the run."

He started forward, but the other guard lowered his spear.

Simeon swung on him angrily. "Tribune Didius wants the Greek woman he made prisoner. Now!"

"Oh." The man stepped back, cowed by Simeon's anger.

Without another word, Simeon passed and entered the darker interior. He understood that the prison was in the basement, but he had never been inside this garrison. Moving swiftly, he ran along the hall that went the length of the building. Nothing. He turned and raced back the other way. At the end was a broad staircase leading up and down. He turned and went down, taking the steps three at a time. At the bottom there was another long hallway, with dozens of alcoves. About midway down the hallway, a man sat on a low chair against the wall. When he saw Simeon, he got to his feet. He was barrel chested and wore only a short tunic, with a leather strap across his chest.

That was what Simeon was looking for. He broke into a trot. As he approached, the man put a hand on the hilt of his sword. "What do you want? You're not authorized to be down here."

"Tribune Didius wants the woman."

"What?"

Simeon had reached the man's side. He was contemplating how he would strike if this man refused to cooperate. He was huge and very powerful looking. It would not be easy. Simeon thought quickly. "The tribune has a pocket of Galileans cornered. Most of them are already dead, but one group is still fighting. The prisoner is the wife of one of the leaders. He'll use her to make them surrender."

The man began to nod.

"Move!" Simeon shouted. "Lives are at stake here."

The man jumped guiltily, then snatched a large iron ring with several keys attached. "Wait here," he said.

Almost collapsing with relief, Simeon nodded and stepped back. Then he realized that he had another problem. When Livia saw him . . . He looked around quickly, stepping into one of the alcoves behind where the guard had been sitting. A moment later, footsteps sounded, and the guard reappeared. Behind him came Livia, her wrists manacled.

The guard gave a soft grunt when he saw the empty hallway, but then Simeon stepped out, moving directly behind the prisoner. "Thank you," he said roughly. He touched the point of the sword to Livia's back. "Start walking!" he commanded.

Not until they had rounded the corner and started up the stairs did Simeon stop. "Livia!" She whirled and gave a low cry. He clamped a hand over her mouth. "Shhh!"

Livia nodded, her eyes wide with joy.

He removed his hand and motioned for her to keep moving up the stairs. "This was all an elaborate trap," he whispered. "There's a major battle raging outside of the fortress."

Livia turned, color draining from her face. "Yehuda?"

"He's out there." Breath exploded from him. "It's bad, Livia. I don't know."

Before she could cry out, he stopped her with a chopping motion of his hand. They were almost to the top of the stairs. "There are still guards. Look frightened."

She gave a wan smile. As if he had to ask.

They stepped into the long hallway and started for the main entrance. Simeon still held his sword at Livia's back, but it was not touching her.

"Hey!" one of the sentries said as he saw Simeon. "She's good looking!"

"Yeah," the other one grunted. "Maybe when the tribune is done with her, he'll give her to us for a day or two."

The first sentry gave a hoot of laughter and made a bawdy comment, which Simeon didn't answer. They marched down the stairs and out into the courtyard. "Straight for the gate," he hissed. "Don't look around. Keep your head lowered."

XII

JERUSALEM, AT THE GATE BEAUTIFUL ON THE TEMPLE MOUNT

A mighty shout went up from behind the Zealots. Yehuda swung around. What he saw dashed all hopes he might have had. A band of legionnaires had broken off the battle and raced around the flank. Now they were coming in from behind. Their only route of escape—out the Golden Gate and into the Kidron Valley—was cut off.

Yehuda groaned. "Into the Court of the Women," he shouted. "Get the gates shut." He turned to follow his own command, wincing in pain as he did so. His left arm hung loosely at his side, blood streaming from a gash made by a Roman broadsword. A broken shaft extended from high in the back of that same shoulder. He had taken a Roman arrow in the first volley and nearly went down. It was Barabbas who had grabbed him, yelled at him to hang on, then snapped the shaft off, causing Yehuda to scream in pain.

He looked around. Barabbas was a few feet away. He had a deep cut on one cheek, and blood was seeping into his beard. He dragged one of his men, moaning piteously, across the paving stones.

"Where's Gehazi?" Yehuda shouted.

Barabbas shook his head. "Down!"

"Into the court. It's our only chance."

Barabbas started screaming at the men around him. "Fall back! Fall back! Inside the gates. They can't follow us in there."

As Yehuda reached the top of the stairs, he saw a man on hands and knees, a large dark stain covering the back of his tunic. "Elihu!"

The head came up. "I'm hit, Yehuda. Help me."

Yehuda stuck his sword into his belt and reached out with his good hand. It was like lifting a very large sack of grain. Elihu grunted with pain; then, just as he got to his feet, his face contorted in horror. "Yehuda!" he screamed.

Yehuda spun around. A legionnaire was running up the stairs, blade gleaming red in the sunlight. Shocked that the Wall of Partition had been breached, Yehuda lunged backwards. He tripped and went down. He rolled, but not quickly enough. Fire shot through him as he felt a powerful blow strike his right side. Fortunately, the soldier's charge had thrown him off balance, and he stumbled over Yehuda's legs and went sprawling. His sword skittered away. A scram of rage burst from Elihu's throat as he whipped out his dagger and fell on the man.

XIII

"Sextus! Demas!"

Sextus turned, looking for his commander. Then he saw him. His helmet was gone, and one side of his tunic was ripped away, but Sextus could see no wounds on the tribune. "Here!" Sextus yelled, waving an arm and darting forward.

"Where's Demas?" Marcus called as Sextus reached him. Demas was another of the senior centurions.

"Maybe dead. I saw some of his men dragging him away."

Marcus pointed. "They're going inside the Court of the Women. We've got to stop them."

Sextus stared at him. "Inside, sire?" In the heat of battle, no one was paying much attention to the *soreg*, but to go into the inner courts of the temple itself? Such a thing had never happened, not even in previous riots.

Marcus swore. "Knock down the whole complex if you have to.

Don't let them shut those gates." Without waiting, he raced away, screaming at the men around him.

Sextus didn't hesitate. "Defend the gates. Defend the gates."

XIV

JERUSALEM, IN THE COURT OF THE GENTILES
ON THE TEMPLE MOUNT

David waited another full minute, then jumped up. The battle had moved to the area in front of the temple entrance. He felt sick. The sounds of the conflict had sharply increased a few minutes before, and he knew the Romans sensed victory.

He looked around one last time. "All right, let's go."

They ran west. "Stay in the shadows," he hissed over his shoulder. Above them arrows were flying. That meant the archers were still atop the ramparts of the massive fortress, watching for anything that moved. But there was no way they could see the two running figures directly below them.

"How will we find him?" Ephraim cried in a hoarse whisper.

"I don't know. Pray for a miracle."

They slowed as they approached the end of the portico, where the gate opened into the central court of the Antonia Fortress. David had his sword out, fully expecting to find sentries there, but none were in sight. They passed through without a challenge.

Then David pulled up short, unable to believe his eyes. Two figures were coming toward him, a man and a woman, hugging the wall.

He peered more closely. It was Livia, her head down. Neither had seen them yet.

At that instant, the soldier looked up and shouted. He ripped off his helmet. "Father!"

"Simeon!"

"Help me," Simeon cried. "We've got to get Livia out of here."

They raced forward, and Ephraim took Livia's hand. "Quick. Stay with me."

David grasped Simeon's arm, noting an ugly bruise on the back of his head. His relief was so intense it was almost crippling. "We came from the porticoes," he said, pointing toward the north. "There's no one there."

"Go! Go!" Simeon urged.

XV

JERUSALEM, IN THE COURT OF ISRAEL ON THE TEMPLE MOUNT

The Court of the Women was raised twelve steps higher than the main level of the Temple Mount, or the Court of the Gentiles. The Court of Israel was raised even higher, fifteen additional steps above the Court of the Women. And the temple itself was raised higher still, set on a platform twenty or more feet above the Court of the Gentiles. Yehuda had made it to the level of the Court of Israel before collapsing. He lay there, holding his side, trying to staunch the bleeding. From this vantage point, he watched as legionnaires stormed the first set of steps and drove the Galileans back from the massive gates. Yehuda knew they had lost.

"Come on," he said to Elihu, who had made it that far with him. Their only hope was if the Romans hadn't yet thought to guard the side gates that led from the Court of Israel back onto the Temple Mount.

He staggered to his feet, weaving back and forth, feeling light-headed. He reached out a hand for Elihu, but the other man shook his head. "I can't. Go!"

Yehuda knew that there was no way he could lift him. He nodded. "Throw down your sword. Don't try to fight them." And with that he lumbered away.

As he stumbled across the Court of Israel, he looked around anxiously. Animals were bleating madly. Men who had come for the afternoon sacrifices and had been trapped when the fight erupted, cowered in corners, eyes wide with terror. Yehuda stared at them, making sure the place held no enemies, then promptly forgot them.

Two men he thought he knew, though he wasn't sure, raced past him, faces bloodied, swords hanging loosely at their sides. They too looked around, then fled through the gates on the south.

Through the gates, out in the Court of the Gentiles, Yehuda saw people running everywhere. The flanking group of soldiers had moved to the south. He turned the other way. No one stood at the north gates. Here the battle had emptied the courtyard. There was no one in sight. Hobbling painfully, Yehuda made his way to the nearest opening and peered around the post. Still no one. He waited a moment, then looked again. Another man raced past him, weaponless and likewise bloodied. He bounded out the gates, taking the steps three at a time. Yehuda heard a sharp snapping sound, and an arrow bounced away, barely missing the running figure. The man ducked behind the Wall of Partition, then ran hard toward the west.

Yehuda looked up. The archers were still on the wall. That was bad. And then he stiffened, barely aware of the pain that shot through him. Four figures had suddenly appeared, coming out of the gate to the

Antonia Fortress. They were running hard, headed for the columned porches. They were fifty, maybe seventy-five paces away, but they were in full sunlight, and he recognized them instantly. In the lead was David, sword up. Next came Ephraim. Then his breath caught. A sob of joy was torn from deep within him. Ephraim was holding Livia's hand, helping her along. Her long blond hair bounced wildly as she ran. Simeon was right behind them. In a legionnaire's uniform, of all things. How strange.

"Livia!" It was a hoarse cry, barely heard above the roar of battle. He leaned heavily against the post, closing his eyes. "Lord God of Hosts," he whispered, "he did it. Simeon did it. Thank you."

He considered stepping out and shouting at them, but the archers were still there. They were looking for stragglers in the battle and not straight down, and he didn't want to call anyone's attention to the escaping figures. As he watched, they disappeared into the shadows of the portico. He closed his eyes. They were clear. "Thank you," he breathed again.

As he debated what to do next, suddenly Yehuda's legs refused to obey him. He felt them buckle and tried to catch himself. His left hand left a bloody smear on the flawless marble post. It took him a moment to realize he was sitting, his back against the post. The world in front of his eyes was swimming, making him dizzy. He sat there for a moment, looking surprised, trying to figure out what had just happened.

Very slowly, he toppled sideways. He uttered one last soft moan of pain, and then he lay still.

CHAPTER NOTES

There is an intriguing, little-noticed reference in Luke, which serves as the basis for the events in this chapter. Luke wrote: "There were present at that season some that told him [Jesus] of the Galileans, whose blood Pilate had mingled with their sacrifices" (Luke 13:1). No further detail is given by Luke.

The contemporary historian Josephus gives two accounts in his history of the Jewish people of major political blunders Pilate committed as governor of Judea, both of which were discussed earlier. The first was when he marched his soldiers into Jerusalem carrying the Roman standards. The second was when he tried to take money from the temple treasury to finance the building of an aqueduct (see notes for chapter 10).

Since neither of these seems to fit the description given by Luke, most scholars believe this is yet another incident, not included by Josephus. The fact that it was only Galileans who were killed suggests a more limited clash. The comment that Pilate mingled their blood with the sacrifices implies that somehow the Romans breached the *soreg*, or Wall of Partition, and entered the inner precincts of the temple where the altar of sacrifice was located. As governor, Pilate would get the credit (or blame) for whatever his soldiers did, whether he was present in Jerusalem or not.

Adam Clarke suggested that the incident mentioned by Luke probably happened during one of the festivals and somehow involved the Zealot movement, which was centered in the Galilee and was considered a threat by Rome. "The Galileans were the most seditious people in the land: they belonged properly to Herod's jurisdiction; but, as they kept the great feasts at Jerusalem, they probably, by their tumultuous behavior at some one of them, gave Pilate . . . a pretext to fall upon and slay many of them" (Clarke, 3:446–47).

It was from this supposition that the author created the motive for the battle and the resulting ambush.

CHAPTER 16

I

JERUSALEM, UPPER CITY

16 OCTOBER, A.D. 32

Marcus Quadratus Didius sat on the bench, still covered by the dark robe that hid his uniform. He pushed back the hood and let it fall across his shoulders. He had kept that hood pulled tightly around his face on his journey from the Antonia Fortress. Though it was dark and late at night, the last thing he could afford was to have someone recognize who was visiting the home of Mordechai ben Uzziel.

Mordechai was raging, something that Marcus had fully expected, and so he simply hunkered down to let it pass.

"What were you thinking?" Mordechai demanded.

"I was thinking of saving my life and the lives of my men," he said evenly.

Mordechai shuddered. "Your men went into the Court of the Women and the Court of Israel?"

"Yes!" he snapped. "Just be grateful none of the Galileans went into the temple proper, because I would have followed them."

"You go too far, Marcus," Mordechai whispered. "You don't know what you have done."

"I know that Gehazi of Sepphoris and Yohanan the Blind, along with two or three other major Zealot leaders, are dead. So is Yehuda of Beth Neelah. I know that I have Elihu of Gadara, Jonah of Chorazin, Jesus Barabbas, and twenty-three more Zealots in chains. We have decimated the Zealot forces. More than a hundred are dead."

Marcus threw up his hands, thoroughly disgusted. "What? Did you think these men would just stand there and let us slap manacles on their hands when we came out after them?"

"The whole council is baying like a pack of wolves. It is an outrage. Far worse than anything else your stupid governor has done."

Marcus's head came up sharply. "He is still the governor," he said tightly. "Watch yourself, Mordechai."

The Sadducee slammed a fist against the marble table that he was standing behind. "You breached the *soreg!* You took men of war into the inner courts. Blood was shed. Human blood. Did you order that? Are you the one responsible?"

"I am."

"The emperor himself has validated our right to keep our temple unpolluted. The penalty for crossing that line is death."

Marcus stood slowly, his face feeling hot. "I lost eleven men in the Court of the Women alone. Three more in the Court of Israel. Twenty-two fell in the outer courts. I'd say you have your death penalty more than thirty times over."

Mordechai barely heard him. "I'm told that you yourself went into the inner courts."

"I did," Marcus replied coldly. "Are you going to bring me before your council and condemn me to death?" Then he exploded. "My men were dying! It was your people who took the battle inside the temple.

They were getting away. You expect me to honor some ridiculous invisible barrier and do nothing in those circumstances?"

Mordechai threw up his hands. "You could have called for us. Stayed outside the *soreg*. We would have brought them out to you."

"Your council is a bunch of old brood hens," Marcus retorted in disgust. "They couldn't drive a cat out of the house, let alone five hundred Galileans from the temple." Marcus was growing angrier with every word. "Our purpose was to go after the Zealots. We did that."

Mordechai stopped his pacing, for the first time remembering that the man he had been railing at was the second most powerful man in the province. He blanched a little at the thought, but he was so incensed he couldn't bring himself to calm down. "And what of Jesus? I am told he wasn't even there."

The tribune shook his head and sat down again. "I think he left the city. When word went out that we had arrested the Greek girl, things were immediately out of our hands. We had to take whoever that brought in. It's not like we could send for Jesus and say, 'Would you mind coming up to the Temple Mount? We're planning to kill some Galileans.'"

Mordechai snorted in disgust. "All of that, and we didn't get the one man we were after."

"*You* were after," Marcus shot back. "As far as I'm concerned, we were successful. It will take years before the Zealots recover from this."

"Successful?" Mordechai cried. "You made a blood bath in the temple. You didn't tell me that was your plan." He sat down heavily, his chest rising and falling.

Marcus didn't say anything. Let the old fool rage. Pilate would be pleased. Marcus had accomplished what he had been ordered to do.

"I am facing the most intense battle in the council I have ever seen," the Sadducee said, more subdued. "Our people are shocked more deeply than you can imagine. They are outraged. I personally am under severe criticism for moving the temple guards out to the gates. If it comes out that I did that at your request and helped you desecrate our temple, I'm finished, Marcus. It could topple our whole government."

Marcus sighed, realizing that for all his anger, Mordechai was right. "No one is going to know."

"The council is talking about drafting a letter to Caesar."

Marcus straightened.

"I'll try to deflect it, but I've never seen them this angry. They want to ask the emperor to remove Pilate."

"That would not be a wise move," Marcus said slowly.

"Really?" Mordechai shot back. "I'll tell them that. I'm sure that will change their minds."

Marcus got to his feet, his eyes like cold steel, his face hard. "I must go. There is still much to do before we start back to Caesarea."

"Just like that?" Mordechai demanded. "Haven't you forgotten something?"

Marcus looked away. He hadn't forgotten it, but he had hoped Mordechai wouldn't bring it up. He should have known better.

"There is one name you didn't mention. Or did you feel it was not my affair?"

Marcus met the other's challenging gaze. "Simeon ben David was the first man arrested. I took him myself."

"So why didn't I hear his name among the dead and the captured?"

So he had heard. He was hoping that word of Simeon's escape would not get out for another day or two, long enough for Marcus to be gone. "I left him in bonds and went to take command of the battle. Somehow he overpowered his guard and escaped."

"Just like that." It was a sneer of absolute contempt.

Marcus's lips were pressed into a tight line. "Yes, just like that. And he went into the prison and freed Livia."

"You think I care about her?" Mordechai shouted. "You promised me Jesus. You promised me you would also take Simeon down in all of this."

"I did take him. The man who allowed him to escape now lies in a cell, his back a bloody mass of flesh. Along with those who let Livia escape."

"And that's supposed to make me feel better?"

Marcus stood again. He was done with this. "If you need a reason to worry, O wise and powerful member of the Great Sanhedrin, you'd better stop worrying about people finding out about why you transferred those guards. You'd better worry about your son-in-law finding out your part in all of this. Yehuda was Simeon's best friend. His newly made widow is your daughter's best friend."

It gave him great satisfaction to see Mordechai's face. Good. He had understood exactly what Marcus meant by that. "If a letter should be sent to Caesar," he went on softly, "there will be a full investigation. You never know what might come out in a full investigation." He felt like laughing aloud as Mordechai turned a chalky color. "Or who might come to know about it."

He pulled the hood up and over his head. "Don't bother seeing me out. I know the way."

II

OUTSIDE JERUSALEM, THE MOUNT OF OLIVES

As the first shovelful of dirt fell with a soft thump on the stiff form wrapped in linen, Livia cried out in intense pain. Simeon held out his arms, and Livia turned and buried her face against his chest. She sagged against him, her body wracked by one shudder after another as the men continued to shovel the dirt into the grave.

Shana had begun sobbing too. Samuel stood beside her. He put an arm around her shoulder, his eyes filled with pain. Leah, who was standing back with her parents, also moved up to comfort her friend. The left side of Samuel's head was swathed in bandages, and there was an ugly red gash down his cheek.

Fortunately, Shana's husband had fallen beneath the first wave of Romans. Seeing the blood, they had passed over him, in anxious pursuit of those still standing. When Samuel regained consciousness a few minutes later, the battle was raging inside the temple courts. Seeing the carnage all around him, he knew that there was nothing he could do. He hobbled away, passing out the Golden Gate to safety.

That was the only bright spot in a black day. Including Samuel and Yehuda, fifteen men from the village of Beth Neelah had answered Yehuda's call for help. Eight, counting Yehuda, had not been as fortunate as Samuel. There would be a long period of mourning in the highlands of the Galilee.

As the men patted the rounded mound with their shovels, Livia bit back the tears. She stepped back and looked at Miriam and Simeon. "If only he could have known that I got away." Her lip started to tremble, and she knew she couldn't go further down that path. She forced a wan smile. "Who would have thought that he would be buried here on the Mount of Olives? Not him, certainly. Now he will come forth in the resurrection before I will." (It was a common belief among the Jews that those privileged to have their final resting place on the Mount of Olives would be the first to come forth in the resurrection when the Messiah came.)

"No one deserves a place here more than Yehuda," Miriam said. Simeon, still struggling with the knot in his own throat, could only nod.

"But he wanted to be buried at Beth Neelah," she said. "He even showed me the spot on the hillside where his grave should be." Her face crumpled. "Oh, Simeon," she whispered, "what am I going to do?"

"You're going to come live with us," Miriam said. "When the baby comes, we'll be there."

"And we will always be there to support and help you," Deborah said, coming forward to stand beside them.

To their surprise, Livia shook her head.

"Why not?" Miriam asked in surprise.

"Yehuda would want me to go back to the vineyard. It was his life."

"But—" Simeon wasn't really surprised to hear her resolve, but it still set him back. "Livia, I know how you feel, but the vineyard takes a man. You can't possibly take care of it by yourself."

"She has a man."

They turned as Samuel stepped forward. "Livia belongs to Beth Neelah. We will take care of her."

"Samuel—" Simeon started.

But the man whirled on him, eyes blazing. "That tribune knew full well Livia was a free woman. He knew it! But he didn't care."

"I know," Simeon said quietly.

"No!" Samuel said fiercely. "*You don't know!* You joined us yesterday, Simeon, and we are grateful for that. We are grateful that you were able to get Livia away from them. It was the old Simeon we used to know. But you are not one of us anymore. We did nothing wrong. This was all a ploy to draw our people into an ambush. And now a payment will be made."

Shana came forward to stand beside her husband. She brushed the tears away with the back of her hand. "And they will pay," she said bitterly. "They will pay dearly for what they have done. I have lost every single member of my family to those Roman pigs. My father, my mother, Daniel. And now Yehuda."

"This is not the answer," Simeon said.

She jerked away. "You've made your choice," she said. "Don't try to make ours."

Livia started to shake her head, her face twisting. "I do not want to be part of revenge."

"No one is asking you to," Samuel said gently, "but you are one of us now. Beth Neelah is your home, and you will be safe there. You are right, Livia. This is what Yehuda would want you to do. Raise him a son who can take his father's land and keep it in the family."

She stood looking at him, her lips quivering, then finally nodded. "Yes," she whispered. She turned to Miriam and Simeon. "I owe that to Yehuda."

CHAPTER 17

ANYONE CAN STOP A MAN'S LIFE, BUT NO ONE HIS DEATH;

A THOUSAND DOORS OPEN ON TO IT.

—*Seneca*, Phoenissae, *152*

I

BETH NEELAH, IN THE UPPER GALILEE

8 MARCH, 33 A.D.

Samuel of Beth Neelah, like most of the men of his village, was a husbandman. He owned a sizeable vineyard, which had been in his family for five generations. His great-great-grandfather had purchased the land from a man who had used the hills as grazing land for his sheep. His great-grandfather, as a young lad, had cleared the land and piled the rocks into the walls that still separated his vineyards from the others of the village. Samuel's grandfather had spent his whole life pruning and dunging the vines and turning the grapes into wine. It was during his lifetime that the Romans came and things began to change. Samuel's father, and then Samuel himself, added a second occupation to that of husbandman. They took up the sword in the cause of the Zealots. Now Samuel had a son—the sixth generation. What lay in store for him? Would more than a hundred years of tradition carry on, or would the cause that inspired such passion in them change everything?

Five generations of stability, but no one could predict what the future held for the sixth.

Samuel was the oldest of two sons and three daughters borne and nurtured by his parents. He was twenty-eight years old. His sisters were all married and lived with their husbands—one in Nazareth, one in Sepphoris, and one still in Beth Neelah. His only brother, the youngest in the family, had married before Samuel; he and his wife and daughter lived in a small stone house just west of Samuel's and helped him tend to the vineyard.

That was good. Samuel needed time for his new responsibilities as leader of a Zealot band. Not that there was much to lead yet, he thought with a frown. In the four and a half months since the disaster in Jerusalem, they had done little more than start a slow and painful rebuilding. It would take years to get back to full strength again. Beth Neelah had about a hundred families. Eight of those had lost men in the slaughter on the Temple Mount—almost one in ten. The bitterness, the passion, the commitment for revenge was there. It would just take time to recruit enough to the Band of Barak to become a real force again.

He felt a quick satisfaction as he thought of the name. They no longer called themselves the Band of Ha'keedohn, the Javelin, not since Simeon, whose title that was, had abandoned them. That new name was ironic, he thought. Small or not, weak or not, Samuel had told his men there had to be at least some retaliation so the Romans would know they had not worked their will with impunity.

In a daring raid, they had struck a Roman patrol one day in broad daylight. They killed three soldiers and captured a small box of gold and a cart filled with bows and a thousand or more arrows. When they heard that the Romans were saying they had been struck like lightning from a clear sky, Samuel knew they had their name. Lightning, in Hebrew, was *barak*.

"Samuel?"

Samuel turned and saw his wife at the door of their house. She had the baby, just two weeks old, in one arm but was waving with the other. "Samuel!"

He lifted a hand. "What is it?"

"Simeon and Miriam are here from Capernaum."

Samuel frowned and set down his pruning knife. He broke into a trot toward the house. When he reached her, he asked, "Here?"

"No, they're at Livia's." She was scowling deeply as she said it.

"All right. We should at least say hello."

"I've got things to do," she muttered.

"Shana," Samuel said, chiding her gently, "you know I don't agree with what Simeon has done either. I think this whole thing with Jesus is pure folly, and I still find it hard to believe the man I once followed has changed so much. But Simeon is no coward. He stood by Yehuda when the trouble broke out. He went into that prison at terrible risk to himself and brought Livia out."

"And Yehuda died while he did so."

He sighed. "If you had a chance to ask Yehuda, what would he say? Try to save me, and probably get killed in the process, or save my wife?"

Shana finally nodded. "I know, but . . ." She wasn't sure what she wanted to add so didn't finish. "Tell them the baby is not well, or that I'm still not getting around much."

He cocked his head at her.

"I don't want to see him," she said stubbornly. "Or Miriam either."

He sighed again. "All right. I won't stay long."

II

"How are you feeling, Livia?" Miriam asked.

Livia rested a hand on the roundness of her stomach. "Quite good, actually. Except when he kicks me hard enough that I can't sleep."

"It's a boy?" Simeon teased. "You're sure?"

"It has to be," she said, pulling a face. "It's like I've got a mule inside me." She turned to Miriam. "And what of you? Any news you can share?"

Miriam blushed. "Not yet, but we're hoping."

"And it has to be a boy too, I suppose," she said to Simeon.

"Not necessarily. If we could get an Esther or a little Miriam, I would be perfectly content."

Miriam nodded. "If it is a girl, Simeon insists that she be named after me. I'm trying to convince him that, with Lilly's baby, we already have two Miriams in the family. We don't need three. I would like to call her after her grandmother."

"That would thrill Deborah," Livia answered.

"Yes, it would," Simeon agreed, "so I'm not opposed to that." Then he peered more closely at her, his eyes sobering. "How are you doing, Livia?"

She looked away, biting at her lower lip. "All right." Then she added quietly, "The nights are the hardest. If we hadn't been so happy, it . . ." She couldn't finish and dropped her head.

Miriam reached out and squeezed her hand. "I know." More than once in the previous four months, she had wondered what it would have been like if it had been Simeon who had been killed and herself left as a widow. Each time she had those thoughts, the pain was sharp enough to make her gasp.

"Any more word from Drusus?" Simeon asked.

Livia looked up, grateful for the change of subject. "I wrote him about everything that happened. He was deeply shocked. He says that when he finishes out this year of his apprenticeship, he's coming here."

"Really?" Miriam exclaimed. "To live?"

"That's what he said."

"Wonderful," Miriam said. "That would be so good for you and for him."

"Yes. I don't know how he'll take to the life of a vineyard keeper, but it would be good to have him with me."

"Especially after the baby comes," Miriam agreed.

"How has the village . . . ?" Simeon took a quick breath. "They don't blame you for Yehuda's death, do they?"

"No. Some still blame me for his decision to turn away from the sword, but no, I love it here. I'm happy. They treat me well."

"They'd better," Simeon growled.

Livia nodded slowly, then forced a smile. "Come. Enough of this. Tell me about the family. What about Leah? Has anything more happened with that young man and the betrothal?"

Simeon smiled back. "Yes, Leah and Jonathan will be betrothed after we return from Passover."

"Wonderful. Is she happy?"

"We can't get any work out of her," Simeon said gruffly, "if that's what you mean. She's like a little bird. Flitting here and there all day long."

"Well, I'm happy for her."

Just then a knock sounded at the door. Livia started to stand, but Simeon jumped up and went to get it. It was Samuel. They shook hands, and he came in. Livia gave him a questioning look. He excused Shana, saying that the baby was fussy. They talked for several minutes about his new fatherhood, about the prospects for the grape crop this year, about things in the village. No further mention was made of Shana.

Finally, Simeon glanced briefly at Livia, then turned to face Samuel. "We had something we wanted to propose for Livia," he said, "and would like to know what you think. It has implications for you as well, Samuel."

Now Livia was curious. "What?"

Miriam answered for her husband. "We would like you to come to Jerusalem with us for Passover."

Samuel immediately frowned. "Do you think that is wise?"

Simeon knew exactly what he meant. Not only would it take Livia back to the scene of the tragedy, but Samuel was apparently wondering if it might also put her in danger of being arrested again. "We have quietly been looking into things there," Simeon said, choosing his words carefully, his eyes moving back and forth between Livia and Samuel. "It was exactly as we suspected. Livia's arrest was nothing more than a way to bait the trap and draw in as many Zealots as possible. Unfortunately for the Romans, they opened Pandora's box when they did so. They—"

"Pandora's box?" Samuel said, looking puzzled.

Livia smiled and explained. "It's a very old Greek myth," she explained. "Pandora was the first woman. The gods endowed her with all of the graces and good gifts of femininity. They also gave her a box that contained all the evils of the world, knowing that with her curiosity she would be unable to resist seeing what was inside. When she gave in to her inquisitiveness and opened the box, evil was loosed into the world."

"Oh."

"And that's what Marcus did that day—opened a box of trouble. Yes, he did great damage to the Zealots, probably setting back the movement ten years, but—"

"Not ten years," Samuel growled. "One, maybe two."

Simeon went on without responding. "But when he sent his soldiers into the inner courts of the temple, it changed everything. The Sanhedrin are still raging about that. We've learned from a good source that the garrison in the Antonia has been given very strict orders. No provocation of any kind."

He looked at Livia. "Are you feeling well enough to travel? That's the first question."

"I feel fine. I've still got three more months before the baby comes. It's just that . . ."

Simeon nodded, guessing what she was about to say. "We understand. It has to be hard to return to Jerusalem. On the other hand, Jesus has not been back to Capernaum since *Sukkot*, so our family plans to leave in a few days and meet him as soon as possible. That will give us a chance to spend a lot of time with him before the crowds swarm him during the feast days."

"In fact," Miriam added, "we stopped at Nazareth to visit with Mary. Her sons and their families are going up, but not until just in time for the feast. So she'll be traveling with us too. She hasn't seen Jesus since the Feast of Tabernacles either."

Livia was pleased at the prospect. "It would be wonderful to be with her again," she said.

"Who is Mary?" Samuel wondered.

"The mother of Jesus," Miriam explained. "She is about the same age as Simeon's mother, and a wonderful woman."

Livia turned to Samuel wistfully. She didn't relish going back onto the Temple Mount where Yehuda had been killed, but neither did she have a morbid fear of being there. And to see Jesus again. To be with him. And not just with him. To be in company with the women she had come to love—Miriam and Deborah and Leah, Mary the mother of Jesus, Mary Magdalene, Anna, and the other wives of the Twelve. In that moment, she realized how keenly her soul hungered for those associations. She didn't need his permission, but she hoped for his approval.

Samuel saw all of that in her eyes. He waved a hand easily. "We have already finished pruning your vineyards. Go with them." He turned to Miriam and Simeon. "Shana and I are not going to Passover this season. The baby is too tiny yet, and Shana is still not strong enough for a journey. We'll watch things here for Livia."

Actually, the more Samuel thought about it, the better he liked the idea. He worried about Livia. He had come to respect her deeply and admired her courage in all that had happened. She needed something like this. "I think it would be good for you."

"Really?"

"Yes. It is a good idea."

"Marvelous," Miriam exclaimed. "Esther and Boaz will be so excited to see you again. As we left, Boaz said, 'You tell my Livie I miss her.'"

"Oh," Livia said softly, "I've missed them too."

"Not all of the family are going up with us," Simeon explained. "Lilly, as you know, is with child again, and, being older, she is having more difficulty this time. She's sick quite a bit, so she and Ezra will be staying in Capernaum. She offered to keep Esther, Boaz, and little Amasa with them so Rachel and Ephraim can spend more time with Jesus and not have to worry about the children."

"I see," Livia said. Then she smiled. "I'll bet Esther set up an objection to that idea."

Miriam laughed softly. "At first, but Lilly told her she needs her to help with Amasa and little Miriam, and that made her feel better. She's become quite the little mother. Rachel and Ephraim won't leave early with us. They'll stay and go up just in time for Passover."

"Even Joseph has decided to stay," Simeon said. "Ezra has promised to make him a new bow and teach him how to shoot if he'll stay and help with the children."

"But I'll get to see them all before we leave?" Livia asked.

"Of course," Simeon said. "We'll be in Capernaum a couple of days, then leave after that."

"Come," Miriam said, standing up. "I'll help you get some things together. We'll leave first thing in the morning."

"No," Livia said, surprising them both. "Let's go now. It's only midday."

Samuel hadn't expected that either, but immediately nodded.

"Don't worry about closing up the house. I'll see to that." He started to move toward the door. "*Shalom*, Livia. Have a good journey."

Simeon stood and went out with him. "Thank you, Samuel," he said softly.

"For all that the village has gathered around her, it's not the same," he replied. "She still feels a bit like an outsider. It will be good for her to have a break."

III

As they left the village, turning southeast on the road that led to Nazareth, Livia stopped and turned back. This was the same road they had come up on the first day she and Miriam had been brought here by Simeon and Yehuda. Her eyes suddenly burned and her lip started to tremble as the vivid imagery of that day sprang to her mind—Yehuda bragging shamelessly about the beauty of the village, Shana tearing pell-mell down the hill to greet them.

Miriam, sensing what was going through her mind, stepped over to her and slipped an arm around her waist. They stood quietly for almost a full minute, Simeon standing back, not wanting to intrude.

Livia finally turned to him. "If he were here," she murmured, "you know what he would say to you for coming into the prison to get me?"

"I was only the instrument," Simeon said somberly. "It was the Lord's hand that delivered you."

"I know." She took a deep breath and let it out slowly. It was a sound of great pain. "I only wish Yehuda could have known," she whispered. "It still haunts me that he died thinking I and our baby were in the hands of the Romans."

"He knows now," Miriam said, near tears herself. "He knows that you are all right and that he is going to have a child to carry on for him."

"Yes," she said softly.

Simeon suddenly looked at her in wonder. "Not only that," he said. He stopped, not sure he should say it. But he couldn't help it. "He knew."

Livia's eyes widened slightly. "*Knew?*"

Simeon nodded slowly. "Yes. I don't know how, but he knew about you getting free. Before he died, he knew. I feel that very strongly."

Her eyes filled with tears, for she also knew. "Thank you, Simeon."

He stepped to her and took her in his arms. "You didn't have a long time together, Livia, but it was so good that you had what time you did. You were the best thing that ever happened to him."

CHAPTER 18

WHAT LACK I YET?

—*Matthew 19:20*

I

IN THE JORDAN VALLEY, NORTH OF JERICHO

15–17 MARCH, A.D. 33

The group traveling from Capernaum had no problem finding Jesus and the Twelve. The whole countryside was ablaze with talk of the man from Nazareth. Virtually every traveler coming north on the highway that led up the Jordan Valley had seen him or heard of his whereabouts. As the group neared Jericho, there were almost constant reports that Jesus was east of the Jordan in Perea. When the travelers reached the site just north of the city where they had camped on their way to the Feast of Tabernacles, they stopped. Several of the brethren, including David and Simeon, left the main body the next morning, turned east, and crossed the river to see if they could find exactly where Jesus was.

The second night after their departure, they returned just before sundown. With them were Jesus, Peter, the rest of the apostles, and a small group of additional disciples.

II

17 MARCH, A.D. 33

They sat around the fire in circles, two and three deep. There were a few children, but not nearly as many as when they had been there before. Like Deborah and David's family, people sensed that things were not the same with Jesus now. They wanted time with him without having to worry about their families. There were a few younger children in the camp, but most of the children had come with their parents from Jericho and the surrounding villages.

Jesus was not there, so they talked quietly among themselves. After supper was finished, Jesus had gone off by himself into the darkness, and Peter asked that he be given some time alone. The Master looked tired, and though many had come specifically to hear him, they honored the big fisherman's request.

As they talked quietly, a man appeared out of the darkness and moved toward the fire. "Excuse me!" he called.

Everyone turned as a man entered the circle of firelight. "Pardon, but I am looking for the one they call Jesus of Nazareth."

Miriam was surprised as she looked him up and down. Jesus was always drawing people to him. Usually they were of the poorer classes. Often they were sick or afflicted in one way or another. But this man was unlike most of those Miriam had seen in the crowds before. He was richly dressed. He wore a turban that flashed in the firelight. It was encrusted with jewels. His robe looked like it was of the finest linen and was heavily embroidered with gold. The sash he wore was fastened with what looked like a solid gold clasp. There was a flash of red, and Miriam saw that he wore an enormous ruby on one finger. There were several other rings as well, in addition to gold bracelets. She could scarcely believe it. She had grown up among wealthy people and did not remember seeing anything quite like this. The man was wearing enough wealth to feed a small village for several months.

Miriam thought of the night Marcus Didius had told her about the Latin word *luxus*, from which came the word "luxuries." *Luxus* referred to a wild, uncontrolled profusion of growth, a garden gone totally to weed, a bush that had never been pruned. Here was visual evidence of that original meaning. The man was luxurious, wealth gone to seed.

Peter got to his feet. "This is the camp where Jesus is staying, but he is not here at the moment. Can we help you?"

It was hard to tell in the firelight whether the man's expression was one of anxiety or annoyance. "Could you tell me where he is, please? I must speak with him."

"I'm very sorry, but—"

"It's all right, Peter. I am here."

Every head jerked around as Jesus came walking toward them. He moved through the seated people until he stood next to his apostles. The ornately dressed man did the same, only from the other direction. They came face to face near the fire.

"You were inquiring for me?" Jesus asked.

"Yes, I was. I have a question."

"Say on," Jesus replied.

"Good Master, what good thing shall I do, that I may have eternal life?"

The question startled Miriam. It was simple, and certainly a good question, but . . . Then she realized what had struck her as odd. It was the "good thing." The man had put the question in the singular. He wanted to know what one single act would earn him life everlasting.

If Jesus had noted the oddity, he said nothing. "Why do you call me good?" he asked kindly. "There is none good but one, and that is God."

The man squirmed a little at what was clearly a gentle rebuke for his obsequiousness.

Sitting beside Miriam, Simeon's thoughts were going in a different direction. He was remembering the first time he and his parents had been at the home of Mary and Martha in Bethany. There a lawyer had accosted Jesus with a similar question. That had brought forth the parable of the good Samaritan, and Simeon half expected that Jesus might tell that story again. Good. It would be well to hear how he had expressed it before. But he was wrong. Jesus' response totally surprised him.

Jesus looked thoughtfully at the young man. Though his eyes never left the other man's face, Jesus seemed to take in his whole personage in that single look. Then he spoke. "If you would enter into eternal life, keep the commandments."

The young man seemed disappointed. "Which?" he asked.

Livia was seated next to Leah. "I thought we were expected to keep all of them," she whispered.

Leah giggled softly. That was an excellent insight. Her mother, hearing the laughter, turned and gave her a warning look.

"Sorry," Livia mouthed.

"Thou shalt do no murder," Jesus was saying, quoting from the Ten Commandments. "Thou shalt not commit adultery. Thou shalt not steal. Thou shalt not bear false witness. Honor thy father and thy mother. Thou shalt love thy neighbor as thyself."

The young man threw back his shoulders, clearly disappointed in such a predictable answer. "All these things have I kept from my youth up," he exclaimed confidently. "What lack I yet?"

"A little humility, I would think," Leah said out of the side of her mouth. Now it was Livia who had to stifle a laugh. This young man was so arrogant that both women found him irritating.

To Livia's surprise, Jesus did not. Instead of condemnation or criticism, what Livia saw in the Master's eyes was more like sorrow and compassion. His face, in the firelight, was infused with love. For a moment, Livia thought he might reach out and put an arm around the young man.

Then in a low voice, Jesus said, "If you would be perfect, go and sell that which you have and give to the poor."

The reaction was instantaneous. The young man's jaw sagged, pulling his mouth down. He drew in a long, painful breath, all the time staring at Jesus.

"If you do that," Jesus said with a sad smile, "you shall have treasure in heaven. Then come and follow me."

The young man's face was pale, the only color two spots high on his cheekbones. He searched Jesus' eyes, as if hoping he might find something there that would let him know Jesus had spoken only in jest, that he didn't—couldn't!—really mean what he had just said.

Everyone's eyes were fixed on the young man, waiting to see what he would say.

Then a second thought struck Miriam with great force. The young man wanted to know what *one good thing* he could do to inherit eternal life? And Jesus had just told him. He had given him *one thing* to do. Just one.

For what seemed like a full minute, Jesus and the young man stood there, searching each other's souls. The richly clad young man opened his mouth, as if he might speak again, but he did not. His hand lifted, and it passed across his eyes before dropping again. After a moment, he turned slowly and, without raising his eyes to look at anyone, walked back the way he had come. In a moment, he disappeared into the darkness.

Not until the sound of his retreating footsteps had completely died away did Jesus turn and let his eyes sweep across the group of upturned faces. The sorrow in him seemed to deepen. He moved over and sat on a stone before the fire. Peter did the same. Again Jesus searched the surrounding faces before he spoke. "Verily I say unto you, how hardly shall they which trust in riches enter into the kingdom of God. I say unto you, it is easier for a camel to go through the eye of a needle than for a rich man to enter into the kingdom of God."

Low exclamations of surprise and dismay erupted from the group. Peter jerked around and stared at his leader in astonishment. Could Jesus really mean what he had just said? One had to accumulate some things even to live. That was something everyone did in life. It was, for most, the sole pursuit of mortality. "Who then can be saved, Lord?" he asked.

Jesus looked at his chief apostle, then at his closest brethren. "With men this is impossible, but with God all things are possible."

Peter looked like he had stepped in front of a runaway cart. He examined his hands, hands that had pulled thousands of fish from the sea so that he could sell them in the market and buy food for his family. The income from his fishing had helped him buy the materials and build the comfortable house he and Anna had in Capernaum. He glanced quickly at Andrew, then James and John, his partners in that endeavor. He had so many questions, and yet Jesus had spoken. He had learned, sometimes painfully, not to question what Jesus taught them.

Finally, he turned back to Jesus. "Master, behold, we have forsaken all and followed after thee." His voice became beseeching, almost pleading. "What shall we have then?"

It was a fair question, Miriam thought. They *had* forsaken all when Jesus had said to them, "Come, follow me." For example, tonight was the first time the Twelve had seen their families in almost five months. The apostles sent a little money when they could, but for the most part their wives were coping on their own.

The four partners had left a lucrative fishing business. Matthew had been a very well-to-do publican; now he earned nothing.

Jesus smiled, a soft and gentle smile that was once again filled with love. "Truly I say unto you, my brethren who have followed me, in the regeneration, when the Son of man shall sit in the throne of his glory, you also shall sit upon twelve thrones, judging the twelve tribes of Israel."

It was an astonishing declaration. These men would become judges of the house of Israel in the life after this! Miriam looked at her husband, seeing if he had heard it the same way she did. He was as speechless as she was.

Jesus lifted his eyes from the men who were seated immediately around him and spoke to the larger group. "Every one of you that has forsaken houses or brethren or sisters—" his eyes fell on Miriam and she felt a thrill of exultation—"or *father* or mother or wife or children or lands, for my name's sake, you shall receive an hundredfold, and shall inherit everlasting life."

Jesus sat back and looked into the fire. No one spoke. Their minds were swirling. Why hadn't the rich young man stayed long enough to hear the promise? He wanted everlasting life; now Jesus had just told them how to get it.

Suddenly Jesus got to his feet. He looked down at Peter. "I am weary," he said.

Peter scrambled to his feet. The rest of the Twelve quickly did the same. "It has been a long day, Master."

Jesus said nothing. The sorrow that Miriam had seen on his face when the young man had earlier turned away was back, only even more than before. He seemed weighted down with a tremendous burden.

"Soon we shall go up to Jerusalem," he said quietly. "Then all things that are written by the prophets concerning the Son of man shall be accomplished." His head turned, and he stared out into the night. "He shall be delivered unto the Gentiles. He shall be mocked and spitefully entreated and spit upon." There was a long, painful silence; then, his voice dropping even lower, he finished. "And they shall scourge him and put him to death."

Amidst the gasps of shock and the soft exclamation of protests, one face drew Miriam's gaze. Mary, mother of Jesus, had sat quietly through all of it, as she usually did. She was always content to watch her son, but rarely spoke out lest she interrupt him or draw attention to herself. Now she stared at her son, her mouth twisting in horror.

Jesus turned, looked deeply into her eyes, then moved away, stopping only for a moment to lay a hand on her shoulder. He smiled down at her and squeezed her shoulder. "But he shall rise again the third day," he said. Then, without another word, Jesus gathered his robes about him, as though suddenly cold, and walked away.

"Master, I—" Peter had one hand up to call him back, but Jesus didn't stop.

As the shadowy figure receded into the darkness, the Twelve erupted. "Peter," Andrew said sharply, "we can't let him go up to Jerusalem. They're waiting for him."

"Who is this Son of man he keeps talking about?" someone farther back in the circle asked.

Peter turned for a moment. "It is a title he often uses for himself," he said gloomily.

"What did he mean about being delivered up to the Gentiles? Did he mean the Romans?" That was from Bartholomew.

"But how can that be?" That sounded like John, but Miriam couldn't be sure. "He's the Messiah. We are eyewitnesses to his power. What Roman—which ten thousand Romans—has more power than that?"

Thomas stepped forward, his hand on his sword. "I don't know what all of this means, but if that is what he wishes, then we shall go up with him." His lips pursed together. "And if necessary, we shall die with him."

III

When the group coming down to meet Jesus had left Capernaum, there had been a light rain and a cold wind, so each night they had erected their tents for shelter and warmth. This day had dawned clear, and in the lower elevations of the Jordan Valley, the air quickly warmed. Once they reached the highlands around Jerusalem, it would be cool again, but tonight the air was pleasant, and the family had decided to forgo setting up the tents and to sleep under the stars.

Most of the camp, including the rest of their family, were asleep, but not David and Deborah. "I saw you talking to Mary afterwards," Deborah finally said in a hushed voice. "How is she? That must have been terrible for her to hear those words tonight."

"Yes," David replied. "But it didn't surprise her."

That brought Deborah over on her side so she could look at him. "You mean she knows?"

"She's heard Jesus talk about it before, just as we have, though never quite so directly."

"Poor Mary. How does she bear it?"

"She told me something I didn't know before, something that happened when Jesus was born."

"What?"

"After the shepherds came that night, she said she and Joseph had a lot of time to think about what all of this meant: Gabriel coming to each of them, the star, the angel appearing to the shepherds, and the singing of the heavenly chorus. But then, as life continued, things settled back to a more normal pace. On the eighth day, they took him up to be circumcised, of course. Then . . ." He stopped, trying to remember all of her words. "After the days of her purification were completed, she and Joseph took him to the temple to present him to the Lord, as the law requires for a firstborn son."

Deborah nodded. She and David had done exactly the same thing with Ephraim.

"They went to the temple and offered their sacrifices as required. As they were finishing, an old man came up to them. They learned later that his name was Simeon. He was of great age, and he had been promised by the Lord that he should not see death before he was allowed to see the Messiah."

Deborah's eyes were wide with wonder. "And he came just then? How did he know?"

"Evidently by the Spirit," David answered. "They had just finished their sacrifices when Simeon stepped forward, holding out his arms. Surprised, but somehow instantly trusting him, Mary handed Jesus to him."

"And what did he do?"

"He blessed him. Mary can't remember all of it, but one thing she does remember is that he said, 'Lord, now you can let your servant depart in peace, for mine eyes have seen thy salvation which thou hast prepared, a light to the Gentiles and a glory to thy people Israel.' It was definitely a prophecy of the Messiah.

"Mary said he handed Jesus back to her and then spoke to her and Joseph. At that point, he said something like this: 'This child is destined to make many fall and many rise in Israel and to set up a standard which many will attack, for he will expose the secret thoughts of their hearts.'"

David paused, then went on. "Then he said something that she remembers very clearly, because he spoke directly to her and his voice was so serious that it sent chills through her."

"What?" Deborah whispered.

"He said, 'Yea, and a sword shall pierce through thine own soul also.'" He took a deep breath. "She said that for all these years, she hasn't been sure what that meant. Now she's afraid she does."

For a long time they lay there together, their thoughts keeping sleep far away. Deborah wondered if her husband had finally drifted off, but then he stirred.

"David?"

"Yes?"

"I've been thinking about Aaron."

"Oh?"

"If Jesus . . ." She couldn't say it. "Suppose something *is* going to happen, even while we're in Jerusalem for Passover, then . . ." She shuddered and pulled the blanket up around her to ward it off.

"Go on."

She decided to say it a different way. "While we are in Jericho tomorrow, I want to try to find someone."

He turned in surprise. "In Jericho?" He and Simeon and Ephraim had business relationships in the city, but as far as he knew, Deborah didn't know anyone there.

"Yes."

"Who?"

"Hava's brother's mother-in-law."

There was a long silence.

"If something *is* going to happen to Jesus, we've got to convince Aaron to come with us, David. He's got to be with him, listen to him, see for himself what Jesus is. Before it's too late."

David reached out and took her hand. "Of course. We'll ask around first thing tomorrow."

IV

JERICHO

18 MARCH, A.D. 33

Being the center of three lucrative industries—dates, the aromatic resin made from the dried gum of the balsam trees, and salt from the Dead Sea—Jericho was a prosperous city. Between its own goods and the caravans that passed through it, Jericho moved a lot of valuable products. Thus, from the Roman point of view, there was another primary industry: taxation. Where most cities had only one or two, Jericho had a cadre of six *publicani*, or publicans, rivaling such major commercial centers as Caesarea, Ptolemais, Antioch, and Damascus.

And the chief of those publicans in Jericho was Zacchaeus.

It was a warm day. Even though spring was just arriving in the highlands on either side of the Jordan Valley, down in Jericho, near the lowest spot on the face of the earth, summer was already flexing its muscles. And even though it was not yet midday, Zacchaeus was already starting to sweat. He was a short, round man, with chubby cheeks and a thin beard. Some joked—never to his face, of course— that if one measured the length of the sash that girded his ample waist, it would nearly equal his height. That was not completely accurate, but neither was it too much of an exaggeration. Therefore, it didn't take much to get him perspiring.

"Chronicus!"

His chief bookkeeper, a native Greek who had once been a Roman slave, appeared at his doorway. "Yes, sire?"

"Open all the windows and prop open the doors."

"But, sire—"

"I don't care about the flies. We'll live with them. It's getting hot in here."

"Yes, sire." Chronicus backed out. He never won this argument, though he never failed to lodge at least a protest.

The customs house Zacchaeus oversaw was one of three in the city, but it was the largest and busiest of them all. Like Zacchaeus, the other publicans in Jericho were independent contractors hired by the governor. Technically, they did not answer to him, but Pilate, within a year of his appointment as governor, had come to realize that Jericho was a major source of revenue for the province. He also learned that the man named Zacchaeus was primarily responsible for maintaining the smooth flow of funds. He pronounced him to be the "chief publican." The others didn't have to work with him—or better, under him—but they quickly learned that not only did Zacchaeus have the procurator's ear if something went wrong but also that under his management all were prospering.

Except for the owners of the largest of the merchant houses, and the remnants of the royal family that owned the vast date palm plantations, the publicans were Jericho's richest citizens. And Zacchaeus was the wealthiest of them all.

He felt a slight breeze stir the room and heard the sound of shutters banging. He reached for a small towel he kept hanging beneath his table and mopped at his brow. As Chronicus passed the door, headed for the other end of the building, Zacchaeus called out to him again. "No word yet?"

This time Chronicus didn't stop. "No, sire."

Zacchaeus rose and walked to the door. He stepped out into the hall and watched as his servant pushed open the shutters and propped them. "You're sure he's coming?"

The Greek shrugged, pretending boredom. In actuality, he also was curious about this man from the Galilee, and he planned to accompany his master when word came. "He crossed the river from Perea late yesterday afternoon and is camped with a group from the Galilee just north of town."

"And you've—"

Chronicus cut in quickly. "Yes, sire. I've got three men who will let us know immediately as soon as Jesus comes to town."

Zacchaeus grunted and went back into the room, half smiling to himself. Chronicus was like that. They had worked together for so many years that it was like the man was an extension of Zacchaeus's own mind. He typically anticipated what Zacchaeus wanted before he could express it, and sometimes he even finished his sentences for him.

The two men had been at the synagogue several months before when Jesus had gone through Jericho the first time. Their curiosity had been piqued. Jesus' fame had preceded him—he was the subject of every conversation; his name was on everyone's lips. They had both watched in absolute astonishment as old crippled Huldah had come shuffling into the courtyard of the synagogue, and Jesus had healed her. Zacchaeus and Chronicus were at the edge of the large crowd and too far away to see Jesus clearly or to hear what was said, but that didn't matter. What Zacchaeus did see that day had stayed in his mind as vividly as if it had just happened.

Since then there had been many other reports of healings, most notable of which was that a man born blind had been given sight in Jerusalem. But Jesus had not been seen again. He passed by Jericho several months earlier, going into Perea, but by the time Zacchaeus had learned of it, Jesus was gone again.

Now at last he was back. Had it not been for a major banquet Zacchaeus had been hosting for three distinguished guests from Jerusalem, he would have gone out to the camp last evening.

He sighed. Well, if Jesus didn't come to the city in the next hour or two, Zacchaeus would go to him.

V

"Do you see him?" Zacchaeus jumped up and down, trying to see over the heads of the crowd in front of him. "Where is he?"

Chronicus, who was a full two hands taller than his master, went up on tiptoes, craning his neck. "It looks like there is a crowd of people just coming around the corner, down by the weaver's shop. But there are a lot of people. I can't tell yet."

Highly frustrated, Zacchaeus moved forward. "Excuse me," he called. "Excuse me, please." When no one moved, he shifted to his left, searching for any opening at all. "Please! May I come through?"

He may as well have put his hand out to open a passage through a wall of stone. No one budged. It was as though they hadn't even heard him. And more people were pressing in all around. He lowered his shoulders and began to make his way slowly southward, hoping he could find a place. Chronicus, who was still on his toes peering forward, didn't turn until it was too late. When he went to speak to his master, Zacchaeus was gone.

The little publican didn't make it far. Soon he was wedged into the crowd and could barely move. He turned his head. Chronicus was no longer in sight and therefore couldn't help him. Ready to scream in exasperation, Zacchaeus felt a sense of despair. After all of his planning, he was going to miss Jesus.

But Zacchaeus had not become one of the richest men in Jericho and the chief of the publicans by simply giving in when things became difficult. As he elbowed his way back from the street to a place where there was a little breathing room, his eyes were caught by something above him. The main road of Jericho was lined with dozens of massive old sycamore trees. They provided dense, badly needed shade in a climate where the summer heat could become deadly. Fifty or sixty feet high, with thick, outspreading branches, the nearest one loomed over Zacchaeus like the bottom of a great house built on stilts.

He started. *An elevated house! A house well above the heads of this crushing mass of people.*

He didn't excuse himself this time. He just lowered his head and plowed forward. He ignored the grumbling and muttering he created and only frowned at a man who swore at him. In moments, he was at the base of the tree. Eyeing the branches, he saw that they were low enough for him to touch, but he didn't have sufficient strength to pull himself up without help. He looked around. Set back from the road, just steps from him, was a small stone house. A three-legged stool sat near the front door. In three steps he reached it, then darted back to the tree. It was enough. Zacchaeus climbed onto it, then scrambled upwards, unmindful that the skirts of his robe were hiked up past his knees.

In a moment, he settled himself in a crotch where one of the main branches divided. He looked down, deeply pleased with himself. He was a good five or six feet above the heads of the crowd and was nearly over the street itself. *Perfect!*

Now he could see what Chronicus had seen. To his left, still almost a hundred paces away, a crowd of people was slowly making its way toward his perch, moving down the center of the street. At first it was difficult to make out anything. People crammed the streets, trying to see better. But they began to give way as the oncoming group reached them.

The noise was deafening. People who couldn't see what was happening shouted at others to tell them what was going on, just as Zacchaeus had done with Chronicus. Near the center of the oncoming throng, people were clapping their hands and shouting out comments to a man who had to be Jesus.

Finally, Zacchaeus saw that man. Though people were all around on every side, basically one person led them, and the crowd flowed in behind him. The publican noted that several men were on both sides of him, helping to hold back the people from rushing in and crushing him.

By the time the distance to his perch had been cut in half, Zacchaeus could see Jesus clearly. Amazingly, he did not seem to be bothered by the press. He smiled as he reached out and touched people's hands or spoke to individuals. Once he stopped, bending down to talk to a young boy. After a moment, he took the lad's face in his hands and shook him gently. They both laughed together. The boy was clearly thrilled, and as Jesus stood again, the lad turned to his mother and apparently began to tell her what had just happened, as though she hadn't been watching the whole thing proudly.

As the day began, Zacchaeus had entertained hopes that he might even have a chance to speak to Jesus, but as Jesus drew near, Zacchaeus knew that wasn't going to be possible. There were too many people. Not that he knew what he would say if he had the chance, but he felt a strange sense of sadness. He had truly hoped for a chance to speak to this man.

Now Jesus was just ten or fifteen paces from his position. Zacchaeus studied him closely. So this was the man everyone was talking about. There was nothing particularly unusual about him. If he weren't in the front of the entourage that strung out behind him, you would have never picked him out of a crowd. And yet . . .

Zacchaeus couldn't take his eyes from the man's face. The hair, shoulder length, was pulled back, revealing clear, wide eyes, a pleasant mouth, a full but neatly trimmed beard. But there was something compelling about his gaze. Zacchaeus grabbed onto the branch and leaned forward to see better.

As he did so, his eyes suddenly widened. A familiar face had jumped out of the crowd. He leaned forward even farther, peering. It was true. He recognized the face of Matthew the Publican, a colleague from Capernaum. He was one of those men nearest to Jesus, trying to control the crowd so Jesus could keep moving. So it was true. Jesus had actually chosen a publican as one of his leaders. When Zacchaeus had first heard that, he had scoffed openly. Publicans were detested by their own people. What religious leader would dare become affiliated with anyone of that class?

Zacchaeus drew back a little when Jesus stopped directly below him. Maybe he would be able to hear what Jesus was saying. He was no more than two or three arm lengths away. Then, to the little man's utter surprise, Jesus looked up. Zacchaeus was surprised when Jesus' eyes fell squarely upon him.

A broad smile slowly stole across the face looking at him. "Zacchaeus?"

Zacchaeus nearly lost his balance. *You know my name?*

The entourage in the street had ground to a stop around Jesus, and every head tipped back, looking up into the tree. The waiting crowd also turned to see what Jesus was looking at. Zacchaeus's face flushed. Here he was, one of Jericho's wealthiest citizens, a man in his early fifties, a man of influence, sitting in a tree like a little boy who had sneaked away from his mother.

"Zacchaeus?" Jesus said again, more insistent this time.

Half dazed, Zacchaeus bobbed his head. "Yes, Lord?"

"Make haste and come down now, friend, for this day I shall abide at your house."

People on every hand gasped. They knew who he was. They knew *what* he was. Was Jesus aware that he was speaking to a publican?

His ears ringing, his heart pounding with the unexpected joy of that declaration, Zacchaeus scrambled down, sure that once he reached the ground, Jesus would take one look at his expensive robes and change his mind.

"Lord," he said, ignoring the angry mutters breaking out all around him, "you do me a great honor this day."

Jesus laughed softly and clapped him on the back. "Come," he said. "This day my disciples and I shall sup at your table."

The muttering exploded into an ugly rumble. "This man is a sinner!" someone shouted.

"Do you not know he is a publican?"

"Take care, Jesus! To even be seen with such a man is a defilement."

Zacchaeus's head flitted back and forth, seeing the twisted faces, the sneering lips, the smoldering eyes. His chin dropped to his chest. What would surely follow was censure and rejection. But Jesus didn't remove his hand from his shoulder.

For years Zacchaeus had been inured to the contempt of his fellow citizens. He had grown so accustomed to their hatred and rejection that he thought he had reached the point where he was impervious to it. He looked up, and in that instant, when he saw neither contempt nor censure nor rejection, but a warm, open acceptance in the eyes of the man who stood before him, something happened to Zacchaeus. Something deep down inside of him broke wide open.

He bowed his head. "Master," he said, speaking softly so the crowd would not hear, "behold, I shall give half of all my goods to the poor."

There were gasps of astonishment from those closest around. Zacchaeus barely heard them. It was as though his heart had suddenly swelled to many times its original size, like it was going to crack his ribs as it broke out of its confinement. He was filled with such a burst of gratitude and purest joy that he wanted to throw back his head and shout to the heavens. Instead, with trembling voice, he added, "And if I have taken anything from any man by false accusation, I shall restore it unto him fourfold."

Those who heard responded with more gasps, more soft cries of astonishment. But Jesus said nothing. Finally, Zacchaeus looked up, dreading what he might see. But he had to know.

To his amazement, there were tears in the eyes of Jesus. He reached out and put both hands on Zacchaeus's shoulders. "Zacchaeus, my friend, this day is salvation come unto your house."

Before the people could react to that, Jesus turned to them, his gaze instantly cutting off their protests. "This man, too, is a son of Abraham," he said, challenging any to disagree with him. "Know you not that the Son of man is come to seek out and to save those which are lost?"

Chapter Notes

The story of the rich young ruler and the Savior's commentary on riches is included in three of the four Gospels (Matthew 19:16–30; Mark 10:17–31; Luke 18:18–30). It is Mark who adds two details, used here, that enrich our understanding of what was said. Mark states that "Jesus beholding him loved him" (10:21). He also adds the clarification, "How hard is it for them *that trust in riches* to enter into the kingdom of God" (10:24; emphasis added).

There have been several attempts to explain the phrase about a camel going through the eye of a needle. Some have speculated that there was in some cities a small, side gate through which a camel might squeeze with utmost difficulty. This gate was supposedly called "the eye of the needle." While this is a possibility, there is no confirmatory evidence that such was the case (see Farrar, p. 476).

In Greek, camel is *kamelon* and "cable" or "rope" is *kamilon*, a difference of only one letter. Some New Testament manuscripts read *kamilon*, making it a rope going through the eye of a needle, but since the best manuscripts have *kamelon*, it is more likely that *kamilon* came through transcribers changing the original, thinking it made more sense metaphorically (Clarke, 3:193).

In addition, the expression of a camel going through a needle is found in the Talmud and other sources, so most agree it was a common proverb of the day, expressing the idea that something was virtually impossible, like our own phrase of "shooting for the moon" (see Edersheim, *Life and Times*, p. 710; see also Clarke, 3:193). When one remembers that the Savior earlier taught, "Enter ye in at the strait gate" (Matthew 7:13), *strait* meaning narrow, as in the Straits of Gibraltar, not *straight*, the meaning seems clear and the metaphor is a powerful one. The camel anciently was a pack animal. Trying to enter the strait and narrow gate of eternal life while burdened down with an accumulation of worldly things is no more possible than a camel squeezing through the eye of a needle. We express the same idea today in a far less colorful way when we say, "You can't take it with you."

We have no record that Mary traveled with Jesus during his ministry, though we know that on at least some occasions he went up to Jerusalem for feast days with his family (see John 7:2–9). We also know that Mary was in Jerusalem when Jesus was crucified (see, for example, John 19:25), so it seemed reasonable that she may have been with him as he went up to the Passover festival. It is Luke who tells us of the aged Simeon's prophecy in the temple (Luke 2:25–35). Though typically the author has used the King James Version in this series, the wording of Simeon's prophecy is more obscure in that version, so the Phillips translation was used in this instance (*The New Testament in Four Versions*, p. 169).

Luke is the only Gospel writer who records the story of Zacchaeus, the man in Jericho who was "chief among the publicans" and "was little of stature" (Luke 19:2–3).

CHAPTER 19

THE FEAR OF THE LORD IS THE BEGINNING OF KNOWLEDGE:

BUT FOOLS DESPISE WISDOM AND INSTRUCTION.

—*Proverbs 1:7*

I

JERICHO

18 MARCH, A.D. 33

David and Deborah walked slowly down Jericho's main street, which was mostly empty as evening came on. They were alone. Most of their party was still at the house of Zacchaeus with Jesus and would return to camp once they finished there. David and Deborah, when they had a moment alone with Zacchaeus, had asked if he knew the woman named Huldah. Filled with excitement, he told them what he witnessed at the synagogue when Huldah was cured of her infirmity. Though he didn't know the exact house where she lived, he gave them directions on how to find her.

"I just had a strange thought," Deborah said.

David turned his head. "What is that?" he asked.

"I was thinking about that young man at the camp last night and Zacchaeus today. It's an interesting contrast. The one who should be most likely to accept Jesus, being a leader in our religion, turns away in sorrow because the Master asked too much of him. The hated, contemptible publican accepts in a matter of moments even though Jesus asked nothing of him."

David had been thinking about that too. "The rich young ruler came to Jesus wanting salvation, and went away, as you say, sorrowing. Zacchaeus came only wanting to see Jesus and, because he was willing to offer so much, came away with salvation for him and his house." He slipped an arm through his wife's. "Every day is a rich learning experience with Jesus, isn't it."

Just then they saw a man and woman coming up the street in the opposite direction. David stepped forward. "*Shalom*, excuse me. We are looking for the street where Huldah lives, the woman who was once called 'Huldah the crippled one.'"

"Ah," said the man, a bit put out, "everyone wants to meet Huldah these days."

His wife shot him a critical look, then smiled at David. "Huldah lives with her daughter, Ruth, and her husband, Joash. It's the third street down on your right. She lives in the second house from the end."

"*Todah rabah*."

"You are welcome."

This was certainly not the section of town where the wealthy lived, but the houses were made of stone and were definitely more than mere hovels. Each looked as if it had two, three, or four rooms, and a few had small enclosed courtyards. The streets were clean, and here and there small plots of flowers and vegetables were visible. For some reason, Deborah had just assumed that Huldah would be poor. She was a widow, living with her daughter and her husband, and Aaron had talked about sending them money. They were not well off, but neither were they living in abject poverty. Perhaps the money Aaron was sending them was more generous than Deborah had supposed. Perhaps

Hava's brother did better as an overseer for one of the big date plantations than she had assumed.

They turned down the correct street, and David pointed as they approached the second house from the end of the street. To Deborah's further surprise, the house was one of the nicest on the street. The golden glow of lamplight shone behind the shuttered windows. "This must be it." He raised a hand and knocked.

A moment later the door opened, and a man stood before them.

"*Erev tov*," David said. "Good evening. We are looking for the house of Joash and Ruth."

"I am Joash," the man said.

Suddenly there was a cry from behind the man. "David?" Another figure appeared, rushing toward the door. "Deborah!"

"Aaron?" Deborah said, completely dumbfounded. "Is that you?"

Joash moved back, and Aaron stepped outside and opened his arms. In a moment he held his sister in a tight embrace. "This is a welcome surprise," he said. "I was going to come out to the camp to try to find you tonight."

"You were?" she said, still completely taken aback by this unexpected turn of events.

"Yes. Come in. Hava's here. Let me introduce you to her family."

II

"How did you know we'd be with Jesus?" Deborah asked. They were settled on benches, chairs, and stools, all facing each other.

"I didn't, not for sure," Aaron answered. "But I thought you might join up with him, coming with him to Passover as you did for *Sukkot*. Only when Hava and I arrived in Jericho yesterday afternoon did we learn that Jesus was coming to Jericho."

"The family would love to see you. Perhaps you and Hava can still come out with us and see them. You could even stay with us for a time, if you'd like. Jesus hasn't said how soon we'll be going up to Jerusalem, but I'm sure it's soon."

Aaron shook his head, causing his *peyot* to bounce lightly. "No, we need to return to the city tomorrow."

"Aaron has been given a seat on the Great Council," Hava said proudly.

"Really?" Deborah exclaimed.

"Yes, I am the most junior member," he said, trying hard not to look too pleased. "But it is a full seat and a great honor to me."

"That's wonderful, Aaron," David said. "Congratulations."

"Thank you."

"Would you take supper with us?" Ruth asked. "We'd love to have you join us."

Hava's sister-in-law was a plump woman about ten years younger than Deborah, with a pleasant smile and a gentle disposition. She had welcomed Deborah and David warmly into their home. Joash seemed a little more withdrawn, but he was still cordial. Huldah, who had said little to this point, was a woman in her late sixties or early seventies. Her eyes were clear and bright, and her face seemed to reflect a deep repose.

"Thank you, but no," Deborah said. "We ate not long ago at the house of Zacchaeus."

Joash's eyes darkened. "That's what we heard."

Aaron frowned. "You actually went in and ate with him?"

"We did," David said easily. "As you may have heard, he became a follower of Jesus today."

"He's a publican," Joash spat. "The chief publican here. First of all, I can't believe your Jesus wouldn't know that. Second, once he was told, I can't believe he didn't change his mind."

Deborah was about to make a comment about his use of "your Jesus" and what he had chosen to do, but Huldah spoke first. "Joash!"

He turned, surprised. "Yes, Mother?"

"When I was twisted, deformed, and in constant pain, you sorrowed for me, did you not?"

As Deborah watched the older woman's face, she suddenly realized she might not be as old as Deborah had first supposed. And then Deborah realized that her physical sufferings had probably added greatly to her aged condition.

Joash instantly nodded. "We did," he said softly. "We sorrowed greatly for you."

"And when Jesus commanded me to be healed, to be straightened, you rejoiced greatly with me also."

There was a tremor in her son-in-law's voice. "We did, Mother Huldah."

"More than we ever thought possible," Ruth agreed.

"They why can you not rejoice over Zacchaeus? He has a reputation for being a fair and honest man, even though he is a publican. But even if he had been twisted and deformed and pained spiritually, could you not rejoice that he has been healed? Jesus laid his hands upon me, and I was loosed from the burden I had carried for eighteen years. Is it not possible that Jesus could speak a word to Zacchaeus and loose him from whatever burdens him down?"

Joash said nothing, but Ruth was nodding. Deborah felt her eyes burning. It had come out with such simplicity and yet had struck them all with such power.

"Well?" Huldah demanded, peering at her son-in-law.

"I suppose," Joash finally admitted.

"Then rejoice in that as well," the old woman said. She turned and looked at Deborah and David. "If Aaron and Hava can put up with an old woman, I shall come out and see Jesus too. I would be honored to have a chance to thank him again for what he did for me."

"I will tell him as soon as we return tonight."

"Thank you."

Aaron stood abruptly. "I must speak with you and David," he said. "There is a matter of some urgency. Let's step outside."

David and Deborah glanced at each other quickly, then stood as well. They had been there only a few minutes, but clearly Aaron was suggesting that they leave. Had Huldah's comments made him uncomfortable?

But once they were outside, Deborah didn't have time to wonder about it any longer. Aaron turned to face her, his face earnest, his eyes grave. "Deborah, before I say what I am going to say, you need to understand something."

"All right," she said slowly.

"When I married Hava, her family, including her brother Joash, lived in Garis, a village about five miles east of Sepphoris." He was speaking to both of them. "Huldah's husband was still alive then, and they lived in the same village with Ruth and their other children. After we became part of their family, Huldah was wonderful to me, even though I was only a brother-in-law to her daughter." He looked at Deborah. "She became like the mother you and I lost."

"She seems like a wonderful woman," Deborah acknowledged.

"Then her husband died and, a short time after that, Ruth and Joash moved to Jericho. They took Huldah with them. When they wrote to tell us of her growing infirmity, we were much saddened, as you can imagine. But the first time we were here and I saw her, many years ago, it nearly broke my heart. She was suffering so."

Neither Deborah nor David spoke. Aaron had not asked for a response, and it was clear he was searching for words. Finally, he went on, more slowly and obviously struggling to express himself. "So when we learned that Jesus had healed her, I couldn't believe it. When she came up to Jerusalem for the Feast of Tabernacles, it was the Huldah I had once known. I wept for joy just to watch her."

Deborah had to swallow quickly. The emotion on her brother's face touched her deeply.

"Why does he have to be so maddening?" he suddenly exploded.

"Who?" Deborah exclaimed in dismay.

"Jesus! He performs an incredible miracle, one that blesses the life of an old woman who has endured far more than her share of sorrow. That's wonderful! But he does it on the Sabbath. He violates the very laws he claims to uphold."

"Aaron, I—"

He rode over her. "As you remember, I was there that day in Capernaum, in the synagogue, when Jesus healed the man with the withered hand. That was another marvelous demonstration of power. But again, it was on the Sabbath. There are six days in the week. Why can't he work his miracles on those days? He claims to honor the Law, but he criticizes the Pharisees, the very ones who most carefully guard and protect that Law. He condemns our practices, calling us hypocrites. He treats sinners as if they were righteous and holy saints. He has, this very night, shared the table of a publican." He spat out the term with complete disgust.

"You heard what Huldah said," Deborah said, fighting to keep the tartness out of her voice. "Why can you not rejoice in the fact that Zacchaeus had his heart changed today?"

Aaron hooted aloud. "His heart was changed?" he scoffed. "From what I was told, the man was so flabbergasted that Jesus would condescend to speak to one such as him that he blurted out that nonsense about giving half of his goods to the poor and recompensing those he'd wronged. Give him a week, and all of that will be forgotten, I can promise you that."

"Aaron," David cut in, "for someone who claims to be a man of faith, you are very cynical about human nature."

The Pharisee in Aaron flared, and he swung on his brother-in-law.

But as quickly as it came, it left again. He waved a hand. "I didn't come to debate or argue with you, David. Nor you, Deborah."

"Why did you come?" Deborah asked. "You said it was a matter of some urgency."

"It is," he nodded, reaching up to pull at his beard. He paused, again apparently searching for words. "Every time I look at Huldah, I realize that our family owes Jesus a great debt. Whether I agree with him or not, whether he drives me to exasperation every time I see him or not, that doesn't change."

"Go on," Deborah said.

"You have to tell Jesus not to come up to Jerusalem for Passover," he said.

Deborah's eyes widened.

"He's in great danger," Aaron went on, lowering his voice and looking around. "I run the risk of being banned from the council for telling you all of this, but the Sanhedrin is determined to arrest Jesus and try him. They are in an uproar. Even Azariah says he's never seen them so determined."

"What do they plan to do?" That was from David, who was very grave.

"I'm not sure," Aaron answered. He shook his head. "I'm not sure they are sure. But Caiaphas and Mordechai and the other Sadducees are livid. They're afraid that if there is another demonstration like the one on the Temple Mount during *Sukkot,* the Romans will move in again. And this time it won't just be against the Galileans."

"This is insane," David said. "Jesus is not fomenting rebellion. Just the opposite is true."

"Like I said, David, I didn't come to debate this with you. I'm not saying what is right or wrong. I am just telling you what is. Hava and I owe Jesus that much."

Deborah reached out and touched her brother's arm. "Aaron, will you come and listen to Jesus? Stay with us when we get to Jerusalem.

Watch him for yourself." As Aaron started squirming, she knew she had lost. "Just find out for yourself," she pleaded. When he didn't answer, she said, "We will tell Jesus what you have told us. Thank you, Aaron."

"It probably won't make any difference," David said.

Aaron swung on him. "Well, tell him!" he cried. "Tell him what I said. This isn't just talk, David. If he comes to Jerusalem, they're going to kill him. Not *try* to kill him. They *will* kill him! Make him understand that."

Deborah felt a great sense of desolation. "I think he already does."

Aaron looked furtively around once more. "This is all I can do," he said mournfully. "We owe him that much." With that he went back in the house, leaving them to look at each other in wonder and concern.

III

NORTH OF JERICHO

18–19 MARCH, A.D. 33

By the time they reached the house of Zacchaeus, Jesus and the others were gone. Deborah and David hurried on, arriving in the camp and seeking out Peter immediately. They reported what Aaron had said and asked what they could do. Peter said he would share the report with Jesus, but it was obvious he was not very hopeful it would make a difference.

The next morning, shortly after arising, Peter came to where they were camped with the family. Deborah was up in an instant. "What did he say?" she asked.

Peter looked very tired. "He said he would like you to convey to your brother his appreciation for his concern and the risk he took in sending word to us."

"That's all?" Livia cried. "Is he going to change his mind about going up for Passover?"

Peter shook his head slowly. "I doubt it." Then he brightened a little. "But he is talking about staying on in Jericho for a time. There is much work to be done here, and Jesus has said nothing more about going up to Jerusalem."

David wasn't quite so optimistic. "Passover is still two weeks away. And we're just a day away from Jerusalem."

"I know," he sighed. "But at least every day we're here is a day he's not there."

With that he again expressed his thanks and returned to his own camp.

About half an hour later, as the camp was starting their cooking fires, a cart rolled into camp; it was pulled by two bullocks and driven by a man and his son. Two other sons followed behind—one led four goats on a tether, and the other drove three yearling sheep before him. It was a gift for Jesus from the house of Zacchaeus, the man explained.

It was amazing. The goats would provide milk, butter, and cheese for as long as they stayed in Jericho. The sheep would provide fresh meat. In the cart was enough food to meet the camp's needs for the next several days. There were more than two dozen large round loaves of bread, several bricks of cheese, crate after crate of the latest crop of dates, dried figs, and jars of honey. Eight live chickens squawked from pens. Two boxes filled with straw protected several dozen eggs. There were boxes of dried apples and a cask of olives. Half a dozen smaller sacks contained various spices: salt, cummin, anise, cassia or cinnamon, dried berries from the bay tree, and coriander seeds. In the front of the cart were two large jars of wine and a smaller jar of fresh olive oil. And just in case something had been forgotten—an unlikely possibility—there was a small pouch filled with gold coins.

The camp watched in amazement as the man and his sons unloaded the cart and then left the way they had come. The travelers had planned to have a breakfast of hard bread, olives, and water from the nearby spring, but now they were going to have a veritable feast. The gifts put the entire camp in a festive mood. This only lifted higher when Jesus announced that they would be staying at least two more days. That meant no folding up of tents, no packing of bedding, no spending a hot, dusty day on the move again.

Immediately several men set about digging a small pit. It would be filled with hot coals and a spit erected over it. The population of sheep in the camp dropped from three to two within an hour after the man and his sons left. Two hours later, the skinned and washed carcass was turning slowly over the coals. By sundown it would be dripping juices and filling the air with the most delicious of aromas. It would be their first fresh meat since leaving Capernaum.

It was decided that even though Jesus would go into Jericho with the Twelve, most of the group would stay behind. The food needed to be distributed and cared for. And, if they were staying in the same camp for a couple of days, there were things that needed to be tended to, things that couldn't be done while they were on the move: fixing harnessing, mending blankets, doing laundry at the Springs of Elisha.

As Peter, Thomas, Bartholomew, and Andrew were putting a few things in the bags they carried slung over their shoulders, a rider on horseback appeared, and for a time it looked as if all of their plans might change.

The man pulled his horse to a halt in a spray of dust and pebbles and flung himself down. "Master," he cried, running directly up to Jesus. Jesus had been speaking quietly to Zebedee, his wife, and their two sons, James and John. He immediately got to his feet and turned to face the man.

"You are Micah of Bethany, neighbor to Martha, Mary, and their brother, Lazarus."

"Aye, Lord," the man said between breaths, grateful that he had been recognized. "I bring a message from them."

"You came here from Bethany alone?" Andrew asked, moving to stand beside Jesus.

The man nodded.

There were murmurs at that. The road from Jerusalem to Jericho—Bethany was just on the eastern outskirts of the larger city—was only about sixteen or seventeen Roman miles, but it was one of the most dangerous roads in all of the province. Dropping steeply from the heights of Jerusalem to the shores of the Dead Sea, the road was narrow and dangerous. It wound its way through narrow canyons, skirting precipitous cliffs. It was also infamous for another kind of danger. It was infested with thieves and robbers, and anyone traveling in groups of less than ten risked being set upon. This very stretch of highway had been the setting for the parable of the good Samaritan that Jesus had given some time before.

"The matter is urgent, Master," Micah said. "Lazarus, whom you love, is very ill."

Jesus straightened slowly.

"Yea, Lord. Both Martha and Mary are very concerned. Their brother has a raging fever, and it has left him completely without strength. He has been confined to his bed for several days. He grows weaker with every hour."

He paused, but Jesus said nothing. He was looking away to the southwest, in the direction of Jerusalem. There was a distant look in his eyes.

"Word had come to us that you were in Jericho. Martha asks if you will come as quickly as possible."

"Thank you, Micah," Jesus said. "Return to our dear friends and tell them all will be well. I shall come."

The man's head bobbed, and he started to turn toward his horse again. Jesus stepped to where Peter and the others had been working and picked up one of the sacks of food they were preparing. "Take this, and ride with care."

"Thank you, Master. They will be greatly relieved."

He hung the sack over the saddle horn, then swung up. In a moment he was gone, leaving only a thin trail of dust behind him. No one moved. Every eye was on Jesus. What would they do with the sheep now roasting over the fire? What about the women who had already left for the springs with their clothing to wash?

To everyone's surprise, however, Jesus did not begin giving orders. Nor did he turn to the Twelve to give them direction. He sat back down again, perfectly calm, and motioned for Peter and the other three to finish what they had been doing. "We shouldn't need a lot," he called out to his chief apostle. "We shall return in time to eat supper here."

Peter came slowly forward. "But Lord . . . ?"

Jesus looked up at the burly fisherman who stood before him.

"Are we not leaving to go to Lazarus's side?"

Jesus shook his head. "This sickness is not unto death."

Peter's eyebrows lifted in surprise.

Jesus shook his head again. "It is for the glory of God, that the Son of God might be glorified."

Peter just stood there, not sure what that meant. He glanced quickly at Andrew, who gave him a puzzled shrug. Then he asked, "So you do not wish to leave for Bethany immediately?"

Jesus cocked his head and gazed at him steadily for a long moment. Peter immediately grew flustered and started to back away. "Yes, Master, I understand. The food for today is almost ready." He swung around to the others. "That's enough," he called. "The Master is ready to go into Jericho."

IV

21 MARCH, A.D. 33

Miriam was really quite surprised that nothing more was said of Lazarus—not that day, nor the next. On the morning of the third day, there was still no talk of the sick man. Miriam knew full well how much Jesus loved this family. Almost always when he went to Jerusalem, he would stay at the home of Martha and her younger sister and brother.

If Miriam had been Micah, the neighbor sent to let Jesus know of the crisis, she would have gone back to Martha and told her that Jesus was on his way to Bethany that very day. That was what Jesus seemed to have told him. Yet here it was two full days later, and Jesus acted like he had forgotten all about the visit and his promise. She knew that wasn't the case. Jesus didn't forget things. Perhaps he knew, through his keen sense of discernment, that Lazarus had recovered. At that thought, she felt herself relax somewhat. That was the most logi-cal explanation for his lack of haste. Jesus had said the sickness was not unto death. If Lazarus was better, there was no need for haste.

As they gathered around the fire for yet another ample breakfast, thanks to Zacchaeus, the group was strangely quiet. Was this the day they would finally move on? Was Jesus going up to Jerusalem after all, or had the reports about the dangers there finally changed his mind? No one knew, but neither did anyone dare to ask him about it. They kept stealing surreptitious looks in his direction, dropping their eyes quickly if his head turned in their direction.

It was only when the women and older girls began cleaning up the meal that Jesus stood. He looked around, then stopped when his gaze reached Peter. "Let us go up to Jerusalem again," he said.

Several stiffened. Then one of them blurted out, "Master, the Jews tried to stone you the last time we were in Jerusalem, and you want to go there again?"

"Are there not twelve hours in a day?" Jesus asked calmly.

The disciples weren't quite sure what to make of that question and just stood there.

"If any man walk in the day, he will not stumble, because he sees the light of the world. But if he walks in the night, he will stumble, because there is no light." Jesus smiled briefly, looking around at the disciples. "Our friend Lazarus sleeps," he said. "I go to him that I may awake him from his sleep."

Matthew stepped forward, clearly relieved. "If he sleeps, then it shall be well with him."

Jesus turned to the publican, who was one of the older men of the Twelve. "Lazarus is dead," he said bluntly.

Matthew rocked back as the shock hit him and all who had heard what Jesus said.

"Dead?" Peter echoed.

Jesus nodded. "I am glad for your sakes that I was not there. This way you may believe."

Peter did not answer. No one else spoke either. Miriam felt a sense of horror. So Lazarus had not gotten better? He was dead?

Jesus spoke to Peter again. "But even though he is dead, let us go to him nevertheless."

Jesus waited for a moment, but when no one said anything more, he left the group and moved to where his bedroll was laid out on the ground. He knelt down and began to fold his blankets.

CHAPTER NOTES

It is John who records the sending of a messenger from Martha's household with the report that her brother, Lazarus, was seriously ill (John 11:3). The details of the Savior's lingering for two more days, including his clear declaration that Lazarus was dead, are all part of John's account (John 11:6–16).

CHAPTER 20

I

ON THE ROAD TO BETHANY
21–22 MARCH, A.D. 33

Even after making the shocking declaration that Lazarus had died, Jesus seemed in no great hurry to leave. Though she said nothing to anyone in the family, Livia was greatly disturbed. She knew, with a pain that was still keen and fresh, what it meant to lose a loved one. And while nothing could make that pain go away, she had also learned what it meant to have those you loved and trusted come forward and put their arms around you. It didn't bring the lost one back, but sharing grief lessened grief. To have people lend their strength when there was none left inside of her had become an important part of her healing process. Livia ached for Martha and Mary. True, Lazarus was not a husband, but she knew how she would feel if it had been Drusus who had died. They needed Jesus now. They needed the comfort and assurance that only he could bring to them. And yet he tarried.

It took a good part of the morning to pack up the camp and get started. As they made their way through Jericho, once again the throngs pressed in, and it took them another two or three hours to complete their journey through the city.

By the time they were out of the city, the sun was halfway down in its western descent. Peter recommended that they camp in the lowlands for the night rather than travel the dangerous narrow canyons in the dark, risking serious falls or attack from bandits. Livia overheard Peter's suggestion and fully expected Jesus to say no, that they had to make haste now that Lazarus was dead. But he didn't. He accepted Peter's suggestion with a nod of his head, and they bedded down less than a mile from where the road began its climb to Jerusalem.

Again, come morning, Jesus showed no signs of urgency. They ate a leisurely breakfast, and by the time they rolled up their beds and started off again, the sun was high. Livia was more and more saddened by the pace of the journey, and she began to withdraw into herself. She felt guilty for harboring feelings critical of Jesus' decisions, and yet she could not understand why he couldn't sense the needs of those two grieving sisters.

But it was more than just that. There were other troubling things about this situation. Why had Jesus said Lazarus was only sleeping if he knew he was dying? True, it was common to refer to death as "sleeping in the grave," but the way Jesus had said it had implied that Lazarus was resting because of the sickness. And what of his comment about this being for God's glory? What did that mean? Especially now that Lazarus was dead. Did a man's death bring glory to God? That thought really stabbed at her heart. She still struggled with one simple but devastating word that rose again and again in her mind. *Why?* Was Yehuda's death in the inner temple courts God's will or just the blind and terrible finger of fate? He was a good man. He honored her choice to follow Jesus. Why hadn't God intervened to save her husband? *Why? Why? Why?*

The persisting relaxed pace brought the questions surging back with renewed vigor. Livia didn't know exactly how Jesus knew Lazarus was dead, but she did not doubt that he spoke the truth. Did he feel it was too late, eliminating the need for haste? Or was he reluctant to face those who grieved, because of his great love for the family? Speaking of grieving, it seemed odd to her that Jesus showed no signs of grief himself. He was mostly quiet as they marched along, speaking only occasionally to those walking beside him, but he did not seem downcast or morose. He was just pensive, far away in his thoughts.

Livia said none of this to Miriam, or to Simeon and his family. They all had concerns of their own. And the men of the company were focused on another, more serious problem. What was going to happen when the Sanhedrin found out Jesus was coming? How could they make sure Jesus was protected without having him feel they were interfering with his ministry?

She sighed deeply and trudged on, her head down. Perhaps her feelings were heightened because she was tired. What had once been a strenuous but achievable journey was much complicated by the child she carried inside her. She knew that she tired more quickly than before, which was true emotionally as well as physically. There was only one thing to do with all of this, she decided, and that was to push it out of her mind and wait to see what happened. Her lips pulled down. *As if it were that simple.*

II

BETHANY

23 MARCH, A.D. 33

Bethany was on the eastern slopes of the Mount of Olives. It was roughly a two-mile walk from there to the Temple Mount in

Jerusalem—a steep climb to the top of the Mount of Olives, and then a steeper descent to the Kidron Valley, then up again into the city.

Jerusalem was at the top of the hill country of Judea. The higher elevations tended to scrub the moisture from the clouds coming off the Mediterranean Sea, leaving little for the deserts that lay beyond. The Mount of Olives was the easternmost and highest of the ridges, and its eastern slopes took the last of the rains. The village of Bethany was a fertile splash of green on the edge of a vast expanse of browns and greys. Flat-roofed stone houses were scattered about on the hillside, almost hidden by small groves of fig and olive trees. Here and there were neat rows of lighter green, signifying grape vineyards just coming fully into leaf.

By the time Jesus and his followers approached the outskirts of the village, it was nearing the ninth hour of the day. The afternoon sun was hot and shining directly into their eyes. Simeon and Miriam were walking beside Livia, somehow seeming to sense her inner turmoil, though so far they had not spoken of it. She knew that Simeon kept glancing at her out of the corner of his eye, and she was afraid that he would either ask her what was on her mind or how she was doing physically. She didn't feel like answering either question.

Just then they heard a shout up ahead of them, and their heads lifted. The first of the villagers, mostly young boys and girls, were coming headlong down the hill towards them, waving their hands and shouting joyfully.

Here we go, Livia thought. *Now we shall see.*

The shouts brought others out too. People were streaming into the main road. In a village the size of Bethany, word spread quickly, leaping from rooftop to rooftop, through the markets, over the stone fences that marked people's property. By the time the travelers actually reached the village, Jesus was surrounded again. He greeted the children with smiles and extended hands, ruffling hair, lifting one of the younger ones into his arms. As the first adult reached them, a man in his early forties, Peter stepped forward quickly. "What news of Lazarus?" he asked.

The man's expression changed from joy to sorrow. "Ah, a tragedy. Poor Martha and Mary."

"Is he dead then?" Peter persisted.

Jesus shot him a look, but the man didn't notice. "Aye," came the reply. "He's been in the tomb four days now."

All around there was a stunned silence. *Four days!*

Livia calculated quickly. They had been two full days on the road, and they had lingered two full days in Jericho after the messenger had come with news of Lazarus.

Livia turned to see if Jesus had heard. He had. He was watching Peter and the man with an expression that was difficult to read.

"Deborah!"

Simeon turned in surprise. Coming down the hill, skirts clutched in one hand, was Simeon's Uncle Aaron. Leah, Deborah, and David moved up beside Simeon and Miriam. Deborah called out and began to wave.

Livia knew she ought to join them, to extend her greetings too, but she didn't feel like it.

Aaron slowed his pace at the sight of Jesus. He was puffing hard, and perspiration formed a sheen on his forehead. Jesus nodded as Aaron started to move around him to get to his sister. "*Shalom*, Aaron of Sepphoris."

Startled, Aaron nodded back. "*Shalom*, Jesus of Nazareth."

"Deborah told me of your message," Jesus said. "I thank you for your concern, and for taking the trouble to come to Jericho."

Aaron wiped his brow with his sleeve, then blurted out, "Things haven't changed, Jesus. There is danger waiting in Jerusalem."

"Thank you for the warning." Then the crowd, which was swelling with every passing moment, moved between them.

Aaron went to his sister. "We need to talk," he said bluntly.

David motioned them to the side of the road away from where Jesus was standing. They would not be alone, but they would be apart from the heaviest concentration of people. The entire family moved over with Aaron except for Livia, though she was close enough to hear their conversation.

"Did you stress to Jesus how serious things are in the Great Council?" Aaron demanded.

"We did," Deborah replied.

He half turned. "Then why—"

"Jesus does what he feels he has to do," Simeon came in. "He knows of the danger, but that doesn't alter what he feels he needs to do."

"Right now, he's come because of Lazarus," Deborah explained.

"Yes, we heard."

"We?" Miriam echoed.

"The Sanhedrin. There are two of us from the council in the village. We've been here since late yesterday."

"To do what?" Deborah asked sharply.

"To learn of his whereabouts, mostly." He looked around quickly, suddenly nervous. "To report back to the council." His hand shot out, and he gripped Deborah's arm. "If Jesus comes to Jerusalem for Passover," he said urgently, "you have to stay away from him. If trouble breaks out, it could engulf those around him."

Deborah was shaking her head. "Aaron, we can't do that. I—"

Just then there was a change in the sound of the crowd. A cry went up. They all turned to see what it was. A small group was coming down the hill at a swift walk. In the lead was a woman.

"It's Martha!" Leah exclaimed.

Aaron barely glanced in that direction. "I have to get back to my associate," he hissed. "Please, Deborah! If he does go to Jerusalem, stay clear of him. Especially when he's on the Temple Mount."

Before she could answer, he whirled and started back up the hill, pushing his way through the people until he disappeared.

David and his family moved back over to Jesus so they could watch the interchange that was about to take place. Martha was close enough that they could see that her eyes were swollen and her cheeks tear stained. The villagers fell back to make a path for her, and a hush quickly fell over those assembled.

Jesus watched the oncoming woman. When she reached him, his eyes softened, and he stretched out both hands to her.

A sob wrenched from her throat as she took his hands. "Oh, Lord," she cried, "if you had been here, my brother would not have died."

Several looked surprised at that. Was Martha criticizing Jesus for not coming sooner? Livia didn't think so. It was a cry torn from a grief-stricken heart, and at the same time an affirmation of her faith in the Master.

As if to prove Livia's conclusion, Martha added, "But I know, that even now, whatsoever you will ask of God, God will give it to thee."

"Where is Mary?"

"When I heard that you were coming, I came to meet you," Martha answered, "but Mary remained at the house." She swallowed quickly. "She misses him so," she whispered. "She still grieves deeply."

Jesus squeezed her hands, deeply solemn. "Your brother Lazarus shall rise again, Martha."

She sniffed back tears, fighting for composure. "Yea, Lord, I know that he shall rise again in the resurrection at the last day."

Jesus leaned forward slightly, peering into her eyes. "I am the resurrection and the life. He that believes in me, though he were dead, yet shall he live. And whosoever lives and believes in me shall never die." He let those words sink in, then asked, "Can you believe this?"

Martha straightened, her shoulders pulling back. She wiped quickly at the tears. "Yea, Lord. I believe that thou art the Christ, the Son of God, who should come into the world."

Livia felt a surge of shame. Was that how she would have answered that query? In her grieving, had she forgotten for the moment who Jesus was and, more importantly, *what* he was?

Jesus looked as if he were close to tears himself. He squeezed Martha's hands again, then stepped back. "Tell Mary we are coming."

"Thank you, Lord." And without another word, Martha turned and hurried back up the hill to take word to her sister.

III

Though Mary was in a back room reclining on her bed, at the sound of the front door opening and closing, she sat up. She could hear her sister's footsteps on the stone floor and got to her feet, pushing back her hair and wiping at her eyes.

A moment later, Martha appeared at the door. "Is he . . . ?" Mary started, but she couldn't finish.

Martha nodded joyfully. "Yes. The Master is come. And he calls for you, Mary."

"Where?"

"He has just entered the village. Come quickly. We must go to him."

When Martha and Mary passed through the courtyard of their home a few moments later, it was filled with people. More were coming all the time. Word had spread that Jesus had come to see the two sisters. People were talking in low tones to each other. The sight of the two grieving sisters had tempered the mood of the crowd. Martha's hasty departure and then return a few minutes before had them watching intently. She had pushed past them without an explanation.

Now, as the two sisters did the same again, pushing through the crowd without answering their questions, the somber mood deepened. "They go to the tomb," one woman whispered.

"That is good," said another. "Mary needs to let her grief come out."

"Let us go with them," a man suggested, "so that we may comfort them."

To Martha's surprise, Jesus was still in roughly the same place where she had met him earlier. The crowd, now swelled to well over a hundred, pressed in around him, impeding his progress. But when the people saw Mary and Martha approaching, they moved back to make way, falling silent so they could overhear.

When they were just a few feet away from Jesus, Martha stopped, motioning her sister to go forward.

Mary was weeping openly at the sight of Jesus. She came forward slowly, then dropped to her knees before him. Her whole body was trembling. Finally she looked up. Two glistening streaks ran down her cheeks. Though she had no way of knowing what Martha had said when she met Jesus, Mary used exactly the same words as her sister had done: "Lord, if you had been here, my brother would not have not died."

All around, the sound of weeping could now be heard. The sight of these two beloved sisters—so honored and revered in the village—stricken with grief, was too much for others, too. The women of the village and the women who had journeyed with Jesus wept together.

Jesus looked down on Mary for a moment, then gently lifted her up. He looked around at the crowd. Several men looked as if they were on the verge of tears as well. He started to say something, but the words choked in his throat. He groaned, and it was a sound of such pain, such anguish, that the women began to weep more copiously.

"Where have you laid him?" Jesus finally asked, speaking to Mary and Martha.

Martha half turned and pointed up the hill. "Lord, come and see," she managed.

As Jesus turned, Livia was astonished to see that his cheeks were wet too. Jesus was weeping, something she had never before seen. And that opened the wells deep within Livia's heart. It had been months since she had been able to cry. She had decided that tears did nothing for her but leave her weak and exhausted. But she could not have stopped them now if she had wished to.

Jesus motioned for the two sisters to lead out and take him to the grave site.

Livia almost bumped into Miriam as she turned to follow. Miriam looked at her and wept all the more. "Oh, Livia," she said softly, "oh, how Jesus loved Lazarus."

IV

There were two common forms of burial prevalent among the Jews. Which form was used depended largely on the economic class of the individual who had died. The poor were buried in graves, usually in small cemeteries just outside their villages. For families with greater means, tombs were used as the final resting place. Some tombs were made out of natural caves; others were carved into the numerous out-croppings of soft limestone common to Judea. Sometimes these tombs were large enough to accommodate several family members; sometimes they were just big enough to hold one body. Once burial was complete, the tomb was sealed, generally with a large, flat stone. A stone track was often carved at the base of the opening. In these cases, the flat stone was shaped like a wheel and, once placed in the track, could be rolled back and forth to open or shut the tomb. This was the case with the tomb of Lazarus. The tomb site was near the road and not far above where Mary and Martha lived.

Preparation of the body was essentially the same for all the dead, except that the upper classes used expensive ointments and perfumes as part of the preparation. The body was laid out on a table, with the hands to the side. The dead, except for the very poorest, were then anointed with various spices and ointments. Substantial sums of money were spent by the wealthy on these preparations. Next, a cloth or napkin was laid over the face. Then the entire body was wrapped— or more aptly, bound—by a long, wide strip of linen. Generally, this took at least two people, for one had to lift various portions of the body enough for the linen to be passed underneath. The end result was much like the mummification of the Pharaohs in Egypt, though not nearly so elaborate.

Occasionally, the body was then placed in a simple wooden coffin and buried in a grave. But in a land where wood was scarce and there-fore expensive, the most common practice was to use a bier to trans-port the body to the place of burial. The bier was nothing more than a wooden pallet with handles on its four corners, much like a litter. The body, bound tightly in its linen wrappings, would be placed on the bier, then lifted by four men who were either family members or close friends, and taken off to be buried.

At the first word of someone's passing, the family or closest neigh-bors began the death wail. A shrill, ear-piercing shriek, it was the com-munity's way of spreading the word that someone had died. This was also accompanied by a mournful wailing. Common expressions in the lamentation included such phrases as, "Alas, my brother!" or "O my son, my son!" These were repeated over and over in a singsong fash-ion. Some individuals perfected this lament to the point of an art and became professional mourners. Even poor families often hired these people to mourn the loss of a loved one until the body was finally buried.

All these customs were four days in the past in the case of Lazarus. The bier had long since been removed. The mourners were no longer present to fill their role. Instead, there was a quiet, reverential hush from the villagers as Jesus and those with him followed Mary and Martha to the tomb site. Jesus wanted to see where his friend was laid, and the people wanted to honor his time to grieve.

The tomb was set back from the road half a dozen paces. Judging from the size of the sealing stone, the opening into the final resting place was not much taller than Livia or Miriam. Small clay pots filled with flowers and small boughs of evergreens lined the ground on both sides of the stone.

Martha stopped directly in front of the tomb. She turned to Jesus. A strangled sob shook her body, and she averted her face. "That is where my brother was laid," she whispered hoarsely. Mary moved up beside her, and again both women began to weep.

Jesus took several steps forward, looking carefully at the tomb and its sealing stone. Then he turned back. "Martha?"

She fought her emotions for a moment, then looked at Jesus. "Yes, Lord?"

"Have them take away the stone."

Martha stiffened. The reaction from the crowd was a collective gasp. Mary's face had a look of horror. Martha's went completely pale. "But, Lord," she cried, "he has been dead four days."

Jesus said nothing, just waited, as if what she had said was not in any way relevant to his request.

She wiped at her eyes with the sleeve of her dress. "Lord, by this time he will have started to stink."

When Jesus still said nothing, just watched her steadily, she said again, "It has been four days."

Jesus moved to the two women. He reached out and took Martha by both shoulders. "Did I not say unto you," he said in a low, but clear, voice, "that if you would believe, you should see the glory of God?"

For what seemed like an eternity, Martha stared at him. Then, finally, her head moved up and down. "Yea, Lord."

Jesus stepped back, turning toward the tomb again. The people had gone utterly silent, shock registering on their faces. This was unthinkable. Under the Mosaic Law, to come in contact with the dead was to bring upon oneself spiritual contamination. The Pharisees held that even being this close to a burial site was enough to require extensive ablution. And now he wanted to open the tomb?

Livia felt someone at her side and turned to see that Leah had joined her. They looked at each other, dismay and consternation clearly written on their faces. Did Jesus want to actually see the body so that he would know for himself that Lazarus was truly dead? How bizarre! Something was terribly wrong here.

And then Livia heard Deborah give a low cry. She turned and saw why. On the opposite edge of the crowd, Aaron was standing with another man. There was a curious mixture of revulsion, horror, and wonder on his face. He was not looking in their direction and did not see them.

Then, before Livia could process what Aaron must be thinking, she saw Martha step back from Jesus' grasp. Still looking bewildered and confused, Martha turned to the nearest man. Livia saw that it was Micah, the neighbor who had brought word of Lazarus's illness to Jericho. Martha motioned for him to roll back the sealing stone.

For a moment, Micah just gaped at her.

"Do it," she commanded. "Do as Jesus says."

"No, Martha!" The cry came from someone in the crowd. "Don't do this."

"Open it!" she commanded, more firmly. Beside her, Mary was nodding.

Micah jumped forward until he stood directly in front of the round stone. He reached up, took the top of it with both hands, and leaned into it. It didn't budge. Two other men moved forward to join him.

They threw their shoulders against the stone's edge. There was the soft rumble of stone on stone, and the seal slowly began to roll. In a moment, it was fully moved to one side, revealing the blackness of the tomb's interior.

The entrance was low and narrow, even smaller than Livia had guessed. It was also narrow enough that a full-grown man would have to turn his body slightly sideways to enter.

Micah stepped away, looking to Martha for further instructions. She motioned him back. Jesus nodded at Martha. As Livia watched what passed between them, she sensed that Jesus was acknowledging that her obedience had taken great faith in him and that he was grateful for her trust. Then he looked at Mary, smiled briefly, letting her know it was all right. Finally, with slow deliberation, he walked to the tomb's entrance. He didn't go in but stopped about three paces back from the opening.

For several seconds, he stood there; then slowly his head tipped back, and he looked heavenward. "Father," he said in a voice firm enough for all around to hear him clearly, "I thank thee that thou hast heard me." He paused. "I know that thou hearest me always. But I say this because of the people who stand by here. I say it that they may believe that thou hast sent me."

And then his voice shouted out so sharply that everyone jumped. "Lazarus! Come forth!"

There was not a sound. Every eye was locked on that dark opening. No one breathed. Without realizing it, Livia had grabbed Leah's arm, her fingers digging into the flesh. Leah was barely aware of it. Miriam moved closer to Simeon. Deborah had taken David's hand.

For a long, tense moment, nothing happened. The sun was low in the sky and at a vertical angle to the tomb's opening, so that it illuminated nothing inside. And then there was a low, almost imperceptible whisper of sound from inside the tomb. Livia drew in her breath sharply. Chills coursed through her body. For a moment, she thought her knees were going to buckle, and she clung to Leah desperately.

The gasps of astonishment were like a series of soft explosions all around them. There was movement in the darkness. Something white and tall was there, just inside the tomb's opening. And then, like a mighty blast of wind had struck them, the half circle of watchers staggered backwards. A figure appeared in the opening, paused for a moment, then shuffled out into the bright sunlight. The figure was totally wrapped in white and without specific form. The arms were bound tightly to its side. The legs and feet could only move a few inches at a time. The face was wrapped as well, but the contours of nose, mouth, and chin were clearly evident.

Somewhere to their left, a woman gave a low cry and sank to the ground. Another exclamation was cut off as abruptly as it had started. Behind them someone began to weep in sheer terror. Livia felt suddenly dizzy herself. Her eyes stared but could not comprehend. There before them, standing erect and tall in the full light of day, was a dead man, bound hand and foot with grave clothes. But he was not dead! He was alive. Moving. Waiting for someone to help him.

Seemingly unaware of the reaction around him, Jesus turned to the men who had rolled back the stone. Their faces were white as they stared at the figure before them. "Loose him," Jesus said quietly, "and let him go."

V

Deborah and David found Aaron seated on a rock wall about fifty paces from the tomb. There were people all around him, but he was unaware of them. His head was in his hands, and he was staring at the ground. Jesus was gone, though no one seemed to see him leave. Once

Lazarus had been freed, the people watched his tender reunion with two women stunned and breathless with joy. A short time later the sisters had left to take Lazarus back to his home. Only the Twelve went with them.

Not many others had left, though it had been several minutes since Jesus had disappeared. They stood in small clusters, talking quietly. Some, like Aaron, were by themselves, still trying to comprehend what they had just witnessed. There was no sign of the other man who had come with Aaron to learn more of Jesus' whereabouts.

"Aaron?"

For a moment he didn't move; then his head slowly raised.

Deborah sat down beside him. "Are you all right?"

He stared at her as if she were a stranger. He lifted a hand and rubbed at his eyes. "Did you . . . ?" he began, but then shook his head. His eyes were haunted. His mouth worked silently in the depths of his beard.

David squatted down directly in front of him. "Yes, Aaron, we were here. We saw what you saw." And then, very gently, he asked, "Now what say you about this man we call the Christ? Is he the Messiah or no?"

Finally, Aaron's eyes registered on David. For a moment, David wasn't sure if he was going to bolt and run or start to weep. After a long moment, Aaron slowly shook his head. "I can deny it no longer," he whispered. He reached up and began to rub at his eyes. "Four days," he said, speaking to himself. "*Four days!*"

Deborah hesitated for a moment, debating whether she should say what she felt had to be said. He was still so dazed. But then she couldn't hold back. "He is more than just the Messiah," she said softly. "He is the Son of God, Aaron."

He turned to face her. "I don't understand. We are all the sons of God."

"No, Aaron. He is literally the Son of God. Mary is his mother, but

God is his Father. Remember what Isaiah said? 'A virgin shall conceive and bear a son, and they shall call his name Immanuel.'" She paused for a moment, then with deep reverence added, "You know as well as I do what that name means: God is with us."

She stopped, because Aaron's eyes were suddenly filled with tears. "What?" she asked.

"Yes," he said in wonder. "That would explain it. The Son of God. That would explain it all."

Deborah gave a low cry and threw her arms around him. A cry of joy and pain rose up from deep within him as he embraced her. "Oh, Deborah," he finally said in a strangled voice. "What shall I do now?"

VI

Beneath a large pomegranate tree, Livia also sat alone. She stared at the ground, seeing nothing.

"Livia?"

She didn't raise her head as Miriam sat down beside her.

"Are you all right?"

She didn't answer. Couldn't answer. How could she put into words what was in her heart at that moment?

"It's Yehuda, isn't it," Miriam declared.

Finally Livia's head came up. "If Jesus had been on the Temple Mount that day, he . . ." Her lips started to tremble, and she had to look away again.

Miriam sat down beside her and put an arm around her. "Yehuda still lives, Livia. You know that. You will see him again in the resurrection."

"I need him now," she said, her voice so low Miriam could barely hear her.

"I know, I know. But you heard what Jesus said. He is the resurrection and the life. If we but believe in him, then we all shall live again. You do believe that, don't you?"

There was no answer for a long time, and Miriam felt herself go cold. "Livia, you have to believe. Think of what we just saw. Jesus raised a man from the tomb. He raised the dead, Livia! Think about it! Doesn't that fill you with hope?"

She shook her head. "I'm so tired, Miriam. I miss him so."

"As you should."

"I don't know what to believe anymore. All I know is that if Jesus could have been there that day, Yehuda would still be alive. Or even if Jesus had called Yehuda forth from the dead four days later!" Then she forced a smile. It was thin and held no cheer of any kind. "I'll be all right. Go be with your family. I'll just wait here."

"You have to believe, Livia," Miriam cried. "You have to believe that Jesus can make everything right."

"Oh, but I do, Miriam. You see, that is my problem. If he can, as I know he can, then why didn't he do it for me as he did for Mary and Martha?"

CHAPTER NOTES

The story of the raising of Lazarus, one of the most remarkable evidences of Jesus' power, is recorded in John's Gospel (John 11:1–45).

The burial customs and practices associated with death are taken from numerous scriptural references. Many of these customs can still be seen among the peoples of the Middle East today (see Wight, pp. 142–46).

CHAPTER 21

LAWS ARE LIKE SPIDERS' WEBS: IF SOME POOR WEAK
CREATURE COME UP AGAINST THEM, IT IS CAUGHT; BUT A
BIGGER ONE CAN BREAK THROUGH AND GET AWAY.

—*Solon, in Diogenes Laertius*, Lives of the Eminent Philosophers, *1:58*

I

JERUSALEM, IN THE CHAMBERS OF THE
SANHEDRIN ON THE TEMPLE MOUNT
23 MARCH, A.D. 33

Mordechai ben Uzziel shot to his feet. "Silence!" he roared.

The tumult of voices was cut off as though the entire assembly had been struck dumb. Those who were standing moved quickly to their seats. Every eye turned to Mordechai as he leaned forward, hands on the table where the presidency of the Great Council sat. Caiaphas, the current sitting high priest, sat beside him. On the other side of Caiaphas sat Azariah, chief of the Pharisees and the other member of the presidency of the council.

"Enough of this babble," Mordechai said angrily. "We are in crisis, and you wring your hands like a child who has broken a toy. Sit down and speak only when you have something to say."

He turned and glared at Azariah, daring him to contradict. But for once, Azariah was of the same mind. He was as shaken by events as Mordechai. For once, they stood united.

Mordechai lowered his voice, but only slightly. "All right, that's better. We have heard the report now. No good will come of trying to explain it or make as if it did not happen. Perhaps this is some elaborate hoax foisted upon us by the followers of Jesus. They could have slipped this Lazarus into the tomb earlier in the day. Who actually knows for sure that the body they carried on the bier several days before was actually him? It would be an easy thing to come at night and make a switch."

Several hands shot up, including those of Joseph of Arimathea, Nicodemus of the Pharisees, and Aaron of Sepphoris, the newest member of the council. Mordechai ignored them. "I don't know what happened, and *I don't care!* The issue at hand is not Lazarus. The issue is Jesus."

"We would be heard," Joseph called out, getting to his feet. "Let us speak." He was the most supportive voice on the council for the preacher from Nazareth, and he obviously had deep feelings.

"*No!* I am not finished."

The wealthy merchant sat back down, his face dark with anger.

"What are we going to do?" Mordechai went on. "The people are completely dazzled by these so-called miracles Jesus keeps working. They are flocking to him by the thousands. And we cannot forget that this man is a Galilean. The Galilee has long been the seedbed for revolt. The Romans know that and are already expressing concern. If *we* don't intervene, we'll lose the entire population to him. And that will surely bring the Romans down upon our heads!"

"They'll disband this council, for one thing," Azariah exclaimed.

"Yes, and much more," Mordechai said. "Rome will not—cannot!—tolerate another Zealot uprising. And this time it won't be just Pilate who comes against us. Not if Jesus has thousands of followers.

The legate of Syria will send every legion at his disposal. If that happens, we shall cease to exist as a nation."

Caiaphas got to his feet. He was almost ten years older than Mordechai. Through his office, which held tremendous prestige, he wielded considerable power, but sometimes he could be little more than a doddering old fool. Mordechai tensed a little as he deferred to him.

But this time, Caiaphas fully understood the gravity of the situation. "Brethren," he began, "on this council we seldom have to deal with matters of life and death. But when the very existence of our nation is at risk, we cannot shrink from our duty." His eyes swept around the half circle of men. "Even if it means someone has to die."

No one stirred. And no one wondered who he was talking about.

"If you think this is not a serious matter, you know nothing at all. We must take action. It is expedient that one man should die to save the people so that the whole nation does not perish."

That did it. Joseph and Nicodemus leaped to their feet, along with several others. Men were waving their hands wildly, shouting for recognition. Caiaphas sat back down again, and Mordechai leaned over and whispered something to him. Then Mordechai straightened, looking up and down the clamoring circle. He ignored those who were the moderates, especially those who would surely speak in favor of Jesus. Instead he pointed to Menachem, a fellow Sadducee and Mordechai's protégé and strongest ally in the Sanhedrin. "Menachem of Bethphage. You may speak."

Menachem made no effort to hide his fury. "Things have progressed beyond the point of debate. As our high priest has said, Jesus must die. It is the only way to save ourselves."

"Hear, hear!" Azariah cried out.

"Fortunately for us, Jesus knows he is in danger," Menachem continued. "We learned just this morning that he left Bethany at dawn.

Reportedly, he has gone into the wilderness of Judea where he will be safe from any attempts on our part to seize him."

The council responded with cries of dismay. This was news even to Caiaphas and Azariah. "Why do I say 'fortunately'?" Menachem went on smoothly. "Because this will give the council time to lay careful plans. Jesus will be back for Passover."

"How can you be sure?" another of the Sadducees called out.

"Because we know," he shot back. "His followers are trying to convince him to stay away, but he will not. He will be back."

"Menachem is right," Mordechai said. He was feeling smug, because Menachem had said only what Mordechai had carefully coached him to say. "We must plan carefully. The people are against us. We can't risk an uprising. We have to take the man by stealth, seize him when the crowds are not with him."

"The Romans do not allow us to put a man to death," another of Azariah's colleagues said, "even if we say he is worthy of death."

"This is true," Mordechai said grimly, "but there are ways around that obstacle. If we plan very carefully. We must find a way to take the man without starting a riot. And yet we must convince Pilate that he is a direct threat to the peace. This is our task. How can we accomplish this without creating greater problems for ourselves?"

"Objection!" It was Joseph of Arimathea. "Our law does not condemn a man without a trial."

"Oh," Mordechai sneered, "he shall have a trial."

"I wish my objection to be registered," Joseph persisted. "I demand a hearing from the council."

"The council's will has been made clear by our high priest. Anyone who cannot sustain our esteemed leader is excused from further deliberation. If you have no stomach for what must be done, then go!"

As one, five or six men stood up, Joseph and Nicodemus among them. So was Aaron, Mordechai noted. He started to turn to see if

Azariah was watching. After all, it was he who had nominated Aaron for the recent vacancy on the Great Council.

But Azariah was already on his feet. "President of the council," he shouted, "before these dissenters leave, I have another matter for us to deal with. It is the matter of Aaron of Sepphoris."

As Caiaphas waved at him to proceed, the departing men stopped. Aaron turned slowly, suspecting what was about to happen.

"I publicly declare before this council that Aaron of Sepphoris has turned against the very body on which he sits, that he has turned traitor and is an enemy of the council."

This was really not much of a surprise to anyone. As testimony was being given about the raising of Lazarus, Aaron had calmly declared his own witness to the reality of the miracle. But he had done more than that, even more than the sympathizers and moderate voices were doing. Azariah, shocked at the unexpected change in him, had blurted out, "You speak as if you believe he is the Messiah." Aaron had straightened slowly. "No," he said, "I don't believe. I know."

Caiaphas was pleased with Azariah's accusation of Aaron and spoke up sharply. "Bring him forward and let us hear the charges."

Mordechai gave Azariah a long look. He had planned to use Aaron's defection to embarrass Azariah. But now? He sat down, motioning for the chief of the Pharisees to proceed.

"Aaron of Sepphoris, you are charged with actions disloyal and contrary to the will of the council. You have publicly stated your full support for the rebel and false teacher, Jesus of Nazareth. Come forward."

Aaron made his way through the seats and benches until he stood in front of the table where the three men sat. Those who had started to leave hung back, watching the events helplessly.

Azariah went on coldly. "As head of the party of the Pharisees, I am charged with maintaining order and discipline in our ranks. I would ask you some questions."

"Let me save this august body the effort it will take to do what you are already committed to do," Aaron said wearily. "I hereby publicly declare that I was witness yesterday to the raising of Lazarus from the dead."

Mordechai shot to his feet. "The 'so-called' raising of a dead man," he corrected.

"I was there, not ten paces away," Aaron went on calmly. "When the men rolled back the stone, I was close enough to catch a whiff of the smell of death. Before that moment, I had closely questioned people in the village about this man. I talked with men and women who helped wrap his cold and lifeless form for burial. I listened to the men who carried his body to the tomb. That was four days before Jesus came to Bethany."

He directed a scornful look at Mordechai. "This is no hoax. No switch was made. I have no doubt of that." He stopped, the awe that he had felt the day before sweeping over him again. "I saw with my own eyes a dead man come forth from his tomb. I saw him wrapped in his burial clothes—alive, healthy, walking. And it was Jesus of Nazareth who made it happen."

"Enough!" roared Azariah. "You will speak only to answer the questions you are asked."

"Yes," Aaron went on, knowing what the next question would be. "I am a follower of Jesus. Yes, I believe him to be the promised Messiah. I love Pharisaism and all that it stands for. It has been my life, and no one can question my dedication to it. I have not, as you say, been unfaithful to my commitments in any way, nor have I done anything contrary to the laws which this council is sworn to uphold."

"Away with him!" Menachem yelled. "He speaks heresy. Silence the man."

Aaron went on quickly, knowing his time was short. "But I believe Jesus to be the Christ. If that makes me unworthy to sit with this group—" he smiled faintly, thinking of the irony in those words—"then so be it."

"You have heard for yourself this outrage," Azariah said, spitting out his words like stones from a sling. "I hereby propose that this man be stripped of his seat on the Great Council and that all income derived therefrom be instantly halted. Further, the council demands that previous monies paid to this traitor be returned. He shall no longer be considered a Pharisee or a believer. Let him henceforth be known as a sinner and a traitor. I so move."

Mordechai had planned to be the first to raise his voice in support, but as he spoke half a dozen others shouted out at the same moment. "Let it be so. Vote! Vote!"

Mordechai leaned forward. "All those who favor the proposal before us, let your voice be heard."

"Aye!" It was thunderous.

Aaron stood quietly, his head up, watching Mordechai.

"It is done as has been proposed."

"Call for the negative vote!" someone shouted. Mordechai was not sure who said it, and he hesitated for a moment. By their law, he was required to see who gave their voice to both sides of an issue. And in his position as Father of the House of Judgment, second in authority on the council, he was charged to see that all things were done in order. But it galled him to do so. There was no question but what the motion had carried. The dissenters would be a small minority and couldn't change the outcome. He didn't want to give them the satisfaction of letting their voices be heard. He picked up his walking stick and smacked the table with a resounding crack. "The proposal carries." He looked at Aaron. "Be gone! The voice of the council has spoken."

As Aaron turned and rejoined the others who were walking out in protest, the council chambers erupted again. This time Mordechai let it roll.

Azariah sidled over to Mordechai. "Thank you for your support," the old Pharisee said grudgingly.

"Thank *you* for taking action with such dispatch."

"We have another problem," Azariah said. He lowered his voice, though it was doubtful anyone more than two seats away could hear him over the uproar.

Caiaphas and Mordechai leaned closer. "What do we do about this Lazarus? They say hundreds are flocking to Bethany to see the man."

Mordechai's brow lowered ominously. "There is only one thing for it."

Azariah looked mildly shocked, though in actuality, he had come to the same conclusion himself.

Mordechai didn't flinch from what needed to be said. "He'll draw people to Jesus like spoiled fruit draws flies." His lips pinched into a hard line. "Lazarus must die."

II

BETHLEHEM

23–30 MARCH, A.D. 33

When Aaron and Hava moved to Jerusalem, they were given a house not far from the Temple Mount. It was owned by the Pharisees and rented out to Aaron and his family at a nominal cost. It was one of the perquisites of power. But by the time Aaron returned home on the afternoon the council expelled him, there were already two armed men at the house demanding that he leave immediately. He and Hava gathered up what few things they could, put those belongings in a hand-pushed, two-wheeled cart, and, with their three children, left their former life behind. Not knowing what else to do, Aaron took his family to Bethlehem, to the house of David's cousin, Benjamin the Shepherd.

It was just as well that Lilly and Ezra had stayed in Capernaum and kept Rachel's three children and young Joseph with them. The home of Benjamin and Esther was comfortable but hardly ample. Rachel and Ephraim had arrived the day before, filling every extra sleeping space. The coming of Aaron's five left the house bursting beyond its capacity.

Not that anyone complained. The joy of Aaron's conversion took precedence over all other considerations. Deborah considered it to be a miracle almost as great as straightening Huldah's back, giving sight to a man born blind, or raising Lazarus from the tomb.

Three days later, Aaron returned to Benjamin's house from a trip to Jerusalem and suddenly announced that he was taking Hava and the children to Jericho. There they would stay with Hava's brother, wife, and mother-in-law. David suspected that something had happened while Aaron was in the city, though Aaron would not say either way. In truth, he had been openly jeered as he passed a group of Pharisees. Five minutes later, someone had thrown a rotten melon at him. It missed him, but the attempt had been enough. He feared that the council's vindictiveness might spill over against his family.

Hava, who was coming to enjoy her deepening relationship with the women of the family, started to protest at his announcement, but then she saw something on her husband's face that changed her mind. She and the children packed quickly, and they left within the hour. Deborah and the others promised to stop in Jericho to see the family on their return trip to Capernaum. Aaron said he would return as quickly as possible to provide one more man willing to stand by Jesus in case of trouble.

With Passover drawing near, the family debated whether to go into the city. Word had come that Jesus was going to stay in Bethany for a time. No further explanation had been given, but the family rejoiced.

That was better than him being in Jerusalem. It also solved another problem. Benjamin needed help. David's cousin was not just any shepherd. He was of the house of Levi and of the priestly order whose job it was to care for the flocks destined for sacrifice at the temple.

Central to the celebration of Passover was the eating of the ritual meal. And central to that meal was the paschal lamb. Thirteen hundred years earlier, Moses was told by the Lord to have the children of Israel take the blood of a lamb and smear it on the doorposts of their houses. When the angel of death came and slew the firstborn of the Egyptians, it "passed over" those houses where the blood was seen. The Hebrew word for "passover" was *pesach*. Thus, the sacrificial lambs eaten in the Passover meal were called *paschal* lambs.

The Law of Moses stated that every part of the lamb had to be consumed that night, so smaller families or individuals often joined together for the Passover meal. On the other hand, the total number of people who could consume the lamb was also restricted so that each person could have a significant portion of the meat. No sheep with any blemish or deformity was allowed to be used in the ritual meal, so each sheep had to be examined for defects. A major function of the priests at Passover was the examination, killing, cleaning, and sale of paschal lambs to the residents of Jerusalem and the tens of thousands of pilgrims who had come to the city for the Passover.

There was no busier time of year for the priestly shepherds who watched over the flocks of the temple. Each day Benjamin and his fellow shepherds, and their sons, started out shortly after dawn with a large flock of sheep. They led them to the outskirts of Jerusalem, where they were put into large holding pens on the northeast corner of the walls, just outside the Temple Mount. There they would wait their turn to be offered up to the Lord.

In the end, it was decided that the men would help Benjamin with some of the more mundane tasks that did not require priestly authority, and the women would stay home. There was no need to go to

Jerusalem on that particular day. On the morrow, they would all go to Bethany in time to accompany Jesus into the city.

III

BETHANY

31 MARCH, A.D. 33

Jesus seemed to be in no hurry to leave for Jerusalem. He sat in one corner of the courtyard outside Martha's house, speaking earnestly to James and John and several other brethren. Lazarus was the focal point of a separate group. Even though several days had passed, everyone still wanted to speak to a former dead man.

The women were congregated near the courtyard gate. There were a goodly number of them, including three different Marys. In addition to Martha's sister, Mary, the mother of Jesus was staying in Bethany with her son, and Mary Magdalene was also present. Several wives of the apostles were there, of course. There was also Joanna, wife of Chuza, Herod's steward, who had been converted at the same time as Mary Magdalene. She stood with Jael, wife of Luke the Physician. Ruth, who had been healed of an issue of blood by touching Jesus' robe, spoke quietly with a longtime friend, Hagith, wife of Jairus, the ruler of the synagogue in Capernaum.

It was still fairly early when the group from Bethlehem arrived. Livia had not gone, claiming she was too tired. Miriam sensed there was more to it than that but did not pry. Benjamin had not gone either; he had to deliver another flock to Jerusalem that morning.

As introductions were made, Miriam's attention was caught by one of the women. Anna, wife of Peter, introduced the woman as Judith, but said nothing more about her than that she was from Jerusalem. Miriam's eyes kept going back to her. She was sure she had met her somewhere before, but she could not remember where. Judith was a woman in her early thirties, of pleasant countenance but with lines in her face that suggested a difficult life. She spoke up from time to time, but for the most part she sat back and listened, smiling and laughing with the others but saying little herself.

Then suddenly Miriam had it. She leaned over to Deborah. "I know who Judith is," she said.

Deborah gave her a curious look. She hadn't known there was a question about it.

"I knew I had seen her once before, but I couldn't think where."

Leah overheard them and moved closer. "And?" she asked.

"Do you remember Livia and me telling you about that day in Jerusalem when we came across Jesus?"

"When he cleansed the temple?" Deborah asked.

"No. That was another time. On this occasion, Azariah and some other Pharisees had brought a poor wretched woman to Jesus to see what he would say."

Deborah began to nod and turned to look at the woman. "That was Judith?" she asked softly.

"Yes," Miriam said. "Isn't it wonderful that she's here? Jesus told her to go her way and sin no more. Her presence means that she didn't just forget him."

Deborah felt a sudden constriction in her chest, remembering the day she and little Esther had met Jesus in the marketplace in Capernaum. On that day, Jesus had reached out to her too. To that point, Deborah had rejected him openly. She had scorned some of his teachings. But none of that mattered to him. He had reached out and touched her heart, accepting her as she was, not as she should have been.

"I wonder how many of us are here today because of a similar miracle," she murmured.

IV

Simeon stood to one side of the main body of men. They spoke quietly together while they waited for the signal to leave, but he did not join them. He was in a curious mood, feeling an odd mixture of emotions. One part of him chafed at the delay. They had left Bethlehem very early to be sure they would not miss Jesus before he left for Jerusalem. So one part of him was ready to act, to move, to face whatever the day held in store. On the other hand, he wasn't sure he wanted it to begin. There were so many possible dangers. First and foremost was the danger to Jesus. But that was not all. For all the assurances he had given Livia about things being safe for them in Jerusalem, now he was starting to worry. What if Miriam's father decided to finally take his revenge? And what of Marcus? There was surely a desire on his part to get his hands on the man who had walked into his prison and taken Livia out, making fools of the best Rome supposedly had to offer. If Marcus saw Livia, would he make another try for her? Simeon didn't think so, but he couldn't be sure. Though Miriam was upset about Livia's refusal to go to Jerusalem on this particular day, Simeon had been relieved. That was one less thing to worry about.

He was ready for whatever came, but he felt a deepening sense of gloom. Since his decision to turn from the life of a Zealot, Simeon had found something he had not even realized he was missing. He was at peace. He had a wife he loved more intensely and deeply than he had ever thought possible. His family stood around him in full and loving support. Soon, the Lord permitting, he and Miriam would have a child of their own. He would be a father. Life was good, and it saddened him to think how easily it could all be lost. Yehuda was a grim reminder of that possibility.

He looked around and noticed that Peter also stood by himself. He too seemed deep in thought. Perhaps his mind was also assessing the potential for this day. Simeon straightened and moved over to stand beside his longtime friend and associate. Peter grinned. "Too much thinking time for men like you and me, right?" he said.

Simeon nodded. "Way too much." He turned and looked to where Jesus still sat in a circle of men. "But *he* doesn't seemed concerned," he noted.

"No," Peter said thoughtfully. "He's not concerned. It's more that . . ." He shook his head as he blew out his breath. "I don't know. He's been more pensive, more withdrawn. More . . ." He stopped. "I don't know how to describe it."

"Is he still talking about his death?"

Peter's head came around, and he gazed into Simeon's eyes. Finally, he nodded. "It happened again last night."

"What did he say?"

Peter turned so his back was to Jesus and lowered his voice. "We had supper here in Bethany with a man named Simon. He was one of the lepers Jesus cleansed some time ago. Martha, Mary, and Lazarus were with us. There were just a few of us and our wives—plus Mary Magdalene, and, of course, his mother. The conversation was relaxed and pleasant. And then . . ."

"What?"

"After supper we were still reclining around the table, just talking. You know how it is after a big meal. Then Mary, Martha's sister, got up and left the table. I thought she was going to clear away the dishes, which seemed odd, since we weren't at her home, but I didn't pay much attention. A few moments later, she came back. In her hands, she carried an alabaster box." Peter held out his hands to indicate the size of the container. "It was very beautiful. She must have brought it with her when we came."

"What was in it?"

Peter seemed not to have heard. "At that, all conversation stopped, and we turned to see what she was doing. She drew a jar from the box, took the lid off the jar, and instantly the odor of spikenard filled the room."

"Spikenard?" Simeon echoed.

"Yes, there must have been a pound of it."

Simeon whistled softly. Spikenard, as the Greeks called it, or *nard* in Hebrew, was one of the most expensive of perfumes. Like balsam, frankincense, and myrrh, the other costly aromatics, spikenard was not something that would commonly be found around the house. Not unless that person was very rich. Mary and Martha and Lazarus were prosperous, but they certainly were not wealthy.

"To our complete amazement, Mary came and kneeled down beside Jesus. Since we were still reclining around the table, his feet were extended outward, toward the room. Jesus sat up, but otherwise he didn't move."

Peter was quiet for several moments, and it was obvious that he was moved by the memories in his mind. Finally, he looked at Simeon. "She poured the ointment into her hands and then began to rub it very slowly and very gently on his feet."

Simeon's eyebrows lifted.

Peter nodded. "It was a most solemn moment. She anointed every part of both of his feet. She never spoke a word, just looked up at Jesus from time to time with those large eyes of hers. They were filled with love and sorrow and joy, all at the same time. When she was done, she bent down and wiped his feet with her hair." Peter's eyes were suddenly shining in the morning light. "It's probably the most sacred act of pure devotion I have ever witnessed. I shall never forget it."

"What did Jesus say?" Simeon was a little puzzled. This was very unusual.

That brought Peter back from his emotions. "Well, we were all dumbfounded, shocked even. Philip looked at me and I at him. Thomas was staring. We all were, I guess. And then Judas broke the spell. He was the first to speak. To everyone's surprise, he was upset."

"Upset? About what?"

"As you may know, Judas has been appointed among us as keeper of the bag. Of course, sometimes we have more than enough for our needs. Other times, especially when we are in areas where the people haven't heard of Jesus, things get pretty tight. If there is no money or food in the bag, we go hungry. And Judas is the one who is responsible for all of that.

"Anyway, you could see he was deeply shocked by what he thought was an incredible extravagance. He spoke to Mary, rather sharply, I'm afraid. 'Why was not this ointment taken and sold?' he demanded. 'We could have received three hundred *denarii* for it. Then the money could have been given to the poor.'"

Peter looked down for a moment, lost in thought. "John doesn't think Judas was worried about the poor at all. He thinks he just wanted that money to go into the bag. Think how that would make life easier for him. Three hundred *denarii*. That is no small amount."

"So did Jesus say anything?" Simeon wondered.

"Yes, and that's the answer to your original question. Mary was clearly hurt by what Judas said. But Jesus came to her defense immediately. It was a rather pointed rebuke. 'Leave her alone, Judas,' Jesus said. 'Why do you trouble her? She has wrought a good work on me.'"

Peter's mouth pulled down into a frown. "And then he said—" He took a deep breath. "He said, 'She has come beforehand to anoint my body for the day of my burying.'"

"Oh, Peter, no," Simeon breathed.

"That's what he said, and with about the same gravity as I just said it."

Simeon didn't know how to respond.

"Then," Peter went on, "Jesus said to all of us, 'Wherever this gospel is preached throughout the whole world, the thing that Mary has done shall be spoken of as a memorial to her. The poor you have always with you, but you shall not always have me with you.'"

Peter sighed, and his voice was heavy with concern. "So there it was again—talk of burial, suggestions of coming tragedy. I'll tell you, Simeon, for me it was a chilling moment. I can't get it out of my mind."

"Do you think he knows what's going to happen?" Simeon asked, feeling a chill in his own soul. "Just like when he knew that Lazarus was dead?"

Peter shook his head. "It seems clear he does."

They lapsed into silence, both retreating into their own thoughts. Twice, Simeon started to ask another question, but then thought better of it.

Two or three minutes later, as the two of them still stood quietly together, a cry from the women brought them both about. Miriam was staring at the gate to the courtyard. With another cry of pleasure, she started forward, moving swiftly.

Simeon and Peter were standing by the outer wall of the courtyard, down a few paces from the gate, and for a moment Simeon could not see what had drawn Miriam's attention. Then, to his surprise, Livia stepped through the doorway. In a moment, she and Miriam were in each other's arms.

Simeon looked at Peter, then moved toward them so he could hear what was going on.

V

"So," Miriam asked carefully, "do you want to talk about it?"

Livia shook her head. They had moved away from the other women and were speaking quietly. "I just realized that it doesn't matter if I'm troubled or not. I want to be with Jesus. I need to be with Jesus."

"That's good," said a man's voice. Both women turned as they realized Jesus had come up behind them. Livia's face flamed scarlet almost instantly. "*Shalom*, Master," she murmured.

"*Shalom*, Livia of Beth Neelah. I take it from Miriam's reaction that your presence here is a surprise."

Livia smiled wanly. "Even to myself."

"Welcome," he said. "And are you well?" He didn't have to explain his meaning. The roundness of Livia's stomach could no longer be hidden.

"Yes, Lord." She hesitated for a moment, then added, "As well as can be expected."

He nodded with understanding. "We were greatly saddened to learn of Yehuda's death." He paused for a moment, looking deep into her eyes. "I am the resurrection and the life, Livia. He who believes in me, though he were dead, yet shall he live."

Livia stared, first at Jesus, then at Miriam. Those were the very words Jesus had used with Martha when she met them at the outskirts of Bethany a few days before. They were the same words Miriam had repeated to her following the raising of Lazarus.

Jesus leaned forward slightly. "Can you believe this, Livia, widow of Yehuda?"

Tears filled her eyes. "I—" She swallowed quickly. "I would like to believe it, Master," was all she could say.

He searched her face for a long moment; then, seemingly satisfied, he smiled. He reached out and briefly touched her hand. "It pleases me that you would come at such a time as this. Thank you."

Then, before she could respond, he looked around. When he saw Peter, he motioned to him. "It is time, Peter. Let us be on our way."

CHAPTER NOTES

Immediately following his account of the raising of Lazarus, John described the turmoil this miracle created in the Sanhedrin. When Caiaphas made his statement about its being expedient that one man should die to save the nation, he seemed to have been steeling the council to take drastic action. But John saw the statement as unknowingly prophetic on Caiaphas's part (see John 11:50–51). Then John added two chilling insights into the heart of the council at that time: "From that day forth they took counsel together for to put him [Jesus] to death" (John 11:53). "The chief priests consulted that they might put Lazarus to death; because that by reason of him many of the Jews went away, and believed on Jesus" (John 12:10–11). The New Testament gives no additional information about whether or not the council took further action on this latter matter.

All four Gospels contain an account of a woman anointing Jesus (Matthew 26:7–13; Mark 14:3–9; Luke 7:37–50; John 12:1–8), and differences in the accounts may indicate that such an incident occurred on more than one occasion. Only John gives a name of the woman, indicating it was Mary, the sister of Martha and Lazarus. Luke puts it early in his Gospel, but the other three have it in the last week of Christ's life. It should be remembered, however, that the Gospel writers wrote their records to bear witness of Christ's divine Sonship, not to catalog a precise chronological outline of his life.

CHAPTER 22

O DAUGHTER OF JERUSALEM: BEHOLD,
THY KING COMETH UNTO THEE.

—*Zechariah 9:9*

I

ON THE ROAD FROM BETHANY TO JERUSALEM
31 MARCH, A.D. 33

They were passing the village of Bethphage, which was not far
from the top of the Mount of Olives. Another quarter mile and they
would crest the hill and be looking down on the city of Jerusalem from
across the Kidron Valley. From there it would be downhill and give
everyone a chance to rest their legs. Good. Simeon was working up a
sweat, and his legs were starting to feel the long, steady climb.

"Simeon, hold up!"

Simeon looked back over his shoulder. To his surprise, he was
ahead of the group by fifty paces or more. He stopped. Ephraim stood
in front of the group and motioned for him to come back. Puzzled,
Simeon turned and started back down the hill.

He had gone out ahead of everyone else for a reason. His years of
being on the run from Roman patrols had prompted him to suggest to
Peter that someone go before the main party to watch for any potential

trouble—to be an advance scout. Nothing unusual had happened, but it was clear to Simeon that they weren't going to enter Jerusalem quietly. Word was already racing out ahead of them. Jesus was coming! The man who had brought Lazarus from the tomb was here. Word of that incredible miracle had spread far and wide. People were streaming from their houses and fields to see for themselves the man who worked such wonders. Others, who somehow knew he was staying in Bethany, had gone out from Jerusalem and went running eagerly when they saw the oncoming company. Their numbers had already swelled to more than double what they had started with. And more were coming all the time. There was no question about it. Long before Jesus reached Jerusalem, Mordechai and Azariah and the Great Council would know that he was back.

"What's the matter?" Simeon asked as he reached Ephraim.

His brother shrugged. Behind them, the whole group had stopped. Jesus was talking with Peter and James, with others of the Twelve standing close by listening. Peter seemed a little puzzled by what he was hearing, but finally nodded. Then he and James moved forward.

As Peter reached them, Simeon asked in a low voice. "What's going on?"

Peter motioned for him and Ephraim to fall in with them. "We have to go to Bethphage."

"Oh?" Simeon said. Bethphage was nearby, but to the right some distance from the main road.

James looked somewhat perplexed too. "He wants us to get a donkey."

"For what?" Ephraim asked.

Peter shook his head. "He didn't say. We were walking along, just talking, when Jesus suddenly stopped. Then he asked James and me to go over into Bethphage." The fisherman's frown deepened. "He says that as soon as we enter the village, we'll find a donkey and her colt tied there. The colt will be an animal that no man has yet ridden. We are to loose the colt and bring it to Jesus."

Simeon just looked at him. "He said all that?"

"Yes," James said.

"But how could he know that?" Simeon started to say. Then he stopped. How did Jesus know there would be a coin in the mouth of a fish? How did he know Lazarus was dead when they were almost twenty miles away and had no word? How did he see into the hearts of men and women?

Ephraim, always of a more practical mind, had a different question. "You are just going to walk up and take someone's animal?"

James nodded, as if grateful that someone else had seen this potential difficulty. "Jesus said that if anyone questions us about what we're doing, we're to say that the Lord has need of it." His look made it clear he wasn't sure that would make any difference.

"We'll come with you," Simeon suggested. Peter, still puzzled, only nodded.

They turned off the road and started up the narrow lane that led toward the village. Bethphage meant "house of figs," and there was no question about where it had gotten its name. Large fig trees lined both sides of the road. It was yet too early in the spring for them to be in leaf—the fig tree was one of the last of the trees to come into full foliage—but it was obvious that in the summer this would be a very pleasant walk.

They rounded a bend in the path and saw a cluster of houses just ahead of them. Then James stopped. "There!" he said, pointing.

Sure enough, standing behind one of the first houses, tethered to a railing, were two donkeys. The one was a hand or two taller than the other and was a female. The smaller was a yearling, nearing its full height but not yet completely mature.

Peter looked at his fellow apostle. "So, do we just take it?"

James's shoulders lifted and fell. "He told us what to say *if* anyone challenged us, so . . ." He shrugged again.

That was enough for Peter. Hesitating no longer, he strode to the two animals, reached over and untied the yearling, and started back toward the other three men. Simeon was looking around, a little nervous about simply walking off with someone's animal.

They had barely started back down the path when a man's voice yelled out. "Hey!"

They stopped and turned. A bearded man in a simple brown tunic was running toward them, waving his arms, coming from the house where they had just been. He looked more than a little angry. "What are you doing with my donkey?" he demanded.

Peter turned to face him. The man stopped a few feet away, his body tensed, his jaw tight. "The Lord has need of him," Peter said quietly.

The man didn't move. He stared at Peter for a long moment. Then, to everyone's amazement, his jaw relaxed and his head bobbed. "Oh," he said, seeming surprised at himself. "All right." He looked at them for another moment or two and then turned and started back for his house.

The four men looked at each other, hardly believing what had just happened. Then Peter gripped the tether and turned back around again. "Come. Jesus is waiting."

II

To Simeon's surprise, when they came in view of the road where Jesus was waiting, the size of the group had almost doubled again. It now numbered somewhere between three or four hundred people.

Closest around Jesus were his trusted friends and loyal disciples, but streams of people were coming from every direction.

As the four men appeared with the young colt, Aaron and David went to join Simeon and Ephraim. Aaron sidled up to Simeon as Peter and James took the animal forward. "What happened?"

"It happened exactly as Jesus said it would," Simeon said.

"But why does he need a donkey?" Aaron wanted to know.

David answered. "I think he plans to ride it into Jerusalem."

"But why?" Simeon said. "Jesus never rides. He walks everywhere."

"It's a steep climb," Ephraim suggested. "Perhaps he's tired." But even as he said it, he shook his head. Jesus often stayed in Bethany with Martha and her family while he was in the Jerusalem area. He walked back and forth between the village and the city often. They had never known him to seek a ride.

David turned to watch Jesus as they brought the animal to him. The Master said something to Judas and Thomas, who were closest to him. Judas took off his outer cloak and spread it across the back of the animal. It was clear that David's assumption was about to prove true. He turned back to the others. "Matthew and I were talking about this while you were gone," he went on. "You know how Matthew is with the scriptures."

"Yes." Simeon knew that well. Matthew loved the writings of the prophets. He was continually pointing out things of significance from them.

"When a visiting king wishes to enter a city on a peaceful mission, how does he do it?"

Simeon had started to move forward again. He stopped and swung around to his father. "He rides on a donkey," he said slowly.

"Yes," David said, his voice low with excitement. "So the people will know he comes in peace. If he planned war, he would come astride a horse or in a chariot."

"Are you saying—" Ephraim began, but his father went on, cutting him off.

"Matthew reminded me of a prophecy about the Messiah given by the prophet Zechariah. It's one I haven't thought about for a long time. Zechariah said, 'Rejoice greatly, O daughter of Zion. Shout, O daughter of Jerusalem. Behold, thy King cometh unto thee. He is just, and having salvation; lowly, and riding upon an ass, and upon a colt, the foal of an ass.'"

Simeon's surprise was complete. He had heard that prophecy before, of course, but he hadn't made the connection to what was happening that very day.

David spoke with great earnestness. "Matthew thinks Jesus is about to enter Jerusalem as her king."

"But that's a Messianic prophecy," Ephraim said. Then his eyes widened even further. "He *wants* the people to know he is the Messiah?"

David nodded. "Matthew believes that we are about to witness the fulfillment of a prophecy that is more than four hundred years old."

They turned as one. Jesus was standing beside the yearling donkey, smoothing out the cloak that covered its back. He looked around for a moment at his followers, then swung one leg over and mounted the animal. For a moment, the colt was startled, and its large ears flicked back and forth nervously. But then it steadied.

Simeon had a sudden flash of insight. He swung around, snatching out his dagger. "Ephraim, quickly! Get some palm fronds."

Ephraim looked at him blankly.

"Quickly," Simeon said. "If he is going into Jerusalem as a king, let us greet him as a king."

With that explanation, David saw it instantly, as did Ephraim. At the Feast of Tabernacles, Jehovah was welcomed as King of Israel by the waving of palm fronds. "Of course!" he exclaimed. He pulled out his own knife, moving forward quickly. Judea was a warm, semitropical climate, and mingled with the olive and fig orchards were half a dozen different species of palm trees. Some were the towering date palms; others were squat and fat, not much taller than a man.

Simeon raced to the nearest one and slashed at the base of the frond. It fell to the ground with a soft thud. He cut off another, then another.

"Simeon? What are you doing?"

He turned. Miriam was just behind him. Leah, Esther, Deborah, and Rachel were coming too, giving the men strange looks.

"Quickly," David said. "Take these."

"But—"

Ephraim was a few paces away. He had cut several too. "Here, Rachel," he cried. "Jesus is going to Jerusalem as the Messiah, as the King of Israel."

He was so excited he spoke loudly. The waiting group heard him clearly and turned in surprise. Then they saw it as well. Men and women leaped into action, running to the closest palms. Jesus watched gravely. Peter stepped to him and whispered something in his ear. Jesus smiled and nodded.

Suddenly worried that Jesus might not approve, Simeon caught Peter's eye, then pointed to the fronds on the ground. He didn't say anything, but his expression was clear. *"Is this all right?"* Peter nodded vigorously, motioning with his hands to proceed.

Soon the entire hillside was bustling with activity. Branches were stripped off of bushes, and myrtle, willow, and citron trees. People plucked up wild flowers that grew among the spring grasses along the roadside and threw them in front of the slowly moving animal. Almond trees were in blossom, and people broke off branches heavily laden with flowers and did the same.

The women of David ben Joseph's family grabbed the palm fronds their men had cut for them and raced forward, getting out ahead of the donkey. Then they turned to face each other a few paces apart. Other men and women joined them quickly, forming a corridor for the donkey to pass through. It was as though a forest had instantly sprung up in the center of the road. The mass of green waved back and forth as if stirred by a gentle wind.

As the first of the group came running back with the fronds in their hands, the chief apostle picked up the donkey's tether and started forward. At that moment, something else happened. Mary Magdalene had been standing near Jesus, watching with large, wondering eyes. Then, as Peter moved forward, she swept off her outer cloak, running forward a few steps, maneuvering around the people with the palms and branches. The cloth billowed outward, then floated softly to the ground directly in front of the colt. Martha and Mary saw it and quickly followed suit. In a rush, others began to join in. Some fell in behind Jesus, palm fronds waving slowly back and forth majestically. Others leaped forward to throw their cloaks in front of the procession. In moments, the donkey was no longer walking on dirt, but on a carpet of robes.

A mighty shout went up. Simeon whirled around, a thrill of elation shooting through him. "Hosanna!" came the cry. "Hosanna! Hosanna to the Son of David!"

"That's enough fronds," David said to his two sons. He snatched up one for himself and raced away. Simeon and Ephraim followed. Aaron stood there for a moment, staring. The hosanna shout had come as a shock. Then, feeling something he had never experienced before, he grabbed up a palm frond from the ground and started running after his brother-in-law and two nephews.

The shout was like a torch of fire in a sheaf of grain. The cry leaped from lip to lip. In moments, the crowd was ablaze with the joyous chant. "Blessed is he that cometh in the name of the Lord. Hallelujah! Hosanna in the highest!"

All waved their branches joyously. "Hosanna! Blessed be the kingdom of our father David."

By the time they neared the top of the Mount of Olives, the increasing accumulation of the crowd was like a flash flood in one of the dry wadis of the desert. With such a flash flood, out of a seemingly clear sky drops begin to fall. Drops become puddles, puddles become rivulets, rivulets become streams, streams become torrents. In the same way, people poured out of every path, every track, every lane, every road. First it had been dozens, then hundreds. As they reached the top of the ridge, it was well over a thousand. The road was lined ten or twelve deep on both sides, providing a living passageway of shouting, cheering, exuberant, exultant humanity.

Though they had come nearly a quarter of a mile since Jesus had mounted the colt, the roadway had been covered for that entire distance. Flowers and greenery showered like rain around Jesus. Every person close enough to see Jesus seemed to want to have his or her cloak be one of those that softened his way. And all the time, the chant rose and fell. "Hosanna! Hallelujah! Praise be to Jehovah. May Jehovah save us."

III

JERUSALEM, THE TEMPLE MOUNT

Mordechai looked up at the sound of running feet. It was Menachem, and he was coming as quickly as his ample girth would allow him to move. Caiaphas shot Mordechai a hard glance. This was a private meeting of the presidency of the Great Council. They were discussing things of the utmost confidentiality. "What is he doing here?" he snapped.

Azariah the Pharisee, the third member of the council leadership, frowned as well. He didn't like Menachem. The man was Mordechai's lackey, always fawning around trying to carry out his mentor's will. But one look at Menachem's face cut off Azariah's protest. His expression was a mixture of shock, horror, and revulsion.

Mordechai leaped to his feet. Something was obviously terribly wrong. "What is it?" he exclaimed.

"You'd better come," Menachem said, puffing heavily. "All of you."

Before they could ask him anything, Menachem swung around and took off again. "This way!" he called over his shoulder.

"Menachem!" Mordechai shouted.

"You must see for yourself," came the answering shout. Then he was gone, shouting for them to hurry.

The chambers of the Great Sanhedrin of Jerusalem were beneath the apse that was on the eastern end of the massive Royal Portico, the covered colonnade that occupied the entire south side of the Temple Mount. Muttering angrily, Mordechai moved as quickly as he could after his aide, with Azariah and Caiaphas following close behind. They came out into the sunlight and stopped, half blinded by the sudden glare.

"There!" said Azariah, pointing. All around the other three sides of the Court of the Gentiles were lesser porticoes, but the one on the east was known as Solomon's Porches. Menachem was standing just outside those porches, waving wildly to catch their attention. When he saw that they had seen him, he turned and disappeared into the deep shade beneath the overhanging roof.

Cursing quietly, Mordechai headed in that direction.

Because the Temple Mount capped the summit of Mount Moriah, in every direction except the north there was a precipitous drop off to the surrounding valleys. The view from the top of the walls was spectacular, and so openings had been designed all along the walls to allow people to see out. From the eastern wall, one could see almost straight down to the Kidron Valley and then across to the great mass of the Mount of Olives.

As the three leaders entered the shade of the eastern portico, Menachem called out to them. "Over here!"

Puffing heavily, Mordechai moved forward, his brows lowering darkly. This had better be important, or Menachem was going to get his hide taken off him. And then he saw that there were groups of people standing at every opening, pointing and crying aloud.

"What is it?" he demanded when they reached Menachem. People standing nearby, seeing who it was, moved quickly to another opening.

Menachem raised a hand and pointed. "Look!"

For a moment, Mordechai wasn't sure what he was supposed to be seeing. Then his eyes caught movement. He leaned forward, squinting a little. *What in the name of heaven?* It was like some giant, multicolored caterpillar was oozing its way slowly over the topmost ridge of the Mount of Olives, then flowing downward, completely filling up the lighter slash that marked the main road from Jerusalem to Jericho.

Then, as his brain finally registered what he was staring at, he drew in his breath sharply. It was a huge, flowing mass of people. At that same moment, his mind also heard a distant roar coming from the same direction. It was the roar of a thousand voices.

"What is it?" Azariah cried. "What's happening?"

Caiaphas stood rooted to a spot just beside Mordechai, his jaw slack, his eyes vacant with shock.

"Listen!" Menachem hissed. "Can't you tell what they're saying?"

Cocking his head to one side for a moment, Mordechai focused intently on the sound itself. And then he felt suddenly sick.

"Hosanna! Hosanna!" And it was like the rumble of thunder, so many were the voices joining in the triumphant shout.

Mordechai turned to his man. "Jesus?" he said in astonishment.

"It has to be," Menachem said. "We got word more than an hour ago that he was coming." He turned to look again, his eyes panicked. "It has to be."

"What do you mean?" Caiaphas burst out. "You mean that it's that madman from Nazareth?"

"That's exactly what he means," Mordechai snarled. He turned back. *Unbelievable!* Even as he watched, he could see streams of people running up the hill to join the group.

"I don't understand," Caiaphas said in alarm. "What are they doing?"

Azariah turned and looked at Mordechai. He was as pale as a sheet of bleached muslin. "They're greeting him like a conquering king," he breathed.

"No," Mordechai hissed. "Not *a* king. *The* King!"

IV

By now Simeon had given up any thought of trying to stay out in front of Jesus and watch for trouble. The multitudes were so thick that there was barely room for the donkey carrying Jesus to keep moving forward. Simeon and his father and the other men had formed a rough circle around Jesus, holding out their arms simply to stop the throngs from crushing in on him and stopping their progress altogether. The people filled the road as far ahead as Simeon could see.

As they topped the ridge and started to descend down the west slope of the Mount of Olives, Jesus called to Peter, who was still leading the donkey. The apostle stopped. For a moment, Simeon thought Jesus was going to dismount, but he did not. He sat there, gazing steadily on the spectacular sight that lay before them. The entire city of Jerusalem lay spread out before them in the morning sunlight. Closest to them, almost as if it were at their feet, was the Temple

Mount, enclosed by the massive walls built by Herod the Great. And in its exact center, gleaming brilliant white in the sunshine, beckoning all to come unto it, was the temple of the Most High God.

Simeon would not have thought it possible for people to be any more stirred with excitement than they already were, but the sight of the city affected them as well. If anything, the roar of the crowd rose even higher. "Blessed be the King that cometh in the name of the Lord," they chanted. "Hosanna! Peace in heaven and glory in the highest."

Suddenly, there was a disturbance heard beneath the tumult. Then Simeon saw why. Four men were pushing their way through the crowd, coming up the hill from the direction of Jerusalem. They were shouting and yelling as they elbowed people out of their way.

"Oh, oh," Simeon cried to Aaron and his father. "This could be trouble."

There was no mistaking who the men were. They wore the robes of the ruling class of the Pharisees. And they were angry. The disciples leaped forward, pulling in tighter around the Master.

The shouts of people around Jesus began to lessen. Further out, where people couldn't see what was happening, the cries continued, and the noise was still thunderous, but in the center the cries quickly ceased. People began to fall back to make way for the four approaching men.

The man in the lead, the most ornately dressed and obviously their leader, came right up to the donkey, ignoring Peter. He leaned forward, his jaw thrust out. "Master! Rebuke your disciples. Do you not hear what they are saying? You must stop this!"

Jesus looked around at the people on every side, then turned back to face the man. "I tell you that if these—" one hand swept out to include the multitude—"should hold their peace, the very stones would immediately cry out in their place."

The man's face instantly flamed. His head bobbed spasmodically up and down, causing his beard and side curls to dance. He was so horrified at this audacity that he couldn't speak. Finally, he spun away. "Come," he said to his companions, "we must report this to Azariah and the council." He glanced back over his shoulder, muttering imprecations under his breath, as they hurried back the way they had come.

Peter watched them until the crowd closed in behind them, then looked at Jesus. "Shall we go on, Lord?" he asked. Others of the Twelve had moved up as well, and they leaned forward to learn what he would have them do.

But Jesus was not looking at them. He wasn't looking at Peter. And he didn't seem to hear the question. The road sloped downward rather sharply, and while there were people blocking the way itself, they could not block the view of the city that lay spread out before them.

Simeon was just ahead and to the right of Jesus. He had moved there to jump in if the four men had meant trouble. To his astonishment, as he turned to see why Jesus hadn't answered, he saw tears in his eyes. He could scarcely believe it. Moments before he had been smiling and waving to the cheering crowd. Now he was weeping!

Others saw it too and began to shush the crowd. "Quiet! The Master would speak! Hush!" The commands rippled outward and gradually the shouts of acclamation began to die. The silence spread outward from Jesus' person. The palm fronds slowly stopped their motion. The cloaks and scarves and veils being waved back and forth like banners were lowered. Jesus seemed unaware of any of it. His eyes never left the scene before him.

And then he took a deep breath and, struggling to speak, exclaimed, "O Jerusalem! If ye only knew the things which belong unto thy peace! But now they are hid from thine eyes."

It was such a remarkable change that shock registered on every face. In an instant, they had plunged from euphoria to gloom, from gladness to crushing sorrow. Even Peter seemed a little dazed by the complete and sudden change.

But still Jesus seemed unaware of anything around him. He was transfixed. He saw something as he looked out on the city that no one else was seeing, and it clearly was affecting him profoundly.

"The days shall come upon thee," he said, "that thine enemies shall cast a trench about thee, and compass thee round, and hedge thee in on every side. They shall lay thee even with the ground, and thy children within thee." The tears spilled over his eyelids and washed down his face. "And they shall not leave in thee one stone upon another; because ye knew not the time of your visitation."

No one moved. Every eye stared at the figure sitting astride the young donkey. Simeon felt a sense of deep foreboding sweep over him. Jesus was speaking to the city as if it were a woman standing before him. He spoke of siege and destruction and death. A moment before, they were shouting their hosannas to the King of Israel. What was the meaning of this remarkable shift of mood and focus?

Before Simeon could make any sense of it, Jesus lowered his head. For a long moment, he stared at the ground, one hand twisting in the animal's mane. Then he looked at Peter. "It is enough," he said. "Let us go on."

V

By the time they reached the Golden Gate, the eastern entrance onto the Temple Mount, the crowd was nearly exhausted from the walking, shouting, and waving. Many had joined in along the way, but others had come the full way from Bethany, a distance of almost two miles, all of it either going up or down hill. Some had dropped off after Jesus had passed, returning to their homes, but there was still a huge throng surrounding Jesus as they reached the open square in front of the gates.

Jesus raised a hand, and Peter and the surrounding protective circle of men stopped. Sensing that something was happening, the crowd quieted quickly. And gratefully so. Their voices were hoarse, arms tired from waving the branches and palm fronds, brows perspiring from toiling up and down the hills.

Jesus dismounted and stretched for a moment to get the stiffness out of his body. He had been astride the animal for almost an hour. Peter removed the cloak on the donkey's back and handed it back to Judas. Then he motioned to a young lad nearby and gave him instructions for returning the borrowed donkey to Bethphage, slipping him a coin for doing so.

An air of expectancy mixed with uncertainty seemed to hover over the crowd. David's family moved closer to hear. If Jesus was going onto the Temple Mount, the danger would multiply exponentially, but no one was of a mind to point that out to the Master. But Jesus seemed content to stay there by the gate, shaking hands, talking one on one with people. Gradually, seeing that the excitement was over, the crowd began to drift away, some going into the temple grounds, others returning to their homes. In twenty minutes, all that was left was the core group of disciples that had started with him in Bethany, plus a few others.

Finally, Jesus turned to Peter and spoke softly. Peter looked relieved, and as Jesus started towards the gates the chief apostle motioned for the others to come closer. "Jesus would like to go in and walk about for a short time on the Temple Mount. Then we will return to Bethany."

"Good," Andrew said. "After what we've just witnessed, it seems best not to stay here today."

Several of the women had come up as well, including Jesus'

mother. Her face was lined with concern. "He looks very tired," she said.

"I can only imagine," answered Mary Magdalene. "I'm exhausted, and all we did was come along with him. This was a very emotional experience, very draining."

Simeon and Miriam were standing together. He leaned over to her. "You stay close by. I'm going to circulate around and see if there is anything to be concerned about."

Miriam's mouth pulled down with worry. "Be careful, Simeon."

He knew what she was thinking. Marcus Didius could very possibly be inside, taking the pulse of the city. "I will," he said and squeezed her arm. Before she could say more, he hurried after Jesus, entering through the massive gates that led to the temple.

CHAPTER NOTES

Approximately one third of the content of the four Gospels focuses on the last week of Christ's life (beginning with the triumphal entry) and the events surrounding his resurrection (see Matthew 21–28; Mark 11–16; Luke 19–24; and John 12–22). This creates some unusual challenges in making chapter notes. The following summary relates to the remainder of the book.

All four writers cover most of the events of this week, though there are some things unique to each. There are small differences in details provided and the amount of space devoted to different events (for example, while Matthew, Mark, and Luke devote a few verses to the Last Supper, John devotes five chapters to it). There is not consistent agreement in the sequence in which events transpired.

The author combines and blends details from different writers to provide the fullest picture of what happened. Trying to document where each detail comes from would become very tedious; therefore, unless there is a particular issue that needs to be addressed, scripture references will not be provided. The reader who is interested in such detail is encouraged to read the parallel accounts and compare them for himself or herself.

With that much content, many things had to be left out of the novel. The choice as to what to exclude was often based on keeping the flow of the story moving forward; it should not be viewed as an evaluation of what things were of greater or lesser significance.

Dummelow notes the significance of entering Jerusalem on a donkey: "An ass [is] the symbol, not of lowliness, but of peace, as the horse was of war" (*The One Volume Bible Commentary*, p. 607). In the conflict over who would be his successor to the throne, King David caused Solomon to make his entry into the city riding a mule (see 1 Kings 1:32–40).

CHAPTER 23

FOR THE ZEAL OF THINE HOUSE HATH EATEN
ME UP; AND THE REPROACHES OF THEM THAT
REPROACHED THEE ARE FALLEN UPON ME.

—*Psalm 69:9*

I

ON THE ROAD FROM BETHANY TO JERUSALEM
31 MARCH–1 APRIL, A.D. 33

When Jesus finished his brief walk around the Temple Mount and started back to Bethany, David's family met in a quick conference. They determined that the women would return to Bethlehem, while the men would accompany Jesus back to Bethany, where they would stay overnight at the home of Martha. Since Jesus had declared his intention to return to Jerusalem the following day, the family would meet up again then.

There were two reasons for the men to stay with Jesus. First, they were concerned about the sheer logistics of traveling all the way from Bethlehem to Bethany in time for an early morning departure every day. Second, though it was unlikely that the Sanhedrin would come looking for Jesus, having a group of armed men sleeping in the court-yard where Jesus was would be a major deterrent to any trouble. What it came down to was that the climate was too laden with the possibility of trouble, and they were not willing to take any risks. So David, Aaron, Ephraim, and Simeon returned with Jesus and the other disciples to the village on the east side of the Mount of Olives.

Back in Bethany, once supper was over, Jesus retired early, and the rest of them enjoyed a quiet, peaceful night.

On the next morning, there was no lingering. Shortly after sunrise, Jesus announced that he was ready to leave. Martha was a little dismayed because she had not yet prepared breakfast. Jesus assured her it would be all right, and they all set off. Once again Simeon took point, staying far enough ahead that he could spot any potential trouble before they reached it. The other men in the family stayed back, but since Jesus was walking with his mother everyone left them alone to have time together.

It was a quiet entourage that made its way toward the top of the Mount of Olives. A few people saw them coming and went out to wave or call out to Jesus, but there was none of the unrestrained exuberance and celebration of the day before.

They made their way to the city without incident, except for one brief but strange occurrence. As they neared the spot where the path turned off to Bethphage and where the group had stopped the day before, Jesus noticed a fig tree that was in full leaf. That was unusual because it was still early in the spring and most fig trees were just coming into bud; it was yet not the season of figs. The fig tree was such that leaf and fruit came on together. If there were leaves, there would be fruit. Having left without breakfast, the travelers were pleased at the unexpected find. The figs would be a way to tide them over until they got onto the Temple Mount, where they would find food vendors.

Jesus turned aside to pick some figs from the tree. But to everyone's surprise, there was no fruit on the tree, not one fig. Then there came a bigger surprise. While everyone was mumbling their disappointment,

Jesus looked up and said, "Let no fruit grow on this tree henceforth and forever." Then he walked away.

Even Mary, his mother, seemed taken aback by that. Had Jesus just cursed the tree?

But he said nothing further, and no one felt inclined to ask him about the odd happening. In another half hour, as they approached the city, the entire incident was forgotten.

II

JERUSALEM, THE TEMPLE MOUNT
1 APRIL, A.D. 33

Though Passover was still a few days away, the temple courtyards were already crowded. As the group pushed their way through the Golden Gate and up the stairs into the Court of the Gentiles, Simeon's eyes swept the throngs. Most heads turned at the sight of their group, and it was clear many people instantly recognized Jesus, smiling or poking their companions and pointing. There were a few Pharisees who glared as they went by—some of the anger focused on Aaron—and several priests in their white robes stared with open curiosity, then averted their eyes and hurried on.

"Pardon! Make way! Make way!"

Simeon turned at the cry. Behind them, just coming through the gates and up the small side ramp alongside the stairs, were a man and a boy of fifteen or sixteen. They had a small pushcart on which was a large vat of what Simeon guessed was wine or, possibly, olive oil.

The group started to fall back, but Jesus moved directly in front of the cart as it reached the main level of the courtyard.

"Hey!" the man shouted. He was swarthy in complexion and heavily bearded. He looked as if he was from Gaza or Hebron, one of the southern cities of Judah. "Make way!"

"What is it you carry?" Jesus asked.

"Wine!" the man snapped. "And what is that to you?"

"Is this wine destined for the temple?"

"No," the man sneered, "it is destined for the bellies of the Romans in the Antonia Fortress." The sneer turned mean. "And the Romans don't like to wait, so I suggest you step aside."

Seeing the man's anger, the disciples began to edge closer. People coming into the temple turned to watch, drawn by the bite in the man's voice.

If Jesus saw any of this, he gave it no heed. "The House of the Lord is not a thoroughfare of merchandise," he said firmly. "It is a house of prayer. Are there not other entrances to the fortress?"

The man let the cart drop. The handles clunked heavily on the paving stones. He began to push back his sleeves, a threatening gesture if Simeon had ever seen one. Simeon too moved closer, prepared to intervene. "The way around is twice as far, and this cart is heavy," the man growled. "This is a convenient shortcut."

The Master's demeanor was calm, his manner unruffled. Quietly he repeated the words he had just said. "The House of the Lord is not a thoroughfare of merchandise. It is a place of prayer."

His eyes never left the man's. After a moment, the wine merchant had to look away from the penetrating gaze. Muttering something under his breath, he turned to his boy. "Back," he snarled. "We'll go around."

Jesus said nothing more. He simply watched as they wheeled the cart back down the ramp, then out the gates. Only then did he turn. He was looking toward the southeast corner of the Temple Mount.

There the crowds were the thickest, and there was the sound of the lowing of cattle and the bleating of sheep and goats.

Jesus' eyes darkened, and Simeon saw that his jaw was set in a hard line.

Peter also saw the look in Jesus' eye and sensed what was about to happen.

III

Miriam, Deborah, Livia, Leah, and Rachel did not bring Aunt Esther with them when they returned to Jerusalem. Benjamin had been assigned to stay with the flocks in the hills outside of Bethlehem through the night, and he arrived home just as the women were preparing to leave. Esther decided she would stay behind and see to his needs. She promised they both would come later.

The rest of them left after breakfast was finished; they reached Jerusalem about the third hour of the morning. The road from Bethlehem entered Jerusalem on the west side of the city. From there they worked their way through the crowded and narrow streets, then crossed the great arch that led from the Upper City to the Temple Mount. As they entered the Court of the Gentiles, they stopped to rest for a moment in the shade of Solomon's Porches.

"Do you see them?" Miriam asked, her eyes searching the crowds that half filled the great courtyard.

"No, but we agreed to meet them near the main gate of the Court of the Women," Deborah said. "I told David we'd look for them there first."

"If they're not here yet, they'll be coming through the Golden Gate," Leah noted. "But if Jesus went somewhere else, they'll stay with him. So they could be anywhere."

"Well," Deborah suggested, "let's start there and see what happens."

As they started forward, moving out into the open, Leah suddenly pointed. "Look at the crowds. I wonder if Jesus is over there." She gestured toward the southeast corner of the great court.

Leah was right. A tight cluster of both men and women were moving slowly across the line of their vision. To Miriam's relief, there were no signs of the temple guards with their long spears, and the people didn't seem agitated.

"I think I see Andrew," Rachel exclaimed. "And there's Luke and John. That must be them."

"Well, that was simple enough," Livia said.

"Yes, let's go," Deborah replied.

The width of the Court of the Gentiles from west to east was about six hundred paces. As the four women began working their way through the crowds, angling to intercept the moving group, Miriam kept going up on tiptoe to see better. She was relieved to see that the group had completely stopped, still some distance from the towering Royal Portico on the south end of the courtyard. That was good. For a moment, she had feared that Jesus might be under guard and on the way to the Sanhedrin's chambers.

Suddenly a shout went up from the crowd. It was instantly followed by the bawling of cattle and a loud crash. Miriam grabbed Leah by the hand, motioning frantically to the others. "Come," she cried. She broke into a run, pulling her sister-in-law forward. "He's with the moneychangers again."

They ran as quickly as they could across the courtyard. Livia, hardly up to running, waved the others to go ahead, but they wouldn't leave her. It helped that they no longer had to fight the crowds. Others had heard the clamor and were running in the same direction to see what was happening.

By the time they crossed the great plaza, people were already standing four and five deep, blocking access to the area where the moneychangers did their business. At that instant there was another loud crash, and a roar of approval went up from the crowd. As the sound died, Miriam heard a shout from off to their left, and she saw Simeon waving at them through the crowd. "Miriam! Mother! We're over here."

"Excuse us, please," Miriam said as she pushed her way through the crowd. "I have to get to my husband. Make way!" She elbowed people aside as gently as she could.

Muttering and grumbling, the people made way. In a moment, they were standing beside David, Aaron, Ephraim, and Simeon. Miriam grabbed Simeon's arm and squeezed it in greeting, then turned to see what was going on.

It was as though she had, in one instant, been transported back almost three years to when she and Livia had happened on this same scene. The images had been indelibly etched into her mind on that day, and they were almost identical now. Small, makeshift pens of ropes and rickety fencing held hundreds of sheep, goats, and bullocks. The courtyard was covered with their droppings, and the stench was heavy in the air. Beyond the penned animals, rows of tables held small wooden cages filled with doves, the men selling them sitting on stools behind them. Since the dove was an acceptable substitute for those too poor to purchase a lamb or bullock, the merchandisers were doing a brisk business. Some tables held only empty cages. Down the center of the whole madhouse, a large aisle had been left to the money-changers. Here were the men who made small fortunes changing coinage from all over the empire into shekels, the only money accepted for the temple tax and in the temple treasuries.

Then Miriam saw Jesus. He was moving down the row of tables. Men scattered before him like frightened chickens. He paused at a heavy wooden table, bent over, grasped the edges, and heaved upwards. There was a resounding crash. Bags of coins hit the pavement and sprayed outward. Again the crowd roared its approval. With one kick of his foot, the next table, much flimsier than the first, collapsed. Its owner howled something at Jesus even as he scrambled backward to get out of the way.

On that first occasion when Jesus cleansed the temple, he had braided a whip of cords and used it to drive the men and animals before him. Now he had nothing but his bare hands. It made little difference. No one had questioned his authority then, and no one was questioning it now.

A burly man in a filthy tunic dove to one side as Jesus gave one of the pens a swift kick and the fencing collapsed. Bleating wildly, half a dozen sheep bolted through the opening, their hooves skidding on the stones as they tried to turn too quickly. Two of the animals slammed into the next pen. It went down and three young bullocks joined the stampede.

Jesus reached the first of the tables with cages. These were all empty. The table went flying, the wooden cages shattering as they hit the ground. At the next table, where the cages were still filled with birds, the man threw out his arms, as if he would stop a tidal wave. "Please, Lord," he blurted. "Not my birds."

"Take these out of here," Jesus snapped. The man and the others behind them leaped from their stools and frantically began loading the cages into their carts. As they did so, Jesus began kicking their stools aside, sending them clattering away.

Another pen collapsed and more sheep bolted through the opening. Their keeper gave a strangled cry and dove at one of them, trying to corral it with his arms. It nimbly leaped to one side, and he went crashing onto the courtyard floor. Some of the crowd cheered and broke into applause. They were loving this. But others looked dismayed—they had come to exchange their money or purchase what they needed for their sacrifices.

Jesus pulled up, turning to survey the damage he had wrought. His eyes were blazing, daring anyone to challenge him. The money-changers and owners of the various merchandise had withdrawn into the shadows of the nearby Solomon's Porches. They were muttering and shaking their fists at him, but not one of them came out to confront him.

Jesus turned to face them. "Is it not written in the scriptures, 'My house shall be called of all nations a house of prayer'?"

The cravens shrank back deeper into the shadows as the crowd turned to see what answer they would give.

Jesus shook his head in disgust. "Instead of a house of prayer, you have turned it into a den of thieves."

IV

The hot debate going on in the Sanhedrin was instantly cut off when the first roar of the crowd went up. Mordechai and half the others shot to their feet, staring out into the courtyard. They heard a loud crack as something heavy hit the ground; then came the wild bleating of animals.

"What is it?" Caiaphas blurted out. "What is happening?"

"It's a riot!" someone cried. "Call out the guards!"

"The Romans are upon us!" someone else screamed.

Mordechai didn't wait to see if either was right. He was up and running as fast as his overweight and underworked body was capable of going. Azariah fell in behind him, as did others.

"Bring Caiaphas!" he shouted over his shoulder.

As they entered into the Court of the Gentiles, Mordechai saw the crowd. Another roar went up; he could tell it was more of a cheer than a cry of alarm. Something else cracked sharply. A moment later, Caleb, Azariah's chief associate and a senior member of the Great Council, raced past them, followed by Menachem. "Make way!" they screamed. "Make way for the council."

V

Miriam looked up as the crowd gave way. Her heart froze. There, his face mottled and angry, exactly as it had been the last time she saw it, was her father. He was with Azariah and several other richly dressed men. She shrank back against Simeon, averting her head.

But her father was not looking at the people around him. He and Azariah, with Caleb, Menachem, and the other council members, pulled up short. Tables were overturned, pens were down, animals were racing away, darting here and there through the crowds. People were on their knees, scrambling for the coins that lay everywhere. And in the midst of it all, there stood Jesus, his chest rising and falling, his hair somewhat in disarray.

At the sight of the delegation he turned slowly to face them.

Mordechai's face went purple. *Again! The man had dared to do this again?*

He strode forward as a low mutter swept across the crowd. Suddenly, four temple guards appeared, running hard, hastily trying to catch up to their employers. But seeing that, several in the crowd rapidly closed the opening behind the men from the Sanhedrin, cutting the guards off on the periphery. Mordechai and Azariah and their cronies were on their own.

Mordechai suddenly felt his hair prickle. While clearly many people were troubled by what Jesus was doing, a far greater number were ecstatic. Their faces turned ugly at the sight of the council members. They detested the moneychangers. They detested these oily men with their corrupt weights and their lightning-fast hands. They detested the Sanhedrin, who gave them license and profited from their filthy lucre.

But then anger overrode any hesitation Mordechai felt. He stepped forward in a fury. Azariah was right beside him. For all his strutting and posturing, the chief Pharisee was not a coward.

"What is the meaning of this?" Mordechai cried.

"You dare to disrupt the services of the temple?" Azariah shouted.

"It is written that God's house shall be a house of prayer, and yet you—" and now Jesus was not looking at the craven men cowering in the shadows; he was looking directly at the leaders of the two most powerful religious bodies in Judaism—"you have made it into *this*."

"By what authority do you take upon yourself to act in the name of the Sanhedrin?" Mordechai shouted, his whole body trembling with rage. "Answer, or face immediate arrest and imprisonment."

"Are you mad?" Azariah joined in, screaming, drops of spittle flying from his mouth and lighting on his beard. He spun around, looking at the wreckage around them, then spoke to the crowd. "The man is insane. Absolutely mad! He desecrates the sacred temple precincts."

To his relief, Mordechai saw more than a few heads begin to nod. There were some here who were not in favor of what was happening. Others were still shouting angrily, but Azariah's accusation had garnered at least some supportive reaction. Mordechai decided to press his advantage.

Pulling himself up to his full height, he also spoke to the crowd. "I am Mordechai ben Uzziel, of the presidency of the Great Council. We demand to know by what authority this man takes it upon himself to create a riot here. Here! In the temple of God." He swung back around. "Explain yourself, Galilean. You have gone too far. By what authority do you dare to act in such a manner?"

Jesus seemed almost amused by the question. Mordechai was instantly wary. The man was obviously not worried in the slightest about this challenge.

"Well," Mordechai said loudly, but a little more hesitantly, "are you going to answer or not? The Great Sanhedrin demands to know."

Jesus leaned forward slightly, speaking in a clear voice for all to hear. "I would ask you one thing, which if you tell me, I in like manner will tell you by what authority I do these things."

Mordechai hesitated. He had seen even old crafty Azariah bested by this man, but there was nothing for it but to agree. "Ask on," he snapped.

"The baptism of John. Tell me from whence it was? Was it from heaven or of men?"

Mordechai flushed. He instantly saw the snare. Fumbling, he decided to stall. "May I consult with my colleagues? Since we speak for the council, we must be united in our answer."

Jesus nodded, smiling faintly.

The delegation huddled together. "What do we say to that?" Mordechai whispered.

Azariah was pulling at his beard, clearly troubled. "It is a dangerous question," he noted.

"If we say it was from heaven," Caleb pointed out, "then he's going to ask us why we did not believe in John?"

"And if we say he was of men," finished Mordechai, clearly seeing their dilemma, "then the people will turn against us."

"It would be very dangerous right now," Menachem agreed nervously. "The common people all hold John as a prophet of the Lord."

"Exactly," Mordechai said shortly. "So then?"

Azariah was shaking his head. "So then we can't answer him, or he'll have us either way," he muttered.

Mordechai nodded and turned to face Jesus again. "We cannot tell whether John's authority be from heaven or from men."

There was a fleeting moment of sadness on Jesus' face; then his expression became determined. "Neither then can I tell you by what authority I do these things."

There was a low murmur of approval from the crowd. These arrogant toads had been bested, and the common people loved it. One man even guffawed out loud.

But before Mordechai or Azariah could say anything, Jesus went on. He had turned away from the delegation and spoke directly to the surrounding people. "What think you? A certain man had two sons. And he came to the first, and said, 'Son, go work today in my vineyard.' And the boy answered and said, 'I will not.' But afterward he repented and went as he was told. And the man came to the second son and said likewise. And this son answered and said, 'I go, sir.' But he went not."

Jesus swung back to Mordechai and Azariah. "Tell me. Which of these two did the will of his father?"

Realizing that they were only being drawn in deeper, Mordechai hesitated. He looked at Azariah. There was no choice but to answer, and there was no answer but one. "The first," he said.

Jesus' expression turned cold. "Verily I say unto you, that the publicans and the harlots will go into the kingdom of God before you, for John came unto you in the way of righteousness, and you believed him not. But the publicans and the harlots, whom you call sinners, believed him. But even then, you repented not, that you might believe him."

Azariah was shocked right down to the tips of his richly embroidered velvet sandals. "Harlots!" he sputtered. "In the kingdom of God? *Publicans!*"

"That is a most ridiculous and insulting idea," Caleb snarled, jumping in to support his master.

Jesus went on quickly, again turning away from them and talking directly to the crowd.

"Hear another parable. There was a certain householder which planted a vineyard, and hedged it round about, and dug a winepress in it, and built a tower. Then he let it out to husbandmen and went into a far country. And when the time of the fruit drew near, he sent his servants to the husbandmen, that they might receive the fruits of the vineyard. And the husbandmen took his servants and beat one and killed another and stoned another."

The unruly crowd settled down rapidly, sensing that in this story something very important was being said. Every person was listening intently, suspecting that once again this story was directly aimed at the leaders who stood before Jesus.

"Again," Jesus continued, "the householder sent other servants, more than the first. And they did unto them likewise. But last of all he sent unto them his son, saying, 'They will reverence my son.' But when the husbandmen saw the son, they said among themselves, 'This is the heir. Come, let us kill him, and let us seize on his inheritance.' And they caught him and cast him out of the vineyard and slew him."

Simeon went rigid. Miriam looked up at him in surprise. "What?" she whispered.

"He's talking about himself. *He* is the son." He felt sick. Here it was again, the talk of death. Miriam's eyes went wide, and then, in horror, she looked at her father. There was no understanding in his eyes. He looked puzzled, almost bored. *He didn't see it!*

"When the lord therefore of the vineyard comes," Jesus asked, turning again to Mordechai, Azariah, and the men who had come with them, "what will he do unto those husbandmen?"

The members of the council looked at each other. What did this little story have to do with what was going on here? Menachem, half sneering, answered the question. "He will miserably destroy those wicked men, and will let out his vineyard unto other husbandmen, which shall render him the fruits in their seasons."

Jesus nodded thoughtfully, letting the significance of that answer sink in. Azariah saw it first. "You speak of us?" he said shrilly. "You're saying . . ." He stopped, the enormity of the words hitting him hard.

"Did you never read in the scriptures," Jesus went on, "'the stone which the builders rejected, the same is become the head of the corner'? Therefore say I unto you, the kingdom of God shall be taken from you and given to a nation bringing forth the fruits thereof."

"How dare you!" Mordechai hissed, his voice trembling with fury. "You would—"

But Jesus cut in sharply, overriding him as his own voice cried out like the blast of a trumpet. "And whosoever shall fall on this stone," he said, "shall be broken. But on whomsoever this stone shall fall, it will grind him to powder."

Miriam's father's face was completely white, and she saw that his hands were shaking violently. For a moment, she was afraid that the two leaders were going to hurl themselves at Jesus. Then her father turned to the crowd, his eyes flitting from face to face. Any sign of support for the council members was shrinking fast. Most of the faces were hard, cold, contemptuous.

Suddenly Mordechai visibly jerked. Miriam drew in her breath sharply. He had seen her! His eyes had stopped on her and Simeon. Slowly he straightened to his full height, his face like stone. It was as though she was staring at the face of a stranger. Then without a word, he turned away from her and haughtily stomped away, the others falling in behind him.

The crowd fell back, making way. The only sound now was the shuffling of feet on the pavement. Eyes burning, Miriam watched until they disappeared, and the throngs closed in again. Simeon put his arms around her as silent sobs began to wrack her body. In that moment, all hope of reconciliation was dashed forever.

VI

Mordechai said nothing as he walked stiffly away from the crowd. His head was high, and his eyes never strayed from the front, but he was keenly aware of the hostile stares and the whispering that took place behind cupped hands. They were making fun of him. Mordechai ben Uzziel, one of the most powerful men in all of Judea, was being mocked like a beggar in the streets.

Once they were clear and the people were behind them, he stopped and whirled on his companions. "Menachem!" he barked.

His aide leaped forward. "Yes, sire?"

"There's something I want done immediately."

"Whatever you command, sire," Menachem said. His voice revealed how deeply shaken he was too.

Mordechai glanced at Azariah briefly. "There is no way we can take this man when the people are with him. You saw it. They would have stoned us if we had tried."

"So what do we do?" Azariah asked.

"Spread the word," came the hard, cold answer. "Put it out on the streets. Send it to every thief and harlot and brigand you can find." His eyes bored into Menachem's. "Let it be whispered in the halls where supposedly respectable men gather. And most especially, spread the word to those who claim to be followers of this charlatan from Nazareth."

"Yes, sire?" Menachem waited expectantly, not sure exactly what word he was expected to spread.

"Let it be known that a very rich reward awaits any man who can deliver Jesus at a time and place where there aren't ten thousand people howling his praises."

A look of pure admiration bathed Menachem's face. Was it any wonder he had placed his fate with this man? "It shall be done, sire," he barked, and he turned and darted swiftly away.

"Well!" Azariah snarled.

Caleb jumped guiltily. "What, sire?"

"You heard Mordechai. Why are you standing there with your tongue hanging out? Go!"

CHAPTER NOTES

Many are not aware that there were two cleansings of the temple, one at the beginning of Christ's ministry and one just prior to his death. The Gospel writers indicate that the second cleansing happened shortly after the triumphal entry (Matthew 21:12–13; Mark 11:15–17; Luke 19:45–46). It is Mark who gives us this detail: "And he would not suffer that any man should carry any vessel through the temple" (Mark 11:16).

Some Gospel accounts also place the second cleansing of the temple on the day before the parable of the wicked husbandmen (Matthew 21:13–24; Mark 11:15–20, 27–33). Luke is less clear, but he indicates that Jesus taught in the temple daily (Luke 19:47); he also places the den of thieves event earlier (Luke 19:46) than the other exchanges with the Pharisees (Luke 20:1–19).

When one reads the Savior's scathing denunciations of the Jewish religious leaders, it isn't surprising that he triggered such murderous fury. We are given some insights as to why they didn't take him immediately: "And they sought to lay hold on him, but feared the people" (Mark 12:12). "The chief priests [the Sadducees] and the scribes [allies with the Pharisees] and the chief of the people [the Sanhedrin] sought to destroy him, and could not find what they might do: for all the people were very attentive to hear him" (Luke 19:47–48).

CHAPTER 24

IT IS AN EASY THING FOR MANY TO BE SHUT UP IN THE HANDS OF A
FEW, AND THERE IS A DIFFERENCE IN THE SIGHT OF HEAVEN TO SAVE
BY MANY OR BY FEW; FOR VICTORY IN BATTLE STANDETH NOT IN THE
MULTITUDE OF AN HOST, BUT STRENGTH IS FROM HEAVEN.

—1 Maccabees 3:20

I

1 APRIL, A.D. 33

After the confrontation between Jesus and the Jewish leadership, the men of the company went on high alert, expecting at any moment to see the temple guards rushing in to arrest Jesus. But they never came.

Jesus left the Court of the Gentiles and went into the Court of the Women. As soon as he seated himself on a bench and began to speak with the people, Peter called for a quick conference to discuss the likelihood of more trouble. Aaron stood back a little, not feeling like he was part of this inner circle, but finally he spoke up. "They're not going to come," he said.

Everyone turned in surprise. Simeon and David gave him questioning looks.

"They fear the people," Aaron said, a little awkwardly. "You saw what happened. They saw that the crowd was with Jesus, and they didn't dare to do anything."

Aaron knew only too well the mentality of the members of the Great Sanhedrin. They were like boys wetting their fingers and sticking them up to determine which way the wind was blowing. And this wasn't just a wind; it was a hurricane. The crowds flocking to Jesus were tremendous, and his popularity was growing every day. And why not? Every day brought some new and wondrous report. A man born blind now saw. Aaron's own relative was straight and whole after eighteen crippling years. And then there was Lazarus. That had set the whole countryside aflame. And all of that had come out when Jesus mounted a donkey and rode into Jerusalem as a king.

The capstone had been his cleansing the temple of the money-changers. Here was a group universally hated by the common people. Not only was the system corrupt and exploitive, but everyone knew that the Sadducees, who controlled everything having to do with the temple, permitted it because they were reaping huge profits from it. Nor were the Pharisees innocent. Though they outwardly condemned any dishonesty, it was common knowledge that Azariah and his brethren quietly looked the other way as they received a healthy share of the take under the table as well.

"Our people are too volatile," Aaron went on. "They're highly emotional. If Mordechai had called for the guards, he and Azariah would have been the ones in trouble, not Jesus. These men are far too shrewd to make that mistake."

The men saw that Aaron was right and relaxed their vigilance somewhat. The Twelve stayed close to Jesus to help manage the crowds, but many of the other men wandered away, glad for the opportunity to walk around the magnificent environs of the temple. David and his family went to see if they could find Benjamin and Esther, who had promised to come as soon as the flocks were delivered to their pens.

An hour passed. Aaron sat on a bench on the opposite side of the courtyard, deep in thought, absently pulling at his beard as he pondered the previous few days. In a way, this had been a troubling day for Aaron. Still bitter over his dismissal from the council, it was not that he harbored any sympathy for Azariah and his fellow Pharisees. Nor was there any faltering in his conviction that Jesus was the Messiah. But Aaron had committed his life to the Pharisees. How many thousands of hours had he spent in the *yeshiva* studying the Torah? How many times had he gone through the meticulous process of washing and purification so that he could be worthy of God's approbation? He had carefully counted out his steps on the Sabbath lest he violate the limitations of a Sabbath day's journey. He had strenuously avoided any contact with the Gentiles lest he be defiled. He watched what he ate, how he dressed, what he did almost hour to hour. Convenience had long since been pushed aside to make way for commitment. Wasn't there some justification in taking pride in that kind of commitment? If Simeon and David and Deborah had seen that as some sort of spiritual elitism, then so be it. In a way, he *had* achieved a spiritual superiority over those who couldn't be bothered with the burdens of the Law.

His change of heart about Jesus hadn't simply wiped all of that away. Aaron was still a Pharisee down deep in his soul. So when Jesus had said that the publicans and the harlots would enter the kingdom of heaven before the Pharisees and the chief priests, that had hit him hard. Harlots in the kingdom of God? And yet, even as those doubts arose, back would come the other. A man born blind. Huldah and her deliverance. And Lazarus. He shook his head, sighing deep within his soul. One didn't simply set aside Lazarus. Not after seeing him shuffle forth out of that tomb wrapped up in his burial clothes. It was incredible. Who could doubt this man's power? How could Jesus be anything but the Messiah?

A disturbance across the way pulled him out of his thoughts. He could no longer see Jesus. People were moving in swiftly around the spot where Aaron had last seen him. Something was up. Feeling a sudden foreboding, he hauled himself up and hurried in that direction. Perhaps his help would be needed.

As Aaron pushed his way forward, he saw immediately what was drawing the people in. Jesus was still in his earlier position on a bench, but four other men now stood directly in front of him. Aaron felt his heart jump a little. They were Pharisees, and though Azariah was not one of them, Aaron recognized Caleb. If Caleb was there, it was because Azariah had asked him to be there. The other three were all prominent in the hierarchy. One of them also had a seat on the Great Council with Caleb and Azariah. He had been one of those who voted that Aaron should lose his seat on the governing body.

One of the men moved slightly, and then Aaron saw a fifth man. It was Menachem the Sadducee, Mordechai's number one lackey. *So,* he thought, *the battle had not been conceded.* Of course not. The issues were too deep, the outcome too important to men like Azariah and Mordechai and Caiaphas. They had sent in another team for the next round.

Caleb stepped forward, smiling unctuously. Jesus did not rise.

"Master?" His voice oozed warmth and cordiality. "We would ask some questions of you. We hope you can help us understand things better."

So that was it. Aaron should have guessed it. The Great Council feared Jesus' popularity with the people, so they were launching a new offensive. These crafty wordmongers loved to debate. The more twisted and convoluted the question, the more they loved it. Aaron himself had been a master of it. That was one of the reasons he had risen so rapidly in the movement. He could carry on for hours with the best of them, debating every nuance, raising every obscure and arcane argument he could muster.

It was a continuing strategy of Jesus' opponents. The questions were brilliant. Was it lawful to pay tribute money to Caesar? If a woman was married to more than one man, whose wife would she be in the resurrection? Which of all the commandments is the greatest? Each question was like a sharp sword, designed for one purpose and one purpose only: to expose Jesus for what he really was in the eyes of these men—a country peasant with no formal learning, no sophistry, no experience in the Law.

It was a trap that backfired on them in every case. Jesus wouldn't be led into their snares. Instead, he turned the question around, taking them in completely different directions than they expected. Time after time, the questioners became the questioned, and the learned became the fools.

The crowd loved it. On this occasion, Menachem looked like he had been skewered with a lance. Caleb was sweating heavily and kept mopping at his brow, even though the day was relatively cool. The people began to openly jeer. They loved seeing these pompous donkeys bested in verbal battle. They loved seeing them twist like rags in the wind. They loved their dismay when Jesus didn't fall into the pits they had dug for him, but instead tripped and tumbled into those pits themselves. The end result was that the delegation actually did more to endear Jesus in the hearts of the people than they did to discredit him.

By the time they were ready to quit, Aaron was filled with hot shame. To think that he had presumed that he might step forward and help Jesus, that his mind was better at this than the Messiah's. He felt as much the fool as Menachem and Caleb and their associates.

Caleb shot Jesus one last searing look in an attempt to mask his retreat. He threw his cloak around himself and whirled away in a huff. "We don't have to sit here and be insulted in this manner," he muttered to his companions. They stalked off, the crowd opening a way for them to pass. They slunk away like some nocturnal animals caught suddenly in the glare of the sun.

Once they were gone, the people turned back to see what Jesus would say next. After several moments, his head lifted, and Aaron was surprised to see a touch of fire in his eyes. He let his gaze sweep over those gathered around him, and then he began to speak.

"The scribes and the Pharisees sit in Moses' seat," he said. To everyone's surprise, he chose to use the Greek word *kathedra*. It carried much deeper significance than the idea of a mere place to sit. The *kathedra* was the official seat of high office, especially religious office, from which pronouncements and declarations were made.

By choosing that word, Jesus had made his meaning unmistakable. The Pharisees claimed for themselves the "seat" of Moses. They spoke as if they sat in his chair as prophets and servants of God.

"Therefore, whatsoever they bid you to observe, that observe and do. But do not after their works, for they say, and do not."

Aaron leaned forward, feeling his heart drop. Not again. Not more condemnation.

"They bind heavy burdens on you which are grievous to be borne. They lay them on men's shoulders, but they themselves will not so much as move them with one of their fingers. All their works they do to be seen of men. They make broad their phylacteries and enlarge the borders of their garments."

Aaron winced. That one hit too close to home. It had become a kind of silent contest among his group to try to visibly outdo one another to prove their commitment and faith. The phylacteries, or *tefillin* as they were known in Hebrew, were small leather boxes worn on the forehead and forearm in response to a commandment in the Book of Deuteronomy. They had no set size defined in the Law. But in recent years, some of the leading Pharisees had begun to order larger phylacteries for themselves. Feeling somewhat pressured, Aaron himself had put aside the set that had been in his family for four generations and purchased a set half again as large. It had cost him dearly, for phylacteries required considerable attention to detail and laborious handwork.

He looked down, feeling his face burn a little. Along the bottom of his robe was a thick ribbon of blue. Again, this was in response to a commandment in the Torah. Blue was the color of the sky, and therefore, by extension, the color of heaven. It symbolized spirituality and purity. Here, too, the latest fashion among the Pharisees was to put wider and wider trimming on their garments. Some robes, such as the one Azariah wore to the council meetings, had trim a full hand-span wide. It was a way of saying to the world, "Look at me. See how spiritual I am."

He glanced up to see if Jesus had singled him out, but Jesus wasn't looking at him at all.

"The Pharisees love the uppermost rooms at feasts," Jesus was saying, "and the chief seats in the synagogues. They love the greetings in the markets and to be called of men, 'Rabbi, Rabbi.' Be not called Rabbi: for one is your Master, even Christ; and you are all brethren."

He paused for a moment, then went on. His voice elevated sharply, startling those around him. "Wo unto you, scribes and Pharisees—hypocrites!" The words were like hornets spilling out of a nest that had been disturbed. "You shut up the kingdom of heaven for others, but do not go in yourselves. Neither will you suffer them that are entering to go in. Wo unto you, scribes and Pharisees—hypocrites! You devour widows' houses, and then for a pretense of righteousness make long prayers. Therefore, you shall receive the greater damnation."

Aaron could feel the color draining from his face. This was a withering, scathing attack. The words almost smoked, like they were being drawn from the bowels of a fiery furnace.

"Wo unto you, scribes and Pharisees—hypocrites! You compass sea and land to make one proselyte, and when he is made, you make him twofold more the child of hell than yourselves. Wo unto you. You are blind guides. You say, 'Whosoever shall swear by the temple, it is nothing; but whosoever shall swear by the gold of the temple, he is a debtor! You fools and blind! Which is greater? The gold, or the temple that sanctifies the gold?

"Wo unto you, scribes and Pharisees—hypocrites! You pay tithe of mint and anise and cummin, but omit the weightier matters of the law: judgment, mercy, and faith. These ought you to have done, but not to leave the other undone."

Aaron wanted to crawl into a hole. It was as though every word was directed squarely at him. He swore by the gold of the temple to give added significance to his oaths. He had sat more than once at his table and carefully counted out every tenth leaf of a sprig of mint and set it aside for tithing. It was as though Jesus had secreted himself in Aaron's house, in his very life, and watched him in his religious devotions. Aaron felt his ears flaming with every new condemnation.

"You blind guides!" Jesus cried, his eyes flashing. "You strain at a gnat and yet will swallow a camel. You make clean the outside of the cup and platter, but inside them, they are full of extortion and excess. O blind Pharisees, cleanse first that which is within the cup and platter, that the outside of them may be clean also.

"Wo unto you, scribes and Pharisees—hypocrites! For you are like whitewashed sepulchres. They indeed appear beautiful outward, but within they are full of dead men's bones and of all uncleanness. So it is with you. You outwardly seek to appear righteous unto men, but within you are full of hypocrisy and iniquity. You serpents! You generation of vipers. How can you escape the damnation of hell?"

Jesus stopped, breathing hard. Gradually the passion in him subsided. His jaw relaxed, his eyes softened. And then, as surprising to the listeners as had been the explosion of indignation, sorrow followed. His shoulders slumped forward. His mouth pulled down. He was no longer looking into the faces of the people, but staring off into space, suddenly far away from them.

When he spoke again, his voice was hushed and heavy. "O Jerusalem, Jerusalem," he cried, "thou that kill the prophets and stone them which are sent unto thee. How oft would I have gathered thy children together, even as a hen gathers her chickens under her wings? But you would not! Behold, this generation shall not all pass away before your house is left unto you desolate. And I say unto you, you shall not see me henceforth, till you shall say, 'Blessed is he that cometh in the name of the Lord.'"

He fell silent, his head dropping until his chin nearly touched his chest. His fingers rubbed softly against his robes. All around there was not a stir. The words had been too shocking. Even his closest disciples had not been prepared for what had just happened. Then, at last, Jesus looked up. His eyes fell on Peter. "I would spend time with the Twelve," he said quietly. He stood and moved away.

II

Aaron was surprised when he felt someone sit down beside him. He looked up. Deborah had joined him on the bench. David stood directly in front of him. He looked away again. "I'd rather not talk right now," he said.

"Aaron," David said. "We saw Luke. He told us what happened here."

Aaron just shook his head.

"He wasn't condemning you, Aaron," Deborah said. "He was condemning some of the excesses that have crept into Pharisaism."

"Don't patronize me," he snapped. "I know what Jesus said. You were not here." He got to his feet, not meeting her eyes.

David stepped back as Aaron pushed past him. "Aaron?"

He stopped, not turning.

"It is not what Jesus says or does that makes him the Messiah, Aaron."

Aaron's head came around slowly.

"It is because he *is* the Messiah that he says those things and does those things."

"I'm not sure I see the difference."

"Let me tell you something, Aaron, something that I have told very few people. It happened more than thirty years ago, while I was staying in Bethlehem with Benjamin and his family."

In spite of his desire to escape, Aaron didn't move. "What?"

David told him. He spoke quietly and without dramatics. He told him of the angel appearing in the fields, of the glorious song of exultation that burst from the heavens, of going to the manger and seeing the newborn baby. Then he told him what Mary, the mother of Jesus, had told them, of Gabriel and his declaration that the child born of her would be of God.

For a long moment, neither of them spoke. Aaron looked at his sister. "Is that what you meant the other day?"

"Yes," she exclaimed. "He is the Son of God, Aaron. True, he is the Messiah. Yes, he is the Prophet foretold by Moses. But above all that, he is literally, in every possible way we can imagine, the Son of God."

He began to shake his head, not able to take in what that might mean.

David stepped closer to him. "If that is true," he said, "and I testify with all the power of my being that I know it is true, then, whether it hurt you or not, whether it enrages the Pharisees and the Sadducees or not, who has a better right to declare what is pleasing to God and what is not?"

He was finished. He stepped aside for Aaron to pass. For a long time Aaron just looked at him. Then, lowering his head, he turned and walked away.

"Oh, David," Deborah said, moving up beside him. "He's hurting so much." When David didn't answer, she looked up into his face. "Will he be all right?"

He hesitated momentarily, then looked down at his wife. "Why do we love Jesus so, Deborah? Why are we willing to follow him anywhere, do whatever he asks, even put our lives at risk to protect him if necessary?"

"Because of who he is."

"Exactly. Not just because of what he *does*, but who he *is*."

She began to nod slowly. "Aaron has come to Jesus because of what he did, is that what you're saying?"

"Yes. Think about it. There was Huldah and Lazarus. The man with the withered hand. All of those things were so overwhelming that Aaron couldn't deny them. And it's true, the miracles can draw people to Jesus so they can begin to learn more about who he is. But if miracles are the only basis for what we believe . . ." He shrugged, not needing to finish.

She turned and looked in the direction where Aaron had disappeared into the crowds, her eyes troubled. "What can we do?"

"Pray for him. Pray for his faith. And pray for Hava. Sharing his feelings with her may be exactly what he needs right now."

Deborah studied his face, this man with whom she had shared her bed and her life, childbirth and sickness, joys and sorrows. "Do you know what else?" she said in a half whisper.

One eyebrow lifted. "What?"

"You are exactly what *I* need right now, too."

III

2–3 April, a.d. 33

Again that night, the women of the family returned to Bethlehem and the men went to Bethany. The sun was down by the time Jesus finally gave the signal that he was ready to leave the city, and so it was full dark when they made their way over the Mount of Olives.

The next morning, as they once again made their way toward Jerusalem, they received another shock.

It had rained during the night, and the morning was cool and pleasant. They moved at a leisurely pace, enjoying the freshness of the air. Simeon, David, and Ephraim walked together near the back of the group. Aaron had not appeared again, and no one knew where he was. David hoped he had gone to Jericho to talk to Hava. She was wise and steady. And she, too, believed in Jesus. She would be good for Aaron.

Then, for the third time in as many days, the group came to a stop near the spot where the lane that led to Bethphage branched off from the Bethany-Jerusalem road. Simeon looked around and saw where they were. "Not again," he groaned. "What is it now?"

Then his eyes grew very wide. Those in the lead had come to a stop in front of a large dead tree.

Ephraim gave a low cry. "Look!" he said in awe.

It took Simeon a moment to realize what he was staring at. Then he gulped, feeling a sudden prickling down his back. It was the same tree! He was looking at the fig tree they had stopped at just twenty-four hours before to see if they could find fruit.

His head tipped back as his eyes took in every detail. The limbs were bare and shriveled. Here and there a solitary leaf twisted slowly in the breeze, but the luxuriant foliage of yesterday was gone. He looked down. The ground was a thick carpet of brown, dead leaves.

Ephraim fell back a step, his eyes darting here and there. Perhaps they had stopped at a different tree. It couldn't be the same one. "Even if someone poisoned it," he breathed, "it couldn't have died that quickly."

"Master!" It was Peter who spoke. "Master, look. The tree."

Jesus turned and let his eyes run up the height of the fig tree, then turned to his chief apostle. "Yes?"

"This is the tree you cursed just yesterday," Peter said. "Look how quickly it has withered away, even down to its roots."

Jesus nodded, not at all surprised by this phenomenon. For a moment it seemed as if he was going to say nothing more. Then he turned and looked around at the circle of his disciples. "Have faith in God. Truly I say unto you, if you have faith, and doubt not in your heart, and believe those things which you say shall come to pass, you shall not only do this which is done to this fig tree, but also if you should say unto this mountain, 'Be thou removed, and be thou cast into the sea,' behold, it too shall be done."

He looked around at his dumbfounded followers, then nodded thoughtfully. "Therefore I say this unto you. Whatsoever things you desire, when you pray, believe that you shall receive them, and you shall receive."

With that, he lifted an arm and motioned for them to proceed. They did so, but one by one, as each man passed, they paused for a moment before the tree, deeply sobered. Time after time they had seen Jesus' power used for good—to still the storm, heal the sick, bless the infirm. The skeletal form that loomed above them showed them something else entirely. For the first time in their experience with Jesus, his power had been turned against something.

No one spoke as they made their way slowly up and over the Mount of Olives toward Jerusalem.

CHAPTER NOTES

Since Jesus spoke in Aramaic, it is unlikely he would have used the Greek word *kathedra*, which is translated as "seat" in Matthew 23:2. But since the New Testament was written in Greek, and *kathedra* is the word used in the Greek, this device was used by the author to explain the significance of what Jesus was actually saying (see Thayer, p. 312). Interestingly, those buildings that housed the highest officers of a religion came to be known as cathedrals, or the place of the *kathedra*.

The fullest account of the Savior's denunciation of the Pharisees is given by

Matthew, which is the version used here (Matthew 23:1–39). Knowing the tremendous pride the Pharisees took in their commitment and almost obsessive obedience to the Law, is it any wonder that as Jesus criticized them again and again their leaders were eventually willing to join in the conspiracy to put Jesus to death?

However, it must be remembered that the condemnation was not a universal one. It was aimed at those who *were* hypocrites, those who *did* pose as the pious and spiritually superior, but who in actuality used their religiosity as a cloak for deep wickedness and spiritual corruption. Such was not the case with all the Jewish religious leaders. We are told, for example, that Nicodemus was a Pharisee (John 3:1). Mark calls Joseph of Arimathea an "honourable counsellor" (Mark 15:43), suggesting he was a member of the Sanhedrin. And John says, "Nevertheless among the chief rulers also *many* believed on him; but because of the Pharisees they did not confess him, lest they should be put out of the synagogue" (John 12:42; emphasis added). After Christ's death, we are told a "great company of the priests were obedient to the faith" (Acts 6:7) and that there were "certain of the sect of the Pharisees which believed" (Acts 15:5).

In Matthew's account, it says that the fig tree withered and died "presently" (Matthew 21:19), making it sound as if the cursing and the resulting death of the tree happened all at once. But in Mark's account, he explains that it was the next day when they came upon the tree again (Mark 11:12–14, 20).

This miracle does seem somewhat strange at first, for it seems to be a use of Christ's power not to heal or lift, but to destroy. However, knowing that Jesus never misused his power or did anything without specific purpose, one has to ask about the significance of this event. One commentator suggests that the miracle provided a unique teaching opportunity directly related to his teachings about the Jewish leadership at that time.

"In order to understand the case of the fig-tree, the first thing to attend to is the fig-tree's law of growth and fruit-bearing. What is it? It is that leaves and fruit appear together and disappear together. As soon as the leaves begin to bud the figs begin to form. . . . But with regard to the tree on the Mount of Olives, we are told that it was not yet the time of figs (Mark xi.13). This fact, which seems at first to excuse the tree, was what really led to its condemnation. If it was not the time of figs, it was not the time of foliage. The tree was in advance of its companions as to leaves, and by its own law of life, that is, the custom of having foliage and figs at the same time, such leadership in outward show should have been accompanied by a similar forwardness in fruit bearing. But 'he found nothing thereon, but leaves only.' *It was a vegetable Sanhedrin.* It seemed to be possessed by the spirit that created the long robe and the large phylactery-box. Sins against God were bad enough, but Pharisaism claimed to be for God. Pharisee and fig-tree were alike as to profession without practice. It was the only thing which called forth the stern indignation of Christ. 'Scribes, Pharisees'—and this unnatural fig-tree—'hypocrites!'" (Mackie, pp. 52–53; emphasis added).

CHAPTER 25

THEN SHALL THE KINGDOM OF HEAVEN BE LIKENED UNTO . . .

—*Matthew 25:1*

I

JERUSALEM, THE TEMPLE MOUNT
2 APRIL, A.D. 33

Peter was in turmoil. Every day seemed to bring a new clash, seemed to heighten the tensions, seemed to create greater danger. As he and the other apostles followed Jesus around the great openness of the Court of the Gentiles, his eyes darted here and there, watchful for trouble. And each time they stopped on the east end of the Royal Portico, home to the council chambers of the Great Sanhedrin, he felt a disturbing tightness in his chest. And yet Jesus had more than once made it very clear that he was not going to walk away from all of this.

From the time he had become a disciple, Peter had seen Jesus criticize the pomposity of the Pharisees, condemning their hypocrisy. But what had happened yesterday in the Court of the Women was like nothing he had ever seen before. It was the first time he had witnessed such a vitriolic attack. The Master's words had been scalding, enough to blister the flesh. What he had said was more than criticism; it was confrontation. It was an open declaration of war. And Peter could just imagine the reaction when Caleb and Menachem had returned to the Sanhedrin with their report.

He suddenly felt very old. Jesus kept talking about the possibility of his coming death. Now for the first time, Peter understood how that might happen. He had seen hatred in its purest form, and he knew it was deep enough to lead to murder.

And yet, Jesus *was* the Messiah. He had to keep reminding himself of that. Jesus *was* the Son of God. He could still a storm with a word, cleanse a leper with a touch, give sight to the blind who had never before seen, and beckon the dead forth from the tomb. That was the only thing that gave the fisherman any hope. The Great Sanhedrin wielded enormous power, but compared to the power Jesus controlled? His breath leaked out in a long, drawn-out sigh. Compared to the Son of God, the Great Council was no more than the seed of the thistle being carried along in the breeze. No power on earth could take Jesus' life from him.

"Master?"

The voice of Simon Zelotes brought Peter out of his thoughts. He turned to watch.

"Yes?" Jesus said.

"The temple and all of its buildings are indeed wondrous, are they not?"

Like Peter, everyone in the group, including Jesus, seemed to have been lost in his own thoughts as they walked slowly along. They had not said anything for several minutes. Now Jesus nodded, almost absently.

Guessing what his fellow apostle was trying to do, Peter was glad. They needed to get their minds off this looming sense of disaster, move away from this deep foreboding they were all feeling. If some light conversation would help them do that, all the better.

"It is no surprise that it has taken forty-six years to build it, and it's still not finished," Peter chimed in. "Think how many stones had to be cut and placed just for the surrounding walls. And some of those stones are absolutely massive."

Jesus was giving them his full attention. He let his eyes take in the mass of the temple with its walled courts and inner sanctums. "You see all these things?" he said thoughtfully. "Well, truly I say unto you, soon there shall not be left one stone upon another here that shall not be thrown down."

The Twelve stopped walking, almost as one. Jesus smiled sadly, looking from face to face, then turned and started walking again, his hands behind his back. They fell in behind him, looking at each other in complete perplexity. Not one stone upon the other? That was like saying that tomorrow there would be no sunrise, no wind, no flowers. It had taken more than four decades with thousands of workers to create this complex. Surely he couldn't be speaking literally.

"Did I hear what I thought I just heard?" Matthew said in a low voice, looking at Peter.

Bartholomew was nodding, his eyes wide. "Not one stone upon the other? That's what he said."

"I think the sun has . . ." It was Judas speaking, and he caught himself quickly. He had been about to say, "left him somewhat addled," but decided it was imprudent to complete his thought.

"Surely he wasn't speaking of *these* stones," John ventured. "Maybe he misunderstood what we were talking about."

Andrew shook his head. "Don't you remember what he said the other day?"

"When?" Simon Zelotes asked. He was the most troubled. It had been his comment that had brought forth the stunning response.

"The day of his triumphal entry, just after we crossed the top of the Mount of Olives."

John began to nod. "When he wept for Jerusalem."

"That's right," Andrew said in a low voice. Jesus was a good twenty-five or thirty paces away from them and hadn't noticed that all of his disciples were not right behind him, so Andrew hurried on. "He said that the days were coming when our enemies would cast a trench about us and compass us round about."

"That sounds like the Romans," James ventured. "That's how they lay siege to a city."

"And then," Andrew went on, "if you remember, he said something like this: 'And they'—our enemies—'shall lay you even with the ground and will not leave one stone upon the other.' I can remember feeling a chill come over me as he said it."

They all nodded soberly. Then Peter glanced up and saw that the Master had stopped and was watching them.

"Come," he said with a start. "He's waiting for us."

As they hurried forward, looking somewhat embarrassed, Andrew sidled closer to his younger brother. "Ask him, Peter," he said in a hushed tone. "Ask him what he meant."

Peter shook his head. "I'm not sure that's a good idea," he whispered back. "At least, not now."

II

OUTSIDE JERUSALEM, THE MOUNT OF OLIVES

They left the Temple Mount by the eastern gate, crossed the Kidron Valley, and started the long climb up the west-facing slope of the Mount of Olives. Jesus didn't speak the whole way. He didn't ask what they had been talking about or open an opportunity to ask him questions. He seemed far away, lost in his own thoughts.

To Peter's surprise, about three quarters of the way up the hill, Jesus turned off the main road, taking a narrow path that led past two or three small stone houses, then petered out into an olive grove. Though the air was still pleasant, the western sky was clearing, and the sun had come out. They were all perspiring from the steepness of the climb. Jesus stopped, looked around for a moment, then moved into the shade of one of the larger olive trees and sat down. As the apostles looked for places of their own, Peter realized that Jesus had chosen a spot where the hillside dropped away sharply enough that it left them a spectacular view of the city.

In a moment, everyone was settled and silence fell over the group. Jesus leaned forward, his arms folded on his knees, and rested his chin on his arms. In that position, he gazed out directly on the temple. If they had expected him to speak, they were disappointed. Jesus still seemed distant and withdrawn. After almost five minutes, Andrew nudged Peter. "Ask him!" he mouthed. John and James nodded their encouragement.

Still worried that he might be intruding when Jesus was looking for some peace, Peter shifted his weight uncomfortably. The sound brought Jesus' head up. His expression was hard to read, but it seemed open and inviting. Peter swallowed quickly and plunged in. "Master, in the temple, you spoke of what sounded like great troubles for Jerusalem. Tell us. When shall these things be?" And then on impulse he added: "You have taught us previously that you will come again before the ending of the world. Tell us also, if you will, what shall be the sign of your coming and of the end of the world?"

Andrew shot Peter an admiring and grateful look. Peter was far more daring than his brother had thought he would be.

Jesus sat up straight, looking at these, his closest followers, one by one. Seeing that he was going to answer, Philip, Judas, and James changed positions so everyone was in a tighter circle, facing Jesus.

"Take heed that no man deceive you about this matter," Jesus began, "for many shall come in my name, saying, I am the Christ, or the Messiah. And they shall deceive many. And you shall hear of wars and rumors of wars. See that you are not troubled, for all these things must come to pass, but that does not mean the end is here."

He paused. He seemed pleased by their attentiveness and went on more slowly. "For nation shall rise against nation, and kingdom against kingdom. There shall be famines and pestilence and earthquakes in divers places. All of these are but the beginning of sorrows."

His voice became low and heavy. "Then shall they deliver you up to be afflicted. And you shall be betrayed by parents, brethren, kinsfolk, and friends. And some of you shall they cause to be put to death."

Peter looked at Andrew in open dismay. This was not what he had expected.

"And you shall be hated of all men for my name's sake, but there shall not perish even one hair of your head. So in patience possess your souls." He drew in a deep breath. "At that time, many false prophets shall rise, and shall deceive many. And because iniquity shall abound, the love of many shall wax cold. But he that shall endure faithful unto the end, the same shall be saved."

His eyes closed momentarily, as if there had been a sudden pain. When they opened again, they were dark and gloomy. "When you shall see Jerusalem compassed with armies, then know that the desolation thereof is nigh. Then let them which be in Judea flee into the mountains. Let him which is on the housetop not come down to take anything out of his house, neither let him which is in the field return back to take his clothes. Wo unto them that day that are with child, and to them that give suck, for these be the days of vengeance, that all things which are written may be fulfilled.

"Then shall be great tribulation, such as was not since the beginning of the world to this time, no, nor ever shall be again. There shall be great distress in the land, and wrath upon this people. They shall fall by the edge of the sword, and shall be led away captive into all nations. And Jerusalem shall be trodden down of the Gentiles until the times of the Gentiles be fulfilled. Except those days should be shortened, there should no flesh be saved. But for the elect's sake, those days shall be shortened." He looked up, letting his eyes move from face to face.

Peter knew his own face must mirror the pain on Jesus' face. His heart clenched with horror at the imagery of Jesus' words. There before him lay the Holy City in all its glory. What Jesus had just described was almost impossible for Peter to even imagine.

Peter cleared his throat, a dozen questions tumbling in his mind. But before he could speak, Jesus continued. His voice was so low they had to lean forward to hear him. "Immediately after the tribulation of those days shall the sun be darkened, and the moon shall not give her light. The stars shall fall from heaven, and the powers of the heavens shall be shaken. Then shall appear the sign of the Son of man in heaven. Then shall all the tribes of the earth mourn, for they shall see the Son of man coming in the clouds of heaven with power and great glory. And he shall send his angels with a great sound of a trumpet, and they shall gather together his elect from the four winds, from one end of heaven to the other."

Peter broke in, unable to stop himself. "How shall we know when these things shall be?"

Jesus turned and looked at this apostle he loved so deeply, nodding at the appropriateness of the question. "I would have you learn a parable of the fig tree. When its branch is yet tender and puts forth leaves, you say that summer is nigh."

Peter nodded. The fig tree, of all trees in their country, was the last to come into full leaf. Somehow it always knew if there was one more cold snap yet to come and waited until it had passed. It was a common saying among the people that if the fig tree was in leaf, then you knew that summer had come.

"So likewise shall you," Jesus continued, "when you shall see all these things, know that the time is near, even at the doors. But of the day and the hour, no man knows, no, not even the angels of heaven, but my Father only. Watch, therefore, for you know not what hour your Lord doth come."

"Lord?" It was John, who sat just to the left of the Master.

"Yes?"

"How then shall we prepare ourselves for these tribulations?"

The silence stretched on for a very long time as Jesus looked first at John, then at Peter, then at Judas and the others, and finally out on the city and the temple.

Jesus nodded gravely. John's was perhaps the best question of all. "At that time," he began, "when I shall come in my glory, then shall the kingdom of heaven be likened unto ten virgins, which took their lamps and went forth to meet the bridegroom. And five of them were wise, and five were foolish. They that were foolish took their lamps and took no oil with them."

Peter smiled as he thought of his own wedding to Anna years before. Anna's aunt had misplaced a jar of oil, and it was only later that Peter learned how frantic the women had been to find enough to share. The wedding had been a glorious affair, and the many handheld lamps in the crowds had shimmered like a canopy of stars. Peter had even kept one lamp as a memento of that special, sacred evening.

"But the wise took oil in their vessels with their lamps. While the bridegroom tarried, they all slumbered and slept. And at midnight there was a cry made, 'Behold, the bridegroom cometh. Go ye out to meet him.'"

Yes, Peter thought. *That was exactly how it happened.* When he had been the eager young bridegroom, his family had gone out into the streets lighting the lamps. Then the cry went up from mouth to mouth until the whole town was alive with it. "Here he comes! Here comes the bridegroom."

Jesus went on. "Then all those virgins arose and trimmed their lamps. And the foolish said unto the wise, 'Give us of your oil, for our lamps are gone out.' But the wise answered, saying, 'Not so, lest there be not enough for us and you as well. But go to them that sell and buy for yourselves.' And while they went to buy, the bridegroom came. And they that were ready went in with him to the marriage, and the door was shut. Afterward came also the other virgins, saying, 'Lord, Lord, open to us.' But he answered and said, 'Verily I say unto you, I know you not.'"

Jesus' eyes once again moved from face to face. "Watch, therefore," he said again with great solemnity, "for you know neither the day nor the hour wherein the Son of man cometh."

Peter swallowed hard. He looked at Jesus, whose attention remained fixed on the Holy City. He opened his mouth to ask a question, but Jesus spoke first.

"The kingdom of heaven is also like a man traveling into a far country, who called his servants and delivered unto them his goods. And unto one he gave five talents, to another two, and to another one—to every man according to his several ability. Then straightway he took his journey.

"Then he that had received the five talents went and traded with the same, and increased them by five talents. And likewise he that had received two, he also gained another two. But he that had received one went and dug in the earth and hid his lord's money.

"After a long time the lord of those servants returned and called for a reckoning. And so he that had received five talents came and brought five more talents, saying, 'Lord, you delivered to me five talents. Behold, I have gained beside them five talents more.' Then his lord said unto him, 'Well done, thou good and faithful servant. Thou hast been faithful over a few things, so I will make thee ruler over many things. Enter thou into the joy of your lord.'

"He also that had received two talents came and said, 'Lord, you delivered to me two talents. Behold, I have gained two other talents beside them.' His lord said unto him, 'Well done, thou good and faithful servant. Thou hast been faithful over a few things, so I will make thee ruler over many things. Enter thou into the joy of thy lord.'"

He had their rapt attention. Even though this was likely another parable, they listened as intently as if it had just happened.

"Then," Jesus went on, "he which had received the one talent came and said, 'Lord, I knew that you are a hard man, reaping where you have not sown and gathering where you have not strawed. And I was afraid and went and hid your talent in the earth. Lo, here is what you gave to me.'

"His lord answered and said unto him, 'Thou wicked and slothful servant. You knew that I reap where I sowed not, and gather where I have not strawed. At the very least, you ought to have put my money to the exchangers. Then at my coming, I should have received mine own with usury. Take therefore the talent from him, and give it to him which hath ten talents. For unto every one that hath, it shall be given, and he shall have abundance. But from him that hath not, it shall be taken away even that which he hath. And cast this unprofitable servant into outer darkness where there shall be weeping and gnashing of teeth.'"

No one spoke. Peter tried to understand how these two stories answered John's question about preparing oneself. Finally Matthew raised a hand. "Master?"

"Yes, Matthew?"

"We know that the oil in the sacred lampstands of the temple represents the Spirit of God, giving out light and understanding for all to see."

Jesus nodded in encouragement.

"So would not the first parable then suggest that only as we have the Spirit will we be ready to meet the Bridegroom when he comes?"

"Without the Spirit we can do nothing," James came in. "It is the only way we can know the will of the Lord for us."

Jesus smiled. "Go on."

Andrew ventured a guess. "Would not the talents given to the servants by their lord represent the blessings and gifts that are given us of God? If we do not use those gifts in serving him, if we do not give our best efforts to building up the kingdom, then the Lord has good reason to call us slothful servants."

Jesus was pleased. "You have all spoken well. Now I would speak one more parable to you."

Peter leaned forward, eager to be taught more.

"When the Son of man shall come in his glory, and all the holy angels with him, then shall he sit upon the throne of his glory. And before him shall be gathered all nations, and he shall separate them one from another, as a shepherd divides his sheep from the goats."

Even though Peter was a fisherman, he clearly understood the vivid image. The hillsides of the Galilee were dotted with black and white sheep and goats grazing together. From a distance, the animals appeared similar in temperament, but Peter, having once ended up in a ditch from the hard head of a goat, could testify that goats were independent, aggressive, and combative. Sheep, on the other hand, were much more gentle. Sheep were completely dependent on the shepherd for guidance and protection from the triple dangers of being lost, scattered, or killed.

"And he shall set the sheep on his right hand," Jesus continued, "but the goats on the left. Then shall the King say unto them on his right hand, 'Come, ye blessed of my Father. Inherit the kingdom prepared for you from the foundation of the world, for I was an hungered, and ye gave me meat; I was thirsty, and ye gave me drink; I was a stranger, and ye took me in; naked, and ye clothed me. I was sick, and ye visited me; I was in prison, and ye came unto me.'

"Then shall the righteous answer him, saying, 'Lord, when saw we thee an hungered and fed thee? or thirsty and gave thee drink? When saw we thee a stranger and took thee in?'"

Jesus leaned forward, speaking very earnestly. "And the King shall answer and say unto them, 'Verily I say unto you, Inasmuch as ye have done it unto one of the least of these my brethren, ye have done it unto me.'

"Then shall he say also unto them on the left hand, 'Depart from me, ye cursed, into that everlasting fire which is prepared for the devil and his angels, for I was hungered, and ye gave me no meat; I was thirsty, and ye gave me no drink; I was a stranger, and ye took me not in; naked, and ye clothed me not; sick and in prison, and ye visited me not.'

"Then shall they also answer him, saying, 'Lord, when saw we thee an hungered, or athirst, or a stranger, or naked, or sick, or in prison, and did not minister unto thee?' And the king shall answer them, 'Verily I say unto you, inasmuch as ye did it not to one of the least of these, ye did it not to me.' And these shall go away into everlasting punishment, but the righteous into life eternal."

Peter looked down at his hands. He had been a fisher of men for three years now, but he still had a fisherman's hands—strong, scarred, and supple. He slowly clasped them together in his lap. Jesus had given him much to ponder and understand. Peter hoped his hands, and his heart, would be strong enough to bear the coming burdens.

Chapter Notes

In what has come to be known as the Olivet Discourse, because it was given while Jesus was on the Mount of Olives, Jesus outlined the events that will precede his second coming and told the disciples how to watch for the time (see Matthew 24:1–51; Mark 13:1–37; Luke 21:5–38). The account given here is greatly shortened.

In Matthew's account, Jesus then gave three parables: the ten virgins, the talents, and the sheep and the goats (Matthew 25:1–46). Considering the context in which they were given, these parables have been called by some the "Parables of Preparation." Having Peter and others speculate on the meaning of the parables is a device of the author to help the readers better understand the significance of the stories and is not part of the scriptural record.

The prophecy given by Jesus had both immediate and long-range aspects. Some things, such as his promise to come in the clouds of glory, related to his second coming at the end of history. But others had direct reference to the Jewish nation. Some of those living at the time he spoke would live to see these prophecies fulfilled. Thus, Jesus' prediction, "This generation shall not pass, till all these things be fulfilled" (Matthew 24:34).

In the thirty years that followed Christ's death, conditions deteriorated in Judea. The Jewish leadership continued to persecute the followers of Jesus, even killing some of the disciples (see Acts 7:58–60; 12:1–3). Pilate was recalled in A.D. 36 and disappeared from history. The Roman procurators became more and more corrupt, and resentment among the Jews intensified until the Zealot factions in the Galilee became extremely violent and radicalized.

In A.D. 66, Gessius Florus, the Roman governor, demanded a huge bribe from the Jews for a concession they wanted, then refused to honor the agreement. A riot broke out in Caesarea, which was brutally suppressed. That spark lit a much greater conflagration. Rebellion spread across the land like a mighty windstorm. The swiftness and the intensity of the revolt caught the Romans by surprise. Several important garrisons fell to the Jews, including the ostensibly impregnable Masada and the Antonia Fortress in Jerusalem. The Zealots persuaded the Romans at Masada to surrender, then massacred them. They likewise slaughtered the Romans stationed in Jerusalem. In cold fury, the Romans retaliated, annihilating the entire Jewish population in Caesarea. Twenty thousand Jews were killed in the ensuing riots.

Finally, Cestius Gallus, the legate of Syria, realized he had full-scale war on his hands and sent in a legion under his command. At that point, the prophecy of Jesus became particularly significant. Gallus sent his XII Legion south. It was hardly sufficient, but resistance collapsed before the disciplined troops. Within a few months, Gallus secured the coast and marched on Jerusalem. He hastily threw up a sedge wall around the city, trapping the inhabitants. By this point, the Zealots were battling fiercely among themselves as much as they were fighting the Romans. The chaos was complete. Then, remarkably, Gallus lost his nerve. Though no one knows for sure why—perhaps because winter was approaching— Gallus suddenly decided to withdraw his armies back to Caesarea. They started back down the Beth Horon Pass. Scarcely believing their incredible good fortune, the rebels poured out of Jerusalem and fell upon the retreating legion. It was an utter disaster for the Romans. The XII Legion was so thoroughly annihilated that it was taken out of commission and never reconstituted. Vast stores of arms and siege machines fell into the hands of the Zealots.

It was at that time that the Christians in the land remembered Jesus' words, "And when ye shall see Jerusalem compassed with armies, then know that the desolation thereof is nigh. Then let them which are in Judaea flee to the mountains" (see Luke 21:20–24). Heeding the warning, the Christians fled the country to Pella, a city of the Decapolis on the east side of the Jordan. Thus, they escaped what was about to come.

After such a crushing defeat, Rome could no longer ignore the Jewish rebellion. The full power of the empire was sent to stamp it out. By the time Titus, the commanding general, finally conquered Jerusalem in A.D. 70, over a million Jews had been killed, many of them slaughtered on the Temple Mount itself. In the final, desperate hours, the Zealots fled to the inner courts of the temple for defense. Once he finally rooted them out, Titus, determined that never again would these massive stoneworks be used for defense, ordered the temple and all of its buildings leveled. He left only the western wall of the Temple Mount as a witness to the defenses his armies had to overcome. Jesus' promise that they would see the day when not one stone was left upon the other was literally fulfilled.

Two years later at Masada, near the shores of the Dead Sea, in the last holdout of the resistance, almost a thousand Jews committed suicide rather than surrender to the Romans. Judea, as a nation of Jews, had ceased to exist. (For an excellent summary of the Jewish revolt, see Frank, pp. 254–73.)

CHAPTER 26

I

JERUSALEM, UPPER CITY

2 APRIL, A.D. 33

Mordechai ben Uzziel was brooding. His heavy eyebrows were pulled down, creating deep lines in his forehead. His eyes scowled darkly as he looked around at the empty room, not seeing anything. His mouth, nearly hidden by his thick, well-trimmed beard, was pinched and hard.

This mood had been on him for some time, and it took only one word to explain why. Jesus! The carpenter from Nazareth had turned the city upside down. His name was on every set of lips. The people flocked to him like he was some kind of Greek oracle. The Sanhedrin was in chaos. The Pharisees were in disarray. His own Sadducees, who had more direct governing power than anyone other than Pilate, were like paralyzed old men unable to move without aid. They fluttered about, wringing their hands and wailing piteously, but doing nothing.

Thrice in the last few days, Mordechai had been on the verge of sending a messenger to the Antonia Fortress, asking for a conference with Tribune Marcus Didius. Each time he had finally backed away. The last time he had brought the Romans in to help solve this problem, it had proved to be disastrous. They had a role to play, of that he had no doubt. But their involvement had to be carefully orchestrated, played with meticulous finesse only when the timing was perfect.

In the meantime, Mordechai brooded.

His head came up slowly when he heard a soft knock at the door. The scowl became a glare. "What is it?" he snapped. Levi knew full well that his master didn't like to be disturbed when his door was shut. Unless doing their assigned tasks or otherwise summoned, the dozen or so servants were to stay in their basement quarters and leave the rest of the massive house to its lone family member.

The door opened a couple of inches. Levi was there—nervous and twitching anxiously.

"Yes! Yes!" Mordechai's voice cracked like a whip.

"Sire, Menachem of Bethphage is here."

Sitting back, Mordechai flicked a finger. The door opened a little further. "He says he has a matter of utmost urgency," the steward said.

"Then why haven't you shown him in?"

Levi disappeared again, and Mordechai heard the slap of sandals walking rapidly across marble. A moment later, heavier footsteps sounded. Mordechai stood up, waiting. He curtly cut off Menachem's apologies and motioned him in. "Shut the door," he commanded.

His fellow Sadducee and protégée on the Great Council stepped inside and shut the door. He was breathing heavily, and beads of perspiration stood out on his forehead. Deciding he was grateful for any diversion, Mordechai's mood softened a little. He motioned to a chair, waited for Menachem to be seated, then returned to his own chair.

"Sire?" Menachem began. He was nervous too. Obviously Levi had told him of the dangers of interrupting Mordechai at such times as this. "I have some good news."

"Really?" There was no hiding the skepticism in his voice.

"So far our promise of reward for anyone who can deliver Jesus to us has brought in only pimps and harlots and beggars."

"This is good news? You had better not have paid out anything to such residents of the dung heap."

"Not a shekel," Menachem agreed, licking his lips quickly. "But . . ."

Mordechai leaned forward. He could see the eagerness in Menachem's eyes. "What?"

"I have someone outside in the courtyard."

One eyebrow came up.

"His name is Judas of Iscariot."

"I know of no one by that name."

"No, nor did I." Menachem flashed a momentary grin of triumph. "But Jesus does. Judas is one of his so-called Twelve Apostles."

II

"So," Mordechai said, holding out a silver cup of wine to his guest. "I understand you are a disciple of this Jesus."

"I am." He took the cup and drank deeply, eagerly.

Filling his own cup but merely sipping at it, Mordechai sat down again. His eyes studied the man, who accepted the penetrating gaze as if he expected nothing less. The face was intelligent, almost handsome. His robes were not expensive, but they were clean, not shabby in any sense of the word. His face was narrow, giving the dark eyes a more sober look, but when he smiled, that impression immediately disappeared. He seemed pleasant and amiable.

"You are one of what Jesus calls his Twelve?"

Judas nodded, ignoring the soft contempt in the other's voice.

"I am. I have been with him for three years now. I am at his side almost every waking hour."

"I see. But not tonight."

Judas flushed a little, clearly understanding the implied question. "By assignment of the Master, I am the keeper of our bag. It is my duty to procure food and lodging where required."

"And you are here now to add to the bag?" Mordechai had to force himself to keep the disgust out of his voice. For all his revulsion at what this man was doing, this was exactly what he had been hoping for. He couldn't alienate him.

"Sir, this is not about money."

Mordechai nodded solemnly. It never was.

"I—I have grown concerned about the way things are going. It is like Jesus has . . . has . . ." His voice trailed off.

"Has what?" Mordechai was interested.

"It's like he's not himself. Perhaps the adulation of the crowd has turned his head. Perhaps he is just tired. But he seems to have lost his better judgment. It's like he's looking for trouble."

"And finding it," the Sadducee drawled laconically.

"The other night a woman anointed his feet with spikenard, probably three hundred *denarii* worth." There was almost a horror in his eyes. "She just poured it out over his feet. Think of what that kind of money could do for the poor."

And for the keeper of the bag, thought Mordechai. But he made a sympathetic sound. "Shameful," he said.

"It's more than that," Judas went on. "He's making statements about Rome destroying the temple and about his kingdom coming in power. I fear that the Romans, hearing of that, might take action against our people."

There was a long silence, and Judas's eyes dropped as Mordechai watched him steadily. "So?" Mordechai finally asked.

"When I learned that the Sanhedrin was looking for someone who could help, I decided this might be the answer. Perhaps if he is kept in a cell until Passover is completed and the tension subsides a little . . ."

"It would have to be done when he is not with the people," Mordechai suggested. "That's our problem, to say nothing of merely locating him among the hundreds of thousands of pilgrims who have come for the festival. We can't afford to have a riot."

Judas's dark eyes became shrewd and calculating. "I am always with him, and because I have responsibility for our needs, I can slip away at any time without arousing suspicion."

Perfect! Mordechai felt like shouting it. So, what to offer the man? He sensed that this was not a time for haggling. The man was wrestling with his conscience, and it wouldn't take much to scare him off.

Then he had his answer. One of the statutes in the Law of Moses specified what payment was required if a man's ox went berserk and killed another man's manservant or maidservant. It was about double the price Mordechai had thought he might first offer, but the irony of it was too delicious to pass by. He leaned forward. "This has to be done quietly and competently. Could we expect more than simply information? Would you be willing to actually lead us to him?"

Judas nodded but said nothing.

"Then you bring more to the table than we had hoped."

Judas gave him a look of anticipation, but still he remained silent.

"What would you say to thirty pieces of silver?"

In spite of himself, Judas rocked back a little. Greed was evident in his eyes. "Thirty shekels?" he exclaimed.

"Yes."

The calculations going on in Judas's mind were obvious.

"It would be paid when you deliver the man to us," Mordechai added.

Judas instantly shook his head. "No."

Seeing his mistake immediately, Mordechai corrected himself.

"You're right. We can't be handing you money in front of the others. Payment will be made when you bring us the information we need."

After a long time, Judas's eyes dropped. "Done," he said quietly.

Mordechai stood. "Come, let us go to the house of the high priest. As head of the council, he must approve this agreement, but it is only a formality." He suppressed a smile of satisfaction. "The deal, as you say, is done."

III

JERUSALEM, THE TEMPLE MOUNT
3 APRIL, A.D. 33

"Are you sure, Peter?"

Peter nodded glumly. "Yes."

Simeon blew out his breath in exasperation, then looked at his father. David was watching the senior apostle carefully, trying to read from his expression what was really going on. "Do you think this is wise?" David asked.

Peter held out one hand imploringly. "David, you have families. Passover is a time for families."

"I know, but—"

Peter cut off his old friend and former fishing partner quickly. "What I'm trying to tell you is that Jesus has said he wants to have the Passover meal with just the Twelve."

"Oh?" David said, taken aback by that.

"Wait a minute." Ephraim interrupted. "Jesus is going to celebrate with just you?"

"Yes, that's what he said."

Simeon saw the oddity of it too. "What about his mother? What about Mary and Martha and Lazarus?"

"They'll stay in Bethany and have their own celebration." The burly fisherman shook his head at the surprise on their faces. "That's what he said."

"Where will you be?" Simeon asked.

Peter shrugged. "He says that will be determined later today."

"Well," Simeon said grudgingly, "at least no one will know of his whereabouts in advance."

"But if trouble starts, Bethlehem is six miles away," David pointed out. "It will take three or four hours to get word to us and have us get back."

"There are twelve of us," Peter noted. He touched the sword hanging from his belt. "We're not totally helpless, you know."

David sighed. "And these are the wishes of Jesus?"

Peter did not hesitate. "Exactly as he asked me to convey them to you. He wants you with your families. He wants to be alone with us."

The three men of the family looked at each other, then over to where Jesus stood talking with a small crowd. The day had been a quiet one. There had been no further confrontation with the Pharisees, nor had they seen anyone from the Sanhedrin. Even the crowds were down, most likely preparing for the Passover meal, the most important meal of the year.

There was also the matter of cleansing the house from any trace of leaven, or yeast. The Feast of the Passover was combined with the Feast of Unleavened Bread. During the festival, the Jews were not allowed to eat any breadstuffs made with leaven. In addition, according to the book of Exodus, the feast required not only an abstention from leavened bread but also the purging of the house of any and all leaven. Since the old dough used as leavening spoiled quickly, this was the Lord's way of suggesting symbolically that Israel purge itself of all that was corruptible. From that requirement had evolved an important ritual involving the whole family. The previous evening, the women of the house—in this case led by Esther, wife of Benjamin—would hide small bundles of the leavening dough throughout the house. This afternoon the hunt would begin. The children would race from room to room, cupboard to cupboard. Every bundle had to be accounted for and carried out of the house. If David and his sons were going to be part of that ritual, they would have to leave for Bethlehem soon.

"You will send for us if there is trouble?" Simeon pressed.

Peter grimaced. "Count on that," he said.

David spoke for the rest of them. He put out his hand and gripped Peter's, locking their hands over the other's wrists. "Then, *shalom*, old friend," he said. "You know we will come at a moment's notice."

"Yes, and so does Jesus. He is much appreciative of your concern."

"Then, good Sabbath, Peter." It was not Saturday, but the festival days were considered holy days, or Sabbaths, as well. In a few hours, the Passover Sabbath would begin.

"Good Sabbath, David. Convey my best wishes to Deborah and the rest of the family." And with that, he turned and walked back to join the others.

IV

BETHANY

Peter was fretting. He knew he should just relax. If the Master was not concerned, then why should he be? Jesus knew what he wanted and when he wanted it. But Peter fretted nevertheless. It was midafternoon. At sundown the first day of Passover would begin. Not only did they need to find a place to meet, but all of the arrangements for a Passover supper had to be made. They had no lamb, no bitter herbs, no . . .

He looked up as Mary passed by the window above him. She and Martha were doing exactly what he should be doing. They were bustling about to complete their preparations for the evening. They had been at it all morning. It would be so easy if Jesus changed his mind and agreed to stay with them. Martha would be pleased. Mary and Lazarus would be pleased. And Peter and his brethren would be greatly relieved. It would be so much more simple. He blew out his breath in frustration.

"Peter?"

He turned, half startled to see Jesus watching him steadily. "Yes, Master?"

"Take John. Go and prepare us the Passover that we may eat."

He leaped to his feet. *At last!* "And where would you have us prepare this, Master?" He motioned to John, who was sitting across the courtyard with Andrew and James in the shade of an olive tree.

"Go into the city," Jesus answered. "As you enter, you will meet a man carrying a pitcher of water."

John had come over beside Peter. Peter glanced at him, trying hard not to show his dismay.

"When you find him," Jesus went on, "follow him. When he enters into his house, then speak with the goodman of the house and tell him that the Master saith unto him: 'My time is at hand. I will keep the Passover at your house. Where is the guest chamber where I may eat of the Passover with my disciples?'"

The two men stared at each other. Had Jesus already made arrangements? He spoke of this "goodman of the house" as if it were someone who knew him, yet he did not give his name. John started to ask for further clarification, but Peter tugged at his sleeve, motioning with his head for them to leave. "Yes, Master," Peter mumbled, and turned and followed his younger companion out the gate.

The main road between Bethany and Jerusalem ran directly in front of Martha's house. Once out into the street, Peter and John turned west, moving up the hill toward the city. Finally, after a minute, John blurted out: "I didn't think it wise to ask the Master this, but how are we to find this man and follow him? There are hundreds of thousands of people in the city today."

That had been Peter's first thought too, but he didn't admit it. He merely grinned, enjoying John's discomfort—Peter had felt that same way more than once himself.

"So how are we supposed to find this man?" John repeated. "How in the world are we supposed to find who to follow?"

"Because he will have a pitcher of water," Peter answered.

"Well," John growled, "that should eliminate all but a thousand or two."

"No," Peter responded, "because *he* will have a pitcher of water. Jesus said to find a *man* carrying a pitcher of water."

John stopped short.

Peter's grin broadened. "If Jesus had said a woman, then we would have a problem. But how often do you see a man carrying water?"

John's face showed his dawning comprehension. "Oh," he said slowly.

Slapping him on the shoulder, Peter started off again. "You are wise beyond your years, old friend. So let us go and see what we can find."

John watched his associate for several steps, then ran to catch up with him. "Does he do this just to teach us to have faith in him?"

Peter laughed. "You had too many words at the end of your sentence. He does this to teach us."

V

Jerusalem, the Temple Mount

They were both still sweating from their journey. The road from Bethany to Jerusalem climbed the full height of the Mount of Olives, the highest elevation in the area, dropped down into the Kidron Valley, then climbed back up Mount Moriah to the Temple Mount. But they had not stopped there. They crossed the great Court of the Gentiles and went out the south gates. There they stopped to consider their alternatives.

There were fountains and public cisterns in several places around the city, but the Pool of Siloam, at the western end of Hezekiah's Tunnel, was the most popular one. Should they start there or find something closer to the center of the city? Even as they debated, their eyes followed the streams of people passing them in both directions.

"There!" John grabbed Peter's arm, pointing.

Peter just shook his head in amazement. He should have known. About a dozen paces away, a man was coming slowly up the hill. On his head, in the fashion of women, he carried a clay pot, cushioned on a folded cloth. The sides of the pot were dark from being dipped in water. He was obviously coming from the Pool of Siloam.

Peter glanced at John. "What did I tell you? He's always teaching us."

"Do you think this is the one?"

Peter looked around. "How many other men do you see carrying water?" he asked lazily. And with that, they began to follow the man, a few paces behind and out of his line of sight.

It soon became obvious that the man was headed toward the Upper City of Jerusalem. At first this surprised Peter a little. That's where the elite neighborhoods of the city were. Would Jesus know anyone up there? But then he remembered that Jesus had mentioned an upper chamber. That should have alerted him. The poor were lucky to have a house with a room big enough to divide with a curtain. Upper chambers came only with some degree of wealth.

The farther they moved away from the temple complex, the more the crowds thinned. As they entered a long, narrow street, the man finally realized he was being followed. He kept glancing back at the two men, once giving them an inquisitive raise of an eyebrow. But Peter only smiled and continued to follow, staying far enough back so that the man wouldn't feel threatened.

The house the man approached was not one of the great palatial homes that dotted Mount Zion—homes like those of the high priest and the other rulers of the Great Council—but it was impressive nevertheless. It was two stories high, made of finely cut stone, with a high wall to shut out the noise of the street. The two apostles stopped as the servant reached the heavy wooden door, raised a knocker, and rapped sharply three times, then turned his head to watch them warily.

In a moment, the door opened and the man went through, removing the pitcher before entering. The door shut again; there was a solid thud as the bar behind it was dropped into place again.

Peter looked at his friend and companion, who just shook his head. This was amazing. They walked to the gate, and Peter lifted the heavy knocker. Following the example of the water carrier, he rapped it three times. In a moment, a face appeared at a small opening. "Yes?" It was another man, with dark, beetle-black eyes.

"We would speak with the master of the house," Peter said.

The eyes stared at them for a moment; then, to Peter's surprise, there was a scraping sound as the bar on the other side was lifted. In a moment, the gate swung open. "Wait here, please," the man said as they stepped inside the spacious courtyard. He was older than the servant they had followed. "I will fetch my master."

They didn't have long to wait. The man who came out of the house was not dressed for the street, but his light robes were made of expensive linen and were elegantly trimmed. "Yes?" he said, eyeing the two of them curiously. "May I be of assistance?"

Peter took a breath. For all his trust in the Master's abilities, he still had a lingering wonderment about whether this was going to work. "We have come from Bethany," he began. "We represent the Master."

"The Master?" the man seemed surprised but not puzzled.

"Yes," Peter said. "He asked that we give you the following message. 'My time is at hand. I will keep the Passover at your house. Where is the guest chamber where I may eat of the Passover with my disciples?'" Peter smiled amiably. "Those are his words."

It was hard to tell what was going on behind the man's eyes, and that seemed a little odd to Peter. He had expected surprise, or even consternation. Two complete strangers appear at the gate, invoke only the word "Master," and request to take over a part of the house? How could this have been anything but a startling announcement. But the man hesitated only a moment, then nodded, and to their complete surprise extended an arm in an invitation. "Come," he said. "I will show you."

They went through the front door—heavy wooden planks with gleaming brass hinges, a solid door opener, and a finely crafted mezuzah. The man immediately turned to the left and took them up a narrow set of stone stairs. At the top was a short hallway with two doors. He opened one at the end and stepped inside, moving back so they could follow.

Peter stopped, and John nearly bumped into him. It was a large room with windows on two sides, the one with a spectacular view of the Temple Mount. There were stools, chairs, and padded benches around the walls. In one corner was a large basin with towels folded and neatly stacked on each side. A pitcher of water stood beside it.

These items were for guests to wash themselves prior to a meal. A large U-shaped table stood in the center of the room. It was low, just three feet off the floor and surrounded by benches, which were wide, padded couches a foot lower than the table. These would provide a comfortable place for the guests to recline as they ate. Most surprising, the table was already set with copper plates and cups.

Peter's eyes widened as he saw the loaf of *matzah,* or unleavened bread, wrapped in a white cloth. Beside it was a dish of celery stalks in water, and beside that, the small bowl of salt water. There was no roast lamb as yet, and the large silver pitcher from which the wine cups would be filled when the appropriate time came was still empty. These would be provided later, once the people arrived, but it was clear that not just any meal was going to be served here. This table was laid in preparation for the Passover.

Turning slowly, Peter gave their host a questioning glance.

"Will this be sufficient?" the man asked.

John could scarcely believe what he was seeing. "But this is ready for the . . ." He shook his head, turning back to look at the table. He counted quickly. Ten place settings.

The man sensed what he was doing. "How many will there be with the Master?"

Peter felt like laughing aloud—once again the Master had taught them an important lesson—but he maintained a grave demeanor. "Twelve others," he said.

"Very well," came the reply. "We will have all in readiness. When may we expect him?"

"Before sundown," Peter answered.

The man bowed his head deferentially. "Until then, may peace be with you and with him."

"We will convey your good wishes and also the fact that all is in readiness for him. Thank you."

CHAPTER NOTES

John gives us the only insight from the Gospel writers as to what motivated Judas Iscariot to seek out the chief priests and elders with his offer to betray Jesus into their hands. He records that it was Judas who was offended when Mary anointed Jesus' feet with the precious ointment, then adds this: "This he said, not that he cared for the poor; but because he was a thief, and had the bag, and bare what was put therein" (John 12:6). The implication seems to be that Judas, still smarting under what he saw as profligate waste and the resulting rebuke from the Master for his criticism, decided to take action of another sort.

The record is clear, however, that Judas initiated the contact, going to the rulers and not the other way around. Matthew tells us that after the agreement was struck, "from that time he sought opportunity to betray him" (Matthew 26:16). Thirty pieces of silver was the price specified in the Law of Moses to be paid in reparation should one's ox gore another man's manservant or maidservant to death (see Exodus 21:32).

CHAPTER 27

I

BETHLEHEM
3 APRIL, A.D. 33

The unfolding of the Passover meal followed a very specific and defined ritual, repeated not only in every household in Jerusalem but throughout the province, and indeed, wherever observant Jews were to be found.

The person appointed to lead the service for the family was generally the head of the house. In Bethlehem, in the house of Benjamin the Shepherd, that was not so easily determined as one might think. Technically, five heads of households were present: Benjamin himself; Benjamin's son, Joab; David ben Joseph; Ephraim; and Simeon, as a newly married husband. Benjamin was the logical choice since it was his house, but he reminded them that he had led the service the last three times they had been there. It took only a moment to convince David that since he was the next oldest male present, it should fall to him.

Deborah had hoped that Aaron and Hava and their family would return to have Passover with them, but they had not seen him since he had left them on the Temple Mount, dispirited, dejected, and hurt. She had sent word to Jericho inviting them to join them in Bethlehem but had heard nothing.

The Passover service consisted of four major divisions, each carried out with precise and solemn attention to detail. In the first portion, the person in charge of the service opened the meal with a blessing and prayer. This was followed by the drinking of the first of four cups of wine. Then the family partook of the celery sticks dipped in salt water. This was to remind them of the tears shed by the Israelites while slaves in Egypt.

Next came the retelling of the Exodus story. This always began with the youngest male present who was capable of understanding asking this question: "Why is this night different from all other nights?" In previous years, that part had been taken by Ephraim's son, Boaz. But since he and his sister and baby brother had remained in Capernaum with Lilly and Ezra, this year the task fell to Seth, Benjamin's nine-year-old grandson. Once the story was finished, the group sang the psalm of David that began with the words, "Praise ye the Lord. Praise, O ye servants of the Lord, praise the name of Jehovah." Then the second cup of wine was poured and drunk.

Next came the formal meal. Here the Paschal lamb, the bitter herbs, and the unleavened bread, or *matzah*, were consumed. Generally parsley, watercress, or horseradish was used. Even the tiniest portion of any of these herbs left the mouth stinging and the stomach twisting a little. What better way to signify the bitterness of their bondage in Egypt than to partake of these bitter herbs each year? Another brief prayer and the third cup of wine followed.

Finally, the person leading the services sang some additional psalms. The meal concluded when the participants drank the last of the ritual cups of wine. It was as David was chanting the last of the psalms that something very unusual happened. David had a deep, sonorous voice, and he sang the measured words with great solemnity. Then suddenly, right in the midst of the singing, he stopped, staring at the scroll with the texts of the psalms that was in his hand.

Every eye turned to him, shocked that he would stop during the ceremony. Deborah started to rise, thinking that something was wrong, but he waved her back down. Looking very strange, he went on, speaking now instead of continuing with the traditional singing. *The stone which the builders refused is become the head stone of the corner.*

All around the table, faces showed surprise. Those were the words Jesus had used in reference to himself in his confrontation with the Pharisees a few days before. That was partly what had offended Aaron so deeply.

David's head lifted. "Do you remember what comes next?" he asked quietly.

The adults looked at each other, then finally shook their heads. The songs used in the last part of the Passover service were songs of praise and adoration and remembrance, but they could not specifically remember what came immediately following the passage David had just read.

David lifted the scroll again. *Save now, I beseech thee, O Lord. Blessed be he that cometh in the name of the Lord.*

Deborah drew in a sharp breath. Miriam reached out instinctively and gripped Simeon's hand. Livia and Leah, who were sitting together, turned to each other in surprise. Memories of a few days before flooded back with perfect clarity. They had been with Jesus, traveling on the road from Bethany to Jerusalem. The Master had stopped and sent two of his disciples into Bethphage to find a donkey. What had followed would never be forgotten. Suddenly a spirit had swept over the crowd. The people had cut down palm branches. They had laid their outer clothing at the feet of the donkey. They had strewn flowers and greenery in its path. As Jesus started forward again, now mounted, a mighty shout went up, as if torn from a single throat. *Hosanna! Hosanna! Blessed is he that cometh in the name of the Lord. Hallelujah! Hosanna in the highest!* Then, just moments later, it was followed by one of the most sacred of all shouts in Judaism. *Hosanna! Hallelujah! Praise be to Jehovah. May Jehovah save us.*

David stopped, his eyes swimming. He started to say something, then looked away. Slowly he lowered the scroll back to the table. Every aspect of the Passover feast was always carried out with great solemnity, but now, David's gravity had deepened even more. He took the pitcher of wine and refilled each cup. He lifted his cup high, and the rest followed suit. What came next was not part of the usual text for the service, but no one cared.

"For over twelve hundred years," David said, his voice low and filled with awe, "our people have celebrated this night of deliverance. But we have never truly been free. First it was Assyria that conquered us, then Babylon and Persia. Next came Greece, and now, finally, Rome. We have not been free for many centuries."

He paused. "I don't know who first added the singing of the psalms to the Passover service. But somewhere back in time, some wise man decided to include a psalm that David wrote under the inspiration of heaven. It is a Messianic psalm."

He had to stop, swallowing hard. Deborah's eyes had filled. Miriam and Rachel and Leah were crying with quiet joy. Livia and Aunt Esther were close to tears as well.

"On this night of nights, after more than a millennia of waiting, we no longer pray for the Messiah to come and deliver us. On this night, we sing, not a prayer for deliverance, but a hymn of praise. The Lord God has come down from heaven. The Son of God has come to earth to save us all." He brought the cup to his lips and took a sip. The others did the same.

"*Hallelujah!*" David said softly. "*Hosanna* and *hosanna!* Blessed is he that cometh in the name of the Lord."

"Amen!" exclaimed the family with equal softness. "Amen and amen!"

II

JERUSALEM, UPPER CITY, AN UPPER ROOM

The first intimation Peter had that this was not going to be a completely traditional Passover supper came in the third portion of the feast. The inaugural blessing and prayer had been followed by the first cup of wine and then the eating of the celery stalks dipped in salt water. So far there had been nothing out of the ordinary.

In the second part of the supper, the retelling of the Exodus story, John, the youngest of the Twelve, led out with the age-old question, "Why is this night different from all other nights?" Jesus was serving as the leader of the service, and for a moment, Peter thought he wasn't going to answer. The question seemed to have struck him with a deep melancholy. But after a moment, he looked up, smiled wanly, and answered with the words that had been recited for hundreds upon hundreds of years. "On all other nights, we eat leavened bread and *matzah*; on this night, we eat only *matzah*. On all other nights, we eat all kinds of herbs; on this night, we eat only bitter herbs."

It was in the third phase of the meal that things changed. Normally, at the appropriate point in the meal, the leader of the service uncovered the loaf of unleavened bread, broke off a piece for himself, then passed the loaf down the table for each individual to do the same. Then everyone would dip their pieces of bread in the bowls of sauce made from the bitter herbs and eat them at the same moment.

Things did not proceed normally at that point. Jesus reached over and took the loaf from the center of the table, laying aside the white cloth that had covered it. He took it in both hands, paused for a moment, looking up into heaven. His lips moved silently for a moment as he offered thanks to God. Then, to Peter's surprise, Jesus got to his feet. He broke off a piece of the flat, hard bread and handed it to John, who was sitting at his right. Surprised, John took it, looking at Peter, not sure what to do with it. Before John could decide, Jesus took another step, broke off a second piece and handed it to Peter. One by one, he went around the entire table, handing each apostle a piece of the bread. When he returned to his place, Jesus broke off one final piece, then set the remainder of the loaf back on the plate. The apostles looked at him expectantly, holding the pieces of bread in their hands.

Jesus straightened again, holding his piece of bread in front of him. Finally, he lifted it to his lips and put it into his mouth. "Take," he said, motioning to the circle of disciples. "Eat."

As they did so, he said, very seriously, "This is a representation of my body, which is given for you. This do in remembrance of me."

John turned to Peter. "What is he doing?" he mouthed.

Peter could only shrug. He was as perplexed by the change in tradition as the rest.

To their further surprise, Jesus then leaned forward and took the pitcher of wine and his cup. He filled the cup, but instead of filling all of the other cups, as was the tradition, he set the pitcher down. Again his eyes lifted, and he offered a brief prayer. Then, once again, he looked down on the twelve men seated around him. He lifted the cup to his lips, sipped briefly, then held it out to John. The young fisherman took it, again not sure what was expected of him. Jesus nodded his encouragement. "Drink," he said gently. "All of you drink from it.

This cup is representative of my blood, even the blood of the new testament, or the new covenant, which is shed for you and for many. This, too, do in remembrance of me."

John took a sip and handed the cup to Peter. One by one, it went around the circle, finally returning to Jesus, nearly empty. His shoulders lifted and fell, and once again there was a sense of great sorrow in his face. "Verily, I say unto you, I will drink no more of the fruit of the vine until that day that I drink it new with you in the kingdom of God."

And with that, he returned his cup to the table and sat down again.

No one spoke or made a sound. Every eye was on Jesus. The Passover meal had just undergone a dramatic change, and they weren't sure exactly why or what it meant. Jesus' head was down. He seemed to be staring at nothing, his thoughts apparently far away from them.

Normally, the meal would have closed with the singing of psalms and partaking of the final cup of wine. But normal was no longer the order of the evening.

After several long moments, Jesus straightened, turned, and moved across the room to the table in the corner where the basin of water and the towels had been placed. As they had entered the home a little before sundown, the master of the house had, as custom required, stationed one of his servants at the door to help the arriving guests remove their sandals and wash and dry their feet in preparation for entering the home. But this pitcher, basin, and towels were in this inner room and had been left untouched. Peter had assumed this chamber was often used as an eating hall for guests, and the washing facilities were left there for that purpose. Now, as Jesus moved to those items, Peter wondered if they had been specifically requested.

When he reached the table, Jesus slipped off his outer tunic and set it on a stool. This left him dressed in the shorter inner tunic, which came to his knees. He picked up a folded towel, stuffed one end of it into the belt around his waist, then, using both hands, picked up the heavy basin and carried it back to the table.

Peter and John exchanged puzzled looks. Now what? This was certainly not part of the Passover tradition.

Jesus stopped at John's place at the table and carefully set the basin on the floor. Then he returned to the table and retrieved the pitcher of water. With the movement of Jesus away from the table, John and the others on his side of the table had sat up, turning their backs to the table so they could watch what Jesus was doing. Now that he no longer was reclining, John's feet hung over the outer edge of the low couch on which he was seated, almost touching the basin.

To the young apostle's utter astonishment, Jesus knelt before him, reached out, gently took him by both ankles, and swung his feet up and over the lip of the empty basin. He removed the towel from his belt, laid it across his knee, and lifted the pitcher of water. With great soberness, Jesus poured a small amount of water over John's feet. He set the pitcher down, and, using both hands, began to gently wash John's feet.

The others began to stir. If they had been surprised at what Jesus had done before, now they were shocked. What was the Master doing? This was servant's work, and it had already been performed. Jesus was no servant. He was the Messiah. This was the Son of God. The sight of him at John's feet was so disturbing that murmuring could be heard around the table.

Jesus never looked up. He again lifted John's feet and placed them on the towel. With that same infinite care, he dried them. Only then did he look up into John's eyes. His expression was grave, his demeanor filled with reverence.

Simon Peter, sitting next to John, was staring with a mixture of amazement and horror. When the Master slid the basin over and then knelt in front of his chief apostle, Peter recoiled. He drew his feet up, tucking them under his legs. "No, Lord!" he cried.

Jesus' head came up slowly as he looked at Peter.

A little embarrassed at his vehemence, Peter backed down a little. "Lord, you would wash *my* feet?"

Jesus spoke quietly, as if only the two of them were in the room. "What I do, you know not now, but you shall know hereafter."

Peter's feet were still drawn up beneath him, and he wasn't about to move them. "You shall never wash my feet," he began. He was about to suggest that he and the others should be washing Jesus' feet, not the other way around.

Jesus sat back on his heels. He took a quick breath and released it, and his voice became firm and resolute. "Peter, if I wash you not, you have no part with me."

Peter looked as if he had been slapped. He had been sharply rebuked once before for not accepting what Jesus was saying. His face went red, and his chin dropped. Slowly he straightened his legs again, letting his feet come down to the floor. "If that is the case, Lord, then wash not my feet only, but also my hands and my head."

Jesus gave a momentary smile, filled with great love for this big, rough man whom he had called as first among the apostles. "Peter," he said softly, "he that is washed needs not but to wash his feet." He placed Peter's feet in the basin and poured water over them. As Jesus began to wash them with his hands, he looked up again. "If that is done, he is clean every whit."

He began wiping Peter's feet with the towel. When he was finished, he looked around at the others, his eyes stopping on the man who had been sitting directly across from him at supper. "And ye are clean," he said, looking at Judas Iscariot, "but not all."

No one said anything more as Jesus proceeded around the table, stopping in front of each apostle, always on his knees, always working quietly and with great reverence. When he finished, Jesus returned the basin, the pitcher, and the towel to the side table. He took up his outer robe again and slipped it on. Only then did he return and take his place at the table again, sitting down with the others.

Every head was turned toward him as these closest of his disciples waited to see what was to happen next. Jesus let his eyes move from face to face. "Know you what I have done to you?" he finally asked. "You call me Master and Lord, and in this, you say well, for so I am. If I then, your Lord and Master, have washed your feet, you also ought to wash one another's feet. For I have given you an example, that you should do as I have done to you.

"Verily, verily, I say unto you, the servant is not greater than his lord. Neither is he that is sent greater than he that sent him." He paused for a moment before adding. "If you know these things, happy are you if you do them."

He stopped, looking down at his hands. Once again a deep sorrow seemed to have swept over him. "I speak not of you all," he said in a low voice. "I know whom I have chosen. But the scripture must be fulfilled: 'He that eateth bread with me hath lifted up his heel against me.'"

That evoked yet another reaction from his listeners. They looked at each other in dismay. Jesus' next words answered their unspoken questions. "I tell you this before it comes," Jesus went on in that same low voice, "so that when it is come to pass, you may believe that I am he. Verily, verily, I say unto you, that one of you shall betray me."

Dismay turned to stunned disbelief.

Jesus nodded. He looked around, his eyes dark and sorrowful. "Behold, the hand of him that betrays me is with me at *this* table."

That did it. The room erupted. "Betrayal?" Thomas blurted out. "But who?"

Then Matthew, he who had once been a publican and hated by most of the population of Capernaum, asked a question that touched all their hearts. He, too, had been completely taken aback by the prophecy of betrayal. His first impulse was disbelief, but he had learned long ago to trust in whatever Jesus said. So his next reaction was to turn inward. "Lord?"

Jesus turned to look at him.

"Is it I?"

Shamed by the simple honesty of the question, the others responded in kind. Were there seeds of treachery and weakness and disloyalty within them? How could one be sure of what lay inside the heart? "Could it be me?" asked Andrew in barely a whisper.

"Or I?" asked a very subdued James.

Jesus let them question for a moment, then looked around. "The Son of Man goes as it is written of him," he said slowly, "but wo unto him by whom the Son of Man is betrayed. It would be better for him if he had never been born."

Directly across the table from Jesus sat Judas Iscariot. His face was flushed, and he had suddenly gone very still. When Jesus' eyes fell upon him, Judas started; then, quickly, he added his voice to the others. "Is it I, Lord?"

"Thou sayest," Jesus said quietly. The others were still in a turmoil, and no one but Judas seemed to have heard it. But there was no mistaking the answer.

Judas flushed even deeper and looked away.

Two seats down from Jesus, Peter jabbed at John, who was talking across the table to Philip and Thomas. When John turned, Peter leaned closer. "You are closest to Jesus, John," he whispered. "Ask him who he is talking about. *Who* is going to betray him?"

John thought for a moment and decided he would ask. He was close to Jesus not only in the seating arrangements, but he also felt emotionally close to him. On one or two occasions Jesus had even called John his beloved disciple. So John turned back to face the Lord. "Master?"

"Yes, John."

He kept his voice low, barely loud enough for Jesus to hear, but no one else. "Who is it of whom you speak? Who is it that shall betray you?"

Jesus thought for a moment, then nodded. "He it is to whom I shall give a sop after I have dipped it."

John sat back, watching. With the table being large enough to seat thirteen men, not everyone could reach the center of the table, and it therefore was not sufficient to have only one bowl of the sauce in which they dipped their bread. So their host had placed several small bowls of the sauce up and down the length of the table. After a moment, Jesus reached for the loaf of *matzah*, broke off a piece and leaned forward. He scooped up some of the sauce on the end of the bread; then, to John's surprise, he leaned even further across the table and offered it to Judas.

To dip bread into a soup or stew from a common pot was the customary way of eating. To dip the bread and offer it to someone at the table was a mark of honor and respect. When it came from the host or the leader of a banquet, it was an especially valued compliment. Judas, completely caught off guard by the offer, hesitated for a moment, then smiled, obviously relieved. He took the bread and put it into his mouth.

"That which thou do," Jesus said softly, "do quickly."

Any comfort that had come to the man instantly disappeared. He stared at Jesus. Could Jesus know what Judas had done? He felt a bead of sweat break out on his upper lip.

Across the table, John turned back to Peter. "It's Judas," he said in astonishment.

"But . . ." Peter stared across the table at his fellow apostle. The man looked very uncomfortable, almost feverish. Then, suddenly, Judas abruptly rose to his feet. Mumbling something about having to make some purchases, he walked to where he had left his bag, picked it up, slipped his feet into his sandals, and hurried out the door.

Jesus watched him go, sadness deepening in his eyes, but said nothing more. The others were a little surprised at the departure but then shrugged it off. Judas was keeper of the bag. They had seen Jesus speak quietly to him. Perhaps Jesus had instructed him to procure something more for the supper. Only Peter and John noted the departure with a deep sense of foreboding.

Jesus sat quietly after the door shut. The apostles visited quietly with one another. Finally, realizing that Jesus was waiting for them, the disciples grew quiet again, turned their faces to him, and prepared to listen.

"Now is the Son of man glorified, and God is glorified in him." He looked on them like a father looking upon his family. "Little children," he said tenderly, "yet a little while I am with you. You shall seek me, but as I said unto the Jews, whither I go, you cannot come. So now I say to you, a new commandment I give unto you, that ye love one another, as I have loved you, that ye also love one another."

He paused momentarily, and he seemed pleased with their attentiveness. "By this shall all men know that ye are my disciples, if ye have love one to another."

This had been a troubling night in many ways for Peter. At these words he could no longer hold back. "Lord, where are you going?"

Jesus turned. "Where I go, you cannot follow me now. But you shall follow me afterwards."

Peter was shaking his head before Jesus even finished. "Why can't I follow you now? I will lay down my life for your sake."

The Master drew in a deep breath as he looked over at the fisherman who had left his nets to follow him. His eyes held an infinite sadness. "Simon, Simon," he said with obvious pain, "behold, Satan has desired to have you and to sift you as wheat. But I have prayed for you, that your faith will fail not."

Simon Peter rocked back, his face twisting with pain. "Lord, I—"

"When you are converted," Jesus went on before he could finish, "then strengthen your brethren."

Peter came up on his knees on the low bench, his mouth twisting in his beard. "Lord, I am ready to go with you, whether it be in prison or in death."

There was a heavy silence as the eyes of the others in the room flitted back and forth between Jesus and their senior brother.

Jesus finally just shook his head, the sorrow only deepening. "Will you lay down your life for me?" he asked softly. "Truly I tell you, Peter, the cock shall not crow before you shall have thrice denied that you know me."

CHAPTER NOTES

The Passover ritual was treated in great detail in volume two (see pp. 424–34, 441–42). The psalms that are part of the service are Psalm 113, which is sung in connection with the telling of the story of the Exodus, and Psalms 114–118, sung as the concluding portion of the service. It is in Psalm 118:22, 25–26 that the words Jesus used of himself and which foreshadowed the triumphal entry into Jerusalem are found.

In all three of the accounts of this first sharing of the sacrament, the Gospel writers have Jesus saying, "This is my body," and "This is my blood." The author took the liberty of adding, "This is a *representation* of my body," and "This is a *representation* of my blood," because this more accurately conveys the idea of the original Greek. Clarke notes that Hebrew and Aramaic evidently did not have a way of saying "This signifies, or represents" something else. So the common way of expressing that concept was to say, "This is" or "These are." For example, when Joseph interpreted Pharaoh's dream of the seven kine, or cattle, he said, "The seven good kine are [i.e., signify or represent] seven years" (Genesis 41:26) (Clarke, 3:252).

Chapter 28

I

Jerusalem, Upper City, an Upper Room
3 April, A.D. 33

Peter had been in turmoil many times in his twenty-six years. A fisherman's life—especially when it was spent on the Sea of Galilee where violent storms could arise in a matter of minutes—was not one for the faint of heart. He knew full well that by nature he was impetuous and prone to action before he had thought things through, and that had brought him trouble numerous times. In the last three years, turmoil had become a regular experience for him, and it had nothing to do with fishing. He was forever asking what he thought was a profoundly important question, only to realize when Jesus answered it that he was still very much a little child. He would take action in a way that he thought would please Jesus, only to be corrected, and occasionally, openly rebuked. He alternated regularly between deep joy, great satisfaction, feeling like a fool, and utter melancholy.

But he had never felt quite like he was feeling right now. His head was down; he stared at the table, not daring to lift his eyes to see if his companions were looking at him. Why shouldn't they? And he could imagine the look in their eyes. Jesus had just declared that before this night was over, he would deny even knowing Jesus!

I am ready to die for you! The thought was so powerful it was like a piercing pain. *I am. I will!*

And that was part of the turmoil, too. For the past several months, Jesus had talked of his coming death, much to his disciples' dismay. In the past few days, he hinted at it again and again. But tonight it seemed to lace every part of the conversation. And now it was more than just words. Jesus acted like a man who was about to die. Peter could never remember seeing him so morose, so filled with sorrow, so . . . He searched for the right word. So fatalistic. Before the cock crowed. That's what he had said. Sunrise was less than twelve hours away; then every rooster in Jerusalem would begin their morning wake-up call. What did it all mean? What was *he* to do?

Suddenly, Peter was aware that no one was speaking, that the room was utterly quiet. He looked up, startled a little. Jesus was looking at him. His eyes were soft, his expression filled with compassion. In that instant, Peter knew that Jesus understood the pain he was feeling, the embarrassment, the humiliation at being told he would lose his courage.

"Let not your heart be troubled," Jesus said, a smile pushing back the sorrow a little. "You believe in God. Believe also in me."

"I do believe in you, Master," Peter said.

Jesus nodded but went right on. "In my Father's house are many mansions. If it were not so, I would have told you." He looked around at the others. "I go to prepare a place for you. And if I go and prepare a place for you, I will come again and receive you unto myself. I will do this, that where I am, there you may be also."

Several apostles stirred at that statement, but Jesus continued in the same calm, peaceful voice. "And whither I go you know, and the way ye know."

That seemed confusing. Across the table, sitting next to where Judas had been, Thomas leaned forward. "Lord, we know not whither you go. And how can we know the way?"

Jesus let the question hang in silence for several moments; then with slow and precise words, he answered: "*I* am the way, the truth, and the life. No man cometh unto the Father but by *me*. If you had known me, you should have known my Father also. But from hence-forth, you know him and have seen him."

Philip, who was seated beside Thomas, raised his hand. "Master, show us the Father, and it will suffice for us."

Jesus turned to face him fully. "Have I been so long time with you, Philip, and you have not known me? He that has seen me has seen the Father. How do you say then, show us the Father?"

Philip looked only the more perplexed by that answer.

Jesus leaned forward, even more earnest than before. "Don't you believe that I am in the Father, and the Father in me?"

Several men, including Philip, nodded quickly.

"The words which I speak unto you I speak not of myself. The Father dwells within me, and it is he that does the works that I do."

He sat back, again letting his gaze sweep around the circle of eleven men. "Verily, verily, I say unto you, he that believeth on me, the works that I do shall he do also. Yea, and greater works than these shall he do, because I go unto my Father. And whatsoever you shall ask in my name, that will I do, that the Father may be glorified in the Son."

That brought an instant reaction. It was an incredible promise. They would have the power to do even greater works than they had seen the Master do? They looked at each other in amazement.

Jesus seemed pleased, and sat back, letting them digest what he had just taught them.

II

BETHLEHEM

With the Passover feast completed, the tables cleared, and the dishes washed and dried, the family of David ben Joseph moved outside into the courtyard to visit. The heat of the past few days had dissipated, and the evening air was cool and pleasant. It would likely be cold by morning, with the promise of rain later in the day. It was full dark, but Benjamin had lit oil lamps and hung them around the walls of the courtyard.

They were still settling in when Miriam, instead of taking a stool along with everyone else, moved over to the small fountain. There she stood, silently watching the others. After a moment, Simeon went over to join her.

Deborah noticed them first and assumed there were not enough seats for them. When she looked around and saw that there were more than enough places, she gave her son an odd look. He just smiled at her with an expression that looked suddenly suspicious. Then she looked at Miriam, who colored slightly under her gaze and dropped her eyes. Deborah puzzled about it for a moment, then suddenly sat straight up, her eyes widening. "Really?" she mouthed to Miriam.

Miriam's face went even brighter, but she nodded.

"Quiet, everyone," Deborah called. "Quiet! Miriam has something to say to us."

They all turned as one.

Miriam laughed softly. "We didn't mean that you all had to stop talking."

"What is it?" Leah asked.

"Well, first of all," Miriam began, turning to Esther and Benjamin, "from all of our family, a hearty and sincere thanks to Uncle Benjamin and Aunt Esther for once again letting us spend Passover with them."

"Hear, hear!" Ephraim called out, slapping his leg with one hand to show his enthusiasm. The others clapped their hands as well.

"It is our pleasure," Esther said. "We love having you all here."

Miriam hesitated a moment, then went on, her blush rising quickly again. "We—Simeon and I—decided that perhaps it might be well to let you know that next year . . ." She smiled softly and turned to her husband.

Simeon stepped forward. "Next year, Uncle Benjamin, you may have to make room for at least one more at the table."

Leah leaped to her feet. "Really?" she shrieked.

Miriam laughed at her excitement. "Yes, really. We are going to have a baby."

"Oh, Miriam," Livia cried. She awkwardly got to her feet, following close behind Leah. As they threw their arms around each other, Miriam drew Livia to her, feeling the swelling in Livia's belly. "We think it will come in mid-September," she whispered, "so your little one and my little one should be only three or four months apart."

"How absolutely wonderful."

As the women swarmed in around Miriam, Simeon stepped back. He motioned to his father, then walked to a place behind the rest of the family. When David reached him, he extended his arms for an embrace. "This is great news, Son," he said. "Congratulations."

"Thank you, Father." He took a quick breath. "There's something else."

The look on Simeon's face caused David to draw back. "Is something wrong with Miriam?"

"No. Miriam feels a little sick at times, but she is really doing quite well."

"What, then?"

"I'm going to take Miriam into Jerusalem."

David's head cocked to one side. "Now?"

"Yes." Simeon's voice lowered even more. "I'm going to tell the others that we're going for a walk. You can tell Mother after we're gone, if you'd like, but I think it's better if the rest don't know. At least for now. They'll just worry."

"Looking for Jesus?" David said, not hiding his own concern.

"No." Simeon's shoulders lifted and fell. "We're going to Mordechai's house."

For a long moment, David just looked at his son.

"It will probably do no good, but this will be his first grandchild. Miriam wants to tell him herself, not have him hear the news from someone else, or even try to tell him in a letter."

"Do you think that's wise?" David said, guessing what the answer would be.

"No," Simeon said flatly. "And I told Miriam that, but . . ." He shrugged again. "If that's what she wants, then I'll be there with her."

There was another long pause; then David put his hand on his son's shoulder. "Perhaps it will be enough to soften him a little. Perhaps I should come with you."

Simeon immediately shook his head. "No. It will hurt her terribly if he refuses to listen to her, but that's the only real danger." He reached up and gripped his father's arm. "But thank you. We'll slip out in a few minutes. I've hired a light cart and horse so we don't have to walk. It may be midnight before we get back." Then he grimaced. "Of course, that's being optimistic. If he refuses to talk to us, we'll be back in a couple of hours."

"May the Lord go with you, Simeon. And may your good news

touch the heart of a bitter old man. I can't think of anyone who so much needs someone to love and cherish."

III

JERUSALEM, HOUSE OF MORDECHAI BEN UZZIEL

Levi made no effort to hide his distaste as he held the courtyard door only partially open. "My master is not here."

The man at the door frowned deeply. "Where is he?"

Levi shot him a withering look. The man acted like he was *his* servant.

"Speak, man!" Judas barked. "This matter is of the utmost importance, and it cannot wait. Your master told me to seek him out be it day or night."

The chief steward of the house of Mordechai ben Uzziel would have given much to be able to slam the gate in the man's face. Levi cared not one whit for the rabble rouser from Nazareth called Jesus, but this man—supposedly a close friend and trusted associate—was willing to sell his loyalty for money. Loyalty had always been something very important to Levi.

"He's at the palace of Annas," he snapped. "Do you know where that is?"

"Two houses up from that of Caiaphas?"

"That's right." Levi started to shut the gate, then stopped. "You'd better have something more than promises. The group my master is with tonight includes some of Jerusalem's most powerful and important men. They will not appreciate being disturbed in the midst of the feast."

Judas glared at him, seemed about to make some kind of retort, but then spun on his heel and trotted away.

IV

Jerusalem, Upper City, Palace of Annas

A look of annoyance flashed across Mordechai's face, and the girl serving the wine shrank back a little in the face of his irritation. "The man said you left word that you wanted to see him, sire."

Mordechai took a sip of wine, fighting back a temptation to swear at the girl and send her running. "What is his name?"

"He wouldn't give it, sire," she said. "But he said—" She stopped, turning her head. "There he is, sire. By the side door. You can see for yourself."

In an instant, Mordechai was up. "Take him into the library." He whirled, snapping his fingers at Menachem, who sat across the table from him, laughing gaily with a woman half his age. Menachem's smile froze, and he scrambled to his feet, cutting the woman off in mid-sentence, making no apology.

"Get Annas," Mordechai hissed. "And Azariah. Bring them into the library."

"What about Caiaphas?"

"Of course, Caiaphas, you fool. Move!"

V

JERUSALEM, UPPER CITY, AN UPPER ROOM

Around the banquet table in the upper room, Jesus had fallen silent. He seemed far away from them for a moment. Then he turned and looked at them and smiled softly. After a moment or two, the disciples realized that they had interrupted Jesus' instructions. They fell silent again and turned back to face him. As they did so, they sensed that he had not been displeased with their reaction.

"If ye love me, keep my commandments," Jesus began again, "and I will pray the Father, and he shall give you another Comforter, that he may abide with you forever, even the Spirit of truth. This Spirit of truth the world cannot receive, because it sees him not, neither knows him. But you know him, for he dwells with you, and shall be in you."

John turned to Peter, nodding. They had talked about this just a few nights before, about this feeling of inner power and enlightenment that had come upon them since they had left their nets and followed Jesus, especially in the last few months.

"I will not leave you comfortless," Jesus explained. "I will come to you."

Judas, a member of the Twelve with the same name as Judas Iscariot, raised a tentative hand. Jesus nodded for him to speak.

"Lord, how is it that you will manifest yourself unto us, but not unto the world?"

"If a man love me, he will keep my words, and my Father will love him, and we will come unto him and make our abode with him. The Comforter, which is the Holy Ghost, whom the Father will send in my name, *he* shall teach you all things and bring all things to your remembrance."

Once again the men around the table began to nod their heads. This was beginning to make sense to them.

"Peace I leave with you," Jesus said quietly. "My peace I give unto you—not as the world gives, give I unto you. Let not your heart be troubled, neither let it be afraid. Hereafter, I will not talk much with you, for the prince of this world comes." He took a quick breath, as though struck with a sudden pain. Then he sighed softly. "But he has nothing in me."

VI

Jerusalem, House of Mordechai ben Uzziel

Levi, chief steward of Mordechai ben Uzziel's house, jerked the courtyard gate open with a vicious yank. He wanted no more to do with the feral-looking man who was selling out his master for a purse full of money. "What is it?" he snarled. Then he stopped, his mouth dropping, his eyes flying open. "Mistress Miriam?"

"*Shalom*, Levi."

He threw back the gate and did something that was most unlike the staid and somber chief servant of that great household. With a cry of joy, he threw his arms around her. "Oh, child!" he cried. "I can't believe my eyes."

He pulled back, realizing what he had just done. His face flamed as he fought to regain the outward aloofness that he had practiced for so many years. Miriam smiled, watching it happen, understanding exactly what was going on his mind. But she didn't care. His first reaction had told her all that she needed to know.

"It is so good to see you again, Levi. Is everything well with you and your wife?"

"It is," he said. "We just recently had our third grandchild."

"Wonderful!" Miriam exclaimed. "Tell Naomi how much I have missed her, will you?"

"I will. She will be so happy to know that you came. Are things well with you?"

"They are." Miriam turned, took Simeon by the arm, and pulled him forward. "This is my husband, Levi. Simeon ben David of Capernaum."

Levi bowed his head respectfully. "We have met before," he said.

Miriam seemed surprised.

Simeon explained quickly. "Remember? Yehuda and I came to the house to meet with your father before the whole Joknean Pass debacle."

"Ah," Miriam said. "That's right."

Levi was suddenly uncomfortable. "We would have you know, sir," he said to Simeon, choosing his words carefully, "that not all in this household received the news of your marriage with . . . uh . . . regret."

Simeon was touched by the sincerity in the man's words. "Thank you, Levi. That means much to Miriam and me."

Miriam's eyes filled. She reached out and touched the arm of this man who had seen her come into the house as an infant and had been with her to adulthood. "Yes, Levi. Thank you very much for that." She took a quick breath, looking past him toward the house. "Is he here?" she murmured.

Levi shook his head. "He is at the palace of Annas, for the Passover."

Miriam's shoulders sagged a little. She had been afraid of that.

Simeon touched her arm. "Do you know where that is?"

She nodded, biting her lip.

"I'm not sure going there would be wise," Levi cut in, anxious.

"He—" He shook his head. "Your father will not even allow us to speak your name here, Miriam."

"I know." She looked up at him through her tears. "But he is going to be a grandfather, Levi."

Again Levi's eyes widened in surprise.

Miriam laughed, touched by his joy. "In September. I think he should know, don't you?"

Putting aside all reserve, he took her in his arms again and held her tightly to him. "Of course," he said huskily. "Bless you, my child. I am so relieved to know that you are all right."

"And happier than I've ever been," Miriam added.

"Then go to him," Levi said, pulling back. "Don't let him turn you away." Then he looked at Simeon. "But take care. There are—" He broke off, unable to say more without betraying confidences with which he had been entrusted. "Take care."

Miriam took Simeon's hand, still looking at the servant. "We shall, Levi. Good-bye, dear friend. Thank you for all you have meant in my life."

"Good-bye, my child," he managed, fighting back a great lump in his throat. "Go with God."

VII

JERUSALEM, UPPER CITY, PALACE OF ANNAS

"Twenty-seven. Twenty-eight. Twenty-nine. Thirty!" Mordechai let the last coin drop into the small leather purse. It clinked softly. He pulled the string tight, hefted the purse for a moment, then placed it in the outstretched hand.

"Thank you," came the murmured reply.

Azariah was almost gleeful. "All right. Where is he?"

"He's not more than a ten-minute walk from here. He's in the upper room of a house just three streets down from here."

Caiaphas looked horrified. "Here? In the Upper City?" How did a Cretan like that come into their neighborhood without being noticed?

Mordechai frowned. "Whose house?"

Judas shrugged. "I do not know his name. Evidently the Master knows the man and made prior arrangements for us to have Passover there."

"Describe it!" Mordechai snapped.

"As I said, it is three streets below us, fourth house on the left as you go up the hill toward Herod's Palace. There are several tall cypress trees in the courtyard."

"The house of Jephunah ben Asa," Azariah muttered. "I had heard he might be a sympathizer to Jesus."

"This is not good," Annas said half to himself.

Mordechai nodded, having already reached the same conclusion himself.

"Why not?" Judas asked in bewilderment. It was so close. It could be done in a matter of minutes.

"We can't risk an uproar right here in our own precincts," Annas replied. "We are only a few streets from the palace of Herod. The last thing we need is to have that old meddler learn of this."

"It has to be done somewhere else," Mordechai agreed. "And with the least amount of notice."

"Is he going to spend the night there?" Azariah asked Judas.

He shook his head. "No. I heard Peter tell our hostess in Bethany that we would be back tonight, though it might be late."

"If he's going back there, we could take him in the Kidron Valley," Caiaphas mused. "That will be isolated enough."

Mordechai considered that idea. Being Passover, the moon was full, but it wouldn't reach its zenith until close to midnight, so at the bottom of the ravine, it would not get full light until much later. On the other hand, if Jesus was on the main road between Jerusalem and Bethany there would be other people returning to their homes as well. During the holiday there were always people about.

Judas jerked up. "I know just the place. It is a favorite of Jesus'. There is an olive grove with an olive press near the bottom of the Kidron Valley. I'm sure you know it. It's off to the left of the road, not far from where the road begins to rise again."

"Gethsemane?" Mordechai asked.

"Yes, that's it. We often stop there to rest as we pass back and forth to the city. I would wager a shekel that we will stop there again tonight, if only for a moment."

Mordechai wanted to hoot in derision. He was willing to wager a whole shekel? How daring! The man had just received thirty shekels. But he said nothing. He turned to Azariah. "How soon can we have a contingent of our temple guards gathered?"

The old Pharisee pulled at his beard. "This is a feast night. Perhaps an hour. Maybe a little longer."

Judas slipped the purse into the bag he carried over his shoulder. "If you know where it is, then I will wait for you there. I'd better get back."

"Oh, no," Mordechai cut in sharply. "You're staying right here until the guards come."

"What? But I've already been gone half an hour. They'll—"

"Part of that thirty shekels was to have you lead us to him. Even with the full moon, we could pass right by him or take the wrong man by mistake. No, you're going to lead the contingent."

Judas shrunk back, looking slightly sick. "The Master might suspect something. He already—" He shook his head and looked away.

"While you're waiting, you might consider how exactly to do this," Mordechai went on, completely ignoring what he had heard. "We don't want him being spooked before we're sure we've got him." He turned to Azariah. "Tell your guards to stay back until this man tells them to come." Then to Judas, he went on. "You have to remember, these Galileans all look alike, especially in the dark. Work out some kind of signal once everything is in readiness so they'll know exactly which man is Jesus."

"But—" Judas's face was gray.

Mordechai had started to turn away. Now he came back around slowly, his eyes glacial. "But what?" he asked coldly.

Judas licked his lips once, then just shook his head.

VIII

JERUSALEM, UPPER CITY, AN UPPER ROOM

The gladness that had been with Jesus as he spoke of his Father slowly died away. He looked around on these faces that he loved. His eyes became troubled. "This is my commandment to you, that you love one another, as I have loved you," he repeated. "Greater love has no man than this, that a man lay down his life for his friends." He had to stop, and his eyes were glistening in the lamplight. "You are my friends, if ye do whatsoever I command you.

"You have not chosen me, but I have chosen you and ordained you, that you should go and bring forth fruit."

He stopped, his eyes dropping to look at his hands. A sigh sounded from deep within him. It was a sound of immense pain. Finally he looked up. "If the world hate you, know that it hated me before it hated you. If you were of the world, the world would love its own. But because you are not of the world, but I have chosen you out of the world, therefore the world hates you."

There it was again, Peter thought. He felt the darkness and gloom settling in again.

"Remember the word that I said unto you: The servant is not greater than his lord. If they have persecuted me, they will also persecute you; if they have kept my saying, they will keep yours also. But all these things will they do unto you for my name's sake, because they know not him that sent me."

Peter wanted to blurt out the question he knew everyone wanted to ask. *What, Lord? What will they do to us?* But he said nothing, holding his peace, half afraid that Jesus was going to tell them anyway.

"If I had not come and spoken to them, they would have no sin. But now they have no cloak for their sin. He that hates me, hates my Father also. These things have I spoken unto you, that ye should not be offended. But know this." He raised a hand, one finger pointing at them to emphasize what he was saying. "They shall put you out of the synagogues. Yea, the time is coming that whosoever puts you to death *will think that he is doing God a service.*"

A chill shot through every man around the table. Jesus had used a plural form of "you." He had not been looking at anyone in particular when he said it. That single choice of words hit them with tremendous force. "Whosoever puts *you*—any or all of you—to death."

Jesus' eyes dropped again. Barely audible, he added one last thing. "And these things will they do unto you, because they have not known the Father or me."

The silence in the room deepened. Finally, after almost a full minute had passed, Jesus looked up. "Let us sing a hymn together, and then we shall depart."

IX

JERUSALEM, UPPER CITY, PALACE OF ANNAS

The servant who opened the heavy gate to them was surly at first, but when Miriam told him she needed to see Mordechai ben Uzziel on an urgent matter, a flash of recognition crossed his eyes, and he motioned them inside. The courtyard was large, probably twice the size of most people's entire property. The garden was immaculate, with not one but three different fountains that splashed softly in the night air.

"Wait here," the man said deferentially. "I will inform my master of your presence."

As the servant moved away, Simeon looked around and whistled softly. "So this is what our temple tax buys," he drawled.

"Simeon," Miriam said with mock severity. "How dare you? You know that those are sacred funds and are to be used only for God's purposes."

He laughed softly, remembering that while he might be surprised with all of this, his wife was not. She had grown up in this neighborhood, had eaten banquets in these lavish palaces. She knew firsthand how wealth could corrupt. That was one of the reasons she had been attracted to Jesus—he clearly knew the same. Further, her early life had been filled with guilt because she knew from whence much of the money that supported her luxurious life had come.

469

"Do you think the servant recognized me?" Miriam asked anxiously. "If he tells Father it is me, perhaps he won't even come out."

"Then we will go in," Simeon retorted. "But no, I think he recognized that you were someone he should know, and someone of importance, but he's not sure who you are."

"Oh, Simeon, is this a mistake?"

He took her hand. "It is not. It could turn out to be very painful, but no, your father has the right to—"

He stopped, his attention taken by something behind Miriam.

She turned, surprised at the startled look on his face. "What is it?" All she could see was a cluster of men near the front entrance to the great house.

"I thought I just saw—" He shook his head, as if trying to clear his vision. "No, it couldn't be," he said, shrugging it aside. But in a moment, he was looking past her again. "Wait here," he said after a moment. "I'll be back."

In surprise she watched him move away. He didn't head directly for the cluster of men. He angled off to the left, past the largest of the fountains. And then she realized what he was doing. He was getting a closer look while keeping himself unobtrusive. She saw him stiffen, lean forward even further, then finally turn and hurry back to her.

"What is it?" she asked.

"I can't believe it. Judas is here."

"Judas?"

"Yes, Judas Iscariot."

Her lips parted, registering her shock. "*Here?*"

"Yes. He's talking with Caleb and a couple of other men."

"Caleb?" The name didn't register. Miriam was still whirling a little with the news. What would one of Jesus' apostles be doing here?

"Yes, Caleb. You remember him. He's Azariah's chief assistant on the Sanhedrin."

"But—" Her eyes searched his, troubled. "But why would one of the Twelve be here?"

"That's what I'd like to know," he said grimly. "And I'm going to find out."

But before he could follow up on that promise, the servant returned. He faced Miriam. "Follow me, please."

Miriam suddenly felt her knees go weak, and she had to reach out and clutch Simeon's hand. He squeezed it tightly, and they fell in step behind the servant, who was already returning toward the house.

Inside the palatial structure, they could hear the noise of a crowd off somewhere in the house, but that was not the direction they were heading. The servant led them down a narrow hall, then opened the door to a side room and gestured for them to enter. "Mordechai ben Uzziel will be with you shortly."

"Thank you," Miriam managed. She gripped her husband's hand even more tightly than before. The man shut the door again, and they heard him walk away.

"Oh, Simeon? What am I doing?"

Before he could answer, they heard footsteps in the hall again. In a moment the door opened, and Miriam's father stepped in, his face a hard mask. He shut the door behind him with a sharp crack, then stood where he was. "I thought it might be you," he said, his voice like a cold wind off the snows of Mount Hermon.

"*Shalom*, Father," Miriam said quietly.

"*Shalom*, Mordechai ben Uzziel," said Simeon.

"What do you want?" he snapped. "How dare you come here?"

Simeon felt his anger rising. "It didn't take any courage at all," he said, giving him a mocking smile. "We just knocked on the gate and came right in."

"Don't be impudent," Mordechai cut in. "I don't find it amusing in any way."

"And I don't appreciate your rudeness," Simeon shot right back.

"This is your daughter. I don't care how you feel about the choices she has made. She is your flesh and blood and—"

"Simeon, please." Miriam nudged him gently and stepped in front of him. She turned to her father, whose face had gone purple at the confrontation with Simeon.

"Father, I'm not here to ask anything of you. It saddens me more than I can say that we have been estranged from each other. I love you and always will."

Mordechai responded with a soft snort and a toss of his head.

"I do, but I didn't come here to try to convince you of that. I came because something has happened that I felt you needed to know. Then we will leave, and we will not bother you again."

His eyes narrowed a little. He said nothing, but she could see his interest.

"You are going to be a grandfather."

Simeon had wondered what Mordechai's reaction would be when he first heard the news. Would he be his usual grim self? Would there be so much as a flicker of pleasure in his eyes? What Simeon saw completely surprised him. Mordechai actually fell back a step. His eyes were large and shone brightly in the lamplight. And then he looked away, not wanting them to see how he was responding.

"It will come in September, about six months from now," Miriam said. She too had been caught completely off guard by his response, and she was near tears. "If it's a boy, Simeon and I plan to call him Mordechai."

"Don't try to influence me in that way," he said gruffly.

"Mordechai is a noble name," Simeon said slowly. "One of my favorite stories is of how the Mordechai of long ago helped Queen Esther save our people in Persia. I have no reluctance to name a son after you."

Mordechai was staring at the floor. Finally, he spoke without looking up. "It is not a good thing that you are here."

Simeon felt the anger flash again. That was it? That was all he had to say?

"I understand," Miriam said dispiritedly. "We'd better get back to Bethlehem, Simeon."

As they started toward the door, Mordechai moved aside.

"*Shalom*, Father," Miriam whispered as she passed him.

"*Shalom*, Mordechai," Simeon said coolly.

Mordechai said nothing. Then, as Simeon pulled the door open, he spoke. It came out sharp and hard. "Simeon!"

Simeon turned back, tensing a little. "Yes?"

His voice was stiff. "This is not a good time to be in Jerusalem."

That surprised Simeon, and it showed.

"Not for a woman, especially." Then his eyes moved to Miriam. "Not for a woman with child." He gave just the slightest hint of softening. "Tomorrow, keep her in Bethlehem where she will be safe."

The tears in Miriam's eyes spilled over. It wasn't much, but for him, it spoke volumes. Impulsively, she ran to him, went up on her toes, and kissed him on the cheek. "Good-bye, Papa."

One hand came up, hovering above her shoulder for a moment; then it dropped to his side again without touching her. "Good-bye, Miriam."

X

Outside, Simeon held his wife for a time, letting the shudders gradually exhaust themselves. The night had turned cold, and her breath came out in soft puffs of mist. When she was finally spent, Simeon helped her into the seat, then moved around to untie the horse. At that moment a noise brought his head up. From out of one of the side gates of the massive complex, a double column of men was emerging. They were in full uniform and carried spears at their sides. Clouds were scudding across the sky, momentarily hiding the moon, but still Simeon could see.

When the column turned in their direction, Simeon moved behind the horse, still holding the reins. "Keep your head down," he whispered. "Don't let them see who you are."

But if the soldiers saw them, they gave them no heed. They filed past, marching in step, moving briskly but not in quick time. Simeon counted as they passed. Twenty. Twenty plus the three men who led them. He climbed up onto the seat beside Miriam.

"Where do you think they are going at this hour of the night?" she asked.

His lips were pressed together in a tight line. So this was what Mordechai had meant. "I'm not sure," he finally said. "I'm going to take you back to Bethlehem; then I've got to come back to try to find Jesus."

"Back to Bethlehem?" she exclaimed. "But that will take you two hours or more. You have to find Jesus quickly. I can go by myself."

"I won't let you go alone. Not tonight."

She didn't want to, either, but didn't know what else to do. Then an idea came to her. "I'll go back to my father's house and ask Levi if he'll send one of the servants with me to drive the cart. You saw his reaction to our visit. I'm sure he'll do it."

Simeon considered that. He didn't like it, but she was right. He couldn't wait two more hours. "All right, but only if Levi agrees."

Miriam grabbed him tightly by the arm. "Oh, Simeon," she cried. "Do you think they really want to—" She couldn't put it into words.

"Did you see who was leading them?" he asked.

She nodded. "I recognized one of them. I didn't get a clear look at the other two."

"Which?" he asked.

"The man closest to us is named Malchus. He is the servant of Caiaphas, the high priest."

Simeon was nodding. That made perfect sense. The temple guards were technically under the auspices of the high priest, though the Pharisees, because of their numbers on the council, handled much of the funding and control. "The one just behind him was Caleb, the aide to Azariah I told you about. He's probably the designated commander of the detachment."

"And the third?"

He turned his head, feeling a deep chill run through him. "The third was Judas Iscariot."

CHAPTER 29

BETRAYEST THOU THE SON OF MAN WITH A KISS?

—*Luke 22:48*

I

OUTSIDE JERUSALEM, IN THE KIDRON VALLEY

3 APRIL, A.D. 33

Peter, James, and John were at the back of the group. The twelve of them, including Jesus—Judas had not yet returned—were strung out for perhaps a hundred paces as they walked along, but these three had lagged behind deliberately so they could talk.

"It's going to be close to midnight by the time we reach Bethany," James noted. They had just reached the bottom of the Kidron Valley. They still had the climb up the western slope of the Mount of Olives and then most of the way down the other side to the village. "Let's hope that the Master doesn't plan an early start in the morning."

"Personally, I feel like I could sleep until noon," Peter agreed, pulling his tunic more tightly about him. It was getting cold enough that they could see their breath, and he was anxious to reach the house of Mary and Martha and get out of the night air. "Surely Jesus must be as tired as we are."

"No," John said quietly.

Both of the others turned to him. "Why?" James asked.

"He's more tired," John said. "Haven't you watched him? His step is slow and heavy. His shoulders sag. It's like he's carrying this great burden inside him. I've never seen him look so utterly drained. He's much more tired than we are."

"You are right," Peter responded.

"And wasn't that a remarkable night?" Andrew, who was just in front of them, had overheard them and drifted back to join them. "Here we went expecting the normal Passover and—"

"I doubt I'll ever be able to even think of tonight without weeping," James said.

"Parts of it were so sacred we may never speak of them," John added.

They were silent for a few moments.

"Some sacred, some frightening," Peter finally said. "I'm worried about tomorrow. It almost seemed like Jesus was bidding us farewell, like he was telling us he was going to . . ." he paused. "Going to die soon."

"I felt the same way," John said. "I can only hope we're misinterpreting."

"Still, tomorrow could be critical," Peter concluded. "I told Simeon and his family and Luke and all the other men to be at Bethany first thing."

"Good," Andrew said. "We're going to need every man we can find to stand with us. The more we have, the less likely it is that the Sanhedrin will try something."

II

BETHLEHEM

"Where will you look?" Miriam asked, not able to keep the worry out of her voice. "Simeon said that even Peter didn't know where they were going to hold the Passover tonight. He could be anywhere. Jesus could be anywhere."

David ben Joseph pulled the cinch on the saddle down with a jerk, then buckled it. "I'm not sure. I'll ask around. Someone surely has seen that many soldiers. Maybe I can follow their trail. That's likely what Simeon will do." He realized that mentioning the soldiers was not the best thing to say. "We're not going to confront them, just see what is going on."

David finished saddling Benjamin's horse. He took the reins and swung up into the saddle. "Ephraim, Benjamin. We'll send word back the moment we learn anything. If you don't hear anything by dawn, then go to Bethany. Whether I find Simeon or not, I will go there. Whatever happens, hopefully they'll know by then where we are."

Deborah moved up beside her husband. "May the Lord smile upon your efforts. Be careful."

He nodded. He wasn't very confident about having good fortune on this night. It was about the second hour of the second watch. Midnight would be almost upon him by the time he reached Jerusalem. But one could only hope.

"We'll pray for you," she whispered.

"No," he responded. "Not for us. For Jesus."

III

Outside Jerusalem, the Mount of Olives

Something ahead of them caught Peter's eye, and he slowed his step. "What now?"

The other three looked ahead as well. In the near total darkness—the moon was covered for the moment by a large cloud—they could see their companions turning off the road to the left.

"It's the garden." Peter groaned. "I was hoping we might bypass it just this once."

"He probably needs to rest for a few minutes," John suggested. "Don't say anything to him."

Peter shot him a hard look. As if he would do that.

The olive grove was near the base of the Mount of Olives, just where the mount started sloping upwards. Because the owner of the grove had not only an olive press but a small cistern to provide the necessary water for washing the olives and cleaning the press after each day's harvest, the people of the area called the grove a garden. Cisterns were not that common, especially on the side of a hill, and most olive groves were just that, groves only. The press, a large stone device, was a commercial one. The owner of this grove, who was better situated than his neighbors, offered to press their crops for a small portion of the resulting oil. Sometime in the past, the garden had been given the Greek name for olive press, *Gethsemane*.

Jesus stopped beneath one of the first of the olive trees and waited for them all to join him. When the last four were there, he looked around, his face barely visible in the darkness. "Tarry here while I go yonder to pray."

They looked at each other, nodding. In light of the mood that had come upon Jesus in the upper room, this was not a surprising announcement. They started to look around for a place to sit.

"Peter?"

Peter turned back. "Yea, Lord?"

"I would like you and James and John to accompany me."

The two sons of Zebedee seemed as surprised as Peter, but instantly moved over to stand beside him. Without another word, Jesus moved deeper into the olive grove. The three men fell into step beside him. They moved slowly, picking their way over the rocks and through the weeds. Then, to Peter's pleasure, light suddenly flooded softly through the leaves above his head. The cloud obscuring the moon had moved eastward, letting its light bathe the earth. It was clear and full, and the effect was as if someone had instantly lit a hundred lamps with soft silvery flames. Trees and rocks stood out in sharp relief.

If Jesus noticed the change, he said nothing. He moved forward about a stone's throw until he came to one of the larger trees of the orchard. He motioned with his hand. "My soul is exceedingly sorrowful," he said, taking them by surprise, "even unto death. Tarry here and watch with me."

The three of them nodded, and he moved off again. He went only a little farther before he found a large, mostly flat rock and sat down. His head was bowed, his hands clasped together.

Peter watched him intently, his concern like the dark cloud that had blocked the light a moment before. *Even unto death?* He didn't like that. What did Jesus know? And would he tell them in time so they might prepare?

Peter's two companions looked around, found a place, and sat down. John patted a bare spot beside him. "Come, Peter," he said. "Rest your feet."

He waited another few moments, but seeing that Jesus had not moved, went over and joined the two brothers. He let out a long sigh. "I must admit," he said in a low voice so as not to disturb Jesus, "it does feel wonderful to stretch out for a time."

For almost ten minutes they sat there. John's head began to droop, and soon it was on his chest. James was not far behind him. He kept jerking his head up, fighting it, but finally lost. He shifted his weight so that he could use the rock for a pillow and closed his eyes.

Peter felt the weight of his own eyelids. It had been a long and grueling day, both physically, and, even more, emotionally. He blinked quickly and pinched his leg, hoping that would push back the weariness a little. Then, a movement out of the corner of his eye brought his head around. Jesus was getting up. He leaned forward, prepared to stand again. But no, Jesus had just shifted his position. He was on his knees, elbows leaning against the rock, his head bowed.

Once again Peter felt a deep longing to know what was going on inside the Master's head. How else could he, the one in whom Jesus had put the trust of leadership, know what he was to do? He stared morosely at the kneeling figure, lost in his own musings.

After a time, another movement caught his attention. Jesus' arms were outstretched. His fingers were clawing at the surface of the rock, as if he were slipping over a cliff. His body was rigid, his face pressed into the stone. Peter could hear the murmur of his voice. He sat up straighter, straining to hear.

What came next made him jump. It was a cry of agony, of pain so deep and intense that it sent chills shooting through him. "O my Father!"

Peter felt tears spring to his eyes. Never had any child cried out with more pleading, more yearning for a parent.

"If it be possible, Father, let this cup pass from me."

Peter got to his knees, leaning forward. The words had stopped.

Was Jesus saying more, or had the agony overcome him? Peter started to rise, then froze as the next words came.

"Nevertheless—" there was a tremendous weariness amidst the pain—"not as I will, but as thou wilt."

The figure slumped forward. Peter was on his feet instantly, ready to sprint across the narrow distance. But something stopped him. "Tarry here" had been the specific instructions. Jesus clearly wanted to be alone. Now Peter understood why. This was a time between Father and Son. Did he, Peter, in all of his earnest efforts to do good, dare to intrude at such a sacred moment? Slowly, he sank back down again. He folded his arms on his knees and laid his head on them, brooding, troubled, disturbed.

IV

Outside Jerusalem, in the Kidron Valley

Judas held up a hand and came to a stop. Caleb swung his head back and forth, searching the wayside nervously, and nearly bumped into him.

"What?" Caleb hissed.

"The entrance to Gethsemane is about a furlong from here. Hold the men in that stand of sycamores while I go forward and see if they are there."

"They'd better be there," Caleb muttered darkly. He still didn't completely trust this man. He had a gnawing worry that Judas might be leading them squarely into an ambush.

Judas didn't answer as he moved off. In moments he was a dark, nearly indistinguishable figure moving up the moonlit roadway.

V

The Garden of Gethsemane

"Peter."

Peter's head came up with a jerk, and he looked around wildly for a moment. Then shame washed over him as he realized Jesus was standing directly in front of him, looking down with reproachful eyes.

Peter heard a shuffling sound and saw out of the corner of his eye that James and John had come awake just as he had.

Peter scrambled to his feet. "Yes, Master?"

"What?" Jesus said sadly. "Could you not watch with me for one hour?"

Peter hung his head. He didn't need to see if his two brethren were doing the same.

"Watch and pray," Jesus said, peering into his disciple's face, "that you enter not into temptation." Then his eyes softened in the moonlight. "The spirit is indeed willing, but the flesh is weak."

"Yes, Lord," mumbled the fisherman. "I'm sorry, Master."

Jesus turned and walked slowly back to the rock. Only then did it register with Peter that Jesus' face had been wet with perspiration and that his hands had trembled slightly as he spoke.

The shame rose up like bile in his mouth. He sat back down again and dropped his head into his hands. When would he learn?

VI

OUTSIDE JERUSALEM, IN THE KIDRON VALLEY

Caleb waited in the shadows until he was certain it was Judas. Then, with a wash of relief, he stepped out and waved. "Over here!" he quietly called.

Judas made a sharp turn and trotted over to join them.

"Well?" Malchus, Caiaphas's servant, asked. He was with the group as a representative of the high priest and spoke with authority of his master.

"They're there," Judas said, grinning wolfishly in the moonlight.

"Jesus, too?"

"I assume so."

Caleb drew in a sharp breath. "You assume so?" he asked incredulously.

"There are eight or ten of them asleep just a few rods into the grove," he explained. He enjoyed making these men squirm. They were so condescending, so contemptuous of him. "I thought I could make out a few others a little deeper in, but I didn't want to risk waking anyone."

"And you're sure it's them?"

"Of course," he said diffidently. "I told you it was a favorite place for Jesus to stop."

Malchus snapped his fingers, and the captain of the guard lumbered to his feet. "Get the men ready," Malchus commanded. "And tell them to keep their hands on their swords. I don't want any rattling or clinking." He turned to Caleb. "All right, let's go."

"Remember," Judas warned. "Don't act until you see my signal."

VII

The Garden of Gethsemane

From somewhere far, far away, Peter thought he heard someone speaking to him. He fought to climb out of the deep, black pit he was in, fought to claw his way upward towards the light. But he kept slipping back. He was so tired. It felt like great millstones were tied to his ankles.

He mumbled something, forcing his eyes open for a moment. Someone was standing in front of him. Someone important. He fought harder. But then his feet lost their hold, and he plummeted down again. It felt good to be down again, off the slippery wall. So good.

Jesus stood motionless, looking down at his sleeping apostles. For a moment, he almost spoke again, but then he just shook his head and turned and went slowly back to his place by the rock.

VIII

For the third time in less than an hour, Jesus stood in front of the three sleeping figures. He looked down on them with a mixture of disappointment and understanding. "Sleep on now," he said quietly. "Behold, the hour is at hand, and the Son of man is betrayed into the hands of sinners."

He reached up and wiped at his forehead with the sleeve of his tunic. Even in the moonlight, it was clear that his body was visibly trembling, as if he had taken a severe chill. His face was pale, drawn, and lined with pain.

He bent down, reached out, and shook Peter's arm. "Peter!"

The fisherman jerked up, arms thrashing wildly. "What! What is it?"

Jesus laid a hand on his shoulder. "Peter! It's me. Wake up."

It took several seconds before comprehension dawned; then the apostle got quickly to his feet. His face was dark with embarrassment. "Oh, not again, Master. I'm sorry. I—"

Jesus brushed it aside. "Come! The hour is at hand."

John and James were up, and a short distance away the others were sleepily getting to their feet too, having been awakened by the sound of voices.

Peter stiffened, then shot John a look. Jesus had turned to watch the others start to assemble. His face was fully illuminated by the moonlight. What Peter saw were dark streaks running horizontally across the Master's forehead. It was if someone had smeared . . . He peered more closely. It was as if someone had smeared blood there.

John had seen it too. He cocked his head slightly, motioning toward Jesus' robe. Peter's dismay only deepened when he saw what his younger associate was seeing. There was a dark stain along one sleeve. It was what would happen if one wiped sweat away with his sleeve. But this was not just sweat. It looked very much like blood.

Jesus turned and saw them staring at him. He met their gaze for a moment, then reached up with his other sleeve and wiped his forehead again. When his arm dropped, the smears across the skin were mostly gone.

"The Son of man is betrayed into the hands of sinners," Jesus said, loudly enough that all of them would hear. "Rise up. Let us be going. He who shall betray me is at hand."

IX

Judas held up his hand and put a finger to his lips. "Shhh!" he said in a sharp whisper. "I think I just heard the Master's voice."

Malchus and Caleb moved up beside him. "Then go!"

Judas nodded. "Wait until I give you the sign."

"Go!" Caleb hissed, giving him a shove. "Get on with it, man!"

The western half of the sky was now completely clear of clouds, and the moon hung like a great silver orb above them. Pushing aside the misgivings he had been fighting for the last hour, Judas strode forward. "Ho!" he called.

He saw the figures ahead of him stiffen and spin around, dropping into a half crouch. "It's me," he said. "Judas."

"Oh," Philip exclaimed, straightening in relief. The others did the same. "We were wondering if you had gotten lost."

"Hardly," Judas laughed. "But I've been looking all over for you." He turned, searching their faces. "Where's the Mas—" But then he saw him. Jesus was coming toward them with Peter and two others.

Judas moved forward, smiling broadly. "Hail, Master!" He ran to him, took him by both shoulders, and kissed his cheek in greeting.

Jesus looked at him for a long, searching moment. "Judas," he said slowly, "would you betray the Son of man with a kiss?"

Judas turned away, his face hot with shame, but there was no time to do more than that. He heard a shout from behind him and the sound of pounding feet. He turned. Malchus and Caleb were coming towards them, with the double column of soldiers right behind them. The disciples gaped at them in astonished bewilderment.

Jesus looked at Judas, his face calm and unruffled. "Friend," he asked quietly, "is this why you have come?"

The double columns had reached Jesus. On both sides, the apostles were edging back, stunned to be awakened to this development. Malchus ran up, jabbing his finger at Jesus' chest. "This is the man!" he bawled. "Seize him!"

Two soldiers darted forward and grabbed Jesus roughly by the arms, pinning them back.

Whatever kind of day Peter had experienced thus far—tiresome, depressing, discouraging, bewildering, exhausting—it did not slow his reaction. When Jesus had said that the one who was to betray him was at hand, it had sent the hairs on the back of his neck prickling and put him on full alert. Then suddenly, there was Judas, coming out of the night. Judas, who had left the supper early. Judas, to whom Jesus had handed the sop of bread as a sign of his betrayer.

The chief apostle had started to shout a warning but had been momentarily put off when Judas came forward and kissed the Master in greeting. Then his blood froze as the night erupted.

"John! Andrew!" he shouted, pulling out his sword. "Get the Master!" He raced forward, but he was already too late. The soldiers who had grabbed Jesus were starting to march him away. Another man was shouting commands at them, screaming hysterically at them to bind him tight.

With a mighty shout, Peter lunged forward. There was a flash of steel in the moonlight, followed by a shriek of pain. Malchus stumbled back, grasping at the side of his head. Caleb fell back as blood spurted from between the man's fingers. Malchus swayed back and forth, moaning horribly, then dropped to his knees. His face was white with shock. He removed his bloodied hand and stared at it. The soldiers uttered loud gasps. Malchus's ear dangled loosely on a thin strip of flesh.

"Peter!"

The fisherman jerked around at the sharp command.

Jesus jerked one arm free from the soldiers. He motioned vigorously to Peter. "Put your sword away."

Peter swung around, not sure he had heard right.

"Put your sword back into its sheath," Jesus said again, speaking more slowly so there would be no misunderstanding. "All they who take the sword shall perish by the sword." Then he gave a wan smile. "Think you not that I could pray to my Father and that he would presently send me twelve legions of angels? But how then shall the scriptures be fulfilled?" He shook his head slowly. "The cup that my Father has given me—shall I not drink it?"

The words Peter had heard the Master cry out in the garden earlier flashed into his mind with searing clarity. "If it be possible, let this cup pass from me." Feeling sick, he slowly returned his sword to its sheath.

Jesus nodded his approval. "Thus it must be."

Jesus pulled free from the dazed soldiers and stepped in front of the moaning, wailing figure of Malchus. The man's hand was clapped over his ear again, and he rocked back and forth, wailing and moaning and writhing.

Without a word, Jesus bent down. Malchus saw him and shrank back. But Jesus reached out with one hand and grabbed his shoulder, holding him in place. Then with the other, he reached for the mangled ear.

"No!" Malchus screamed.

But Jesus wouldn't let him draw away. Holding him firmly with one hand, he placed the other over the cupped and bloody hand of Malchus. Another scream started deep in Malchus's throat, but it was cut off as his eyes flew open and his jaw went slack. Slowly his head came up until he was looking straight into Jesus' eyes. And then, dazed to the point of being almost incoherent, he pulled his hand from beneath Jesus' hand. It left a bloody smear on his cheek. No one noticed. Every eye was on the hand of Jesus, still cupped over the horrible wound.

And then Jesus straightened, withdrawing his hand from Malchus's face.

Astonishment exploded from every side. One soldier dropped his spear, clapping a hand over his mouth. "O Lord God of Heaven!" the soldier nearest to Malchus exclaimed, "Praises be to thy name."

"It's healed," cried another, his voice hoarse with shock. "Look! The ear is healed."

Caleb, trembling with amazement, stared dumbly, his mouth open and slack. His eyes were telling him something that his mind would not accept. As Malchus got shakily to his feet, Caleb leaned toward him, peering at the ear with wide, frightened eyes. It was perfectly normal—no bleeding, nothing hanging grotesquely by a shred of flesh. The Pharisee turned slowly back to Jesus, his eyes bulging, his mouth working but nothing coming out.

"Whom do you seek?" Jesus asked, speaking to Caleb, who had taken charge now that Malchus was no longer functioning.

"Uh . . ." Caleb was finding it hard to bring himself back to the situation at hand. "We seek Jesus of Nazareth," he finally mumbled.

"I am he," Jesus said calmly.

Caleb glanced at Malchus for help, but it was clear he was on his own. He looked as if he had just realized it was his task to do something about this man.

Jesus asked again. "Whom seek ye?"

"I told you," he stammered. "We seek Jesus of Nazareth."

"And I told you that I am he." His eyes swept the soldiers as well as their two leaders. "Are you come out as against a thief with swords and staves to take me? I sat with you daily in the temple, but you laid no hold on me there."

"You are under arrest by the order of the Great Council," Caleb finally blurted, getting back a little of his courage now it was obvious that Jesus was not preparing to fight.

"If it is me you seek, then let these go their way." He motioned with his head toward Peter and the others.

For the first time, Caleb turned to look at Judas. Judas's face was pale, and his eyes were deep in their sockets. "Well?" Caleb asked him. "What about that?"

Judas wasn't sure why he was suddenly being consulted. "The council asked only for Jesus," he suggested.

"Of course," Caleb said with relief. He wasn't sure that either he or the soldiers were up to taking the others, not in light of what had just happened. "Agreed," he said to Jesus.

Jesus turned to look at his followers, but they had already heard. For all their earlier protestations of courage, events were happening too quickly. They reacted from shock and fear and started moving away.

Caleb, regaining his confidence quickly, jerked his head at the two men who still stood beside Jesus. "Take him to the house of Annas."

Chapter Notes

Luke, who interestingly enough was a physician, is the only one who records what has come to be called "the bloody sweat." He, like Matthew and Mark, records Jesus' pleading with the Father to let the "cup" pass from him, but adds this: "And there appeared an angel unto him from heaven, strengthening him. And being in an agony he prayed more earnestly: and his sweat was as it were great drops of blood falling down to the ground" (Luke 22:43–44).

Because of the words, "*as it were*," some commentators have tried to explain this away as a mere simile, saying that the agony he was enduring caused him to perspire copiously, and in the moonlight the drops of sweat appeared to be drops of blood. Many others, including the author, strongly disagree with this suggestion, seeing it as an attempt to dilute and weaken the significance of the atoning sacrifice. In the first place, "bloody sweat," or perspiration mingled with blood, is not an unknown phenomenon. There are recorded cases where, under severe stress, the vessels inside the body rupture and blood oozes from the body like beads of sweat (for examples, see Clarke, 3:257; Edersheim, *Life and Times*, pp. 846–47; Farrar, p. 577).

More to the point, the Greek word which Luke uses and which is translated as "drops" is *thrombos*. It was an ancient medical term and means "a large, thick drop of clotted blood" (Vine, p. 341). It was not used to describe normal perspiration. Even today, *thrombosis* is the condition where there are blood clots within the veins.

Accepting it as blood raises questions of another sort. After the experience, surely Christ would have been at least partially covered with blood. Did he wipe it off somehow? Were his clothes bloodstained? Were the apostles that night aware in any way that something remarkable and terrible had just happened? To all of this, Luke is silent.

Here again the author used a device (Peter and John seeing remnants of blood on the Savior's forehead and stains on his robe), not to propose that this is what actually happened, but only to call attention to Luke's important addition to the record of this night.

Though we do not have a full understanding of what happened that night, it is clear the sweating of blood was highly significant. James E. Talmage summed it up this way: "Christ's agony in the garden is unfathomable by the finite mind, both as to intensity and cause. . . . It was not physical pain, nor mental anguish alone, that caused Him to suffer such torture as to produce an extrusion of blood from every pore; but a spiritual agony of soul such as only God was capable of experiencing. No other man, however great his powers of physical or mental endurance, could have suffered so; for his human organism would have suc- cumbed. . . . In that hour of anguish Christ met and overcame all the horrors that Satan, 'the prince of this world' (John 14:30), could inflict. . . .

"In some manner, actual and terribly real though to man incomprehensible, the Savior took upon Himself the burden of the sins of mankind from Adam to the end of the world. . . . The further tragedy of the night, and the cruel inflic- tions that awaited Him on the morrow, to culminate in the frightful tortures of the cross, could not exceed the bitter anguish through which He had successfully passed [in the Garden]" (Talmage, pp. 613–14).

It is of interest to note that the place where Jesus was pressed down by the sins of the world to the point that he bled from every pore was Gethsemane, a place where the olives were pressed until the oil was squeezed from the flesh of the fruit.

CHAPTER 30

IF I HAVE SPOKEN . . . WELL, WHY SMITEST THOU ME?

—*John 18:23*

I

JERUSALEM, UPPER CITY, THE PRAETORIUM

3 APRIL, A.D. 33

Marcus Quadratus Didius, tribune of the tenth legion, senior tribune in the province of Judea, second only to the procurator, Pontius Pilatus, in the line of command, groaned softly and rolled over. He cracked one eye open enough to see that the only illumination in the room was slivers of moonlight coming through the shutters and not dawn's first light. He shifted his weight until his body found the right position, then settled back again.

"Marcus?"

He turned his head. Diana had come up on one elbow. He could see only the shadow of her head in the faint light.

"Someone's knocking," she said sleepily, then fell back again on her pillow.

On cue, the sharp rapping sound that had first awakened him sounded again. "Tribune Didius," came a muffled voice.

Marcus groaned aloud and hauled himself up into a sitting

position. Why wasn't there a guard outside his door? "One moment," he called. Swinging his feet over the side of the bed, he reached for his night robe, slipped his feet into woolen slippers, and stood up. He felt the chill in the room and quickly pulled the robe around him, then padded softly to the door. He opened it a finger's width, squinting at the sudden brightness from the flickering light of the torches in the hall. Then he understood. Centurion Sextus Rubrius was standing there, his helmet under one arm. The guard had moved back out of the way. "Yes." Marcus said, stifling a yawn.

"My apologies for disturbing you, sire," Sextus said in a low voice, "but we have received word that the temple guard has just been called out."

Marcus had reached up to rub at his stubbled chin, but his hand stopped in midair. "For what purpose?"

Sextus shook his old grizzled head. "I am trying to ascertain that now, sire."

Marcus opened the door a little wider. "What time is it?"

"Approaching midnight."

"How long ago did this happen?"

"About an hour ago, according to the report."

"Where did they go?"

"They were seen crossing the Temple Mount toward the east, but we are seeking to learn that as well, sire."

"Have you told Pilate yet?"

"No, sire. That was one of my questions. Would you like me to inform the governor?"

Marcus considered the idea, then shook his head. "Not yet. Let's get more information first."

"Very good," Sextus agreed. "Would you like me to bring you further word when it comes?"

Marcus sighed reluctantly. For a moment, he considered the offer.

He thought about how good the bed had felt, how deeply he had been sleeping. He yawned again, this time giving it full sway. "No," he said, "I'll be down in a few minutes."

"As you wish, sire." His officer turned to leave.

"Sextus?"

He turned back. "Yes, sire?"

"Have my horse saddled and waiting, just in case."

"As you wish, sire."

Shutting the door, Marcus moved back across the room and sat down on the edge of the bed. Diana was sitting up. "Trouble?" she asked.

He shrugged. "Probably not. The festivals here are always like this. Something going on all the time that you have to keep an eye on."

She reached out and began to rub his back. "Do you have to go?"

He laughed softly, leaning over to kiss her bare shoulder. "A good Roman matron would ask her man, 'What can I do to help you get ready?'"

"I'm still learning about all of that," she said, pretending to pout.

He kissed her again and stood up. "Unfortunately, the answer to your question is yes, I'd better go down. Hopefully, it will prove to be nothing, and I'll be back in an hour or two. But if not, Pilate would have my head if I slept through it."

She lay back down and pulled the covers up around her with a little shiver. "Does a good Roman matron have to still be awake when her husband returns?"

He took off his robe and moved to the wardrobe where his uniform hung. "Not if she's still learning how to be a good matron," he answered. "I'll see you in the morning."

II

JERUSALEM, THE TEMPLE MOUNT

David entered Jerusalem through Zion's Gate, the most direct route into the Upper City. That was where Simeon had left Miriam. Even though David knew that the temple guards would not likely be anywhere near where Simeon and Miriam had seen them, it was a place to start. Hopefully someone would have seen which way they went.

He rode slowly, stopping to ask the few people who were still out and about if they had seen the double column of guards. No one had. When he finally reached the western side of the temple complex with no more success than when he started, he found a place to tie his horse and climbed the great staircase up to the Temple Mount. To his immense relief, as he neared the top of the stairs, he heard a shout and looked to see Simeon waving at him.

Simeon, greatly relieved himself, explained quickly that he had had no success and finally decided to wait for his father, knowing that he would eventually come to the Temple Mount.

They strode swiftly across the plaza of the Court of the Gentiles as Simeon told him what little he knew. Passing through an opening in the *soreg*, or "wall of partition," they turned slightly and headed for the eastern gate to the inner temple complex. Though the gates to the city remained open twenty-four hours a day, by this time of night the side gates to the inner courts of the temple were shut and barred and would remain so until morning. Only the main entrance on the east, the Gate Beautiful, remained open all night. Since it opened into the

Court of the Women, the court that held the large brass chests into which contributions and the temple tax were thrown, Simeon assumed it would be guarded.

As they came around the corner of the temple complex on the east side, Simeon was gratified to see that his surmise was correct. There were two guards, leaning on their spears, talking lazily to one another, clearly bored with their night duty. But at the sight of the two approaching men, they both straightened.

"*Shalom*," David called as they drew closer. "Good Sabbath."

The men relaxed. These two were well-dressed men and seemed unlikely to pose a threat. "And good Sabbath to you." The nearest one grinned mischievously at them. "You two are out pretty late. Too much celebration after the feast?"

Simeon laughed and pointed his finger at the man, as if they were sharing a private joke. "Well, something like that."

"You here to make a contribution?" the other one asked sarcastically.

"In a way," David answered back. "Actually, we're looking for information, and if you happen to have it, the contribution would be for the two of you."

Both men perked up noticeably. "Such as?" asked the second of the two.

Simeon grew more earnest. "About three hours ago, maybe more, a double column of your men left the palace of Annas. We were wondering if they had come by this way."

The first man started to nod, but the second was suddenly suspicious. "Who wants to know?" he asked.

"We're looking for a friend of ours who hasn't returned home as yet." David reached in his tunic, brought out two shekels, and began to slip them back and forth between his fingers so they made a metallic clinking sound. "I can't imagine that the soldiers were after him." He gave them a knowing look. "He's basically harmless. But his family and friends are getting worried, if you know what I mean."

The younger of the two hooted softly. "Too much wine, eh?"

David held out the coins, shrugging enigmatically. "It *is* Passover," he noted.

The two coins were snatched away and quickly disappeared. The nearest man, who was the older of the two, answered. "They passed this way about two hours ago."

Father and son exchanged quick glances. "Headed east?" Simeon asked.

"Well, they went out the east gate of the city headed for the Kidron Valley."

"But you don't know where they were going?" Simeon persisted.

The second shrugged. "Kind of hard to see through stone walls from here." The first man guffawed loudly.

"Did they have anyone in their custody?" David asked.

"Not when we seen 'em," came the reply.

Simeon and David exchanged another glance; then Simeon started backing away. "Thank you for your help. We'll keep looking."

"*Lailah tov*," the one called out cheerfully.

"*Lailah tov*," David said over his shoulder.

"Yes, good night," said Simeon. They moved eastward, heading for the steps that led down to the Golden Gate and out of the city into the Kidron Valley.

Once the two strangers were out of earshot, the first man turned to his partner. "Why didn't you tell them that we saw the detail again just an hour ago, headed back for the palace? And this time they did have someone in custody."

"Because they only gave us one shekel apiece," the other said. He grinned, but it faded quickly. "Shekel or no shekel, we'd best not be too loose with our tongues. Besides," he went on, "didn't you notice anything about those two?"

"What?"

"They were Galileans."

"Well, of course. I could tell that the moment they spoke. So?" And then understanding came. "Oh," he said slowly.

"What if this so-called friend they were looking for is that Jesus of Nazareth?"

"It could likely be," the other replied thoughtfully. "Well, if so, they're too late to do anything for him now."

III

JERUSALEM, UPPER CITY, THE PRAETORIUM
4 APRIL, A.D. 33

It was just at the changing of the second watch, almost precisely at midnight, when the runner returned. He was not in uniform and wore a light cloak. Sextus had told Marcus that the runner, a Greek named Atticus, had been chosen for two reasons: he was known for his endurance and therefore was often used to send messages back and forth, and he also spoke fluent Aramaic, so he could make inquiries without meeting the resistance that faced all Romans.

Both tribune and centurion got to their feet as the man was ushered in by one of the guards at the front door. His face had a light sheen of perspiration on it, but he wasn't breathing that heavily.

"Well?" Marcus demanded, before the man even stepped up before him. "Any success?"

"Aye, sire. I found them."

"Good work. So what's going on?"

"It was a column of twenty or so men, sent out by the Great Council as you had heard," he reported. "They have arrested a man from Galilee by the name of Jesus of Nazareth."

Sextus visibly started, but Marcus didn't see it. He was too pleased with the news. "Jesus of Nazareth? You're sure of that?"

"I saw him for myself," came the reply. "They were on their way back to the Upper City. I was told they are going to put him on trial."

"Tonight?" Sextus exclaimed.

The messenger half turned. "Yes, that is what the soldiers told me."

"But the Sanhedrin is not supposed to be seated at night. Especially not during a feast day. It is considered a Sabbath to them."

Marcus turned to his old associate, one eyebrow arching. "Really?" he said mildly. "I didn't know that."

"It's part of their laws about the council, sire," Sextus said, concerned that he had spoken before thinking.

Marcus nodded absently, then looked at the runner again. "Did they arrest anyone else?"

"No, sire. They only had the one man."

Marcus bit his lip, thinking. So old Mordechai had finally gotten his way. They had Jesus. Well, good. He had wondered what was happening. Since that night following the disaster during the Feast of Tabernacles, he and the head of the Sadducees had not spoken. Relations between him and Mordechai were still strained.

He turned to his centurion. "I'm going back to bed for a while, Sextus."

"Very good, sire."

"But there could be trouble come morning when word of this gets out. Wake me precisely at dawn. Have the men up and ready. I'll report to Pilate on the whole matter at breakfast."

Sextus slapped his arm across his chest in salute. "Yes, sire." He motioned to the messenger that he was no longer needed.

"Well done, Atticus," Marcus called after him. "Sextus, see that he is given a suitable reward."

"Of course."

"Thank you, sire," Atticus exclaimed.

"Let me know if there are any further developments," Marcus said to Sextus. "Otherwise, I'll see you in a few hours."

IV

ON THE ROAD TO BETHANY

"Surely they wouldn't dare attack the house," Simeon said, puffing heavily as they toiled up the steep slope of the Mount of Olives.

David slowed his step and pointed to a rock wall. "I need to rest for a moment, Simeon." As he moved over to sit down, he continued, "I find it hard to believe that the Sanhedrin would send a contingent very far outside of the city. It's not like them. And yet . . ."

Simeon nodded. He knew what David was thinking. If the temple guards had gone out the east gate, the most likely destination was Bethany and the house of Martha. Surely they would know by now where Jesus was staying. Simeon sat down by his father and wiped his brow. Even though their breath showed in the night chill, they were both perspiring from the swiftness of their walk.

"Maybe we should have gone back for the horses."

Simeon was leaning forward, hands on his knees, drawing in deep breaths. "This was quicker."

David nodded. He hadn't really meant it. Horses were not allowed on the Temple Mount. It would have taken them a quarter hour to walk back to where they had left their animals, then another half an hour to ride them around the outside of the walls to the point where they now were. As it was, it had been only ten minutes since they spoke with the guards.

They sat quietly for a time, catching their breath; then David got to his feet. "I'm ready."

"We can't keep up this same pace," Simeon said, standing beside his father. "Not up the hill anyway."

"Agreed." They fell into step together and started upward again, trudging with heavier steps.

They were no more than halfway up the western slope of the Mount of Olives when Simeon stopped, reaching out to grab his father's arm. "Someone's coming," he whispered. He pulled, and they quickly stepped off the road into the shadows of a large olive tree.

For a moment, Simeon's hopes soared. He could tell from the crunch of sandals on gravel that more than one man was approaching. But a moment later, his hopes plummeted again. A dozen or so men approached the olive tree, but none of the men were soldiers. They were walking swiftly, talking in great animation to each other.

David stiffened. "That's Andrew," he said when a deep voice boomed out.

With a soft exclamation of pleased surprise, Simeon stepped out into the moonlight again. "Ho!" he cried. "Andrew, it's Simeon and David ben Joseph."

At the sight of a figure suddenly appearing out of the night, the men coming down had stopped short. But with Simeon's call, they hurried forward.

Simeon's face fell as he scrutinized each face and realized that Jesus was not among them.

"Simeon," Andrew said, clasping hands firmly, "I'm so glad to see you." He half turned. "*Shalom*, David."

Simeon peered at the men in the faint light. There were no

women, and Simeon realized it was the inner circle of disciples who had been with Jesus during the last few days. The apostles were there, of course, as were Luke the Physician, Matthias, Joseph Barsabas, John Mark, and several disciples from the Galilee. Then with a start, Simeon realized that Peter was not with them. Nor John.

"There's been bad trouble," Andrew said, noting Simeon's dismay. "Jesus has been arrested."

Simeon fell back. That was the news he had dreaded most. "I saw some of the temple guards. Judas was leading them."

Philip stepped forward. One hand passed over his eyes. "At the supper, Jesus warned us that one of us would betray him. We had no idea what he meant."

"Judas led them straight to Jesus," James said bitterly.

"Where's Peter? Did they take him too?"

"No," Andrew said. "They let us all go. Peter and John are following after the Master to see where they are taking him. We went back to Bethany to get help."

"Any idea where they might be going?" Simeon asked.

"Nathanael overheard them say something about the palace of Annas."

"Yes," Simeon blurted. "That's where I first saw the guards."

David turned to his son. "You go with them. I'll cut around and get the horses and ride back to Bethlehem. I can be back with more helpers by first light."

"The women in Bethany, along with some additional men, will be coming in to Jerusalem at the same time," Andrew said. "Right now they are spreading the word. We want to have as many come into the city as possible."

Simeon hesitated only for a moment. They needed Ephraim and Benjamin, every man they could muster. And his mother and Miriam and the others would never be content to stay in Bethlehem once they heard the news. Andrew was right. The more people they had, the better. "All right. Come to the palace of Annas first. We'll watch for you or leave someone to tell you where we are."

As his father broke into a trot down the hill, Simeon turned back to the group. "All right. Tell us what you want us to do."

V

JERUSALEM, UPPER CITY, PALACE OF ANNAS

For a long time after Simeon and Miriam left, Mordechai stood alone in one of the side rooms of the palace of Annas. He went out briefly when the contingent of guards finally came, making sure that Malchus and Caleb were properly instructed and that the Judas fellow was with them; but then he returned to the darkened room and stood staring at the window.

His emotions ran the gamut. It was a rare man who didn't want to see his family perpetuated, spreading from children to grandchildren and then to great-grandchildren. But in the Jewish culture, having lineage took on special significance. Having seed to carry on your name and your property and your legacy was one of life's highest goals. If a man had a wife who was barren, he could divorce her and no one would question it. So as Mordechai thought about having a grand-child, he felt a deep relief and a quiet satisfaction. With it, however, came the bitter realization that this would be his seed in a literal sense only. He doubted that the rift between him and his daughter could ever be healed now. Her betrayal was too deep, too final, too utterly treacherous. And when this night was over, assuming things went as planned, Miriam would know that it was her father who had been the chief architect in the destruction of Jesus. There would be no reconciliation after that. The only thing that gave him a kind of savage satisfaction was knowing that, with the death of Jesus, his grandson—or granddaughter—would not be raised as a follower of the Nazarene.

Menachem came in once to report that they had heard nothing as yet, but Mordechai suspected that he also wanted to make sure everything was all right. Annas himself came a little while later. Mordechai put them off, letting them think his obvious anxiety simply grew from what was happening. No one besides the servant knew about Miriam's visit, and he wanted to keep it that way.

His head came up as he heard a disturbance outside in the courtyard. He pulled back the drapes, then opened the shutters wider so he could see what was going on below. A man was running toward the house. "They're coming!" he called to the servant watching the door. "Tell Annas that they're back."

Mordechai drew the shutters in, yanked the drapes back into place, then left the room, walking swiftly. Any thought of his daughter was, for the moment, forgotten.

VI

The first thought Mordechai had was that the soldiers were being very sloppy. Jesus stood between two men, with several others behind him. They hadn't even tied his hands. It was like they were escorting an honored guest to a banquet, not guarding the most dangerous man in Judea. Then something else caught his eye. As he looked more closely, Mordechai wondered if there had been a struggle. There were bloodstains on the prisoner's sleeve and what looked like faint smears of dried blood on the man's face. But he could see no wounds.

They were standing in the main entry of the palace. Everyone at the banquet was gathered behind them, but only four men had come into the entry to meet the returning party: Annas, whose house they were in; his son-in-law, Caiaphas, the present high priest; Mordechai, who was head of the Sadducees; and Azariah, chief of the Pharisees. Menachem, Mordechai's trusted aide, hovered just behind them in case he might be needed.

"Where did you find him?" Annas asked.

There was no answer. The servant of Caiaphas was staring at Jesus, and it seemed as if he had not heard.

"Malchus!" Caiaphas barked.

The man jumped guiltily and spun around. "Yes, sire?"

"Annas asked you a question."

He turned to the older man, twitching nervously. "Pardon, sire," he mumbled. "What was it you asked?"

Mordechai peered more closely at Malchus. The side of his robe also had bloodstains on it, and there appeared to be dried blood around one ear. And yet, again, there were no wounds, not even a scratch. What had happened out there this night?

Disgusted, Annas started to ask his question again, but then stopped. He stared at Malchus's ear, then his hand. The palm of it had dark smears across it. "What happened?"

The servant, seeing the direction of Annas's gaze, lifted his hand and stared at it stupidly. "I . . ." Then he just shook his head. "I'm all right, sire."

Caleb stepped forward, snapping to attention in front of the four leaders. "We found him in Gethsemane," he explained. He glanced quickly at Jesus, then away again. Mordechai saw a flash of something in Caleb's expression, and his puzzlement only deepened. Was it fear he had just seen?

"Were any others around?" Annas demanded. "How many saw the arrest?"

"Only the guards and a few of his closest disciples. One of them tried to resist, but then he backed down again." Caleb swallowed quickly, not feeling it wise to add that Jesus had made him do so.

Mordechai was troubled. Something had happened that wasn't being reported. Even the soldiers seemed dismayed. Malchus was in a daze. Caleb, who was normally as cold as tempered steel, seemed deeply shaken. But then Mordechai's eyes rested on the captive, and he forgot about his questions. Here was his quarry at last. He felt an immense satisfaction. All of his careful planning, all of his meticulous laying of snares had paid off. They had him.

Jesus stood quietly, not bothering to follow the interchange with his eyes. He seemed to be looking past them, staring at nothing in particular.

Mordechai leaned forward a little. "You are Jesus of Nazareth?"

The eyes finally came back, focusing on Mordechai's face, but he didn't answer.

Annas moved up beside Mordechai, also staring at the Galilean. "Tell us," he sneered, "tell us about your disciples and your doctrine. What is it you have been doing that has stirred up the countryside so?"

Jesus looked at the graying old aristocrat. "I spoke openly to the world." The calmness in his voice was startling. He seemed to be the only man present who wasn't shaken, and he was the prisoner! "I ever taught in the synagogues and in the temple," he went on, "where it is common for our people to resort. I have said nothing in secret. Why do you ask this of me? Ask of those who have heard me what I have said. They will tell you."

Caleb, who had noticed the puzzled look on Mordechai's face, leaped forward, eager to reestablish his control. He swung hard, striking Jesus with the back of his hand across the cheek. Jesus' head snapped back, and instantly there was an angry red mark where flesh had struck flesh. "You would answer the high priest so?" he shouted.

Behind his father-in-law, Caiaphas grimaced. Not at the violence—he had expected that. But Caleb had called his father-in-law *the* high priest. It had been some years since Caiaphas had been appointed to replace Annas, but everyone still referred to the older man by the title. And part of Caiaphas's frustration was that he, most of all, knew who really controlled the office, and it wasn't him.

Jesus turned to Caleb, still unruffled, though the blow must have been very painful. The splotch on his cheek was a deep red. "If I speak evil," he said, "then bear witness of the evil. But if I speak well, why do you smite me?"

Caleb fell back a step under the penetrating, probing look that was directed at him.

"Enough!" Azariah exclaimed, stepping in to cover for his associate. "We know what you have both said and done. We need not ask anyone what you are up to."

Mordechai nudged Annas and moved to one side, turning his back away from the others. Annas followed, seeing that Mordechai wanted to speak with him. "What is it?" he asked. Azariah, not willing to be left out of anything at this point, quickly joined them. Mordechai also motioned for Menachem.

"If we conduct any kind of examination or trial here," Mordechai pointed out, "we could be criticized." He shot Annas a quick glance. "Some might say it was not done under the proper authority."

Annas frowned, irritated by the suggestion, and yet he had been around too long not to know exactly what Mordechai meant. For all his power and influence, he did not officially hold the office of high priest any longer. "So?" he snapped. "What shall we do?"

"Let's take him to Caiaphas's palace. As high priest, your son-in-law has every right to conduct an interrogation."

"Agreed," Azariah jumped in. "Caiaphas's palace is the place for it. We don't want to give anyone an excuse to question what we are about to do."

What we have already determined to do. Mordechai almost corrected the Pharisee aloud, but did not, of course. He only nodded.

Annas nodded as well, then turned back to the others. "This man is charged with blasphemy," he said loudly. "He must be tried before the council. Take him to the palace of Caiaphas."

"Now?" someone from behind them exclaimed in shocked disbelief.

Mordechai swung around, eyes blazing. The crowd almost shrank back in the face of his fury. Then the voice, coming from a man near the back of the group, meekly added, "I thought the council could not convene at night."

Mordechai went up on his toes, trying to see who was speaking. Not that it mattered now. The damage had been done. It was true, and if he and the others were worried about proper protocol, they would be well advised to take especial care.

Azariah came to his aid. "The trial will not start until dawn," he barked, "but there is much to do to prepare. Rest assured, all will be in order."

Mordechai shot a scathing look at the crowd, daring them to say anything more. He feared that someone might remember that this was a high holy day and a day when the council normally would not be convened. His coldness worked. Heads dropped and looked away. No one else spoke.

Caleb turned to the soldiers. "You heard Annas. To the palace of Caiaphas."

"And bind the man's hands," Annas snapped angrily.

As the guards leaped to obey, Mordechai beckoned to his assistant, moving away from the others. Menachem moved in close.

"There are three things I need you to do. Take whomever you need to help you."

"Yes, sire."

"First, most of the council members are here already—they were told to be ready for an emergency session. But I need you to send the word out and get the others here right away. Of course, as before, there are some we need not worry about awakening."

Menachem accepted the assignment without comment. They had already discussed it, and he knew what to do.

"Second, we're going to need those witnesses we talked about. Have them at Caiaphas's palace at least half an hour before dawn."

Menachem nodded curtly. That was not a surprise either. Things had been carefully orchestrated long before this night had come.

"The final thing is the most important, and I want you to see to this yourself."

"What is it, sire?"

"Once word spreads that we have Jesus, his followers are going to gather to support him."

"Yes?"

"We need some strong support of our own—a large crowd that can make their will known as well."

Menachem grinned. "Their 'will' being whatever we pay for, of course."

Mordechai shrugged blandly.

"What we need is a mob," Menachem suggested.

Pretending shock, Mordechai reared back a little. "Whatever possessed you to use that word?"

Menachem's grin only broadened. "Sorry, sire. I don't know what came over me."

Chapter Notes

Though Annas is sometimes called the high priest, a more accurate term would be high priest *emeritus*. He served in the first role from A.D. 6 to A.D. 15, then was replaced by his son-in-law, Caiaphas. He obviously still wielded tremendous power and influence during the time of Christ's ministry (see Hastings, s.v. "Annas," p. 34).

CHAPTER 31

HE WAS OPPRESSED, AND HE WAS AFFLICTED,

YET HE OPENED NOT HIS MOUTH.

—*Isaiah 53:7*

I

JERUSALEM, UPPER CITY, PALACE OF ANNAS

4 APRIL, A.D. 33

"Can you tell what they're doing?" Peter hissed, looking up. He had John on his shoulders so John could peer over the lowest part of the wall.

"Most of the guards are still outside," John whispered. "The front door is open, and it looks like they have Jesus just inside. There are quite a few people there, but I can't tell what they're doing."

Peter staggered a little under the weight of his companion but planted his feet more firmly. "Can you hear anything?"

"No. Just mumbles." Then he jerked up. He put his hands on the top of the wall and hoisted himself up a little higher. "Wait! They're coming out again."

He climbed up on top of the wall. "Don't let them see you," Peter warned urgently.

But John didn't hear him. He had his head cocked to one side, trying to hear. Someone was barking orders, and the guards were coming to attention. Then he caught a momentary glimpse of the Master being marched between two men. The temple guards closed in around him, forming a hollow square. A man ran down the steps, and the door closed behind him. He went to the head of the column and motioned with his arm. "To the palace of Caiaphas," he commanded.

John swung his legs over and dropped down beside Peter. "Good news," he said. "They're taking him to Caiaphas's palace."

"That's good?" Peter said in dismay.

"Yes," John said, his face grim. "I have a friend there who is one of the household servants to the high priest. We'll have to hurry, but maybe we can get in and see what's happening."

II

JERUSALEM, UPPER CITY, PALACE OF CAIAPHAS

"They're coming here?"

John nodded, looking around furtively. "They should be at the front gate any moment. Can we come inside?"

The young maidservant looked around with the same nervousness that John was feeling; then she opened the gate more widely. "Word is spreading that Jesus has been arrested. There is already a crowd gathering in the courtyard, expecting that eventually he'll be brought here for trial. I dare not let you into the house—someone might recognize you. But I'll take you to the courtyard if you wish."

"The courtyard is fine," John said quickly. "Thank you."

She hurried away again, and John motioned for Peter, who came forward swiftly. They slipped through, and John closed the gate firmly behind them. "Down there," he said, pointing.

Because the palace of Caiaphas was built on the eastern slope of Mount Zion, the house itself was on three levels. Thus, the large courtyard covered three levels as well. The two men passed through the smaller upper two courtyards quickly, then slowed as they came down the steps. Evidently, the Sanhedrin had put the full contingent of temple guards on alert, for another dozen or so soldiers were on the lowest level of the outer court. They were lounging in one corner around a fire, warming themselves. Their spears were stacked neatly against the one wall.

Some few paces apart from that group was another cluster of people—mostly men, but one or two women as well. They too had a small fire, and several held their hands out to its warmth. John searched their faces quickly as they approached, hoping they might find some fellow disciples. No such good fortune. From their dress, he guessed that several were off-duty household servants or were staff to the Great Council—the ones who did much of the mundane work of running a large city. Obviously they knew that something important was about to happen and that it would likely happen at the house of the high priest, for they were settled in to wait. Unlike the soldiers, who were laughing and enjoying themselves, this group wasn't saying much to each other.

As the two newcomers approached, they were examined closely, then greeted with brief smiles and several nods of acknowledgment. The group had seen the woman bring John and Peter to the courtyard, so they assumed the two men had a right to be there. John smiled back, murmured a brief greeting, and took a place beside the fire, turning to face Peter and discourage any possible conversations.

They were barely settled when they heard a commotion above them. A group of soldiers, led by Caleb and Malchus, appeared in the upper courtyard, followed by more soldiers, then Jesus. His hands were tied, and one of the soldiers had him by the elbow, half dragging him along.

John reached out and steadied his companion with a light touch on the arm, silently warning him not to give themselves away.

The highest, or westernmost, part of the house contained the living quarters for the high priest and his family. These were sumptuous, palatial, and luxurious. The middle level contained offices and work areas for those who served the council. The lowest was fully dedicated to the judicial functions connected with the office of president of the Great Council. In that section was a large room filled with benches and chairs. In inclement weather, the Sanhedrin would meet there, rather than on the Temple Mount. More frequently, however, it was used as a chamber for hearings and judgments. To the immediate left of this room was the pit prison, a deep, narrow room cut into the limestone bedrock. The only entrance to the pit was a small round hole at the top, just large enough to lower or raise a person through it with a rope. The pit was used to hold prisoners who were awaiting trial or interrogation.

Beyond the pit prison were two or three additional cells and a scourging room. Under the Mosaic Law, certain of the more grievous crimes were punishable by whipping. The Law allowed forty stripes, but with their usual meticulous attention to detail, the Pharisees had reduced that to thirty-nine to ensure that the person administering the punishment did not accidentally exceed the Law and face punishment himself. Thirteen lashes were laid across the back, thirteen across the right breast, and thirteen across the left. Like the pit prison, the scourging room was cut from the native limestone. Two pillars had been left in place in the center of the room; there the prisoner was tied and held fast during the administration of the punishment.

With Caleb at the head, the column of men marched down the steps to the main level of the courtyard. They apparently planned to take Jesus through the west doors directly into the judgment chambers. The Pharisee barked a command, and all but four of the soldiers split off and marched over to join their waiting comrades, who stood at rigid attention.

Fortunately, even though the night was cold, the large shuttered doors to the lower level were left open. Evidently the servants had been told to expect a large crowd that might spill out onto the courtyard. The open doors would allow those in the overflow to follow the proceedings as well. With all the lamps and torches lit and the room stuffed with people, it would also provide some needed ventilation.

With the doors open, Peter and John could see clearly as Jesus was taken inside and brought before the table where the presidency of the council normally sat. Caleb required Jesus to stand before the table, even though it was empty, and then Caleb settled back to wait.

Nearly half an hour passed before the upper gate banged again. Both apostles instinctively ducked their heads when they saw who it was. Coming through the gate, lit by both the moonlight and torches placed along the courtyard walls, was the ruling body of the council. They walked in single file, with Caiaphas at the head. Mordechai ben Uzziel came next, with Azariah, chief of the Pharisees, third. Everyone watched quietly as, one after another, the council members who had been summoned filed after their leaders.

Inside, Caiaphas took the center chair but didn't sit down. He looked at Jesus for a moment, then flicked a finger. A servant jumped forward. "Put him in one of the cells," he said. "We can't start for a few more hours. We'll call when we are ready."

III

JERUSALEM, UPPER CITY, PALACE OF ANNAS

Simeon came back, moving swiftly with long strides. The moment he rounded the corner, the others stepped out of the shadows. "What?" Andrew demanded.

"He's not here," Simeon answered. "They've taken him to the palace of Caiaphas."

"But why?" Philip exclaimed.

"For the trial," came the flat reply. He took a quick breath. "They say they are going to try him for blasphemy."

"Blasphemy!" Matthias said in horror. "But that's punishable by . . ." He stopped, his eyes haunted.

Simeon looked up. The moon was low now. He turned to Andrew. "They can't start the trial before dawn. I'm guessing that's in about an hour or so. What do you want to do?"

James came forward. "We have to get in there," he said, "to see what is going on."

Andrew slowly shook his head. "No, the risk is too great." He motioned for the others to gather in more closely. "Simeon's right. By law they cannot start the trial until daybreak. The more people we can have here with us at that time, the better it will be. This place here is good. We're off the street and out of sight, yet we can see the front gate to Caiaphas's compound from here."

He looked at Simeon. "Your family is coming here, right?"

Simeon nodded. "They will come up here if they don't find us on the Temple Mount. I suggest we just settle down and wait." He looked around and when everyone seemed to agree with that, he leaned back. "At least we've found him."

Luke raised a hand. When Andrew nodded at him, he sighed. "Jesus' mother will be with the women," he murmured. "This is going to be very difficult for her."

Andrew lowered his head. "I fear this is going to be a very painful day for all of us."

IV

Jerusalem, Upper City, Palace of Caiaphas

John moved closer to Peter and nudged him with his elbow. The chief apostle was staring moodily into the fire, which was now mostly glowing coals. When Peter looked up, John motioned with his head toward the large building before them. "I think they're getting ready to start," he whispered.

Peter half turned and immediately came to the same conclusion. For the last hour or so, not much had been happening inside. People sat talking quietly. The presidency of the council had moved to the middle level of the palace and were no longer in sight. But people began to find their chairs.

"There he is!" Peter exclaimed.

He was right. The four guards had reappeared with Jesus between them. Once again they placed him before the council table. A moment later, Caiaphas and the other leaders could be seen coming down the stairs. Everyone in the room stood as the leaders moved behind the table and took their seats.

"Let's get closer," Peter suggested.

John hesitated, glancing around at the crowd. This was a hostile and dangerous place for them. Then he started a little. The maid-servant who had let him in at the gate was standing behind a guard at the door to the judicial chamber. John stood too. "Come on," he said.

The young woman seemed a little surprised to see John, as if she had forgotten she had let him in before, but then she smiled at him and whispered something to the guard. He stepped aside. Peter was close behind John and went to follow him in, but the guard immediately cut him off. The girl looked up at him, searching his weathered face.

John came back quickly. "It's all right," he murmured.

But her eyes didn't look away. "Aren't you a disciple of this man Jesus?" she asked.

Peter looked like a goat suddenly confronted by a lion. "I am not!" he said, more loudly than he had intended.

Others turned at the sound. The maid continued to question him, looking doubtful, then turned to John, who was holding his breath. Finally, she nodded and motioned for Peter to enter. "Thank you," he said, greatly unnerved. As they moved through the crowd, however, looking for a place to stand, Peter's nerves got the better of him, and he changed his mind. He reached out and touched John's shoulder. "I'd better wait outside." Before John could reply, he was gone.

With his head down, Peter pushed his way back out into the night. The first brushes of light were softening the eastern sky. Keeping his head averted, he returned to the fire and turned his back to it. Part of the reason for his position was to allow him to see what was going on inside the palace—but he was also afraid someone had watched the little interchange at the door.

He jumped as a hand was laid on his shoulder. He turned to see an older man peering at him. "You're a Galilean too, aren't you?" the man asked roughly.

From the fineness of his dress, Peter wondered if the man might be one of the minor officers of the council.

"Don't deny it," the man prodded. "Your speech betrays you. Are you a follower of this Jesus?"

"Of a truth," Peter said angrily, "I am not."

Cowed by the bigger man's vehemence, the officer backed away, but it was clear that he wasn't convinced. Peter turned back towards the house, feeling his stomach starting to churn.

V

It was probably just as well that Menachem hadn't returned. He was still out seeing to the final task Mordechai had given him. If he had been in the judicial chamber, he might have become the focus for Mordechai's disgust. Under the Law, especially in crimes serious enough to warrant possible capital punishment, testimony from at least two witnesses was required for a conviction. Three was better, but two was the absolute minimum.

Mordechai sat back fuming, ready to leap up and throttle Azariah's prosecutor. There was no shortage of witnesses. That was hardly the problem. In that regard, Menachem had done well. More than one coin had crossed palms this night. But to get two of them to agree, even on the broadest of the accusations, seemed beyond the man who was taking their testimony. One had heard Jesus say a certain thing, and the witness swore to it on the temple, or on his grandmother's grave, or whatever else might convince the court that he was telling the truth. The very next witness would disagree, saying no, that wasn't exactly what Jesus had said, and then give another version that was just different enough to render the previous testimony unacceptable.

Azariah had vouched for the prosecutor, saying he was one of his most skilled questioners, but the man didn't seem capable of even noticing the contradictions, let alone steering his witnesses around them.

And this was what Menachem had paid for? And yet, even as Mordechai asked the question, he knew that wasn't the problem. These people were so patently eager for the reward that had been offered, they were trying to anticipate what the prosecutor wanted before he could even ask them a question. If he asked any follow-up question, their story would instantly change as they tried to guess what he was looking for and altered their testimony to fit it. It was an embarrassment, and Mordechai felt like standing up and screaming. Jesus, who said nothing through the procedure, from time to time would look at the bench where they sat, as if to say, "And this is how you hope to condemn me?"

"Did you hear this Jesus preach anything contrary to the Law of Moses?"

This was the eighth or ninth or twentieth man who had been brought forward, and Mordechai barely paid him mind. His mind was racing, searching for some other alternative.

"I certainly did." The man was middle-aged, with crooked teeth and a complexion scarred by the pox. He tried to look indignant. "I heard him say that he would destroy the temple which was made with hands, and then in three days he would raise up another one made without hands."

Immediately something happened in the room. This was something new to the council. Mordechai, who had heard Jesus make this statement some time before, had forgotten it. He pulled himself up. "Say again," he called.

The man looked triumphant. He knew he had struck something with his words. "He said he was going to destroy our temple and then in three days he would raise one up that was built without hands."

"Only a god could do such a thing," the prosecutor exclaimed.

"Well, that's what he said."

"When you say 'he,' you mean Jesus of Nazareth?" That was from Azariah.

"I do. Him right there. I heard it with my own ears."

Caiaphas leaned forward, his attention directed at Mordechai, one eyebrow raising. Could this be what they had been looking for?

Mordechai raised from his chair. "I would ask the witness a question."

"Of course." The prosecutor bowed obsequiously.

"Was there anyone else with you when you heard him say this?" he asked.

"Of course, sire. There were a lot of people. But a friend of mine, Saul the Candlemaker, was there with me. He can tell you as well, if you like."

Before Mordechai could ask him if Saul the Candlemaker might be present, a man in the back started waving his hand.

"That's him," the witness said. "That's Saul right there."

"Come forward."

The hush in the room deepened as another man of about the same age as the witness made his way to the front. Outside, the people pressed in closer, sensing that something important was happening.

When the man stood beside his companion, the prosecutor stepped in front of the two of them. "Your name is Saul?"

"Yes."

"Do you know the penalty for bearing false witness, Saul?" the prosecutor asked unctuously. It was the first time he had brought it up.

"Aye, it is punishable by death."

"Well and good then. You have heard the testimony of this man." He motioned toward the witness. "Were you there on the day of which he speaks?"

"I was."

"And you heard this man teaching?" He pointed at Jesus.

"I did."

"Tell us what you heard. Put it in your own words. Don't try to say it as your friend here has said it."

"Well," he began, scratching at his beard, "some of the people round about where this Jesus was preaching had been talking about the temple, about how beautiful it was and all of that. Someone suggested that the stones were so great and so expertly placed that the temple might stand forever. Then this man—" he turned and pointed at Jesus—"he said that he could destroy the temple in one day, but if he did, he could build another without hands in three days."

The room began to buzz. Here, at last, was something they could get their teeth into, something that reeked of real blasphemy.

Mordechai was exultant. The first man had said he *would* rebuild the temple in three days. This man had said he *could* do so. But that was splitting hairs. Either statement implied that Jesus wanted to suggest he was divine. It was enough.

The chamber was in an uproar. Caiaphas banged the table with a heavy gavel. "Order!" he shouted. "Order."

VI

Peter edged as close to the open doorway as he dared, trying to hear over the shouts. "What's happening?" he called to the man nearest him.

"They've just had their two witnesses," the man shouted back. "I think they've got the madman finally."

Peter was about to say something more when he felt someone

tugging on his arm. He turned and felt his stomach drop. The man yanking on his sleeve was the same one who had confronted him a few minutes before about being Galilean. He had another man with him, one dressed in uniform. It was one of the soldiers.

"This is the man," the first one said.

The soldier peered at Peter. "My name is Balthar. I am one of the captains of the guard."

"Yes," Peter said, his voice barely audible, even though the people inside the chambers were quieting again under the pounding of the gavel.

"Malchus, servant of the high priest, is my kinsman."

Peter went completely cold.

"I was there last night when they arrested the Galilean." He squinted a little. Fortunately they were not directly under a torch, and Peter's face was partially in shadow. "You look familiar to me." Then his eyes widened perceptibly. "Didn't I see you there in the garden with him?"

Peter swore at him. "Fool!" he hissed. "Of course I wasn't there. *I am not one of them!*"

He had spoken sharply enough that people around them, both inside and outside the room, turned to look. Peter started to fall back. The silence was absolute. At that very moment, not far away, a cock crowed, joyfully greeting the growing light in the east.

Peter jerked as if he had been hit by a javelin. He turned his head, looking past the people all around him. Inside the council room, Jesus stood in front of the table where his accusers sat. But his head was turned, and he was looking directly at Peter.

Before the cock shall crow this day, Peter, you shall deny me thrice. The words flashed across his mind as if written in white hot flames.

With a strangled cry, Peter whirled and plunged past the two men who had come to accuse him, plunged past the staring crowd in the courtyard, plunged through the gate into the street. Weeping bitterly, the fisherman and chief apostle stumbled away into the gloom.

VII

Caiaphas got to his feet. His eyes were cold, and his lips pressed together into a hard line. He leaned forward, hands on the table, glaring at Jesus. "Well?" he said.

Jesus watched him steadily, but his lips never parted.

"Do you answer nothing!" the high priest roared. "What do you have to say about what these men witness against you?"

The eyes never flickered, and Jesus still stood speechless.

Caiaphas was livid. He stalked around the table and walked right up to Jesus. He was two or three inches shorter than the Galilean and so had to look up into his face. His hands were clenched into balls, and his lower lip was trembling with rage. "I command you in the name of the living God, tell us under oath whether or not you are the Christ, the Son of God."

There was a sharp gasp from the watching crowd. Even those who had sat on the council for many years had never heard the high priest, the presiding officer of the body, demand something in the name of the living God.

A man beside John turned to him. "He can't do that," he whispered. "A man cannot be forced to testify against himself. And if he does, that testimony cannot be used in a conviction."

Before John could respond, several others turned and shushed the man. It was clear that they didn't want to hear about legal technicalities. The noise that had burst out with the shocking demand of Caiaphas went as quickly as it came. Every eye was on Jesus and the man who confronted him.

And then Jesus stirred. His chin lifted a little. John held his breath. The regal dignity in his Master's bearing was striking. He stood there, hands bound together, in a room of men who hated his very name, and yet the feeling was that it was not Jesus who was on trial, but his accusers. Then his lips parted, and he spoke in a clear ringing voice. "I am," he declared.

Once again the chambers exploded. Men shouted and stamped their feet on the floor in protest. Some shook their fists at Jesus. Others stood with their mouths open in shocked disbelief. Caleb, who had moved over to stand behind Azariah, shouted hoarsely, "He makes himself a God."

Jesus' voice rose sharply, echoing off the stone walls and drowning out the cries and exclamations. "And henceforth," he cried, "you shall see the Son of man sitting at the right hand of power and coming with the clouds of heaven."

Caiaphas fell back, throwing up one hand across his face, as if to ward off an evil spirit. And then, in a night of shocking happenings, he did the most shocking thing of all. He reached up with both hands, grabbed the edge of his robes—the robes that were worn only by the high priest and revered almost as much the Torah scroll—and yanked downward. There was a sharp tearing sound as the fabric split from his neck to his chest. The bedlam in the room was snuffed out like a candle pinched between wet fingers. The high priest had rent his garments. There was in Judaism no sign of greater horror, deeper shock, or more piercing grief than to rend one's garments. But for it to be done by the high priest, and for the tear to be made in the sacred garments . . . Even Mordechai gaped in astonishment.

In an instant, the bony old man straightened to his full height. "You have heard it for yourselves," he shrieked at the crowded room. "Does not the man blaspheme? What further need do we have of witnesses?"

His head jerked and bobbed as he stared wildly at the men in the room. John had the fleeting image of a stork or heron, searching the beach for dead fish. "What say ye?" Caiaphas thundered.

Mordechai shot to his feet. "He is worthy of death!"

"Yes!" came the answering roar.

Azariah was up, shaking his fist toward the man who stood there so quietly. "Death to the blasphemer!" he screamed.

Jesus gave no further response. He was done. He said nothing more. He just continued to look forward, calmly and with quiet dignity. He was like a mountain in the midst of a raging thunderstorm: quiet, majestic, barely aware of the puny forces raging around it.

"Kill him!" Caleb shouted.

John, son of Zebedee, the one whom Jesus had called his beloved, dropped his head and stared at the floor. Now he understood. Jesus was not going to save himself. He wasn't going to use his limitless powers to stop this travesty. This is what he had meant by what he had said earlier that night. This is what he had tried to tell them the night before. His hour had truly come. The Son of man had been delivered up to the Prince of Darkness.

CHAPTER NOTES

A word about Peter's denial is in order. Almost universally, commentators attribute Peter's denial to cowardice. Some have even referred to it as a shameful lapse of character. They grudgingly note that he later repented and went on to become a strong and effective leader, but only when he overcame this "flaw" in his character.

It is true that on the surface, the record of Peter's thrice-repeated denial might suggest that. However, depicting Peter as a panic-stricken, trembling coward who slinks away at the first threat of danger doesn't square with the rest of the picture. Did he simply buckle under the tremendous pressure of that night? Is it simply that when the chips were down, he couldn't take it and scrambled away in an effort to save himself?

Think for a moment of what had happened just hours before in the Garden of Gethsemane. When Judas led the soldiers to the Savior, he didn't go alone.

Both Matthew and Mark tell us that he brought a "great multitude" and that they were armed with "swords and staves" (Matthew 26:47; Mark 14:43). What did Peter do when he saw this very real and dangerous threat—a much more direct threat than was presented to him in the courtyard? Did he bolt and run? Did he slither away into the darkness? No. Of all the apostles, he alone sprang into action. He whipped out his sword and waded in swinging. Malchus lost his ear that night. To a craven coward? The idea is ridiculous. Peter stopped only when the Lord himself told him to put away his sword. Yet these commentators would have us believe that just hours later, he is paralyzed with fear. It just doesn't add up.

Or consider this. Matthew tells us that after Jesus was arrested, the rest of the twelve "forsook him, and fled" (Matthew 26:56). But Peter and John followed after Jesus, even though he was under armed guard. That surely wasn't the safest course of action. If Peter was so petrified with fright, as some would have us believe, why would he go inside the courtyard at all? Why not just stay away and hope things would work out?

Yes, Peter did three times deny knowing Christ. There is no doubt of that. Yes, he did weep bitterly over his denials. But should we not be a little cautious about imputing motive and mental state to Peter when the Gospel writers themselves do not do so?

There is another possibility we should consider. Several months before, when Jesus had told the apostles of his approaching death, Peter tried to dissuade him from that course. In a stinging rebuke, Jesus chastised Peter for what he was trying to do (see Matthew 16:21–23). Then, just hours before the three-fold denial, Peter took up the sword in Jesus' defense. Was Jesus pleased with this show of courage? No. Again Peter was rebuked and was specifically commanded to stop interfering. Did not Jesus tell Peter that if he needed help, he could call down twelve legions of angels? Isn't it possible that Peter backed down that night, not because of fright, but through reluctant obedience to what was clearly the Master's will?

True, it does say that after the third denial Jesus turned and looked on him, and then Peter went out and wept bitterly (Luke 22:61–62). "Isn't that proof of his shame and remorse," some would say? But why must we assume that the look Jesus gave Peter was one of condemnation? The scriptural record gives no such description. Perhaps Jesus looked at his apostle with approval. Perhaps it was his way of acknowledging that Peter was doing what he wanted him to do. Wouldn't

Peter weep just as bitterly knowing that Jesus was going to die and that he was prevented from doing anything to try to stop it?

The author is not taking the position that these possibilities are what really happened, only that there may be other explanations for the denials than fear and cowardice. If Peter turned coward that night, it was a strange contradiction in his character. Let us not rush to judgment based on a limited account of what happened. The Gospel writers make no attempt to explain the whys of Peter's behavior that night. If they do not, perhaps we too should be a little more cautious before doing so. (For a more extensive presentation of this issue, see Kimball, pp. 1–8.)

CHAPTER 32

ALREADY IT IS TIME TO DEPART, FOR ME TO DIE,
FOR YOU TO GO ON LIVING. WHICH OF US TAKES THE BETTER
COURSE, IS NOT KNOWN TO ANYONE BUT GOD.
—*Socrates*, Plato's Apology, *42a*

I

JERUSALEM, UPPER CITY, PALACE OF CAIAPHAS
4 APRIL, A.D. 33

A great sense of euphoria filled the judgment hall. The sound was deafening. Everyone was shouting and laughing raucously, fueled largely by a huge sense of relief. It was done. The many contradictory witnesses had pretty much subdued the watching crowd. It appeared that Jesus was going to slip out of their hands. Then the unexpected occurred before their eyes. The fool had blurted out his own condemnation. The high priest had put it exactly right. What need was there for further testimony? They had three dozen eyewitnesses. Four dozen maybe. The man had sealed his own fate.

Caleb leaned over and whispered something to Azariah, who was still seated at the table with Mordechai and Caiaphas. The old Pharisee looked up, then nodded curtly. Caleb turned to the man standing just behind him and whispered again. He gave a momentary look of surprise, then grinned fiendishly. Motioning for others to follow, the man moved around the table, his eyes fixed on Jesus.

The Galilean still stood quietly. His head was up, but his eyes were focused somewhere other than in the room. It was if he stood alone in a quiet forest.

The approaching men slowed as they reached the prisoner. They had hoped he would turn and cower at the sight of them. The lead one, whose name was Eliad, stopped directly in front of Jesus. Finally, Jesus' eyes focused on him, but Jesus offered no change of expression.

Several in the crowd noticed what was going on and began shushing the others. In a moment, the room was quiet. "Heretic!" the man suddenly screamed into Jesus face. "Blasphemer!" He made a hawking sound in his throat, then lunged forward. The spittle caught Jesus squarely on the left cheek just below the eye. It slid slowly downward, leaving a wet streak that glistened in the lamplight.

A roar went up, and people pounded their hands together in approval.

A second man followed suit, this time hitting Jesus' beard. The phlegm hung there like an accidental spill of food not yet seen.

"Death to the blasphemer!" Eliad shouted. Spinning around, he lifted his arms. "Death to the blasphemer!" He waved at the people, much like a choral director. "Death to the blasphemer!"

"Death to the blasphemer!" It was ragged, but the crowd quickly caught the rhythm. "Death to the blasphemer! Death to the blasphemer."

Mordechai watched from beneath hooded eyes. The crowd was loving it. The chant made the very floor tremble.

He motioned to his two associates, and they leaned in closer to him. Annas, who stood discreetly behind his son-in-law, came forward as well. "We have a problem," Mordechai said.

"What?" said Caiaphas.

Azariah didn't need to ask. He just said, "The Romans, right?"

"That's right," agreed Annas. "We cannot carry out a sentence of death without their approval."

"After what happened at the Feast of Tabernacles," Caiaphas snorted, "Pilate and his Roman tribune owe us a favor. They'd better give us license to do whatever we need to do."

Mordechai nodded, but it was only a thin courtesy. He saw a touch of disgust in Annas's eyes as well. Caiaphas had so much to learn about how the power game was played. Mordechai spoke to Azariah, but he was loud enough for the other two to hear. "You know what they'll say if we come to them with a charge of blasphemy."

Azariah jeered at the very idea. "Those heathen dogs have no concept of the word. Their gods are so twisted and corrupt, blasphemy would be a joke to them."

Annas was nodding, and Caiaphas finally understood as well. "Do we have to tell them what our ruling is?" he asked. "Can't we just tell them that we have just cause for putting him to death?"

Turning, trying to hold his patience, Mordechai started to explain, but the chant filling the room stopped abruptly, turning into applause. They turned to look. Another man had come up to Jesus. His name was Johanan. He placed both hands on Jesus' shoulders. He straightened him as if he were a clay statue, then took a scarf, quickly rolled it into a narrow strip, and blindfolded Jesus. The applause quieted as the crowd watched.

Johanan finished securing the blindfold. It didn't hide the angry red mark on Jesus' cheek. It still glowed a dull red from when Caleb had struck him at Annas's palace. Mordechai watched with curiosity, not sure why they wanted the prisoner's eyes covered.

He quickly found out. The crowd was completely quiet. It was Eliad who came forward, moving with exaggerated slowness. He crouched down, peering up into the face of Jesus to determine whether he could see out from beneath the blindfold. He lunged forward, his fist clenched, stopping just a hair's breadth from Jesus' face. Jesus didn't flinch at all. The blindfold was doing its work. Laughter rippled through the appreciative group. Eliad was playing to his audience.

Then, quick as a cat, he again lunged forward, and again there was a sharp crack. This time the back of his hand caught Jesus squarely in the face. Johanan cackled in delight. "If you are the Christ, tell us who it is that struck you."

"Yes!" cried the crowd.

A third man jumped in. Crack! Jesus' head rocked back again. When his head came up, Mordechai saw that his nose was starting to bleed. "Prophesy unto us," the man shrilled. "If you *are* the Messiah, prophesy. Tell us who strikes you."

"Prophesy! Prophesy!" screamed the crowd.

Mordechai turned back to his associates, raising his voice to be heard over the bedlam. "There are too many followers of this man," he explained. "Even if Pilate gives us permission to kill him, the people will blame us for his death."

Annas grunted his agreement. "The Romans have to take the blame."

Mordechai turned and looked behind him, toward the hallway that led to the upper floor of the palace. "You haven't seen Menachem yet?"

Azariah shook his head. "No. Where did he go?"

"I sent him on some errands, but he should have been back by now."

"He's over there." Caleb, still hovering behind Azariah, was pointing. Just inside one of the shuttered doors open to the courtyard, Mordechai's aide was watching the proceedings.

Exasperated that Menachem hadn't come immediately to report, Mordechai half stood, waving an arm. Menachem jumped when he saw him and started pushing his way through the crowd towards them.

"Well," Mordechai snapped when his assistant reached him.

"Done, sire," Menachem said, flushing a little. "The men you requested are awaiting our signal."

"Very well. We need you to go to the Antonia Fortress as quickly as possible. Tribune Marcus Didius is there. You must speak to him directly. Tell him we are bringing a prisoner to them."

One eyebrow arched slightly in response, but Menachem nodded. "How soon shall I tell him to expect you?"

"We won't be far behind you. Ask him to alert Pilate. We'll need a hearing."

"He'll want to know who and what the charges are."

"Oh," Mordechai said slowly, "my guess is that Tribune Didius already knows who we have in custody. The charges will be treason against the empire."

Caiaphas came around with a jerk. "Treason?"

Azariah was staring at him too, but then a slow grin stole across his face.

Annas nodded in admiration. "Treason," he mused. "Of course. What else?"

Mordechai snapped his fingers, and Menachem darted away. He turned back to watch the crowd making sport of the prisoner but felt a tap on his shoulder. To Mordechai's instant annoyance, Menachem was back. "The assignment I sent you on is urgent, Menachem," he barked. "What are you—"

"Sire," he said in a low voice. "He's here. He wants to see you."

"Who's here?"

"The betrayer. Judas of Iscariot."

"*Here?*"

"He says he has made a terrible mistake. He wants to give the money back."

The other three men were listening intently. "Send him away," Caiaphas said flatly. "The matter is done."

Menachem didn't even glance at the high priest. "He's very insistent. He could make trouble."

"Where is he?"

"In the main entry hall upstairs."

"Go! Find the tribune," he said. "We'll take care of this."

II

Judas looked gray. There was a sheen of perspiration on his face, which only added to his pallid complexion. In one hand, he held the leather purse he had been given earlier that night. His eyes flicked back and forth among the four men but finally stopped on Mordechai.

"What do you want?" Mordechai made no attempt to disguise his utter contempt.

The disciple of Jesus held out his hand, letting the purse dangle from it. "I have made a terrible mistake. I have sinned in that I have betrayed innocent blood."

"What is that to us?" Annas sneered. "That is your affair, not ours."

"I didn't know you planned to kill him." It came out almost as a whisper.

"Then you're a fool!" Azariah exclaimed. "Out, before we arrest you too."

Like a deer trapped in a thicket, Judas looked back and forth, eyes wide and haunted, seeking some mercy, searching for any sign of softness in their faces. There was none. With a strangled cry of pain, he dropped the purse, letting it hit the floor with a heavy clunk; then, hunched over as if in terrible pain, he turned and plunged out the door.

"Prophesy, O Jesus of Nazareth!" someone below them shouted.

"Death to the blasphemer," the crowd roared back. "Death to the false Messiah!"

III

As the gate to the courtyard of Caiaphas's palace swung open, James and Andrew and the men who waited with them a short distance up the street jerked to attention. It was still a quarter of an hour or more before full daylight, but there was enough light that they could see clearly.

James leaned forward, staring. Then he called out. "Judas?"

The man spun around, looking like he had been struck with a well-aimed shaft.

James stepped out fully into the street. "Judas! It's me, James. And Andrew!"

"No!" The cry was muffled but clearly audible. Then the figure turned and broke into a stumbling run in the opposite direction.

James took a few steps, then stopped. He turned back to look at the others, his expression grim. "It's Judas."

Andrew was shaking his head. "So he's still here working his treachery. This is not good, brethren."

Thomas shook his head. "Where is Peter? And John?" He looked up at the walls to the sumptuous building across from them. "What is happening in there?"

IV

Azariah bent down and picked up the purse. He hefted it in his hand thoughtfully, then looked at the others. "I think it's all here, the full thirty pieces."

"What do we do with it?" Caiaphas asked. He didn't like this turn of affairs, none of it. It was complicating things just when they were finally moving forward.

"Put it back in the treasury," Mordechai answered, not really caring.

Azariah reacted strongly to that. "We can't do that."

"Why not?" Annas asked.

"Because this money was paid as the price of blood. It would pollute the treasury."

Mordechai scoffed loudly. "You didn't blanch at paying out blood money," he said derisively. "Why the scruples all of a sudden?"

Azariah shook his head stubbornly. "We can't pollute the treasury with blood money."

"Then use it somewhere else," Annas snapped, done with the matter.

"Where?" Caiaphas wondered. On this matter, he was in agreement with the Pharisee. The temple funds were sacred.

Ever the one to worry over details, Azariah was thinking hard. "Legally, the money still belongs to this man. If he gives it back, then it has to be used to foster the public good somehow."

Mordechai couldn't believe it, but he knew that the old goat wasn't going to let it go until he had a solution. "We've been talking about the need to extend the *alcedama*." *Alcedama* was the Aramaic word for field of blood, a euphemism for a place of burial. "We've talked about purchasing that potter's field in the Hinnom Valley." He looked at Azariah, barely hiding his scorn. "Would it offend your tender sensibilities if we used the money for that?"

Azariah flushed, but nodded. "That would be an appropriate way to deal with this matter."

"Then let's get back down there. We need to call the council to order and ratify the verdict." He turned as the noise coming from the stairwell surged up again. "I hate to spoil their fun, but it's time we got on with this."

V

"Here they come." Simeon saw the approaching group, stepped back out into the street, and waved his arm. "Father, we're over here."

The group of waiting disciples moved out into the street to welcome their comrades. On seeing Simeon, Miriam broke free and ran to him, throwing herself into his arms. Between the traveling and her worry, she had not slept the entire night. "What's happening?" she said. Her eyes were red and swollen. Her face was lined with concern.

He shook his head. "We're not sure. They have Jesus inside. Evidently they're trying him before the Great Council."

The other family members had come up in time to hear his answer. "But no verdict yet?" David asked.

Simeon shook his head. "They're not letting anyone inside, so we don't know." He told them briefly about seeing Judas a few minutes before.

They joined the waiting disciples. Andrew immediately faced David. "We're also waiting for a group to come in from Bethany. I suppose you didn't see any of them?"

Simeon's father shook his head, but it was Ephraim who answered. "No, we watched for them, but we came in through Zion's Gate. If they're coming from Bethany, they'll be coming from the east, from the Temple Mount."

Benjamin stepped forward. "I can go look for them if you'd like."

Andrew immediately shook his head. "We sent Philip off about a quarter of an hour ago to take a look. He'll come back here to report." He looked around nervously. "Let's get out of the street. We don't want to call too much attention to ourselves. So far the streets are quiet, but let's not take any chances."

Simeon watched his family as they began to move toward the trees. They were all in shock. His mother had been crying. Rachel hung on Ephraim's arm heavily. Leah was pale as a sheet of papyrus. His younger sister had always been especially sensitive to the pain of others. Aunt Esther was—and then it hit Simeon. He turned to his wife. "Where's Livia?"

Miriam sighed. "She didn't come."

His mother moved up beside them. "She was deeply disturbed by the news," Deborah explained. "After what happened to Yehuda the last time we were here, the talk of arrest and soldiers was too much for her." She made a soft sound of distress. "She was almost physically sick. We felt it best if she stayed home."

"Good," Simeon said. He had not thought of Livia until this moment, but he knew instantly that this would be especially hard on her. He was glad they had prevailed on her. She was only a few weeks from bringing her child into the world. No one wanted the shock of this night and what yet may lay ahead to bring that child before its time.

VI

Philip returned about ten minutes later. The path that ran between the palace of Caiaphas and the next palatial home led down toward the main part of the city. The hillside was steep at that point, and stairs had been built to smooth the way a little. By the time Philip reached them, he was puffing heavily. Andrew went to meet him, as did many others, filling the street. Fortunately, that early in the morning no one was out and about as yet.

"I found them," Philip exclaimed as he ran up. "Mary, Martha, Lazarus—there are a dozen or more, including several more men."

"Good," James said. "Are they coming?"

"No. They're waiting outside the lower gate of the courtyard. We need to go down there. We could hear what sounded like a riot inside. People were shouting and screaming."

That startled Andrew. "Shouting? What kind of shouting?"

Philip scanned the faces of his brethren for a moment, then lowered his head. "'Death to the blasphemer,'" he said in a bare whisper. "That's the one that we could hear the clearest."

VII

Jerusalem, Upper City, the Praetorium

"Sire?" Marcus pulled back the linen curtain, leaned forward, and laid a hand on the governor's shoulder.

Pontius Pilate came awake with a start. He let out a low cry and jerked to a sitting position, eyes darting wildly about. Finally they settled on Marcus. "By the gods!" he snapped, "Marcus? What are you doing here?" He glanced towards the windows. "The sun isn't even up yet."

"No, sire. I'm sorry to disturb you. Your servant didn't want to let me in, but there's trouble brewing. I thought you'd better hear it from me. You'd better come down to the judgment hall."

VIII

JERUSALEM, UPPER CITY, PALACE OF CAIAPHAS

The disciples from Bethany were waiting outside the lower gate to the palace compound. The women immediately moved together, gathering around Mary, the mother of Jesus, to lend their strength and support to her. Though not weeping openly at the moment, she looked terribly drawn. It was as though she had aged ten years in one night.

The men drew into a tight knot and began discussing what action they might be forced to take. James and Andrew took the lead in the discussion, which centered around what Jesus expected of them. James told them about Peter's attempt to protect the Master and what Jesus had said to him. "It was like he wanted us out of the way," Andrew broke in. "Besides, what can we do in the face of such a large body of armed soldiers?"

Simeon nodded. "If we're not careful, this could turn into a bloodbath like it did a few months ago."

As the men debated, the women kept turning to look at the gate and the walls of the palace. The shouting that Philip had described had been silenced. From time to time they could hear the murmur of voices, but nothing more. Finally, the group lapsed into a worried silence, fearing what was happening to Jesus. A second, unspoken fear was that Peter and John had been arrested too. A growing feeling of gloom and depression settled on the group.

Not more than five minutes later, they heard a soft creak as the gate swung open, and John appeared. He blinked in surprise for a moment to see thirty or forty people waiting for him, but quickly recovered. He swung the gate shut again and motioned everyone to

gather around. It was a superfluous gesture. Everyone was already pressing in to hear what he had to say.

"What's happening?" James asked. "Is Jesus all right?"

John's face was grim. "They've convicted him of blasphemy."

The other disciples responded with gasps and exclamations of
shock and dismay.

"They've sentenced him to death," he went on doggedly. He
stepped to Mary and put an arm around her, pulling her close as he
spoke. "However—" He wished there were a way to soften this, but
they had to know. She had to know. "However, they know they can't
get the Romans to approve a death sentence for a religious violation.
They're getting ready to take him to Pilate at the Praetorium. They're
going to charge him with treason."

"Treason!" It was Bartholomew who had burst out.

John's head bobbed once. "They'll be leaving here in just a few
minutes. We need to get over to the Praetorium so we can be there
and give Jesus our support. Our only hope now is that Pilate will see
this for what it really is—a sham. The council has trumped up the
charges because they hate Jesus' popularity with the people. That's all
there is to this. Pilate needs to know that."

Andrew reached out and grabbed John's arm. "Where's Peter?"

The young apostle looked around quickly. "He's not with you?"

"No. We haven't seen him since you left us at the garden."

John's gloom deepened. "I know a servant here. She let us in, but
we got separated. Half an hour ago, maybe more, I saw some men talking with Peter. He seemed angry. I couldn't tell what was happening.
He jerked away from them and ran out. I was coming out to look for
him."

"Have they hurt him?" It was Mary. She was looking at John with
imploring eyes. "Have they hurt my son?"

John looked away for a moment, his own face lined with pain, then finally answered. "They've struck him in the face a few times," he said slowly.

She winced but did not turn her eyes away.

"They've been mocking and ridiculing him, but no, so far they have not seriously hurt him."

CHAPTER 33

ART THOU A KING THEN?

—John 18:37

I

JERUSALEM, UPPER CITY, THE PRAETORIUM

4 APRIL, A.D. 33

Pilate was fumbling to buckle a gold band around his wrist as he descended the stairs. Marcus snapped to attention, as did Sextus and the four soldiers with him.

The procurator stopped in surprise and looked around. "Where are they? I thought they were clamoring for a hearing."

"They're outside in the courtyard, sire," Marcus explained. He wore a sardonic expression. "Being the Passover and a high holy day, they won't defile themselves by coming inside."

Pilate reached the bottom of the stairs, hooking the clasp. He snorted in disgust. "These people! Can't risk pollution by a Gentile, but they are not squeamish about putting a man to death on manufactured charges."

"Agreed, sire. They are an unusual lot."

"Well, I ought to tell them that they either come inside or forget it, but I suppose we'll have to humor them."

As he started for the door, he stopped. "Marcus?"

"Yes, sire."

"Tell me what you think of this whole matter. Is this Jesus really a problem for us?"

Marcus hesitated. "Would you have me speak forthrightly, sire?"

Pilate gave an impatient flick of his hand. "Of course."

"I think our sally against the Zealots last fall has pretty much defused our problems in the Galilee. Everything we are hearing is that this Jesus does not preach rebellion or uprising. Just the opposite, actually."

"So?" Pilate barked sharply. Being awakened early had left him grumpy and short-tempered. "Give me a conclusion."

"Jesus is very popular with the common people, sire. I think if we intervene and punish him in some way, we could create more problems than if we just tell him to keep his mouth shut and let him go."

Pilate swung on Sextus. "Do you agree with that, Centurion?"

"I do, sire," Sextus replied quickly. "The tribune has assessed the situation accurately, in my estimation. Jesus is no threat to us."

"So what are the formal charges against this man?"

Marcus couldn't help but smile. "Blasphemy, sire."

Pilate turned in disbelief. "Blasphemy? Surely you jest."

"Sextus has eyes and ears within the high priest's staff. That's what we were told."

Pilate moved over in front of a full-length mirror made of cloudy glass. "Blasphemy," he muttered, half to himself, as he turned back and forth checking to make sure every fold in his toga was just right. "Well, this shouldn't take long then." Satisfied, he turned to his men, waving an arm. "All right, let's get it over with."

When they went out on the balcony that overlooked the courtyard, they stopped in surprise. It was completely full. People were standing in groups, milling around, glaring at the sentries at the doors. And more were coming in even as they watched.

Pilate gave Marcus a sharp look. "You didn't tell me we were going to have half the city here," he grumped.

"I didn't know we were," Marcus answered. He jerked his head at Sextus. "Get some men down there. Have them ready for trouble."

Sextus slapped his chest in salute and walked swiftly away, motioning for the four soldiers to follow. A moment later, soldiers began filing quietly out into the courtyard, taking places all around the walls. It had an instant, subduing effect upon the crowd.

Pilate moved to the marble balustrade and looked down. Marcus moved with him and fell in just behind his elbow, his eyes taking in the situation quickly. "There's Mordechai," he pointed out to Pilate in a low voice. "Directly below us. And Caiaphas and Annas."

"Who is the plump one? I've seen him before, but—"

"That's Azariah, chief Pharisee. He's third in terms of position on the Great Council."

"Yes, that's right."

"And where is—" But then Pilate saw the prisoner. There was a phalanx of temple guards with their spears raised in neat rows. Inside the hollow square they formed stood a man. He was bareheaded and clothed in a simple robe. He stood quietly, his hands tied in front of him.

"So that's him?" Pilate asked.

"Yes. That's Jesus."

Pilate looked more closely. The sun was just coming up over the eastern hills. It would be another hour before it penetrated the courtyard, but the light was good, and Jesus' head was up. Pilate could see the discoloration on his face and grunted. So they had been having a little fun while they waited. No surprise there.

He leaned out, both hands on the railing, looking down at the four leaders. "Speak! What is it? What accusation do you bring against this man?" His tone let it be known that he was in no mood for trifles.

It was Mordechai who took a step forward and bowed slightly.

"Excellency," he said smoothly, "if he were not a criminal, we would not have delivered him to you."

So, Pilate thought, that was how it was going to be. They were not cowed by the presence of the governor. "Criminal?" he said coldly. "Then take him and judge him according to your laws."

"By Roman decree," Mordechai replied smoothly, "it is not lawful for us to put any man to death."

Caught by surprise, Pilate turned to Marcus. "Death? They're talking about a capital crime here?"

"Under their law, blasphemy is considered a capital crime, yes, sire."

Mordechai, watching carefully from below, guessed what was going on. "Excellency, we found this person perverting our nation."

Pilate's eyes narrowed. "How's that again?"

"This man is guilty of rebellion and sedition, sire. He has been forbidding his followers to pay tribute to Caesar. He claims that he is the Messiah and seeks to make himself a king."

Pilate turned to Marcus again. "Is that true?"

Marcus was a little taken aback. His information, not yet an hour old, came from a pretty good source inside the high priest's household. Jesus had been convicted of blasphemy. Nothing had been said about treason. "This is news to me, sire," he said lamely.

Pilate turned back, his eyes searching. When he saw Marcus's centurion, he waved a hand. "Sextus Rubrius! Bring the prisoner to me."

II

"That's not true!" Miriam grabbed Simeon's arm as the Romans took Jesus from the temple guard and marched him up the stairs to the balcony. "Jesus didn't forbid us to pay tribute. He said, 'Render to Caesar the things that are Caesar's.'"

"I remember," Simeon murmured. They were standing back in one corner where the shadows were deepest. His eyes kept moving nervously back and forth between Pilate, Marcus, and the crowds around them. In a way, it was insane for him to be there. If Marcus saw him and Miriam, he might take action. Mordechai was another threat. He had warned them last night to stay away—now the reason was evident. He would not be happy to see that Simeon had ignored his warning.

On the way over, the disciples had debated about going inside the Praetorium. James and the other apostles were worried too. The temple guard had seen them last night, even though it had been only in the moonlight. If the guards recognized them, would they seek to arrest them as well?

However, when the group arrived they were surprised to see how many people were already at the Roman headquarters. Finally, they decided they would slip inside, but scatter among the crowd and stay back, staying as inconspicuous as possible. Even the family had split up. David and Deborah were a few feet away from Simeon and Miriam. Ephraim, Rachel, and Leah were beyond that. Simeon couldn't tell where Benjamin and Esther had ended up.

Simeon looked at Miriam, frowning deeply. Something was wrong, and he wasn't sure yet what it was. But all he said to Miriam's comment was, "They have to manufacture something against Jesus; otherwise the governor will send them away."

His head turned, and he watched as five or six more men entered through the gate. Like most of the crowd around him, these were a tough looking lot. They had that hard look that men of the streets have. Their tunics were ragged and dirty. Their hair and beards were a tangle. As three passed by right in front of them, Simeon caught the offensive whiff of strong body odor.

Motioning for Miriam to wait where she was, he moved over to slip up beside Andrew, John, and James. "There shouldn't be this many people here," he whispered. "Not this early."

John nodded grimly. "Only about a quarter of them came from the Hall of Judgment," he noted. "The rest . . ." He looked around in distaste. "Who are they?"

"Have you noticed the way they recognize each other when they come in?" Simeon had spent his life in situations where assessing the enemy and the situation you were in was critical to one's survival. "They know each other. But they don't know Jesus. Most of them seemed to examine him pretty closely when they brought him in."

"Well, they're definitely not part of Jerusalem's upper crust," John added. "So where are they coming from?"

James was thoughtful. "I saw Mordechai's assistant a few minutes ago. What's his name?"

"Menachem," Simeon supplied.

"Yes, that's the one. He was standing near the gate. The men seemed to be looking to him for direction when they came in."

Simeon stared at him. He hadn't seen that. "What kind of direction?"

James shook his head. "He didn't say much. Mostly it was a nod of the head, or pointing where they should go."

Simeon's lips pressed into a tight line. "This is not good, brethren, not good at all."

III

Pilate sat in the marble chair. It was placed at the head of the assembly room that opened directly out onto the balcony. He watched curiously as Jesus was led in by Sextus and another guard. The bruises on the man's face were evident, and the governor noticed drops of blood on the front of his tunic and a smear of blood on each sleeve.

Sextus stepped back, leaving Jesus alone in front of the procurator. Marcus stood behind Pilate, near enough to receive instructions but far enough back to make it clear who was in charge. Suddenly, he saw a movement out of his eye. He turned and saw Pilate's wife standing at the doorway. Marcus could scarcely believe his eyes. Fortunata Cassandra Drusus Pilatus was rarely up before the third or fourth hour of the day, and that was when they were in Caesarea. Up here in the Jewish capital, it was not uncommon for her to not be seen all day. She hated Jerusalem and made no secret of it.

She caught Marcus's eye and motioned frantically for him to come over. He did so, walking swiftly.

"I must speak with Pilate," she exclaimed, before he had even reached her.

He didn't try to hide his surprise. "M'lady," he said, as politely as he could, "the governor is in the midst of a hearing."

"I know that," she hissed. "That's why I have to talk to him. Now!"

Marcus backed away, nodding. "I'll tell him," he said.

Pilate rose to his feet as Marcus returned. He slowly walked around Jesus, examining him with careful scrutiny. He was about to speak when he saw Marcus. Irritation flashed across his face when he saw Marcus signaling to get his attention.

"Sire, your wife is here."

Pilate turned and looked, as surprised as Marcus had been.

"She says she has an urgent matter."

Frowning, Pilate walked swiftly to his wife.

As he approached her, she ran to him, grabbing his arms. "Pontius?"

"What is it, my dear? What has gotten you out of bed at this hour?"

Fortunata was a delicate woman, one who would rather be inside the marbled halls of a palace than strolling outside in the sunshine. But she did not lack courage or fortitude. She had stayed at his side in this and other unpleasant assignments like any good Roman matron would do. Even though they had separate chambers and didn't spend much time together during the day, Pilate was glad for his wife and felt a fond affection, almost a fatherly protectiveness, towards her.

She turned, trembling a little. "Is that him?"

"That's Jesus of Nazareth," he replied.

"You can't have anything to do with him," she said with sudden fierceness.

It was so totally and completely unlike her that he rocked back a little. "What?"

"He is a just man, Pontius, and you can have nothing to do with him."

He didn't know what to say. When had she ever cared about the affairs of state or for the welfare of a common prisoner?

Her eyes dropped, not able to meet his. "I have suffered many things in a dream this night because of him, Pontius. Please! Don't have anything to do with this."

And then, before he could get over his astonishment, she went up on her toes, kissed him on the cheek, and turned and strode back inside.

Troubled more deeply than he was willing to admit, Pilate walked slowly back to Jesus. Marcus gave him a questioning look, but the governor ignored it. He sat back heavily in the chair, brooding sullenly, thinking of Fortunata's dream. From birth, Romans were taught to look for portents and deep meaning in their dreams. This was making him increasing frustrated. Finally, he looked up. "Are you the king of the Jews?" he growled darkly.

Jesus' head came up to look at him. "Do you say this of yourself, or did others tell you that?"

Leaping to his feet, Pilate lashed out. "Am I a Jew?" He began pacing back and forth in front of him. "It is *your* nation and *your* chief priests that have delivered you to me. What have you done?"

Marcus leaned forward, curious to hear the answer to that.

"My kingdom is not of this world," came the calm response. "If it were, then my followers would fight for me, that I be not delivered into the hands of the Jews. But my kingdom is not from here."

Marcus felt himself relax. Just as he had said. This man was no threat. But to his surprise, Pilate seemed only the more troubled by that answer. "So are you a king then?" he pressed, staring into those fathomless eyes.

For a long moment Jesus seemed to be taking the measure of his accuser, but then finally he nodded. "Yes, it is as you say. To this end was I born, and for this cause came I into the world, that I should bear witness of the truth." He paused. "Everyone that is of the truth hears my voice."

Pilate stiffened at the implications of that. "What is truth?" he snapped angrily. He turned to Sextus and flipped his hand. "Hold him in the corridor," he said. Then he motioned Marcus forward.

"Yes, sire."

Pilate sat down in the judgment seat, not looking up. "Do you find this man a threat to Rome?"

"No, sire. As I said before, I believe the greater threat would be stirring up the people against us. He's very popular."

The older Roman took a deep breath, his eyes half closing as he considered. Then he stood and strode back out onto the balcony. The people milling around below went quiet again. Pilate looked directly down at Mordechai, Caiaphas, Annas, and Azariah. "I find no fault in this man," he called loudly.

A howl of protest exploded from many lips.

"There is nothing here worthy of death," he shouted over the noise.

"Not so!" Azariah bellowed. "This man has been stirring up the people from the Galilee to Jerusalem. Thousands flock to him saying he is the King who shall deliver them from Rome's oppression."

The last was meant to serve as a barb to the procurator, but Pilate hadn't heard it. At the mention of Galilee, he spun back around to Marcus. "He is a Galilean?"

"Yes, sire. He's from Nazareth. That's in the upper Galilee."

"And Herod is here in Jerusalem for the feast?"

"Yes, Excellency, he is."

Pilate pulled at his chin. After the breakup of the kingdom of Herod the Great, Emperor Tiberias had divided up the kingdom among Herod's sons. Some had lost their portions through mismanagement or falling out of favor with the emperor, and those areas had become the province of Judea, governed directly by Rome. But the tetrarchy of the Galilee, which had gone to Herod Antipas, had remained intact. Antipas and Pilate had fought many a battle over who really had primary responsibility there, and Pilate detested the man. But . . .

"The Galilee is his territory, as he continually likes to remind me." He made up his mind. "Take the prisoner to Herod's Palace. Let that old weasel take jurisdiction here."

IV

"Wait here," Simeon murmured, touching Miriam's arm.

Her eyes widened. "You're not going to try to—"

He gave her a comforting smile. "No, I'm not going to follow them. I just want to get a better idea of what is going on. I'll be right back."

When the soldiers marched Jesus out the gate with the Jewish leaders hard behind, word spread that Pilate had sent Jesus to Herod. A few people filed out after the soldiers to see what would happen with Herod, but Menachem, after a whispered word from Mordechai, stopped at the gate and turned most of the crowd back. They were to stay where they were. The delegation would be back, he promised.

That's when Simeon knew for sure that something smelled bad, very bad. The Sadducee who served Mordechai moved among the people—or rather, among a select group of the people—there in the courtyard. He would join a group, whisper briefly to them, wait for the nod of acknowledgment, then move on. His contacts were always with the men who made Simeon's flesh crawl a little. None of them were the kind of men you wanted in the house when you were trying to sleep.

Certain that Menachem wouldn't recognize him—Simeon had always been in a crowd when he had been in Menachem's presence—he pushed his way through the people, going at an angle so he would intercept Menachem as he met the next group. On reaching them, Simeon turned his back, bending down, pretending to lace his sandals up more tightly. Menachem was right behind him.

"You know what to do?" Menachem asked softly.

There was a mutter of agreement.

"Good. Just follow my lead."

"And when do we get paid?" another voice demanded.

"Shut up, you fool," Menachem warned. "You'll get paid when you've done what you were brought here to do."

He moved off again. Simeon stood and, without turning to look back, started a large circle around the court to the place where James, John, Andrew, and the others had gathered. As he did so, he saw the group of women who had come from Bethany. They too were deep in the shadows. He saw that Mary Magdalene and Martha were standing beside Jesus' mother, holding her by both arms to help steady her.

V

Pilate was waiting for them, drumming his fingers rapidly on the arms of his seat. At the sight of Jesus, he stood up. "What is this?" He pointed at Jesus, who now had a gorgeous, full-length scarlet robe draped around his shoulders.

Marcus motioned for Sextus to stand Jesus where he had been before, then turned to his commander. "Herod put it on him."

The governor reached out and fingered the material. It was beautiful. The cloth was thick and finely woven. Such color came from a dye made by crushing a rare species of shellfish in Phoenicia. It was rare enough that only the wealthiest could own such fabric. This was not an insignificant gift.

Marcus sensed what was going through the governor's mind. "Jesus refused to answer any questions, which annoyed Herod. But some of the people started calling Jesus the king. That amused Herod greatly, and he called for the robe to be placed on Jesus' shoulders."

Though they were speaking in Latin, and Pilate assumed this simple Galilean could not understand their words, Jesus' steady gaze made Pilate uncomfortable. He moved back and then said, "So? Herod didn't pronounce sentence?"

"No, sire. It was a waste of time. The Jewish leaders were there, making the same accusations they did for us. As I said, the king questioned Jesus at some length, but he never once opened his mouth. Finally, Herod turned him back to me, saying that he didn't find anything in him worthy of death." He smiled ironically. "Sire, the king expressed his deep appreciation for your consideration in sending Jesus to him. He has heard much about him and wanted to meet him. It was a wise courtesy. He said he hopes this leads to a more amicable relationship between the two of you in the future."

"Good." Pilate turned back to look at Jesus. "But he made no judgment?"

"None. He said it was in your hands."

Pilate snorted softly. So Herod didn't want this hot coal thrown into his bag either. He stood there, deep in thought for a moment, then strode past Jesus and out onto the balcony again. "Bring him out here," he said to Marcus as he passed.

The people, who had waited lazily while the soldiers were gone, had come fully awake again. Jesus was back. They looked up at the governor, waiting for his word. Once again Mordechai and the other leaders stood directly below him.

Pilate put his fists on the marble railing and leaned far out. "Leaders of the Great Council of Jerusalem," he intoned, "you have brought me this man—" he gestured with a hand to the figure just behind him—"and say that he has been perverting the people. Behold, I have examined him and have found no fault in this man touching the things of which he is accused."

His voice rose sharply as an angry rumble erupted below him. "I sent this man to Herod Antipas, and, as you can see, he has returned. Neither did he find anything worthy of death in him."

The rumble became a roar before he had finished speaking. People screamed up at him, shaking their fists, shouting insults.

Pilate flushed and turned to Marcus. His tribune moved up quickly beside him. "Sire, I have a suggestion."

"Yes?"

"Remember that it is our tradition to release a Jewish prisoner during Passover."

Pilate's eyes lighted. "Yes," he mused. "Near the end of the feast."

"We have been holding the three Zealot leaders we captured last fall and planned to crucify them this week as a reminder to the people of what happens to rebels."

Pilate turned slowly, suddenly interested. "Yes, go on."

"I mentioned to you the other day that the Jews want us to release the chief of them, the one called Barabbas, in keeping with the custom."

"Barabbas?"

"Yes, sire. He is a murderer and a dangerous man. I think it is a mistake to release him. So what if we released this Jesus instead?"

Whatever feelings of frustration Marcus had from time to time with his commanding officer, he had never considered him dull witted or slow of perception. Pilate saw immediately the advantages of what Marcus was suggesting. "Hmm," he mused. "As popular as Jesus is with the people, they should love that."

"It would extricate us from a sticky situation here."

"Good thinking, Marcus." He turned back and looked into the faces of the people, holding up his hands. They quieted somewhat, but not totally. They were getting restless, and an ugly undercurrent of anger was swelling, which worried Pilate a little. "Citizens," he said loudly, "as you know, it is our custom to release a prisoner to you during this festival time. Since neither I nor Herod find any fault in Jesus, I will chastise him and then we will release him as—"

"No!" It was Mordechai who shouted it, but others had cried out as well. "Away with this man!"

Several days before, as the council discussed the possible release of a prisoner during the feast and settled on Jesus Barabbas, Mordechai had objected. He hated the Zealots and knew they represented a very real danger to the nation. Their blind fanaticism threatened to bring down the wrath of Rome on their heads. To set one of the most dangerous leaders free was a mistake. But the people's love for the Zealots was in direct correlation to their hatred of Rome. A large majority insisted on asking for Barabbas. And so he had finally backed down.

Mordechai exchanged a glance with Menachem. "Barabbas," he whispered. Then he looked up at Pilate. "We don't want this man. Release Barabbas unto us."

"Barabbas!" Menachem shouted, whirling around. "We want Barabbas!" He pumped his hand. "We want Barabbas!"

Then men in his pay saw what he was doing and joined in immediately. It spread quickly through the whole group.

"We want Barabbas! We want Barabbas!"

For a long moment, the procurator stared down into the faces of what was very quickly becoming a mob. Then, shaking his head, he turned, motioning with his finger for the guards to bring Jesus back inside. The thundering chant followed after them.

He dropped into his chair and put his head in his hands, pressing his fingers against his ears. When he looked up, Marcus was watching him. "We can disperse them if you wish, sire."

Pilate shook his head. "No, that could quickly get out of hand. What is it going to take to satisfy them? Their heads are like blocks of granite."

Marcus said nothing. After a minute or two, Pilate stirred. "Take the prisoner downstairs and scourge him. That will show them we're not being soft with him. Then bring him back to me."

Marcus was surprised. There had been no determination of guilt. But he didn't feel it wise to point that out to Pilate. He turned to Sextus. "You heard the governor."

Sextus, uncharacteristically subdued, answered with a nod, but his eyes were on the ground and he didn't look at the tribune.

"Sextus?" Marcus warned in a low voice, guessing what was causing his hesitation. Sextus turned before Marcus could say more and started barking orders to the guards. Four of them surrounded Jesus and marched him out. Sextus followed behind, not turning to look back as they left the room.

VI

No one was exactly sure who had first devised the scourge as an instrument of punishment, but, as they had with so many other things, the Romans had perfected it. Whips of one sort or another were initially invented to control animals. When men began viewing other men as animals, it was not surprising that the whip should find a new application.

The Roman *flagrum*, or *flagellum*, had a hollow wooden handle through which passed several leather strands. The length of these thongs could be shortened or lengthened as desired by pulling them one way or the other through the handle.

Three was the most commonly favored number of strands, but Sextus had seen as many as nine. A strip of dry rawhide, even when wielded by a powerful man, usually left only angry red welts. So the Romans had developed an enhanced version of the instrument for use when more severe punishment was required. Three very thin strings of leather were braided together, with pieces of bone or shards of metal added every two or three inches. With that, there was no longer any question of damage. The flesh was ripped and torn even with a light blow.

Sextus stood back as the soldiers prepared the prisoner. The centurion watched Jesus, wondering if he remembered him from Capernaum. How could he not, when Sextus had spoken to him face to face and asked him to heal his servant? But if Jesus recognized him, he gave no sign. Jesus had not looked at him directly at any time since being brought to the Praetorium.

In almost thirty years of service, Sextus had watched more scourgings than he could count. Some he had administered himself, usually to a legionnaire who had fallen asleep on duty or lost his courage and fled during battle. He had never liked it, but this was the first time he was sickened by it.

The soldiers, bored after several days of barracks duty, were eager to carry out the sentence. They had heard that the prisoner was accused of being a king. His being clothed in the scarlet robe only piqued their curiosity the more. They found the whole idea hilarious. It had not been their privilege to scourge a king before. They called him, "Your grace," or "Your majesty," bowing low in exaggerated homage, treating him with mock deference. Someone found an old dried reed and stuck it in his hand as a scepter. All of this was punctuated with raucous peals of laughter and slaps across his face, blows to his head, or savage kicks to his ankles and shins. Jesus submitted without protest or outward sign of response.

Then two of the men had an idea. They ran to the garden that was at the back of the Praetorium. There a large thorn bush grew. Its long willowy branches were studded with two-inch spikes that could draw blood like the point of a knife. They cut off two or three branches and trooped back to the dungeon. Then, as their comrades shouted encouragement, they wove the branches together to form a "crown."

Preparations for an actual coronation could not have been done with more care. The gorgeous scarlet robe was removed with great ceremony and laid aside. The crown and scepter were placed neatly beside it. Next, the outer tunic was removed. Finally, the inner garment was pulled down over the shoulders so that Jesus' body was bared to the waist. Long leather straps were fastened to his wrists, which were still bound with cords. Two of the men shoved him roughly forward, while two more lashed the leather straps to the scourging post, cinching Jesus' body tightly against the post so he could not pull away from the blows.

A powerfully muscled legionnaire with a pockmarked face walked over to the bench and picked up the scourge. The laughter died away. No matter how hardened a man might be, there was rarely much laughter during the actual punishment.

As the man reached Jesus and planted his feet, checking the thongs on the scourge to be sure they were the proper length, Sextus raised a hand. The legionnaire stopped, clearly surprised. All heads turned to their centurion, waiting expectantly. Sextus paused, then shook his head, dropped his hand, and turned away. "Bring him back up to the judgment chambers when you are finished," he said.

VII

The crowd had been getting restless, and Pilate had finally sent Marcus out to tell them that the target of their hatred was undergoing a Roman scourging. That brought a ragged cheer, and they settled down again somewhat. But some of the people had been there for almost three hours, and Pilate could sense he wasn't going to be able to pacify them much longer.

He jumped to his feet when the door opened and Sextus came in. Behind him came the first two legionnaires, then Jesus. Pilate started toward the balcony, then stopped again, turning back. Jesus was still in shadow, but something caught Pilate's eye. Then as Jesus came forward, Pilate's breath drew in sharply. The prisoner was still clothed in the scarlet robe, and his wrists were bound together. But his face was streaked with blood. That puzzled Pilate for a moment. A scourging did not involve the head. Then he saw it. A cleverly woven crown of thorns had been pressed deeply into Jesus' hair. Blood glistened on several of the tips, and Pilate winced involuntarily as he realized what his soldiers had done.

Seeing the governor's eyes fill with comprehension, the guard behind Jesus grinned impudently. "Here's your king back, sire. He's been properly coronated."

Sextus swung on the man, but Pilate waved him back. "It's all right. The men need to have their diversion." Then he was back to business. "Bring him outside."

Marcus, sensing that Pilate was growing impatient, moved forward and took Jesus by the elbow. The guard stayed on the other side but let Marcus lead out.

At the sight of Jesus crowned and bleeding, the crowd exploded with approval. They stamped the pavement with their feet, clapped their hands, whistled, cheered.

Mordechai stood up. He too was growing impatient. Pilate was stalling. Mordechai knew that as surely as he knew he wasn't going to let Pilate get away with it.

Pilate brought Jesus forward to the balustrade. He stepped back so Jesus stood alone, a pitiful, solitary figure. Mordechai saw the red stripes on the prisoner's shoulders. And yet his head was high and his eyes, though dark with pain, were clear; they showed no signs of madness, a common result of a thorough scourging.

Gradually, when neither man on the balcony moved or said anything, the crowd subsided. When it was finally quiet, Pilate straightened and held out one hand, pointing to Jesus. "Behold the man!" he called out loudly.

For a moment, the people gave no response as every eye looked up. Mordechai, sensing an opportunity, tipped his head back. "Crucify him!" he shouted.

Menachem, recognizing his mentor's voice, immediately took it up. "Crucify him! Crucify him!"

Caleb, mingling in the crowd, added his voice. "Crucify him!"

As the chant quickly spread and became a roar, Pilate, rankled, leaned over, peering down at Mordechai and his associates. "*You* take him and crucify him," he yelled. "I find no fault in this man."

Mordechai bristled at the insult. Pilate knew they couldn't carry out that sentence. Only the Romans could. He waved at Menachem, who, surprised, began shushing the crowd again. "We have a law," Mordechai called up at the procurator when he could be heard, "and the emperor has said that you are sworn to honor our laws. This man claims to be the Son of God, and by our law, he must die for such an outrage."

Pilate stepped back, his lips pulling down into an angry grimace. The old Jew was trying to force his hand. He was right, of course. As long as a people peacefully accepted Roman rule, the head administrator was instructed to support and uphold their laws, unless they contradicted Roman law. It didn't matter whether Pilate thought the laws were ridiculous or not.

But even as the anger boiled up in him, he felt a deeper reaction, one of dismay, perhaps even a touch of fear. The Son of God? Once again he strode back inside the judgment hall. Marcus and the guard took Jesus and followed after him.

VIII

Outside the gate to the Praetorium, Miriam stood beside Simeon, watching Deborah and Martha and Mary Magdalene kneeling beside the mother of the Master. Mary had crumpled to the ground at the sight of her son, then began to sob as the chant swelled.

Andrew was there too. John held her up, steadying her. Any concerns about their being recognized were gone. The shock was too deep, too total, placing their entire focus on Jesus and what was happening to him. The women were weeping bitterly. Every new cry brought further horror. Surely this couldn't be happening!

Then Simeon felt Miriam sag beside him. He flung an arm around her and held her up. Her shoulders started to shake convulsively as great sobs tore through her body. He pulled her closer to him. "Miriam! What is it?" He knew she was in shock. The cry for crucifixion hit them all like a massive blow. But this was something more.

She looked up at him. Tears streamed from swollen eyes. "Didn't you hear him?"

He reared back a little. "Hear him? Who?"

She just shook her head, unable to speak. He felt a movement and turned. Leah was beside him. She too was weeping, but she was somewhat in control of herself. He gave her a searching look. "Who, Leah?"

But Miriam knew she had to be the one to say it. No one else had caught it. "My father," she blurted between her tears. "It was my father's voice who first shouted it out."

IX

Once they were inside again, Pilate whirled on Jesus. "From whence do you come?" he demanded, his voice sharp and almost frightened.

Jesus turned his head enough to look at him but said nothing.

Pilate turned and kicked at a footstool, sending it crashing away. "You won't answer me?" he bellowed. "Don't you know that I have the power to release you or crucify you?"

Jesus watched him steadily, completely unaffected by the outburst. Then he spoke. "You could have no power over me at all if it weren't given you from above." His head turned, and he looked toward the balcony. "However, he that delivered me up to you has the greater sin."

Pilate felt something cold brush across his soul. It had been spoken with such unruffled majesty. This man spoke of power and unseen things and the consequences for sin as if all of those were his to give or withhold. At that moment, Fortunata's frightened face passed before his mind. *He is a just man, and you can have nothing to do with him.* He felt a prickle at the back of his neck.

Swearing softly, he turned and strode back outside. Again he leaned out, shouting down at the four men below him. "I find no fault in this man! I shall release him, as is the custom."

"We want Barabbas," Mordechai shouted.

"Barabbas!" screamed Menachem.

"Barabbas! Barabbas! Barabbas!" The building trembled beneath the pounding words. Swallowing hard, Pilate turned his head. "Marcus!"

Marcus stiffened and saluted. "Yes, sire."

"Do we have Barabbas here?"

"Yes, sire, in one of the cells down below."

"Release him."

The response was deafening. A mighty shout of triumph reverberated off the walls.

"And what would you have me do with Jesus?" Marcus asked, turning back.

"Crucify him!" shouted Azariah.

"Crucify him!" Caleb echoed.

"Crucify him! Crucify him!" roared the crowd.

Pilate was trembling with anger. "Would you have me crucify your king?" he screamed at the crowd.

Annas looked up in disgust. "We have no king but Caesar," he shouted back.

Mordechai took a step forward and cupped his hands to his mouth to make himself heard above the crowd. "If you let this man go, you are no friend of Caesar's. Any man who makes himself a king speaks directly against Caesar."

Pilate paled and fell back a step. That was no accidental phrase Mordechai had invoked. *Friend to Caesar* was a formal title given to provincial governors, especially provincial governors who were in particular favor with the emperor.

Pilate knew that Mordechai ben Uzziel understood the procurator's tenuous standing with the emperor right now. Three different times during his reign he had undertaken to put these intransigent Jews in their place, and three times disaster had resulted. The last time, a delegation from the Great Council, perhaps even Mordechai himself, had written a letter of protest to Rome. A few weeks later, Pilate had received a terse reprimand from the legate in Syria. The message was blunt and to the point. "If you wish to keep your position as governor, make peace with the Jews. The emperor does not want any trouble in the east right now."

The procurator moved away from the balcony, looking trapped. His mind was racing. But there was no way out. That last threat had just overturned everything, like a chariot hitting a stone at full speed.

Marcus watched the governor in surprise. He had seen him leaning over, obviously talking to the four council leaders below him, but he was shocked to see his commander's face when he straightened again. He came forward quickly.

Pilate barely saw him. He dropped into his chair and buried his head in his hands. After a moment, he began to massage his temples. Marcus waited, not sure he should disturb the procurator.

After what seemed like several minutes, the leonine head came up, the eyes defeated but defiant. "Marcus?" He had lost sight of him.

Marcus sprang closer. "Yes, sire?"

"Have the servants bring me a pitcher of water and a basin."

Marcus stared at him for a moment.

"A pitcher and a basin," he snapped. "And a towel. Now!"

But Sextus had already heard it and was moving towards the door, calling for one of the servants.

As they sat back and waited, Pilate started to chuckle. It had a strangled quality to it and sounded like it came from a mad man. Marcus stared more closely, feeling a sense of uneasiness.

"Have you ever studied the Jewish law?" Pilate asked suddenly.

Marcus slowly shook his head. "No, sire. I have not."

"A labyrinth," he said to himself. "Totally incomprehensible." He smiled again, a secretive, sly smile. "But sometimes understanding the folly of one's enemy has its advantages."

"Oh?" Marcus didn't dare say anything more than that.

"Yes. They have rules to cover every possible situation. Did you know they even have a commandment that tells them what to do when someone is killed and they can't find the guilty party?"

"Really?" This was growing stranger by the moment.

The smile broadened, a smile of triumph. "The law says that if they wash their hands of it, it signifies there is no guilt."

Marcus felt instant relief. Pilate was troubled, but he was still in possession of his senses. Then Marcus smiled as well as he thought about the implications. "I understand, sire. Excellent idea." His admiration went up a notch. This was the crafty old politician he had come to know. You didn't count this one out too easily.

"Move that small table out here. And a chair." As Marcus jumped to obey, he added. "And I want you to help me, not the servant."

"Yes, sire."

The crowd sensed something unusual was occurring and quieted quickly. They watched as the large basin was set on the table. The servant laid a towel over Marcus's arm, then handed him the heavy pitcher. Pilate took the chair and sat down carefully. He held out his hands and nodded at Marcus.

Marcus poured a stream of water over Pilate's hands. The splash of the liquid in the basin could be clearly heard throughout the courtyard, so total had become the silence. Pilate rubbed his hands together with exaggerated slowness as the water continued to hit them. Then he nodded, and Marcus stopped.

Marcus handed the pitcher to the servant, who stood off to one side, then extended the towel to Pilate. He took it and stood up. Lifting his hands high for all to see, he dried them with that same slow, ritualistic movement. Then he tossed the towel to one side.

"I am innocent of the blood of this just person," he said solemnly. His head dropped, and he looked directly at the four leaders who waited below him. "You have your crucifixion. See you to it."

He spun on his heel and started toward the door to the inner hallways. Over his shoulder he barked a command. "Marcus. Send for the cross beam. Take him to Golgotha."

"What about the other two, sire?"

Pilate didn't break his stride. "Of course," he flashed angrily. "Crucify them all."

Chapter Notes

Though Matthew, who describes the washing of the hands, does not say that Pilate was aware of the Mosaic Law about hand-washing, this was a well-known custom, and after being in Palestine for several years, it is likely that Pilate was aware of exactly what he was doing. One commentator put it this way: "The hand-washing was a Jewish custom to signify the removal of guilt (Deuteronomy 21:6; Psalm 73:13), but Pilate may have used it either in desperation or in mockery" (Guthrie, p. 849).

An oft-asked question is, "How come there were vast multitudes swarming out to wildly welcome Jesus as the Messiah at the triumphal entry, then just a few days later, those same people are howling for his blood?"

Perhaps there are better explanations than having the Sanhedrin "seed" the crowd, as is shown here, but there are some peculiarities in the brief descriptions of that morning. First, we know that the Great Council went to great lengths to take Jesus secretly so as not to stir up the crowds. Second, it was early in the morning when they went to Pilate. Obviously, the disciples had spread the word of Jesus' arrest during the night, but likely that only went to their own small circle. So where did the crowds come from at such an early hour? And why were they so hostile to Jesus?

Manipulating events by controlling a mob has long been a device used by evil men to accomplish their own purposes, and that tactic makes good sense in this setting. There is one phrase in Matthew that hints that undue influence was being exercised that morning. Matthew says that the chief priests and elders "*persuaded* the multitudes that they should ask [for] Barabbas and destroy Jesus" (Matthew 27:20; emphasis added).

One note of interest about Barabbas. Little is known about him other than what is given in connection with the trial of Jesus. In one of the ancient manuscripts, however, his name is given as *Jesus* Barabbas. That would not be surprising, since Jesus (*Yeshua* in Aramaic) was a common name at the time. Barabbas is a patronymic—*bar* meaning "son of," *abba* or *abbas* being the word for "father" (Hastings, p. 84). Thus Pilate, probably without knowing the significance of what he was saying, asked the crowd, "Do you want me to release to you this brigand, Jesus, son of the father, or shall I release your Messiah, Jesus, the Son of the Father?"

CHAPTER 34

I

JERUSALEM, UPPER CITY, THE PRAETORIUM
4 APRIL, A.D. 33

Marcus looked up and saw Sextus watching him steadily. He looked away and refilled his cup. He emptied it again. When he glanced up, his centurion's gaze had not shifted. "What are you looking at?" he snarled.

Sextus's expression never changed. "The detachment is ready when you are, Tribune Didius."

"Oh," Marcus said, mocking his tone, "so now it's Tribune Didius, is it? And why the formality all of a sudden? It wasn't my decision to crucify your Jesus."

Sextus acknowledged Marcus's disclaimer with a quick bob of his grizzled head. "I've called out the full century, sire. I thought we'd send eight quarternions ahead of you to keep the crowds back." His expression darkened momentarily. "The word is out. There are large crowds in the street."

That was enough to bring Marcus out of the alcoholic haze that was starting to fill his head. "Already?"

"Yes, sire. And now most of these seem to be Jesus' followers."

"Is a century going to be enough?" He could tell his voice was getting a little thick. He didn't care. He poured another half a goblet and took a drink.

"Unlike the bunch down below, the crowds out there seem to be more in shock than anything."

"Good."

Sextus went on as if there had been no interruption. "I've detailed eight men with each of the prisoners. The rest of the company will bring up the rear, again to make sure the people are kept back."

Marcus stared at the fire in the grate in one corner of the room.

"Sire?"

He didn't look up.

"Would you like me to send word to Lady Diana that you will be gone for a time?"

He jerked up. He had completely forgotten about his wife. What would she say if she knew what he was about to do—not once, but three times? "No," he blurted. Then, more calmly, "She's used to waking up and having me gone."

"As you wish, sire." Sextus started to turn, his eyes still completely inscrutable. "I'll be with the men."

Marcus got slowly to his feet and had to reach out and steady himself against the wall. "You have the crossbeams?"

"Yes, each prisoner has his own."

Marcus took a quick breath, his mind already racing forward, feeling the dread welling up again. "Mallets and spikes?"

"All is in readiness, sire," came the quiet reply.

Marcus slammed down the cup, splashing wine across the table and his hand. "Then let's be done with it."

II

Miriam was sickened at the sight of Jesus, staggering under the weight of the thick beam lashed across his shoulders. His face was bloodied from the lacerating thorns, and on his bare shoulders she could see the dark stripes from the scourging. Numbed beyond anything she had ever experienced, she didn't even think to avert her face as the soldiers passed.

Marcus was on his horse, staring straight ahead, holding the reins tightly as the animal pranced nervously among the crowd. Then he saw Miriam's face in the crowd. He stiffened, his eyes widening. They narrowed instantly when he saw Simeon beside her. But Miriam saw none of that. She did not take her eyes from the prisoner.

Only when she heard her name spoken sharply did she turn. The Romans had required the leaders of the Great Council of Jerusalem to walk directly in front of the prisoners. She fell back half a step when she looked directly into the cold, hard eyes of her father. In one instant, her face registered the revulsion she was feeling. He was largely responsible for this scene, and she knew it as well as he did. She looked away, the tears coming even more heavily than before.

He made as if to speak to her, then jerked angrily to look at Simeon. "I told you to stay away!" he exclaimed. "Get her out of here. This is a dangerous situation."

Simeon was as pale as death. Over and over as the horror of the night had progressed and deepened, he kept waiting for that moment when it would be enough, when Jesus would finally unleash his awesome power in his own behalf. Simeon had seen with his own eyes a mature, healthy fig tree completely wither away in less than twenty-four hours. He had been on the ship when a raging storm was stilled with a single word. He had watched in stunned astonishment as Lazarus, four days dead, came forth from the tomb. One word from Jesus and the Roman guards surrounding him could be blown aside like dry leaves before a whirlwind. One blink of his eye, and the entire Sanhedrin would wither away, just as the fig tree had done. But only now, as Simeon watched the grim procession passing, was it finally clear to him. Jesus was not going to act. He was not going to call down power of any kind in his own behalf. For reasons that Simeon could not fathom, he was submitting to this gross injustice. He had accepted his fate as calmly as does an animal being led to the slaughtering pens. He had placed himself— him, the Son of God—completely in the control of evil, wicked men.

All of that had been tumbling through Simeon's mind when Mordechai appeared before them. For a moment, Simeon wanted to scream at him, lash out for what this man was doing, strike him down for the damage his monumental pride was doing to the Messiah *and* his own daughter. But he pushed it all back. "You don't know what you have done this day," he said softly. "May God have mercy on your twisted soul."

Going instantly purple, Mordechai spun away in a swirl of robes, striding out swiftly to rejoin Annas, Caiaphas, and Azariah.

Simeon and his family, along with the group of apostles and disciples from Bethany, pushed in behind the last of the soldiers. Simeon was not surprised when many of the crowd in the courtyard began to dissipate. They had done their work, made their influence felt with the governor. This unknown man was going to the cross now. They could go home and drink off their ill-gotten wages.

III

The streets of Jerusalem

When they came out of the courtyard of the Praetorium and into the streets, trying to stay close to the column of Roman soldiers, David ben Joseph looked around in surprise. The streets were packed with people. He turned to James and John. "The word is out," he said.

John nodded, his face grim. There were a few angry faces around. One or two jeered or spit at the prisoners as they passed. But for the most part, the crowd was not hostile. The loudest sound was the wailing and weeping of the women. On every side, eyes were sunken and haunted, faces showed the horror, stiff bodies were evidence of the disbelief. Here was the man they had listened to raptly on the Temple Mount. Here was the Prophet whom they had gone out to see less than a week before, throwing their garments at his feet and waving the palm branches wildly. Here was the Messiah, who had merited their shouts of hosanna and hallelujah. He moved slowly, his head down as he struggled to carry the cross beam. Could this truly be their Deliverer?

"Look!" Andrew called out, bringing Simeon's head around. "There's Peter."

It was true. Ahead of them, standing on a low stone wall, leaning out to see better, was the chief apostle. He hadn't seen them yet; his eyes were fixed on the Master, who was moving slowly past him.

"Peter!" Andrew started forward, waving his arm. "Peter!"

Peter turned, searching the crowd, then saw his brother. He dropped to the ground and started pushing his way against the flow of the crowd. In moments he had reached the other apostles. Crowding around him, the disciples moved to one side of the street to escape the crush of people.

Peter's first thought was for Mary. He went quickly to Jesus' mother and took both of her hands. "I am so sorry, Mary," he said, his voice thick with emotion. "I never dreamed it would come to this."

She clung to him. Her tears had long since been exhausted. She was now just pale and drawn, hunched over with the never-ending pain. "Thank you," she murmured.

"Pilate wanted to release him," Matthew explained. He was standing just behind the women. "But the Sanhedrin forced his hand. They're going to crucify him."

No one needed to tell Peter that. He turned as Anna came up and threw her arms around him. "Oh, Peter," she cried. "We've been so worried about you."

He took his wife in his arms and held her tightly. "It's all right. I'm here now."

"Where did you go?" John asked. "I went looking for you."

"I—" The fisherman shook his craggy head, not finishing. He looked around. The procession had slowed to a bare crawl as the soldiers tried to clear the streets ahead of them. Word was spreading rapidly. The Messiah was being crucified. Hundreds of people were streaming in to see what was happening. Peter grunted. He didn't want to get too far behind, but he saw they could tarry a little longer. Out of long habit, he immediately began taking back his position of leadership.

The apostle motioned for the men around him to move in closer. "I assume they're taking him to Golgotha?"

Simeon nodded, as did several others. That was not a difficult guess to make. The primary value of crucifixion for the Romans was its power to deter future crime. Part of its deterrent value was that it was designed to be a lingering, excruciatingly painful form of death. Often, victims could live as long as two or three days on the cross, alternating between periods of unconsciousness and extreme agony. But even the most fiendish form of execution didn't carry much deterrent value unless it was well known and vividly implanted into the minds of the population. So it was common practice to choose as the site of crucifixion the sides of heavily traveled roads. Thus, the maximum number of people could become eyewitnesses of this, one of the cruelest ways man had ever devised to end the life of their fellow human beings. Golgotha, which in Hebrew meant "the skull," signifying it as a place of death, was just outside the northern walls of the city. It was set back only a short distance from the well-used road that led to the northern environs of the city. Everyone in Jerusalem knew about Golgotha.

"When we start moving again, let's try to push our way forward a little," Peter went on. "It will be difficult, but let's stay as close to Jesus as we can." He arched his neck, looking out ahead.

David blanched a little. "You're not thinking of trying to—"

Peter cut him off quickly. "No, the Master has forbidden us to intervene. But we can let him know we're here."

"We saw Judas," Andrew said as they began moving forward, closing in on the last of the soldiers. "He was coming out of the palace of Caiaphas early this morning."

"Judas is dead," Peter said flatly.

The group responded with gasps and exclamations of astonishment. "Dead?" Deborah cried. She walked beside David, holding his hand for strength. "Where? How?"

"I saw one of the disciples just a few minutes ago. Someone found him at the base of a tree this morning. There was a rope around his neck that had snapped in two. He evidently hanged himself."

John passed a hand across his eyes. "Because of the betrayal, do you think?"

Peter shrugged, his expression moody. "We may never know. The man who found him said it was clearly done by his own hand."

A shout up ahead caused them all to turn. The column of soldiers was moving again. "Come on," Peter said. "Let's split up and go on either side of Jesus."

IV

The typical cross was made of two pieces: the *stipes*, or vertical beam, usually planted deep into the ground and left in place between executions, and the *patibulum*, or cross beam, the thick plank to which the victim was affixed before it was hoisted into place atop the *stipes*. This was called the *tau* cross, after the Greek letter of the alphabet that corresponded to the Latin T, because once the *patibulum* was in place, that was what the cross looked like.

The cross beam was generally about four fingers thick, a little more than a hand-span wide, and about four cubits long—roughly six Roman feet. Stout enough to take the spikes driven through it and to hold the weight of a man, it generally weighed upwards of about a hundred pounds. The Roman practice was to place the cross beam over the condemned man's shoulders, with his arms extended along its length; the beam would be lashed into place with ropes around both elbows.

At the sound of a solid thud behind him, Marcus turned in the saddle. It took a moment for his eyes to locate the source of the sound, but when he did he grunted softly to himself. The street through this section of the city rose up a set of six or seven stairs. Jesus had not made it. Halfway up, he had slipped and gone down. The heavy plank had slammed into the pavement with the thud Marcus had heard.

He reined around, but before he could get moving, the nearest legionnaire waded in on Jesus with a short whip. "Get up, fool!" he screamed, lashing at Jesus' back. "On your feet."

Jesus uttered a soft moan as new stripes were laid on his already mangled flesh.

Marcus spurred his horse, but Sextus was quicker. The centurion leaped in, yanking the soldier back and sending him spinning away. As

Marcus reached them, Sextus had an arm under Jesus and was trying to help him to his feet. With a superhuman effort, Jesus made it almost to his knees, shouldering the weight of the cross, wincing sharply with the pain. Then his knees buckled, and he went down again. He lay there, panting heavily, his limbs trembling with shock and the loss of blood.

Sextus looked up. "He's too weak," he said to Marcus. "He can't carry this any farther."

Head pounding, wishing he either had not drunk as much wine as he had or that he had drunk much more, Marcus nodded. He looked around at the crowds pressing in around them. There were numerous women, peering through the arms and spears of the legionnaires who were holding them back. Their shrill wailing was grating terribly on Marcus's already jangled nerves. Then he saw a large, dark-skinned man wearing a brightly colored turban around his head. The man was half a head taller than anyone else in the crowd, and powerfully built.

"You!" Marcus jabbed his finger at the man.

The man looked up, his eyes flying wide open. He fell back a step. "Me?"

"Yes. Come forward. You're going to carry this man's cross for him."

Two legionnaires darted over and grabbed the man and dragged him forward. He was close to panic, Marcus saw. As they passed beside his horse, he leaned down. "Settle down, man!" he commanded. "We're not going to crucify you. Just carry that man's cross."

With the weight removed, Jesus slowly got to his feet. As he stood there, his whole body visibly shook. His head was down. Sweat darkened his hair, and the dried blood from the thorn crown was starting to streak where it mingled with his perspiration.

The sight only seemed to send the watching women deeper into their grief. Their cries lifted sharply, reverberating off the walls of the narrow street. Marcus wanted to clap his hands over his ears and shut it off.

V

Simeon, David, and Ephraim had pushed their way forward until they reached the last of the three prisoners. But that still left them ten or fifteen paces behind Jesus, who had been placed in the lead. Leah, Miriam, Deborah, and Rachel were right behind them. Benjamin and Esther had chosen the other side and were no longer visible.

The forward movement suddenly stopped. Ephraim jumped up and down in place, trying to see over the crowd. "Someone's gone down," he said. "I think it's Jesus."

"Let's go," David said, taking Deborah's hand. "We've got to get closer."

Ignoring the angry looks and muttered curses, the seven of them forced their way forward. Suddenly, Miriam felt a hand on her arm, gripping it tightly. "It's Marcus, Miriam." Simeon was at her elbow, whispering urgently in her ear.

"I don't care," she cried. "Jesus needs us."

Simeon felt a wash of shame. At the sight of his old enemy, he had, for a moment, been distracted from his greater purpose. "Yes," he said, and pushed forward with greater vigor.

To their surprise, when they were finally close enough to see Jesus clearly, he was upright and no longer carried the wooden beam. Another man was down on one knee, bent over as two soldiers tied the cross beam to his arms.

"Jesus!" It was Leah. She was sobbing hysterically. "Oh, Jesus."

He turned at the cry, and then his eyes found the familiar faces. A look of recognition flashed in his eyes, and he nodded.

"We're here, Master," Miriam called out. "We're here."

All around them weeping tore the air. A woman next to the wall of soldiers dropped to her knees and wrung her hands. She began the death wail, the funeral dirge used by professional mourners to lament the passing of a loved one.

To everyone's astonishment, Jesus lifted his head and cried out. "Daughters of Jerusalem!"

It came as such a surprise that the surrounding crowd instantly went silent. Sextus Rubrius swung around, not sure who had spoken. Marcus, turning back to his place at the head, also jerked around.

"O daughters of Jerusalem," Jesus said in a trembling voice, "weep not for me, but weep for yourselves and for your children. For, behold, the days are coming, in the which they shall say, 'Blessed are the barren and the wombs that never bare, and the paps which never gave suck.'"

Marcus was staring at the man. At a time like this, he was warning them of potential danger?

"At that time, then shall they begin to say to the mountains, 'Fall on us.' And to the hills, 'Cover us.'"

He looked around, his eyes moving from woman to woman. They lingered for a moment on Leah, then moved to Deborah, Rachel, and Miriam. Then his head slowly lowered again. "For if they do these things in a green tree, what shall be done in the dry?"

Then, without waiting for a signal from his captors, Jesus started moving again, his step heavy, his shoulders sagging under the sorrow that was upon him. He gave one last look at the four women who had been with him so often in Capernaum, then turned his head back to the front and moved on.

Chapter Notes

Certain traditions have become so fixed in Christianity that they have taken on the stature of scripture. An example of this is the idea that *three* wise men came to Bethlehem to visit the Babe; in actuality, Matthew does not specify a number. So it is with the Crucifixion. The Romans had several different kinds of crosses that they used in crucifixion. They did use what they called the *crux capitata,* commonly called the Latin cross, which had the vertical post rising above the cross beam. This is the shape so familiar to all Christians. But such an arrangement required a more complicated construction in order to secure the cross beam to the upright.

The far more common form used, especially in the time of Christ in Palestine, was the *crux commissa,* or the *tau* cross. In this case, the uprights were put permanently into the ground so that the cross beam had only to be placed on top and fastened into position. The upright then carried the weight of the cross beam and the prisoner (Edwards, pp. 1455–57).

For that same reason, the common depiction of Christ carrying the full cross on his way to Calvary is likely not how it happened. It is much more probable that he carried only the cross beam, which, even then, was too much for him in his condition of physical shock and exhaustion. Likewise in paintings, Simon of Cyrene, the man who was impressed into duty to help Jesus carry the cross, is often shown as a black man. That is possible. Cyrene was in what we today would call North Africa. There were likely many from black Africa living in Cyrene at that time. But even at that time, North Africa was made up of Arabic peoples, and this is why the author chose to depict him as such in this chapter.

Finally, the depiction of the crosses being on a hilltop, while aesthetically and dramatically impressive, is probably not the case either. There are two traditional sites of Golgotha, or Calvary, in Jerusalem today. One is inside the walls of the Old City, the other outside the northern walls near the Damascus Gate. Both are small knolls or hills. However, it is more likely that the crosses were at the base of the hill, near a well-traveled roadway, as is depicted in this novel. That would be the Roman way. It also would better explain Matthew's comment that "they that *passed by* reviled [i.e., mocked] him" (Matthew 27:39; emphasis added).

CHAPTER 35

IT IS FINISHED.

—*John 19:30*

I

GOLGOTHA

Sextus Rubrius had been a legionnaire for nearly thirty years. He had participated in some fourteen major battles and countless lesser skirmishes. He had administered the lash to lax or rebellious legionnaires more than a score of times and had been lashed twice himself. He had seen more gruesome sights than any man should see in three lifetimes. He had learned how to steel himself against it, but he had never learned how to revel in it as some did. Once, in Thracia, when a particularly stubborn town had finally been overrun, his commander had ordered every surviving male—more than two hundred of them—crucified. Thankfully by then, like Marcus Didius, Sextus had learned the value of getting drunk before the executions ever began. When they were done, he and his men were given a week's leave with unlimited access to the spoils of the vineyard. It was then that he learned that not even a week spent in a drunken stupor was enough to blot some things out.

He knew with exact precision how to carry out the execution to achieve the maximum effectiveness, and his mind ran over those procedures by habit of long training. First, a mild narcotic made of a mixture of wine and myrrh was given to the victim. Though in a way this was an act of mercy, that was not what prompted the practice. The physical pain was so horrible, so intense, that the writhing and twisting and jerking of the body made it difficult for the soldiers to manage the execution. The narcotic dulled the victim's pain enough that they could maintain at least some control.

The condemned was laid flat on the ground with his arms outstretched on the cross beam. Spikes created especially for this purpose by garrison blacksmiths were used to secure the outstretched arms. A full hand-span long, the spikes were square with a heavy rounded head, but they tapered sharply from the head to their pointed ends. Nails in the palms alone would tear free, so a second set of spikes were always driven through the wrists, just above the fleshy heel of the hand. Placing the spikes required the greatest care. They had to go between the two bones of the lower arm, thus providing the stability needed to hold up the weight of the body. Care had to be taken not to pierce the major artery between the arm and hand. If so, the victim would bleed to death quickly, and that wasn't acceptable. It was far too merciful.

Once the man was fastened securely to the cross beam, it was lifted up and placed on the upright. If the uprights were short, about the height of a man, this could be done by a couple of soldiers. With taller uprights, as were used at Golgotha, the soldiers used block and tackles to raise the condemned man into place. Then a man with a ladder would climb up and, with other spikes, fix the cross beam firmly to the upright.

That done, the feet were nailed to the cross as well. Generally this required only one spike. It was driven through both heel bones, again to prevent the softer flesh from tearing through. Midway on the upright, a small, triangular block of wood was nailed to provide a crude seat for the condemned. This, like the drink of wine and myrrh, helped carry out the goal of the crucifixion, which was prolonged, sustained agony. By sitting on the seat for short periods of time, the man could relieve the constriction in his chest, which was caused by the intense pain, and thus avoid suffocation.

Fortunately for Sextus Rubrius, on this day he had a commanding officer who had no more stomach for crucifixion than Rubrius did. Once they had arrived, Marcus had barked out some orders, retrieved another flagon of wine from his saddlebags, and gone up the little knoll above them to watch it all from a distance.

Sextus gave his orders, then turned away. By now he had seen several faces he recognized in the crowd: David ben Joseph and his wife, Deborah; Simeon and his new wife; Peter the Fisherman; Matthew the Publican; and Luke the Physician, who more than once had treated Sextus or his household servants.

He couldn't meet their eyes. He was sure they recognized him, just as he had them, but he kept his gaze fixed on the ground or directly on the soldiers carrying out his orders. With a deep sadness, he realized that never again would he be free to return to Capernaum, where he had spent some of his best years as a Roman soldier.

A disturbance erupted behind him, and Sextus turned. The first prisoner was already up on his cross, moaning and writhing in pain. The second Zealot was on the ground. He fought violently as the soldiers pinned his arms. He cursed and spit and shouted every obscenity he could bring to his tongue. He kicked out at one of those who held his feet and sent him sprawling. Three more soldiers leaped in to hold him fast. When the mallet struck the first spike, the curses turned into a shriek that rent the air. These were the sounds of Sextus's nightmares, placed there by crucifixions in the past. They never went away. Perhaps they never would. The man's body twisted and turned as the waves of pain shot through him. Sextus watched only long enough to make sure his men had the situation under control, then turned away.

A few feet from the second Zealot, Jesus stood quietly, waiting his turn. Sextus moved a little so that one of his men blocked him from Jesus' sight; then Sextus studied him with dark, moody eyes. What was going on in Jesus' mind? What was he thinking, now that he was just minutes from going to the cross? The crowds had mostly broken up and gone back into the city, not having the stomach for what they knew was coming. About a dozen of the Sanhedrin remained, however, including the four leaders. They stood in a tight cluster. There was no horror in them. Their faces were hard as flint. Their voices were low and angry. They would see this out, make sure that nothing went wrong at the last minute.

The rest who were present were mostly loyal followers of Jesus. The women were huddled together, shawls pulled up and over their heads. They were not talking, and they had become too numbed and exhausted for tears. The men were a short distance away, looking as if they were the ones who had been sentenced to die.

Sextus grimaced at the sudden irony of it all. Loyal disciples, bitter enemies, hardened and apathetic soldiers—a strange fellowship had gathered to watch this man die. Yet if Jesus was aware of any of them, he didn't show it. He still wore the scarlet robe and the crown of thorns. His hands were no longer bound—they had been freed when the cross beam had been tied onto his shoulders back at the Praetorium—but they hung limply at his side. The trembling in his body, caused by loss of blood and the terrible pain of the scourging, had steadied. His face was drawn and haggard, but his eyes were calm. His gaze was fixed on some far distant point.

In spite of himself, Sextus turned and looked where Jesus was looking. There was nothing to see, of course. The green hills of Jerusalem were in the foreground. Beyond that, the sky was gray, covered by a high, thick overcast. The air, though not particularly warm, was already heavy. It was muggy, and by the time the afternoon came it would likely feel quite oppressive.

"All right, your royal highness," barked a voice. "It's your turn."

Sextus turned back. Two soldiers were standing before Jesus, removing the robe from his shoulders. For a moment, the old centurion was tempted to bolt up the hill, find Marcus, and blurt out whatever excuse it would take to allow him to stay there with him. Then the sense of duty that had been Sextus's lodestar for the last thirty years overrode the desire. Only this time it wasn't duty to the empire that moved him; it was his sense of duty to the man who was about to be nailed to the cross. This man had once treated him as an equal, had healed his servant from a distance, even though Sextus was a hated Roman. There was nothing Sextus could do to stop what was happening, but he could see to it that Jesus had at least one person who viewed him with respect and dignity as he went to the cross.

He turned and walked swiftly, his sandals crunching on the gravel. The men looked up in surprise. They were removing Jesus' tunic, stripping him down to the inner garment that covered his loins, but leaving him otherwise naked. Jesus winced and grunted softly as the fabric was pulled away, tearing at the dried blood and flesh of his lacerated back.

One of the soldiers dropped to his knee and swept out one arm. "Right this way, your majesty," he cawed.

"That's enough!" Sextus snapped.

The three men looked at him quickly, surprised by his anger.

"Get on with it. The time for making sport is over." Without waiting to see their reaction, he walked to the jar that held the wine and myrrh and filled the cup. By the time he turned back, they had Jesus on his back and were stretching his arms out across the long beam. Sextus knelt beside Jesus. He wanted to avert his face, to avoid looking into the eyes that had once looked into his with respect and acceptance, but he couldn't. He lifted Jesus' head and brought the cup forward. Seeing what it was, Jesus raised up hungrily. But the moment he tasted it, he jerked away and refused to drink any more of it.

Sextus let go of his head and stood up. He wanted to speak, to say something. Anything. But nothing came out. He shook his head. What could you say to a man whom you were about to crucify?

Then he looked down, starting a little. Jesus was looking directly up at him. His eyes were bright and alert and, in that instant, Sextus realized why Jesus had turned away from the cup. He would meet this day with full faculties. And then he saw something else in the man's eyes. He nearly fell back a step, realizing that it was exactly what he had once seen there before—respect, acceptance. And understanding.

"We're ready, sir," a voice beside him said. Sextus turned. The soldier in charge of placing the nails stood directly behind the cross beam. In his hand, he held a large wooden mallet with steel bands around the head, and a sackful of spikes. The two soldiers who had stripped Jesus of his clothes still knelt, holding his hands and arms.

"Take care," Sextus said gruffly. "No mistakes." He owed Jesus that much. He stepped back, forcing himself to not turn away, forcing down the sickness in the pit of his stomach.

Jesus gasped as the first blow of the mallet sounded dully. His body jerked violently. His eyes glazed over momentarily, and Sextus thought he might faint. But he did not. As the nail was driven deep into the wood, the chest rose and fell in great heaves. A second nail went through the palm, and Jesus groaned in agony. Then his eyes came open again. He was staring straight up into the heavens. And, to the astonishment of those who stood or knelt around him, the prisoner spoke.

"Father!" It was a strangled cry torn from parched lips. "Father, forgive them, for they know not what they do."

II

Sextus felt a rough hand on his shoulder and turned around. "You can't put that up there."

Sextus frowned. It was Azariah, the pompous old Pharisee who was one of the leaders of the Great Council. Right behind him were Mordechai ben Uzziel and the two high priests. Their mouths were twisting in indignation.

With a grim smile, Sextus turned back and handed the *titulus* to the nearest soldier. "Make sure it's secure," he commanded.

The soldier, grinning at the discomfiture of the old Jews, took the sign and scrambled up the small ladder that had been placed against the back of the cross. He reached around, placing the sign over the head of Jesus, and quickly tapped two nails through it to hold it in place on the cross beam.

"You can't say that," Azariah protested shrilly. "Don't say that he was King of the Jews."

Sextus glanced quickly at the title board, though he knew very well what it said. The same simple sentence was written in Hebrew, Greek, and Latin. "Jesus of Nazareth, King of the Jews." Now Sextus understood why Pilate had been so specific about it, which had surprised him at the time. The Romans always placed a *titulus* on the cross, a board that carried the criminal's name and crime for which he was being punished. When Marcus had asked the procurator what title he wanted over Jesus' head, Pilate gave him a crafty smile. The Jews had insisted that Jesus was making himself a king, and that was treason. So Pilate had rubbed their noses in it. A king he would be.

"Say not, 'The king of the Jews,'" Caiaphas suggested, "but only that he *claimed* to be the king of the Jews."

"It was the governor who wrote that," Sextus said coldly. "If you wish the title changed, then take it up with him."

"We shall!" Mordechai snapped right back at him. He didn't like the insolence of this Roman centurion. "And we shall report your unwillingness to cooperate. Come," he said to the others. "There are other matters we must discuss with the governor as well."

He started away, but Azariah didn't move. He was staring up into the face of Jesus, now about two or three feet above him. His lips twisted into a mocking sneer. "Jesus!" he called out sharply.

The head lifted, the eyes slowly coming into focus.

Azariah moved a little closer. "You said you could destroy the temple and rebuild it in three days," he taunted. "Well, *if* you are the Son of God, as you claimed to be, let us see you come down from the cross."

Caleb, who was nearby, hooted in delight at Azariah's joke. "Yes, Jesus," he called. "You claim to be the Messiah. Surely you can save yourself."

Mordechai stopped to watch, not pleased. It was a juvenile thing to do. They had gotten their wish. Their enemy was hanging from the cross. It was done. Yet he was not surprised when Caiaphas turned back and joined Azariah and Caleb. "He saved others," Caiaphas cackled wildly, "yet he cannot save himself."

Others from the council moved in. It was obvious the Romans weren't going to interfere. Even the centurion had moved back in disgust, but he made no effort to stop them.

"He is the king of Israel," one of the Sadducees cried, pointing to the title sign. "Let him come down from the cross, and then we will believe."

"Hear, hear!" cried another. "Come down, Jesus, and we will worship you."

"He trusted in God," Caleb said gleefully, "let us see if God will now deliver him."

"All right," Mordechai said, his temper growing short. "We have things to do. Let's be on with them."

Still laughing, the group moved away. As they reached the road, Azariah looked back again. He raised a fist and shook it in the direction of the crosses. "Save yourself, Jesus," he called. "Then I will believe."

III

Peter put his hands over his ears, trying to shut out the jeering and the mockery. His hands twisted in his hair as he stared at the ground. Andrew sat beside him, staring blankly at nothing. The other apostles stood or sat in small groups. Some could not take their eyes away from the horrible scene before them. Some could not bear to look and had turned their backs to the crosses. Mary Magdalene and Martha had their arms around each other, swaying slowly back and forth as if that might assuage the pain somewhat. Lazarus and his sister Mary stood together, staring across the road at the city walls. Luke sat alone. Matthew and Thomas and Philip were together, but no one spoke. Anna, Peter's wife, sat on the ground. Jesus' mother had her head buried in her lap, and Anna stroked her hair gently again and again. John knelt beside them, steadying Mary's arm as she fought her grief.

In Simeon's family, it was no different. His mother and Rachel clung to each other. Leah was prostrate on the ground, her face buried in her arms. From time to time, silent shudders would sweep through her body; then she would lie still again. Simeon knelt by Miriam, who sagged heavily against him. She had a double burden on this day. She was staring at her father, who stood near the cross with the others.

Simeon put a hand on her cheek. "He's not part of the mockery, Miriam," he whispered. "You can see he doesn't approve."

She had seen that, but it was little comfort. Jesus was dying right before her eyes. Perhaps her father wasn't willing to taunt him now, but he was glad. That showed in every movement, every expression of his face. What did a little reticence about mockery count for at this point?

Then finally, thankfully, the jeering, taunting group moved away, turning back toward the city gate. To Simeon's surprise, however, another voice took up the cry. His head lifted, searching for the source of it. To his shock, it was the Zealot who hung to the left of Jesus. "Art thou the Christ?" His voice was hoarse and strained. "If you are, save yourself and us."

Jesus turned and looked at him, but then the third man spoke. He was not looking at Jesus, but at his companion. "Leave him alone," he cried. "Do you not fear God, seeing that we are under the same condemnation as this man? But we indeed suffer justly, for we receive the due reward for what we have done." He turned to look at Jesus. "But this man has done nothing amiss."

There was a long silence. Every eye had turned to the three men. Every person there listened intently to the interchange.

"Jesus?" The second man's voice grew softer, almost pleading. "When you come into your kingdom, will you remember me?"

The head of the Master lifted painfully. "Verily I say unto you, on this day, you shall be with me in paradise."

IV

John came up with a start. The flash of light was followed almost instantly by a crack of thunder, which shook the ground and bounced off the stone walls of Jerusalem. He tipped his head back, astonished at what he was seeing.

Just an hour before, the sky had been overcast, with little threat of rain. Now it was as black as a beetle's belly. The clouds were low and visibly rolling toward them from the west. Lightning flickered in the roiling mass, and a rumble sounded in the distance.

Mary's head came up too, and she looked around anxiously. John put his arm around the Master's mother. "It's all right. A storm is brewing, that's all."

She scanned the sky even as the first puff of wind stirred her hair; then she put her head back down again in Anna's lap.

"John!"

The youngest of the apostles leaped to his feet, staring upward. He walked swiftly to the foot of the cross. "Yes, Master?"

The tortured eyes lifted. John turned. Mary was sitting up again, her hand to her mouth. When she saw that Jesus was looking directly at her, she rose and walked quickly to stand beside John. "What is it, my son?" she asked, tears spilling over again as she looked up into his face.

The love she saw there, behind the pain and the agony, made her draw in her breath involuntarily. The tears poured out, and her shoulders began to shake.

"Woman," he said, using the title that connoted the greatest respect and honor a child could extend to a parent. "Behold thy son."

Her eyes widened; then she slowly turned to John. But John still had his eyes fixed on the man above him.

More quietly now, as if that first effort had nearly spent him, he spoke again. "John, behold thy mother."

John's head dropped. His eyes were burning. Finally, he lifted his head again. "I understand, Master," he whispered. And with that, he put his arm around Mary and helped her back to rejoin the others.

V

JERUSALEM, UPPER CITY, THE PRAETORIUM

"This is an outrage," Azariah spluttered. "An insult."

"It was you who said he was a king." Pilate turned and gave

Mordechai ben Uzziel a long, hard look. "And it was *you* who suggested that if I didn't do something about this man who would be king,
you would complain to Caesar."

Mordechai said nothing. If he had been close enough, he would
have grabbed Azariah by the throat and tried to choke off the idiocy
coming from the man's mouth. They were out in the courtyard. The
wind was howling around them, and blowing dust stung their eyes.
Pilate had come to them, irritation and distaste written all over his
face. Mordechai had tried to convince Azariah to go inside and not
make Pilate go out into the storm, but the stubborn old fool wouldn't
budge on that either. If they entered the house of a Gentile during the
Passover festival, an elaborate ritual of purification would be required
before they could be clean. No wonder Pilate was not cooperative.

"Then at least say he *claimed* to be a king." Azariah was not one to
let things go easily.

"What I have written, I have written," Pilate said shortly, ending
the debate.

Mordechai glanced at Annas, signaling for him to join in.

"We have another matter," Annas came in smoothly.

"Oh?"

"Yes, Excellency. As you know, today is Friday. That means the
Sabbath begins at sundown."

"After nine years in Judea," Pilate observed curtly, "I think I have
learned a thing or two about the Hebrew calendar."

Annas flushed a little but went on. "By our law, it is unlawful to
leave a dead man unburied on the Sabbath."

The governor offered them a thin smile. "Then we're all right.
Jesus won't be dead until day after tomorrow."

Mordechai hid his irritation. Pilate was being intractable and
enjoying it. "Even if they have not died, it would be a violation of our
law to leave them suffering on a holy day."

Pilate laughed right out loud. "Oh, that's right. Now that you've put this man to death, you can't pollute yourselves by having him hang on the cross on a holy day." He shook his head in open contempt. But before they could respond, he snapped his fingers. "Scribe!"

A man darted in with a sheet of papyrus, quill pen, and small jar of ink. "Take an order for Tribune Didius."

The man sat down at the small table, dipped the pen, then poised it over the paper.

"Tribune Marcus Didius. By order of His Excellency the Governor, the prisoners are not to be left on their crosses after sundown. See to it that they are dead before that time."

He snapped his fingers again, and the man picked up his things and beat a hasty retreat.

"You have your order. Now go."

"Excellency?"

But before Azariah could do any more damage, Mordechai grabbed his arm and dragged him away. "Thank you, Excellency," he called back.

VI

It was not even ten minutes later before Pilate's chief servant was again back at the door. "Sire?"

"Yes, yes," he snapped irritably. "What is it now?"

"There's a member of the Great Council asking to see you, Excellency."

"Again?" He slammed down his fist against the table. "I'm tired of those fools."

"This is one that has not been here before," the man said nervously. When the governor started into one of his tempers, it was best to walk carefully.

That stopped Pilate. "Oh?"

"He says his name is Joseph of Arimathea, sire."

VII

GOLGOTHA

Centurion Sextus Rubrius sat on the ground a few feet away from the center cross. His knees were up, his arms folded on them, and his head lay on his arms. The gravel beneath him stung through his tunic, making him very uncomfortable. He was barely aware of it. Time seemed suspended. It felt as if he had been stuck in this dreary place of death for days, and not just hours. The thought of staying there until the prisoners died was almost more than he could bear.

He heard a soft moan, only barely discernible over the sound of the wind. Sextus straightened, looking up. Jesus had gone rigid. His legs twisted to one side to give him leverage, and his body arched upward. His chest rose and fell in great heaves. The pain must be excruciating.

Sextus leaped to his feet and took a step closer. What was he doing? Was he even conscious? Then he saw Jesus' eyes. They were huge and staring upward into the angry clouds. Sextus jumped back as a great cry was torn from the Galilean's lips. "*Eloi! Eloi! Lama sabachthani!*"

The nearest of the guards came running over. "What did he say?"

Sextus could not take his eyes away from Jesus' face. It was transfixed, looking up into the heavens.

The guard leaned forward. "What did he say?"

594

"'My God! My God! Why hast thou forsaken me?'"

"Ha!" another man said with great relief. "If his God has abandoned him, then he can't be some great magician like everyone says."

Sextus didn't deem that worthy of a reply. He turned as some of the onlookers came up. "He called for Elias," one of the men exclaimed. "He's delirious. He needs something to drink," said another.

"Leave him alone," cried a third. "Let's see if Elias will come and save him."

Sextus was still looking at Jesus. Suddenly Jesus' head slumped to his chest, and his body sagged down again. "I thirst," he said in a muffled voice.

"Get me a sponge," Sextus commanded. Even as he barked out the command, he darted to where the soldiers had a jar of sour wine. He looked around, then saw a stalk of hyssop lying beside the other things. He snatched it up as the soldier brought a sponge and handed it to him. Thrusting the sponge onto the end of the hyssop stalk, Sextus plunged it into the jar of wine, bracing himself against the wind. Carefully, he extended the sponge until it touched Jesus' lips, now cracked and bleeding. The eyes opened in surprise, then closed again gratefully as he opened his mouth and sucked hungrily on the liquid-soaked sponge.

After a moment, he turned his head away. Sextus waited, the sponge just inches away from Jesus' mouth, but he didn't open his eyes again.

Finally, after a full minute, Sextus turned back around. To his surprise, David ben Joseph was there waiting for him. "Thank you, Sextus."

Sextus nodded, not trusting himself to speak. Then, as the two of them stood awkwardly together, Jesus lifted his head, his eyes again looking toward the sky. "Father." It came out from a depth of weariness unlike anything either of these men had heard in a lifetime. "Into thy hands, I commend my spirit."

The head slowly began to lower, the eyes closing again. A great shudder ran through his body. Then, in one final sigh, Jesus spoke his last three words in mortality: "It is finished."

The chin dropped onto the bare chest. The body went limp, pulling against the nails in the hands and wrists. The face gradually relaxed, the lines of pain smoothing out.

And then David could see no more through the sudden blur of tears that swept up like a flood from deep within his soul.

VIII

Sextus turned in surprise when he saw two of his soldiers spring to attention and slap their arms up in salute. When he saw the reason for their salute, he got an even greater surprise. Marcus was standing there, weaving back and forth as the wind, which was howling around them now, tore at his uniform.

"Sire?" Sextus exclaimed.

"I have received two orders from the governor." His tongue was thick, and he was clearly struggling to make himself coherent.

"What kind of orders?"

"First, Pilate has granted permission to a man named Joseph of Arimathea to take the body of Jesus and bury it."

Sextus was both surprised and relieved at that. "Very good, sire. And the second order?"

"Pilate wants the prisoners dead before sundown."

"Pardon, sire?"

"You heard me!" Marcus screamed at him. "Break their legs." He spun around and strode to where a legionnaire was holding his horse. "The matter here is done," he called back over his shoulder. "I'm going back to the Praetorium. See to it, Sextus."

Sextus was too flabbergasted to even respond. He watched silently as Marcus galloped away, then finally turned to his men. At the sight of their commander, they had gathered around to await their orders. Sextus took a deep breath, then looked at his senior noncommissioned officer. "You heard him. You know what to do."

The nails driven through the wrists of those crucified pierced the great medial nerves that ran up the arms. This caused such intense pain that the muscles of the upper torso would begin to violently constrict. This, in turn, squeezed the lungs until the victim began to suffocate. To ease that pressure, horrible as it was, the person being crucified could stand on the nail in his feet enough that he could rest himself on the small seat for a time. When the pain became unbearable, he would slump down, and the cycle would begin all over again.

Thus the life of the victim would be preserved through many hours, even days, of inconceivable pain.

But with their usual careful attention to the art of suffering, the Romans had also devised a way to hasten death when it was required. Near the place of execution, they kept a long piece of rough oak with a handle carved on one end to provide a grip. The man in charge of the execution walked swiftly to where the mallet and spikes lay on the ground. He found the oak club and hefted it expertly. Then, without waiting for a further signal, he walked to the first Zealot. Without so much as a glance upward, he swung the club, striking the man's legs squarely across the shins. There was a dull thud, then a terrible scream. The man's body dropped sharply now that he could no longer support himself. Death would come in minutes.

The second rebel was dispatched with equal swiftness. When the man approached the center cross, however, Sextus stepped forward. "He's already dead," he said.

The man shot him an incredulous look. Was he somehow trying to protect the man? These criminals had been on the cross only about three hours. Already dead? Not a chance.

Not asking permission, the soldier jerked the spear from the nearest legionnaire's hand, and with one swift movement thrust the point upward into Jesus' side. The point, sharpened to the fineness of a keen dagger, buried itself a full hand span into the prisoner's chest. There was no response. No cry of pain, no violent jerking of the body. Astonished, the man yanked the spear out again. A mixture of blood and water poured out as Jesus' followers stared in horror at what had just happened.

Sextus had started forward when he realized what his man was about to do, but he had not been swift enough. He stepped back, his face gray. "I told you he was dead." He swung around. "All right, get them down from there. Someone get the pinchers so we can pull those nails."

As they sprang into motion, Sextus turned to see what had happened to David ben Joseph. He had returned to his position with the others. Their faces looked like spectral spirits as they gaped at the Romans. In a day of one staggering emotional blow after another, here was yet another bitter and terrible act, and their faces showed it.

Well, it was done with. Never had he been so glad to see an assignment finished. He would—

A cry was ripped from his throat as Sextus was suddenly thrown off his feet and slammed to the ground. Pain shot through his arm and the side of his face as he hit the gravel hard. Dumbfounded, thinking he had been struck from behind, he started to get up. He shook his head, faintly aware that all around him people were screaming. But as he got to his knees, the earth beneath him bucked like a wild horse. He bounced once, then went down hard again. He rolled over, gasping with the pain. He saw that he had scraped a two-inch patch of flesh off his elbow. He touched his cheek with his fingers, and they came away red.

Coughing violently, Sextus pawed at his nostrils, trying to clear them to breathe. Dust was everywhere—thick, choking, blinding dust.

He covered his mouth, fighting for breath. He got to his knees, looking around wildly, trying to maintain his balance on the undulating earth. In quick succession, his mind registered the images that were all around him. The ladder he had been on just minutes before toppled sideways and crashed to the ground. It didn't lay still, however. It continued to bounce up and down as though it were possessed by something alive. Two of his legionnaires were clinging desperately to each other as they swayed crazily back and forth, as though they were on the deck of a ship in a violent storm. One of them screamed as he was torn loose from his companion and hurled to the ground. Somewhere behind Sextus a tremendous crack sounded, as though some gigantic wine jar had split in two. He turned and saw a fissure the width of his hand snaking away from him. At the same time, a thunderous roar sounded all around him, like a thousand chariots bearing down. The earth bucked and heaved and trembled like a tortured monster trying to break free.

Later, he would try to calculate exactly how long it lasted and conclude it probably was no more than a minute. But while it lasted it seemed like an eternity.

Finally, the earth subsided. The groaning softened; the trembling steadied. With a start, Sextus felt something wet on his face, then realized the heavens had unleashed a slashing, driving rain. It was almost as dark as night, so thick were the clouds overhead. In seconds, the air was cleared of dust, and the ground turned into a quagmire. Sextus got unsteadily to his feet. Lightning was flashing almost continuously. The thunderclaps were so violent he could feel his eardrums compress with the concussion.

For a long moment, Sextus stood there, heart pounding, gasping for breath, feet spread wide apart, hair plastered to his head, water streaming off his face into his suit of armor. Slowly, so filled with awe that he felt he could barely breathe, he turned and looked up into the face of Jesus of Nazareth. The eyes were closed in repose; the face had found peace at last.

And then the grizzled veteran of nearly thirty years of army service slowly sank to his knees. He bowed his head. "Truly," he whispered, "truly this man was the Son of God."

CHAPTER NOTES

In 1968 archaeologists found the bones of a crucified man at Giv'at ha-Mivtar, a Jewish settlement just north of Jerusalem. These belonged to a man about twenty-six years old and were dated to the time of Christ. The shin bones had been broken, and a spike was actually still affixed to both heel bones. The lower end of one of the bones in the arm showed the marks of a nail at what would have been the wrist. This confirmed in a dramatic way what was known from other sources, namely, that the description of the crucifixion as given by the Gospel writers is accurate. It is later writers and artists who have assumed that the nails were put in the palms only and not through the wrists (see Connolly, p. 51; Edwards, pp. 1458–62).

The author debated about how much detail to give on the crucifixion. It was gruesome and horrible, a fiendish way to die. Yet the Gospel writers did not pass over it lightly to spare us the horror. In our secular, modern world, some skeptics have suggested that Jesus didn't really die on the cross, that he was drugged in order to endure the terrible pain. When the disciples took him down, these detractors say, Jesus was still alive. The disciples nursed him back to health and then presented him to the world as the "resurrected Christ."

Partly to show how utterly fantastic such a hypothesis is, and also to help the reader better appreciate the terrible price paid by the Savior for all mankind, the author concluded that there was value in describing what crucifixion was actually like.

The King James Version of the Bible says that Jesus was given vinegar to drink, which seems odd to modern readers. It was likely a sour wine.

Also, it seems odd that if the two thieves crucified with Jesus were Zealots, as suggested in the novel, that the one would say that they were being executed justly. However, the author sees two possibilities: (1) He was simply saying that they were being crucified for actual acts they had committed, whereas Jesus was not; (2) That facing death, he wondered if their violent life had been justified after all. The Romans viewed the Zealots as *lestai*—bandits or criminals—and indeed, the Zealots felt that they should use any means at their disposal, including violence, theft, or murder, to bring to pass God's will.

Obviously, Sextus Rubrius is a fictional character in the novel, and there is nothing in the scriptures to suggest that the centurion who asked Jesus to heal his servant in Capernaum was the same as the centurion at the cross. But it is recorded by Matthew, Mark, and Luke that the centurion at the cross, after experiencing all that had happened, declared Jesus to be the Son of God.

John is the only one who records Jesus' admonition from the cross for him (John always refers to himself in the third person in his Gospel) to take Mary and care for her. John then adds, "And from that hour that disciple took her unto his own home" (John 19:27). One very ancient tradition states that Mary died in Ephesus some thirty years later while still living with John (Fallows, 2:1124).

John is also the only Gospel writer who gives an account of the spear thrust into Jesus' side and the resulting blood and water that came from the wound (John 19:34). Evidently this was not just a minor detail in his mind, for after describing what happened, John states: "And he that saw it bare record, and his record is true: and he knoweth that he saith true, *that ye might believe*" (John 19:35; emphasis added). What was it about the blood and water that caused John to bear such a solemn witness of it?

One medical expert noted the following: "The Greek word (*pleura*) used by John clearly denoted laterality and often implied the ribs. . . . The water probably represented serous pleural and pericardial fluid . . . [signifying] acute heart failure. . . . Jesus' death after only three to six hours on the cross surprised even Pontius Pilate. The fact that Jesus cried out in a loud voice and then bowed his head and died suggests the possibility of a catastrophic terminal event. One popular explanation has been that Jesus died of cardiac rupture" (Edwards, pp. 1462–63).

The Psalmist, under the power of inspiration, wrote: "Reproach *hath broken my heart*; and I am full of heaviness: and I looked for some to take pity, but there was none; and for comforters, but I found none" (Psalm 69:20; italics added). Thus, though the *form* of death, crucifixion, fulfilled one set of prophecies about the Redeemer, how he actually died fulfilled another. It appears as though Jesus literally died of a broken heart.

CHAPTER 36

I

BETHLEHEM

5 APRIL, A.D. 33

In the house of Benjamin the Shepherd, on the hillside overlooking the fields of Bethlehem, the Sabbath day passed with infinite slowness. The family had barely made it back to Bethlehem before sundown the night before. With unspoken consent, they had bypassed the traditional Sabbath day ritual, where the holy day was welcomed like a visiting queen. They had no desire for food. Each couple retired immediately to their assigned sleeping spaces and tried to work through the grief that hung like a great lead weight on their hearts. By full dark, the house was quiet except for the occasional sound of weeping coming from within the house.

It was late into the night when the family members finally fell into an exhausted, troubled sleep, and the sun was fully up when they finally gathered for a cold breakfast. Since it was the Sabbath, no fires could be kindled. Little was said. Recounting the events of the day before would only bring back the horror with unbearable sharpness. No one was ready for that yet.

After breakfast, Simeon, David, and Ephraim helped Benjamin see to the needs of the sheep. It didn't take long. The flocks had been greatly diminished after providing the Paschal lambs for Passover. When they were done, the couples once again found places to be by themselves, trying to cope with the awfulness of the change that had descended upon them.

When, just after midday, a loud pounding sounded on the gate to the small courtyard, it immediately sent tremors of fear through the household. Had the Romans finally decided to act against the followers of Jesus? Had Mordechai convinced the Sanhedrin to arrest Simeon and Miriam for being Jesus' disciples?

Telling the women to stay out of sight inside the house, Benjamin, David, and their sons went to the gate, hands on their swords. Benjamin opened the peep hole, then with a cry of relief threw open the gate. There, to their astonishment, stood Aaron and Hava.

"*Shalom*," Aaron said solemnly. "Good Sabbath."

Simeon was staring in disbelief. "Uncle Aaron?"

"Very perceptive," Aaron said dryly.

"But . . ." Simeon's mind was racing. He had thought his uncle and aunt were in Jericho. Today was the Sabbath. A Sabbath day's journey was only two thousand paces, or about a mile. Jericho was sixteen or seventeen miles from Bethlehem. Even if Aaron had come only from Jerusalem, that was still six miles away. "What are you doing here?" Simeon asked incredulously.

Aaron guessed at what had triggered that question. "I thought you might be a little shocked. Actually, Hava and I have indeed come up from Jericho. We left about midnight."

Deborah had been watching from the window, and the rest of the family came pouring out. As the women greeted Hava, Simeon pressed the issue with his uncle.

"On the Sabbath?" Simeon exclaimed. "You came from Jericho on the Sabbath?"

Aaron grinned, but it was grim, with no humor in it. "I know, I know. That says a lot about the state I'm in, doesn't it." Then without waiting for Simeon's response, he turned to David. "I need to talk to Jesus as quickly as possible, David. Do you know where he is staying?"

Aaron fell back a step at the look that came over his brother-in-law's face. "What? What's wrong?"

"You haven't heard?" Benjamin whispered.

"Heard what?"

David's head came up slowly. "Jesus is dead, Aaron."

II

While David quietly recounted the terrible events of the previous two days, Aaron sat motionless, staring at the ceiling, his mouth working silently but his eyes showing no expression. Hava sat beside Deborah, weeping silently as David's words battered at her consciousness. She was not alone. To hear the terrible details again in David's low, dispassionate voice had set all of the women to tears again.

When David finished, Aaron was quiet for a long time. His fingers plucked at unseen threads on his robe. Finally he looked up. "I had to talk to him, David," he said. "I had to ask him why he so savagely condemned the Pharisees. I know we're not perfect, but our desire has always been to serve God. Why—"

Everyone in the family gaped at him. It was like he hadn't heard anything David had said. Surprisingly, it was Ephraim who reacted first. He leaped to his feet. "Uncle Aaron!"

Aaron turned slowly to look at his nephew.

"Jesus is dead! What does it matter now what he said about the Pharisees? He's dead, Aaron. Dead!"

Rachel reached out, took her husband's hand, and pulled him back down again, then put an arm around his shoulder as his body began to tremble.

Aaron slowly nodded. "I have so many questions, Ephraim. I just wanted to ask him—" Then, suddenly, his head came up. "How can he be dead?"

Simeon felt his own anger flare. What was the matter with this man? "Because they nailed him to a cross, Uncle Aaron. Then to make sure, they thrust a spear into his chest."

"Don't, Simeon!" Miriam cried.

He turned. Miriam and Livia were sitting together on a low wooden bench. Livia's face had drained of color.

Simeon was instantly contrite. Ironically, it was Livia, who hadn't even been with them in Jerusalem, who had taken the news of Jesus' death the hardest. She had collapsed in a near faint and had withdrawn into a silent shell ever since. "I'm sorry," Simeon murmured, moving over swiftly to comfort her as well.

Aaron looked at David, his eyes wide and disbelieving. "I know he's dead. But why? He was supposed to be the Messiah, David. The Deliverer. That's what you said. That's what I came to believe. He can't be dead."

David sighed, and the pain in him was like a knot twisted tight. "I know," he said. "We thought the same thing. Right up to the very last we thought he would save himself."

"But—" Aaron's eyes turned to Deborah. "How can he deliver Israel if he can't even deliver himself?"

"He said it was necessary for him to die so he could save us all," she whispered, not understanding any more than her brother.

Aaron's head dropped into his hands, and he began to shake it back and forth, as if trying to make a petulant, insistent child go away from him. Then he looked up at his wife, his eyes dark with anguish. "I should have listened to you, Hava. Why am I such a fool? We could have been here in time to talk to him."

Hava got to her feet and went to Aaron, but it was to the others that she spoke. "When we got your message inviting us to have Passover with you," she explained, "I wanted to come. Though my brother and his wife and Grandma Huldah were planning to have us celebrate the feast with them in Jericho, I felt like Aaron needed to be here. He's been so torn since hearing Jesus that last time. I thought that if he could see Jesus again he could resolve this bitterness he was feeling."

"But no," Aaron cried out, "not me. I was too stubborn to come back. Who was Jesus to condemn everything for which I have given my life? I would show him! So I went away to let him know of my deep disapproval."

Hava, her face gentle and full of love, knelt beside him, but he went on, the passion in him making his voice rise. "But I couldn't get the other things out of my mind—his teachings, the power and majesty of his bearing, Grandma Huldah, completely whole. Mud smeared over the eyes of a man born blind, and he comes back see-ing." He stopped, and his voice went soft with reverential awe. "Watching as a man wrapped in his burial clothes came out of that tomb."

"And that's how you know he was the Messiah! It's not just what he did—marvelous and miraculous as his deeds were—but it was who he was. How he made us feel when we listened to him. How he made us want to be better." David was quiet for a moment, then went on. "Maybe we don't understand what's happened yet, but that doesn't change what Jesus was: the Son of God. That's what you need to hold on to, Aaron. That's what you need to believe."

Aaron didn't even look at him. He just closed his eyes and again shook his head.

From the time he had come into his teen years, Simeon had found his uncle's narrowness, his intransigence, his sense of mental and spiritual superiority over the rest of the family more than he could bear. But he could see that now Aaron was struggling, grieving in his own way. "When Jesus died," Simeon said softly, "the heavens wept, Aaron. We have never seen such a terrible storm. And the earth shook so violently that we could not stand. It groaned as if it were a living thing." He paused. "The Son of God died, Aaron, and all of nature cried out in agony. The very heavens and earth wept at his passing."

Aaron's head came up, his eyes wide. "That was when he died? We felt the earthquake. We couldn't believe the storm."

To everyone's surprise, Livia spoke up. She removed Miriam's arm from around her shoulder. Her voice was husky and strained, but she was under control again. "Aaron?"

He turned to her.

"I understand what you are going through."

"You could not," he snapped back. "No one understands the turmoil inside me right now."

Her voice dropped to a hush. "I was here, Aaron. While the Roman scourge was flaying the skin from the Master's back, I was here, sitting beneath the shade of the pomegranate tree, drinking a cup of cold water from the well. And while he was being nailed to the cross and suffering pain beyond my comprehension, I went inside the house, lay down, and took a nap." Her eyes bored into him. "Don't tell me I don't understand your pain."

"Livia, you don't have to—" Miriam protested, but Livia ignored her.

"I told the others that it was because I was tired, that I didn't think I could face more violence. But do you want to really know why I stayed behind? Because I had a bitterness of my own. I don't care what Jesus said to you about the Pharisees. What I wanted to know was this: If Jesus was really all powerful, and full of love, as I had been taught to believe, then why didn't he save my Yehuda?" Tears started to trickle down her cheeks. "When we took my husband to the Mount of Olives and laid him in the grave, why didn't Jesus come and call him forth, as he did Lazarus?"

No one made a sound. Miriam stared at her friend in deep sympathy. Even Aaron's eyes softened as he watched her.

"I didn't fully realize it then, but I do now. I wasn't sure if I wanted to see Jesus anymore. I was afraid I might suddenly scream out at him, 'If you are the Messiah, why did you let the Romans kill Yehuda?'"

"And why did he let them kill *him?*" Aaron murmured. But he wasn't trying to disagree with her. She did understand. She was probably the only one, but she understood what was tearing him apart inside.

"Those are terrible, terrible words, Aaron. *If* he is . . . *If* he was . . . I see that now, but it is too late. Too late for me to go back and be there for Jesus. Too late for you to ask him your questions." She buried her face in her hands. Her shoulders began to shake. "I told him I believed in him, and then all I could do was ask why. *If* he truly was the Son of God, why? why? why?"

Miriam took her in her arms and tried to steady her, weeping as freely as Livia. Leah moved over beside them and took Livia's hand.

David sighed deeply. This had been a long day, a day filled with despair and darkness, with weeping and self-recrimination. Aaron and Livia weren't the only ones torturing themselves over the events of the past days. He and Simeon and Ephraim should have stayed with Peter and the Twelve instead of returning to Bethlehem. Perhaps they could have stopped the soldiers from arresting Jesus. Miriam was convinced that if she had gone to her father and begged for mercy, perhaps the outcome of the trial might have been different. Deborah was torturing herself for not doing more to help Jesus' mother in her devastation. Leah had almost gone up to Jesus the day before Passover to tell him how much she loved and admired him for what he had done for her. But she hadn't, and now she never could.

Livia had said it for them all. *What if* were terrible words, and they were doing nothing but causing pain for the family. It was time to stop.

It was time to focus less on the pain and the grief and try to remember the powerful and positive things Jesus had brought to them. As the scriptures said, it was time to rely on the arm of the Lord. David stirred as the words flashed in his mind. Unconsciously he spoke them aloud, "To whom is the arm of the Lord revealed?"

Deborah looked at him. "What did you say?"

David started. He looked around at his family. He loved them all so much, and he hurt not only for himself but for them as well. He wanted to find a way to help them begin to heal. A warm feeling started in his heart and spread through his whole body. "As we've been talking, I've remembered something I'd like to share with you all. Maybe it will help."

He looked at Aaron. "It's from the prophet Isaiah. And I think it means more to me now than ever before."

David stood and moved to the center of the room. His voice naturally fell into the rhythm of words long repeated but only now fully understood.

"Who hath believed our report? and to whom is the arm of the Lord revealed?" he began. "For he shall grow up before him as a tender plant, and as a root out of a dry ground: he hath no form nor comeliness; and when we shall see him, there is no beauty that we should desire him. He is despised and rejected of men; a man of sorrows, and acquainted with grief: and we hid as it were our faces from him; he was despised, and we esteemed him not.

"Surely he hath borne our griefs, and carried our sorrows: yet we did esteem him stricken, smitten of God, and afflicted. But he was wounded for our transgressions, he was bruised for our iniquities: the chastisement of our peace was upon him; and with his stripes we are healed.

"All we like sheep have gone astray; we have turned every one to his own way; and the Lord hath laid on him the iniquity of us all.

"He was oppressed, and he was afflicted, yet he opened not his mouth: he is brought as a lamb to the slaughter, and as a sheep before her shearers is dumb, so he openeth not his mouth. He was taken from prison and from judgment: and who shall declare his generation? for he was cut off out of the land of the living: for the transgression of my people was he stricken. And he made his grave with the wicked, and with the rich in his death; because he had done no violence, neither was any deceit in his mouth.

"Yet it pleased the Lord to bruise him; he hath put him to grief: when thou shalt make his soul an offering for sin, he shall see his seed, he shall prolong his days, and the pleasure of the Lord shall prosper in his hand. He shall see of the travail of his soul, and shall be satisfied: by his knowledge shall my righteous servant justify many; for he shall bear their iniquities.

"Therefore will I divide him a portion with the great, and he shall divide the spoil with the strong; because he hath poured out his soul unto death: and he was numbered with the transgressors; and he bare the sin of many, and made intercession for the transgressors."

David's words fell away into silence. Tears streamed down everyone's faces.

"Come," David reached for Deborah's hand. "There is still much we can do to help our friends." He pulled his wife close. "And to help Jesus."

Several nodded, but Aaron and Hava looked puzzled, so he went on quickly. "There is a man named Joseph; he is originally from Arimathea. He—"

"Joseph?" Aaron exclaimed. "But I know him. He is a member of the Great Council."

"Yes, it is the same man. He went to the governor and asked permission to see to the burial of Jesus' body. He arrived at Golgotha with the written order from Pilate just before Jesus died. It was nearly sundown by then. We had to act in great haste before the Sabbath began—we knew the Sanhedrin would use any excuse to arrest more of us, including the argument that we were violating the Sabbath by burying Jesus then. Joseph has a garden that, gratefully, is just a short distance from Golgotha. A few months ago, he had his workman start carving a large tomb that could serve as his family's burial place. He told us to bring Jesus there. Joseph provided fine linen, and Nicodemus brought myrrh and aloes to help anoint the body."

"I wonder what the council will do if they find out," Aaron said, not trying to hide his bitterness.

"I think they think it's over now," Miriam said. "My father and Azariah and the others didn't even let Joseph, Nicodemus, and the other moderates know about the trial until it was done. They finished their work without them and now sit back in satisfaction."

"Anyway," David came back in, "because of the rush, we didn't have time to finish preparing the body properly."

Deborah suppressed a shudder. She had been one of the women asked to accompany the body into the tomb and begin preparing it for burial. She would always remember the coldness of the flesh, wiping the dried blood from the gaping wounds, trying not to touch the lacerated back, even though Jesus was then beyond any pain. She and Mary Magdalene and Anna, Peter's wife, had taken the precious ointment brought by Nicodemus and did the preliminary anointing of the body. Then, as the men carefully lifted the body off the stone slab enough to pass the roll of linen beneath it, the women had wound the cloth around and around until Jesus was completely encased in white. It was then that it had hit her with full force that Jesus truly was dead, that no miracle was going to happen.

He was gone. When Deborah had left the tomb, David almost had to carry her until they were out of the garden.

She took a breath and, speaking mostly to Aaron and Hava, explained what David meant. "We need more spices and perfumes, more ointments. And we need to place Jesus in the receptacle that has been carved inside the tomb. We had to leave his body lying on top of the slab until we could return."

Aaron was greatly sobered. "I understand. And I agree totally."

David spoke again. "We promised Peter and the others that we would go to Jerusalem by sundown this evening. As soon as the shops reopen after Shabbat, we're going to buy what we need, then go to the tomb and finish what we started."

He turned to Livia, and his voice softened. "If you are feeling up to it, Livia, we'd all like for you to come with us."

She did not hesitate. "Of course I'll come," she said firmly.

David looked at Aaron. "You and Hava have had a long journey. And it still is the Sabbath. We can't wait until the Sabbath is over and then leave. You can stay here and rest if you would prefer, and—"

"I'm coming with you," Hava said quietly.

Aaron jerked around. "No, Hava. It's too late now. And there could be danger."

Hava then did something that shocked Aaron so deeply that he was completely silenced. Hava had spent her life almost worshiping her husband, serving him in glad adoration, accepting his counsel without question, letting him take the lead in their marriage in every way. But this was a decision she would not bend on. "You do as you wish, Aaron, but I am going with the family."

She watched him for a moment, seeing the astonishment in his eyes. "I, too, have seen Grandma Huldah's straightened back," she said softly. "I, too, have talked with Lazarus, who once was dead. And I, too, have felt my heart stirred within me when I've listened to Jesus teach." She took a deep breath. "I cannot speak for you, my husband, but I can speak for myself. There is no *if* in my mind. *Jesus was the Messiah!* And I am going with the family to see to it he is given a proper burial."

III

JERUSALEM, HOUSE OF MORDECHAI BEN UZZIEL

Mordechai looked up as Levi ushered Menachem of Bethphage into the garden area of his spacious courtyard. The older man set the scroll he had been reading to one side and motioned his assistant forward. "I thought you would be resting on this Sabbath afternoon."

"I've been worried," Menachem said, dropping onto a marble seat across from Mordechai.

Mordechai grunted. "Good. I pay you to worry. What is it?"

"I was seeing to the remuneration of those who helped us at the trial and at the Praetorium and I—"

"Why, Menachem," Mordechai said, feigning horror. "On the Sabbath day? How could you?"

Menachem grinned. "Actually, I thought of stopping by Azariah's house just to see if he would go into an apoplectic fit." Then, instantly, he sobered. "One of those I saw today was the man who testified for us about Jesus destroying the temple."

One eyebrow raised questioningly. "Don't tell me he wants to change his story now."

"Oh, no. But he said something that troubled me. He said that what Jesus was talking about was not the Temple of Herod but the temple of his body."

Leaning forward, his mouth pulling down into a frown, Mordechai had gone very quiet. "Say that again."

"This man claims that his disciples knew that Jesus wasn't talking about the actual temple. One of them told this man when he questioned him about it that of late Jesus had been speaking a lot about his imminent death. According to this man, Jesus said that even if they destroyed his body, he would rise again in three days. That's what Jesus meant. It was the temple of his body."

"Ridiculous," Mordechai said.

"You know that, and I know that," Menachem said, picking his way carefully, "but I haven't been able to get it out of my head."

"It's twaddle," Mordechai exploded. "Don't give it another thought." His irritation was rising. He expected better than this from someone he had handpicked to eventually replace him. "Surely you don't give any credence to the idea that Jesus can raise himself from the dead?"

Menachem flushed a little. "Of course not, sire." His eyes darkened. "But suppose, just suppose, that his disciples decided to convince the people that it was true."

"Let them talk until they are blue in the face. No one will listen to that kind of drivel."

"I'm not thinking about them just talking, sire."

Mordechai's eyes narrowed. "Then what *are* you saying?"

"The garden where they took the body—do you know of it?"

"I've not been there, but, yes, I know where it is. Joseph of Arimathea has a house nearby."

"It is a very private place, Master. It's outside the walls of the city, off away from any roadway." He drew in a breath, not sure if he should say what he was thinking.

"What?" Mordechai snapped.

"Suppose the disciples were to remove the body."

Mordechai sat back very slowly, staring at his associate.

"It would be easy enough. Sometime during the night they roll the stone back, take the body and dispose of it, then . . ."

He didn't have to finish it. Mordechai was far too shrewd not to see immediately what Menachem was saying. He shot to his feet. "Levi!"

His chief servant instantly appeared at the door of the house. "Yes, sire?"

"Get my sandals. Menachem and I are going out."

IV

JERUSALEM, UPPER CITY, THE PRAETORIUM

"I don't give a fig whether the governor wants to be disturbed or not, Marcus. We have to see him immediately. This is a matter of the utmost urgency."

Marcus winced and half closed his eyes. "You don't have to shout, Mordechai." He began to rub at his eyes. They were bloodshot and had heavy dark circles beneath them.

Taking his measure, Mordechai guessed that the tribune had been drinking heavily. That would explain the rumpled uniform, the stubble on his jaw, the hair that badly needed a comb run through it. It made Mordechai all the more disgusted. "We have to see him, Marcus. We could have a serious problem on our hands." Then, speaking slowly and evenly, he outlined Menachem's theory.

Bleary-eyed or not, Marcus was no fool. He saw the implications of the situation as quickly as Mordechai had. "Wait here," he said, and strode out.

Three minutes later Pilate came into the room, his face dark and stormy.

"Excellency," Mordechai said, his voice respectful, almost soothing. "Thank you for taking—"

"What's this about Jesus being raised from the dead?"

"He's not been raised from the dead, Excellency. However, we fear that his disciples may try to steal the body and then claim that he was."

"Did he really say that he would rise again in three days?"

"Evidently, sire," Mordechai replied. He didn't like the look he saw in Pilate's eyes. It was genuine fear. "If that rumor gets started among the people, it could be—"

Pilate cut him off shortly again by spinning around to Marcus. "Fortunata is not to hear a word of this, Marcus. Not a word."

"Of course not, sire."

"She's already begging me to take her back to Caesarea. This thing with Jesus has rattled her nerves."

"Yes, sire. I'll see to it that she does not hear any of this." Marcus was thinking he wasn't about to tell Diana either.

"So what do we do?" Pilate said, turning back to Mordechai.

Mordechai was incredulous. He had to ask? "He said it would happen in three days, Excellency. Perhaps you could put a guard at the tomb until that time has passed."

Pilate seemed relieved with that suggestion. "Yes, that would do it." He snapped his fingers. "Marcus, see to it immediately."

"Yes, sire." He turned and left the room.

Pilate was staring at the floor, his fingers working nervously. Finally, he looked up, seeming surprised to see the two Jews still standing there. "Well," he barked, "you have your guard."

"Yes, Excellency. Thank you." Mordechai started to back away, bowing as he did so. "Thank you for granting us audience."

The governor stared at him balefully. "On your way. You have your watch. Make it as sure as you can." And with that, he flung his toga over one arm and stalked out of the room.

As they left the palace and crossed the courtyard of the Praetorium, Mordechai looked at Menachem. "I want you to make sure the guards really get there."

"Of course."

"And take some men with you and seal the tomb. Do you understand me? Guards or no guards, I want that tomb sealed up tight."

"Yes, sire," Menachem said firmly. "I'll see to it right away."

V

JERUSALEM, UPPER CITY, HOUSE OF JEPHUNAH BEN ASA

Though the afternoon had become muggy and warm, in the house of Jephunah in the Upper City of Jerusalem the door to the courtyard and all the outer doors of the house were shut and barred. Servants guarded the outer gate and the main entrance to the house. On the first level, the windows were left open—no one was down there to be seen from the outside—but in the upper room, the same upper chambers where Jesus and the Twelve had observed the Passover, the shutters were pulled and latched. That left the room in near darkness, even though outside the daylight still lingered. Oil lamps hung on chains from the ceiling, giving light, but their smoke left the air even more thick and heavy than it was outside.

This near paranoia said much about the mental and emotional state of the disciples who gathered together that evening. Once Jesus had been arrested by the Sanhedrin and then passed to the Romans, there was little evidence that anyone was concerned about his followers. The Sanhedrin apparently assumed that these crude and unlearned Galileans had scattered like chicks when the mother hen was taken by the fox. Nor was there any real threat from the Praetorium. Rome paid the disciples of the rebel king no more mind than if they had been children watching the mighty legions marching through their village.

But Peter, James, and John, who had definitely taken over the reins of leadership, were not taking any chances. The Romans had a reputation for cutting a broad swath when they felt a need to eliminate any threat to their security. And no one dared to predict what the Sanhedrin might do. Though no one openly expressed it, there was still some concern that having the daughter of one of the most powerful men on the council as part of their group might trigger a reprisal on anyone who dared to shelter her.

Simeon looked around the room as Peter gave out various assignments for what had to be purchased. Simeon was surprised that more people were not present. The room could easily hold a hundred or more, but there were only a little more than half that. But then, as he thought about it, it really wasn't that surprising. The events of the previous day had been like the explosive eruption of a nearby volcano, which had sent everyone scurrying for safety. It would be days—or perhaps weeks or months—before the numbing effects of the tragedy wore off.

He let his eyes move across the faces. No children were present, with the exception of one or two like Leah, who were young adults but still single; and he saw that quite a few of the wives were not there. The men had felt compelled to come, but they didn't want to put their families at risk too.

There, at the head of the room, were the apostles—now just eleven of them—with all but two or three of their wives. To the left was most of what Simeon thought of as "the Bethany contingent," that is, the ones who had been with Jesus in Bethany—Martha, Mary, and Lazarus; Mary Magdalene; Joanna, the wife of Chuza, and a close friend of Mary's; Luke the Physician with his wife and a son about Leah's age.

Then there were the others from Capernaum. Jairus, ruler of the synagogue in Capernaum, was there alone. Zebedee, father of James and John, was there with his wife, Salome, but their younger children had been left with relatives. There were three or four other Galileans whose names Simeon didn't know.

From Jerusalem, in addition to Jephunah and his wife and daughter, were Joseph of Arimathea and Nicodemus, sitting together. John Mark and his mother, who were close friends of Peter and who owned a home not too far from where they were, talked quietly together. Again, half a dozen others were unknown to Simeon.

What was most surprising to him was to see the four young men at the far end of the room. These were the four younger brothers of Jesus—James, Joseph, Simon, and Yehuda. Their mother, still in a state of complete collapse, was in another room, cared for by her two daughters. What surprised Simeon was that the last he had heard, which was several months ago, the siblings were still struggling to come to terms with the idea that their elder brother was the promised Messiah. Simeon was glad to see them there. They would be a great comfort to their mother.

He turned to watch Aaron for a moment, wondering what was going on in his mind. He had to suppress a smile of gratitude as his eyes shifted slightly to his aunt. Hava had startled them all earlier that afternoon, but it had thrilled him to see her stand her ground, especially in defense of Jesus. Livia, to his relief, was much better now. She didn't say much, but she was no longer withdrawn and distant. She and Miriam even smiled occasionally as they talked.

Just as Simeon started an examination of the rest of his family, a voice brought him back to the present. "Any questions?"

Peter stood at the end of the room, his eyes sweeping over the assembly.

Mary, sister of Martha, raised a tentative hand. She still showed the ravages of grief, as did most of the others in the room. Peter nodded at her, his eyes softening. "Yes, Mary?"

"Once we have made our purchases, should we come back here or go straight to the tomb?" Then before Peter could answer, she added, "It's going to be very dark soon. We'll need torches to find our way."

Peter shook his head. "Not to the tomb. Not tonight. We're all exhausted, and you're right—it is growing dark quickly."

Simeon nodded, along with many others. That was wise. It would be much better in the morning.

Mary sank back into her chair, relieved and yet clearly disappointed, too. Anna moved over and slid an arm around her.

Peter went on quietly. "Bring everything back here. James has made sleeping arrangements for all of us here and nearby. We'll meet back here first thing in the morning to finish what needs to be done."

John came in now. "Probably all of us should not go to the tomb. We don't want the Romans thinking they're under attack."

"I would suggest that only some of the women go," Andrew spoke up. "They are the ones we need to prepare the body anyway, and if the Sanhedrin is watching the tomb, the women shouldn't pose any threat to them."

Peter nodded, then looked around. When there were no further questions, he went on. "All right then. Once the burial preparations are completed, we'll return here for a last meal together." His shoulders lifted and fell. "And then, Passover or not, my family and I are going to start for home. We are done with Jerusalem."

"Amen," someone behind Simeon said softly.

CHAPTER NOTES

The Gospel accounts do not specifically say that meetings held by the disciples after the death and resurrection of Jesus occurred in the same house where the Last Supper took place. However, many assume so because Mark tells us that the Passover meal was celebrated by Jesus in a "large upper room" (Mark 14:15), and in Acts, not long after the resurrection, the disciples again met in "an upper room" (Acts 1:13).

CHAPTER 37

I

JERUSALEM, HOUSE OF MORDECHAI BEN UZZIEL

6 APRIL, A.D. 33

"Sire! Wake up." Levi hesitated, then bent over and shook his master's shoulder.

Mordechai gave a moan, then half turned.

"Wake up, Master!"

Squinting against the light of the small hand lamp that Levi carried, Mordechai raised up on one elbow. "Levi?"

"Yes, sire. I'm sorry, but there's a messenger here from Caiaphas."

Turning his head enough to see that it was pitch black outside the window, Mordechai muttered something under his breath. "What time is it?"

"Well into the third watch, sire. Maybe three hours until dawn."

He sat up. "Caiaphas?"

"Yes, sire. The messenger says it is of the utmost urgency."

II

Mordechai was still muttering to himself as he banged the heavy door knocker loudly. Spineless old fool. What had got his heart fluttering at this hour of the night? Had someone peeped into his window? Had he heard something creak in the house?

When the servant opened the door, Mordechai strode past him without so much as a word. "They are in the council chambers, sire," the man called after him.

Mordechai stopped. "They?"

"Yes, sire. Annas is here, and Azariah."

Wary, Mordechai took the stairs two at a time, dropping from the upper level, past the level where the offices of the high priest were, down to the lower level. He stopped dead when he saw two Roman legionnaires standing behind Annas and Caiaphas. Two more legionnaires were just outside the door that opened out onto the courtyard. Azariah was talking earnestly to them.

As he moved forward again, Mordechai saw that Caiaphas was pale and trembling. Annas's mouth was pinched and his visage grim, as if he had just looked death in the face.

On seeing Mordechai coming, Caiaphas turned his head. "Azariah. He's here."

Annas motioned to the two soldiers. "We need to be alone."

The older of the two men nodded brusquely, and they went out to join their companions. Azariah pulled the door closed behind him as he came in.

"What is going on?" Mordechai demanded. "What are they doing here?"

"You'd better sit down," Annas said.

"I don't want to sit down," Mordechai retorted. "What's happened?"

It was Azariah who answered. "We have a problem."

"What?"

"The body is gone!"

Mordechai fell back a step. *"What?"*

"That's right," Annas said. "It's been stolen."

The rage inside him exploded. "How could that be? Pilate put a guard on it." He stopped, staring at the men outside. "Are they—?"

Azariah nodded. "I think you'd better hear this for yourself." Without waiting for permission, he went to the door and pushed it open a foot or two. "Soldier, come back in here."

The older of the two who had been inside before stepped back into the room. One look at his face and Mordechai could tell he was badly shaken.

Mordechai moved over and dropped into a chair. The others did the same, and the soldier came and stood before them.

"All right, tell him what you told us."

The man took a deep breath, then, not meeting Mordechai's eyes, began to talk rapidly. "Excellency, as you may know, the governor asked that a guard be placed at the tomb of one of the prisoners who was executed on Friday, the one they called the King of the Jews."

"I know that," Mordechai said shortly. "I'm the one who made the request of the procurator. Go on."

"Well, we were the fourth set of guards to be stationed there, sire. We came on at the beginning of the third watch. Everything was fine. The others had not had any problems. They hadn't seen anyone, in fact."

"All right, all right," Annas snapped. "We don't need all of that."

The man swallowed nervously but nodded. "We had been on duty about an hour or so, I'd say. Everything was quiet, and—"

"Were you sleeping?" Mordechai cut in sharply.

The man's face flushed. "The penalty for sleeping on guard duty is very severe, sire."

"So? Were you sleeping?"

"Absolutely not, sire. The four of us were sitting around a small fire, talking. We had heard that the governor was going back to Caesarea soon, and we were wondering if we might be assigned to go with him."

"Come on, man!" Azariah growled. "Get to the point!"

"Sorry, sire." He looked directly at Mordechai. "Suddenly there was an earthquake, sire."

"An earthquake?" Mordechai asked incredulously. He looked to the others. "Did you feel another earthquake in the night?"

They shook their heads.

The man stubbornly refused to budge. "It shook the ground something fierce," he went on. "I was knocked back. One of the men cracked his head on a stone when he was thrown to one side. You can see the knot he got. It's a bad one."

"What happened?" Mordechai's exasperation had vanished. He had been expecting some fantastic excuse for falling asleep on duty, but this had completely taken him by surprise.

The man was fumbling for words. "You won't believe this, sire, but—" He took a quick breath and let it out noisily again. "I was lying there on my back, trying to figure out what had just happened." He looked away. "Suddenly, there was this brilliant light above me in the air. It was like the sun had suddenly appeared, only it was white, pure white. It was descending towards me—towards us. I screamed; I couldn't help myself. The other men were scrambling too, trying to get out of the way."

"A light? What kind of a light?"

"You're not going to believe this, sire, but it was a man."

Mordechai shot forward. "What did you say?"

"There was a man in the light, sire. He was coming down from heaven." His eyes got a faraway look in them. "I never saw such a thing before, sire. His face was like lightning. His robes glistened like a snow field in the sun. The night was suddenly brighter than noonday. It was—I had to put my arm up to stop from being blinded."

Mordechai just stared at him. An angel? He was describing an angel?

"Go on," Annas urged, more kindly now. "Tell him the rest."

"We were terrified, of course," the man continued. "I was trying to get my sword out. But the man didn't come to us. He floated to the ground in front of the tomb, sire. Then—" He stopped, shaking his head, still incredulous. "He lifted one hand. There was a tremendous crack, and the ground shook again. The sealing stone rolled back, revealing the opening to the tomb."

"And?" Mordechai said roughly when he didn't continue. "What happened next?"

"I don't know, sire," he said sheepishly. "The next thing I knew, we found ourselves on the ground again. We had, each of us, fallen like dead men. It was all dark again, and everything was quiet. I grabbed a torch and ran to the tomb to look inside. That's when we saw that the body was gone."

Mordechai sat back and closed his eyes. This was unbelievable, so fantastic as to be ludicrous. Except for one thing. This man was telling them the truth. There was no question in Mordechai's mind. You could see the terror in his eyes as he relived the experience. You could hear the absolute awe in his voice.

"Why did you come *here?*" Azariah finally asked.

Relieved to be on safer ground, the man turned. "We'd heard the detail had originally been requested by the Sanhedrin. And to be honest, sire, we didn't know what else to do. If we go back and tell this story to the centurion, or to Tribune Didius, we're dead men. We'll be the next ones to go to the cross. We decided that maybe you could help us." Suddenly he was pleading. "You've got to believe us. I've told you the absolute truth."

Mordechai's voice was very low. "Thank you, Sergeant," he said. "We appreciate that. Now, could you give us a few minutes? We need to talk about this."

"Of course, sire."

III

It was a full ten minutes before Azariah called the soldiers back, this time motioning for all four to come. By unanimous agreement, it was decided that Mordechai would be their spokesman.

"Sergeant?"

"Yes, sire?"

"This story is too fantastic for anyone to believe. You know that, don't you?"

The head dropped a little. "Aye." Then it came up again, and the eyes were defiant. "But that is exactly what happened. You can question us individually if you'd like, even put us under the lash, but—"

Mordechai held up a hand. "We believe you. But no one else will."

"Aye, sire." It came out very forlorn.

Mordechai reached for the sack of coins Caiaphas had fetched from the strongbox in his office. He tossed it, and the man deftly caught it. He stared at it in disbelief.

"Here is what you are going to do," Mordechai said evenly. "If you don't, you *will* end up on the cross. We'll see to that. Understood?"

"Yes, sire." The other three soldiers were nodding vigorously as well.

"Here is what you're going to say. You are going to say that you were very tired, that your eyes grew heavy."

"But, sire," one of the others blurted, "that is punishable by—"

The sergeant cuffed him sharply. "Just listen!"

"Your eyes grew heavy, and you fell into a deep sleep. Perhaps you had too much wine. But while you were asleep, someone came—the disciples of Jesus surely. They rolled back the stone, and they took the body of Jesus."

The man was nodding, relief evident in his eyes. "What about Pilate, sire?"

"We'll see to it that there are no reprisals against you. But only if you all tell the same story and never change it."

"Yes, sire."

The others bowed their heads in acknowledgment. "Never," they murmured.

"All right. Make sure no one sees you leaving here. Go directly back to the Praetorium and report what happened." He pulled out the letter they had hastily drafted. "Give this directly to Tribune Didius."

"Thank you, sire." The sergeant took it, tucking it into his tunic, then stepped back.

Azariah moved to the door and opened it. Without another word, the four men disappeared into the night. As he closed it again, he turned, staring at the others. None of them spoke.

Finally Caiaphas raised his head. "Do you really believe them?" he asked anxiously.

Mordechai was brooding, his lips pursed and his fingers pressed together, forming a steeple.

"Well?" Caiaphas cried, almost in a panic. "Tell me. Could it be true?"

Mordechai looked up. "Don't be ridiculous," he said. Then, forestalling any further discussion, he rose and quickly went up the stairs.

*

IV

JERUSALEM, UPPER CITY, HOUSE OF JEPHUNAH BEN ASA

Mary Magdalene suddenly stood up. "I'm sorry," she said in a strained voice, "I can't wait any longer. I'm going to go ahead. I'll meet you there."

"But it's barely coming light," Martha answered. "The others will be here shortly."

"I know, but—" She pulled her shawl up around her head, reached out for one of the jars of myrrh that had been purchased the previous evening. "I'm sorry. I'll see you there."

Miriam started to rise. "I'll go with you," she volunteered, but Deborah quickly pulled her back again, shaking her head.

"She needs to be alone," she whispered.

Mary, overhearing Deborah's comment, gave her a grateful smile and hurried out. It wasn't two minutes later when the door opened again and Philip and Bartholomew entered. They had been with the group of men assigned to sleep in the courtyard. Seeing the women standing there, they went over. "Mary just left," Martha said.

"Yes, we talked to her for a moment." Philip looked around. "Are all of you going?"

They looked at each other, not sure how to answer.

Bartholomew, who was an older man with a kind face and gentle personality, smiled. "I'd say no more than four or five of you."

Anna, Peter's wife, stepped forward. "I agree that we shouldn't take so many that the guards get nervous, but we may need to lift the body to make sure the linen is properly wrapped. Perhaps seven or eight would be ideal."

Both apostles accepted that. Philip made the decision. "Mary has already gone, so Joanna, it might be well if you went too. She's still pretty distraught, and you're closest to her."

Joanna nodded without comment. She had been worried about Mary's precipitous departure, so this relieved her mind somewhat.

"Anna, I think you should go." He was still searching their faces. "Martha and Mary, you helped yesterday, so why don't you go again."

"So did Deborah and Miriam," Anna said.

"Good, the two of you as well then." He counted quickly. "That would be seven."

Leah raised her hand just enough to catch his eye. "I can go."

Philip smiled kindly. "If you wouldn't mind, could you stay here with the others and help prepare a meal? We've got many mouths to feed."

Leah, trying not to show her disappointment, accepted with a nod. Livia and Rachel were just behind her, but neither of them volunteered in her place. Rachel already had too many horrible images in her mind from the crucifixion. She would go if asked, but she didn't feel a need to volunteer. Livia, for all her determination to make restitution for having stayed home two days before, could not face the prospect of actually being in the tomb with Jesus' dead body.

Philip looked around at the women once more, then selected Salome, wife of Zebedee and mother of James and John, to go as well. As the two brethren left and the seven women prepared to depart, Deborah noted that except for Mary, sister of Martha, and Miriam, the others were all older, more mature women. She suspected that was not simply by accident. Philip understood full well the toll this would take on their already fragile emotions.

They gathered up the purchases from the night, then looked at each other. "All right, then," Anna said, looking a little wan. "Let's get started."

V

The Garden Tomb

As Mary of Magdala made her way slowly along the rocky path, she began to have second thoughts. Perhaps she should have waited for the others. And she hadn't even thought to bring a torch or a lamp. The eastern sky was showing the first glow of dawn, but here in the trees and undergrowth it was still so dark she wasn't even sure she was on the right path. She stopped, debating about whether to wait here for the rest of the women to catch up with her.

What would she say to the guards? Could she, being alone, convince them to let her in? She felt a quick chill. She knew that she was not an unattractive woman. Would they, seeing that she was alone, feel free to make unseemly advances?

She stepped off the path, fear clutching at her heart, and felt the branches of a tree brush against her face. She jumped and let out a low cry. Then, realizing what it was, she felt like such a fool that it brought her back to reality. The other women wouldn't be far behind her, but she didn't want to wait any more now than she did back at the house. She wanted this over with. Only then could she begin the long process of healing.

Clutching the jar she carried more tightly to her body, she stepped back out onto the path and started moving again.

Five minutes later she was relieved to realize that the dark shapes around her looked familiar. Here was a rock wall and, a little farther on, a small outbuilding. Farther back and to the right, the dark roundness of the hill that rose behind Golgotha was barely discernible against the sky. Then she heard the soft splash of a fountain and turned towards it. This was it. She passed through a stone arch and was in the garden of Joseph of Arimathea.

Cautiously, placing her feet with great care, straining to hear every morning sound, she moved to the left, down the path that led to the tomb. She stopped again, her eyes searching carefully for any movement, her ears listening for any voices.

There was nothing. Feeling a growing sense of uneasiness, she moved forward a few more steps. She could barely make out the lighter hues of the rock face into which Joseph had cut his tomb. Then she made out the shape of the great circular stone that sealed the tomb. There was no movement of any kind.

Suddenly her heart plummeted. The stone? How was she supposed to roll back that massive stone? It had taken four men to put it into place. Greatly dismayed, she took a few more steps in the near darkness. She could make out the stone track in which the stone rolled back and forth, but something didn't seem right. It wasn't where she had remembered it should be. Then, just beyond the stone, she could just make out a deeper patch of darkness, oblong and slightly less than the height of a man. She drew in a breath sharply as she realized that the stone was already rolled back. She was staring at the opening of the tomb.

With her heart pounding so hard she felt like she was going to be sick, she set the jar of myrrh to one side and moved forward slowly. When she reached the opening, she remembered how it had been constructed when they had been there before. She stepped carefully over the lip of the track, and then again over the threshold to the tomb, which formed part of the back side of the trough, and entered the tomb.

Instantly she realized her mistake. It was dark inside. She stepped to one side, letting the faint light from outside come in. Gradually her eyes began to adjust a little. She was surprised to discern something white to her left. She moved closer, bending down a little. When she realized what she was seeing, she gasped again. With a low cry, she backed hurriedly outside, nearly tripping on the track for the sealing stone. She stared numbly at the opening for several seconds; then, with a cry of anguish, she turned and started running.

VI

NEAR GOLGOTHA

Anna and Salome were in the lead. Suddenly Salome held up a hand. "Shhh!"

The other five women stopped abruptly. Then they heard it too, the sound of running footsteps on gravel, coming towards them. "Quickly!" Anna hissed. "Into the trees."

Anna's heart beat wildly as she stepped into the deeper shadows of a small olive grove, gathering in tightly with the other women for courage and defense. And then, with a huge sigh of relief, she heard the footsteps fading again. They were passing them on the left, some distance away now, and growing more muffled by the moment. In less than a minute, they had died away completely.

"Whoever it was, they took another path," Miriam said. "I remember from last night, the path splits somewhere just ahead of us."

Anna started forward again. "Let's go, but be careful."

VII

JERUSALEM, UPPER CITY, HOUSE OF JEPHUNAH BEN ASA

The morning dawned bright and clear. Though the air was still quite chilly, it was going to be a beautiful day. Peter stood in the courtyard. He tipped his head back and breathed deeply, then let it out slowly, savoring the moment. It felt good. He filled his lungs again. After the last forty-eight hours, anything clean and fresh was a welcome relief.

Then he swung around. This was not a time for savoring life. "Jephunah!"

The master of the house appeared at the door.

"Let's eat out here in the courtyard. We'll keep it simple so we can get to the tomb and get this done."

Then, before Jephunah could answer, a sharp banging was heard from the direction of the gate. Those who were outside all turned. Men froze, hands resting on daggers and swords. The women paled and moved quickly toward the house.

"Let me in. It's me. Open the gate."

With a rush of relief, Peter recognized the voice. He waved a hand at the servant stationed as a guard there. "It's Mary Magdalene," he called. "Let her in."

The man lifted the heavy bar and pulled the gate open a foot or two. In a moment Mary was inside, and he slammed it shut again. A few of the women started toward her, then stopped again as they saw the look on her face. The men moved in closer as she ran up to Peter. Her chest was heaving as she gasped for air. Her hair was tousled and her face flushed.

"Mary! What's wrong? What happened?"

She straightened, still drawing in huge breaths. Her mouth was pinched into a tight, hard line. "He's gone, Peter."

"Who's gone?"

"Jesus. His body. Gone."

"*What?*" He was aghast.

"I saw inside. Burial clothes, but no body." She bent over, holding her side. "The tomb has been opened." She burst into tears. "They stole his body, Peter. He's gone!"

Peter swung about. "John! James!"

John was right behind him. "James isn't here yet."

"We can't wait. Let's go." In three steps, Peter had reached the gate. He flung the bar back and jerked it open. Then he turned back. "Simeon, David, Thomas. Stay here until we find out what has happened." He started away, then turned back again. "Have everyone get ready in case we have to leave immediately." Then he was gone, with John following behind.

"Peter, wait!" Mary darted forward, still holding her side. "I'm coming too."

The guard had started to close the gate again but stepped back when he saw her coming. She cupped her hand to her mouth as she stumbled forward. "Take the path to the left. It's much shorter." Then, between breaths: "Wait for me. I'm coming."

VIII

The Garden Tomb

John was three years younger than Peter. Not only was he lighter in build, but he hadn't had the "benefit" of eight or nine years of being fed solid meals every day by a wife. He was lean as a willow and lithe as a cat. By the time he passed beneath the arched gateway and saw the fountain, Peter was so far behind he was no longer in sight. Slowing to a walk, John moved forward more cautiously, searching through the trees for any signs of movement. There was nothing. As he came out into the open area in front of the tomb, his eyes took in the scene quickly. No one was there, but off to one side wisps of smoke rose from a pile of ashes, and there were chicken bones scattered on the ground. A few feet farther on he saw a burned-out torch, and beyond that, a Roman helmet on its side. So there had been a guard. But where were they now? Judging from the smoldering ashes, they had been gone for several hours.

He half turned. In the dim light of early morning, he saw the massive stone in its track, but it was five or six feet back from where they had left it after sealing the tomb, just as Mary had said. Moving slowly, he approached the entrance to the tomb. Then he stopped. He could hear Peter's footsteps. They were faint, but they were coming, definitely slower than when they had left the Upper City.

The young apostle stooped down, peering into the deeper shadows of the inner tomb. He could see some white cloth there, but nothing else. He wanted desperately to step inside, to see what was there—or not there—but something held him back. He and Peter had been fishing partners for several years and were more like brothers than just friends. But Jesus had set Peter apart from the rest of them when he made him the chief apostle. There was great equality in that brotherhood of twelve, but unquestionably, Jesus looked to Peter to serve as their leader. So now, John held back. He would not go in before his leader.

He moved closer to the stone. Around the edge there was fresh cement, now torn and jagged. The tomb had been sealed, but the seal had been broken. That was a bit of a surprise. It would take more than four men to break the seal and roll it back. What had happened here?

Then the slap of sandals on gravel brought him around. Peter slowed to a walk as he came into sight, puffing hard. "Is he there?"

"I haven't gone in," John said simply.

Peter strode past him to the opening cut into the rock face. It was only chest high, and he had to stoop to go inside. Once inside, he stopped and uttered a low grunt. John couldn't tell what that meant. He moved to the door, then went in as Peter stepped to one side.

The tomb was empty. Though the light was dim, John's eyes saw that in an instant. From where he stood he could easily see into the small antechamber to the back and the chamber to the right. Mary had spoken true. Jesus' body was gone. John turned to say something to Peter. Peter's eyes were wide, fixed on something in front of him, and enlarging even as John watched.

John turned slowly and immediately saw it too. At the base of the wall of the inner chamber, a large protrusion of stone had been left jutting into the room. The top had been left in place to form a table for preparing the body, but beneath the table surface the stone had been hollowed out to make a place for the body's final resting place. A stone slab would be fixed in place over the opening to seal the body in.

It was the top of the coffin that Peter was staring at. John saw the long splash of white. He had noticed it from the outside. It was the linen in which the body had been wrapped. Then, suddenly, he noticed something very odd. He took a step forward, but Peter's hand shot out and stopped him. John wasn't sure why, but he didn't protest. His eyes ran along the length of the cloth, trying to understand what was bothering him about what he was seeing. His head shifted slightly to the right. At the head of the flat platform, but separate from the linen, was another cloth, this one much smaller. He recognized it as the square napkin, or face covering. The women

IX

THE GARDEN TOMB

Mary Magdalene had to stop when she reached the point where the path split. She was feeling lightheaded and dizzy, and her breath was becoming more and more labored. She had lost sight of Peter and John shortly after going back out into the street and quickly realized there was no way she was going to catch them. She finally faced the fact that she had to catch her breath or she was going to faint.

She stood there for several minutes, haggard, exhausted, drained beyond her ability to comprehend it any more. What more could happen? How much more horror and degradation and humiliation did they have to endure? She could sense she was very close to the breaking point but fought it back. She had to hold on until she had found Jesus. Hold on until she had cared for his needs this one last time.

She jerked up as she heard the soft murmur of men's voices. A moment later, she gave a soft cry of relief. Peter and John were coming up the path towards her. They were hurrying but no longer running.

"Did you find him?" she cried, going forward to meet them.

Peter was sweating heavily, and he wiped his forehead with his sleeve, then shook his head. "The body *is* gone, Mary."

"No!" It was a strangled cry.

He glanced at her briefly, almost as though he had barely taken notice of her response. "But it's all right," he said, smiling.

John took her by the arm. "It wasn't stolen, Mary."

She just looked at him stupidly.

"It wasn't the Romans, nor was it the Jews." He glanced at Peter, who was moving away rapidly. "Come back with us," he said. "We need to talk."

had wrapped that cloth over the face and head of Jesus before they started wrapping the body. Now it was in a neat square and set to one side, as if someone had carefully removed it from the body, then folded it up before leaving the tomb.

And then, with a start that sent his heart racing, John realized what it was that had caught his attention. The linen used to wrap the body had come from a large roll brought by Joseph of Arimathea. As was traditional, the corpse had been completely encased in the burial shroud. John had been one of the men who had lifted the body so the women could pass the linen beneath it each time. Now the cloth lay flat on the stone table, still showing the overlapping pattern created during the wrapping. That was it! The linen had not been cut nor torn. It had not been crumpled as it was removed and tossed in one corner. The neat, overlapping folds were the length of a full-grown man.

His mouth slowly opened as the realization of what that meant sunk into his heart. It was as if the linen had been carefully wound around a bubble of air, and then the bubble had been burst and the cloth simply collapsed in on itself.

John turned slowly, his mouth agape. To his surprise, Peter was not there. John had been concentrating so intently on the cloth, he hadn't heard his fellow apostle leave. He turned once more, staring at the cloth in wonder, then hurriedly backed out of the tomb.

Peter was just disappearing at a trot around the path that led out of the garden. "Peter!"

He stopped and waited for John to catch up to him.

"No one stole Jesus' body, Peter. Did you look at that cloth?"

Peter's eyes were like great mirrors, and John saw registered in them his own shock, wonder, fear, and puzzlement.

Peter started to say something, then just shook his head. "We have to tell the others," he said. And with that, though he was still breathing heavily, he broke into a trot again.

She pulled free. "In a few minutes," she managed, giving him a wan smile. "I just need a few minutes."

John was clearly concerned but finally nodded. "All right, but don't be long, Mary. We need to talk about all of this."

She moved away, head down and shoulders slumped.

X

By the time they realized they had taken the wrong path in the semi-darkness, the seven women found themselves near the Damascus Gate, a good ten minutes beyond their intended destination. Irritated at themselves but glad for the increased light, they retraced their steps and entered the garden of Joseph of Arimathea. As they passed the stone fountain and heard the soft gurgle of water, Anna brought them to another halt. "How are we going to roll the stone back?" she asked.

They looked at each other in dismay. Why hadn't they thought of that sooner?

Anna turned around. "Mary!" she called. She started forward, with the others falling in behind. "Mary, where are you?"

As the path opened up to the area in front of the tomb, Anna stopped in shocked surprise. "The tomb is already open."

"Some of the men must have come after all," Salome suggested.

They stopped about a dozen paces from the tomb, holding their breath. There was no movement, no sound other than the soft chirping of birds somewhere behind them. "Mary?" It was Martha this time, and it came out more hoarsely than she intended. "Mary? Are you in there?"

The stillness only seemed to deepen.

Deborah felt a prickling sensation run up her back. Maybe it was Mary they had heard running past them earlier. What had frightened her?

Joanna had come specifically to see if she might be a comfort to her friend, so when there was no response, she made up her mind. She pictured Mary collapsed in a heap over the dead body, weeping silently. She strode forward, trying to look far more confident than she really felt, and went inside the tomb. A moment later, her head reappeared. Her face was pale and her mouth open. She beckoned frantically for them to come.

As they rushed forward, the terrible news burst from her lips. "The body is gone!"

"Gone!" Martha exclaimed.

"Where's Mary?" Anna cried, rushing to the opening and stepping inside. Joanna just shook her head. In a moment, all seven women were crowded inside, staring at the folded linen in the dim light.

Salome started to weep. "Where could it be?"

Deborah didn't know, but she did know what they had to do next. "We have to tell the others."

Miriam had been the last one to enter the tomb, and so she was the first one out. As she straightened, she let out a scream and dropped the jar of ointment she had in one hand. It shattered as it hit the ground. Where moments before there was only the muted light of morning, now the open area outside the tomb was flooded with a brilliant light. And two men were standing not five feet away.

Deborah was right behind Miriam. She jumped back. Then she, too, saw the men. She fell back against the outer wall of the tomb, one hand flying to her mouth.

"Why seek ye the living among the dead?" one of the men asked calmly.

Three things registered in Miriam's mind at that instant. One was the dimly heard cries and gasps of those behind her. The other was that it had been the figure closest to her that had spoken. The third, and most vivid, was the voice itself. It was low and rich. Instead of terrifying her, suddenly she was filled with a marvelous sense of peace.

She felt Deborah clutching at her robe as she came up behind her. She didn't turn. Lifting a hand to shield her eyes, Miriam gazed at the two figures who stood before them. They wore no sandals and were dressed in brilliant white robes. The cloth was dazzling, so bright as to hurt her eyes. Even the flesh of their faces was radiantly bright, like sunshine reflecting off the water. Then, as her mind finally realized what she had just seen, her eyes flew back down to their feet. They were standing in the air, a few inches above the stone floor in front of the tomb. It was as if they were statues placed on invisible plinths.

As one, the women fell to their knees, throwing their arms across their eyes.

"Fear ye not!" the voice commanded gently. "Be not amazed. I know that you have come seeking Jesus of Nazareth, who was crucified."

Miriam felt as though every cell in her body was on fire. Every nerve was tingling, and she found herself almost too weak to raise her hands. But the fear was gone now. The voice was so calm, so remarkably filled with peace and comfort and consolation that the terror of moments before vanished instantly. She slowly raised her head, still shielding her eyes, but now only with one upraised hand. Out of the corner of her eyes, she saw the others doing the same.

"Why seek ye the living among the dead?" It was the figure nearest to her who spoke again. "Jesus is not here. He is risen. Behold the place where they laid him."

He raised a hand and pointed toward the mouth of the tomb. The inside of the chamber was flooded with that same eerily brilliant light. It was so bright that Miriam could see with perfect clarity the chisel marks on the wall, the rear of the chamber that hadn't been quite finished yet, the stone coffin on which the linen lay.

Feeling as if she was going to faint—or that she was so light she might lift right off the ground herself—she turned back. "Remember," the angel said in that same wonderful voice, "remember how he spake unto you when he was yet in Galilee? Did he not say to you that the Son of man must be delivered up into the hands of sinful men and be crucified?"

Miriam nodded without even being aware she was doing so. Suddenly she remembered how David had once tried to explain to the family what it had been like when he and Benjamin had seen an angel that night on the shepherd fields of Bethlehem. Words had finally failed him as he tried to describe the indescribable. But now she knew.

She turned to Deborah, eyes wide with wonder. Immediately she saw that her mother-in-law was experiencing exactly the same feelings that Miriam was.

"Go," the gentle voice said. "Go quickly and tell Peter and the disciples. Tell them this: 'Jesus is risen from the dead.'" He raised one arm, then finished. "Lo, I have told you so."

And then they were gone. As suddenly as they had come, the angels were gone.

For what seemed like an eternity, Miriam didn't move. Then she heard someone nearby stir. One by one the women got to their feet, staring at each other, not knowing what to say. Miriam could feel her body trembling as if she had sprinted a great distance, and yet she wasn't exhausted. She was exhilarated. This was the most incredible, exultant feeling she had ever known.

Anna was the first to speak. Her voice was trembling. She, too, was still half dazed. "Come," was all she could think of to say. "We have to find Peter."

CHAPTER NOTES

All the Gospel writers agree that it was only women who went to the tomb that first Sunday morning to finish the burial preparations. But who they were and how many there were is not clear. Five are specifically named (see Matthew 27:61; Mark 16:1; Luke 24:10): Mary Magdalene; Mary, the mother of James; "the other Mary" (Matthew 27:61); Joanna; and Salome (whom many believe was the wife of Zebedee and the mother of James and John). Luke also indicates that there were other unnamed women as well (see Luke 24:10). The "other Mary" cannot be firmly identified, though it is possible that she is the same as the mother of James.

There is a discrepancy in the accounts that needs some explanation. John's account, the fullest and most explicit, has Mary arriving at the tomb alone, yet the others say she went with other women. When she saw the empty tomb, she ran back and told Peter and John, who then came on the run to see for themselves. John tells us that he outran Peter. After they left, Mary returned, still alone, and there became the first human being to see the resurrected Lord (see John 20:1–18). Matthew tells us that the other women who came to the tomb eventually saw Jesus as well.

As noted several times before in this series, the Gospel writers were not recording a history, but their testimony of Jesus, and these discrepancies may be the result of considerable compression in the narratives. Some commentators suggest that what we have are two separate visits to the tomb by women. John emphasizes the visit of Mary Magdalene; Matthew, Mark, and Luke emphasize that of the other women (see Edersheim, *Life and Times,* p. 908; Farrar, pp. 660–61). The author took the liberty of using separate paths and different departure times to explain how the three different groups might arrive at the Garden Tomb without seeing each other and getting an updated report.

The scene in the tomb with Peter and John is based on John's unique testimony: "Then cometh Simon Peter following him, and went into the sepulchre, and seeth the linen clothes lie, and the napkin, that was about his head, not lying with the linen clothes, but wrapped together in a place by itself. Then went in also that other disciple [John], which came first to the sepulchre, *and he saw, and believed*" (John 20:6–8; emphasis added). John does not tell us what he saw that brought that sudden understanding, but clearly there was something in the way the linen was arranged that convinced him that Jesus had been resurrected and not just stolen away.

CHAPTER 38

I

THE GARDEN TOMB
6 APRIL, A.D. 33

In the end, Mary Magdalene did not turn back to follow Peter and John. She continued on to the garden. She had pushed aside John's comments, only feeling more confused than before. If the body hadn't been stolen, then where was it? Who had it? If they found it somewhere, could they still take the ointments and the spices and do what they had first set out to do this morning?

She had no answers and so walked on, the tears coming afresh when she came to the great stone that was now rolled away from an empty tomb. For a long time she stood there, swaying back and forth as if in a quiet breeze, her thoughts far away. She was thinking of the day Jesus had come to her and with a word had driven away the darkness that had tormented her for so long. In one instant, light had flooded into her soul, and she had begun a new life—a life of joy, of meaning, of fulfillment, a life where Jesus was the center of everything she cared about.

With slow step, she finally turned and walked into the tomb.

Perhaps she would just sit there for a time. Perhaps being where his body had last lain might give her some comfort.

As she stepped inside, the tears coming ever more freely, she gave a startled cry. "Oh!"

Two men dressed in white robes were sitting at both ends of the coffin. Through her tears, it looked as if the sunlight had somehow penetrated the gloom and fallen upon their clothing. The whole tomb was lit by their presence. She blinked quickly, but their images only blurred the more.

"Woman?" The voice struck her with great force, though it was not frightening in any way. It filled her with a sudden strangeness. "Why weepest thou?"

Confused by this sudden, unexpected development, Mary could think of only one answer: "Because they have taken my Lord away, and I know not where they have laid him." A strangled sob rose up from deep within her.

Suddenly a movement out of the corner of her eye brought her head up. Outside the tomb, in the deeper shadows of an olive tree, a man stood watching her silently. "Woman?" he said quietly, "why weepest thou?"

It didn't register that this man had asked exactly the same question as those inside had asked. This was someone different. He wore a common tunic with sleeves to the wrist.

"Whom seekest thou?"

A surge of hope shot through Mary. Perhaps this was the gardener. It was full daylight, and around the city, workers would be starting the day's work. She exited quickly, the men inside forgotten with this new possibility. If he did work in the garden, perhaps he would know what had happened. "Sir?" She spoke softly, hopefully. "If you have borne him somewhere, tell me where he is, and I will take him away."

For a long, long moment, there was no answer, and Mary's hope melted away. Her head dropped again.

"Mary."

The sound of her name brought her head up with a snap. She stared at the man. She would have recognized that voice anywhere. She had heard Jesus speak her name countless times, with love and compassion and understanding.

"Rabboni?" she cried. "Master?"

With heart pounding, she started forward. Now there was no question about it. It *was* Jesus! Her mind refused to believe what her eyes were seeing. She had watched him die in horrible pain. She had anointed the cold, torn body, then helped the others wrap it in the burial shroud. And yet she could not deny. *It was him!* The joy was dizzying, almost choking off her breath.

With another cry, she rushed at him. Jesus *was* alive!

To her surprise, Jesus stepped back and raised a hand before she could reach him. She stopped, bewildered.

"Mary," he said, ever so gently, "touch me not, for I have not yet ascended to my Father."

He smiled at her, and in that one instant the darkness, the despair, the utter hopelessness of the past two days was banished. Gladness shot through her like a hundred bolts of lightning, causing her to tingle down to her fingertips.

He went on, every word further enlivening her soul. "Go to your brethren and say unto them that I ascend unto my Father and your Father, and to my God and your God."

Mary dropped to her knees, barely able to restrain herself from reaching out to him. The tears, now of unbelievable joy, streamed down her face. "Yes, Master," she whispered, as she bowed her head.

He said nothing more. Finally getting some control of her emotions, she wiped at her eyes with the back of her hand, then looked up. To her astonishment, he was gone. There hadn't been a sound, but he was gone. She was alone again, kneeling on the ground outside an empty tomb.

II

Near the Garden Tomb

"I can't wait to tell Livia," Miriam whispered. She and Deborah were slightly ahead of the other women. They were walking at a brisk pace, speaking earnestly to each other about what they had just seen.

"And Aaron!" Deborah said excitedly. Then her face fell. "I'm not sure he'll believe us."

"He has to!" Miriam cried. "Every one of us saw them. Seven of us. That's testimony that will stand in any court in the land."

Deborah was not quite so sure, but then her mind was swept away again with the memory of what had just happened to them. "'He is not here,'" she murmured, quoting the man with the infinitely gentle voice. "'He is risen!' Oh, Miriam! I can hardly believe it."

Miriam stopped dead, and Deborah nearly bumped into her. "What's the matt—" Then she, too, went rigid. Up ahead, standing just off the path in the deep shadows of a tree, was a lone figure. It was a man, and he was watching them steadily.

Deborah felt a clutch of fear and reached for her daughter-in-law's hand. "It's nothing," she said, forcing a lightness into her voice. "It's just someone coming down the path."

But he was not coming; he was just standing there, his eyes on the group of women. The others came up to them. "Who is it?" Salome whispered.

Miriam shook her head.

Anna sized him up quickly. He was clearly not a Roman. He wore the outer tunic that was worn by common people, so he wasn't from the Sanhedrin either. He wore no head covering. He had a beard, and his hair, what she could see of it, fell down to his shoulders. But his face was in shadow. Like the others, Peter's wife felt a sudden shiver of fear, but she forced it aside. "Come on," she said in a low voice. "Let's stay together. It will be all right."

Then Deborah gasped. The man took one step forward, into a patch of dappled sunlight coming through the trees. She gasped again. "Jesus?"

The blood drained from Miriam's head, and she felt her legs start to tremble. Blindly, she clutched at Deborah's arm, but her eyes never left the face of the man who waited for them. And then, with a thrill ten times—a hundred times—greater than that which they had just experienced outside the tomb, she saw him smile. "All hail," he called, and lifted a hand in greeting.

III

Jerusalem, Upper City, House of Jephunah ben Asa

Aaron was getting angry. Simeon was getting frustrated. Hava grew more anxious as tempers began to rise. Livia, Leah, Rachel, and Ephraim sat back quietly, willing to be no more than spectators. Fortunately, David ben Joseph understood perfectly what was going on inside Aaron's mind and heart and decided to intervene. He held up a hand, cutting off another exasperated retort before it came.

Aaron turned to him gratefully. "I'm not trying to be difficult, David. But I still don't see why everyone thinks that what John saw is so significant. There could be a dozen explanations for it."

"Give us one," Simeon said tartly.

"Simeon," David said, "let Aaron speak."

Simeon sighed. "Sorry."

"I don't blame you for being frustrated, Simeon. I'm frustrated with myself. But I just don't see it." He turned to the women. "Does it make sense to you?"

Hava nodded slowly, knowing she was only going to add to his aggravation.

"Then tell me. You explain it as you understand it."

She took a deep breath, then began talking quietly. "When Mary came back and told us the body was missing, we all assumed it had been stolen. But that doesn't make sense now. First of all, who would steal it?" She waved her own question aside, not wanting to be deflected. "Secondly, if they did, why did they leave the grave cloth behind?"

"Perhaps Joseph of Arimathea decided the body had to be moved. Maybe he wasn't satisfied with what preparations had been made the other night and decided they should start over." Aaron stopped, knowing how weak his argument sounded even as he said it.

"We've already talked to Joseph," David said quietly. "He had nothing to do with this."

"I know that," Aaron said, his impatience showing. "I'm just trying to show that there might be some other explanation."

"Let's say," Hava continued patiently, "that for some unknown reason, the people who took the body did decide to remove the linen. How would they do it? Let's suppose their motive is evil. If they were in a hurry, fearing detection, wouldn't they just rip it off or cut it off and throw it aside?"

"Yes, yes, I see that. But you're still speculating."

Hava gave him a look that silenced him. "Sorry," he mumbled. "Go on."

"But let's assume that these people, whoever they were, were not bad. Let's even say they were disciples. So they would treat the body with respect. Why they would unwrap the grave clothes, I don't know, but when they did, they would do it carefully. Think about it. Once the cloth was off, what would they do with it?"

He frowned. That was something he hadn't considered. "I suppose they would fold it up or put it back into a roll."

"Exactly," she went on. "But the cloth wasn't tossed aside. Nor was it folded or in a roll."

He squinted his eyes. Finally, he was beginning to see where she was going.

Simeon was amazed at Hava's calm, deliberate approach, and though he wanted to clarify some things, he decided to let her finish.

"That's right, Aaron. There are really only four options as I see it: take the body still wrapped in the grave cloth, cut or tear the cloth off and toss it in a corner, roll it up, or fold it up. But *none* of those are what Peter and John found. The face napkin was folded and set aside, but the *linen* was not. That would suggest that no one took the body."

Aaron's mind understood what she was saying, but he struggled to comprehend what it meant. Hava quickly extended one arm out straight in front of her. "Let's assume that my arm here is the body of Jesus. And here, I have here an imaginary roll of linen. Now, I'm going to wrap the body. Watch what happens."

She began to wind the invisible cloth around and around her arm. "Notice how each time when I make the next complete circle, the cloth overlaps the previous layer just a little until the whole arm is encased."

Aaron was watching intently. "Go on."

"Now—" She drew her arm back slowly. "Suppose that somehow my arm was withdrawn without disturbing the linen wrapped around it. What would happen to the cloth?"

"It would collapse upon itself."

"And that would leave the folds of linen in that same overlapping pattern, only now they would be flat." Hava was very earnest. "*That* is what John saw, Aaron. The cloth had simply collapsed in on itself."

He thought about that for a moment, then began to shake his head again. "I know what you're trying to say, and yes, I see that it makes sense. But it is just too fantastic. Poof! and a full-grown body simply dissolves into thin air?"

"Not dissolves," Leah said softly. "It is resurrected. That's what John is saying, Aaron. That's why he was so excited."

"Then where did it go? Where is Jesus now?"

"In heaven," Leah answered. "Where we all go when we die."

"When we die, we don't take our bodies with us," he burst out. "They stay in the grave. Of course, I believe that some part of Jesus, the spirit part of him, is still alive, just as the spirit part of us will live after death. But I can't believe that he took his body with him. That's all I'm trying to say."

Livia had remained aloof from the discussion, watching but not saying anything. "But if he did, Aaron, think what that would mean for us. If he kept his body, maybe we will keep ours when we are resurrected."

He wanted to lambast that idea but didn't because he knew that Livia was thinking about Yehuda, whose body lay in a grave not too far from where they sat.

Simeon was thinking of Yehuda too. "It would mean that we are not some amorphous, shapeless, spiritual mass up in heaven," he suggested. "If we receive our bodies again, then it seems like we will keep our uniqueness, our identity."

Aaron just shook his head. "That's all well and good, and a comforting thought, but what proof do you have of that other than a collapsed piece of cloth?"

David gave his brother-in-law a thoughtful look. "I know it's become popular among our people to speak of the resurrection only in spiritual terms, but that's not what some of the prophets believed."

"What makes you say that?"

"Didn't Ezekiel see a valley of dry bones come together with sinew and flesh coming upon them? And didn't the Lord then say that he would open the graves of Israel and cause the people to come out of those graves?'"

Aaron was taken aback by that example. "Well," he said defensively, "the greatest of the rabbis interpret that metaphorically, meaning the House of Israel will receive new life in the latter days."

"It doesn't sound metaphorical to me," Rachel said.

Leah came in. She knew they were ganging up on her uncle a little, but he was being especially difficult at the moment. "What about Job?"

"What about him?" Aaron shot right back.

"I can't quote it, but he said something like . . ." She stopped, trying to remember exactly how it went.

It was Ephraim who began to quote it. "I know that my Redeemer lives and that he shall stand at the latter day upon the earth, and though after the skin worms destroy this body, yet *in my flesh* I shall see God."

Aaron was trapped, and he knew it, but he never got a chance to wiggle out of it because just then he heard the sound of the gate opening. He turned and was surprised to see Mary Magdalene come inside as the servant guarding the gate held it open. Her face was radiant, in such sharp contrast to her demeanor when she had left that he barely recognized her.

Off to one side of the courtyard, Peter jumped to his feet. "Mary? Are you all right?"

She turned and gave a little cry of joy. "Oh yes!" she exclaimed. "Peter, I have seen the Lord. He lives, Peter. He lives!"

IV

Aaron stood near the back of the crowd that pressed in around Mary Magdalene. He listened intently, searching her face for any sign of—he shook his head. Of what? Madness? He realized what he was doing. There were only three possible explanations for the remarkable change in this woman. Perhaps she was deliberately concocting a story—a possibility that even in his cynicism he could not accept. Though he didn't know her well, he sensed that Mary Magdalene was a woman of the deepest integrity. And the change in her was too dramatic, too complete to be an act. Every part of her was infused with joy.

The second possibility was, of course, that she *was* telling the truth, that she had just experienced something far too wonderful and incredible to comprehend. That left Aaron even more troubled. How could . . . he shook it off.

The third possibility was that somehow she had been deluded. This made some sense to him. He knew she had been so distraught, so near to mental collapse, when she left. Could she have seen something she thought was the risen Jesus? Maybe the play of sunlight and shadow. The eyes could play wonderful tricks on you, especially when the heart and mind were so desperately longing for something.

"How close was he to you?" Aaron was startled when he realized he had spoken out loud.

Mary turned, not sure who had spoken. Aaron recoiled a little. The pure happiness in her eyes and in her countenance filled him with guilt. Did he really want to take that away from her? But he had to know. He lifted his hand to identify himself. "Were you very close to him?"

She turned to Peter, who stood beside her, then took three steps back. "When he spoke my name, I was perhaps ten or twelve paces away, but when I realized who he was, I ran to him. When he stopped me, I was no farther away than this." She indicated the distance between her and Peter.

"Did you touch him?" Aaron knew he had no right to ask these things, but he had to know.

Her head lowered a little, and her cheeks colored. "No. I was so overwhelmed, I wanted to throw my arms around him, but he told me not to touch him. He said he had not yet ascended to the Father. So, no, I never actually touched him. But I don't have to touch Peter to know that he is real."

"So it could have been a specter, an apparition, a ghost of some kind."

Mary just looked at him and didn't answer.

Leah was embarrassed for her uncle and caught Mary's attention. "Mary, where are the other women? Did you see my mother and Miriam and the others?"

Mary seemed momentarily startled. "No. Now that you mention it, no, I didn't. Did they go to the tomb then?"

Leah nodded, a trace of anxiety showing in her eyes. If Mary hadn't seen them, nor Peter and John, where had they gone?

That thought crossed Aaron's mind too, but he was too focused on Mary's report to give it much thought. As other people started firing questions at Mary, wanting to hear every detail of her experience, Aaron leaned in so he could hear better. When he felt a touch on his arm, he turned and found himself face to face with his wife. She searched his face for a long moment, and there was some sense of chastisement in her eyes. Finally, he shook his head and looked away. There was nothing to say. He needed time to sit down and think all of this through. The shocks were coming like a stormy surf at high tide, one battering wave after another. He had to sort out what it all meant.

Hava's disappointment was clear, but she simply stepped back to let him pass. And at that moment, once again, heavy knocking sounded at the courtyard gate. Worried about the absence of her mother and the others, Leah started swiftly toward it. The servant pulled the gate open and Salome and Anna stepped through it, followed by Deborah, Miriam, and the others. Aaron was relieved. So they were back.

Then Aaron stopped. He was looking at Deborah's face. It had that same strange glow of happiness he had seen on Mary Magdalene's face. It was then that he realized he was about to be hit by the biggest and most incredible wave of all.

V

Miriam watched Simeon's uncle with a sense of great love and understanding. How could she condemn him for not believing when she could scarcely believe it herself for joy? It was like a dream, a wonderful, incredible, fantastic, marvelous dream. Her entire body was still filled with a comforting glow, a warmth that pushed aside every sorrow, every concern, every desire to criticize.

"Aaron?"

He turned to her.

"You don't have to decide anything now. Just think about what we have told you."

"That's right," Deborah said. She reached out and took his hand. "How I wish you could have been there."

His head came up. "Did you actually touch him?"

Deborah nodded solemnly. "When we realized who it was, we fell at his feet. We bathed his feet with our tears. It was like nothing I have ever experienced before, Aaron. Nothing!"

Miriam spoke, her voice hushed and reverent. "We saw the wounds, Uncle Aaron."

His head came around slowly.

Miriam nodded. "Yes. We saw where the nail had gone through his feet. We saw the marks in his palms and in his wrists."

"But—" he stammered. "Maybe it was just a spirit. Maybe you were so overwhelmed with the experience that you—"

Tears welled up as the memory flooded back in Miriam's mind.

"We touched him, Aaron. We touched his risen body. It was flesh and bone." She squeezed her own arm. "It was as real as my own. We saw and felt those cruel wounds that took his life and yet knew that he is alive again. He is risen, Aaron. With all the power of my soul, I tell you, Jesus is risen from the dead. I know that with my eyes. I know that with my ears. I know that with my hands." A sob of joy broke off her words. She swallowed quickly, then finished. "And I know that with all my heart."

VI

Livia turned on her side so that her face was close to Miriam's. "Are you still awake?" she whispered.

Miriam's eyes opened immediately, and she nodded. "I'm far too excited to sleep."

"Me, too." Livia went up on one elbow. They were lying on the only bed in one of the back sleeping rooms of Jephunah's house. Leah and Deborah were on a straw mattress on the floor across from them. The two of them had insisted on taking the floor and giving the bed to the two who were carrying children, even though both Livia and Miriam had tried to protest. As Livia studied the two figures, she could see that their breathing was deep and even.

The previous night all of the women of the family had been in the room together, but once there was no need for further burial preparations many of the group had returned to be with their families. Thus, it was no longer necessary to crowd so many people into each room. Rachel and Hava were in the next room with some of the others. That was good, for Livia had been hoping for a chance to be alone with her friend.

"Tell me again, Miriam. Tell me everything."

Miriam smiled, not minding it at all. She found reliving the whole experience to be rejuvenating. And besides that, as the other women had gathered in around Mary and the seven of them, eagerly pressing for details, Miriam had realized that this was a special trust the eight of them had received. It was only right that they share it with the others.

So she began, speaking in soft whispers so she wouldn't awaken the other two. Livia listened quietly, not interrupting once until Miriam reached the point where she had backed out of the tomb and dropped to her knees at the sight of two angels.

"So they *were* angels," Livia said.

Miriam was a little surprised. "Of course."

"Before, you just talked about two personages, or two men dressed in white."

"They were standing in the air, Livia."

Livia's eyebrows shot up. "Really? You didn't say that before."

"I didn't? Well, they were. I remembered looking at their feet. That's when I knew they weren't beings who lived on this earth."

Livia blushed a little. "I've always thought the Jewish concept of angels to be a little strange. I guess I never really could picture them as being real."

"Well, these were real. They were glorious, Livia. It was like . . ." She stopped, looking for some way to express it adequately. "It was like being ushered into a room filled with the softest, most beautiful music, the most exquisite perfumes, the most elegant tapestries and furniture." Then she shook her head. "That doesn't describe it either. But it was marvelous. Even now, just thinking of being in their presence makes me shiver with pleasure."

"And they told you that Jesus was risen?"

"Actually, only one of them ever spoke to us, but yes. And he told us to hurry back and tell the rest of you."

"Oh, Miriam," she exclaimed softly. "Do you think there is any chance that I might see him too?"

"Why not?" she said, not sure if she should be making such a promise.

"Go on. The angels disappeared, and then what happened?"

Miriam paused, struggling with her emotions. It stirred her deeply to even try to put what had happened into words. But she managed to keep her voice steady as she told Livia about seeing the stranger standing near the path in front of them, about their initial fear, and then how they had recognized him as he stepped into the light. At that point, she couldn't hold back, and she had to tell her the rest of it through her tears.

For a long time, Livia lay there, staring up at the ceiling, her own eyes glistening. "Thank you," she finally murmured.

Miriam reached out and squeezed her hand, guessing at her thoughts. "You will see Yehuda again, Livia. And he will be the Yehuda you know, the Yehuda you love. He will get to meet this child, and someday your child will get to meet his or her father."

"I know," she whispered huskily. "I know."

Again the silence stretched on for some time as Livia lay back and closed her eyes, trying to picture what Miriam had described for her.

"Tell me," Miriam asked after several moments had passed. "Tell me what you're thinking."

Livia's eyes opened, then closed again as she chose her words with care. "Since Yehuda died, I have dreaded the rest of my life. Yes, I knew that some part of Yehuda was still alive, but I never pictured *him* still being there, not the Yehuda I knew. He was, in my mind, like some cosmic angel, some being I might not even recognize when I finally saw him. Now, life holds no more fear for me. Even if I live another fifty or sixty years, I can bear it, for I know that someday I will see him again. And he will have a body, just as I will have a body."

Her voice choked for a moment. She fought it back, then finished very quietly. "When we meet again, I know that he will take me into his arms and hold me tight. And that makes everything all right now."

VII

The house of Jephunah was mostly quiet. David ben Joseph stood beneath the deep shade of a fig tree and looked around. Many of the disciples had left once it became clear that they were not needed any longer. Benjamin and Esther returned to Bethlehem. John had taken Mary, the mother of Jesus, and her sons to where he and James were staying so she could rest. Others had simply returned to their families to complete the Passover holy days.

With all of that, the numbers were now less than half of what they had been the previous night. The women were inside the house resting. The men were outside doing the same. Most of them had found places in the shade and were sound asleep. Aaron had finally been able to lay aside his questions about Jesus for the moment and was snoring softly. The events of the day had not been enough to keep Simeon and Ephraim awake, but they were too much for David. He had tried to sleep but had quickly given up on the idea. He stood in the shade and idly gazed forward, his mind repeating all that he had heard.

Once the report of the women had been heard, Peter and the rest of the apostles called a hurried meeting of the brethren to determine what their next course of action would be. Any thoughts of immediately leaving Jerusalem had been put aside. They would stay in the area for at least a few more days, until they knew for sure what was going on. Could it be that Jesus had really risen from the dead? That was the central question, and it was vigorously discussed. Aaron was not the only one struggling with what he had heard. Several others were also trying to sort it out. And even if it was true, then what? What did it mean for Peter and the other apostles? Was their work over? Had it just begun?

The whole experience had left David with a dozen questions too, and he wasn't sure what course of action he should take. He longed to return to Capernaum and let life settle back to normal, but if Peter and John and Andrew were—

A movement caught his eye, and he turned to see Peter appear out of nowhere. He was rubbing at his eyes. He stretched, then quietly found a secluded bench and sat down. So he had not been able to sleep either, David thought. Glad for an opportunity to speak with his long-time friend, David left the shade and walked over.

"Quite a day," he said as he sat down beside him.

Peter nodded but said nothing. He seemed pensive, almost melancholy.

"It will work itself out," David suggested. "Things have happened pretty fast this morning. We all need some time to let it ruminate."

"Do you believe it?" Peter asked abruptly.

David didn't hesitate. "I do. Deborah is the most honest person I know. If she says it happened, then I know it happened."

"Yes, Anna too."

"And Miriam. If there was even a question in their minds. If only one had seen it. If any of them expressed even one tiny sliver of doubt about what they saw, then . . ." He shrugged. "No, I believe them. I can't fully comprehend all that it means, but I believe them."

"As do I." Peter's mouth pulled down. "But I fully empathize with what Aaron is going through. He can't disbelieve—not when his own sister and niece are so adamant about their experience—and yet he can't bring himself to fully accept it either. It is too . . . too—" He threw up his hands.

"Too unbelievable," David finished for him.

"Yes! It is too joyous, too wonderful, too perfect to be true. Life doesn't turn out like this, David. Tragedies don't turn into triumphs. Loss doesn't become gain. One moment I'm saying, 'It has to be true,' and the next, I'm shaking my head and saying, 'How could such a thing be?'"

"We cannot believe for the joy of it," David suggested. "That's it, isn't it."

When Peter only nodded, David added another thought that had been troubling him all afternoon. "And because of that," he said wistfully, "we are all a little envious of these women, aren't we."

Peter grunted. "What makes you say that?"

David was taken aback by the dismay he saw on his friend's face. "Well, aren't you? Doesn't it make you just ache to have been there too?"

"I *was* there," Peter replied softly.

Now it was David who was surprised. "You were?"

"At the tomb," Peter explained. "John and I were at the tomb." He sighed, and it was a sound of pain. "So why didn't Jesus appear to us? Why didn't John and I see those angels? It couldn't have been but a few minutes difference between our being there and Mary and the women. Did we simply have the misfortune of bad timing?"

His hands came up, and his fingers began to massage his temples. "We are his apostles, David. Supposedly, we are his leaders . . ." His voice trailed off. Then almost to himself, he added, "I can't speak for John and the others, but I think I know why I wasn't privileged to see him. I think I know exactly why."

"Peter, I—"

But Peter stood up abruptly. "Luke and Cleopas are going to Emmaus. I promised I would see them off. Then I'm going for a long walk." He managed a smile as he looked down at David. "Don't fret about me, old friend. Jesus is alive. That's all that matters. He is alive again."

CHAPTER NOTES

John gives us the detailed account of Mary's experience with Jesus (John 20:11–18), and Matthew records the appearance of Jesus to several women after their experience with the angels at the tomb (Matthew 28:9–10).

There are a number of discrepancies among the Gospel writers about the events on Resurrection day. For example, Matthew and Mark report only one angel present at the Garden Tomb, but Luke and John specify two angels. Likewise, Matthew places the angel outside of the tomb, while Mark, Luke, and John indicate the angels were inside the tomb (Matthew 28:2; Mark 16:5; Luke 24:4; John 20:12). As noted in the novel, Jesus instructs Mary Magdalene, "Touch me not" (John 20:17), yet shortly after, other women are permitted to touch Jesus (Matthew 28:9). Such minor discrepancies often occur in eyewitness accounts of an event and do not lessen the testimony of the Gospel writers about the miracle of the Resurrection.

CHAPTER 39

IN THE THIRD DAY HE WILL RAISE US UP,

AND WE SHALL LIVE IN HIS SIGHT.

—Hosea 6:2

I

JERUSALEM, UPPER CITY, HOUSE OF JEPHUNAH BEN ASA

6 APRIL, A.D. 33

By the time the sun had fully set, the upper chamber of Jephunah ben Asa's house was shut up tightly again. John had received a report from his contact at the palace of Caiaphas. Now they understood about the Roman guards and what had happened to make them flee. Knowing the Sanhedrin was eager to squelch any rumors of Jesus rising from the dead, Peter had once again ordered all doors closed and the windows shuttered.

They had decided not to set tables in the room, even though it was large enough to accommodate the group. Instead, serving tables were set up on one end of the room, and they were just waiting for the last of those downstairs to trickle in. When Peter came in, he looked around and spotted David sitting with his family against the far wall. He beckoned with his finger, and David immediately went over to join him.

Any sign of the earlier melancholy was gone. Peter was confident now, joyous, greeting people with a firm grip and infectious grin. David wondered what had brought about the remarkable change.

To his surprise, the apostle took him to one side and spoke in low tones. "Do you remember our conversation earlier today?"

"Of course."

"Well," he said, looking around. "I haven't told anyone other than the apostles yet, but I wanted you to know first."

"Know what?" And then David reeled back. "Are you saying . . . ?"

Peter laughed softly. "Yes, David. I went for a walk, to be alone." He bent his head down until it nearly touched David's. "I saw him, David. Jesus appeared to me."

David just gaped at him, feeling that familiar tingle he had experienced as Deborah had recounted in detail the experience she and the others had had that morning. "What did he say to you?"

Peter shook his head. "Many things. Wonderful things." He took a quick breath. "Sobering things." He gripped David's shoulder. "I just wanted you to know. I plan to tell the others once we get started." His grip tightened. "It's all right now, David. Everything is all right now."

II

To the family's surprise, Aaron came through the door about ten minutes later. Hava was on her feet immediately and rushed to him. When she and the other women had come out following their afternoon rest, Aaron was nowhere to be found, which set the whole family to worrying. Aaron was not some little-known disciple. His former seat on the Great Council made him vulnerable to identification and possible arrest. Hava had twice started out to look for him, but David and Deborah had prevailed upon her to be patient.

David waited until he was settled, then simply said, "We're glad you're back safely, Aaron."

Aaron nodded absently, looking around the room.

"Peter saw him," David said, after a moment.

That startled them all, for he had said nothing after Peter had spoken with him.

Aaron's face registered momentary astonishment, then fell dejectedly. "Him, too?"

Then before David could answer, he went on. "Good. If anyone should see him, it would be Peter."

Hava leaned forward. "Does that mean you believe now, Aaron?"

He sighed wearily. "How can I not believe?" he asked. He looked at Deborah. "Otherwise, I must call you a liar." He turned to Miriam. "And you a deluded fool. I can't do that."

"But you are still troubled, aren't you," Livia said, not making it a question.

"Aren't *you?*" he asked.

"No," came the quiet reply. "I have many questions, many things I don't understand yet, but I have never been more at peace."

"May I have your attention, please."

The family turned. Peter was standing at the head of the room.

"Everything is in readiness, thanks to Jephunah and you women who have worked so hard. We shall return thanks for the food; then if you will fill your plates as quickly as possible, we shall begin. We have much to talk about tonight."

III

Peter was right. Jephunah had not spared any expense in preparing the meal. The tables groaned beneath the bounty upon them:

broiled fish, roasted lamb, bowls of olives, round loaves of bread, pocket bread that could be opened on one end and stuffed with meat or vegetables, various kinds of cheeses, pieces of honeycomb, dried dates, shelled almonds. Once everyone had their food, the people spread out across the room, mostly sitting on the floor and using the numerous stools, benches, and wooden chairs as their tables.

The mood in the room was dramatically different from the night before. There was still much perplexity—the various reports of the day had left many filled with questions—but the pall of gloom had lifted. The conversations were still subdued, but they were now filled with hope and excitement, with anticipation of a future that no longer looked totally bleak.

David and his family had been near the front of the line, and so they had time to talk while the others were still getting their food. Aaron, who was carefully stripping the flesh off the bones of the fish he was eating, looked up. "Can I ask a question?"

"Of course," Deborah said.

Simeon frowned. He was not in a mood for any more of Aaron's skepticism. Miriam, seeing that, poked at him, signaling for him to not be so critical.

Aaron noticed none of that. He sat back, putting his plate on the floor for a moment. "Why do you think Deborah and Miriam were allowed to see Jesus, and not John or Andrew?"

Miriam was startled by Aaron's bluntness, though she had been pondering that very question earlier.

"How do you suppose Jesus chooses to whom he shows himself? Is it simply at random? Those who happened to go to the tomb at the right time were the privileged ones, and the rest of us were not so fortunate. Is that it?"

Leah looked at the floor. "I wanted to go," she whispered. "If I had, then I would have been there too."

To her surprise, Aaron went up on his knees, leaned over, and kissed her on the top of her head. "I thought about that, in fact," he said. "It can't just be based on righteousness, can it? They don't come any purer or any sweeter than our Leah."

She stared at him, completely taken aback. Coming from Aaron, that was perhaps the most touching compliment she had ever received.

But Aaron was only momentarily deflected. "It seems obvious why Jesus would come to Peter. But why not the others? Is it because some don't need it as much as others? Or maybe because they have less faith?"

"I've thought it strange that he should first appear only to women," Rachel said. "That is especially remarkable to me."

Livia had a pretty good idea what was behind this line of questioning. She wiped her fingers on a small towel, then looked at Aaron. "What you really want to know, Aaron, is why didn't he appear to you, right?"

Aaron had just started to take another bite of fish and nearly choked on it.

She went on quickly. "That's my question too. When I say, why not Simeon or why not David, what I'm really asking is, why not me?"

Aaron shook his head. "I already have the answer to that." He offered a wry smile. "If he appeared to me, I would probably demand some proof that he was real."

Simeon laughed aloud. It wasn't often that Aaron surprised him, but he did with that.

"Does it really matter?" Miriam mused aloud.

Everyone turned to her in surprise.

"Well," she said, a little defensively. "Of course I am thrilled beyond words to think that I was one of the first to see him. It was the most glorious experience imaginable. But my belief in the living Jesus doesn't rest on that." She stole a glance at Aaron. "Leah wasn't there, and yet she believes."

Aaron's color darkened. There was nothing he could say to that except "Guilty as charged."

"Will Jesus have to go around and appear to every person he wants in his kingdom?" she continued. "I can't imagine that will be the case. What about when we return home? Aren't we going to tell others about this? Can they believe on our words alone, or will Jesus have to appear to them too?"

"Miriam's right," Deborah said. "What matters is not what you see, but what you believe."

"I agree," Aaron finally said. He spoke slowly and with deliberation. "And you are right, of course, Miriam." He blew out his breath, searching for the right words. But he didn't have a chance to find them because Peter was on his feet again.

The conversations quickly died away. As the room quieted, Peter motioned for Luke and Cleopas to come forward.

"I know you're still eating, some of you, but I'd like you to hear what these two have to say. I am tempted to say some things in introduction, but I think it will mean more if they just tell you what they told me when they first arrived here." He stepped back and went over to sit beside Anna.

Luke looked at Cleopas, who was several years younger than the physician, but Cleopas nodded for him to go ahead. Luke cleared his throat and began.

"As some of you know, the two of us left early this afternoon to make the short trip to Emmaus. Cleopas had some business, and I went to help him. As we walked along, you can imagine what the main topic of our conversation was. We talked solely of the events of the past few days, and especially what happened this morning."

"Without us really noticing," Cleopas came in, "a fellow traveler joined us. He listened for a time; then, suddenly, he asked us a question. 'What are these things you talk about with one another as you walk?' he said.

"I could hardly believe it," Cleopas continued. "I asked, 'Have you been here in Jerusalem and yet know nothing of the things that have come to pass these last few days?' He looked at us both, completely unruffled by my question and asked again of what things we spoke."

Luke took up the story again. "So we told him about Jesus, how he was a prophet, mighty in word and deed before God and all the people. We explained how the chief priests and elders had him arrested and then delivered him up to be condemned to death and crucified."

"He didn't say anything to that," Cleopas said. "So we began telling him about what happened this morning." His eyes sought out Mary Magdalene from the rest of the crowd, and he smiled at her, but surprisingly, at the same time, he looked a little sheepish. "We told him about how some of our women had gone to the tomb, then had come back with a report that angels had told them that Jesus was alive."

"Didn't you tell him that we had actually seen Jesus?" Mary asked.

He dropped his head and looked away.

Luke winced but met her gaze. "We did not. We were not sure he would believe us." He gave a short, self-deprecating laugh. "We were not even sure what *we* believed at that point. We did tell him about Peter and John going to the tomb and finding it just as the women said, which only deepened the mystery."

Peter leaned forward. "Go on, Luke. Tell them all of it."

Luke straightened. "Well, it was about then that the man began to upbraid us a little. He spoke very plainly. 'O foolish men,' he said, 'and slow of heart to believe in all the prophets have spoken. Know you not that it behooved Christ to suffer these things and enter into his glory?'"

Cleopas's eyes were bright with excitement. "What happened next was astounding. Starting with Moses, and then from the prophets and the Psalms, he opened the scriptures to us concerning the Messiah."

"Such as?" Aaron called out.

They looked at each other; then Luke took the question. "There were many. They just came rolling out one after another."

"Give us one example," Aaron demanded.

Luke thought for a moment, then nodded. He found John in the crowd and motioned for him to stand. "John, you heard a report on Judas and his betrayal from a source you have at the palace of Caiaphas. Would you tell us what price the Sanhedrin paid Judas for turning over Jesus to them?"

"Thirty pieces of silver," John called out.

Aaron went rigid, his face draining of color. "Thirty pieces of silver?" he echoed hoarsely.

"Yes, Aaron. Would you please tell us why that is so significant to you?"

Aaron got to his feet; then, with his voice tinged with wonder, he began. "The following is written in the words of Zechariah: 'And I said unto them, If ye think good, give me my price; and if not, forbear. So they weighed for my price thirty pieces of silver.'"

"Thank you," Luke murmured. He took a deep breath and straightened. "Hearing him expound the scriptures to us was marvelous. He must have talked with us for an hour."

"Who was this man?" Aaron muttered. "Is he a disciple?"

Luke ignored the question. "By this time, we had reached Emmaus, and it was late in the afternoon. When we told him we were going to stop there for the night, he made as if he had to continue on. But we entreated him to abide with us. It had been such a wonderful experience. Our hearts had burned as he communed with us, and we didn't want that to end. And so he agreed."

He started to go on but suddenly couldn't continue. He motioned for Cleopas to take over. He did so in hushed tones. "It was when we were about to break bread. The stranger took the loaf and broke it for us." His voice caught. "That's when we saw his hands."

Several people around the room audibly gasped.

"It was the Master?" Aaron exclaimed.

"Yes," Luke said. "It was. For some reason, a veil had been drawn over our eyes up to that moment, and we had not recognized him. But all that time, we had been speaking with Jesus."

"As quickly as we recognized him," Cleopas concluded, "he vanished. Just like that, disappeared from the room, and we were all alone."

Luke shook his head, his eyes filled with tears. "That's when Cleopas and I decided to hurry back here as quickly as we could to tell you."

Peter stood again. He embraced both men, then looked around. "Thank you. Now I, too, have something to tell you."

CHAPTER NOTES

There are ten or eleven recorded appearances of Jesus to his disciples following his resurrection from the dead. These took place over a forty-day period (see Acts 1:3) known as the post-resurrection ministry. They are: (1) to Mary Magdalene at the tomb (John 20:11–18); (2) to other women after they had seen the angels and were hurrying back to tell the disciples (Matthew 28:9–10); (3) to Peter (Luke 24:34; see also 1 Corinthians 15:5); (4) to Cleopas and an unnamed disciple on the road to Emmaus (Luke 24:13–32); (5) to a group of disciples on the evening of that first Sunday (Luke 24:36–43; John 20:19–25); (6) to a group of disciples the following Sunday when Thomas was present and was allowed to see the Savior for himself (John 20:26–31); (7) to seven apostles—Peter, James, John, Andrew, Nathanael, and two others not named—on the shores of the Sea of Galilee (John 21:1–25); (8) to the eleven apostles on a mountain in Galilee (Matthew 28:16–20); (9) to five hundred brethren at once (1 Corinthians 15:6); (10) to James, mentioned only once by Paul (1 Corinthians 15:7); (11) at his ascension from the Mount of Olives (Acts 1:3–12). The first five, and possibly number ten, all took place on the day of the resurrection itself.

Some believe the final ascension and the appearance to the five hundred may be the same. If so, this would be ten appearances.

Because all these appearances are not cited in the novel, some parts of what the resurrected Christ said on later occasions are placed on that first night in the upper room.

Luke is the only writer who includes the story of the two disciples meeting Jesus on the road to Emmaus (Luke 24:13–32), though Mark makes brief mention of it as well (Mark 16:12–13). Luke names Cleopas but not the second man. Some believe that this was Luke's way of not taking glory to himself, he likely being the second disciple (see Edersheim, *Life and Times*, p. 912). This would explain why he could give such a detailed account.

No specific scriptures are listed by Luke as being those quoted by the Savior in his discourse to them on the prophecies of his death and resurrection. (The reference in Zechariah is 11:12–13.) Here is a possible list of other references he may have cited, especially focusing on the Psalms, since those are specifically named (see Luke 24:44):

Psalm 22:1. *My God, my God, why hast thou forsaken me?*

Psalm 22:7–8. *All they that see me laugh me to scorn: they shoot out the lip [an idiom for mockery], they shake the head, saying, He trusted on the Lord that he would deliver him: let him deliver him, seeing he delighted in him.*

Psalm 22:16. *The assembly of the wicked have inclosed me: they pierced my hands and my feet.*

Psalm 22:18. *They part my garments among them, and cast lots upon my vesture.*

Psalm 41:9. *Yea, mine own familiar friend, in whom I trusted, which did eat of my bread, hath lifted up his heel against me.*

Psalm 69:21. *They gave me also gall for my meat; and in my thirst they gave me vinegar to drink.*

Isaiah 53:3–5. *He is despised and rejected of men; a man of sorrows, and acquainted with grief: and we hid as it were our faces from him; he was despised, and we esteemed him not. Surely he hath borne our griefs, and carried our sorrows: yet we did esteem him stricken, smitten of God, and afflicted. But he was wounded for our transgressions, he was bruised for our iniquities: the chastisement of our peace was upon him; and with his stripes we are healed.*

Isaiah 53:9. *And he made his grave with the wicked, and with the rich in his death.*

Zechariah 9:9. *Rejoice greatly, O daughter of Zion; shout, O daughter of Jerusalem: behold, thy King cometh unto thee: he is just, and having salvation; lowly, and riding upon an ass, and upon a colt the foal of an ass.*

CHAPTER 40

AND THERE ARE ALSO MANY OTHER THINGS WHICH JESUS DID,

THE WHICH, IF THEY SHOULD BE WRITTEN EVERY ONE,

I SUPPOSE THAT EVEN THE WORLD ITSELF COULD NOT

CONTAIN THE BOOKS THAT SHOULD BE WRITTEN.

—*John 21:25*

JERUSALEM, UPPER CITY, HOUSE OF JEPHUNAH BEN ASA

6 APRIL, A.D. 33

By the time Peter finished his account of seeing Jesus, there was so much excitement in the room that he decided to let it run itself out before trying to conduct any further business. Aaron looked around, then got to his feet, plate in hand. He looked down at his wife. "I'm going to get some more almonds. Would you like anything else?"

Hava retrieved her empty plate and handed it up to him. "No, I'm fine, thank you."

"Anyone else?"

Ephraim got to his feet. "I want some more cheese, but I'll come get it."

"I'll come too," said Leah. The others all shook their heads.

Aaron led out, threading his way around the small groups seated on the floor. The serving tables had been set up near the door, which was barred and locked for security. When the guests had seated themselves, they had left a wide space around the tables to allow others easy access to the food. As Aaron moved into the open space, his eyes were focused on the dish of almonds, noting that there were still plenty of the nuts left.

Suddenly, directly in his line of sight, a figure materialized out of thin air, cutting off his view of the table. Aaron jumped back, screaming aloud. The plates went flying and hit the wall with a shattering crash. Eyes bulging, he started backpedaling and backed straight into Ephraim, who was frozen in place, staring at the personage before them. The figure was dressed in a full, dazzling white robe, with sleeves to the wrists. He wore no sandals on his feet and had no covering on his head.

"*Shalom,*" the figure said in a low, rich voice. "Peace be unto you."

Aaron thought his heart was going to burst inside his chest. He could feel the veins hammering in his throat. Dimly, he was aware of women screaming, men shouting and scrambling to get out of the way. All around him, people were falling to the ground, throwing their arms across their faces. Aaron was rooted to the spot, his eyes riveted to the face of the man before him. It was Jesus. Unquestionably. He was only three or four steps away from Aaron. *It was him!*

And then Aaron realized something else with shocking clarity. The door was still barred. The windows were still heavily shuttered. Jesus had come from nowhere to stand before them.

"Be not frightened," Jesus said, raising his voice enough to be heard by all, but still speaking with great gentleness and perfect calm.

"It's a spirit!" a woman gasped. "A specter!"

"No, it's him!" cried another. "It's Jesus."

Jesus took a step forward. In spite of feeling as if every ounce of his strength had drained away, Aaron stumbled backwards, trying to get out of the way.

"Why are you troubled?" Jesus asked. "Did not the others tell you that I was risen? Why then do you doubt?"

He looked around at the circle of ashen faces, slack jaws, and wide, astonished eyes. "Why do you reason thus in your hearts about whether I am a spirit or not?"

He took another step forward, extending his hands towards them, palms up.

Aaron gasped. The flesh of the palms was torn and scarred. The sleeves of his robe pulled back slightly, revealing the terrible wounds in the wrists, as jarring and vivid and real as those in his hands.

"See my hands and my feet," Jesus said, his voice softer now. The screaming and shouting had stopped, and a great hush came over the room. "It is I myself. Touch me and see, for a spirit hath not flesh and bones as ye see me have."

Jesus turned to one side. Leah had dropped to her knees, her hands over her eyes. He bent down and touched her on the shoulder. "See for yourself," he said, and held out his hands to her.

Slowly she raised herself, staring first at the hands, then up into Jesus' smiling face. He nodded his encouragement. Gingerly, as if she were about to touch a hot coal, she reached out and touched the center of his palm. A sob was torn from inside her and tears burst forth. Clutching blindly with her other hand, the young woman grasped both of the Master's hands and laid them against her cheek. "Oh, Master!" she cried.

Jesus straightened. He looked directly at Aaron, who was right in front of him. Slowly, his eyes never leaving him, he reached up and pulled back the fold in his robe that angled across his chest. Now Aaron dropped to his knees as well. There, just below the rib cage, was a three-inch scar, with the edges of the flesh pulled back a little from the wound, evidence of the reverse force of the spear being withdrawn.

Aaron buried his face in his hands and began to sob. But he couldn't bear to miss seeing what was happening. Through the blur of tears, he saw Ephraim on one knee beside him. He had both of Jesus' hands in his and was tracing the wounds in the wrists with his fingertip. His eyes were huge. His mouth was open in unabashed astonishment.

Did you touch him? Suddenly the question that had been Aaron's obsession flashed into his mind. He had asked it of Mary Magdalene. He had asked it of Miriam and Deborah. He looked up into the eyes of the Master. Jesus gave another radiant smile and then a nod of encouragement. Trembling so violently he could hardly stand, Aaron leaned forward on his knees, reaching out to touch Jesus.

The warmth shocked him. He had expected the flesh to be cold and hard. But the hands were warm and soft. He blinked rapidly, trying to clear his vision. He could feel the roughness of the wounds beneath his own hands. The scarred flesh scraped against his own. In great wonder, he thrust his finger against the wrist and felt the depression there, now healed, but still grim evidence of the driving force of the great nails.

He jerked his hands away, suddenly feeling unworthy and ashamed. "O, Master," he cried. "Forgive me."

For a moment, he felt the gentle pressure of Jesus' hand on his shoulder; then Jesus moved away.

Ten feet away, Livia had to prop herself against the wall to stop from collapsing. It was as though every muscle and sinew and bone in her body had turned to water. Waves of joy washed through her, strengthening and draining her at the same time. She watched with wide eyes as Jesus moved slowly around the room, stopping to let each person touch his hands, or press their hands against his side. Peter cried out in joy and fell at his feet and embraced his ankles, tears streaming down his face and into his beard. James, John, Andrew, Matthew—one by one the apostles dropped to their knees in adoration. Mary Magdalene, who had been forbidden to touch him that morning in the garden, now bathed his hands with her tears. Martha, Mary, and Lazarus, who himself had come forth from the tomb—one by one, with no rush, no sense of urgency, Jesus let each person come to know for themselves.

Livia's heart began to pound ever faster as he came closer. David was drawn to the Master in a long embrace. Simeon bowed his head, sure that he was unworthy to touch the hands, and was pulled to his feet. Jesus drew him and Miriam to him and let them touch his hands at the same time. Ephraim and Rachel knelt together, and Jesus touched them both on the shoulder. Deborah, who had already experienced this once, quietly knelt when Jesus finally reached her. She murmured something to him, and Jesus laughed softly.

Even as he moved in front of her, Livia was afraid that he would look into her eyes, see the weakness that was there, and move away. "Master," she whispered, lowering her head. "I would be a worthy disciple, Lord."

When she looked up, his eyes—eyes that she would never forget—held hers for a long moment. She could feel him search her soul, and then she could feel his acceptance. The compassion that swept through her almost took her breath away, and somehow he let her know that he understood her loss and her pain and her penitence. Ever so gently, he took her right hand and pressed it against his side, over the wound. Her shoulders began to shake convulsively, as the reality of what she was feeling swept over her. He held her hand there for another moment, then let it drop again. Reaching up, he brushed the tears from her cheek, smiled once more, then moved to the next person.

When he had made the full circle, Jesus turned to Peter. "Have you anything to eat?"

That was hardly what Peter had expected, but he nodded. Anna reached the table before he did, however. In a moment she stood before Jesus and handed him the plate. On it was a piece of broiled fish and part of a honeycomb. He murmured his thanks, then began to eat, standing in place. There was not a sound in the room as everyone watched, still too astonished to believe what they were seeing.

When he was finished, he turned and set the plate on a stool. He motioned for Peter and the other apostles to come forward. When they stood around him in a half circle, he spoke. His message was meant for them, but it was clear that he wanted everyone to hear.

"Remember the words which I spake unto you while I was yet with you, how that all things must be fulfilled which was written in the Law of Moses and the prophets and the Psalms concerning me. Thus it is written that the Messiah should suffer, and rise again from the dead the third day."

He paused to let them assimilate that for a moment, then continued. "It is also written that repentance and remission of sins should be preached in the name of Christ to all nations, beginning from Jerusalem. You are witnesses of these things. Behold, I send forth the promise of my Father upon you; but tarry in the city, until you are clothed with power from on high.

"Go ye therefore into all the world, and make disciples of all nations, baptizing them in the name of the Father and the Son and the Holy Ghost. Teach them to observe all things whatsoever I commanded you. He that believeth and is baptized shall be saved, but he that believeth not shall be damned."

His eyes lifted for a moment, and he seemed to be looking right through the ceiling; then they came back to rest on Peter and the men with him. "And lo," he said, his voice thrilling everyone in the room to the very core, "I am with you always, even unto the end of the world."

Then, even as those assembled in the upper room there in the house of Jephunah ben Asa watched in stunned amazement, Jesus was gone, vanishing as quickly as he had come.

> So then after the Lord had spoken unto them, he was received up into heaven, and sat on the right hand of God.
>
> And they went forth, and preached every where, the Lord working with them, and confirming the word with signs following.
>
> —Mark 16:19–20

BIBLIOGRAPHY

Backhouse, Robert. *The Kregel Pictorial Guide to the Temple*. Edited by Tim Dowley. Grand Rapids, Mich.: Kregel Publications, 1996.

Bloch, Abraham C. *The Biblical and Historical Background of Jewish Customs and Ceremonies*. New York: Ktav Publishing House, 1980.

Brandon, S. G. F. "The Zealots: The Jewish Resistance against Rome, A.D. 6–73," *History Today* 15 (Sept. 1965): 632–34.

Buttrick, George Arthur, ed. *The Interpreter's Dictionary of the Bible: An Illustrated Encyclopedia*. Nashville: Abingdon Press, 1962.

Clarke, Adam. *Clarke's Commentary*. 3 vols. Nashville: Abingdon, 1977.

Connolly, Peter. *A History of the Jewish People in the Times of Jesus: From Herod the Great to Masada*. New York: P. Bedrick Books, 1987, 1983.

Dummelow, J. R. *The One Volume Bible Commentary*. New York: Macmillan Publishing Co., 1908.

Edersheim, Alfred. *The Life and Times of Jesus the Messiah*. Revised edition. Peabody, Mass.: Hendrickson, 1993.

———. *The Temple: Its Ministry and Services as They Were at the Time of Christ*. 1874. Reprint, Grand Rapids, Mich.: Wm. B. Eerdmans Publishing Co., 1958.

Edwards, William D., Wesley J. Gabel, and Floyd E Hosmer. "On the Physical Death of Jesus Christ." *Journal of the American Medical Association* 256 (21 March 1986): 1455–63.

Fallows, Samuel, ed. *The Popular and Critical Bible Encyclopædia and Scriptural Dictionary*. 3 vols. Chicago: The Howard-Severance Co., 1911.

Farrar, Frederic. *The Life of Christ*. Portland, Ore.: Fountain Publications, 1964.

Frank, Harry Thomas. *Discovering the Biblical World*. Revised edition. Maplewood, N.J.: Hammond, 1988.

Guthrie, D., J. A. Motyer, A. M. Stibbs, and D. J. Wiseman, eds. *The New Bible Commentary: Revised*. Grand Rapids, Mich.: Wm. B. Eerdmans Publishing Co., 1970.

Hastings, James, ed. *Dictionary of the Bible*. New York: Charles Scribner's Sons, 1909.

Jacobs, Louis. *The Book of Jewish Practice*. West Orange, N.J.: Behrman House Publishers, 1987.

Josephus, Flavius. *Antiquities of the Jews*. In *Josephus: Complete Works*. William Whiston, trans. Grand Rapids, Mich.: Kregel Publications, 1960.

Kimball, Spencer W. "Peter, My Brother." *BYU Speeches of the Year 1970–71*, 13 July 1971, 1–8.

Mackie, George M. *Bible Manners and Customs*. Old Tappan, N.J.: Power Books, 1984.

New Testament in Four Versions, The. King James, Revised Standard, Phillips Modern English, New English Bible. Washington: Christianity Today, 1963.

Talmage, James E. *Jesus the Christ*. Salt Lake City: Deseret Book Company, 1983.

Thayer, Joseph Henry, trans., rev. and enl. *A Greek-English Lexicon of the New Testament: Being Grimm's Wilke's Clavis Novi Testamenti*. Grand Rapids, Mich.: Baker Book House, 1977.

Vincent, Marvin R. *Word Studies in the New Testament*. 4 vols. New York: C. Scribner's Sons, 1887–1900.

Vine, W. E. *Vine's Expository Dictionary of Old and New Testament Words*. Old Tappan, N.J.: Fleming H. Revell Co., 1981.

Wight, Fred H. *Manners and Customs of Bible Lands*. Chicago: Moody Press, 1953.

Wilson, William. *Old Testament Word Studies*. Grand Rapids, Mich.: Kregel Publications, 1978.